Laying a Foundation

&

The Groundbreaking

Love Under Construction Series

Prequel & Book 1

by

Deanndra Hall

The Groundbreaking
&
Laying a Foundation
Love Under Construction Series
Prequel & Book 1

Celtic Muse Publishing
P.O. Box 3722
Paducah, KY 42002-3722

Copyright © 2013-2014, Deanndra Hall
Print Edition
Originally published separately, July 2013
Combined print version, May 2014
Combined ebook version, May 2014

All rights reserved. Except as permitted under the U.S. Copyright Act of 1976, no part of this publication may be reproduced, distributed, or transmitted in any form or by any means, or stored in a database or retrieval system, without the prior written permission of the author.

This book is a work of fiction.

Names of characters, places, and events are the construction of the author, except those locations that are well-known and of general knowledge, and all are used fictitiously. Any resemblance to persons living or dead is coincidental, and great care was taken to design places, locations, or businesses that fit into the regional landscape without actual identification; as such, resemblance to actual places, locations, or businesses is coincidental. Any mention of a branded item, artistic work, or well-known business establishment, is used for authenticity in the work of fiction and was chosen by the author because of personal preference, its high quality, or the authenticity it lends to the work of fiction; the author has received no remuneration, either monetary or in-kind, for use of said product names, artistic work, or business establishments, and mention is not intended as advertising, nor does it constitute an endorsement. The author is solely responsible for content.

Cover design 2014 Novel Graphic Designs, used by permission of the artist.

Disclaimer:

Material in this work of fiction is of a graphic sexual nature and is not intended for audiences under 18 years of age.

More titles in the Love Under Construction Series

Tearing Down Walls (Book 2) – Fall 2013

Secrets – they can do more damage than the truth. Secrets have kept two people from realizing their full potential, but even worse, have kept them from forming lasting relationships and finding the love and acceptance they both need. Can they finally let go of those secrets in time to find love – and maybe even stay alive?

Renovating a Heart (Book 3) – Spring 2014

Can a person's past really be so bad that they can never recover from it? Sometimes it seems that way. One man hides the truth of a horrific loss in his teen years; one woman hides the truth of a broken, scarred life that took a wrong turn in her youth. Can they be honest with each other, or even with themselves, about their feelings? And will they be able to go that distance before one of them is lost forever?

Planning an Addition (Book 4) – Fall 2014

When you think you're set for life and that life gets yanked out from under you, starting over is hard. One woman who's starting over finds herself in love with two men who've started over too, and she's forced to choose. Or is she? And when one of them is threatened by their past, everyone has choices to make. Can they make the right ones?

Also available . . .

The Celtic Fan

Who is Nick Roberts? He wrote a bestselling novel, The Celtic Fan, but no one's ever met him, seen him, even confirmed that he exists. When four buddies take their annual "guys road trip," they set out to find Roberts. Three of the four get distracted, and only Steve Riley, a journalist from Knoxville, stays on track and hunts down Roberts. His search takes him to the address he was given, only to find someone he's sure has no ties to the author. But when a flash flood traps him with the shy and quiet Diana Frazier, the search is almost abandoned until Steve makes a discovery: Nick Roberts might not be as far away as he thinks. And if he finds the elusive author, will he tell? Two books in one, Steve's story is told in his voice as Roberts' original work winds through it. They're sweet, passionate love stories, but one has a tragic end.

The Harper's Cove Series

Come and visit the neighbors of Harper's Cove! From Karen and Brett, to Becca and Greg, to Donna and Connor, every house on the block has a dirty little secret – and individually they think they're the only ones. As they go about their kinky business, sneaky Gloria, the neighborhood busybody and drunk, is determined to know everyone's secrets. As she pokes and pries, she gets a few surprises she never could've imagined. Join in the fun in the fast, nasty little erotica novellas and see how much fun you can have! This series will have seven to nine books eventually, and there's a new one always around the corner.

Adventurous Me

When Trish's husband of almost 30 years decides he's leaving her because she's "boring, tiresome, and predictable," Trish sets out to show him a thing or two. But when her attempts to drown her sorrows put her in the path of a man who can introduce her to adventure she could never have imagined, she steps into the realm of BDSM and finds her place. And when something passing as fate pits her for two solid weeks with the one Dom in the place who seems to hate her, will she survive the adventure of a lifetime?

Support Indie Authors!

Independent (Indie) authors are not a new phenomenon, but they are a hard-working one. As Indie authors, we write our books, have trouble finding anyone to beta read them for us, seldom have money to hire an editor, struggle with our cover art, find it nearly impossible to get a reviewer to even glance at our books, and do all of our own publicity, promotion, and marketing. This is not something that we do until we find someone to offer us a contract – this is a conscious decision we've made to do for ourselves that which we'd have to do regardless (especially promotion, which publishers rarely do anyway). We do it so big publishing doesn't take our money and give us nothing in return. We do it because we do not want to give up rights to something on which we've worked so hard. And we do it because we want to offer you a convenient, quality product for an excellent price.

Indie authors try to bring their readers something fresh, fun, and different. Please help your Indie authors:

- Buy our books! That makes it possible for us to continue to produce them;
- If you like them, please go back to the retailer from which you bought them and review them for us. That helps us more than you could know;
- If you like them, please tell your friends, relatives, nail tech, lawn care guy, anyone you can find, about our books. Recommend them.
- If you're in a book circle, always contact an Indie author to see if you can get free or discounted books to use in your circle. Many would love to help you out. If they help you out, please have circle members review the book(s) to help us out;
- If you see our books being pirated, please let us know. We worked weekends, holidays, and through vacations (if we even get one) to put these books out, so please tell us if you see them being stolen.

More than anything else, we hope you enjoy our books and, if you do, contact us in whatever manner we've provided as it suits you. Visit our blogs and websites, friend our Facebook sites, and follow us on Twitter. We'd love to get to know you!

LOVE UNDER CONSTRUCTION SERIES: PREQUEL

The Groundbreaking

DEANNDRA HALL

The Groundbreaking

Love Under Construction Series

Prequel

by
Deanndra Hall

A Word from the Author...

Welcome to the Love Under Construction series! While there aren't enough changes to call this a new edition, I hope you'll enjoy the combination of this series' prequel and first novel. I decided to make this leap when the decision was made to take this series into print. It only made sense, as the prequel was so short. This way you get all of it at one time!

As I wrote the first book, I realized the characters were far more complex than I ever thought they'd be, and their stories deserved to be told so the reader could appreciate them and how far they'd come to get where they landed. It wasn't easy writing; some of their stories are difficult to read even for me, painful in fact. But as a reader, you'll find it easier to read the subsequent books if you know more about the characters. You'll probably even discover that you have a favorite character (I do have a favorite myself, but I'll never tell – I love them all!).

The most important thing about these books is that, unlike most others, the main characters aren't just barely out of their teens. They're mature adults who would argue that the best portion of their lives is still ahead of them and, if you read these books, you'll find out they're right!

As a reader, you also need to know these aren't stand-alone books. If you skip one, there will be aspects to the next that you won't understand. Also know that they get progressively steamier as they go along – that's something to look forward to!

A special thanks to my loving partner, who has been long-suffering in this effort. In the original version, I promised him that I'd take a break after I finished these five books. He now knows that's never going to happen. So thanks, baby! And thanks too to Kellie at Novel Graphic Designs for the beautiful works of art that grace these books.

Enjoy this volume and keep reading – some of the things that happen will surprise you. I wrote them, and they surprised me!

Love and happy reading,
Deanndra

Visit me at:
www.deanndrahall.com

Contact me at:
DeanndraHall@gmail.com

Join me on Facebook at:
facebook.com/deanndra.hall

Catch me on Twitter at:
twitter.com/DeanndraHall

Find me blogging at:
deanndrahall.blogspot.com

Check out my Substance B page at:
substance-b.com/DeanndraHall.html

Write to me at:
P.O. Box 3722, Paducah, KY 42002-3722

Welcome to the Commonwealth of Kentucky!

The city of Louisville, Kentucky, occupies four hundred square miles of riverfront property on the Ohio River. Even though the city also known as "The Ville" or "da Ville" doesn't seem like a southern city, it is physically below the Mason-Dixon line, the imaginary line of demarcation for the southern states. Most of its residents sincerely consider themselves southerners, and they will let you know that in no uncertain terms.

With a metropolitan area of almost three quarters of a million residents, and the Louisville Combined Statistical Area boasting a population of 1.45 million, it is richly diverse in culture and lifestyle. Louisvillians are surprisingly open-minded, despite the fact that out of its nine colleges and universities, three are religious seminaries. It has micro-populations of virtually every nationality and culture, partially fed by nearby Fort Knox. The dining options are numerous, from Thai to Indian to Mediterranean, Italian galore, and everything in-between. Cultural events are plentiful, and the big event of the year, no surprise here, is the Kentucky Derby on the first Saturday in May.

And if you live in Kentucky, you'd better like – no, love – basketball. While the University of Kentucky Wildcats are legendary, University of Louisville's men's Cardinals won the NCAA Championship for the 2012-2013 season, and their women's team was second in the nation that season. When March Madness hits, households in the Bluegrass State revolve around their local coverage of games, and as Kentucky teams are eliminated, fans of the eliminated teams rally behind other Kentucky teams and will cheer their Kentucky rivals on to the end. When it all shakes out, as long as somebody from Kentucky wins the championship, everybody's happy; well, fairly so anyway.

Hospitals abound. University of Louisville's hospital was the first in the nation to offer a trauma center. Residents from five states come to University of Kentucky's medical facilities and University of Louisville's hospital. Norton excels in spinal surgeries, and Kosair Children's Hospital is a premiere facility drawing patients from all over the country.

Lexington's horse farms are gorgeous, and as the second largest city in

Kentucky, it has a Combined Statistical Area of almost seven hundred thousand people. The metropolitan area has a variety of laws in place to allow it to grow without destroying the horse farms that make it known as "Horse Capital of the World." As cities in Kentucky go, it is the chic place to live and raise kids. The population tends to be wealthier and better educated, and residents of Lexington consider themselves somewhat more sophisticated than most other Kentucky residents.

Shelbyville, by contrast, is a typical Kentucky small town. With a population of barely fourteen thousand, it's known as the "American Saddlebred Capital of the World." Its little main street is quaint, and the county is dotted with horse farms. It lies along Interstate 64, the artery that connects Louisville, Frankfort (the state capitol), and Lexington, known by most Kentuckians as "The Golden Triangle," and, as such, serves as a bedroom community for Louisville. Shelbyville may be small and well north of the triangle, but it carries the flavor of all three of Kentucky's largest cities.

Family is important in Kentucky, and nationwide, Kentucky has the largest percentage of native-born residents still living inside its borders. If you're born in Kentucky, you're pretty likely to be buried there. And for most Kentuckians, that's just fine with them.

Tony

Christmas 2011

The fire was warm and comfy, and so was everyone near it in the huge house not far outside Shelbyville, Kentucky. Drinks were sloshed around, enough food was spread out to feed a university campus, and the holiday music coming from the home theater system was just so much noise in the background.

Tony looked around at the other couples in his big family. Most were touching each other in some way, holding hands or sitting side by side with an arm around the other's shoulder, and it took everything he had not to give in to the dull, persistent ache in his chest. If he lived to be one hundred, he'd never fully understand how someone could be in a crowd and still be so utterly alone.

While everyone else ripped at wrapping paper, he went into the kitchen for another drink. If he were being honest with himself, he did it just to get away for a minute or two, to distance himself a little from all the merriment. A hand on his back caused him to turn, and he looked down to find his baby girl. She might be a grown woman, but she'd always be his baby.

"Dad, you okay?" Her voice was rife with concern.

"Yeah, fine." He popped the cap on another beer. *Not very convincing*, he thought with a sad smile.

"I know it's hard. You'll find someone eventually. I have faith in you." Her hand rubbed small circles between his shoulder blades.

"Don't worry about me, pumpkin. I'm fine." He leaned over and gave her a peck on the cheek.

Her walnut-dark eyes smiled. "I know. But I also know how lonely you are. It hurts to watch." She turned and left the room, and he knew she didn't want him to see the tear that was certain to be trailing down one cheek. He wasn't hiding his misery well enough, and the last thing he wanted was to make someone else miserable.

Standing in the kitchen doorway and looking out into the great room, he watched the whole Walters family. All four of his brothers had beautiful wives, and their kids were something special. His own two kids were in great relationships. His son had married a lovely girl and they were hoping to have a child soon. His daughter had found someone and managed to land in a loving, committed relationship – no small feat for a lesbian in her twenties. Even his mother seemed happy in her widowhood; she'd made it plain that his father had been the love of her life and she would never need another. It would be natural to be happy for all of them, knowing that they were comfortable and loved. But looking at them, watching them, was almost too painful to bear.

After everything was cleaned up and everyone was in bed, he sat on an ottoman in front of the fire. His heart was as cold as the beer he was sucking on. Beams of light from the flood lamps on the patio reflected the snow that was falling even harder now. He thought about his ex-wife, the bitch, and watched the huge flakes fall. Wonder where she was spending Christmas? He didn't care, as long as it was nowhere near him, and he shuddered just thinking about her. She'd ruined everything for him.

I'm fifty-seven and that part of my life, love and happiness and all of that shit, that's all over. The fire was starting to die down, and he contemplated putting another log on. Why bother? Let it die. He poked at the embers to get the last of the heat out of them, then sat back in his chair and glanced down at the front of his jeans – yep, limp and dead, just like it had been for twenty years. Oh, it had a revival a couple of years before, but generally it just hung there neglected, no longer waiting for someone to come along and stimulate it, knowing that wasn't even on the table anymore.

He had his work; that kept him busy. Heading up a large, family-owned construction and contracting business wasn't a part-time job. And he had the gym. He was there almost every day, and his body was a well-tuned instrument. Everyone who saw him thought he was in his early forties, certainly not his actual age, and his genetics helped that along. Women looked at him with longing, but after what that bitch had put him through, no one was getting near him, no way, no how.

The embers in the fireplace seemed to simply wink out of existence, just like his chances at happiness. Everyone under his roof tonight was snug and warm with someone they adored and someone who adored them nearby.

Except for him. And that wasn't likely to change.

New Year's Eve 2011

"Hey, what did you bring?" Tony prowled through the bags that Vic had brought in with him.

"Hmmmm, let's see," Vic said, pulling out a box. "Mallomars and Moon Pies."

"Love 'em," Tony said.

"Yeah. And big bags of m&m's and Skittles."

"Love 'em too," Tony said.

"And," Vic said, pulling out two boxes, "Goo-Goo Clusters!"

"Ah, makes me proud to be a southern boy!" Tony said, ripping a box open.

"And a huge bottle of," Vic pulled it out with a flourish, "Maker's Mark. Plus some cheaper stuff for when we don't care anymore. Which I hope is soon."

"No shit. I plan to get completely hammered." Tony looked at the bottle and gave serious consideration to tearing into it and drinking straight from it.

"Yeah, me too. I looked around the house but I didn't have any weed or I would've brought that too."

"Ohhhh, that would've been sweet. Oh, well, I think we can still do enough damage with the liquor." Tony scrounged around the kitchen and came up with bowls for all of the stuff Vic had brought.

"What else have we got?" Vic asked.

"Well, I've got donuts, the powdered sugar kind and some filled with Bavarian crème, and all kinds of cookies, and chips, my god, every kind of chips I could find, and that great pub mix, you know, the one with all the different little things in it?"

"Yeah, I love that shit!" Vic grabbed two bowls and headed for the great room in the big house. Tony picked up all he could carry and followed.

An hour later, they were well on their way to something much more intense than a buzz. Neither of them did any heavy-duty drinking on a regular basis, and the much larger Vic was faring a lot better. The alcohol was slamming into Tony like a freight train.

"Well, here we are. Two cousins. Alone on New Year's Eve," Tony mumbled.

"We're not alone," Vic reminded him. "We're here together."

"You know what I mean, smart ass," Tony slurred back. "I don't have a woman, and you don't have a woman. So we're alone."

"Yeah. No fun. Hey, how long's it been since you got laid?"

"Couple of years." Tony took a pull off a bottle of bourbon.

Vic's eyebrows knitted. "I didn't know you dated anybody. What was up with that?"

"Didn't date her. Long, sad story." Tony took another hit off the bottle. "Well, the getting there was sad. The being there was awesome. She was a helluva fuck, lemme tell ya. But I've said enough; I really don't want to talk about that. What about you? What happened to that little girl, Carrie? One day you're banging her, and the next, she's gone. Where'd she go?" Tony didn't usually talk so coarsely, but it was just him and Vic and the liquor. Liquor always worked as a solvent on his personal filters, so they were more or less already shot.

"I pretty much ran her off; kinda scared her away. Didn't mean to, but it happened." Vic drained a bottle and looked for another. "I'm a bad, bad man."

"Yeah, right; big, bad teddy bear. That's what you are, my cousin-brother," Tony laughed. "Big ol' teddy bear."

"The teddy bear has a grizzly side. Hey, didn't I see a bottle of Evan Williams around here somewhere?" Vic asked, changing the subject and looking through the pillows on the sofa.

"I think it's in the, the, oh, hell, what's that room called?" Tony slurred, pointing toward the kitchen.

"Can't remember." Vic stuck his hand between the sofa cushions and pulled out a quarter. "Hey, your sofa's throwing up money!"

"Don't be talking 'bout throwing up, what with the power of suggestion and all that." Tony got up to go to the kitchen and staggered a little. "Whoa, damn house must be on one of those tectonic plate fault line thingies 'cause the earth's moving," he giggled. When he came back, he tossed a bottle of Old Granddad to Vic. "Here, more fuel for the fire."

"Thanks, cuz. Seriously, though . . ."

"No 'seriously' now. I can't handle fucking seriously," Tony admonished.

"Okay, just bullshitting you then, isn't there a woman somewhere that you want to ask out?"

Tony thought for a minute. "Yeah, there's this woman at my gym. She's kinda cute. Nice tits, nice ass. Very nice hair. Looks like a sweet one. I've been watching her for four years. But she'd never go out with me."

"Four years? Hell, nobody can accuse you of jumping the gun! You'd be lousy at speed dating." Vic was shocked; why hadn't Tony just asked her out? "Why wouldn't she go out with you? You're a good guy."

"Yeah, and I'm hung, too! But I can't just walk up to her and go, 'Hey there, I'd like to go out with you and guess what? I'm hung!' Probably get ar-ar-arrested, think?"

"You'd better slow down, buddy. You're getting pretty damn polluted." Vic reached for the bottle of Jack Daniels that Tony was sucking on.

"Hey, fuck you!" Tony snapped, snatching the bottle away. "You're damn right I'm getting polluted! I'm here in my own house in my own recliner. So if they wanna ar-ar-ar-arrest me for that damn intoxication bullshit, they'll have to do it between the recliner and the bed, 'cause that's the only place I'm going tonight." He took another draw. "And I'm not asking any woman out. Bitches only break your heart, man. Over and over. All of them. That's no good."

"Wow, you're even more jaded than I thought."

"Yeah, well, uh-huh, yeah, I am. Pre-tteeeee damn jaded." Tony picked up a donut, stuck his tongue through the hole, and tried to pull the whole thing back into his mouth which, of course, failed miserably and made a huge mess. "Boy, Helene's gonna be pissed at me tomorrow," he groaned, his head falling back onto the chair.

"Not as pissed as you're gonna be with yourself, especially since she won't be working because it'll be New Years. That means we'll have to clean up this damn mess ourselves; I can hardly wait. Come on, bud, let me get you into bed." Vic put his arm around Tony's waist and helped him stand.

"You're not gonna take advantage of me, are you?" Tony laughed.

"You should be so lucky," Vic growled as both of them staggered down the hall.

Vic felt like a rhino had sat on his head all night. He managed to get to the kitchen, but he didn't smell any coffee. Tony was there, perched on a stool at the island, head on the counter and arms extended straight out.

"What the hell are you doing?" Vic asked him.

"Am I dead? Because I'm wishing I was," Tony mumbled into the countertop.

"Not unless you're a zombie or a vampire, because you're talking to me, idiot," Vic said matter-of-factly.

"Uhhhhhhhhh, if I was a vampire I could get all the good-looking women. They love that shit," Tony groaned.

"Fuckstick, you couldn't get a woman right now if you were naked on the side of the street and waving thousand dollar bills," Vick laughed.

"Bite me!" Tony growled.

"Won't do you any good. I'm not a vampire."

"Oh, yeah; that's how it works. I forgot." Tony rolled his head slightly to look at Vic. "How much did I drink last night?" He rolled his forehead back to the countertop. He didn't remember a whole lot after they'd opened the second bottle.

"Let's just put it this way – you're now on every whiskey maker's VIP list." Vic was busy trying to figure out the coffeemaker, punching buttons and getting more frustrated by the second. "Why the hell do you have to have a damn three-hundred-dollar coffeemaker? Why can't you just have a simple fifty dollar coffeemaker so we could have some coffee?"

"I don't know," Tony groaned. "I don't know anything anymore."

"That's sure as shit true. What do you want for breakfast?"

"Sleep. And more sleep. And you?"

"Yeah, sleep. I wish I could just sleep my fucked-up life away," Vic muttered as he won the war against the coffeemaker. "Coffee coming up in ten."

"Thank god. I thought I was gonna have to drink more bourbon and pretend it was coffee." Tony tried to sit up and dropped his head back down again.

"No more liquor for you. We've gotta get our shit together because we've both gotta go back to work tomorrow."

"Okay. Hey, wait; I'm the boss. I don't fucking have to go to work if I don't want to," Tony told the countertop.

"Hell, you know that won't fly, boy." Vic shook his head again. "Shit, you're a lightweight drunk," he chuckled.

Tony ignored his goading. "So, you wanna drink some coffee, take a shower, go get something to eat? We probably should." Tony tried to sit up again and this time he succeeded.

"Hope you've got some good dark sunglasses, 'cause you're gonna need 'em," Vic said.

"Darkest Oakleys they make," Tony told him. "Where's that damn coffee?"

Nikki

August 2006

Folding the basket of laundry seemed too hard. Nikki just pulled her things out and threw them in the suitcase. She took the little bit of clothes still in the closet off the hangers and put them in too. Then she threw the dirty stuff into a garbage bag, squished the bag in, and zipped it all shut.

It was late afternoon after the funerals, and the house was quiet; her mind was anything but. She thought about the dirty dishes and garbage she left behind in the kitchen at home when she took off. Thank goodness she'd remembered to take the dogs to the vet to board them; it was a miracle she hadn't just forgotten and left them in the house alone.

The last three days had been a blur. Dozens of people had shown up for the services, which surprised Nikki to no end. It had only been six months since they'd moved away, but longer for the kids because they'd gone away to college and found jobs elsewhere, and yet many of their former classmates had shown up. Interestingly enough, almost no one had even acknowledged her; it was all about her parents. The house was full of food that she wouldn't eat brought by people she didn't know, mostly her parents' friends from their church. It was all so exhausting. If Randy had been with her it would've been much easier, but of course he couldn't be. She hadn't gotten his ashes back yet, or she might've put them in her suitcase just so she'd feel him close to her.

Worse yet, Nikki had gotten the distinct impression that her mother was gaming for a fight. Barbara had been more condescending than usual, and she'd thrived in the attention she'd gotten from everyone who'd shown up. Occasionally she'd taken a sideways glance at Nikki. That meant something was about to happen, and Nikki was certain it wouldn't be pretty.

A noise at the door made her turn and look and, sure enough, her mother stood there, hands on her hips. "What are you doing?" she asked, and Nikki could tell with only those four words that she should steel herself for battle. And she knew it wouldn't take long for the verbal bullets to start whizzing past her head. Her mother was used to getting her way, and nothing would ever change that. Bucking her meant you'd have hell to pay.

"I'm packing." Nikki thought that was pretty obvious. "I've got to get back home and take care of things."

The corner's of Barbara's mouth twitched, and Nikki could almost swear she saw the beginnings of a sadistic smile. "You are home. You're not going back there."

Nikki stared at her, her brow furrowed. "What do you mean, I'm home and I'm not going back? Murray isn't my home. I live in Louisville."

"Oh, for goodness sake, Nikki, give it up! You don't need to go back there," her mother growled. "Your dad and I have made a decision; we'll clean out the spare room and you can live here."

Nikki's mind reeled. "That's not your decision to make. I live in Louisville," she reiterated. "My house is there. My dogs are there, for god's sake. I'm going home," she said again.

"Oh, Nikki, don't be difficult about this. After all, you don't have anyone there anymore, and we don't have anyone here. You can stay here and take care of us! Wouldn't that be nice, just the three of us? It'll be fun!"

As that scenario played out in her mind, Nikki shuddered. No way was she staying in Murray, taking care of them, being shackled to a life of board games, jigsaw and crossword puzzles, church socials, and the fried seafood buffet at the local family restaurant. If she stayed, her life would be over. Oh, it was pretty much over anyway, but at least at home she'd be near Randy, Jake, and Amanda's things. She'd have peace and quiet to think and to heal. She'd have the dogs; Bill and Hillary were all she had left of her little family, and she was anxious to get back to them. "No, Mom, I'm going back to Louisville."

Barbara's face knotted in anger. "You selfish, ungrateful brat!" she snarled at Nikki. "You think you'll go back and have a happy life, but you'll be miserable. I know – you're probably thinking you'll get a man! Well, they're not going to want you. Look at you – fat, pale, short. You're a terrible cook and a horrible housekeeper. And you've got no personality. What man will want you?"

Don't cry, don't cry, don't cry. Don't let her see you cry. "You know, Mom, I'm sorry that you've always been so jealous of me and my relationship with

Randy. I'm not stupid – I know I'll probably never have that again – but if I stay here, I'll never have a chance at anything, and thanks to you and your mouth, I'll have zero confidence and optimism to boot. So no, I'm not staying here."

Nikki felt something in the air shift as Barbara strode across the room and pointed a finger in Nikki's face. "Let me tell you something, missy!" she screamed. "If you leave, that's it! We'll have nothing more to do with you! Don't bother trying to get in touch, because you'll be dead to us, you hear me?" she continued yelling. "And you can pack your stuff up and get out of here this afternoon, go stay in a motel or something, because you're not welcome here!" She stomped out of the room and slammed the door shut behind her.

Nikki stayed in the bedroom with the door closed for the rest of the day; she wasn't hungry anyway, and the guest room had its own bathroom, so she just hid out and stayed in her pajamas. As she was getting ready for bed, there was a knock at the bedroom door. Before she could answer it, the door opened and two uniformed officers stood in the doorway. "Mrs. Wilkes?" one of them asked.

"Yes?" she answered, confused. There was no one else for her to lose, so why were they there?

"We got a call that you were asked to leave this property and refused. Is there a problem?"

Nikki sighed and shook her head. "No, no problem, sir. Let me get dressed and I'll leave. My mother's just . . ."

"Yes ma'am, I don't know the exact dynamics, but this is their home and you need to honor their wishes."

"Again, no problem. I'll be gone in a few minutes. You're welcome to stay and watch me leave if you'd like. But I need to get dressed."

"Not necessary, ma'am." He turned and looked over his shoulder up the hallway. "And, by the way, I'm very, very sorry for your loss," he almost whispered. He looked at the other officer out in the hall, then turned back to Nikki and very quietly said, "And I'm so sorry we had to do this. This is very mean-spirited of your parents, but we're bound by law, you know? So I apologize. Is there anything we can do for you? Help you in any way?" He looked sincerely regretful, and the other officer nodded his agreement.

"No, thanks." Nikki gave them a weak smile. "But I appreciate it. Don't worry about me – I'll be fine as soon as I get back home to Louisville."

"Well, you be careful and safe, ma'am. Again, our sympathy for your loss." He closed the door, and Nikki heard low voices in the front of the house before the front door opened and closed as they left.

Nikki put on her clothes, gathered up her luggage, and made her way up the hall to the front door. She took one last look at the couple sitting in the living room in front of the TV, doing an exceptional job of ignoring her, and wished things could be different. *I need you, your love, so much right now. Couldn't the two of you just love me a little bit, just for a little while?* But no; it was all about them, always had been, so Nikki already knew the answer.

The wheels on the luggage clunked down the sidewalk and she loaded the bags into her car, then pulled away from the curb. Instead of going to a motel, she just got on the road and started driving toward Louisville. There was no reason not to; if she didn't make it, no one would care. The vet would find homes for the dogs, and she'd be free of the pain she knew she'd feel all day, every day, for years to come.

Christmas 2011

In a small house in the Middletown township of Louisville, she finished her leftovers and put the paper plate in the trash. The two little dogs, roused out of their sleep by her movements, followed her from spot to spot, hoping for something to fall from the counter.

The little Christmas tree – she still called it Christmas, even if she celebrated Yule instead of the Christian holiday – was lit and standing by the television. She couldn't bring herself to turn on the TV because she didn't want to see any of the Christmas specials or old movies. Instead, she picked up the few wrapped packages and called the dogs up onto the sofa with her.

"Look! This one is from Dr. Kincaid! What could it be?" she cried in mock excitement. She ripped the paper off as they watched, tails wagging. Gourmet dog cookies; Dr. Kincaid gave tins of those to his clients every year. They went wild until she gave each of them a cookie, then they jumped from the sofa and ran to opposite sides of the room, probably each thinking that would keep the other from stealing their treat.

She opened another small package, this one from her boss, Marla. Inside was a pair of pretty gold earrings and a gift card for the café next door to her work. At least she'd have lunch a couple of times a week for awhile. There was a card from her coworker, Carol, and it had a gift certificate to the nail salon she frequented – that meant she'd get a break on a few of her nail fills.

That was the one thing she'd been able to keep up – having her nails done – since Randy had died, and knowing that she'd at least have that little luxury had kept her going when she would've quit her life otherwise. She hadn't been able to get Marla or Carol anything but cards, couldn't afford to. The only other package had no tag because she'd wrapped it for herself. It was the sweater she'd seen for months in the window at Accoutrements, the consignment store down the street from work. She'd finally talked herself into buying it, then decided to save it for Christmas. It was the nicest thing she owned, so she gifted it to herself.

And with that, Christmas was officially over. No more gifts to unwrap. No family to visit, or have visit her, or even send anything to or get anything from. Against her better judgment, she decided she'd make an attempt and pulled out her cell phone, then dialed the number from memory.

It rang three times, and her mother answered. "Hello?"

"Hi, Mom? It's me."

She heard her dad's voice in the background: "Who is it?"

Her mom answered him. "It's no one." The line went dead.

Well, she'd tried. Even though it was painful, she was pretty sure she'd try again on their birthdays, Mother's Day, Father's Day, and even next Christmas, and probably with the same result.

She went into the kitchen and made herself a cup of hot chocolate. Cuddling back into the sofa, she picked up her old electronic tablet, the one Randy had given her for her birthday years before, and tried to read but couldn't concentrate. In the photo app she looked through the images, bright on the screen. A smiling, happy family looked back at her, and in some of the pictures, she saw her own face, slightly younger and with fewer lines, not to mention lots of extra pounds. It was hard to believe they'd been real; they seemed like a sweet dream instead of the living, breathing people they'd been. But they were gone and she was alone, and likely to stay that way.

A lone tear meandered down her cheek and dripped off her jaw. That was the trouble with grief; there was no instruction manual, no expiration date. She didn't know how long it was supposed to take. When would it be over? Would that day ever come? Even if there was an end, she wasn't certain that she'd live to see it.

She sipped her hot chocolate until it was cold and not very tasty anymore. After she unplugged the small tree, she let the dogs out one last time and changed into her pajamas. A driving snow had started, and the light from the porch reflected on the large, fluffy flakes. It would be pretty in the morning. After the dogs came inside, she turned off the light and locked the door.

Climbing into the empty bed, she pulled the flannel sheets up around her neck. One dog lay next to her, the other at her feet. They were her only family now, and she was glad they were there, but they couldn't tell her that they loved her, or if she looked okay when she got ready to leave for work in the morning, or discuss their opinions on the latest movie they'd shared with her on the sofa. Even with them, she was still so terribly, horribly alone. Just someone to eat dinner with, or to talk to while she was shopping at the grocery, anything or anywhere, really – that was all she wanted, but that part of her life was over. She'd spent thirty years with the love of her life, so expecting to find someone else, especially without making any effort to do so, was asking a little too much. She had her work at the shop, and her books, and the gym. Working out made her feel good about herself, so she just poured any energy she managed to squeeze out into getting fit and feeling better. It would be nice to say the exercise made her feel less depressed, but nothing could do that.

Snuggling down under the comforter and sheets, she tried to think of other things, but kept coming back to those faces. Just when she thought she'd cried so much that she had no tears left, her pillow wound up soaked. She cried until she couldn't cry anymore, and then cried for ten more minutes.

Turning on the light, she grabbed a handful of tissues and blew her nose, then turned the light back off and switched to the dry pillow on the other side of the bed. A weariness spread over her, born of the simple act of continuing on. She thought about lighting her Candle of Intention, but it seemed like too much work, so she shuddered and closed her eyes. As she did every night before she finally drifted off, she asked the God, the Goddess, the Universe, whoever was listening, to please let her just stop breathing in the night. It was simple; just let her heart stop beating. Why not? Her life was pretty well destroyed anyway. Continuing on was too hard. After she'd pleaded for fifteen minutes, she sighed deeply and fell into a restless sleep. She'd sleep all night that way and wake up in the morning as tired as the night before. There was no real rest for her, because there was no escape from the thoughts that drained her, and no one to hold her when she cried.

Vic

September 1974

"*Nipote*, would you like to tell me what happened?" Zio Marco was standing over Vic, and he was furious.

"They called me a dago, so I kicked their asses."

Marco shook his head. "Vittorio, you cannot just go about beating other boys when they call you names. I fear I will not be able to keep you out of the hands of the law if this continues. School has just started for the year, and already you are in trouble? This cannot continue."

Vic hated to see Zio Marco disappointed in him. Zio Marco and Zia Raffaella had been more than kind to him and to his mother, Raffaella's sister Serafina, since they'd run from Italy to his aunt and uncle's home in Kentucky to get away from Vic's father, leaving behind everything they had. The things that man had done were horrible, and Vic had sworn to himself that he'd never be beaten, abused, or mistreated by anyone again.

"But they came at me with a baseball bat, Zio Marco! What was I supposed to do, just let them knock me senseless?" Vic asked.

Marco sat on the side of the bed and put his face in his hands. "I do not know, *nipote*. I just know that this must stop. You have to finish high school so you can go to college."

"Oh, I don't want to go to college," Vic announced, and Marco stared at him, horrified. "I want to join the service."

"Well, *nipote*, the service will not take you if you have a juvenile record. So think about that, young man." Marco got up and walked out of the room, closing the door behind him.

What the hell am I supposed to do?, Vic wondered. *All of the kids at school hate me. I have no friends, no dad, no girlfriend.* In his mind, Vic had no one. He and Bennie were the same age, but Bennie wouldn't have anything to do with him. Bennie was a Walters, and even though Vic had lived in the lap of luxury growing up in Italy, to the Walters boys, Vic was a poor relation. Freddie was only a little older, but he didn't really have anything to do with Vic either. Tony had always been nice to him, but Tony wasn't around; he was in college in Lexington and besides, he was older too.

On top of that, none of the Walters kids had gone to American public high schools; they'd spent their high school years in Italy, living with relatives and learning about their heritage. Vic had never gone to a public school – his years in Italy had been spent in expensive private schools, so an American public high school was like a whole different universe to him. And as if it wasn't bad enough already, Vic had graduated from secondary school at the age of twelve. The last thing he wanted to do was go to school and sit, bored, all day long for no good reason. The only class he even remotely liked was civics; he enjoyed learning more about the United States.

Zio Marco didn't understand what it was like, being dropped into a strange, new world. He'd worked hard to get rid of his accent, but it still crept out from time to time, so he just tried to be quiet and not really talk to anyone. And being so tall made it impossible to blend into the crowd. He was sure he was a pretty good guy and he'd had lots of friends in Italy, but none of the kids would even give him a chance. *I've tried staying to myself, ignoring those people, but they just won't leave me alone. I hate that school. Maybe I should just run away.* It didn't help that he was easily the best-looking young man in the whole school. That only made the other guys hate him even more.

At school the next day, Vic was trying his best to lay low and stay below the radar when Mr. Barnes, the physics teacher who coached the wrestling team, walked up to him and asked, "Vic, can I talk to you for a minute?" He headed to his classroom and Vic followed, wondering what he'd done this time.

Mr. Barnes sat down behind his desk and motioned for Vic to sit. "I wanted to talk to you," he said once they were both seated. "You're a big guy."

"Yeah. I guess I am." He was only fifteen, sixteen in October, and already he was at least six feet and three inches tall.

"Have you ever thought of trying out for the wrestling and the weightlifting teams? I think you'd be pretty good." He smiled at Vic.

"How do I do that?" He'd never tried out for anything in his life. Any kind of sports would have been out of the question for him in Italy – he was supposed to look good and be a politician's son, not an athlete.

"They're holding tryouts tomorrow. Would you like to sign up?"

Vic thought for a minute. Yeah, what the hell? Worst thing that can happen is that I don't make it. "I guess so," he told Mr. Barnes with a shrug.

"The signup sheets are in the office. Just go and ask Mrs. Connors to let you sign them. And good luck." Mr. Barnes stood and when Vic stood, Mr. Barnes shook his hand. It was the nicest anyone at the school had ever been to him.

Vic went straight to the office and asked Mrs. Connors, the school secretary, for the signup sheets. He put his name on both the wrestling team sheet and the weightlifting team sheet. He took a minute to look at the football team signup sheet, then thought better of it. *I don't really understand American football that well. And I'd rather do something where I rely only on myself, not teammates. No one's ever had my back.*

Vic had never wrestled before, so he watched a couple of the other guys at the tryouts the next day. *I can do this*, he thought. *It doesn't look so hard.* When it was his turn, they paired him with the biggest guy on the team. *They're trying to get rid of me*, he thought as he faced the other young man. Something clicked inside him, and when the whistle blew, it took Vic a whole three seconds to solidly pin the guy to the mat. There were gasps and murmurs from the bench. They paired him with another big guy, with the same results. He went through almost every guy on the team, and quickly and efficiently laid them to waste, one by one.

After the tryouts, Mr. Barnes came up to him and said, "Well done, Vic! Did you by any chance sign up for the weightlifting tryouts too?"

"Yes, actually, I did."

"Good. Coach Murdock will love getting hold of you."

By the end of the day, Vittorio Vincenzo Cabrizzi was a starter for both the wrestling and weightlifting teams. He finally belonged somewhere.

July 2009

"Vittorio Cabrizzi?" The police officer stood on Vic's doorstep, another officer standing behind him. They had to look up at the huge Italian; he dwarfed them with his six feet and eight inch frame.

Vic felt sick to his stomach. "Yes, that's me. Can I help you, officer?"

"Yes sir. We got a call from the hospital about some injuries sustained by a Carrie Johnson? They said you were with her. Could we come in and ask you a few questions?"

"Sure. Please come on in and have a seat." *Oh, great — I'm fucked*, Vic thought as he led them into the living room.

"So, Mr. Cabrizzi, the hospital told us that the patient said she'd sustained the injuries during, um, relations, is that right?" the officer asked, trying to be matter-of-fact but still blushing a little.

"Yes sir, that's right."

"And so this was an accident? Because the physician didn't think it looked like an accident. They said it looked like an assault."

Uh-huh, Vic thought, *one look at my height and these muscles and they just assume I beat up on women. This could be really, really bad.* "It was an accident. We just got a little carried away, that's all. Carrie talked to them about it and told them that we . . ."

"Speaking of whom, is Miss Johnson here? Could we talk with her?" the officer asked.

"Yeah. Let me get her." *Damn, this just keeps getting worse*, Vic thought as he made his way to the bedroom.

Carrie was standing by the bed, slowly packing boxes, and the sight broke his heart. Her face was flooded with tears when she turned to look at him. "What?" she asked.

"The police are here. They want to talk to you." Vic's head dropped. "Carrie, you don't have to say anything for my benefit. Tell them whatever you like."

She walked past him and headed to the living room without saying a word. Vic followed her, but the officer looked at him and simply said, "Alone," so he went back to the bedroom and sat on the side of the bed. After about ten minutes, he heard a male voice say, "Well, thank you, miss, and if you need us, please call us."

In a few seconds, Carrie came back into the bedroom. She started packing again, then looked over at Vic, who sat with his head down. "Don't worry. I told them the truth, the same thing I told the people at the hospital. I don't think they'll bother you again. It's not like I want to get you into trouble, Vic."

Vic felt his eyes burning as the tears welled up. "You didn't have to do that, but thanks." He reached over and put his hand on her arm, but she pulled away. "Carrie, I'm so sorry. I just, I don't know what to say because I really don't know what happened. If I could've stopped, I would've, but I couldn't. It was like something just clicked inside me and I lost control and I, I don't know . . ." His voice broke, and he buried his face in his hands.

Carrie sat down on the bed beside him, but she didn't touch him. "Vic, I don't know what to say either. You're a great guy, really, you are. You've treated me like a queen. I'm not in love with you, but I care about you, and I was committed to staying with you, trying to see where this thing between us was going, you know? But now I'm afraid. This is the third time this has happened, and every time has been worse than the one before. And I can't take a chance on it happening again. Next time you could do damage that couldn't be repaired and the injuries could be permanent. That really scares me, because some day I want a family, so I can't take that chance. That means I've got to go. I'm sorry." Still not touching him, she stood and started packing again.

Vic got up and walked out of the room, through the kitchen, out the back door, and sat down on the steps. The moon was bright, and there were so many stars that it looked like the sky would explode with them. *This is it for me*, he thought. *I'm done. I'm going to hurt some poor woman. That can't happen again. Next one might be more than just some stitches; it could be much worse. So that part of my life is over.*

"I'm going," he heard Carrie say from behind him. He turned and looked at her in the doorway. She looked so beautiful there, the lights from the kitchen illuminating her curly red hair, and a deep ache set up in his chest.

She walked up the hallway to the front door, and he followed her, wishing he could come up with something, some reassurance, that would get her to stay. But if he did he wouldn't even believe it himself, because he couldn't guarantee it wouldn't happen again, since he didn't know why or how it happened in the first place. When she stopped at the door, she looked at him with such sadness that his heart broke all over again. He reached to hug her; for a moment, she pulled away, then she stood on her tiptoes, leaned toward him, and wrapped her arms around his neck. His arms closed around her waist, and as she began to sob into his neck, hot, sour tears poured down Vic's face and fell into her hair. They stood like that for several minutes until she finally pulled away and walked out the door without looking back. Vic watched her car roll down the street until the taillights disappeared.

And once again, like always, he was alone.

Laura

January 1996

"So, what did you get?"

Laura opened the package. Even though Christmas was officially over, it had taken a good while for the boxes to reach Bosnia, military mail being notoriously unreliable. Inside the package were socks, her favorite shampoo, and three sticks of her favorite deodorant, along with some feminine products. They'd also tucked four letters in with the personal items; there was one each from her mom, dad, brother, and Charles. "Did you get a box?" she asked Brian.

"Yeah, my mom sent it. A couple of books and some of her peanut butter cookies. Want one?" He held the tin out to Laura.

"Oh no, you save those for yourself," she said, packing away all of the things she'd received.

"You going to the card game tonight?" It was one of the few forms of entertainment they had.

Laura shook her head. "Nah. I think I'll just sit in my bunk and read. Hey, can I borrow one of your new books?"

"Sure!" Brian fished them out. "This one is probably a murder mystery," he offered, holding one out. It had a picture of a knife with a drop of blood on the tip in full color on the cover. "Wanna try it on for size?"

"Yeah, I like that kind of stuff. Thanks." Laura put the book under her pillow and got busy.

Being the only woman anywhere near the location was a challenge. She'd had to learn creative ways to shower and take care of her personal needs because the guys had flatly refused to make allowances for her or show her any courtesy. It was obvious they resented her being there, but they sure didn't want to do her job. The job of a U.S. Navy Explosive Ordnance Disposal Specialist was something most service people wouldn't even consider, but Laura had always wanted to be an EOD specialist. She'd gotten interested in explosives when her dad's department had gotten themselves a bomb squad. The counties around theirs had all pooled their money to start the unit. Since their county was centrally located, they chose her dad's department to house it, and with him being the sheriff of their county, she'd been able to see up close and first-hand how the bomb squad worked.

When she graduated from high school, she hadn't been interested in college; she went straight into the Navy to train as an EOD Specialist. It had been hard; the men didn't want her there. They had no choice but to allow her to do her job, but they didn't have to accept her. In fact, they made her day-to-day life hell, but she was tough and managed anyway. Then she'd been deployed to Bosnia. It was her dream come true, if she could just hang on.

She spent the afternoon checking in equipment for one of the infantry divisions, then went to the mess hall and ate what only passed for food. Dinner was meatloaf and mashed potatoes, which looked and tasted suspiciously like the chicken fried steak and mac and cheese they'd had the night before. After dinner, she showered and climbed into her bunk to read the book Brian had loaned her. It was kind of nice to have her own sleeping quarters; she loved the privacy after being around the men all day.

She could hear the music from the big hall down the way – the poker games were in full swing. Then she heard something else, something closer and quieter, but still audible. She turned on her battery-powered ceiling light and called out, "Hello?"

Her door opened and Brewster, a private she recognized from one of the infantry divisions, came into her quarters.

"Hey, Brewster! Can I help you with something?" Laura asked him.

"I dunno – maybe." Brewster walked closer to her. As he crossed the room, the door opened again and two more men walked in. She'd seen them around, but she didn't know their names. After they'd made it through the door, two more men walked in, two she'd never seen before but also probably from an infantry division. "What are you reading?" He reached over and took the book.

"I borrowed it from Brian." Something felt wrong, and she started to get nervous. "I think you need to leave. You really shouldn't be here," she said forcefully, hoping they'd just go.

"The lady thinks we need to leave," she heard a voice say and, through the group of five men, a sixth man walked in and right up to her. Her heart froze.

Sergeant Wagner stood in the front of the group, a menacing grin on his face. "But we don't want to leave, EOD Specialist Billings. We'd like to have a party, but we don't have any girls to dance with. Do you like to dance?" he asked her, leering.

"Please leave. I really don't want any of you here." She tried to sound brave even though she was terrified.

"She doesn't want us here, guys. What do you think of that?" Wagner asked.

"I think we should make her glad we came," one of the men said.

Wagner walked right up to Laura and grabbed her arm – hard. "I think you're right, Taylor. I think she'll be glad by the time we're finished." With that, Wagner pushed Laura back onto her bunk and told two of the men, "Hold her arms. I'm first!"

Laura started to struggle and tried to scream, but one of the men put his hand over her mouth while Wagner fished around under her bed, found a pair of her underwear, and stuffed them in her mouth. He pushed her tank up until her breasts were exposed, and squeezed both of them hard. Some of the men laughed. After he'd stripped her underwear off, he told two more of the guys, "Hold her ankles. I don't want to get kicked by our mule!" He opened his fly, pulled out his penis, and growled, "Now I'll teach you to dance, Billings!"

Laura struggled, but the men held her firm. The two holding her ankles walked outward and spread her legs as wide as they could, and Wagner drove himself into her. She tried to scream, but she could barely breathe, and the panties muffled any sound she made. *Oh, god, please, Brian, come back to check on me!* Wagner continued to pound into her, and the pain was excruciating.

When he was finally finished, he said, "Here, Brewster. Give me that arm and you take your turn!" The men swapped places, and Brewster freed his penis and pounded into her just as Wagner had. Laura's mind spun out of control, and the pain was so unbearable she hoped she'd lose consciousness. Just as she thought she might actually go out, Brewster finished and swapped out with Taylor, and the process continued.

Laura could hear them laughing, making comments about how tight she was, how her breasts looked, how good it felt to take her, but she felt like she was somewhere else, hearing them from a distance. She felt the pain, but it was dulled somehow, and she felt her body being bumped up and down by their activity. It seemed to go on forever, days and days, and she just floated, feeling completely disconnected from what they were doing to her body.

When they'd all had a turn, Wagner started in on her again, and she wondered if he'd ever finish. Just as she thought he might be done, he did something she never expected: He started to stroke her clitoris, trying to make her have an orgasm. Even though she didn't want to, her body responded, and her hips started to buck of their own accord. She hadn't felt shame until that moment, but suddenly she felt as though she was an accomplice in her own rape, somehow responsible for it. Charles had been the only man who'd ever done that with her, and when her body convulsed and the orgasm hit, it felt like Charles and all the love and tenderness he'd ever given her had been ripped from her.

"See? You liked it, slut!" Wagner snarled, continuing to rub her until the spasms were unendurable. "Now, you listen to me and listen good. You tell anyone, anyone, what just happened here and you'll die. You hear me? You'll be dead before your tongue can wag." He pulled the underwear from her mouth and asked, "You gonna scream?" Laura was too afraid and too exhausted to make a sound. "That's what I thought — liked it too much to tell, didn't you? Hey, maybe we'll be back!" He turned to the other men. "You can turn her loose now. She's not gonna do anything, are you, cunt? Let's go play some poker!" They started out the door, but before they left, one of the men pinched one of Laura's nipples hard and said, "Nice lay, bitch. Nail ya later!" Another slapped her mound and said, "Can't wait to fuck you again, sweetheart." They left her quarters like a bunch of friends walking out of the local bar after a night of playing darts.

Laura lay on her bunk, afraid to move, wondering what she'd find when she looked down at herself. She expected to somehow look damaged and wounded, but when she finally worked up the courage to look, she found she looked pretty much normal, except there was blood on the insides of her thighs. When she finally stood, a tiny trickle of blood made its way down the inside of one thigh. She grabbed her robe and headed to the showers.

There wasn't enough soap made to wash them off of her, but she tried — god, she tried. While she was in the shower, she ran her fingers up inside herself and the pain was so bad that she couldn't stand it. She didn't know what to do. If she went to the medics, they'd ask her what had happened. What would she tell them? No way could she tell them the truth. Wagner would kill her.

By the time she left the shower, she'd devised a plan. She went to the medics' tent and told them that a Bosnian national had somehow gotten into the compound and assaulted her. Dismay mingled with relief as they took the report but didn't really seem too interested, as though it happened all the time and they were powerless to do anything about it. They decided she needed some stitches, then gave her some antibiotics to take and sent her back to her bunk. No psychologist. No chaplain. No concern. Nothing.

When she got back to her bunk, Laura wanted to cry, but she couldn't. She tried, but nothing happened. A numbness set in, and she lay in her bunk and tried to sleep, but that didn't happen either. Instead, she lay there awake all night, and all the nights to follow.

February 1996

"EOD Specialist Billings? Can you hear me? EOD Specialist Billings?" Laura tried to make sense of what was going on around her, but she couldn't. She was cold, really cold, and everything was white. Her head was buzzing, and she couldn't figure out where the sound was coming from.

"She's going into shock," she heard a voice floating somewhere above her say. Then everything got dark.

When she finally woke again, her ears were assaulted by a sound that was so loud it was painful. What had happened to her? Why did she hurt everywhere?

An air medic looked down into her face and saw her open eyes. "EOD Specialist Billings! Hold tight! We'll be off the ground in a few minutes! Are you in any pain?" he yelled over the sound of the helicopter's rotors.

"Wha . . . wha . . ." Laura mumbled, but she couldn't make her mouth form the words.

"We're flying you out now," he yelled. "Do you remember what happened? The ordnance exploded. Remember?" No, Laura didn't remember. She had no idea what had happened.

"We'll be off the ground in about thirty seconds, but you'll be fine — eventually." She heard squawking over his helmet headset, then he said, "Someone wants to see you before we take off. It'll be just a minute."

She tried to remember what had taken place, but everything was fuzzy. Then she remembered the sound — like a cannon going off. There was the sensation of flying, and nothing else. She blinked to clear the blurriness in her eyes, and she heard something, someone, nearby.

Sergeant Wagner looked down into her face. "Well, well, well, EOD Specialist Billings! How are you? You gave us quite a scare!" His voice was sympathetic, but there was something in his eyes that scared the shit out of her. "That was some bomb, huh? It threw you fifty feet! I guess you're kinda sore, huh?" he yelled above the rotor noise, then added, "If you know what I mean."

She knew exactly what he meant. Bastard. Why was he there rubbing it in? It was bad enough that she'd had the accident. Why did he have to come there and make everything worse, remind her what they'd done to her the month before?

"You know, that blast would've killed most people," he yelled. "No one knows how you managed to live through it. Guess you were just lucky." He looked down at her, got close to her face, and spoke low so the medic couldn't hear him. "You won't be so lucky next time. I don't make the same mistake twice." With that, he disappeared from her vision, but she heard him say, "Get well, Billings. The guys are counting on you." Then she felt the chopper wobble as it lifted off.

Laura's heart almost stopped. Wagner had tried to kill her. She didn't know if he'd messed with her body armor or the explosive device, or exactly what he'd done, but he'd done it, practically confessed to it. And there wasn't one damn thing she could do about it.

She tried to quiet her mind, but she was just too scared, and there was no one she could tell. And if she did tell someone, their life would be in danger too. She was starting to feel panicky when the medic broke into her thoughts.

"Billings, you're one lucky young woman, but your injuries are still very extensive. We're taking you to a field hospital, then stateside, and I don't think you'll be seeing any more active duty."

"When are you sending me?" Laura asked. *Oh, please, let it be soon!*, she thought. *Getting out of here is the only thing that will save me.*

"You'll go to the field hospital today and be shipped out tomorrow. In the meantime, try to rest. The trip will be rigorous enough, and pretty painful for you. But you'll be back in the states – we're sending you to the naval hospital in Jacksonville, Florida. They'll take good care of you. Best of luck, Billings." With that, the medic went back to monitoring her vitals, leaving her with more questions than answers, and no energy to ask.

Laura tried to get her wits together and look herself over, but the only thing she could see was a huge bandage all over the front of her torso. It looked almost like a sheet of bandaging, cut to fit her shape. She didn't know what was under that bandage, but she was sure she'd find out eventually.

March 2010

"Laura Butler?" Laura rose from her seat and strode across the room toward the man, then followed him to an office down the hall. He pointed to a chair and said, "Have a seat, please."

"Thank you for calling me for this interview, Mr. Ludlow." Laura straightened her skirt. "I've been wanting to get into the field for awhile. I did very well in the training program and I've been hoping you'd find an opening for me somewhere, something that's a good fit." She'd passed all of the courses with flying colors and gotten all of her arms certifications. Security work was something she thought she'd like. She'd been looking for a position for too long and was getting really tired of working in the bar at a restaurant. It had been years since she'd had a job where she carried a gun, and she was ready.

"I have to say, Miss Butler, your CV is very impressive," the placement counselor told her. "I think we've found a place for you. We got a call from someone who's looking to put together a team of security specialists, and he called us looking for candidates. How do you feel about relocating?"

"That would be no problem, sir. I've got no real ties to this area." After she'd recovered, or at least recovered physically, she'd lived in a half-dozen places, with the most recent being St. Louis. She just kept moving around, and she'd taken her mother's family name, Butler, so it would be harder for Wagner to track her down. "So where would this move be?"

"To Louisville, Kentucky." Laura almost gasped – her hometown was less than thirty minutes away. "Oddly, one of the reasons the gentleman pulled your information and called us was because he's originally from southeastern Missouri, and with you being in St. Louis, he felt you might be a good fit, might be more on the same page with him. Are you interested?"

If Wagner knew she'd grown up in the Louisville area, he might look for her there. Or maybe he'd think that was the last place she'd go because it would be too obvious. She felt like she was pondering iocaine powder in the movie *The Princess Bride*. This move would put her closer to her family; that would be nice. Maybe she could pull herself together enough that they'd want to be around her. "Does he want to interview me too? Because I could go there."

"No. Oddly enough, he said if I found someone suitable that I was to just send you there and he'd hire you on the spot. I'll give you his contact information if you want the job."

"Yes sir!" Laura almost shouted. Mr. Ludlow handed her a sheet with the information. On it was the name *Steve McCoy* – her new boss. "Thank you. I'll call him as soon as I get home."

Steve

April 1975

In the waiting room of a community hospital in Sikeston, Missouri, the tall, lanky teenage boy sat alone, his hands shaking. "Steve?" When the nurse called his name, he rocketed up out of the chair and hurried toward her.

"Now, honey, she won't be with us long, but you can hold her and talk to her until she goes. I know this is hard, but the doctor said you told him that you wanted to do it, so just be brave, okay?"

She took him into the hospital room and pointed to a chair. "Just have a seat right there. Vanessa, honey, Steve is here. I'll be right back with her. Just sit tight." She turned and shuffled out of the room.

Steve looked around. Plain white walls, plain white floors, plain green curtains. Vanessa lay in the hospital bed with her face turned away from him.

He moved to the side of the bed and began stroking her hair. "Hi." She didn't turn to look at him or say anything. "How are you feeling?"

"How do you think I feel?" the girl spat at him. "I'm fifteen, I've just had a baby, and the baby is dying! So how do you think I feel?" she snarled. He reached up again to stroke her hair, but she slapped his hand away. "Don't touch me! My life is ruined! My mom and dad are making me move away, and no guy will ever want me again."

Steve didn't know what to say to make things better, so he sat back down in the chair and waited. In a couple of minutes, the nurse came in with a bundle. "Here you go, honey. Just talk to her and hold her. And call me if you need me." She handed him the bundle, then pulled the call button from the bed over to his chair and left the room again.

Steve opened the blanket and looked in. There, in the folds of the blanket, was a baby – his baby. He knew what they'd told him, that her brain was so underdeveloped that it couldn't make her heart work and she only had a few hours, but she looked perfect. Reaching in with his free hand, he drew his finger under her tiny palm but, unlike most babies, she didn't grasp it. She just lay there, still and quiet, barely breathing. He noticed that she felt cooler than he'd thought she would.

Standing, he crossed the room back to the bed. "Vanessa, do you want to hold her? We've only got her for a little while. Don't you want to see her and talk to her?"

She sat up in the bed, her face a mask of pain. "No! I do not want to hold or talk to that thing! Take it away!" Plopping back down in the bed, she sobbed quietly. Still not knowing what to do, he went back to the chair with his dying daughter.

"I know what they're telling us, but I don't care. Your name is Sarah and I love you." He kissed the small, soft cheek. "I may only be sixteen, but I really do love you and your mommy, and I would've been a really great daddy to you." Steve spent the next two hours telling the pale, still child about all of the things he'd planned to do with her, like taking her fishing and shopping, about the birthday parties she would've had and the pretty dresses he would've bought her. The chair wasn't a rocking chair, so he just rocked forwards and back, holding her and staring down into her face.

Too soon the nurse came back into the room. She pulled the blanket open farther and put a stethoscope against the fragile-looking chest, then moved it around and around, listening carefully, then gave her head a sad shake. "She's gone, honey. I need to take her now. Do you have a preference for arrangements?"

"Arrangements?" he asked, confused.

"You know, a funeral or something?"

"I don't have any money for that. What do I do?" he asked the nurse, trying hard not to cry.

"Well, the county will bury her for free. She won't have a stone or anything, and it'll be in the pauper's cemetery, but at least you'll know where she is. Do you want us to put that on the forms?"

"Yes, please," he told her as she took the bundle from him.

He stopped her just before she made it out the door, and pulled the blanket open one more time, then leaned in and laid a gentle kiss on the tiny, cold forehead. "Bye-bye, sweetheart. Daddy loves you." The nurse sniffled and pulled the blanket closed, and she was gone.

June 1991

We're sorry, but you do not fit our needs at this time. However, we'll keep your application on file in our office in the event that we have a position more suited to your skillset at a later date.

Another one. Steve was running out of options. All the years he'd worked to put himself through college and law school, all the studying, all the letters he'd sent out, and not one bite. Worse yet, he was going to have to tell Sherry that he'd been turned down again, and that wasn't going to go over well. He'd held the envelope until he got to work, hoping against hope that it was good news. Tearing it in half, he threw it in the trash.

He rifled through his pockets; thirty-five cents. Maybe he could find a cheap cup of coffee somewhere for lunch. His clerk's position at the St. Louis County courthouse didn't pay squat, and he was getting desperate. The phone rang and he picked it up. "Clerk's office, Steve speaking."

"Steve," he heard Sherry say, "can you talk?"

"Not really. Can it wait?"

"Steve, damn it, it's waited for two weeks. We've got to talk. What about tonight?"

There weren't any more excuses; he'd run out. "Okay. Seven? I can be home by then."

"Okay. Don't flake out on me, Steve. This is important."

"Okay, okay. See you then." He slammed down the phone, and Phyllis, the woman who worked at the next desk, turned and stared at him.

"Damn telemarketers," he said to her with a small smile. He headed out to find that coffee and didn't come back for an hour and a half.

After work, he piddled around until he ran out of places to piddle and went home about six thirty. Sherry was already there, and she'd cooked something – her dishes were always unidentifiable. Steve threw down his briefcase and looked at her. "What's so important?"

"What's so important is that we're married and we haven't had a conversation in six weeks, that's what." While she talked, she spooned something out of the pan and onto two plates.

All she does is yell at me when we're together, he thought. *No wonder we don't talk.* "So what are we talking about?"

"Did you hear from the firms?" She picked at whatever she'd put on their plates, then took a bite. Even though she'd cooked it, he could tell she didn't like it.

He couldn't find a way to keep the information from her anymore. "Yeah, I heard from them. Got turned down by every one of them." He picked at the food, then tried it. Yeah, inedible.

"God, Steve, every one of them?" she shrieked at him. "You've got to find a firm, and pretty soon. I'm not going to wait forever."

"Wait for what?"

She hesitated for a second, then blurted out, "Wait for you to be successful!" There – she'd said it, what she really meant. Steve felt his face start to burn, and down deep a sort of fury started to brew.

"Wait for me to be successful?" he growled. "Wait for me to be successful? You know, you harp at me every waking minute. It's a miracle I can even hold the job I have!"

"Every waking minute? I never see you! When you're not at work, you're at some bar, or doing something with your friends, or just generally staying away, and I'm sick of it. Are we married or not?" she asked, standing, her hands on her hips.

"It doesn't feel like a marriage. It feels like a death sentence," Steve muttered, throwing the plate into the sink.

"Really? Well, let me tell you, it isn't a marriage as far as I'm concerned. I'm gonna lay it all out, Steve." Sherry took a deep breath. "Here goes: I'm involved with someone else. We've been seeing each other for six months. But you were too busy staying away from me to notice. And yes, we're sleeping together."

Steve felt his insides go cold. "Is this someone I know?"

"None of your business," she told him, throwing her plate into the sink too.

"Oh, really? I told you I wanted to start having kids a year ago, but you haven't seemed to be the least bit interested in starting a family! Do you even care about that?" Steve yelled.

"We can't have kids when you don't have a decent job!" Sherry yelled back.

"We have enough. If I got a good job with a good firm tomorrow, how long would it be until you thought we had enough to have a kid? Two years? Five years? Fifteen years? You just don't want kids – admit it!" Steve was getting really pissed.

Then Sherry dropped the bomb: "Steve, I was pregnant. I had an abortion eight months ago. I can't have kids with you, and I certainly don't want to be married to you anymore. I'm filing tomorrow – I've had enough."

Steve didn't hear anything about not being married anymore or about filing. His comprehension of what she was saying ended when she said the word "abortion." All the years he'd wanted a child, and she'd done this? It wasn't what she'd done; if ever anyone believed a woman had the right to control her own body, it was Steve McCoy. No, it was that she hadn't even told him, hadn't consulted him, hadn't given him a choice, knowing how important it was to him. He felt something deep inside him shutting down, and his face went completely blank. "Go!" she muttered. "Get the hell out. I don't care anymore. It's over." He grabbed his jacket and stormed out the door, slamming it behind him as he went.

By nine, he was so wasted that he couldn't sit on the bar stool, so Sammy, the bartender, moved him into a booth. He tried to make sense of what had happened, but he couldn't. It hurt so much that there was no point. All he wanted to do was numb the pain, but it had been with him for so long that it seemed more like an old friend. It had become the center of his life.

All he'd wanted was a family, a family with a mom who didn't have fifteen boyfriends, a dad who didn't hit anyone, and happy, pretty children. All he'd gotten was rejection and pain. The last person who'd loved Steve was Sarah, a long-gone baby who hadn't even known he existed. It was over forever, and he wouldn't try again.

A cute girl came over and sat in the booth with him, but he didn't really talk to her. She wanted someone to sleep with, and when she left, she took him home with her. He fucked her for four hours, ignoring her requests to satisfy her, just doing what pleased him, and then got dressed and left, with her cursing him as he went. That's how he'd operate from then on, he decided – fuck 'em and forget 'em. It would work better than being hurt over and over.

"McCoy? Steve McCoy?" Two nights into his bender, Steve sat on the curb, too drunk to stand. Who was talking to him? He tried to look up, but the street light above the figure backlit it and made it look totally black.

"Yeah, I'm McCoy. Whaddya want?" he slurred.

"I need to talk to you. Let's get you sobered up." The figure helped him to his feet. "And cleaned up. You smell like a brewery."

When he managed to get himself upright and take a look, he saw that the figure was an older gentleman in a trench coat. The man helped him down the block until they found an all-night diner and ducked in. Once inside, they took a booth and the waitress brought them black coffee and dry toast. In thirty minutes, Steve was able to make a sentence that sounded somewhat intelligent.

"Why do you want to talk to me? And who the hell are you?"

"Who I am is of no concern." The man took another sip of coffee. "But the man for whom I work has been watching you and your career. He would like for you to come to work for him."

"Doing what?"

"The law," the man said plainly.

"Why me?"

"Because you need a position. Because he needs a lawyer. Because he thinks you're the right person for the job. He has a firm but he will be retiring, and he believes you will be the person to take over his practice. He is prepared to offer you this." He slipped a piece of paper to Steve.

When Steve unfolded the paper and looked at it, he almost fell out. He was being offered a brand-new BMW, a four-bedroom house, full benefits, use of a plane, a membership to a country club he'd never heard of, and an income that was close to a million dollars a year. "Holy shit," Steve whispered. "Wait – where is this?"

"Louisville, Kentucky. Are you interested?"

"Hell, yeah! Sign me up!" Steve practically shouted. There was nothing left in St. Louis for him anyway.

"Then be at Lambert, hangar 89A, at six thirty in the morning."

"I'll be there!"

At six thirty the next morning, Steve boarded a small private jet and got comfortable in the leather seat. He hadn't brought anything with him. For what he was about to step into, he could buy all new stuff. Even though he'd never been to Louisville, he was pretty sure he was going to love it.

Kelly

July 1991

"Krystal, goddamn it, get yo ass ovah heeyah. This man be wantin' service," Bledsoe barked, picking sesame seeds out of his grill with a toothpick. The tiny brunette hated his gold caps; she thought they made him look even seedier.

"Hey, cute thing! Let's go party!" The guy oozed sleaze, wrapping an arm around Krystal's waist. They walked along the Hoboken street past dozens of other girls, then turned and walked down an alley, coming out in the courtyard of a pay-by-the-hour motel. He led her down to room one eighteen, took out a key, and opened the door to the shabby hole in the wall.

Everything reeked of cigarette smoke, but that was nothing new. Krystal never knew what kind of rat hole she'd be lying down in from trick to trick. Once they were in the room and the door was closed, the man turned to her and ordered, "Take off everything. I want to look at you."

Krystal did as she was told. She'd lost her modesty years back when she'd come into the life as a runaway at thirteen, and she'd grown used to stripping off so men could stare at her body. When she was naked, he walked over and pinched both of her nipples viciously. Because she'd cried out, the man slapped her across the face, then said, "Nice little tits. How old are you, eleven? Tell me you're eleven."

"How did you guess?" Krystal asked him. She wasn't; she'd be nineteen in two weeks, but he wanted her to be eleven, so for that moment in time, she was. She was whatever they wanted her to be if it would keep them from beating her.

"Oh, I can tell. I've had lots of little girls, and I like me some virgin kiddie pussy." He rubbed his hand roughly up and down her slit, and it burned her skin something fierce, but she tried her best to look like she liked it and it was turning her on. Then he dropped to his knees, spread open her folds, and looked up at her from below. She moved slightly, and he took it to mean she was being uncooperative. Slapping the inside of her thigh, he sing-songed, "You're gonna have to be still for Daddy, sweetheart."

He stood, and his fingers went around the back of her neck, gripping tightly. He forced her to kneel on the floor, then took his penis from his pants and pressed her mouth down over it. She tried to do the job herself, but he wanted to do it for her, wrapping his hands in her hair and yanking her head up and down over him. The head of his penis hit the back of her throat repeatedly, and she gagged and choked, tears streaming down her face.

"Oh, you like that, don't you, little slut? I'm coming; you'd better swallow it all down." He grunted a couple of times and her throat was flooded. She felt like she was drowning, and she tried to swallow, but his penis was buried firmly in her throat, and she was getting closer and closer to fainting.

Finally, he pulled back and she was able to breathe, but before she could really catch her breath, he grabbed her by the hair, threw her on the bed, wrestled her to her hands and knees, and rammed into her rear entrance without any warning. Krystal screamed and begged him to stop, but he just kept ramming her, then pulled out of her, threw her onto her back, and started to plunge into her vagina with all his might. She was crying in earnest, begging him to at least slow down, but he kept going, all the while slapping her face or breasts or backside.

When he was finally done with her, he told her to put her clothes on. Pushing her out the door, he handed her a wad of bills, then slammed the door. She was left to walk back to the strip in the dark by herself. *Oh, well, there's nothing anyone could do to me on the way back to Bledsoe that would be worse than what just happened*, she thought. Everything below her waist still hurt and she was having trouble walking, but Bledsoe expected his money immediately.

She tottered out onto the main street in the ridiculously-high heels that Bledsoe said made her fuckable, and he was on her before she could whistle. "Whayah my money, bitch?" Bledsoe asked her. Krystal handed him the wad of bills. "Sweet! Hey, day a guy ovah dayah want some lovin'. I tole him you'd supply. Getcho ass over dayah and do yo thing." He pushed her toward a blue sedan. Krystal walked up to the window and asked, "Hey, wanna party?"

"Get in," the guy said gruffly. Once she was in the car, he leaned over and pulled her legs apart, then stuck three fingers into her vagina in one shove, and Krystal gasped in pain. "Nice and tight." He drew out his fingers and drove her to a parking lot three blocks away. Dragging her out of the car by her hair, he practically threw her in the backseat, then climbed in and fucked her fast and rough. When he was finished, he didn't even let her back into the front seat, just drove her back to the block where he'd picked her up, handed her some cash, and barked, "Get out, whore!"

Bledsoe appeared out of nowhere. "Hand it heeyah, bitch." Krystal handed him the money and he counted it. "You stealin' from yo ol' man?"

"No sir. What's there is what he gave me," she said, trembling. With his violent streak, Bledsoe could be dangerous when he was crossed.

"Asshole; don't wanna pay fo quality. Times is hard." He pocketed all of the money.

Krystal was hurting. Men violated her all the time, but those two had been particularly rough. She thought the pain would take her down, but before she could even sit and rest, Bledsoe told her, "See dat man ovah dayah? He lookin' fo a good time. Getcho ass ovah dayah and do what he want, heeyah?" Barely able to walk, Krystal tottered over to the car. "Ready to party," she said, wincing.

This guy said, "Get in," but it was softer and gentler than they usually spoke to her. Krystal got in, hoping he'd be something of a human being. He drove them to a park four blocks down the street, parked the car, and turned to Krystal. She expected him to pull his penis from his pants, but instead, he looked at her with a gentleness in his eyes, something she hadn't seen in a long time.

"Do you want out?"

"What?" Krystal replied, confused. What did he mean, did she want out? Out of the car?

"Do you want out of the life? The organization I work for operates a shelter for girls wanting to leave the life. Do you want to leave?" he asked her again.

"Of course I want to leave. But Bledsoe will find me and kill me. I can't leave. And I'm almost nineteen; places like that don't take girls over eighteen who are supposed to be able to take care of themselves."

"We don't care about your age – you still need out. And as for saying 'I can't,' well, yes you can, if you want." By now Krystal was pretty sure it was a trick. "You can have a clean bed and clean clothes, and a good breakfast in the morning. Whaddya say?"

Yeah, he was going to take her to a building somewhere, and he and four of his friends were going to rape her; she was pretty sure of it. But for reasons she didn't understand, she answered, "Yes. I want to go."

"Well, okay then. Let's go."

Once they'd reached the shelter, the man stopped the car. "By the way, I'm Wayne. What's your name?"

"It's Krystal." Not one john had ever asked her what her name was.

"Krystal. That's a pretty name. Well, this is the place. Let's go inside, okay?" He came around, opened the door for her, and helped her out of the car.

Stepping inside, Krystal was instantly excited. The building was clean and well-lit, and she could smell some kind of food cooking. That was when she realized she was hungry. Thinking back over the last two days, she couldn't remember when she'd eaten.

"Let's get you some clean clothes, let you shower, and we'll get you something to eat. But I need to know; are you injured in any way? We have a doctor here who can look at you," Wayne offered.

"Uh, yeah, I hurt. You know – down there." All of a sudden, Krystal felt shy.

"Then come on and let me show you to the shower, get you some clothes, and we'll get Dr. Kurt to look you over, okay? He's a nice guy; you'll like him." Wayne led her down the hall, got her some underwear and a bra, plus sweat pants and a tee-shirt, all from a room full of clothing, and, after finding her some athletic shoes, he showed her to the shower. Once she'd finished and dressed, he led her down the hall to an examining room.

Within a few minutes, a man walked in, tall and nice-looking, and stuck out his hand. "Hi, I'm Dr. Kurt. You're Krystal?"

"Yeah," she said, her eyes wary.

"Okay, well, I'm going to let you undress and I'll do the exam. It'll only take a minute. Let me know when you're ready." Kurt walked out and closed the door behind him.

In fifteen minutes, it was all over, and Kurt pronounced her bruised but otherwise uninjured. She'd thought that as soon as he had her on the table he would probably rape her, but he was very gentle and professional, even using a drape so she wouldn't be quite so embarrassed. She'd never been examined by a doctor before, and it felt strange for a man to look at her undressed and not abuse her.

Wayne let her choose what she liked of the food in the kitchen, then warmed it in a microwave, and she sat down at one of the dining tables with him to eat a chicken drumstick and some mashed potatoes. They tasted so good that she thought she'd died and gone to heaven.

"We have some things to talk with you about, but that can wait until morning," Wayne told her. "But basically, you need to come up with a new name for yourself. And if you don't want to go home to your parents, we'll have to move you to another state to keep your pimp from being able to find you. Be thinking about what you'd like to be called and where you need to go, and we'll all talk in the morning." Krystal didn't know who "we'll all" was, but she was willing to find out.

As she snuggled down in the clean sheets on the small bed they'd given her, she thought about the things Wayne had said. She didn't want to go back home. And she knew what name she'd like to be called: Kelly.

November 2004

"I'm sorry, Miss Markham, but even with your so-called contract, you have no legal claim to anything." The attorney she'd hired wasn't good for anything except taking her money.

Gary had been good to her, but he'd been in his sixties when they'd gotten together, and then he'd up and had a fatal heart attack. His kids hated her, and why not? They were older than she was. They saw her as an opportunistic gold digger. She'd loved Gary, they'd had a lifestyle that had suited them both, and it had been good while it lasted. But now that he was gone, she was left with nothing.

Kelly called her friend who was a headhunter and asked for a favor – find her a job, and make it somewhere other than Nashville. She just wanted out of that town. He found her a job in the insurance industry in Louisville, so she started packing. Most people would've called a family member or friend to tell them about the move, but Kelly didn't have anyone to tell. No one knew where she was, and no one cared where she was going, because no one gave a damn about her, hadn't for a long, long time. The only person who'd seemed to care about her other than Gary was a lady she'd met through a program for alcoholics at a church in New Jersey, but they'd lost touch after she'd moved to Nashville and moved in with Gary.

It had taken her years to start over, then she'd spent eight years with Gary. He'd been a fabulous Dom; she'd never wanted for anything, he'd taken good care of her, and she'd been as devoted as a sub could be. She'd never told him about her past. If he'd asked her to marry him, she would've told him, but he hadn't, so she kept it all to herself. She'd just start over in Louisville. This time she had a leg up; she had a good work history, a nice pair of boobs that Gary had paid for, and some jewelry he'd given her that she could hock. She'd make it in Louisville. It wouldn't be easy, but it would be a damn sight easier than the world she'd grown up in.

Peyton

July 2006

"I have more, I have more! Don't knock me down!" Peyton was laughing as the children crowded around him, yelling and jumping. His body armor made it harder to get to the pocket of his shirt, but he dug around and found two more packs of gum. "Here! Let me get it open and everybody can have a piece!" He broke open both packs and passed sticks around. As they took a stick, they ran away to play. In two minutes, every stick of gum was gone. *I'll have to ask the folks to send more*, Peyton thought.

"Stokes! We're not babysitters!" Sergeant Colson yelled at him from across the road. People were everywhere, walking, running, riding bikes. Kandahar was busy in the mornings, the markets open and locals scrambling back and forth, trying to get good deals on the few goods available before they were all gone. The war had severely limited supplies of everything, and if you couldn't get it early, you probably wouldn't get it at all.

"Sorry, sarge!" Peyton yelled back, but he'd never stop doing that kind of thing. Children always flocked around him and everyone seemed to like him. The blond, blue-eyed soldier couldn't look more unlike the people around him, five feet and eight inches with a bodybuilder physique and a sweet, boy-next-door charm. Even though it was obvious he wasn't a native of the country, he loved the people of Afghanistan and hated the way the Taliban had hijacked their country. His parents had always taught him to remember how he'd feel in any situation and then try to empathize with whoever was in that situation. There wasn't enough gum in the world to make those kids feel better. Many had lost their parents; a good number of them had wounds of some type.

He checked his weapon; matter of fact, he checked it every five minutes. He'd heard Vietnam vets talk about the Viet Cong, and the Taliban operated in much the same way. Every person he passed on the street was a potential enemy, and you could never be too careful.

A knot of young women stood at the side of the road, speaking rapidly and making lots of hand gestures. When Peyton got close, they moved a little to the side, and he brushed past them. As he did, a man brushed against him from the other side and, a split second later, Peyton heard a thud behind him. He turned to look.

The IED was only ten feet from him.

Yelling at the top of his lungs, he dove into the cluster of young women, sending them face down in the dirt, and before they could even fall all the way to the ground, Peyton heard the pop. It didn't sound at all like he thought it would; later, as he thought back, he'd remember that it was an unusual sound, not big, just piercing. A burning sensation hit him like a tsunami, and he screamed over and over and couldn't stop screaming. He heard Sergeant Colson yelling something, saw others from his unit running and pointing, heard them shouting, but everything seemed to be happening in slow motion, and then it all started getting fuzzy.

About thirty hours later, Peyton woke in a hospital. He'd been flown out almost immediately after the bomb blast, and he hurt all over, at least the back half of his body. It was impossible for him to see what was going on because he was face down on a bed, his face in a donut-shaped cushion lower than his body, almost like the massage tables he'd seen at the salon back home where he'd always gotten his hair cut.

He managed to get his forearms on the table and pushed himself up so he could see. There were other people – soldiers, he assumed – in other beds all over the big room. A nurse looked up, saw him looking around, and made her way over to him. She had to be military, because she looked at the chart on the wall beside his bed and said, "Stokes, lie back down. You need your rest."

"What happened?" Peyton asked, his voice groggy and hoarse.

"IED. You probably don't remember. You're going to be okay. You were lucky; they say it mostly propelled itself up into the air, but it still blew. It sent shrapnel all over your back and gave you quite the concussion, so you need your rest." She pushed on his shoulder, and he was so weak he couldn't fight her. "I'm going to ask the doctor to give you some more pain medication."

In less than ten minutes, Peyton saw someone sitting on the floor, looking up at him through the hole in the face cushion. "Hi, Stokes!" a voice said, and a face popped into his field of vision. "I'm Dr. Klein. I'm taking care of you. Are you in any pain?"

"No, I don't think so," Peyton managed, confused and suddenly tired.

"Good. I gave you a little more painkiller. You'll sleep for awhile." The physician smiled. "Before you're back out, do you have any questions?"

"Yeah, how bad . . ."

"Well, the concussion, not so bad. Your back, pretty good, actually, surprisingly so. We'll be able to roll you over tomorrow. But your leg, not so good."

"What do you mean?" Peyton didn't understand. "I can feel my legs, so they can't be that bad, right? I mean, the left one hurts, especially my foot, but not too bad."

"That's phantom pain, Stokes. Your left leg below the knee is gone."

February 2010

Another rejection letter. Peyton slammed the mailbox door shut and limped back into the house. It was the day he had early classes, so he was hurrying to go when he opened the envelope.

"Did you get anything?" his mother asked, excitement filling her voice.

"Yeah." Peyton threw the letter on the table. "I've gotta go. Class in forty minutes. I'll see you guys this evening." He had to go back to physical therapy; his prosthetic just wouldn't stop rubbing his stump, and someone was going to have to help him. Even though they lived only four blocks from campus, he couldn't even walk that distance. Trying to get a job in law enforcement was ridiculous; one look at him in an interview and they'd turn him down cold.

He'd gotten through University of Louisville's criminal justice program in record time. Of course, he'd done it by taking twenty-one hours every semester, but his parents had insisted that he live with them, and he had the money he'd saved while he'd been in the service, so he didn't have to work. Now it was time to find a job in his field, and that just didn't seem to be happening. And forget women – none of them wanted an unemployed amputee, so he didn't even bother to ask. Feeling especially low, he parked the car in the student lot and struggled painfully to walk the half block to class.

As soon as he walked in the door, Professor Augustino stopped him.

"Peyton, see me after class, please." *Oh, god, wonder what I've done wrong,* Peyton thought. It was too close to graduation to screw anything up.

After class, he hung back. When the room was empty, Professor Augustino motioned for Peyton to follow him to his office. Once inside, he closed the door and pointed at a chair for Peyton.

"Gotten any positives?" the professor asked him.

"Not a single one – another rejection this morning."

"That's what I wanted to talk to you about. I got a call from a guy here in Louisville, an attorney, who's looking to put together a security team to hire out to his clients who need shadowing, protection, whatever. I know it's not what you had in mind, but it's a job, and it would give you experience until you can, well, you know." Professor Augustino smiled at him and tried to look hopeful.

"I'm not kidding myself anymore." A gloomy look passed over Peyton's face. "No police department is going to hire me. And I'm still having trouble with my prosthetic. I don't know what to do at this point."

"So do you think you might be interested in working with this guy? If you are, I'll give you his contact information."

"Yeah, sure, why not? I don't have any other prospects. Might as well." *Oh, great – a life of following cheating housewives around.* He took the contact information and put it in his binder.

"Have a seat, Mr. Stokes. Mind if I call you Peyton?" The tall, blond, muscular attorney pointed to the sofa in his office, and Peyton had a seat.

"No sir, feel free." *Pretty nice digs,* he thought. Steve McCoy's office was big and very tastefully decorated, with what looked like extremely expensive art scattered about here and there. "So, I understand you're just trying to get this off the ground?"

"Yeah. I have clients who are wealthy and they need protection sometimes; not all of my clients, but a few. They sometimes have, how can I say this delicately, questionable business practices, and they make enemies. That's where we come in."

Spectacular – career criminals and mafia moguls. No wonder he has a nice-looking office, Peyton thought. And it wasn't just the office; it was obvious to Peyton that McCoy knew he was a good-looking man and felt he was somewhat superior to most of the people around him. This was an interesting-looking situation, and Peyton decided maybe this would be a good place to get his feet wet; well, foot wet.

"So, I hear you have a slight difficulty." McCoy looked at Peyton with a steady eye.

"I have a below-the-knee prosthetic, left leg." Peyton walked to the side of McCoy's desk to show him. "I'm having a little trouble with it, but it'll get worked out, I'm sure. I've just got to work with my physical therapist and the orthotist, and it'll be fine."

"Well, frankly, I hope so, because I think you'd be great in the field. Until you can get that ironed out, I'll put you in the office, helping me get everything up and running. There's a future here for you, if you want it, maybe as a supervisor for the other mercenaries!" McCoy laughed.

"I'd be interested in helping out, especially with startup. I'd really like to help hire the other workers, you know, interviewing and things like that."

"Good! You know, I like you, Stokes. You seem like an honest guy, and I need that with some of the people I deal with. Plus you were career military and you're not a kid." McCoy extended his hand. Peyton took it and shook it firmly. "So, when can you start?"

José

February 2010

"The crowd's getting rowdy, my man. Time to get out there and do your thing." Jorge slapped José on the shoulder as the younger man rose. José could hear the crowd, stomping their feet and screaming. He'd both looked forward to and dreaded this night, and it was finally here.

José pulled his waist-length, jet black hair back, and Jorge braided it to keep it out of the way. He twisted his long goatee into a corkscrew and looked in the mirror. The cut above his right eye was healing nicely; he sure hoped it didn't get reopened.

They took the last walk down the hallway and when the doors opened, José was floored. There had to be five thousand people there, all for the hottest ticket in cage fighting: José Flores versus Devon White. The federation had been promoting it for months and they'd done a good job – every seat was filled. It might not have been the biggest, most prestigious federation, but the fights he won paid the bills.

The spotlight hit him, and José's whole demeanor changed. What had been an average guy walking down an average hallway suddenly turned into a raging lion, muscles swelling and tingling. He loved the adrenalin rush he got from the crowd, the music, the cage cuties, all of it.

And then there was the cage.

When the fighters walked in and that gate slammed shut, José always felt more alive than anywhere else. It meant that all the work, all the training, and all the frustration and pain he'd lived with all his life had come down to that one slice of time, and he made the most of it. But tonight would be different.

Two of the men Devon White had fought had died. The guy was enormous, a foot taller than José and tough as a Sherman tank. And he'd made it clear: He wanted to fight José Flores, the only fighter on the circuit that he'd been told might actually kick his ass. In White's mind, this was a night to make sure everyone knew how tough he was. There would be no smack-talking, no dancing around, just fighting and fighting hard. He wanted to take out Flores in the first five minutes, had to, to make sure everyone knew he was the champ.

When José saw the huge guy, something in his gut turned. This would be the defining moment in his life. If he won this fight, he'd finally know that he'd shown all those assholes who'd beaten him, lied to him, cheated him, and generally treated him like shit, that he was one tough motherfucker and not somebody to be messed with. And he was fucking sick and tired of being messed with.

They came to the gate and shook hands. José almost laughed when White tried to give him the evil eye. He wanted to say, *You don't scare me, punkass*, but the time for that was later. Now it was time to fight.

The cage gate slammed shut, and it was do-or-die time. After sparring a little, they got down to business, and that's when José noticed something: White was favoring his left shoulder ever so slightly. It wouldn't be noticeable to most people, but it was a blinding red light to José. He let White hit him twice; that would get him in close, lull him into a false sense of security. White tried a roundhouse kick, which José deflected easily; that would send him back to using his upper body, which was exactly what José wanted. José decided to do something bold; he reached out and slapped White with an open hand, just like a parent would slap a smart-mouthed child. José could tell that it had the desired effect when White glared at him and growled, "I'm gonna kill you, spic!" Then José turned the screw: He smiled at White. A look of deep-seated fury passed over the bigger man's face, and he came after José like a wrecking ball.

José let him get so close that he could see the veins in White's eyes, and then he struck, grabbing the bigger man's left arm and twisting hard. Then the unexpected happened – José heard a snapping sound, like a branch being twisted in a violent storm, and White's face contorted in agony. He went down with a thud, screaming in pain. If he got free now, he'd be more than dangerous; he'd be a killer. José continued to torque his arm, leaned down to him, and whispered, "You stay down and I'll turn loose." Instead, White growled again, and José gave the arm another little twist. As the pain doubled, then tripled, White's eyes rolled back in his head and he was gone, passed out cold.

The house was coming apart, the screaming so loud that it overpowered the sound system. Jorge came to the gate and opened it, and José walked out to cheering and shouting the likes of which he'd never heard. White's team had headed into the cage to carry him out, and Jorge and José walked back through the double doors and down to his warm-up area.

"*Mi dios*, that was awesome!" Jorge yelled. "You took him down so fast that he didn't know what hit him!"

"Is he okay?" José asked, the raging lion gone and the kid from Englewood on Chicago's south side back in the house. "I hope he's going to be okay."

Jorge's eyes went wide. "What the hell, man? Why do you even care?"

"Because. Because I never thought something like that would happen." José shook his head sadly. "That's just not who I am." *My madre and padre didn't work themselves nearly to death to see me be a total asshole*, he thought.

"He wouldn't have hesitated to kill you if he got the chance," Jorge reminded him. "Shake it off."

But José wasn't wired that way. He went down the hall to White's camp and knocked on the door. White's manager came out into the hall. "What the hell do you want? Gloating?" the man asked.

"No, man, I came to check on him. Will he be okay?"

White's manager stared at him in disbelief. "Seriously? Are you for real?"

"Yeah, man. I just wanted to check on him."

The man's face softened. "Yeah, I think he'll probably have to have surgery, but he'll be okay. But I doubt he'll ever be able to fight again." He was surprised at the look of pain that flitted across José's face. "I'll be sure to tell him you asked, okay?"

"Thanks. I appreciate it. I wish him the best," José turned to walk back down the hallway to his area. Photos were taken, autographs signed, and it was time to go home.

Two days later, José went to the hospital to check on White. When he got to the hospital room, two men blocked his way in. "Where the hell you think you goin', spic?" one of them asked José.

"I wanted to talk to White. I'm . . ." José started.

"We know who you are," the man spat. "You really wanna go in there?"

"Yeah, I do. I'd like to tell him how sorry I am for what happened."

The men laughed. "Sure, go on in." One of them held the door and José walked in.

A hush fell over the room. Everyone moved away from the bed, and when White saw José, he couldn't believe his eyes. "What the hell you doin' here?" White yelled. "You think I can't get outta this bed and kick yo ass? You crazy?"

"I just wanted to see how you were, tell you that I'm sorry for what happened. I know all's fair in fighting, but I hate hurting anyone." José's voice was steady and clear. "Is there anything I can do for you? Need anything?"

White was seething. "Are you serious? Getcho damn wetback ass outta here. I never wanna see yo punkass again, motherfucker. You hear me?"

José turned to leave, and he heard White say, "I'm gonna get outta this bed and when I do, I'm gonna hunt yo spic ass down and kill you." José just kept walking.

When he got out into the hall, one of the men watching the door grabbed his arm. José drew back to defend himself, but the man yelled, "Hey! Hey! Don't hit me! I just wanted to tell you that I heard you in there, and that was classy, man. Very classy." The other man nodded in agreement. "Don't worry about Devon. When he cools off, it'll be okay. He's just pissed and in pain. Hey, congratulations on your win and good luck, okay?" The man extended his hand.

"Thanks." José took the man's hand and shook it. Then he walked down the hall and out the door.

That's it, he thought. *No more fights. I don't want to hurt anyone like that ever again.*

March 2011

"I can't do this anymore," the stocky blond said. "I can't support us both, and you just can't seem to find anything that's permanent or steady. And this relationship isn't going where I'd hoped it would either. I think we need to see other people."

"Please, Braden, don't do this!" José pleaded. "We're good together, you know we are!" José felt like his whole world was cracking apart. He'd worked so hard to find a job and just hadn't had any luck. And now Braden was breaking up with him? That just wasn't fair. It wasn't his fault that the economy was down, and it wasn't like they were hurting; Braden made good money, and José supplemented it when he could find work.

Then something flitted through his mind. "Have you met someone?" José whispered, not really wanting to know.

Braden looked away. "Yeah. I have. And I still care about you, but I don't love you and I'm not in love with you."

José's heart sank. Well, that was it. Relationship over. "Fine. I'll be out by tomorrow." *Where the hell will I go?*, he thought. He'd call Vivica; maybe she knew someone who needed a roommate. But he didn't have a job, so how could he make rent?

He packed all of his stuff and put it in his van. *I wish I'd taken better care of this van; I might have to live in it*, he thought, looking at the dust and rust.

A call to Vivica took care of his housing dilemma. "I don't have anybody in my extra bedroom. Come on over and crash until you can find something. Don't worry about rent; we can take it out in trade!" she laughed. Until José met Braden, he and Viv had been sleeping together on a regular basis. She was pretty and fun, a great fuck buddy, and she didn't want a commitment. He'd never expected to fall for Braden, but when he fell, he really fell. He and Viv had continued to talk frequently, but they'd stopped being each other's booty calls. Looked like that was about to change.

Once he'd settled in at Viv's, he set out to really look for a job, but it wasn't easy. Unemployment was high and everyone was looking for work, and most of them had more experience, training, or education than he did. Cage fighting didn't translate too well in the work world either. He'd just about given up when his mother called; his cousin Diego was in town for a visit and was hoping to see him.

When he got to his mom's house, the party was in full swing. He walked in to see relatives he hadn't laid eyes on in years. It had been fifteen years since he'd seen Diego, and José had trouble picking him out of the crowd, but finally found him near the beer tub. They exchanged a bro hug.

"So, I hear you're the big name in cage fighting now!" Diego shouted over the noise. "That's great! I'm surprised I haven't seen your name on the schedule for the federation. When's your next fight?"

"No more fighting," José told him. When Diego realized what he'd said, he grabbed José by the arm and dragged him outside.

"Whaddya mean, no more fighting? You're the champ!"

"Yeah, and I hurt somebody real bad. I'm done, man. That's not my style."

Diego stood for a moment with a strange look on his face. "Man, I can't believe that. What are you going to do now?"

"I have no idea. I can't find a job. It's brutal out there, and I don't really have any skills. I had some money from the win, but it's been a year and I've pretty much gone through that. I don't even have any prospects, and I don't have any income. I lost my place, and I'm living with a friend. Times are hard, man."

Diego smiled. "Do you want a job?"

"More than just about anything." *Well, except for Braden,* José thought, but that was never going to happen.

"The guy I work for would love to get his hands on you. But you'd have to move to Louisville."

"Hell, I've got no reason to stay here. What exactly does he do?" José asked.

"He's an attorney and I work for him as a paralegal, but he's started a security company and he's looking for people who can handle themselves, if you know what I mean. You interested?"

"Hell yeah! Could I stay with you until . . ."

"Of course," Diego smiled again. "That's what family's for, *mi primo*!"

"What do I do?"

"I'll talk to him when I get back, and I'll give you a call," Diego promised.

"I appreciate this, man. I really do."

"Hang in there, cuz. I think he'll jump to get you."

Two weeks later, Steve McCoy called José and talked to him over the phone. The next day, he and his van full of belongings were headed to Louisville.

Molly

June 2002

"Where's your dad?" Molly was tired of chauffeuring both boys around. Even though she was glad to have them home from college for the summer, Freddie insisted that their cars be parked unless they had jobs and money for gas. Problem was, he never seemed to be around when they wanted or needed to go somewhere, even when he wasn't at work, and Molly wound up taking them everywhere. And she was tired of it.

"I dunno," Todd, their twenty year old, mumbled through a mouthful of potato chips. "Last time I saw him he was in the yard."

"I saw him going next door," Jeff, the nineteen year old, told her. "I don't know what he was doing, but he was headed that way."

That same sick feeling came over Molly again. She'd thought it was her imagination, but now she wasn't so sure. Ever since the Morgans next door had hired that sixteen-year-old babysitter, Felicity, Molly's husband of almost thirty years was nowhere to be found. Molly didn't want to think that Freddie was sniffing around an underage girl, but it seemed odd to her that he was always turning that direction.

"Okay, get your stuff. Now where am I going?" she asked the boys. They were just about to tell her when Freddie walked in the back door.

"Where are you guys going?" Freddie picked up an apple from the fruit basket on the counter and bit into it.

Just as she started to answer him, Molly noticed something that made her pulse slam in her temples. "Could you please go and wait in the car for me?" She wasn't asking; she was telling them. Both boys skulked out the door and let it close behind them. When she was sure they were out of earshot, she turned on Freddie with well-deserved vengeance.

"You know, if you're going to screw the next-door-neighbor's babysitter, you could at least hide the fact from our kids," she spat at him.

His look of astonishment didn't fool her for one minute. "How can you say something like that to me?" he cried. "What would make you think a thing like that?"

"Oh, gee, I don't know, maybe because they saw you sneaking over there. And, oh, yeah, there's the fact that your damn shirt is on wrong-side out!" she screamed at him.

Freddie's face turned bright red, and he took his shirt off and turned it right-side out. That was when she saw them – love bites. "My god, don't you have any shame?" she shrieked and headed out the door.

When Freddie looked down to see what had finally given him away, he felt faint. There was no denying what the marks were, or where he'd gotten them. But Felicity was so cute, and her breasts were so big and perky, and she was so hot and tight, and . . . he felt a stirring below his waist just thinking about her. Problem was, if Molly gave him away, he could go to jail for having sex with a minor. And just how would Freddie Walters explain that? The legal system was the least of his worries; two of his brothers would knock the bejesus out of him, and the other two would do the same if they lived there in Louisville.

As Molly drove the boys to friends' houses, she stewed. She was screwed; the only place she'd worked since the kids were born was the boutique Freddie had bought there in town and given to her to run. Unfortunately, she was pretty sure if she left him she wouldn't get the boutique. Then she'd have no job. And she had no other way to make herself a living. She could ask her brothers-in-law, Bart and Tony, if either of their businesses had an opening, but it would be weird to work for her husband's family if she was divorcing him.

Divorce. That was the first time Molly had really given it a thought. Sure, things between them hadn't been perfect, but they'd had a pretty good run. They had four kids, four good kids, with the oldest two, the girls, grown and out of the house, and the two boys almost in the same situation. Regardless what he was dipping his wick into, the kids loved their dad. Problem was, she did too. But she knew she couldn't compete with a piece of high-school-aged ass. She and Freddie had been together since she was seventeen, married at eighteen, and she really didn't know anything else but being his wife. What would she do?

She'd stick it out, that's what she'd do. Eventually he'd tire of being with a kid and he'd come back to be with her. She wouldn't make it easy on him.

If he wanted out, he'd have to come right out and ask.

November 2012

Molly pulled the pins and elastic out of her long, dark hair, then took off her dress and threw it across the chair. Freddie was undressing and getting ready for bed too. It had been a long day. She'd always found Thanksgiving to be a tiresome, thankless holiday, especially for the women in the family.

"I still can't believe the announcement my brother made today. That was a shock."

"Looks like the big family Christmas is going to be quite the celebration." Molly hated the Walters family gatherings. Everybody was always so happy, except for her. *If they had any idea what Freddie was up to, they wouldn't be quite so happy, now would they?*, she thought, fuming. "That's all anybody wanted to talk about today, how wonderful it would be and how happy they are. Blah, blah, blah," she added, sarcasm dripping from her voice.

"No, do you want to know what everyone was really talking about today? They were talking about what a bitch you were. Are. Will be – forever. Why do you have to be such a bitch?"

"Why do you have to be such a pedophile?" she slung back at him.

"Oh, shut up. I'm tired of your barbs, tired of trying to please you, tired of being made to feel like I'm not doing enough. Don't I give you everything you want or need?"

Molly mocked him with a sarcastic grin. "Yeah, everything except a stable relationship."

"What's not stable about it? I mean, we have a good life. We have a home, cars, money, good kids, and you can't say I've ever denied you in bed."

"And your kiddie girlfriend, don't forget her," Molly sniped.

"She's not a kid. She's twenty-six," Freddie shot back.

"Verbage. She was a kid when you first started screwing her!" Molly climbed into bed. "And since she's working with you, I assume you're still screwing her?"

"Oh, come on, Molly, let's not talk about that. I want something from you, and I want to give you something too," Freddie offered, sliding into bed and slipping his hand up Molly's leg to the juncture of her thighs. She didn't tell him not to touch her, and within minutes the deed was in full swing. Her thinking was that if she gave him whatever he wanted, maybe he would leave

Felicity alone and recommit to her. But who was she kidding? It had been going on too long, with no end in sight.

When they were finished, Molly lay staring at the ceiling. She had finally decided to let her anger go for the night and get to sleep when Freddie announced, out of the blue, "Molly, I want a divorce."

It took all she had not to lean over and choke him to death. They'd just had sex, and he'd asked her for a divorce. Talk about poor timing, or maybe he was just more of a bastard than she'd already thought; now, on top of everything else, she felt like a whore. A tear welled in the corner of her eye, but she was determined that he'd never see her cry, especially over him.

"I'm going to hire myself a really good attorney." It wasn't like she hadn't seen it coming, just hadn't seen it coming in the last ten minutes. She'd already been thinking about an attorney, just in case. It looked like "just in case" had finally come around.

"I'm not going to fight you over stuff. I'll give you whatever you want, but Felicity and I want to be together." Freddie rolled over with his back to her. "Do you know what you want? I mean, of our property and such?"

"Yeah," Molly answered, "I want the boutique. I've built it into what it is, and I at least deserve that."

"Sorry. Of all the things you could ask for, I'm not giving you that one. I've already promised it to Felicity."

A scorching wave of rage consumed her. The one thing she would want, and it was the one thing he wouldn't give her, that he was going to give to that . . . Yeah, that figured. She wanted that boutique, but she'd need a good attorney to do it, and she didn't know how she'd pay anyone for their legal services. Unless something changed, she'd be destitute.

"So when do you plan to tell your family? You know, we're going over there for Christmas. What am I supposed to do, pretend that everything is fine?"

"That's exactly what you'll do," Freddie told her, "if you want anything at all. Of course, you're always such a bitch to everyone, they won't know anything's up."

That seems to be where I live, Molly thought, *between a rock and a hard place*. Her mind went wild. What would she do? She hadn't worked anywhere but the boutique since the kids were born. There was nothing else that she knew how to do. How would she make herself a living? Molly's heart nearly stopped when she realized that all of the things she enjoyed were about to be a thing of the past.

"So do you want the house?" Freddie asked. "You can have it if you want it. We want to find somewhere else to live anyway, a place that you and I haven't lived in."

"No, I can't take the house." Molly tossed the last shred of her dignity to the wind. "I won't be able to afford to take care of it or pay the taxes or insurance. I won't have much of anything."

"Suit yourself." Freddie yawned. "Just thought I'd offer. Thought you might want to sell it for the money. But that means I need you to be out by the end of the first week of January so I can list it."

Where in the hell would she go? "No problem." She rolled over with her back to him. She had no idea where she'd go or what she'd do, but she sure as hell didn't want to stay there.

LOVE UNDER CONSTRUCTION SERIES: BOOK ONE

Laying A Foundation

DEANNDRA HALL

Laying a Foundation

Love Under Construction Series

Book 1

by
Deanndra Hall

A Word from the Author...

This might not have been the first volume in the series, but it was the first novel. I think I enjoyed writing this book as much or more as anything I've ever done.

I'd had Nikki in my head for at least 12 years, and I had never had anywhere to put her or people with whom to entrust her. When I started to think about her seriously as the female protagonist of a book, it took less than an hour for Tony to form in my mind, and when his family and friends came along for the ride, I knew I was onto something. I wrote the whole thing, then realized that the character details would be better suited to their own volume. At the time I did this, I'd never seen another writer do anything like it; no one I knew had either. I did eventually find someone who did, and did it well, and I was glad I wasn't the only one. That's how *The Groundbreaking* was born; it was an offshoot of this book. And if you're reading this, you've already had the opportunity to read the prequel. Now the fun begins.

Thanks to my baby, who continues to be my biggest supporter and fan. MSH, you have no idea how much I love you; even though I'm a writer, there are no words. Thanks too to Drue, Alicia, and Felicia for their undying support. I'd have quit if it weren't for the three of you. You love my books and, for that, I love you.

Enjoy this book. It features characters well over 40 having the best sex of their lives, not a bunch of college kids or post-college kids who have no idea what great sex is. They're honest, raw, sometimes raunchy, and very often funny, not to mention willing to explore and have a little frisky adventure. Come along and have one with them!

And now, as Tony would say, "Business is business." Let's get down to it and enjoy our stay in Louisville, Kentucky.

Love and happy reading!
Deanndra

Visit me at:
www.deanndrahall.com

Contact me at:
DeanndraHall@gmail.com

Join me on Facebook at:
facebook.com/deanndra.hall

Catch me on Twitter at:
twitter.com/DeanndraHall

Find me blogging at:
deanndrahall.blogspot.com

Check out my Substance B page at:
substance-b.com/DeanndraHall.html

Write to me at:
P.O. Box 3722, Paducah, KY 42002-3722

Chapter One

How did the glass get so dirty on the inside? It seemed as though she was constantly fighting the grime. Nikki dipped the squeegee into the bucket again, making quick, even passes, wiping the rubber strip with the rag, and dipping again. As soon as the window was clean, she could put out the new display.

"Hey, Nik, about done there? I could use some help," Carol, her coworker at The Passionate Pansy, called out from the back.

"Boxes?" Nikki called back to her. She relished opening the crates, enjoying the beautiful blooms, sorting them, pricing them, and putting them into the walk-in cooler.

"Yeah, fourteen of them."

"Fourteen? Are you kidding? Good grief, it'll take us all morning!" Nikki stepped up her pace and finished with the window. "What in the world did Marla order?" She stared incredulously at the crates. "Where are we going to put all of this?"

"Wherever we can." Carol pulled out her box cutter. "I don't know how the cooler is going to handle all of this. I think she was thinking of the big prom push."

"Oh, that's right," Nikki sighed. "Prom. I'd forgotten." She pulled out a bundle of daisies dyed fuchsia. "Big hair, crazy eye shadow, fake nails, and stilettos on girls barely out of diapers. What fun." She oozed sarcasm when she said, "I can hardly wait."

"It's worse now that they've made it mid-March to avoid spring break and finals. The girls are kinda nuts, what with prom two weeks before the break. I hear the tanning beds around here are booked solid. Hey, you know, you should go over to the school, volunteer to be a chaperone for prom. You might meet a nice algebra teacher." Carol smiled.

"I don't think so. Doesn't sound like fun to me." Nikki pulled out another bundle of daisies; these were dyed a bright, fake peacock blue.

"I don't think you'd know fun if it bit you on the ass." Carol glanced over at her. "You really should get a life."

"I have a life, thank you very much," Nikki responded, expressionless. *But that's not true*, she thought. *I don't have a life. At least not much of one.*

"Aw, honey, you've just got to jump in, you know? You can do it," Carol said, not looking at Nikki. "You just have to want to."

Problem was, she didn't want to. She had no life, and that was fine with her. Just struggling through the day was a small victory. If the dog's not barking and snarling, don't tease it, right? Just walk on by.

The gym Nikki had joined four years earlier was one of the smallest in the Louisville area, but she liked it because it was small, clean, and never crazy-busy. She stowed her gear in the locker and headed out onto the floor. First the cardio theater, then the weights, followed by a stretching routine – her customary drill. No one noticed how she looked, but she felt better when she exercised, so she kept it up.

She looked around briefly; no one unusual. Nikki had made up names for most of the people she saw repeatedly at the gym, usually something to do with their appearance. It was her way of helping herself feel more comfortable in a room full of people she didn't know. There was Baseball Cap; Boobalicious, the buxom, curvaceous brunette next to her on the treadmill; and Fuzzy, the young guy with the enormous afro. Across the cavernous room was Blondie, one of the more appealing guys who showed up at the gym on a regular basis. But he looked like he was twelve years old, at least to Nikki. Beak came over to Blondie and seemingly asked the young adonis to spot him. She wasn't fond of the nickname Beak, but his nose was huge, so it fit.

Frick and Frack were at the smoothie bar, chatting up the young girl who was working that evening. To all appearances they were identical twins, and probably the youngest guys there. Nikki thought they might actually still be in high school.

She didn't see anyone else. It was a pretty quiet evening, even with the televisions blaring in the cardio theater. Over the years, people had come and gone, but she was still there, and why not? She sure didn't have anything else going on.

And then he rounded the corner from the locker room: The Italian. Even though he'd been there the entire four years Nikki had been coming to the gym, every time he strode through Nikki held her breath. Now, *that* was a man. She detected the swivel of Boobalicious's head in her peripheral vision; she was watching too, would have to be dead not to. Of course he probably wasn't Italian, but he certainly looked it. He had dark, wavy hair down to his shoulders, and one lock always escaped to fall over his right eye; the rest he kept pulled back into a stubby ponytail, just tight enough to show off the tiniest bit of gray at his temples. A hint of five o'clock shadow graced his lower jaw, and his lips looked ever-so-soft. Unlike the younger guys who came into the gym, his body wasn't wiry and sinewy; he was built like a man, firm and sturdy, with broad, thick shoulders, and his dark, olive skin showed off every ripple. Even though he probably knew full well how good-looking he was, his eyes were soft and kind, with tiny smile lines at the corners. As he walked past on his way to the free weights, he smiled and nodded at Nikki. She felt her insides turn tingly and warm and her face redden, and she smiled and looked at the floor. *Seems like a nice guy,* she thought. How old was he? Forty? Forty-five? Fifty? It was hard to tell, but it didn't matter. That man was way out of her league.

Wonder what would happen, she thought, if I were forward enough to walk up to him? Talk to him? Find out his name and a little bit about him? That would never happen; after all, she'd been seeing him in that gym for over four years and she'd never worked up the courage. Someone like Boobalicious, beautiful and stacked, might have the nerve, but not Nikki. Besides, people at the gym never talked. They were there to work out, nothing more. They didn't want their workout routines disturbed, and she most certainly didn't want to be rude.

Nikki watched him move across to the weight area and pick up a couple of dumbbells. He stood with his back to the rest of the room, looking in the mirror, checking his form as he curled the weights. She stepped off the treadmill and, instead of going to the weight area, she bolted for the locker room. It was just too torturous to see him there, knowing she'd never have the courage to even speak to him.

Finally home in her little house in the Middletown township, she ate her leftovers out of their storage containers. She fed Bill and Hillary their dinner while she cleaned up her own dinner mess, then wandered down the hallway to the bedroom, the two poodles following at her heels. It had been a long day and she needed to unwind.

Nikki lit her Candle of Intention, curled up in the bed, and drew the dogs close. She was about to open her latest read when something crossed her mind.

Grabbing a slip of paper and a pencil, Nikki crossed the room to the candle. She lit it every night in hopes that something would come to her, some positive move she could make to finally improve what was left of her life. But tonight she wanted to do something different. Which goddess? Clíodhna, queen of the *Bean-sídhe*, the Banshees – she'd do. Nikki hesitated for a few minutes, trying to come up with rhymes that made sense. Then she wrote on the paper:

Clíodhna, queen of the Banshees,
Hear my solemn plea.
Send the Banshees' keening forth
And bring someone to me.
As I ask it,
So mote it be.

Hmmmm . . . would that do it? She tore the corners off of the paper and dropped them into the candle's flame; they flared momentarily and then ashed away. Then she began to read the poem, nine times aloud, visualizing someone coming toward her. She wasn't looking for a lover or another husband, just hoping for someone to maybe go to the movies with her, or on a picnic, or maybe to a ballgame. No big deal. Maybe gay! A gay guy friend would be nice and safe. When she'd finished reading, she rolled the poem up and tied it with a piece of thread from the drawer of the chest on which the candle sat. Then she lit the tiny tube from the candle's flame and watched the paper curl and turn to white ash.

Nikki climbed back into bed. The rest was up to the Universe; she had done her part. All she could do now was think positively and keep her eyes open. She turned off the light and sighed, staring into the darkness until her lids grew heavy and sleep finally found her.

Chapter Two

Blink, and something got screwed up. How exactly did that happen so fast, and how did the guys make it look so easy? Tony drummed his fingers on his desk, listening to Cal tell him the crew had put the wrong kind of reinforcement in the concrete forms and all of it was going to have to come out before the pour the next day.

"And exactly where was the person who was supposed to be supervising this?" Tony asked.

"At the hospital with his wife. They had their baby," Cal shrugged.

"Well, I guess Walters Construction can't compete with a baby," Tony grinned. Cal visibly relaxed. "You know how I feel about this kind of thing. I don't want it to happen, but sometimes it does. We fix it, we go on. And we try not to have it happen again. Right?"

"Exactly!" Cal agreed enthusiastically. Tony had to fight to keep from laughing. The short, bald, stocky guy was definitely the best foreman Walters Construction had ever had, but he was the epitome of high-strung. Tony took everything very seriously too but, unlike Cal, he tried not to give himself a stroke over anything. Virtually everything could be fixed, but the goal was to not have to fix anything.

"Okay, so go pull the mesh, replace it, and get that truck down there. We need that concrete poured tomorrow morning or we're going to be behind schedule." Tony rose from his chair and crossed the room to the coffee pot. "I'd really like to get this job finished ahead of schedule. We've got the possibility of landing the contract for that new hospital in Willisburg and I'd hate to have to pass because we're dragging ass on this job."

"You got it, boss. Anything else before I go?"

"Yeah," Tony turned and grinned. "Tell Matt I said congratulations and I hope Andrea and the baby are doing great. Boy or girl?"

"Girl. Madison Paige."

"Thanks. I'll be out on the jobsite tomorrow morning if I don't see you before then." Tony shook Cal's hand as the younger man headed out the door. He turned back to his coffee, dropped one sugar cube in and stirred.

"Hey, Cheryl?"

"Yeah?" Tony's secretary called back.

"Could you please send flowers over to the hospital for Andrea Fowler?"

"Already done. Took care of it first thing this morning."

"Ah, you're a good one, Cheryl Brooks. Remind me of that on Secretary's Day, would you please?" Tony laughed.

Cheryl called back, "Yeah, I'm on it!" She was still laughing when he closed his office door.

He made a note to himself to find out exactly when Secretary's Day was. He owed it to Cheryl to treat her like the valuable employee she was. She'd gotten him out of more than a few jams over the six years she'd worked there, and she was always one step ahead of him. That was her greatest asset, as far as he was concerned.

Tony sat back down with his coffee and looked at the bid package for the hospital project. Getting the contract would be a plus, but definitely not their bread and butter. Underneath it was the bid package for the new runway and hangars in Lexington; now *that* would definitely be bread and butter. He'd have to hire more employees and buy more equipment if they won that one. Those were the kinds of jobs Walters Construction wanted to reel in. He'd have to see what the acquisitions department could do, have the numbers crunched, run it by Vic.

He glanced up at the clock. If he left in the next ten minutes and got to the gym, he could be home, showered, eating, and parked on the sofa in plenty of time for the tipoff. He rinsed out his coffee cup, grabbed his gym bag, and yelled goodbye to Cheryl as he headed to his truck.

Tony liked the gym. Chris, the manager, always kept it spotless. Tony had a well-appointed workout room in his home in Shelbyville, but the house in the Louisville township of Anchorage where he spent his work week was too small, so the gym was a necessity.

He didn't know any of the others who frequented the gym, but they all seemed friendly. He did know a few of their names, like Todd, the young blond guy. And there was Alvin, who had the most incredibly large nose Tony had ever seen. There were also a couple of twins who came in and out, but he didn't know their names.

As for women, there were only two there on a regular basis. There was Kelly, who had the largest breasts east of the Mississippi. They were fake, had to be. No one had real tits that big. Even in a sports bra, they were enormous. He'd been noticing her there for the last couple of years.

And there was another woman – probably not a lot younger than he was? – who was usually there in the evenings. She was small, fair, blond, and trim. He never spoke to her, even after seeing her there for at least four years, but lately he'd taken to smiling and nodding at her. She always smiled back, but then she'd look down, like she was shy. He'd love to talk to her or Kelly, but that was really frowned upon in gym etiquette – he only knew Kelly's name because she'd been featured in an advertisement for the gym. He'd learned early on that guys who tried to pick up women at a gym were considered creepy. When it came to women, he was shaky enough already – he certainly didn't need the "creepy" label.

Ah, women. They were impossible to figure out. Well, okay, it was probably a little easier when they weren't completely nuts. Nuts like Dottie. Crazy. Certifiably insane. Mentally ill. Chronically mentally ill. How exactly did you describe someone like Dottie? Cunningly insane? Yeah, that was more like it – cunningly, irritatingly insane. Her illness would've been easier to take if she hadn't been such a bitch on top of it. So good riddance.

But it still made him sad to think of all the precious years he'd wasted on her, continued to waste. She was the reason he couldn't seem to bring himself to start over. It seemed like far too much work to try, and extraordinarily scary on top of that. Even if he did try, he was sure wherever he started would turn out to be the wrong spot.

He pulled up in the parking lot and grabbed his gym bag, hoping that maybe just one time when he got there the blond lady would be leaving, and he could stop her and talk to her out in the lot, away from the actual gym and prying eyes. But he wasn't sure he'd have the courage even if that ever happened.

Once changed and out of the locker room, Tony walked to the far end of the main room to hit the free weights. Most of the usual people were there. Kelly and the blond lady were on the treadmills. When he passed, Kelly looked up first and he nodded, only to have her return his greeting with a sexy little wave and a 100-megawatt smile.

Then the blond glanced his way. Tony smiled a small, warm smile and nodded. She smiled back and looked at her feet. She was so cute when she did that — that shy thing, like she'd been caught doing something she shouldn't. He wouldn't exactly call her a beauty, but she was a nice-looking, very well-put-together woman, with decent-sized, real-looking breasts, a nice, tight ass, and not an extra ounce of fat on her, just lean and strong. Tony thought she looked like someone who could hold a decent conversation. He'd really like to find out.

But not tonight. Tonight he'd work out, eat, and watch the game. Then he'd go to bed like he always did — alone — and get up tomorrow and start all over. Tomorrow evening he'd smile and nod, and she'd smile back and look down at her feet. Then same song, second verse.

Like always.

Chapter Three

"We'll get those delivered tomorrow morning for you. Is there anything else I can help you with?"

"No, I think that's everything. She's going to love them!" the young man said, grinning from ear to ear as he turned to leave.

"If she doesn't, you let us know right away and we'll make it right," Nikki replied. "Have a great afternoon."

Nikki turned a bit and noticed the young woman in the far corner. "Miss, is there anything I can help you with?"

"Uh, yeah. I need something for my girlfriend," she said, caressing a large pink rose.

"What's the occasion?"

"Our anniversary," the girl offered. She was petite and lovely, with long, dark hair, golden skin, and soft brown eyes that lit up when she mentioned their special day.

"First? Or long time?"

"We've been together for five years," the girl replied, looking at a crystal vase.

"Well, congratulations to you both! What's her favorite color?"

"Lavender."

"I think I might have just the thing. Let me get them." From the cooler, Nikki brought out an armload of something wrapped in tissue. She opened the tissue to reveal a dozen exquisite lavender-colored roses. "Whaddya think? Think she'd like these?"

"Oh, my god, she'd love those! Maybe in this vase? With some other stuff in them, you know, those little white things . . ."

"Baby's breath? Of course. And some fern. We can do it up right nice. I think you'll be pleased," Nikki smiled at her. "So let's get some information and get started. Your name?"

"Annabeth Walters," the girl replied.

"And they're going to . . ."

"Katie Reynolds. 451 Thrush Lane."

"Oh, she's my neighbor! I live on Bluejay Lane."

"Really? We've lived over there for the last four years, ever since we had our ceremony."

"Commitment ceremony? Wedding?"

"Well, we call it our wedding, but it was a commitment ceremony. You know Kentucky's not that progressive!" Annabeth laughed.

"Don't I know it!" Nikki was impressed with the young woman. She exuded self-confidence. "You're so lucky to find each other."

"Thanks! Yeah, I don't know what I'd do without Katie." A wistful smile stretched across Annabeth's face. "She's smart and funny and beautiful. And she understands me better than anyone."

"Everyone deserves to have someone like that," Nikki said thoughtfully, pulling the crystal vase from the shelf and putting it with the order slip.

"You're the flower shop lady. You're in the business of making love bloom! That makes you an expert – I bet you have a special someone, too."

"Well, I did. But not anymore. Some things don't last forever." Nikki couldn't bear to make eye contact with Annabeth.

"That's so true. Divorces are hard for everyone. My parents are divorced."

Nikki swallowed hard. "Not divorced. My husband, um, passed."

"Oh my god, I'm so sorry! That's awful." The sad look on the girl's face was exactly what Nikki didn't need.

"It certainly has been," Nikki replied. She hesitated before adding, "We'd been married for thirty years."

"Wow. Do you have kids?" Annabeth asked.

"Had." She hesitated again. "They passed as well." Nikki couldn't force herself to look up, to see the look on Annabeth's face. She'd seen it too often, that mixture of horror and pity.

It took a minute before the young woman spoke. "How terrible for you. I'm so, so sorry. It seems like you're doing very well, though. That's good, right?"

"Looks can be deceiving, dear. But enough about me. Planning a big anniversary date?" Nikki asked, smiling.

Annabeth was relieved that the topic had changed. "Yeah, dinner at Brisbane. It's Katie's favorite place."

"I've never been there, but I hear it's really nice." Then Nikki had a thought. "Would you like for us to send them to the restaurant? They'll put them on your table when you come in."

"Oh, that would be great! What a good idea." Annabeth smiled warmly. "You know, it's been really nice talking to you. Most people recoil in horror when they find out I have a girlfriend. You didn't."

"Of course I didn't. The heart wants what it wants. And everyone deserves love, don't they?" Annabeth couldn't help but notice how warm Nikki's eyes were when she spoke.

"Yes, you're right – everyone does. What's your name, by the way?"

"It's Nikki. Nikki Wilkes. And it's been really nice talking to you, Annabeth. Have a great afternoon and let us know if she's not satisfied with the flowers," Nikki called behind her as Annabeth turned to the door.

"At this point, I'm way more concerned about paying for the dinner!" Annabeth laughed, waving as she walked out.

Nikki smiled. What a sweet young lady. She was probably a little younger than Nikki's daughter Amanda would've been. Nikki wondered if Amanda would've found someone special by now. She thought about Jake, too. He'd just gotten the paperwork on his divorce a week before the accident. He might've started over by now.

At that point her mind couldn't help but drift to Randy. Even after five years, she still thought of him almost every second of every day. He'd been ripped from her so violently that she couldn't help but feel life was hemorrhaging from her daily. She couldn't say she hadn't looked at other men since, but she hadn't considered dating anyone. Didn't matter; no one had asked. She wondered if she had that "wounded animal" look that turned men off completely.

The phone rang and interrupted her reverie. She was thankful for every distraction. Another customer, another order. Weddings, funerals, birthdays. Everyone had something special to celebrate, someone's life to commemorate.

Except her.

Chapter Four

"Hi, baby! What can I do for you?"

Tony was always glad when Annabeth stopped by. She was like a ray of sunshine come to sit in his office for a few minutes. "Could Katie and I please use the house in Gatlinburg next weekend?" Annabeth toyed with the tiny Camaro on Tony's desk. The model was painted to look exactly like his car.

"Sure, honey. I'll call Roselle and ask her to have it ready for you. Big occasion? Or running away?" he laughed. The house in Tennessee had long been a haven for his little family when things with Dottie got too difficult in Louisville.

"Running away. Work's been extremely brutal for Katie lately. We just need to go somewhere that isn't 'da Ville.'" Tony didn't like the tired look that passed across her face.

"That bad?" She looked more stressed than he'd ever seen her.

"Yeah. When she took this promotion, she didn't realize she'd be cleaning up some really bad loans the last guy made." Annabeth frowned. "She's working lots of evenings and Saturdays, but she's insisted on being off on Sundays. That's all that's saved us."

"Then of course, use the house; that's why I keep it. Stay as long as you like." Tony came around from behind his desk and held out his arms. "Come here and let me give you a hug." Annabeth stood and let him hug her long and hard, and she rested her face on his broad chest.

"You're the best dad in the world," Annabeth sniffled.

"Aw, thanks, honey. You're the best daughter!" He gave her a big kiss on her forehead. She brightened, and he could see her relaxing, the furrows in her forehead softening.

"Well, I guess I'll see you this weekend some time." Then a perky look came over her. "Oh, and there's something else I'd like for you to do for me," she added.

"Oh? What's that?"

"There's this lady I met at the florist shop, The Passionate Pansy. I really think you need to go by and meet her," Annabeth said matter-of-factly.

"Now, Bethie, we've been over this before . . ."

"Dad, I think you'd really like her." Annabeth put her hands on her hips. "She's seems very sweet, and she's a widow. They'd been married thirty years when he died. Her name is Nikki. Can't you just go by there and check her out? She'd never have to know."

Tony set his jaw. "Annabeth, you know I'm not interested in getting involved with anyone." How many times did he have to go over this with everyone in his family? Why did they keep harping at him?

"Dad, I'm just asking you to . . ."

"Can we drop this? Please? I really don't want to meet any women, period." Tony returned to his chair and dropped in weariness, then turned and put his elbows on the gleaming desktop. "I tried that once. It was a disaster. I'm not eager to try it again." He'd gone out with Elaine Burrows a couple of times and she'd nearly worried him to death, trying to find out how much he made every year, then trying to cajole him into a proposal – all in two dates! He hadn't even slept with her, and he hadn't been out with anyone since. And if Annabeth had any idea how long it had been since he'd had sex, she might've decided there was something seriously wrong with him.

"Okay, Daddy. I love you. But please, think about it." She turned and left, waving to him from over her shoulder.

Tony put his head down on the desk. He couldn't tell Annabeth, his son, Clayton, or Raffaella, his mother, how lonely he was. They'd drive him insane trying to get him to ask out someone, anyone. After all the horrible years with Dottie, there was no way he'd get involved with any woman. His hand was a much better sex partner than Dottie had ever been, and gave him a lot less trouble. And he'd never had to have it committed to a mental ward.

But Annabeth and Clayton both had seen right through Elaine and neither had liked nor trusted her. They were both good judges of character and had good instincts. What made Annabeth sure this woman was different from all the rest?

There was a knock at the door and a ruddy face peered in. "Busy, boss?" Jason asked.

"Nah. Come on in," Tony answered, trying to clear his mind.

"The concrete work looks good. I'm on my way to pick up a replacement fixture for the Brookwood site. Need anything while I'm out and about?"

Jason offered.

"Can't think of anything."

Jason stood staring at Tony for a minute. "You okay? You look kind of, I don't know, rattled maybe?"

"Yeah, I'm fine." Tony sighed. "Annabeth was just here. We were talking about something and then, out of the blue, she announced she wants me to meet this lady she met."

"I know that's hard for you." Jason gave Tony his best sympathetic look. "I have to side with her, though – you need to meet someone nice. Hey, if you don't like this lady, I know someone . . ."

"Oh, for god's sake, you too?" Tony put his head in his hands. "Are you kidding? No. Not gonna happen."

"Well, if you change your mind, let me know," Jason laughed. "She's small, blond, cute, your age range. Very smart. Used to be the secretary of our neighborhood association. I think you'd like her."

"Nope. But thanks." Tony ran his fingers through his hair. "I'll keep that in mind."

"Okay, boss, whatever you say. Just remember I offered to introduce you." Jason waved as he walked out, just like Annabeth had, in that defeated kind of over-the-shoulder gesture.

Tony sat staring after Jason. What was it with everyone he knew? Sure, he was lonely, but did he look that miserable? He wasn't, really. He had a very full life. There were the kids, his mother and brothers, his cousin who worked for him, three homes, and the company. Work took up almost all of his time. It was an effort to maybe have a little bit of lunch and make time for the gym. He had everything he could handle. Why did everyone think he had time for a relationship?

And besides, love was highly overrated. Look what it had gotten him – years and years of pain and suffering. If Dottie hadn't been so damned determined to get crazier than she'd already been, they would've probably still been married. Loveless, sure, but still together.

The life he had was good enough. He didn't need a woman to take up his time. Tony picked up his coffee cup and took a swig, then spit it back into the cup – cold, just like his heart. But being open, letting someone in, would be too hard.

Chapter Five

Nikki hated Sundays. It was the only day of the week she had nothing to do outside the house. She remembered the days when she loved being at home. Now, it was just a place that reminded her of how alone she was. Except for Bill and Hillary, she really didn't have a reason to be there. But she was still lonely, even with them around her ankles.

Sunday morning in the conservative upper South meant the gym would very nearly be empty while everyone was in church; everyone except her, anyway. She dressed in the first gym clothes she could pull out of the closet, and then pulled her hair back in a ponytail and added a headband to keep it out of her face. She looked in the mirror – not very attractive, but no one ever looked at her. After all, she was all but invisible in the world.

Hers was one of only four cars in the gym lot, and one of them had to belong to whoever was working the front desk. Once she'd stashed her things in her locker, she hit the cardio theater. Boobalicious was already on a treadmill and nodded to her as she walked up. Nikki set the treadmill's program and dug in. She looked around. Other than Boobalicious, the only other person working out was a young guy she'd never seen before.

Fifteen minutes in, something caught Nikki's eye, and she looked up to see The Italian walk in the front door. When he strolled out to the weight area, he nodded to Boobalicious. Nikki looked down at her feet, then back up, only to find him looking directly at her. He smiled and nodded, and she smiled back before looking down again. When she looked up again, he was gone, already standing in the weight area with his back to her, curling some incredibly heavy-looking dumbbells.

Nikki could feel her face burning. Why couldn't she smile back with some confidence, make eye contact, and stop being so shy? She was afraid; afraid of being rejected, of looking desperate, or, worse yet, stupid. She got so mad at herself sometimes. Trying to concentrate on the walking program was useless. When she felt hot tears welling up in her eyes, she shut down the treadmill and jetted into the locker room.

Nikki sat on the bench in the locker room and wiped her eyes on her sleeve. No use in crying about it. It was just another wasted opportunity. She heard footsteps and looked up.

Boobalicious walked into the locker room, mopping the back of her neck with a towel. She glanced at Nikki and smiled. "Hi! We've never spoken, but my name's Kelly." She held out her hand.

Nikki shook it. "I'm Nikki. Nice to finally meet you."

"Yeah." Kelly unlocked her locker and started taking shower items out. "I see you here all the time. Nice décor, huh?" Kelly nodded her head toward the exercise area. Nikki looked at her, puzzled. "The guys. We've got some pretty good looking ones here, don't you think?"

"Can't say I've noticed," Nikki bluffed, digging in her purse for her hairbrush.

"Are you kidding me? You had to notice. Especially Tony. You know – Tony Walters." Kelly spoke the words as though Nikki should've known who she was talking about. "I've noticed how he looks at you," Kelly added.

"Me?" Nikki shook her head. "You think someone was looking at me? You must be mistaken."

"Hell no! The good-looking, dark-haired guy? He just nods to me. But he smiles at you every time he sees you. Introduce yourself!"

"Oh, no, I could never do that." Nikki could feel her cheeks starting to burn again.

"Shame," Kelly smiled. "I think he's into you. He'd be quite the catch, you know. Oh, well, nice to finally meet you," the buxom brunette told her as she walked away.

"Yeah, same here," Nikki called after her as Kelly disappeared down the hallway to the showers.

Did he really look at her? Nodding and smiling didn't equal being interested, just being polite. It would be nice, though, if he noticed her. She tried to quickly put him out of her mind. But now she knew his name – Tony, a typical Italian name. She'd never know if he was Italian, but it was kind of a funny coincidence.

As she walked out of the gym, she glanced across at him as he used one of the machines. He stared into the mirror as he monitored his workout but, for one split second, she could've sworn he made eye contact with her in the mirror from across the large room. No, she had to be mistaken; he might've with Kelly maybe, but not with her. She walked to her car, mentally beating herself up for being too damn shy. She'd just go home where she belonged. She'd had love once, but that was over.

Bill and Hillary would have to do.

Nikki pulled the little microwave dinner out and stirred it. In front of the TV, she looked for anything to lose herself in. She ate in silence, Bill and Hillary staring at her, hoping she'd drop something. They each got a dog cookie after she'd finished, then she climbed into the shower.

The warm water washed over her like a steamy embrace, and she let it soothe her. In her mind she saw Tony walking across the gym. He looked so sexy, so dark and dangerous, and yet his eyes were so kind. She felt a tingling between her legs, and her belly tightened. Looking down, she confirmed what she already knew – her nipples were rigid and standing straight out. She reached up, pinching and rolling one between her fingers, and she felt her abs clench. Ah, if only he were there to do that, to wrap those lips around . . .

No, she still loved Randy. But he was gone – forever. What should she do if the moment ever presented itself? Would he forgive her if he knew?

Nikki finished her shower and toweled off. When she chose a pair of panties to put on, she saw her jelly vibrator, forgotten in the drawer. It hadn't been touched in quite some time – after all, she wasn't a sexual being, just a shell of a woman. But something about it called to her, and she touched it, picked it up, hit the switch. It sprang to life. At the feel of the vibration, her nipples stiffened again to the point of hurting.

She lay back on the bed, her towel underneath her, and looked at the vibrator. It had little hearts all over it – how ironic. She looked down the length of her body. A little saggy, but at fifty-one, who wasn't? Maybe she didn't look too bad. When Randy was alive, her mound was always bare, but she'd let the hair grow back. Maybe it was time for a little landscaping. She let the tip of the vibrator trail down her body, between her breasts, and travel down to her mons. The sensation caused her back to arch, and she pressed the tip of the vibrator into the depression right above the hood of her clit. Fire shot through her body as the once-familiar feelings flooded through her, foreign and a little frightening now.

Then she thought about Tony, his smile, his dark hair, those lips. Oh, god, how she'd love to have those lips on her! The tip of the vibrator slid down to her clit, and she dipped it into her juices before bringing it back up and moving it in a circular motion. Tension started to build in her belly, coiling and releasing ever so slowly, and then picking up the pace. Her hips began to rock of their own accord, and she thought of his eyes and moaned quietly. In a few minutes she felt the peak, the heat, and before she even realized what was happening, she cried out through her orgasm, her hips thrusting and stomach clenching, his face in her memory. As the current running through her sex subsided, she plunged the vibrator into her pussy and felt it tighten around the little machine. It had been so long . . .

Shame washed over her. She'd been thinking about Tony when she should've been thinking about Randy. But Randy had left her there all alone, not of his choice, but still alone. Tony was a living, breathing, hot-blooded man. And she wanted him, really wanted him. Tears blurred her eyes, and she cleaned herself up and put on her plain cotton panties. After washing the vibrator with antibacterial soap, she threw it back into the drawer, hoping she'd forget it, and dressed.

She sat back down in front of the TV, but stared into space. Could she really have that again, someone to share her life with? Would a living person be enough to quiet the ghosts that would rise up? Why hadn't she gone in that car with them? Why was she still alive? Hot tears coursed down her cheeks and she felt her heart split open again. They were dead. She'd been dead for quite some time, too, but she wanted to feel alive again. Wouldn't it be nice if the person who revived her was Tony Walters? She knew that was a long shot, but a girl could dream, right?

Chapter Six

Tony walked to his truck on Monday evening, wondering what it was about the blond woman that made him want to get to know her. If he could just get her to hold his gaze for a couple of seconds . . . but she never would. No one at the gym seemed to know her, so he had no in. He'd have to screw up the courage to speak to her and risk being labeled a creep.

He turned his phone's ringer back on and checked for messages. He turned on the truck's heater to make sure his muscles didn't get too cool and stiff too fast, then started listening. Cal looking for a set of keys and finding them before he could even finish leaving the message. The plumbing contractor's office calling about some supplies they needed before starting the next morning. His brother, Bart, asking if Walters Construction was bidding on a job he was thinking about bidding on for his electrical company. Last but not least, Dottie raving about something – he deleted that one without listening to it.

The message from Clayton was not good; those wing nuts from that weirdo environmental awareness group had apparently flattened the tires on one of the company's forklifts, all four tires. It was the fourth sabotage of the month, and it was getting expensive fast. Why was Walters Construction the only company being targeted by these people? Nobody knew.

Listening to the voicemails served another purpose – it gave him a chance to sometimes see the blond lady leaving the gym. She was always so neatly dressed, even at her hottest and sweatiest, and Tony realized she had the look of a woman who was loved and cared-for, cherished even. She probably had someone. No way was she single.

As if on cue, she walked out of the gym and got into her red SUV. He pulled out of his parking space and watched her start her vehicle from his rearview mirror as he waited to turn out onto the street. Thinking about her was probably a bad idea; he should get a new hobby, he told himself.

He stopped at a fast food restaurant on the way home and picked up dinner. Maybe Annabeth, Katie, Clayton, and Brittany would come by later in the week. He could make it easy, pick up pulled pork barbecue and sides. If they wouldn't come for his company, they'd definitely show up for food. They already knew he kept plenty of beer.

He loved having the kids around. Annabeth and Katie had been together for five years, and Clayton and Brittany had been married for eight. Even though he could see some of Dottie's features in Clayton, he was still a Walters, almost as tall as Tony, with a headful of dark, wavy hair, big brown eyes, but with softer features than the Walters men. Katie and Brittany were like daughters to him. Katie's coloring and size were so much like Annabeth's, even though her auburn hair was lighter, that she could've been his own child, and the pale, red-haired Brittany was a porcelain beauty. He hoped they felt like he was an extra father to the two of them. He'd do anything for all four of them if it meant they'd be and stay happy.

As for their mother, Annabeth and Clayton had distanced themselves. She'd never been a real mother to them. Her illness had kept her from being able to love much of anyone – until she and Tony had divorced, at which time she seemed to love everyone, primarily men, and not necessarily in a good way. By then she'd been so busy sleeping her away across Jefferson County that she hadn't had much time for her kids. Because of the way she screamed and swore and ranted and raved, they really didn't want to spend time with her anyway. Tony had been the only parent they'd ever really had, and Tony's mother had been a great help too. Of course, he knew full well he and his mother hadn't been a replacement for a mom. The kids never complained, but he knew it still hurt them.

After he'd cleaned up the little bit of mess he'd made in the kitchen, he turned on the shower to let it warm up and brushed his hair before climbing in. The scalding water felt good on his shoulders, still tight from his workout. He stood under the spray for a good while, letting it run down his body like a warm massage, enjoying the feeling on his skin.

As his muscles warmed, Tony thought about the blond lady. Not the prettiest woman in the world, but there was something about her that drew him in and made him want to reach out and hug her. Then he thought about her face and figured it out: There was a sadness to her smile, something behind her eyes that made his heart ache for her. He wondered what her hair looked like when it wasn't caught up in one of those stretchy ponytail things. Was it soft? It probably smelled good. He was surprised to find he was getting hard just thinking about her. She was thin and fit, but in a soft way, not all sharp and angular. He wondered what she'd feel like under him.

He had to stop it. He didn't even know her and, at the rate he was going, he never would.

Rinsed and dried, he padded naked across the bedroom to the closet. When he passed the mirrored closet door, he stopped and backed up. Tony took a good, long look at himself. *Not too shabby,* he thought. He was fifty-seven, but he was a solid fifty-seven, not paunchy, flabby, or saggy like most other fifty-somethings. His time in the gym had paid off, and he had a body that most twenty-year-olds would envy. Sure, he wasn't thirty, but his waistline was solid, not soft. There was only the tiniest little bit of gray at his temples, and his hair was thick, wavy almost to the point of curls, and almost down to his shoulders. He still looked more than good enough.

Once he'd dressed in a pair of old jeans and a tee, he wandered into the den to watch a game. It was March Madness in the Bluegrass State, and someone had to be playing basketball somewhere.

Tony finished his last beer of the night before bedtime. After throwing the bottle away in the kitchen, he noticed the moonlight on the patio out back. Even though it was early in the year, when he opened the door he was surprised at how comfortable it was outside, and he strolled out onto the concrete and took a seat on the end of one of the chaise lounges.

The March sky was overflowing with stars of all sizes and colors and he chuckled to himself as he tried to count them. He wondered, *What would it be like to be able to sit out here with a woman? My arm around her, her head on my shoulder; that would be nice. Could that really happen?* He looked back up at the stars – there were so many. Were there enough women out there to actually find one who'd love him? Then a strong, hungry voice in his head spoke almost audibly, *Maybe it's time to find out.*

Chapter Seven

"So, what are you doing for Annabeth for her birthday?"

Tony's heart leaped up into his throat. This was why he paid Cheryl the big bucks – she'd saved his ass so many times it wasn't funny. "Don't tell me you forgot," she called from the other room.

"Um, well, no, I hadn't actually . . ."

"Yep, you forgot." He looked up to see her standing in the doorframe of his office, glaring at him, her arms folded across her chest.

"Um, yeah, well." He thumped his pen on the desktop. "So what would you suggest? I could use some help here."

"I'd say . . . start out by ordering her some flowers. That should get the ball rolling." Cheryl piddled in the papers on his desk. "And maybe take her to dinner. Her and Katie. And get her a piece of jewelry – girls like that."

"Jewelry?" Tony didn't even know where to start with that one.

"Something diamond. Doesn't even matter what." That was Cheryl – always practical.

Then it hit him, and he jumped up from his chair and grabbed his jacket. "I'll be back in a little while."

"Where in the world are you going?"

"To order flowers." A plan was hatching in his mind, but he wasn't about to share it with anyone. He'd never hear the end of it, especially if it failed, which was likely.

"Can't you do it over the phone?" Cheryl asked, staring at his back as he dashed toward the door.

"No. I don't remember the name of the shop. Annabeth told me about it. I'll know it when I see it," Tony called back to her.

"So you'll be driving around town for awhile?" Cheryl chuckled. "Well, see you when you get back, boss!" She'd known him too long. He was definitely up to something.

"Yeah, yeah, yeah . . ." Tony waved her off and trotted down the steps.

The plan would work if he could just find the right florist shop.

Ten minutes and several back-tracks later, The Passionate Pansy stood across the street from the little lot where he'd parked his truck. A tiny wave of panic rolled into his chest as he crossed to the storefront. He hadn't talked to a prospective date in a long time, but this was a woman who'd managed to have what sounded like a successful long-term relationship, and that was exactly the type of woman he'd be interested in meeting. What should he say? But she wouldn't know why he was there, so it wouldn't matter. This was a reconnaissance mission, just to check her out. Order flowers, no worries, no stress, get in, get out; over in a few minutes.

A bell jingled on the door when he opened it — no backing out now. He looked around the shop at the colorful arrangements and giftware, then started toward the counter in the back. Behind the counter he could see a woman, or her back at least. She had long, wavy hair, and it was a gleaming gold. Just as he made it to the counter, she turned to speak, then stopped and stared.

It was her — the blond woman from the gym. What the hell? Tony's heart did a double twist and back flip. He hoped the shock didn't show on his face, and he tried to compose himself.

As she turned, she automatically said, "Can I help . . ." Nikki froze. It was him. "You're the . . ." *No, don't say The Italian. He'll think you're nuts.* ". . . guy from the gym, right?" She looked flustered and a little pink.

"Uh," Tony started. Suddenly, he couldn't remember — why was he there? "Uh, yeah, hi! I recognize you too. Um, I need to order flowers for my daughter. For her birthday." *Focus,* he thought. "I'm looking for someone named Nikki?"

"Oh, that's me." Nikki was startled, and it showed. "How did you know my name?"

Tony couldn't believe it — the woman Annabeth had told him about was the woman from the gym? That couldn't be right. "My daughter, um, the one I want to order flowers for? She ordered some here. She said you guys did a really nice job. So I thought I'd come by." There, not so bad — he didn't sound like a complete idiot. But he knew he probably had an odd look on his face. What were the chances that this could happen?

"Who's your daughter?"

"Annabeth. Annabeth Walters."

"Oh, yes! Annabeth! She's a beautiful girl. She ordered them for a friend of hers." Nikki looked down and there it was; that small, shy smile accompanied by the hint of sadness in her eyes. Tony felt the panic in his chest bloom into something very different, something warm and tender and completely unfamiliar. She looked so different, too, with no ponytail, wearing makeup and street clothes. She might've looked good at the gym, but she looked even better up close.

"Katie, her partner. Their anniversary," Tony offered.

"I bet you're proud of her. Sounds like she's made a very happy life for herself." Nikki picked up an order pad and a pencil. She didn't want to look completely stupid. It was so hard to not stare and embarrass herself. Why did he have to be so good-looking? That dark hair and those deep caramel-colored eyes with gold flecks had her so flustered she could barely hold it together. She tried to rein her mind in. "So, it's her birthday. How old?"

"She's twenty-eight," Tony replied. "I was thinking something in a pretty vase, maybe crystal? Would she like that?" He had no idea what to order, but maybe asking enough questions would get her to come out and stand beside him. He wanted that desperately.

"Any girl would like that! Do you know what colors she likes?" Nikki came out from behind the counter just as he'd hoped and sashayed toward a large display. He walked behind, watching with delight. Her gait was very graceful, and she had a small, well-defined waist and a nice sway to her hips. In her wake was a beckoning scent of something dark and warm, spicy even. He felt something stir down deep inside him, like it was stretching and waking from a long sleep. "Here's a pretty vase. Will this do?"

"Oh, yeah, that's great." Tony held the cut crystal, admiring it, then handed it back. "And she likes blue – lots of blue."

"That's very doable. Blue, blue, and more blue, and some white accents. Does that sound good?" she asked. Blue indeed – her eyes were clear and almost turquoise, and he really wanted to get lost in them.

"That sounds great." Tony reached over to touch a plant that looked too perfect to be real and found it to be as alive as the woman he was admiring. The place was so lush, and the flowers were so colorful. Or maybe it was her. She seemed so warm and gentle. It was as though she radiated something he couldn't define and it filled the whole room, touched all of the flowers, made the light softer and warmer and the air sweeter. He didn't want to finish the order because he'd have to leave, and what he really wanted was to stay there and talk to her.

"So let's get this set up for you. What's your name?" She certainly didn't want him to know that she and Kelly had been talking about him in the locker room.

Damn, Tony thought. *I didn't even introduce myself – how stupid.* "Tony. Tony Walters. I'm sorry, you're Nikki?"

"Yeah. Nikki Wilkes." She reached out her hand to shake his and he wished he'd had a chance to wipe the sweat from his palms before they touched. Her hand was small and delicate, with long fingers and beautiful nails, and when their palms touched he got the impression that something more than an introduction had passed between them. When he let go, she wrote the date and his name on the receipt. "And this is going to Annabeth Walters," she repeated to herself out loud as she wrote, "over on Thrush Lane. I'm sorry – I can't remember the house number."

"Actually, it's going to her work, Grayson Motors over on Taylorsville Road. She's their financial agent."

"Good! We have a delivery over on Taylorsville already scheduled for this afternoon, so we'll take hers too. Pick out a card and we'll include it." Nikki pointed to the little rack at the other end of the counter.

Tony picked out a small birthday card and wrote in it:

To my beautiful Annabeth,
I hope you have a happy day today and every day.
I love you,
Dad

"There," he said, handing the tiny card to Nikki. "That oughta do it."

"Beautiful choice," she told him as he handed her his credit card. The transaction was almost over, and so was his contact with her. *Should I ask her out? I don't know what to do.* Indecision swallowed him. He didn't want to leave, but he was afraid she'd laugh and turn him down flat if he asked her out cold turkey. Why could he make a five-minute decision on hundreds of thousands of dollars, but couldn't ask a woman to dinner? Had Dottie really done that much damage?

"Sign right here, please," she said, handing him the receipt. *Do something!* his brain was yelling, but his hands were shaking as he signed and handed it back. "Thanks and let us know if she's not happy, okay? We'll want to make it right."

"Will do." It was all he could squeeze out. He could feel his face getting flushed. And he couldn't think of anything else to say.

"Well, have a nice day, Tony Walters. Guess I'll see you at the gym, huh?" She smiled that smile again and looked down at her feet. His heart was hammering.

"Yeah, see you at the gym," he mumbled. He stood there looking at her for an awkward moment, then turned and hoofed it to the door. When he made it to the sidewalk and the door closed behind him, he realized he'd been holding his breath. Why had he been so nervous? What was it about her that made him feel like a complete imbecile? Had she noticed how tense he was? He'd really screwed up. He hadn't asked her out. But did he want to go out? He hadn't given it serious consideration in a long time.

Once Tony was gone, Nikki finally took a breath. She'd barely been able to slip the receipt in the cash box because her hands had been shaking so hard. He probably thought she was some kind of freak because she'd acted so weird. She'd treated him like any other customer, but she'd wanted so much to talk to him, to find out what he was like. Was he as beautiful on the inside as he was on the outside? She'd never seen a man so gorgeous. But it looked like he was just being kind. She tried to concentrate on how pleasant he'd been, not how disappointed she was. Kelly was wrong – he wasn't interested in her at all, just ordering a gift.

Tony walked across the street and got into his truck, trying to think of an excuse to go back inside, but he couldn't come up with anything. So he sat, head on the steering wheel, mentally kicking himself for not having the balls to come right out and ask her to dinner.

Across the store, Nikki called out to Carol, "Going to the bathroom." She shut the door and let the tears fall. How ridiculous – someone like him wouldn't give her a second look.

Tony started his truck and pulled out onto the street. At least he'd see her at the gym. He had to work up some courage. He never thought he'd want to date anyone, but if there was a chance she might say yes to going out with him, maybe it was time to give it a try.

"Oh, Daddy, the flowers are beautiful!" Annabeth was practically singing over the phone.

"Like them? Send me a picture of them. I'd like to see," Tony grinned into the phone.

"I will!" She hesitated. "So, did you meet Nikki?" Annabeth asked.

She wasn't going to give it a rest, so he figured he might as well tell her.

"Yes, actually, I did," he answered.

"And?"

"Turns out she goes to my gym. I recognized her when I walked into the shop."

"Really? That's cool." It sounded like Annabeth was eating something.

"Are you eating birthday cake?" Tony asked.

"Actually, birthday cupcake. Katie picked them up for us. They're very good. Stop by and have one, why don't you?"

"I think I'll do that." He started straightening up his desk. "I'll be there in a few."

"Clayton and Brittany are here. We'll save one for you. But only one. And if you take too long to get here, well, no promises!" she laughed into the phone.

"On my way!" He shoved his phone into his pocket, snatched his jacket from the sofa, and headed toward Thrush Lane.

Annabeth waltzed back into the living room of the little house, grinning, cupcake frosting all over her mouth.

"Annabeth Maria Walters! What have you done?" Katie cried out. "I can tell you're up to something. Who did you call?"

"Dad." She wiped frosting from her face with her finger and sucked it off. "I called to tell him thanks for the flowers." She grinned even wider. "He got them at The Passionate Pansy."

"Oh my god!" Katie squealed. "Did you . . . ? I know what you did! And?" Clayton and Brittany stared at the two of them.

"It worked! She actually goes to his gym! Can you believe it?" She held up her hand and Katie high-fived her.

"She? Who?" Clayton asked.

"Clayton, I think your sister's playing matchmaker," Katie laughed.

"With . . . ?"

"With Dad!" Annabeth shrieked, jumping up and down.

"No way!" Brittany squealed with delight. "Out with it!"

Chapter Eight

"Boss, I hate to tell you this, but She Who Shall Not Be Named just pulled up." Tony could hear Cheryl rustling around as she talked, trying to retreat to another work space.

"Aw, shit," Tony muttered, throwing his pencil across the room. There went a perfectly good day.

She hit the office door like a bulldozer crashing into the wrong house. "Hey, Cheryl, Tony in his office?"

"Uh, yeah, I think . . ."

"Good. We need to have a little talk." Dottie took two pieces of candy out of Cheryl's candy dish, unwrapped one, and threw the wrapper back onto Cheryl's desk, then walked straight into Tony's office.

"Dottie." He didn't bother to ask how she was; he didn't give a shit. He didn't even stand. He reserved that sign of respect for those who deserved it, and she wasn't included in that group.

She didn't bother to ask how he was either, just threw her sloppy form down into the chair in front of his desk and crossed her legs. "I need two thousand dollars," she announced, unwrapping the second piece of candy and tossing the wrapper onto Tony's desk.

"And you're here why?" He leaned back in his desk chair. God, she was a loathsome creature. He couldn't believe he'd actually loved her at one time.

"Because. You're my husband. You're supposed to give me what I want."

"In case you don't recall, we haven't been married for sixteen years," Tony scowled, refusing to look at her.

"We took vows! We'll always be married in God's eyes," Dottie railed.

"Oh, I see. We're married when you want money and not married when you want to fuck someone else. How exactly does that work, Dot?"

"Do you have to remind me of every horrible thing that's happened between us? God, Tony, you're so hurtful!" Dottie whined and pouted, looking to drop some guilt on him. And she failed miserably.

"I'm hurtful? Me?" He could feel his ire starting to rise. "Look, I'm not giving you any money. Go ask the husband of the week for whatever you want. By the way, who is it this week?" He glared at her.

"Well, that's really nice of you," she spat sarcastically. "You know Hector and I are separated."

"Who's Hector?" That was a name he hadn't heard before. This was her third since him? Fourth? Tony had lost count.

"Oh, you're so damned self-righteous, aren't you?" Dottie turned like the flip of a switch. Her Jekyll-and-Hyde brain was hard to follow. "Just because nobody wants you, you can't believe anyone would want me. I can't help it that you're old and fat and have a big nose."

"Me? That's a joke. Have you looked in the mirror lately?" He knew she was full of shit, that she was sick and made everyone around her sick, but her words still stung. She'd spent so many years tearing him down, no wonder he couldn't bring himself to ask anyone out. He looked in the mirror and saw a guy who looked perfectly fine, but he heard her words in his head and they tore him down again and again. He had to find a way to silence her voice permanently. "Dottie, I'm done. Go. I'm not giving you anything." He pointed at the door.

"And what do you think your kids will say when they find out their mother is homeless because you wouldn't give me a little bit of money, like you don't have it or something?" She rose and shuffled toward the door. On her way out, she stuck out her arm and swept it down his credenza, knocking over framed photos, certificates, and a lamp.

"At least you got the 'my kids' part right. And my kids will say it was about time I told you to go to hell," Tony growled, looking away from her. She cleared her throat and he turned to see what point she was trying to make.

She stopped in the doorway, turned, and pulled up her blouse to flash both of her breasts, leering at him. Tony rolled his eyes. "Oh my god, get the hell out, Dottie." She pulled her blouse back down, shot him a hurt look, and walked out of the office, her ass swaying back and forth, until she finally disappeared out the door.

"Sweet jesus, I saw that. And I wish I hadn't." Cheryl was grimacing when she appeared in Tony's doorway. He folded his arms on the desk and rested his face on them, unable to look Cheryl in the eye. "Did she really . . . ?"

"Yeah. She did." Tony didn't know whether to be embarrassed or sick. He'd almost give Dottie whatever she wanted if it guaranteed she'd leave town and he'd never see or hear from her again, but she'd just come back, wanting more. Homeless? The two thousand was probably for another divorce. "You know how she is. I'm sorry, Cheryl. I'm sorry you have to deal with that, sorry you had to see it, sorry I ever married her."

"Oh, hon." Cheryl sat down in the chair in front of his desk and patted his arm. He looked up at her, his face drawn and tired. "Oh, don't let her rattle you. And don't apologize to me. She's crazy – everyone knows that. And don't you listen to her, you hear me? You'll find someone special, I just know it. Of course, you kinda have to go out and look, don't you?" She smiled warmly at him. If he'd had a sister and could've chosen her, Cheryl would've been his first choice.

"Yeah, right." He shook his head. "I don't stand a chance. Sometimes I don't think I can get out of bed in the morning. I hear her voice in my head and, I don't know, I just . . ." He put his head back down and closed his eyes.

"You've got to get past that. You can do it. You're a good-looking guy and women drool after you. Any woman would be lucky to have you." Cheryl patted him on the arm again and stood. "You don't want to be alone for the rest of your life, do you?" she asked as she walked out.

Did he want to be alone? No. He didn't. He had to find a way to ask Nikki out. He was tired of being alone. He'd do it even if it killed him.

Chapter Nine

"What's the deal with all of this stock?" Nikki called out to Marla. "I've got two cartons of dual-colored mugs here."

"Secretary's Day is tomorrow," Marla reminded her as she came through the stockroom door.

"Oh, yeah. I guess we're going to get hit today, huh?" Nikki took the mugs out of the boxes and put them on the shelf by color. There were pink ones lined with yellow, purple lined with green, and blue lined with orange, sixteen of each – four dozen. "Do you think we'll have enough?"

"Probably. You know guys – they won't all order for their secretaries. Most of them don't even do anything for their wives' birthdays." Marla's ex, Dave, was a rat bastard of the highest order. If Nikki had been married to him, she wouldn't have had a very high opinion of men either.

Once Carol got there, she helped them unpack the cartons of flowers for the morning. They had plenty of containers and fresh cut flowers to do anything anyone could want.

Nikki wondered about Tony. Did he have a secretary? Would he come in to order something? She'd seen him almost every day at the gym in the three weeks since he'd been in for Annabeth's flowers. Every time he came by her, he spoke to her, and she spoke back. She could feel daggers shooting out of Kelly's eyes, and she had to admit, it felt kind of good. No one had ever been jealous of her before. She lived for those moments, a simple "Hey, Nikki, how are you?" or "Hi, Nikki, doing okay?" She was finding it easier to look at him and not her feet. Sometimes she even imagined he'd stop and say, "Hey, Nikki, wanna go for coffee?" That would be nice. Probably never happen, though.

She turned on the OPEN sign and checked the counter to make sure they had all the sales supplies they needed. Good thing, too; within ten minutes, they'd had three customers, two of whom were women ordering for their secretaries. One had a secretary named Chuck who was getting a box of chocolates and dark burgundy calla lilies. He'd like those.

The morning meandered toward noon, and soon it was lunchtime. Nikki chose to work through. It was easier than eating alone.

Clayton stuck his head into Tony's office and spoke low: "Dad, you do know tomorrow is Administrative Professionals Day, right?" Cheryl had gone to the post office, but Clayton was still being careful.

"Huh? What?" Tony's face twisted in puzzlement.

"Administrative Professionals Day. You know, it used to be called Secretary's Day?" Clayton answered.

"Crap, thanks for reminding me. I need to do something for her." Tony wrote FLOWERS FOR CHERYL on a sticky note and stuck it to the front of one of his desk drawers where she couldn't see it. "I'll go take care of that in a little while."

Mission accomplished, Clayton thought. Annabeth had given him strict orders to remind Tony so maybe he'd pay a visit to The Passionate Pansy. Clayton smiled to himself as he walked away from his dad's office. His sister was determined to get Tony together with that woman who worked there. He had to admit to himself that he didn't think it was a bad idea. He'd watched Tony barely shuffling through his existence, numb and alone, and he'd like to see some sign of life creep back into his dad.

And it worked. Tony parked across from The Passionate Pansy and looked around; sure enough, he'd thought he remembered a café next door. The special of the day was a Reuben, so he went in and ordered two sandwiches, two bags of chips, and an iced tea. Then he walked over to the flower shop, wondering if what he was about to do would help him or hurt him.

A dark-haired woman stood at the counter. "Can I help you?" she asked, smiling at Tony.

"Um, yeah, I need to place an order for Secretary's Day, uh, Administrative Professionals Day," he corrected himself. "She, actually," he stuttered, "uh, I sort of know Nikki. Is she here?"

"Oh, yeah. Hey, Nik!" Carol called out. "Customer!"

Nikki stepped out from the workroom and couldn't believe her eyes. He'd asked for her? She smiled. "Hi, Tony!"

"Hey! I'm, well, I need to, um, you did such a good job with Annabeth's flowers that I, um, I thought maybe you could help me with something for my secretary?" He felt his face grow warm. What the hell was wrong with him? Why did he feel so flustered?

"Sure! We've got a lot of really pretty things. What did you have in mind?" She came around from behind the counter, and his heart nearly stopped. She had on a pair of form-fitting, flared-leg jeans and shoes with three-inch heels, and her legs were long and lean. The long-sleeved purple tee she was wearing hugged her torso, and her breasts were round and soft-looking. A beautiful vintage amethyst pendant hung down in the v-neck of the top, lying perfectly against her ivory chest just below her collarbone. And that hair – it cascaded down her shoulders, down her chest, down her back. It positively glittered. He couldn't think, couldn't move, couldn't speak. He wanted to lean in, to sniff her hair, to touch it, touch her, wrap his arms around her waist and bury his face in her neck. He felt something happening in his jeans, and realized he was getting hard. Strangest thing – that kept happening when he thought about her. He hoped she wouldn't notice.

Then he snapped back to reality. "Um, something colorful? She works with a bunch of guys, so she'd probably appreciate something bright and feminine." He wondered how long he'd stood there staring at her, hoping he hadn't made a fool of himself, but she smiled at him like nothing was wrong.

"We can do colorful. Not a problem. How much do you want to spend?"

"Uh, fifty? Is that enough?"

"We can do miracles with fifty! Let me get all of the info." Nikki started writing down the information she already knew; Tony supplied Cheryl's name and his address and phone number. "And where is this going?"

"Walters Construction. Over on Brownsboro Road."

Walters; surely no coincidence. "So, is that family?" She hadn't known where he worked.

"Yes, you could say that," Tony answered.

Too many questions, too forward, she thought. Her insides were turning to mush, and she was getting wet just standing close to him. She wished she'd worn a padded bra, not just so she'd look bigger, but to cover her nipples better. They were hardening, and there wasn't a damn thing she could do about it.

"Looks like I've got all of the information," she said as she took his credit card. "We'll get this out tomorrow first thing. If she's not happy with them, please let us know and we'll make it right."

"Oh, I'm sure they'll be beautiful. You do good work." Tony smiled at her. He'd placed the bag of food on the counter while he ordered, and now it was time for his act. He picked up the bag, looked at it, and shook it, then opened it and peered inside. "Oh no! They gave me two of everything. Have you had lunch?"

"Well, no. I worked through lunch," she stuttered, wondering if he was about to ask her to lunch. She felt kind of giddy at the thought.

"I can't eat all of this. Would you like a sandwich and some chips?" Tony held them out to her.

Nikki's heart sank. "Oh, how kind! Thank you." She reached out for the wrapped sandwich and the bag of chips and, for a split second, their fingers touched. In that moment, she felt like she was about to cry, partially because she wanted so badly to touch him or have him touch her, but mostly because she was so disappointed. She'd so hoped he was about to ask her to spend fifteen minutes with him, eating across a table somewhere; instead, he handed her extra food he'd accidentally gotten from next door. But it was kind of him to offer it. With very little disposable income, she rarely got to eat out. She smiled and looked down at her feet.

"Well, thanks for the help." Tony strolled to the door, feeling pretty good about himself. He might not have asked her out, but he'd given her something to think about for as long as the sandwich and chips lasted. Was it his imagination – were her nipples poking out underneath her tee? He didn't want to stare; well, he wanted to, but not so she'd see. "See you at the gym!"

"Yeah, see ya," she called behind him. When he'd cleared the door, she called out to Carol, "Can you come out and man the counter?"

"Sure." Carol walked to the counter just in time to see Nikki's eyes redden. "Hey, what's wrong?" Carol asked, but Nikki shook her head and took off for the back, food in hand.

"Are you okay?" Carol called behind her.

"Yeah, I'm fine. I just need to eat this before it gets completely cold," Nikki called back, trying to sound normal. The back door banged shut behind her and she plopped down on a crate outside the door. She unwrapped the sandwich, but with the first bite, hot tears sprang from her eyes, and when she tried to swallow, she choked. She worked to get the bite down, and tried for the next one. While she chewed, she told herself, *Tony gave me this sandwich. So maybe he didn't buy it just for me, so what? He could've thrown it away, but he was kind enough to pass it on to me. I should eat it and be thankful for it.* But she so wanted to be eating it somewhere with him, sitting across from him and looking into his eyes. She'd see him at the gym. Maybe someday he'd actually notice her.

For now, the sandwich would just have to do.

Chapter Ten

A plan was hatching in Tony's head. He'd been seeing Nikki at the gym every day, and he always smiled and spoke. It was really getting to Kelly too – he thought that was pretty funny. Did they talk about him in the locker room? The idea made him smile.

And there was the night. Every night. He'd climb into bed all alone and, no matter how much he concentrated on other things, his mind made a three-sixty and came back to her. Before he could draw another breath, he was hard, harder than he'd ever been, and he'd just get harder and harder until it was impossible to think about anything but her soft hair, her pale skin against his darkness, her hard, rosy nipples, and he had to relieve his pain. He'd wrap his hand around his shaft and start to stroke, tight and slow. He wondered how tight her pussy would be, how warm and soft she'd feel in his arms. Her long, beautiful legs would wrap around his waist, and he'd pump into her like a dying man drawing his last breath. In his mind he could see those clear blue-green eyes staring up into his as he fucked her for all he was worth until she'd drawn every last drop of his essence from him. Oh, god, he made a mess every night, but it was worth it to imagine what she'd be like.

Then, every morning, he thought about his plan and wondered if it would work. He sat at his desk and daydreamed about the end result. It surprised him to find that, while it terrified him, it was also exhilarating. The idea that he might actually have a chance with this woman was beyond anything he'd ever imagined.

"Did you hear me?"

"What?" Tony snapped back into reality. Clayton was standing in front of his desk, and Cal was leaning against the door facing.

"I said, is the plumbing firm ready for the Carson project? Geez, Dad, where the hell were you?" Clayton eyed him suspiciously.

"Yeah, yeah, the plumbing. Dalton called this morning and said they're ready to go. Just say the word. Hey, can I ask you something?"

"Sure."

"So, it's been a long time for me. Do women expect to have sex on the first date now?"

Clayton's brows shot up into his hairline. "Shit! Really, Dad? I can't believe you asked me that!"

"But, Clayton, I need to know because . . ."

"Oh, no! I don't want to know! I don't even want to think about that. Aw, man . . ." Clayton looked woefully distressed, and Cal chuckled.

"But seriously, Clayton, I haven't had sex in, well, awhile, and . . ."

"Noooooo! Oversharing! I don't want to hear this! *Please!*" Clayton made a big production of putting his hands over his ears. By then, Cal was barking with laughter in the background.

"Would you guys help me out here, please? I really don't know what I'm doing." Tony sounded exasperated and a little desperate.

"Boss, maybe I can help," Cal offered, taking Clayton by the shoulders and moving him over to the credenza, out of the way. Cal sat down in the chair in front of Tony's desk. "So, how old is this girl? Twenty? Twenty-five? Thirty?"

"Oh, hell no! I'm not sure, but she's at least forty-five, maybe older." Tony made a disgusted face. "What, you think I'm some old man going for a teenage girl or something?"

"No, boss, but you are a man that women want."

"Me?" Tony's eyes went wide with disbelief. "Women want me? What women? Where? On what planet? 'Cause I'm not finding any of them."

"Oh, they're out there. Lots of women," Cal grinned, eyebrows raised. Tony gaped at him, and Cal started again. "All ages, sizes, and types. Do you have any idea how many women see the Walters Construction logo on my truck and ask if I could introduce them to you?"

Clayton had taken his hands off his ears. He nodded toward Cal. "He's not lying, Dad. They do it to me all the time, too. When they're not propositioning me. You know, the apple doesn't fall too far from the tree." He looked positively proud of himself.

Tony was bewildered. "Oh, come on. You guys are joking, right?"

"Hell no! You're considered quite the catch around Louisville." Cal smiled and shook his head. "You really don't know that?"

Tony shook his head. "Do they want my money? I have to assume that's it."

"Among other things," Cal smirked. "Your money doesn't hurt, but they want you too. They wanna jump your bones in the most primitive of ways."

"Oh, my god, here we go again!" Clayton yelled, putting his hands back over his ears. Cal shot him a look. Tony didn't quite know what to say and he turned to Clayton, who took his hands down and, pointing at Cal, added, "Yeah, what he said."

Tony tried to compose himself. "So, back to my original question," he tried again, feeling more than a little disconcerted. "Do women these days want sex on the first date? I know things have changed since I was younger. And I've been out of circulation for a long time."

"Boss, it really depends on the woman. I'd say to not assume that's the case and wait and see. Based on what you know of her, what's your impression?"

"She doesn't seem to me like the type." If his plan worked and he got her to go out with him, he didn't want to screw things up by going too fast.

"Then go with your gut. You know her better than we do." *Actually, I don't know her at all*, Tony thought. *But I want to get to know her.* It would be so easy to sabotage this with sheer stupidity.

All he knew was that, the more time went by, the more he wanted her. He made it a point to speak to her every time he saw her at the gym. A couple of times he'd even stood and talked to her for a minute or two. Sometimes she'd ask him a question about one of the weight machines or a lift she'd seen him do. Once, she'd even asked how Annabeth and Katie were. He was sure she wasn't flirting, just being warm and friendly. Or was she flirting? He couldn't tell.

So, this was it. It was time to fish or cut bait. He had to find out if she was interested in him or not. And apparently, according to Clayton and Cal, if she wasn't, maybe he had options. But he really didn't want options; he wanted her.

Secretary's Day was two weeks in the rearview mirror, and there were no holidays coming up, only a boring Thursday to get through. Nikki sighed as she put up the fresh cut roses that had come in that morning. The last time Randy had sent her roses, they'd still been on the counter when the police officers came by to tell her . . .

Enough of that. She wiped a stray tear from the corner of her eye. Tony still spoke to her at the gym, but he was only being polite. He wasn't really interested. There was not one thing exciting about her to attract a man, especially a man like Tony Walters. Besides, if he wanted to ask her out, he already would've. Guys like him weren't bashful.

She carried the huge watering can from display to display, filling reservoirs and watering live plants. The bell on the door jingled, and she walked to the counter, set the can down, and turned to greet the customer.

It was Tony. Something in her chest tightened, and she smiled at him before looking back at her feet. Then she looked up at him again and he broke a huge smile at her – beautiful! "Hey, stranger! How are you!" she sing-songed, then thought, *Shit, that sounded so lame.* She was embarrassing herself.

"Hey yourself! I'm good. You?"

"Good. What can I help you with today?"

"I want to send something to someone special. I thought maybe you could help me." Tony fidgeted and hoped she wouldn't notice. This was getting real, and he was getting very, very nervous.

"What did you have in mind?" Nikki took out an order book. *Someone special.* So he had a girlfriend; she hoped he couldn't see her disappointment. He was leaning on the counter, closer than he'd ever been to her. She felt her nipples hardening as she took in his scent – he smelled so good, a warm, dark, earthy fragrance like her incense. A glance down the front of her blouse gave her a view that made her blush. Damn – there they were again. Maybe he wasn't paying any attention.

"Oh, I don't know. What do you like?" he asked, looking around.

"I like roses. Pink roses."

"Pink roses it is," he told her decisively. "What about a vase?"

"For long-stem roses you'll need a taller vase than the one you sent to Annabeth. What about this one?" She pulled down a tall, slender, clear glass vase.

"That'll do nicely. And some greenery. And a big pink bow."

"A big bow. Anything else?" she asked, writing as quickly as she could. At least while she was writing, she could pull her arms in a little to cover her nipples, which were getting harder and more noticeable by the minute.

"Nope, I think that'll do it." Tony watched her finish writing the order and noticed the peaks under her thin sweater. He felt his cock growing and tried to stifle the sensation, but that didn't work too well.

"So, where is this going?"

"Um, what's the address here?" he asked.

"Here?" She knew she must've misunderstood him. "The shop?"

"Yeah, here. What's the address here?" he asked again.

"It's . . . 4229 Frankfort Avenue," she answered haltingly.

"Send them to 4229 Frankfort Avenue," he announced, trying to sound nonchalant.

She was confused, but she wrote down the address. "Here? Okay. And to whom should they be addressed?"

"They should go to Nikki Wilkes at The Passionate Pansy, 4229 Frankfort Avenue." His voice was clear and strong. Nikki felt her knees weakening and her mouth going dry. She started her mantra: *Don't cry. Don't cry. Don't cry.* "Oh, and I'm going to need a card, huh?" he added, trying to keep a straight face. He went to the end of the counter and took a small card from the rack. "Can I borrow your pen?"

"Uh, yeah, sure." Nikki handed him the pen, her cheeks blazing. She could feel herself getting wet and hot, and her nipples were so hard they throbbed. As she watched, he wrote something on the card and slipped it into its tiny envelope. Handing it to her, he added, "I know you'll make sure this goes with the flowers." He smiled again and handed her his credit card.

She filled out the rest of the order ticket, her hand shaking almost uncontrollably the whole time. Once he'd signed the receipt, she handed him his copy and gave him a weak, "We'll make sure this gets taken care of right away."

"Oh, yeah, I know, if she's not happy with them, I'll let you know and you'll make it right!" All of a sudden he felt like the smartest man on earth – he'd pulled it off! "Guess I'll have to be sure to ask how she liked them, huh?" Nikki looked so shocked that he couldn't help but smile. "See you at the gym!" he called behind him, waving over his shoulder.

Once he was out of sight, Nikki realized she hadn't been breathing. She gulped in air and her knees buckled, sending her to the floor. Her butt hit it with a "thud" and she sat there in shock.

"What the hell?" Carol cried as she bustled out from the workroom and helped Nikki to her feet. Of course, she'd been trying to listen at the door. "What happened?"

"Look!" Nikki cried out, thrusting the order in Carol's face.

Carol squinted at the writing, and her mouth fell open. "Sweet mother of god, honey, that man wants you!" She squealed and hugged Nikki. "Oh, my god, he's soooo hot!" The way she was laughing and dancing around, anyone watching would've thought he was sending the flowers to her. All the while, Nikki stood in stony silence, almost unable to believe or understand what had just happened. "I'm filling this order right now!" Carol laughed, running to the back.

In five minutes, she was back with a dozen huge pink roses in the glass vase, sporting an enormous bow. A card pick held the tiny card.

"Open the card! Read it! What does it say?" Carol squealed, clapping and bouncing up and down.

Nikki pulled the miniature envelope off the pick and, with trembling fingers, opened it and pulled the card out, with Carol looking over her shoulder in curiosity. He'd written a short message and she read it aloud.

I would very much like to take you to dinner tomorrow night.
You have my number in the order book from my earlier orders.
If you want to go, please call or text me and tell me yes.
We'll go from there,
Tony

"Well?" Carol asked emphatically, hands on hips.

Nikki pulled the order book from under the counter and, flipping back a couple of weeks, found the receipt for the Secretary's Day flowers. She wrote Tony's number on the back of the card and tucked it into her bra, close to her throbbing nipples.

Nikki had to decide – was it a go or a no? She had to admit, it could be a scary thing when your dreams looked like they were about to come true.

Tony sat in the truck, feeling a bit lightheaded, and tried to stick the key into the ignition. Had her nipples really stiffened while he was standing there? He leaned his head onto the steering wheel. Minutes ticked by, and no ringing or text tone. She just wasn't interested; Clayton and Cal were wrong.

He drove back to Walters Construction. The coffee pot was on, and he poured himself a cup and retreated to the safety of his office. His coffee got cold, and he didn't notice. People came and went; he felt like he was walking through deep, deep water, barely moving, while the rest of the world spun around him. He sat in his desk chair, turned around backward and staring at the wall, all afternoon. Cheryl asked him something, but he couldn't think of an answer.

"Are you okay?" she tried again, concern saturating her voice.

"Yeah, I'm fine," he lied, turning back to the wall.

He'd messed up. And now it would be too awkward to even talk to her at the gym. He shouldn't have even hoped – his time had passed.

His phone started sounding off as usual at that time of day. He looked at it, refusing to believe anything would be there from her.

Annabeth, wanting to know if he wanted to have dinner with them.

Annabeth again – Brussels sprouts or green beans?

Clayton, asking if he was planning to come to the jobsite on Saturday to meet with the crane crew.

Brittany, reminding him of Clayton's birthday the following week.

And a text from a number he didn't recognize.

His hands started to shake and he felt like he was choking. This was it – now or never. The screen popped up, and he felt something in his chest break wide open, like all the air in the world was rushing in. One simple word changed his world.

Yes.

Chapter Eleven

It was in the gym parking lot – the big, silver Walters Construction pickup truck. One glance around told her he was already at one of the weight machines. Within a few minutes, Nikki had climbed onto the treadmill next to Kelly's. She smiled and nodded to Kelly, who smiled and nodded back as always.

Head down and headphones on, she walked at her usual vigorous pace. When she glanced up again, Tony was standing right in front of her, grinning. He put his hand up to his head, thumb and pinkie splayed, and mouthed, *I'll call you later, okay?* She smiled wide and nodded, and watched him amble toward the locker room.

A hand on her shoulder brought her back into the moment, and she turned to see Kelly staring at her, her mouth moving, an odd expression on her face. Nikki popped her earbud out. "I'm sorry, what did you say?"

"I said, what the hell was that all about?" Kelly asked, wide-eyed.

"I'll explain later." Nikki was barely able to contain what would've certainly been a cheesy grin.

When she was finished, Nikki found Kelly sitting on the locker room bench with a bottle of water, waiting for her, almost glaring at her. "What?" she asked, sitting down beside the brunette.

"What the hell . . . did he say he'd call you later?" Kelly scowled.

"He, um, he asked me out."

"Are you kidding me? I've been trying to get that man to notice me, and he asked you out? What the . . . ?"

"Hey, hang on for just one damn minute!" Now it was Nikki's turn to be righteously indignant. "I know I'm not as young or firm or well-endowed as some of you, but, hell, I'm not exactly chopped liver either. I work hard to at least look presentable. Some men might even find me somewhat attractive." She felt her eyes burning. *Don't cry!*, she told herself. "I was married to a man who told me every day how beautiful I was. I miss that. I'm not under any delusions, but I'd like to think I have *something* to offer."

Kelly looked sheepish after Nikki's outburst. "I'm sorry. I didn't really mean it the way it came out. You're a very nice-looking woman. But I've spent a lot of money and time trying to get men like Tony Walters to notice me. He's like a goal that women want to reach, and I thought I might actually have a shot, and then you come along and, well, you're not flashy, you don't stand out in a crowd, and wham! He asks you out? You've gotta understand, that hurts."

"Wait. He's like a goal that women want to reach?" Nikki looked at her in confusion. "What exactly do you mean by that? He's just a guy."

"Well, for some of us, he's a god." Kelly was looking down at her hands, picking around her fingernails.

"I don't understand. He's good-looking. I get that. But a god?"

"I mean, he's Tony Walters. *The* Tony Walters," Kelly emphasized. Nikki stared at her, still not understanding. "You know, Tony Walters? Walters Construction?"

"Yeah, I know. He works for Walters Construction. I guess that's his family?"

"How long have you lived here in The Ville?"

"Almost six years, give or take."

"And you really don't know, do you?" Kelly stared at her in disbelief.

Nikki shrugged. "I guess not."

"Well, then, let me educate you," Kelly stated matter-of-factly. "Tony doesn't work for Walters Construction – he *is* Walters Construction. He owns it. All of it."

"Is it big?" Nikki asked innocently.

Kelly looked at her with astonishment. "Big? It's the biggest construction firm in Kentucky, possibly in five states. If there's a major project going on, you can bet Walters Construction is involved. They have hundreds of employees and millions of dollars' worth of equipment and property. It's *huge.*" Kelly threw her arms out in illustration. "I know he has an average-type house here in town somewhere, but he's got a multi-million-dollar spread somewhere out in Shelbyville that was the family farm. Wait," Kelly ran to her locker and returned with a magazine in her hand. "Here, look. You'll see what I mean."

It was a five-year-old copy of Kentucky Today magazine, ragged from being passed around. Nikki stared at the cover in disbelief. The headline read, "The Bachelors of Kentucky." There were four insets across the top of the page and six down one side, all of very good-looking men who were, presumably, bachelors. But the central image snatched the breath from her lungs.

There in all its glory was an enormous photo of an only-slightly-younger Tony. He was wearing a plaid work shirt unbuttoned just enough to show a hint of his muscular pecs. With his arms crossed and his flexed biceps outlined through the sleeves, he exuded pure maleness. The shirt was tucked into a pair of skin-tight jeans, in which the bulge was prominent. Her gaze traveled down his legs; he was leaning against a Walters truck, ankles crossed with one foot on the ground, the other toe down, and sporting black work boots. He practically glared at the camera, his smoldering eyes looking straight into the lens, and every fiber of his being oozed sex. She swallowed hard. If he only had a little dollop of whipped cream on his head, she'd eat the page and beg for more.

"H-h-h-holy shit." It was all she could force out.

"Now you see?" Kelly looked vindicated. "And that was five years ago. I think he's hotter now, if that's even possible."

"So, if he's such hot man meat in Louisville, how many women has he dated in all these years?" Even if she wasn't part of the gossip circles in town, Nikki knew it ran rampant.

"That's just it!" Kelly whispered loudly. "No one. He was married to that hideous bitch all those years and, to everyone's knowledge, he's never dated anyone. All that, well – I mean, look at him – going to waste. Incredible." Kelly shook her head.

Wow. Nikki stared at the magazine cover again. Why her? "I guess you're wondering, why you?" Kelly said in answer to her unspoken question; that was creepy.

"Exactly."

"I gotta tell ya, I have no idea. I mean, you certainly don't look anything like his ex." Kelly rolled her eyes as she muttered, "Thank god."

"That bad?" Nikki asked. Spectacular – an ex-bitch.

"Yeah, that bad. She's, well, I should let him tell you himself. All I know is rumor after rumor. But everyone in town knows about her."

"Except me." The woman must be a real piece of work if she was legend.

"The scoop?" Kelly asked, leaning in. "Tell me, how did this all happen?"

Nikki filled Kelly in on how Tony had come into the shop and ordered the flowers. As she told the story, she realized how clever it had been. It appeared he'd been thinking for awhile about how to approach her. Had he engineered the whole double sandwich thing too? Why? He could've just asked her out. Could he possibly be that scared? Nikki glanced at the magazine cover again. Was it possible someone so sexy and desirable had been as nervous about asking her out as she was about being asked? How could someone like him be anxious about asking out a woman? Good god, they were probably crawling all over him.

She pulled herself out of her head. "So I'm going home. He said he's going to call me. I guess we're having dinner tomorrow night; that's what he asked anyway. Maybe I'll have something to tell you this weekend." Nikki grinned at Kelly. "By the way, can I borrow this?" She pointed to the magazine.

"By all means. Take it home and read it. The article is pretty good. And hey, good luck, girlfriend!" Kelly giggled and slapped Nikki on the shoulder. "Have fun. And tell me how he is, uh, how it goes, okay?"

"Right!" But Nikki's real thought was, *Not on your life*. She might fill Kelly in on the date itself, but not what they would talk about or do. She never was a kiss and tell.

She'd finished her little dinner when her phone rang. It was him; she'd saved his number after her text.

"Hello?"

"Hi! Nikki?" Tony sounded a bit hesitant.

"Yeah! Hi!" She had trouble forcing out the words, almost breathless from the effort.

"Um, thanks for texting me. I didn't know if you'd want to go out or not."

"Sure! Why not?"

"Well, I didn't know if you, I mean, Annabeth told me you were a widow, and I wasn't sure if you dated or not."

"Actually, I haven't up until now. But I thought I'd take a chance. You aren't going to make me regret it, are you?" she asked, laughing.

"Well, god, I hope not!" Tony laughed back. "I think I'm a pretty nice guy. I hope to prove that to you tomorrow night."

"I'd already figured that out or I wouldn't have said yes. After all, you raised a beautiful, gracious young woman! What did you have in mind?"

"I was thinking, since we really don't know each other, maybe you'd like to meet me for dinner? Down the street from your work? Vocelli's Pizzaria?"

Ah, Italian food! Wouldn't it be funny if he really was Italian? "Yeah, that sounds great! What time?"

"You get off work when?"

"Six."

"So would six thirty be too early for you?" Tony asked.

"Nope. Six thirty would be fine. I'll see you there."

"Actually, it'll be getting dark by then. I'll meet you at the shop and we'll walk down together, if that's okay." He didn't like the thought of her walking down a Louisville street alone in near-darkness.

Ah, a gentleman!, Nikki thought. "That would be perfect. I'll see you at the shop at six thirty tomorrow night."

"Great! See you then. Have a good evening."

"You too, Tony." She pressed END and the phone went silent.

Nikki remembered the magazine, so she got it from her bag. Tony's face burned into her from the cover. Bill and Hillary settled in beside her on the sofa as she finally found the right page.

There he was behind a massive desk, feet crossed and resting on its surface while he leaned back in a big chair, hands clasped behind his head. Rolls of blueprints were scattered on the desk along with several books, lots of papers, a telephone, and a coffee cup. The bookcases behind the desk framed a huge window and, even in the photo, the heavy equipment, cranes, trucks, all of the trappings of the construction industry, were visible through the window. He looked so comfortable and at home in that environment. In the photo he was wearing jeans and a form-fitting thermal shirt in dark blue; the color of the shirt made his warm eyes look even more intense.

Nikki forced herself to stop looking at the photo and read the article, and it was revealing. The lead-in was worth the couple of minutes it took to read it. "Take Mel Gibson. Mix in a generous portion of Gerard Butler and a dash of Bradley Cooper. Then give him the largest construction company in the Bluegrass State to own and run. And make him beyond gorgeous and spectacularly single. That's the recipe for this year's *Kentucky Today*'s most eligible bachelor, Tony Walters of Walters Construction out of Louisville." According to what was written there, Walters Construction was enormous, with contracts in at least five states; that meant it was probably even larger at that point. It was worth millions of dollars. There were all kinds of facts and figures, plus a list of some of the larger projects they'd been involved in. Many were newer landmarks there in the area, things even she, as a more recent transplant, recognized.

But then it turned more personal, especially about his divorce. Nikki did the math in her head; if she'd subtracted correctly, he'd been divorced for sixteen years. He had two children; she knew about Annabeth, but he also had a son, Clayton, who was older. And there were five boys in his family. She couldn't imagine having four siblings, much less all brothers. Even though it didn't name her, it did mention his mother – was she still living? It said she lived in Louisville, as did two of his brothers. The brothers were Mark, Bart, Freddie, and Bennie; two were older than him, and two younger. Bless his heart, he was smack in the middle. There was a photo of Tony at a charity event with a woman. She looked older than him, but the photo was so tiny that it was very hard to tell much about it.

She turned a page to find another photo, this one of Tony in white drawstring pants and a white cotton shirt, barefoot, sitting in a cushy armchair in front of a huge fireplace. From the caption, it appeared it was taken at his family home in Shelbyville. In every photo, his hair was pulled back in the ponytail she'd always seen him wear. She wondered what his hair looked like down and she shivered with pent-up tension. Around the photo were more details, charity work in which he was involved, his likes and dislikes – apparently he hated liver – and what he looked for in a woman.

"Walters says he's always been attracted to women who have no idea how beautiful they are. 'I can't stand being around a woman who's sure she's the most desirable thing in the room,' Walters says. 'Down-to-earth, real beauty is a rare commodity. It's hard to find. I'm hoping someday to find it myself in someone who'll rock my world.'" *Well, he'd be avoiding arrogance with me,* she thought. *I'm a lot of things, but sure of myself isn't one of them.*

Nikki put the magazine down and sighed. She stroked his photo on the cover. She knew a little more about him now, but she wanted to know more, and she wanted it to come straight from him.

Chapter Twelve

"Okay, so the guys will be at the Colufab site in the morning with the cranes. I know it's a Saturday, but can you be there at eight thirty? Boss?" Tony snapped back into reality and stared at Cal, who looked concerned. "You okay?"

"Yeah, I'm fine." Tony glanced around furtively and then whispered, "Can you keep a secret?"

"You bet!" Cal whispered back. "What's up?"

Tony's eyes lit up. "I've got a date tonight!"

"No way!" Cal ran to close the door. "Who is she?"

"A lady who goes to my gym. And she works at a florist shop down on Frankfort Avenue."

"Nice looking, huh? Big rack?"

"Uh, no, not an especially big rack. But she is cute. And very nice." Tony pictured her in his mind, and he felt his cock give a little jump.

"Oh, come on, boss. You can have any woman you want, cream of the crop. Don't settle." Cal sank back into the chair.

"I'm not settling. She's a really nice person, very cheery and upbeat. I really like her. Annabeth told me about her, too. So she kind of came at me from two different directions. I took that as a sign, you know?"

"Yeah. But, hey, I'm glad you're getting your feet wet again. It's time." Tony noticed Cal almost seemed relieved. That was curious. "Do you have, you know, protection? 'Cause, I mean, even at our age, you can't just assume . . ."

"Geez, Cal, no!" Tony felt his cheeks overheat. "I mean, I'm not planning on sleeping with her tonight. I'm not even picking her up; we're meeting at Vocelli's. I thought she might be more comfortable that way, seeing as how we really don't know each other that well."

"Yeah, good thinking. So you think this will go anywhere?"

"I have no idea, but I'm willing to find out. She said she doesn't date –

she's a widow – but she was willing to take a chance on me. I want to take a chance on her too."

"Gotta start somewhere, I always say. So, you'll be at the Colufab site tomorrow morning?"

"Yep," Tony answered. "Business is business."

Tony went to his truck, got his clothes, and changed. It was five forty-five, and he didn't want to be late. He'd decided to park in the lot across the street from the shop like he'd done before. That would mean he'd have a chance to spend more time with Nikki when he walked her back to her SUV. He'd thought out everything very carefully; he'd always been that way. Leaving things to chance just wasn't his style.

Cheryl was gathering her things when Tony walked out into her work area, and she looked up in astonishment. "Wow, nice! Going somewhere?" she asked cheerily.

"Yeah" He didn't volunteer anything else.

"Well?" Cheryl demanded, hands on hips. "Planning on telling me where? Or maybe I should ask with whom?"

"Well, I wasn't planning to . . ."

"Out with it!" she barked, pointing a finger at him.

Tony cringed. "Okay. I have a date."

"OH MY GOD!" Cheryl screamed and ran across the room to hug him. "That's GREAT! Who is she? Where are you going? Oh, Tony, I'm so happy!" He looked up at her and realized she was starting to cry.

"Whoa there! It's one date! Shit, I don't have a ring in my pocket or anything!" He looked at her, tears running down her face. Apparently his efforts at hiding his loneliness and misery had been more of an epic failure than he'd even imagined.

"I know, I know, but do you know how much we've all wanted you to find someone? To be happy, not be alone?" Cheryl sniffed. "This is a huge first step for you. Is she nice? I hope she's nice. She'd better not hurt you. If she hurts you, I'll . . ."

"She's very nice," he said, trying to calm her. "She goes to my gym, and Annabeth met her elsewhere and tried to hook us up."

"I trust that girl's judgment; good head on her shoulders. Sure didn't get that from her mother," Cheryl snorted.

"No kidding. Anyway, I asked her out yesterday and I'm meeting her for dinner."

"Oh, I'm so happy!" Cheryl screeched again, clapping her hands. "You'll tell me all about it on Monday, right?"

"Maaaaybeeeee . . ." So much for privacy.

"Okay, well, have a good time," Cheryl called out as she left for the day.

Tony walked back into his office and looked in the full-length mirror on the bathroom door. Dark gray blazer, darker gray shirt. Black jeans, really black, brand new; perfect fit. The black biker's boots he'd bought a couple of weeks earlier were a nice touch. Perfect. He looked in the mirror again. Something wasn't right.

He looked again, then reached up and pulled the band from his hair, and it fell free. He shook his head, and it loosened, just brushing his shoulders. Instead of reaching for his brush, he ran his fingers through it and took another look in the mirror. What he saw there startled him.

The man looking back at him was confident, elegant, and very, very virile. He'd never seen that man before. Was that what women saw when they looked at him? He reached into his bag, brought out the new watch he'd bought, a carbon black Tag Heuer, and strapped it onto his wrist. Then he pulled out his dad's large onyx signet ring with the Walters "W" on it and slipped it on his right ring finger. *There – polished and well-dressed,* he thought. *I need to make a good impression.*

He picked up his work clothes and slipped them into the bag. One last look around the office and he strode out the door, locking it behind him. He wished he'd driven the Camaro that morning, but the truck would have to do, and he climbed in and headed downtown.

Nikki felt herself getting more and more nervous as the afternoon went on. Finally, at four thirty, she couldn't stand it anymore.

"Marla, would you mind if I worked in back for the rest of the afternoon? I can't cope with another customer right now."

Marla looked at her with pity on her face. "Nerves getting to you, hon?"

"Yeah, is it that obvious?" Nikki tried to smile, but only succeeded in making herself look more strained.

"No. And you're bound to be terrified, but it'll be fine."

"I know. It feels right, but I feel so, I don't know, guilty." Nikki pushed a dust bunny around with her toe.

"Now, honey, if Randy could talk to you, he'd tell you to get on with your life. I'm sure all he ever wanted was for you to be happy. And you haven't been, not alone. It's time to explore, see if there's someone out there for you." She put an arm around Nikki's shoulder. "Want to go on home? I can manage."

"Oh, god, no! At least here I have things to keep me busy. And he's meeting me here."

"Really? Hope he gets here early. I'd like to at least catch a glimpse of this guy. Carol says he's like a Greek god." He really had that effect on women, she'd noticed.

"Well, I don't know about that, but he is ridiculously good-looking." Nikki wore a wistful smile as she talked about him. "I have no idea why he'd be interested in me."

"Because you're such a cutie! Now have a good time. Do you have some, you know, protection?"

"Oh my god! I can't believe you just asked me that!" Nikki cried, slapping Marla playfully on the shoulder.

"Well, now, honey, one can't be too careful these days!"

"I have absolutely no intention of sleeping with him tonight. Or anytime soon." Nikki thought for a minute and realized that might not be accurate. Her nightly fantasies told her she did want him. Just maybe not tonight. Definitely not tonight.

"Just checking," Marla laughed. "Get on back to the stockroom. I'll work out here. There's plenty back there to keep you busy."

Nikki worked through the afternoon until about five fifty. She ran to her SUV and got her dressy clothes before Marla left.

"I thought I'd hang around, but I'm getting hungry. I'll see you Monday, okay? You'll fill us in!" Marla hugged her before leaving.

Nikki went to the back and changed. She'd picked out a pair of skinny jeans with jewels on the back pockets and kitten heeled thong sandals. The top she'd chosen had a sweetheart neckline to accentuate what little she had in the boob department. She changed from her regular bra into a more substantial one with a little bit more lift and light padding – something to hide those pesky nipples and give her a tiny bit of cleavage. The jewelry she'd picked out sparkled even through her hair, which she took down and left free. It was her greatest asset, and she wanted it to be front and center tonight.

When she'd dressed, Nikki did a once-over. She'd done her toes the night before, and they looked cute with their bright pink polish. She checked her nails – perfect. Looking into the mirror, she was disappointed. No one special, just a woman pushing the far edge of middle age, breasts no longer perky, and a tiny little bit of a bulge at the waist. Why had she agreed to do this? He wouldn't want her. Tears threatened, and she sniffed hard. Oh, well, she'd said yes. Even if he never asked her out again, she'd have a date under her belt. She hoped she could be something a little better than boring during dinner.

When she walked out into the shop, she noticed that a card had fallen off the counter, and she stooped down to pick it up. At that moment, she heard the door open and turned. When she saw the man standing in the doorway, she almost gasped out loud. He was so beautiful, so unbelievably, incredibly, heartbreakingly stunning, that she shook to her core. And he was looking straight at her! "Hi!" she managed to stammer.

Tony looked her up and down. "Wow – you're the most gorgeous thing I've seen in a long, long time! Ready to go?" he asked, holding out his arm.

In that moment, she knew what the right answer was. "Yes. I'm ready." And she knew she really was.

Chapter Thirteen

"I don't think there's anything you can put on a pizza that I won't eat," Tony announced, looking at the menu.

"Except maybe liver?" Nikki grinned but didn't look up.

Tony frowned. "Oh, my god, did somebody give you that awful magazine article to read? I swear, that horrible thing will follow me to my grave." He feigned horror.

Nikki laughed. "Yes, someone did. It was enlightening."

"Oh, I bet. By the way, major airbrushing there," he grumbled.

"I don't think so. Looked pretty real to me. And it was Kelly who gave it to me, by the way." She snickered as she looked over the menu.

"Great. I'll have to remember to thank her for that. It kinda creeps me out that she's been holding onto it for this long. She must be a literary stalker." He picked up a breadstick and bit into it.

"I'm surprised you asked me out. Kelly has a 'thing' for you, if you know what I mean."

Tony snorted. "Not my type. At all. She's so, well, I don't know, fake?"

"You mean *they're* fake, don't you?" Nikki grinned.

"Guess so. I mean, I'd rather have small and real than big and fake any day." He blushed a little when he said it.

"Let me tell you, mister, when it comes to me, what you see is what you get, good or bad," she told him, still grinning.

"When I look at you, all I see is good." He smiled at her. "Besides, I haven't gotten the impression that anything about you is fake. You don't seem the type. Now, I'm starving. Wanna share a pizza? Or did you have something else in mind?"

"No, pizza's fine." She closed her menu. "Order whatever your favorite is. I'll eat it, I promise. I'm curious to see what you order."

"Okay, then, my choice." He motioned the server over. "We'll have the Adolpho Classic. Anchovies?" he asked Nikki; she nodded. "Anchovies it is.

Thanks." The server hustled away, leaving them alone. *The Adolpho Classic – typical guy,* Nikki thought, *meat, meat, and more meat, with a little cheese for something that might pass for variety.*

"So, here's where I think we're supposed to make conversation. I'm not very good at this, really out of practice, but I'll start. So you're a widow?"

"Yes."

"And you were married for how long?" he asked.

"Almost thirty years," she answered, looking at the tablecloth.

"If this is too painful, we can talk about something else," he said in apology.

"No, no, it's okay."

"So, thirty years is a long time. What was your secret?" He smiled.

A wistful look came over her face. "Communication. In everything, diet, finances, recreation. In bed," she added. *I can't believe I said that.*

That got Tony's attention. "Really? You managed that? That's pretty rare."

"That's what I hear. But I have a simple theory. Wanna hear it?"

"You're talking about sex, so I'm all ears. Well, not all ears, but . . ." He grinned, resting his elbows on the table and his chin in his hands.

"Okay, funny guy! Well, I've always said people can do it, take off their clothes and crawl into the sack with a perfect stranger, perform the most intimate activity two people can perform, and then walk away and never talk about it. And that's just nuts, you know? They can talk about politics, religion, the weather, finances, everything, but not sex. And if they want to have really great sex, they should talk about it, don't you think? At least I think they should." She stopped and noticed he was staring intently at her – sort of awkward for her – and she was rambling, mostly because she was so nervous. "Well? Say something."

"I think," he stated matter-of-factly as he raised his wine glass to his lips, "you are both brilliant and absolutely correct. And I can't say I've ever done that with another human being. Well, with one," he corrected.

"Your wife, um, ex-wife." She took a sip herself.

"Actually, no. But that's a conversation for another time." He set his glass back on the table. "Anyway, you're absolutely right. People should be able to talk about it." He added, "About sex."

"So, what happened to your marriage, if you don't mind my asking?"

"No, I don't mind you asking, but that's a conversation for another time too. Way too dark and intense for tonight. I'd like to keep things a little more cheerful, if that's okay. But I have to tell you, I know about your kids, too – Annabeth told me. I'm so sorry. I don't know what I'd do without my two."

Nikki choked back tears. "Thanks. So, I understand from the article that, besides Annabeth, you have a son?"

"Yes, Clayton." He took another sip of his wine. "He's got an engineering degree from UK. He works for the company too. I guess by now, because of the article, you know about the company . . ."

"You own it."

"Actually, I own seventy-five percent. My family owns the other twenty-five. But they don't have anything to do with the running of it. It's mine. I'm the president; Clayton's the general manager, and my cousin Vic is the general manager of the Lexington office. Clayton and Brittany have been married for eight years now."

"No grandkids?" She chewed on a breadstick.

"No, unfortunately. Clayton and Brittany want one, but they've had problems, lots of failed attempts. Annabeth and Katie want one too, but artificial insemination is expensive and they haven't been able to agree on which one will carry. They're in no hurry, though; they're kind of hoping the state will allow them to marry before too long. I think that's more of a pipe dream – that's not going to happen in the foreseeable future. Of course, if the Supreme Court rules it unconstitutional to deny gays the right to marry, well, then, the states will have to follow their ruling. Problem solved."

"Exactly! I'm hoping that day is soon." Just the way Nikki said it told him her sentiments were genuine.

"Me too. As for Clayton and Brittany, they just keep trying. They really want a baby. They're already happy together, and that would just make them happier."

"That would be so nice," Nikki agreed. Lucky him – she'd never have grandchildren. "By the way, there was a woman with you in a photo in the magazine. Who was that?"

"Oh, that was Cheryl, my secretary. I guess you'd call her the sister I never had. She's the best. Her husband is a great guy."

"Everyone should have one of those, a sister. Or a brother." Nikki wished she had a sibling. "I don't have any."

"Yeah, well, I've got five of those counting my cousin Vic, and sometimes it ain't all it's cracked up to be," Tony laughed.

The pizza showed up at that moment, and it smelled so delicious Nikki decided she could eat some of it even though her stomach was still a nervous, knotted mess. She thought of something and giggled a little.

"What?" Tony asked, a puzzled look wrinkling his brow.

"You'll think I'm crazy, but I have these made-up names for people at the gym because I don't know their real names. Like Kelly; I called her Boobalicious." At that little disclosure, Tony snickered.

"What about me? What did you call me?" He shot her a mischievous grin.

She hesitated – this was so embarrassing. "I called you The Italian." She blushed and looked down at the table.

He stared at her, wide-eyed. "You're kidding, right? It's that obvious?"

"What's that obvious?"

"Nikki, my whole family's Italian. All of them. How did you know?"

"But your last name is Walters. Isn't that German or something?" she asked, not believing what she was hearing.

"I don't know – I was told he was Welsh. That was my great-great-great grandfather's last name, and it's been carried down through the family by the men for all these years. And the region the Cabrizzis came from – my mother's family – in Italy was held by Germany until World War I, so I always assumed he was German, but that's not what I was told. But he was the only one who wasn't Italian – everyone else was Italian. Every last one."

She couldn't believe it. "No! But your brothers? Mark? Bart? Freddie? Bennie?"

"Yeah," Tony nodded. "Marco, Bartolomeo, Federico, and Benecio. My dad was Marco as well. My mother is Raffaella. My name is actually Antonio. How did you know?"

Nikki didn't know what to say. "I didn't. I couldn't," she stammered. "You just looked Italian to me. I don't know why I didn't think Jewish, or South American, or Portuguese, but it was Italian that stuck with me." She looked down at her lap. "Isn't that funny?" she whispered, smiling that small, shy smile at him. His heart was melting and he felt powerless to stop it.

It didn't take long for Nikki to realize that he loved to talk about his heritage. He had the story memorized, starting with his great-great-great grandfather's parents taking him to Italy, home of his maternal relatives, to avoid the Civil War, and moving forward all the way to his own parents' courtship and marriage. She was also surprised to find that his parents had sent each of their sons to Italy for their high school educations, letting them come home in the summers. But they all came back to live in the states to go to college.

Then he told her about his brothers: "Mark is an obstetrician in Portland, Oregon. Bart lives here; he's an electrician and owns one of the electrical companies in town, Pinnacle. Freddie lives here, too; he has a finance degree and he's a commercial banker. And Bennie has a degree in English and owns a bookstore in New York City. They're all married, all have kids. And, well, here I am – The Italian." He grinned at her until his eyes crinkled shut and he looked so cute that she could barely keep her hands off him. "What about your family?"

"Oh, we're Scotch-Irish mutts!" Her laughter sounded like wind chimes to Tony, soft and lyrical.

He couldn't help it; he reached across the small table and put his hand against her cheek. "Show me a mutt whose skin glows like that in this light, and I'll swear there's a pedigree there somewhere!" His heart skipped a beat as she pressed her cheek into his palm. Nikki's eyes closed, and Tony thought he saw a hint of a tear in the inside corner of one of them.

Then her eyes snapped open; she reached up and took his hand from her face, but she held it in hers and dropped them to the table. Her fingers were fine and soft, and he felt a solid, strong energy coming from her, something positive and effervescent. She played with the ring on his finger for a second, then let go and grabbed a piece of pizza.

"So really," he repeated, "what about your family, if you don't mind my asking?"

"Nope, don't mind at all," she said, holding the pizza. "But, as you said before, that's a conversation for another time. Let's eat this before it gets cold." She gave him a wide smile and took a huge bite. He laughed at the pizza sauce in the corners of her mouth before taking his napkin and wiping it off. She laughed too. They were both having a good time and, for that little moment, it was just the two of them. The rest of the world fell away.

They made their way down the block slowly. Tony didn't want the evening to end. They'd had so much fun, laughing and talking. He knew there were lots of important things they probably should discuss, but he just wanted to see Nikki laugh and smile.

Nikki couldn't understand – how had this guy managed to stay unattached for so long? He was perfect in every way – gorgeous, smart, funny, warm, caring. Why hadn't some long-legged, big-breasted bimbo managed to snap him up before now? Was there something really wrong with him? If there was, she couldn't identify it.

She waited, hoping as they walked he'd take her hand. Tony didn't disappoint; halfway back to the shop, she felt his fingers playing along hers. She opened her hand and spread her fingers, and his had wrapped through and around them in an instant, almost instinctively. She'd forgotten how good it felt to hold someone's hand, and she didn't want it to stop.

They got to the parking lot and she led him to her SUV. He took a look at it and laughed. "I see this thing at the gym, but I still can't believe it. I had you pegged for a sports car girl!" He looked it over again and couldn't help but think how cute she'd look in a convertible, her hair blowing back.

Nikki laughed. "God, no. I couldn't get all of my crap into a sports car!" She unlocked the door, opened it, and turned to face him.

"Well, I guess this is it." Tony reached for Nikki's hand again. "I don't know about you, but this was the best evening I've had in, well, maybe ever. It's been so much fun. I'm really sorry it's over."

"Me too." She squeezed his fingers, and he squeezed back. She wondered if he was waiting for her to say that the night didn't have to end, but she wasn't ready for that step yet. Would he kiss her? She was hoping.

"So, be careful. I'll call you in a little while to make sure you made it home okay." He squeezed her hand again. "I'll see you soon, okay?"

"Yeah, sure. I'd like that." *I hope he means that literally,* she thought. "Bye. And thanks for dinner."

"No, thank you!" he called back, waving as he got into his truck.

Nikki started the Escape and pulled out of the parking lot, Tony's truck right behind her. She turned right, he turned left, and she watched his taillights disappear down the street. It had been a perfect night. If he'd invited her to come home with him, she wasn't sure she could've said no. Every cell in her body ached. Her panties were soaked and her nipples were so hard she was afraid their circulation was damaged. Everything about him called to her, to her heart and her body.

When Tony couldn't see Nikki's taillights any more in the rearview, he sighed. He'd wanted so badly to taste her lips, to pull her softness against him, wrap his arms around her waist, let her feel his hardness, how badly he needed her. But he didn't want to scare her or move too fast. It had taken every bit of his resolve to let her get into that car and drive away, but he'd already decided; when he called Nikki later, he planned to ask her out again for Sunday.

"You home and locked in?" he asked when she answered.

"Yeah, I'm fine. Thanks again for dinner. It was..." dared she say it? "magical."

"It was, wasn't it? I didn't know a pizza could taste so good. I guess it was the company I keep, huh?"

"Maybe. That was one very tasty pizza!"

"So, I was thinking. I've got to go to a jobsite tomorrow morning, but I've got no plans for Sunday. Would you like to spend the afternoon with me, maybe drive out through the country, have some dinner?"

She didn't want to sound too eager, but then she decided what the hell. If being honest with him turned him off, at least she'd know sooner rather than later. "I'd love it!" she gushed. "So, what do I need to wear?"

"Dress casual and comfortable. I'll pick you up about one. Hey, you need to give me your address – I don't even know where you live."

"429 Bluejay Lane."

"You live in Annabeth and Katie's neighborhood!"

"Yes. We figured that out when Annabeth ordered Katie's flowers."

"Wait – do you have a neighborhood association?" Tony asked. Seemed he remembered something someone had said – maybe Jason? He lived in Annabeth and Katie's neighborhood too.

"Yes, we do, but I've never seen Annabeth or Katie at a meeting. I used to be the..."

"Secretary?" he interrupted. His heart was about to pound right out of his chest.

"How did you know that?" she gasped.

"Then you know Jason Miller?" His mind was reeling.

"Sure! He lives over here too."

Tony hesitated for a few seconds. Should he say out loud what he was thinking? "I've got something to tell you, but it'll freak you out – it's freaking me out. Do you know why I came to the shop?" he asked slowly.

Was this a trick question? "To buy flowers?"

"Yeah, but I came there to buy flowers because Annabeth had met you. She wanted me to meet you and wouldn't take no for an answer. When I got there, I realized you were the woman from the gym, the one I'd been wanting to ask out." Damn – he hadn't meant to say that.

He'd wanted to ask her out all along? She thought about it for a second, and realized she'd been going to that gym for four years. In that time, he'd always been there. He'd been thinking about asking her out all that time? Four years? "So you didn't know I worked in the shop when you came in?"

"Well, I knew someone named Nikki worked there because of Annabeth, but I didn't know you were the same woman from the gym. But here's the freaky part. Jason works for me. He knew Annabeth was trying to get me to meet someone, and he knew I kept balking." He stopped and took a deep breath. "And he told me if that didn't work out, he'd be glad to introduce me to the former secretary of his neighborhood association."

Nikki was glad she was alone – her bottom lip was trembling and tears were welling in her eyes. "So you're telling me that somehow, some way, from three different directions . . ."

Tony took a deep breath. "Nikki, I don't want to go too fast. And I'm not saying this is anything permanent. But don't you think it's odd that all of this came together, like something, someone, was determined to make sure we met? Don't you think it's funny?"

"It's not funny, Tony. It's called fate." Her voice was failing and the tears were coming so fast that she couldn't stop them. "I can't wait until Sunday," she managed to get out in a whisper.

"Me neither." Tony's voice was low and almost reverent. "Sleep well. I'll be thinking of you until then. Good night, beautiful girl."

Nikki choked and whispered back, "Good night." She pressed END, dropped the phone, and sobbed into her pillow.

He'd called her beautiful. This couldn't be happening. No one got this lucky twice in a lifetime.

Chapter Fourteen

When Tony's number popped up on her phone screen, Nikki decided to be a little bold. "Good morning, handsome!" she answered cheerfully. "How are you this beautiful morning?"

"I'm great, pretty girl. How's your morning?" Tony was more than a little excited that Nikki sounded glad to hear from him.

Nikki had spent all morning boxing up Mother's Day orders, a day she tried hard to forget; it only depressed her. His voice was like music to her. "It's better now that I'm talking to you! What are you up to?"

"Exactly what I wanted to ask you." He poured another cup of coffee.

"I'm at the shop."

"Oh." Disappointment was thick in his voice. "When do you get off?"

"Noon. Why?"

He brightened back up – his idea could still work. "My jobsite trip got cancelled for the day. Want to have a picnic with me?"

"Absolutely! That sounds so good! But I can't fix anything . . ."

"I've got it covered. There's a restaurant down the street from me that specializes in picnic meals. Can I pick up something from them and meet you at the shop at noon?"

"I'd love that! Is there anything I can do?"

"Yeah." Tony's heart was hammering. "Smile when I come through the door. It'll make my day."

"Trust me, that'll happen without you asking! I'll see you at noon – can't wait."

"Me neither. See you then." Tony hit END and put the phone down. He thought about spending the afternoon with Nikki, and everything below his waist tensed. God, he wanted her so much, but he knew if he wanted to have a long-term relationship with her he couldn't rush things.

He took his time getting ready and still left with ten minutes to spare to meet Nikki when she got off work. But before he pulled away from the house, he had a thought: Call Steve. After briefly warring with his conscience, he found Steve's number in his favorites and hit it. It only rang twice before Steve answered.

"Hey, big guy, what's up?" Steve McCoy's deep voice and small-town twang had always felt like order in the midst of chaos for Tony. He was a good friend and an even better attorney, not to mention the fact that if there was dirt, Steve could dig it up.

"I need you to do something for me," Tony said haltingly.

"Just name it." A chewing sound came from Steve's end of the phone. It seemed like he was eating every time Tony talked to him.

"I need you to check someone out."

"Is this a business associate, or a politician, or . . ." Steve fished.

"Neither. A woman."

"Ah! Is that right?" Steve started to laugh. "Finally, the area's most eligible bachelor is . . ."

Tony interrupted him. "Hey, give it a rest, asshole. I've heard it all from my family already. Not you too. Please."

"Sorry. Okay, okay, I'll give it a rest. So who is she?"

Tony filled Steve in on everything he knew about Nikki. Steve was snoopier than a bunch of little old ladies on a church social committee; nothing escaped him. If there was anything about Nikki she wouldn't want known, Steve would find it, and he wouldn't waste any time doing it. And he'd sure as hell have no compunction about sharing.

"I'll get right on it, buddy," Steve assured Tony. "And, for the record, I'm glad you're seeing someone. I hope I don't find anything."

"Thanks. But you'll tell me if you do, right? Even if it hurts?"

"Absolutely. You can count on me. I'll get back with you on Monday afternoon. I should have something by then."

"Thanks, man. I owe you."

"Well, not yet. But you will – I'll bill you!" Steve laughed as he hung up.

Tony stopped at the restaurant and picked up the food, then drove to the shop to meet Nikki. He was a little early, but he'd sit in the car in the parking lot and wait, anything to be a little closer to her. Even though he was alone, his cheeks pinked up. He was acting like a horny adolescent, but he didn't care. For him, it was just exciting to be alive for the first time in a long time.

Nikki heard the door and turned. When she saw Tony, the smile that burst across her face was so huge that it was almost painful, and he looked so delicious that she wanted to lick him. He seemed pretty happy to see her too.

"Hey, about ready? Or do you have to wait until noon straight up?"

"No, I'm good. Let's go." She locked the door behind them and, with no hesitation, Tony took her hand as they made their way across the street. His hand was big and warm, and hers felt safe in it.

She looked around the lot, but his truck was nowhere to be found. Glancing at his face, she didn't see any sign of distress. She was confused – right up until she heard the locks click on a beautiful black Camaro sporting a silver overhead stripe package, sitting on the back edge of the parking lot. He opened the door for her and helped her inside.

"Like it?" he asked, a tiny, sly smile pulling at one corner of his mouth as he got in.

"Like it? It's – wow!" It even smelled brand new. "How long have you had this?"

"About six months. They took almost a year to get it to me, but it was worth the wait, don't you think?"

"It sure was!" she gushed as he hit the button on the key. The engine roared to life, and the six-speed manual barked the tires as they pulled out of the parking lot.

Tony drove straight to the riverside green space and parked. They made their way across the wide lawn to a small grove of trees about halfway to the river. Tony opened the carrying box and, inside the top, there was a red and white checked tablecloth plenty big enough to use as a ground cloth. Nikki helped him unpack the gourmet food and a jug of peach tea big enough to last all afternoon. She'd never seen such a decadent picnic feast.

After they'd cleaned up from lunch, Tony lay down on the cloth and looked up at Nikki. "I don't want to be a buzz kill, but I think we need to talk." Whatever it was, it didn't sound like fun to Nikki.

"Oh? What about?"

"Remember last night when I kept saying that this or that was for another conversation? Well, that conversation is now. I want to hear about your family. And there are some things I need to tell you. They need to be aired before we take this any farther. But you first."

"What do you want to know?" she asked.

"I know you lost your husband and your two kids. No more kids?"

"Nope. Just the two."

"How long ago?"

"Five years," she answered, looking down at the blanket and picking at a thread in the design.

"I know this is hard, but we need to get it out of the way." Nikki didn't look up, but she nodded in agreement. "I think you told me you'd been married thirty years?" he asked.

"We'd celebrated our thirtieth anniversary that year." Thirty years – Tony couldn't even imagine. He thought about how lost his mom had been without his dad the first few years.

"You weren't originally from here, were you?" he asked.

"No. Murray."

"That's in the far western end of the state, right?"

"Yes. Near Paducah. Murray State University is there."

"Right, the Racers." He watched her smile and nod. "And you came here because . . ."

"Randy's job. He got transferred to a loading facility here."

"How long had you been here when, you know . . ."

"Um, about six months."

"How old were your kids?"

"Oh, grown. She was twenty-four; he was twenty-nine. They didn't live with us; they were just visiting." It was all starting to flood back. She held her breath and fought back tears.

"So how about you start at the beginning. It would be easier." Tony rolled over on his side and propped himself up on one elbow so he could keep watch on her face, stop her if it got too painful, or interject something if she got too upset. Nikki had dreaded that moment; she took a deep breath and started.

"Okay. First, you have to understand my family. Everyone in my family was a religious nut. My grandparents, all of them, were cold and distant, and neither of my parents ever felt loved. They had a child, me, because they wanted someone to love them – whether or not they were able to love me never mattered to them. It's always been all about them. They were never supportive, caring, loving, anything."

"And your husband?"

"Randy and I started dating when I was fifteen. By the time I was seventeen, I was pregnant and we got married. I desperately wanted a family, people to love who would love me. Even though we were teenagers, Randy loved me more than anyone else ever had, and I felt like I had a chance at a real life. Jake was born right after I turned eighteen; Amanda came along five years later. Even as young and poor as we were, we were a very happy little family. Randy and I had a few rocky years, but it got better as we grew up. By the time he died, we were crazy mad in love with each other again. He made good money and we were enjoying life. We moved here; we liked the culture of the city compared to all the small-town bullshit. Amanda lived near here; Jake lived in Ashland, so we were closer to him. I was trying to meet people with the same interests as mine."

She swallowed hard. "The kids were here visiting. All three of them wanted ice cream; I didn't, so they went to get some. They begged me to come along, but I said I'd stay behind and clean up the dinner dishes and we'd watch a movie when they came back. But we never got to watch that movie." Nikki stared at the red and white checks as they started to swim in her tears, and she closed her eyes. She felt Tony's hand on hers and started again.

"It happened less than a mile from the house. I heard the sirens and commotion, and I realized they should've already been home. So I started calling their cells, but no one answered. I knew – I just knew . . ." she trailed off. Then she took a deep breath and started again.

"The guy was so drunk that he couldn't understand why he wasn't in the car anymore. He didn't know what he'd done until the next morning. By that time, Randy and Amanda were gone, Randy at the scene and Amanda in the ambulance. Jake died the next day. I ask myself every day why I couldn't have died too." Tony watched tears roll down her face and drip off of her jaw. He wanted to pull her to him, but he knew she needed to finish. "Only someone who's been through it can possibly understand what it's like to walk into that hospital emergency room and see a broken, battered body, tubes and tape and bloody blankets all around, and be told it's your child or your husband, that they're gone, and there's nothing you can do about it. Then having to make the decision to unplug a machine and let what's left of someone you love cease to function." The tears were falling uninhibited, so fast that she couldn't wipe them away.

She shook herself and pulled her shoulders back, taking a deep breath. "So I took them home to bury them. Not Randy; he wanted to be cremated. But the kids . . . So anyway, the day after the funerals, I was packing up to come back to Louisville. My mother walked in and asked what I was doing. She said, 'You're not going back. We've cleaned out the spare bedroom. You don't have a family anymore, and we don't have anyone else, so you can live here and take care of us.' I knew if I did that, I'd never have a life. I'd be that pitiful widow who lived with her folks. I told her thanks, but I was coming back to Louisville to pick up where I'd left off. She called me terrible names, told me I was an ungrateful brat, that I was running from my problems. She said they didn't care if I was their only child – if I didn't stay they'd disown me and never talk to me again. When I told them no, they had the police come and tell me to leave."

"You're kidding! And?"

"When I got back, I called to tell them I was home and safe. She hung up on me. Every time I called, she hung up or wouldn't answer. At one point, my dad answered and yelled into the phone, 'Stop calling!' I'd send birthday cards; they'd mark them 'return to sender' and send them back. Friends who still live there told me they were telling all kinds of vicious lies about me all over Murray, that I was a prostitute in Louisville, that I was dealing drugs, all kinds of horrible, weird things, all because I wouldn't do exactly what they wanted. So I really don't have any family anymore."

Tony was stunned. How could anyone treat their child that way, especially their only child? The pain on her face was heart-rending; it took his breath away. As though she could read his mind, she managed to get out, barely above a whisper, "Sometimes it hurts to breathe."

In an instant, he rose to his knees and took her into his arms, pulling her to his chest. Five years of grief, pain, neglect, despair, and abuse poured out of her and onto his shirt as she sobbed with total abandon. He smoothed her hair and pressed his face into the top of her head. There was a fragrance to her hair that was warm and earthy, kind of exotic, and he breathed it in deep and held his breath before breathing it in again. In a few minutes she stopped gasping and started to breathe more normally, and she pulled back a little, looking up at him.

"I'm so s-s-s-sorry," she stuttered through broken sobs. "I must really look a sight." He handed her a napkin from lunch, into which she promptly blew her nose. He laughed, and she giggled too. "Oh, god, I bet I'm a mess!" she smiled.

"A beautiful mess," Tony whispered into her ear as he stroked her hair. "A truly beautiful mess."

"Aw, you know exactly what to say to a girl, don't you?" Nikki patted her face with the napkin. "You're quite the charmer, aren't you, Tony Walters?"

"One of my many talents," he smiled.

She caught her breath, shuddered a little, and looked at him. "Okay. I think it's your turn. What is it that you think you need to tell me?"

Where to start? "Get comfortable. It's a long story. But first, you should know, I don't believe in any particular religion, but my mother is a typical Italian Catholic mother. She'll grow to love you, but she won't like it if you're not Catholic. And you're not, are you?"

"Nope. I'm Pagan. I've found that's worse than atheist for most people. I guess I'm doomed, right?"

Tony laughed. "No, if you're Pagan, I'm guessing you can handle my mother. What are you, a Buddhist or something?" he asked. She could tell he was clueless.

"Nope. Wiccan, among other things." She paused. "I'm also a witch." Her gaze was steady, and her eyes seemed greener than usual.

"Uh, okay," he responded, his eyebrows peaking. "I'm not going to ask exactly what that means; we can talk about it later. Plenty of time for that. So consider yourself warned." He stopped, then added, "And for the record, it doesn't bother me one bit."

"Taken under advisement. Now, let me get comfortable." She lay back on the tablecloth with her jacket under her head.

"Here, take mine too." Tony peeled off his jacket and handed it to her. "This is going to take awhile."

He sat back, took a deep breath, and started. She watched the muscles in his jaws tense. "You know I'm divorced. But unless you're tapped into the gossip groups, I'm guessing you don't know about Dottie." Nikki shook her head.

"Dottie and I met when we were sixteen. I came back to the states for summer break in high school and met her at the pool in the park. We dated for six years and got married when we were twenty-two. My parents were very disappointed; they'd hoped I'd find an Italian girl during the school year, marry her after I graduated, and bring her back to the states. But Dottie's family was Italian, so I think they just decided she'd do. I'd never had another girlfriend or sex partner; Dottie was all I knew. At the time, I was her first and only too."

"Anyway, she never seemed to like sex much, but I thought that's how it was supposed to be – hell, I didn't know. When we'd been married for a year, she started saying she wanted a baby. I was young; it meant more sex for me, so I decided hey, why not? Took us a few years, but Clayton was born when I was twenty-six."

Nikki interrupted him. "Wait, I'm sorry. I'm fifty-one – fifty-two in

September," she offered. "And you're how old?"

"Fifty-seven – fifty-eight in September." God, he was a good-looking fifty-seven. She nodded for him to continue. "So we had Clayton. He weighed seven pounds and twelve ounces, perfectly healthy. I brought them home from the hospital, and it didn't take long for things to start heading south."

"How so?" Nikki asked.

"When he was two weeks old, I came home one day and found him still in his bed, still in the diaper he'd had on overnight, hadn't been fed, changed, bathed, nothing. Everything was soaked. He'd screamed until he couldn't scream anymore – he was shaking all over and was almost catatonic." Nikki looked horrified. "When I asked Dottie what had happened, she said she just didn't want to be bothered." Nikki's eyes widened. "I cleaned him up, held him, and fed him while she read a book."

"Good god!" Nikki was shocked – what kind of woman was this?

"The next day, I came home at lunchtime to check on them. Good thing I did – same scenario. I didn't know what to do. I asked her again what was wrong. She glared at me and said she didn't want that baby and I should find someone to take him. I was twenty-six. I had a newborn baby and a wife who didn't care if we lived or died. My dad had passed away the year before, and I was trying to keep the company afloat. I really didn't know what to do or what was going to happen.

"I called my mother and asked her to come and get Clayton and some of his things. When I left the office that evening, I went to her house, told her everything, and asked her what to do. She said she'd go every day and stay with them.

"Then things got really dicey. Dottie would curse at my mother, throw things at her. She threatened to kill the baby and blame it on Mamma. It was so bad that Mamma couldn't stay there anymore during the day, so I started taking Clayton to her every morning and picking him up on my way home. The house was a wreck. It was like Dottie was trying to see what kind of mess she could make. It wasn't fit to live in, so I tried to hire a cleaning woman, but Dottie was so horrible to her that she quit after three days.

"By then, it was time for her six-week postpartum checkup. I went with her and told the doctor what was going on while she sat there and swore I was lying. He said he thought she was suffering from classic postpartum depression and gave her medication, which, of course, she wouldn't take. When Clayton was two months old, I had her committed for the first time."

"Oh, god, that's horrible!" Nikki gasped. "I mean, horrible for you. Horrible for everyone."

"Oh yeah? It gets worse. She'd get out and do better for awhile. Then she'd get worse again. When it was bad, she'd disappear for days. I'd come home and find her in bed with anyone she could get to sleep with her. Drunks, drug addicts, anyone. It's a wonder none of them killed her and robbed me, or that I didn't get some kind of disease. No way was I leaving Clayton with her either. He went to daycare. At least that way I knew he was safe and his needs were being met." Tony stopped and took a deep breath. "Then, when he was three, she started saying she wanted another baby. And, once again, still under thirty, I saw it as an opportunity to finally have sex with my wife. So she got pregnant again.

"But the weird part was that, while she was pregnant, she was completely normal. She'd started hearing voices and having hallucinations, but while she was pregnant, she was fine. She kept the house clean, cooked somewhat-edible meals, fixed up the nursery. I thought everything was finally okay. She still wasn't really warm toward me in bed, but she was decent and civil. It was actually more than I'd ever hoped for.

"Then Annabeth was born. She was a beautiful baby, bigger than Clayton had been, and very, very strong; really lively too. And two days after she was born, it all started again. I couldn't believe I'd brought another child into the world to have to live with that. The guilt was devastating, but it was too late; I had to deal with it. So she went to daycare too. My mom helped when she could. Dottie went in and out of the hospital dozens of times. She threatened to kill us, to kill herself, to set the house on fire. I started making myself go numb just so I could deal with her. There was nothing between us, and that was fine, anything to protect myself. She spent most of her time tearing me down, telling me how worthless I was, ugly, totally inadequate in bed. I still hear her voice in my head, every day. It was hard; still is."

After all the years that had gone by, Tony's anguish was still raw and fresh. Nikki found herself holding her breath against his pain.

"About the time Clayton turned thirteen, she started asking me for a divorce. At first, she just hinted at it. Later, she outright asked, demanded even. I wouldn't give her one. Her family was the worst bunch of Italian trash you'd ever find, and even *they* had abandoned her; and yeah, she was a good Italian Catholic. Who would've thought?" he asked sarcastically.

"Anyway, I couldn't just throw her to the wolves. I felt responsible for her; why, I don't know, but I did. She'd come in from sleeping with two or three different guys... I'll spare you the details, but she'd show me the evidence. Some of the things she let them do to her, well, it was horrible. She'd hit me, slap me, kick me, scream at me, trying to get me to give her a divorce. I kept hoping some break would take place. She'd go to the hospital, get out for awhile, go back.

"Then, one day, she went to the hospital on her own and stayed for a year. We'd go to see her, but she told them she didn't want to see us. When she got out, she announced she wanted a divorce because she'd fallen in love with an orderly there. At that point, I'd had all I could take. Clayton was sixteen and Annabeth was twelve. They'd never really had a mother, and I'd never really had a wife. I decided if she was willing to divorce me to marry a fucking orderly at a mental hospital, I'd let her go. That was sixteen years ago."

He stopped and took a deep breath. Nikki reached out and put her hand on the side of his face, stroking down to his chin and raising his face so he could see her expression; the love and admiration visibly bloomed there. "You, Tony Walters, are a saint. I don't know how you were as patient as you were."

"I'm no saint, but I tried. I was desperate." He put his hand on hers and dropped them both to the tablecloth. "Problem is, she's still around. Since then, she's been married, oh, I think four times, I'm not sure. She turned up a couple of months ago, asking for money. She shows up from time to time, making a commotion and hurting everyone, and then disappears again. I can't help it — I hate her. I realize she's sick, but she's just so damn mean." He squeezed his eyes shut, and Nikki could see a tear in the corner of each, then he opened them and blinked, his face suddenly tired and drawn. "So that's my story. A doozie, huh?"

"Sure is." She gave him a tiny smile. "Makes mine pale in comparison."

"Nope. My story is mine; your story is yours. No one is better or worse. It just is what it is."

Nikki smiled at him, but a question popped into her head. "So, how many women have you dated since your divorce?"

"One."

"Who?"

"You. Last night was the first real date I've been on since I was sixteen. Unless you count Elaine Burrows," he laughed.

"Who was she?"

"No one of any consequence, rest assured," he insisted. "I think she wanted to date my bank account. I wouldn't let that happen, so that was that."

"Smart guy." She patted his head in dog fashion and laughed; Tony laughed too. She was so damn easy to talk to, and he felt so relieved to get it all out.

Then she surprised him by asking, "So when was the last time you had sex with anyone?"

His eyebrows shot up into his hairline and he smiled. "Um, a couple of years ago."

"I thought you said you hadn't dated anyone," she queried, her eyebrows knitting into their own question marks.

"That's right." He didn't elaborate, and she waited as long as she could.

"So . . . ?"

"As I said before, that, my dear, is a conversation for another day!" He grabbed her around the waist, rolled her onto the tablecloth, and looked down into her face. "However, I've been waiting to do this, and I think the wait is over."

Tony leaned down to her and kissed her. He didn't just kiss her; he sealed his lips to hers and poured himself into her. Nikki had never been kissed like that, ever, not with that intensity or fervor. He didn't wrap his arms around her or press his body against hers; he just kissed her like he was starving and she was his only nourishment. His tongue explored every fraction of an inch of her mouth, and hers reciprocated eagerly. She felt something stirring deep inside her, a craving she couldn't quite name, and her nipples began to throb and go hard. She was getting wet and hot and, as he plunged his tongue into her mouth, her pussy clenched tight. She reached up and put a hand on either side of his face, and he caressed the side of her face with one hand. He paid close attention and got just what he was looking for – he felt her squirm ever so slightly, and he knew she was every bit as aroused as he was. When he broke away and pulled back, he looked down at her with a dark, smoky gaze that put a flutter in her chest. She took a quick glance and confirmed – the bulge in the front of his jeans was significantly bigger than it had been ten minutes before.

"Wow. For a guy who hasn't been dating, that was some kiss," she whispered, gasping and licking her lips. He tasted like macadamia nut cookie.

"Let me tell you something, baby. I've been saving those up for a long time. I guess I was saving them for you." He kissed her on the tip of her nose and pulled her up to a sitting position. "We'd better get up and walk around before we do something much sooner than we intended. Might even get us arrested!" They gathered the leftover picnic things and put them in the car, then found their way to the walk and strolled out through the green space.

"Yeah, hon, what's up?" Tony had dropped Nikki's hand to dig his phone out of his pocket and answer it; Annabeth.

"Dad, where are you?"

"I'm at . . . dammit. I totally forgot. I'll be there in a few minutes."

"But where are you?" she asked again.

"I'll explain later. There in thirty." He hit END and turned to Nikki. "I promised my kids I'd watch the game with them this afternoon and I completely forgot. I'm so sorry. I've got to go home or I'll never hear the end of it."

"Cards and Reds?"

"Yeah, it's the . . ." He stopped. "How did you know that?" he asked, puzzled.

"We're, um, I'm a Reds fan." She stared at the sidewalk as they walked back toward the car after what had been a blissful hour of strolling and chatting. "I still keep up with all the scores. I used to watch all of the games."

"Used to?" Tony echoed.

"Yeah. Not much fun when you're, well, just not much fun anymore."

"Well, I'd ask if you wanted to . . ." Tony started, then shook his head. "Oh, hell, do you want to come over? I mean, Annabeth already knows you. No big deal."

"I don't want to impose. This is time you're supposed to be spending with your family," Nikki said, a far-away, hopeless kind of look on her face.

"No, no imposition at all. I'd really like for you to be there. I really don't want this to end. We were having such a good time that I forgot about the game, remember? So come, please. It's sort of Clayton's birthday thing and there'll be cake! Please?" Tony put his hands together in a praying gesture and made a big frowny face. Nikki laughed.

"Are you sure?"

"I'm positive."

Nikki stopped and put her hands on her hips. "Will you be so sick of me by evening that you don't want to spend tomorrow with me?" she asked with a grin.

"Absolutely not. Matter of fact, if you're already getting tired of me today, tell me now and I'll insist you go home so you'll be excited about seeing me tomorrow," he laughed.

"No way! I'd love to come over to watch the game. And have cake!" Then she added, "I'd have to drive myself, though, so you'll need to take me by the shop to pick up my car before. I'll have to leave to go home and feed Bill and Hillary."

"The Clintons are at your house?" Tony asked sarcastically, then laughed.

"They're my dogs!"

"Are they Rottweiler's?" He laughed even harder.

"No!" Nikki started laughing too. "They're cinnamon toy poodles!"

"Bill and Hillary? What the hell?"

"Yeah, I know, but that's what my kids named them and it stuck. Even worse, they're brother and sister."

"That's just a little bit strange, don't you think?" he asked, still chuckling.

"Maybe. But they're just Bill and Hillary. You'll understand when you meet them."

"I can't wait," Tony said, and he meant it.

When he walked in the front door, Annabeth rounded the corner. "Where exactly have you been?" She was scrutinizing him a little too closely.

"Out. Where's everybody else?"

"Hey, guys, Dad's here!" Annabeth called out. Clayton appeared in the foyer, followed closely by Brittany and Katie. "So, Dad, where *have* you been?"

Tony thought carefully. "I was out getting some fresh air." That sounded good.

"Alone?" If Annabeth was nothing else, she was persistent.

"I don't have time to answer that. We have a guest coming over." There – it was out.

"A guest?" Clayton jumped in. "Who's this guest?"

"Just someone I know." Tony decided to go for broke and braced himself. "Annabeth knows her too."

For a split second Annabeth looked confused, but then a look of disbelief crossed her face as it sank in. "I know her. I know her? Nikki? The lady from the florist shop?" Annabeth's voice was getting higher and more animated with each syllable.

"Take a deep breath and calm down. Yes. Nikki from the florist shop. She'll be here in a few minutes."

"So you really went over and met her?" Annabeth asked.

"Yes, nosy daughter." Oh, what the hell – he plunged in head-first. "We went out on a date last night."

"OH MY GOD! OH MY GOD! DAD HAD A DATE!" Annabeth started screaming and jumping up and down, grabbing at Clayton, Katie, and Brittany, then turning her attention back to Tony. "You had a date! Why didn't you tell us?"

Clayton moaned and shook his head. "Um, I think I see why he didn't tell us. And I'd say this is exactly what he was trying to avoid."

"Well, she'll be here in a couple of minutes, so for god's sake, calm down, okay?" Tony looked around nervously. "How's the food situation? Is there something I need to do?" He sounded a wee bit frantic.

"Aw, how cute!" Brittany giggled. "Tony's nervous about bringing his girlfriend home to meet the fam." Katie started giggling too. Clayton rolled his eyes and watched Annabeth continue to bounce on her toes.

"We've taken care of all of it, Tony; we'll just pop the casseroles in the oven later. Hey, does she drive a red SUV?" Katie asked.

"Yeah – is she here?"

"Looks like it." Katie let the drape fall back over the front window.

"Okay. Please, everybody, behave. Please?" Tony begged, looking a bit worried.

"Dad?" Annabeth whispered. Tony turned to look at her and she mouthed, *I'm so happy!* She was grinning so hard that her face was bound to ache.

Tony opened the door as Nikki reached for the bell. "Come on in. Let me introduce you to everybody."

They leaned against Nikki's Escape at the end of the evening. It had been a long time since she'd been around that many happy people. Annabeth, Katie, and Brittany had treated her like one of the girls, and Clayton had reminded her a lot of her own Jake. She didn't really want to leave, but she also didn't want to wear out her welcome. They'd watched the baseball game; Cincinnati had won easily. Then they'd eaten the casseroles – poppy seed chicken and broccoli with cheese – that the girls had baked, and sat around for awhile shooting the breeze. And there'd been double chocolate cake! They'd even told her Tony's family nickname, Tookie; seemed he hadn't been able to say "cookie" when he was little, and the two older boys had mocked him with it. He, of course, hated it, but everyone had a good laugh about it. It had been so relaxed, and it felt so right to be there with them. She'd been pretty quiet, just trying to fit in, but they'd made sure she felt comfortable and included.

"So, we're still on for tomorrow, right?" Tony asked.

"I can't believe you still want to take me out tomorrow after you've spent all day with me today." She smiled up at him.

"Unless you're tired of me?" He looked down at her face in the darkness, and she felt something going on inside her, a warming, a thawing of something that had been cold and frozen over for a long time.

She shook her head. "Hell no. Don't think that's possible. I'll see you at one o'clock tomorrow?" In answer, he put a finger gently under her chin, tipped her face up to his, and pressed his lips to hers. She put her hands on his waist and stepped into him, melding her lips to his, moaning softly as his arms enveloped her and pulled her even closer. Tony was surprised by the hunger rolling off of her, the way she met his kiss with her own urgency, no tongue, just a steady pressure that told him she didn't want it to end any more than he did. When he finally released her, he leaned back and took in her face again, the glow he'd left on it and the pretty smile she gave him that told him she felt the same thing he was feeling, even if neither of them was sure exactly what it was.

"I'll be waiting," she whispered, breathless. Tony opened the door for her and she slid into her SUV. "So where are we going tomorrow?"

"That, beautiful girl, is the surprise."

"So, did you like the show?" Annabeth, Katie, and Brittany bit their lips at Tony's question.

"What do you mean?" Annabeth answered with feigned innocence.

"I know damn good and well you were watching us out the window," he grinned.

"We were sitting right . . ." Katie started.

"Oh, good god, how stupid do you guys think I am?" Tony chuckled. "I just want to know – what do you think?"

Clayton was the first one to speak up. Tony could always depend on him for bare-bones honesty. "I really like her. She just has a way about her that makes you feel comfortable. It was like she'd always been here."

"Yeah, I thought so too," Katie chimed in.

"See, Dad, I told you she was really nice," Annabeth added. "You really like her, don't you?"

He thought for a few seconds before answering, then nodded. "Yeah. Yeah, I do. I really do."

It was Brittany who walked right up to him, put her hands on his cheeks, looked straight into his eyes, and told him point-blank, "Tony, do it. Your heart is safe with that woman. I just know she'd never hurt you. Don't you hurt her either, you hear me? I have a very, very good feeling about this."

Tony took a deep breath and let it out. "Okay, guys. I'm going for it."

"Make it home okay?"

"Yeah, safe and sound." After so long of having no one who cared, it seemed odd to have someone care whether or not she got home safely. "Bill and Hillary are fed, and I'm going to bed."

"Did we wear you out?" Tony laughed.

Nikki giggled. "Pretty much! I haven't had that much fun in a long, long time."

"Good. I'm glad. We're pretty good entertainment. So I'll see you tomorrow afternoon. It's going to be hard to wait. Go to bed and get some rest. And think of me a little bit, would ya?"

"A little bit? I won't be thinking about much of anything else. Night, Tookie."

"Oh, god, not you too," Tony groaned.

"Sorry! Just had to do it once. I'll never say it again, I promise," she giggled, making only a tiny attempt at being apologetic.

"I'll forgive you – this once!" Tony chuckled. "Goodnight, beautiful girl," he said and hit END.

She wasn't stupid; she knew she wasn't beautiful. But when he called her that, she felt like she just might be.

Chapter Fifteen

Sometimes she wished she drank coffee. It would be a perfect morning to sit on the porch with a steaming mug. Nikki sat on the glider, drinking ice water and rocking. Her text notification pinged.

Hi, beautiful girl. Having a good morning?

She smiled. It was so gorgeous out for an early-May morning. *It's beautiful out today. I hope we're going to spend some of the afternoon in the great outdoors.*

Yes. My idea of a great afternoon too. See you at 1.

See you then, handsome. That didn't sound very clever, but it was the only thing Nikki could think to say. She'd like to call him honey, or darling, or lover, but that would be too much too soon, although she'd called him all of those things to herself as she burned out more batteries in her vibrator the night before. How many orgasms had fantasizing about him given her? Three? Four? More? She couldn't remember, but she'd certainly been exhausted. At one point, she'd thrown the vibrator aside and plunged in with her fingers, and she'd been surprised at how swollen and hard her clit had been. Her pussy had been aching, wanting to be filled, and that vibrator hadn't been nearly big enough. She needed him badly, but she couldn't say that to him, at least not yet.

"Hi! You're early!" Nikki opened the door and peeked through just enough that Tony could see half of her face.

"Yeah. Guess I was excited to see you." He waited. "Are you going to ask me in?"

Nikki's face turned bright pink. "Oh my god, of course, but I'm not ready. So, close your eyes?" He grinned, then squeezed his eyes shut. "I'm going to take your hand and lead you to the sofa. Don't open them until I say you can." She took his hand and led him inside, backed him up to the sofa, and sat him down. He heard her footsteps cross the room, and then she told him, "Okay, you can open them. I'll finish up in here."

Tony looked around. The living room wasn't large, but it wasn't tiny either. Everything was very neat, tidy, and organized. It was decorated very simply, and it wasn't extremely girly-looking. Some of the toss pillows were floral, but quite tastefully so. On the table were the roses he'd sent her.

Over on the mantel were a half dozen photos of people, so he got up to look at them. A smiling family gazed back at him; a woman, man, and two younger people. Next to it were two pictures in matching frames; each was a photo of one of the younger people in the first photo with a person of the opposite gender with them. On the other side of the mantel was a photo of the man and woman from the first photo, just the two of them. The woman looked familiar, but he couldn't figure out where he'd seen her. "Hey, who's this woman in these photos?" he called out. "You don't have a sister, do you?"

"No," he heard her reply, then there was a long pause before she replied, "that's me."

Tony looked again. The woman looked a little younger than Nikki, but was a good hundred pounds heavier. "You're kidding, right?" he called back. "That's you?"

"That was me," she called back. "That's not me anymore."

"Well, no shit." Tony heard a sound behind him and turned. "Oh. My. God," he murmured. His mouth fell open in shock.

Nikki stood in the open doorway in her gauzy turquoise sundress. The straps of her purple bra showed under the sundress straps, and both showed through the open knit of the cap-sleeved shrug she was wearing over the dress. She had on matching bejeweled flip-flops and a gold ankle bracelet, and plenty of sparkly jewelry. Her hair was pulled back in a half-tail with a turquoise, blue, and purple scarf tied around it. "Do I look okay?" she asked.

Tony chuckled and shook his head. "You have no idea, do you?" he asked her.

"What? What's wrong?"

"You look spectacular. Really, really hot." Tony looked her up and down. "I wish you had some idea what kind of effect you have on me."

Nikki blushed. She wondered if he'd done the same thing last night, alone in his bed, that she'd done in hers. She'd like to think he had. As if to answer her unspoken question, he offered, "Do you have any clue what kind of shape I was in last night after you left?"

"No," she lied. "What do you mean?"

"Let's just say it was a good thing all of the kids went home." He looked down at the floor and blushed, then looked back up at her under his brows. "Ready to go?"

"Yeah, let me say goodbye to Bill and Hillary."

"Can I meet them? Will they eat me?" he asked mockingly.

"Oh, yeah, they'll eat you! Come in here." She motioned for him to follow her into the kitchen, where the two small dogs jumped at his legs as she fussed at them to stop. Tony just dropped to one knee and scratched ears and chins.

After she'd petted them goodbye and closed the gate to the kitchen area, she and Tony made their way out the front door. Before they could get through the doorway, Tony caught her around the waist, twirled her around to face him, and planted a small, soft kiss on her lips, then buried his face in her hair. "You can't know how much I've been looking forward to this."

"I doubt you've looked forward to it as much as I have," she whispered in his ear.

He squeezed her to him and leaned back, his gold-flecked eyes locking with her turquoise-blue ones. "If this day goes as well as I think it will, we're going to have a lot to talk about on the way home." He let her go and swept his arm toward the car. "After you, baby."

"Do you really like dogs?" she asked as she buckled in.

"Oh, yeah, I love them." He looked both ways before pulling out onto the street in the non-existent Sunday afternoon traffic.

"But you don't have one?"

"Nope. I'd love to have one. But I work so much that it wouldn't be fair to a dog. Plus I always had my hands so full taking care of, well, everything, by myself that I couldn't handle a dog too. Maybe someday I'll have somebody in my life to help me so I can have a dog. Or maybe," he said, reaching over to take the hand she held in her lap but not looking at her, "she'll already have dogs and I can love and enjoy them."

"Even if they're weird, yippy little dogs?"

Tony laughed. "Hey, even weird, yippy little dogs need love!"

"By the way, whose car is this?" Nikki ran her hands across the leather seat of the gold Mercedes sedan. It was easily the most luxurious car she'd ever ridden in, and so quiet too.

"Mine."

"This? Where's the Camaro?" Nikki loved the sports car. It was beautiful, fast, and very, very sexy.

"At home in the garage," he told her as he pulled onto the interstate.

She wasn't sure what answer she'd expected, but that wasn't it. "So exactly how many cars do you have?" she asked without looking at him.

"Let's see . . . this one, the Camaro, the work truck, my personal truck, which is a Dodge Ram, a Yukon Denali, and a BMW convertible. Oh, yeah, and a Harley." Tony rattled them off as though it were the most natural thing in the world to have an entire car lot of vehicles.

"Oh. And what about a plane and a helicopter? And the yacht?" she asked, trying to be funny.

"No helicopter or yacht. But I do have a plane," he replied matter-of-factly. "Well, the company has one. It's at our hangar."

Nikki didn't know exactly what to say to that. How do you ask someone why they need six cars and an airplane? And besides, why was it her business? He clearly enjoyed what he was working so hard for. She decided she'd asked all the questions she needed to ask for the time being, so she took a deep breath, sat back in the glove-soft leather, and relaxed. She had a feeling it was going to be a fabulous day.

They hadn't gone very far before Tony signaled and pulled onto an exit ramp. Nikki started to ask where they were going, and then she remembered: The magazine article said Tony's family home was in Shelbyville, and that was the exit they were taking. Was he taking her to his other house?

Within a few minutes they were driving through the middle of Shelbyville. It was small but quaint, with a sparsely-populated main street like so many small towns in the state. Tony kept driving east until they were on the other side of town. There were plenty of fairly average houses, nothing spectacular, but the countryside was gorgeous.

"So you grew up here?" Nikki asked.

"More or less. I think I told you, when I got to high school age, my parents sent me to Italy. I came back here summers until I graduated high school, then I went to UK to engineering school. But I came here almost every weekend during college. I was seeing Dottie. Her piece-of-shit family is here too. So being here seemed like the thing to do." Tony didn't look at her while he was talking. She wasn't sure if that was because he was watching the road, or if he really didn't want to talk about those years. "Now, with the business to run, I don't spend as much time here as I'd like. I like the outdoors, the farm, the land, all of that. But it's easier for me to live in Louisville. And I raised the kids there for that reason too." He turned onto a smaller road, barely big enough for meeting cars to pass.

"Is this where you're planning to retire?" Nikki gazed out the window at the neat white fences along both sides of the road.

Tony's voice sarcasm when he said, "Retire? What's that? I doubt I'll retire until I'm so old that I won't be able to drive all the way out here! Even my weekends are usually pretty jammed up."

Nikki turned to look at him and asked him outright, "So you're sure you'd have time for a relationship?"

Her question caught him by surprise – very direct, but he respected that. He thought for a minute before answering. "I think the right woman could persuade me to spend time with her."

"That's good to know." She was blunt and there wasn't even the hint of a smile. "Because I'd hate to think I'm wasting my time on somebody who wouldn't have time for me. I'm not very demanding and I enjoy my 'me' time, but I miss having somebody to talk to, eat with, that kind of thing."

This time when Tony smiled at her, it was a sad smile. "I'd make time for the right person." He hesitated for a second, then added, "Actually, I scrapped some plans this weekend to come here."

"To come here?" she quizzed. "Or to come here with me?"

"Both. But mostly the latter." He smiled without looking at her; she was tricky, this one. She was just so damned straightforward. He'd have to stay on his toes with her, but he liked a challenge, and it looked like she might offer a lively one.

Nikki looked out the window so he couldn't see her face and broke into a wide grin. He'd had plans, but he'd cancelled them to spend time with her. That was sounding promising.

After they'd gone a couple of miles, a modern ranch-style home appeared on the left a small distance ahead of them, but instead of facing the road, the house sat perpendicular to it. "What a lovely place!" Nikki chirped, noting the carefully manicured lawn and small fish pond out front.

"Looks like Helene is home." Tony pointed at a small gray car in the driveway.

"Helene?" Nikki asked, puzzled.

"Yeah, my housekeeper." He honked the horn twice as he got nearer but, to Nikki's surprise, he kept driving. "That's her house."

"That's your housekeeper's house?" She'd assumed it was his.

"Yeah. Mine is over the hill." They passed the housekeeper's house and started up a long, gradual incline. Nikki looked behind them and saw a middle-aged woman waving at them from the back deck of the house.

"What's the name of this road?" Nikki asked as they continued the gradual climb.

"Oh, this isn't a road." Tony sighed. "This is my driveway."

The Mercedes crested the hill and started down the other side, and Nikki had to stifle a gasp. Ahead of them lay an enormous two-story house. Her brain couldn't quite grasp its immensity; it made the McMansions she was accustomed to seeing look like tract houses. The entire façade was stone, wood, and glass. On the first level, an imposing mahogany front door with leaded beveled crystal sidelights was framed by the columns supporting the second level balcony, which had huge windows looking out over it. Several gargantuan oaks graced the lawn and threw shade onto the house, and a tire swing hung from a branch on the largest tree. Jutting out and back at an angle on either side of the house were two-story wings. The left wing appeared to have windows from the living area; the right one, a five-car garage. To the left and a good quarter-mile behind the house was a large stable, designed to mimic the exterior of the house, and a half-dozen horses grazed on the lush grass in the sunshine beating down on the pastureland around the scene. It was almost too perfect, like an advertisement from a travel magazine.

"Sweet mother of god," Nikki whispered under her breath.

"Like it? My humble abode," Tony announced, pulling up in front to park. "Come on in."

She opened the car door but, before she could get out, Tony was there, holding it for her. He closed it behind her and marched up the steps, her hand in his. She noted he didn't take out a key; the door was unlocked and he simply opened it for her and held it until she was inside.

What the outside didn't do to intimidate her, the interior managed. It was beautiful, crystal entry chandelier and all. Her voice broke as she asked, "How many bedrooms?"

"Eight. Not counting the one for the housekeeper. I can use it as guest housing now that Helene has her own house. So I guess nine." Tony walked into the kitchen with Nikki following. "Would you like something to drink?"

he asked, opening the refrigerator.

"Just water?" Nikki choked out, realizing it came out sounding more like a question. She really didn't know what to say or how to act as she tried to wrap her mind around why a man like Tony Walters would even ask her out. Was he testing her to see if she was a gold digger? Or if she'd be put off by his money? Her head was spinning, trying to figure out why she was standing in the kitchen of a house like that.

"So, listen," Tony said.

"Yeah?" she managed to squeak out.

"No, I mean, listen," he repeated. "It's so quiet."

He was right – there wasn't a single sound. Nikki found herself thinking how she could get used to that, when a woman's voice rang out. "Tony? Why didn't you let me know you were coming?" The woman she'd seen on the deck of the smaller house bustled in through the back kitchen door.

"Hey, Helene! I didn't call because I don't want you to do a thing. Just go on back home. I'm guessing there's some food in the fridge?"

"Oh, yes, some sliced ham, deviled eggs, green bean casserole, and pot roast. I think there's some meatloaf in there too." She had a round, soft, medium build and was slightly older than Tony, with a chubby, ruddy face and no makeup. Her gray hair was cut very short, and she wore the whitest tee shirt Nikki had ever seen.

"Perfect! That'll be fine." Tony busied himself pulling things out. Helene tried to take them from him, but he pulled the containers away from her. "No, you just go on now. I've got this. Take a day off, for heaven's sake. I think we can handle it," he told her and grinned at Nikki. "By the way, this is my friend, Nikki."

"Very nice to meet you." Helene responded with a smile and extended her hand.

Nikki took it. Helene had a warm, firm grip. "And you as well," Nikki replied.

"So where did you two meet?" Helene asked, trying hard not to break into a huge grin.

"And it's time for you to go home. Take the day off. We're going to spend some quality time sitting and talking." Tony pointed at the back door. "I'll answer questions at the press conference." For a moment, Nikki thought he was serious. When he noticed the stricken look on her face, he laughed. "Just joking!"

"Oh! It was . . ."

"Damn that magazine article. Hey, really, nobody cares what I do. That was a fluke." He pushed Helene out the door and closed it behind her, and she stood on the back steps for a second or two before shuffling off. "Now, what's your preference, ham or pot roast?"

"Did Helene cook this stuff? Because it's incredible." Nikki thought about how many calories were probably in the meatloaf and then decided she didn't care.

"Yeah, she's an exceptional cook." Tony forked up more green bean casserole. "I would've starved years ago if it hadn't been for her. Sometimes she makes stuff when she knows I'm coming and sends it back with me. Don't know what I'd do without her."

"Worked for you long?"

"Yep. Her grandparents worked for my grandparents, and her parents for mine, and, well, you get the picture. I finally built the house for her a few years ago. I don't need somebody living under my roof, but this way she's close and somebody's watching the house." He chewed thoughtfully. "But I didn't bring you here to talk about food."

"So why did you bring me here?" She felt her stomach flutter ever so slightly as she waited for his answer.

"Like I told Helene, to talk. Without interruptions." He ate the last bite of casserole, then rinsed his plate and put it in the dishwasher. She tried to finish hers, but her nerves wouldn't let her, so she handed him her plate and he made short work of her leftovers, then rinsed her plate and stowed it too.

"Come on, let's go sit in the great room and do some getting-to-know-you communicating." He took her hand and led her out of the kitchen and into the massive room. Huge French doors led out onto a flagstone patio, and the doors were flanked by two enormous stone fireplaces. Beyond the patio, Nikki could see a large swimming pool surrounded by plenty of space to entertain, filled with lots of expensive-looking outdoor furniture. Under a covered area, a stone grill accompanied by a built-in range dominated a dining area complete with a table that would probably seat twelve. To Nikki, it looked like something straight out of an architectural magazine.

Tony plopped down onto a soft, overstuffed leather sofa, kicked off his shoes, put his feet up on the coffee table, and motioned for her to sit beside him. She kicked off her shoes too, and pulled her feet up onto the sofa. "So, you kept saying we were going to talk. What are we supposed to be talking about?" she asked quietly.

"I just want to know what you have in mind for this relationship." His eyes scanned her face, and she felt her heart flip-flop in her chest.

"What exactly do you mean? Maybe you should tell me what you have in mind so I have a little better idea of what you're looking for in the way of an answer." She hoped he couldn't see or hear her heart pounding.

"Not gonna make this easy on me, are you?" He smiled and she shook her head. "Okay, here goes. Nikki, I haven't dated anybody since my divorce, and I do not engage in casual sex. I don't see dating as a sport. I see it as a way to, I don't know, maybe audition somebody? To see if I'm compatible with them?" Nikki's eyebrows were slightly raised, and she was listening intently, judging by her face. His heart felt like it was going to burst from anxiety. He didn't want to scare her off, but he wanted to be honest with her. "I mean, I wouldn't even ask somebody out if I didn't think I was really interested in them. So I guess what I'm asking is, do you think you're even remotely interested in a long-term relationship with me? I know it's kind of early to ask that and we really don't know each other very well, but . . ."

"No, I don't think it's early. And I don't believe in casual dating either," she answered. "I wouldn't have said yes to a date if I only wanted to see you once or just sleep with you or something like that." She couldn't believe she'd said that, but he was really putting himself out there, so she wanted to honor that by being as honest as she could manage. "I'm most definitely interested in seeing where this goes. But I have to warn you, I'm afraid."

"Of what?" Tony's eyes were sad. "Of me? Of getting involved with somebody? Of getting hurt? Because you couldn't be more afraid of getting hurt than I am. I'm terrified."

"Then why are you doing this? Why scare yourself silly? You have a good life, even without a partner."

"Because," he took a deep breath, "because I'm tired of being alone." There – he'd said it, and she wasn't laughing or running away. She was still gazing steadily into his eyes. He felt his heartbeat start to calm.

"I understand." Nikki looked down at her hands. "I've got my own issues. I'm afraid of getting hurt. I'm afraid I won't fit into your lifestyle, your family, your circle of friends. Look at this place. I'm so plain. I'm no fancy person; I'm just me." She felt tears start to pool in her eyes and she didn't want to draw attention to them, so she fought the urge to wipe them away. "I'm afraid of everything, of being rejected, of finding out you don't want me like you thought you did. I'm not twenty-five; I'm almost fifty-two. Gravity is not my friend; nothing is as perky as it used to be. I'm scared of pretty much everything." She stopped for a second and took a deep breath, her shoulders shuddering. "I guess my question is, why me? What could you possibly see in me? I'm nobody; I'm nothing. You could have anyone you want. Why in the world would you want me? Why am I here?"

Tony reached out and softly placed his hand on her face. His palm was warm and velvety, and when she leaned into it and closed her eyes, she felt a tear spill out and run down her cheek. Before it could get all the way to her jaw, he caught it with his thumb and wiped it away. "Honey, I'm not looking for fancy," he told her in a liquid tone barely over a whisper. "I'm looking for real, and the thing that drew me to you was how real you are. I could buy myself a plastic girl, somebody all pumped up with silicone and Botox and collagen, but that's not me. I just want somebody who'll treat me with some love and respect, somebody who'll be there for me, somebody who'll try their best to make a life with me. And you have a proven track record with a man you loved, and who loved you. What you had with your husband? *That's* what I'm looking for. That's all I've ever really wanted." Tony stopped and looked at her, waiting for her to look at him.

When her eyes finally opened, there was a tenderness and gentleness to their turquoise tint that he'd never seen in another woman's eyes, deep and pure. She gave a little sniffle and whispered out, "I'd like to try to see where this goes. I'd really given up on ever having much of a life again. I don't even know where to start."

Tony shrugged. "I don't really know where to start either, but I think we've gotten off to a pretty good one, don't you?"

"I know I'm having fun. This has been the best weekend I've had in years." She straightened a bit. "I'll be sad when it's over."

"It doesn't have to be. Let's just spend as much time together as we can and see what happens. But I have a rule: I won't sleep with you until you're ready and we've talked about it, about expectations, about limits, about all of it. Just like you said, remember?"

"Absolutely," Nikki agreed. "I'm in no hurry. Well, I mean, I don't want to rush things." She blushed. Nothing was coming out right. "I mean, it's not that I don't want you, because I . . . oh, I should probably shut up now." Her face was growing hot and she wanted to crawl under a rock.

Tony chuckled. "Let me make something clear right now. I want you. I want you bad. But I want us to get to know each other a little better first, make sure we're a good fit, you know? The last thing I'd want would be to find out we aren't compatible and wind up with both of us feeling used and hurt."

"I agree." Nikki felt better. "Make sure we're a good fit. We're grownups. We can do this." She looked up into his face and saw nothing but pure joy there.

Oh my god, Tony thought. *I'm not sure I'm grownup enough to wait.*

"Are any of them yours?" When Nikki approached one of the horses, the bay gelding raised his head for her to scratch his face, then put it back down and started munching on the tender spring grass again.

"No. I lease the barn to a neighbor. Some of them are his, and some are boarders. His wife teaches riding lessons." Tony patted a huge sorrel mare on the shoulder. "Do you like horses?"

"Oh, yeah! I had a couple when I was a kid. I'll always love them." She plucked a yellow dandelion bloom from the ground and twirled it between her fingers. "Do you think I could maybe ride one of them sometime?"

"I think that's completely doable. He's told me to ride them anytime. I've just never had anybody to ride with." Tony pointed out two in the herd. "I think he said that bay and the appaloosa were the two best ones to ride."

"What are their names?" Nikki asked.

"You know, I have no idea. I'll have to find out. I have a key to the tack room, but I'd need to know which saddle and bridle for which horse." Tony smiled: Good. She was making plans to come back.

"Great! Maybe next time I'm here." Nikki reached down for the halter on the big palomino mare, and she raised her head easily and nuzzled Nikki's neck. Nikki giggled and Tony felt a wave of bliss roll over him – she was really enjoying herself. He was so happy to see her as carefree as a child. He'd never really cared about all the stuff his money bought, but being able to make someone else happy, well, that was what he wanted more than anything, and she did appear to be having a good time.

"I don't know when we'll get the chance to come back." Tony tried to look serious. *Uh-oh,* Nikki thought. *I guess I was a little too forward. What was I thinking, assuming he'd bring me back here?* Then he added, "But that won't keep us from spending time together."

"Of course not. At least I hope not." She picked a clover blossom and put it behind her ear, and he couldn't help thinking it was the most beautiful flower he'd ever seen.

He closed the gate behind them and they headed back toward the house. "I don't know how you'll feel about it, but I'd like to see you at some point every day if that's possible. What do you think?"

Nikki was startled, but in a good way. "That would be great! If we can't, can we at least talk on the phone?"

"Of course. Often. I have a good feeling about all of this, I guess because I've enjoyed this weekend so much." Tony pulled her down to sit beside him on one of the gliders on the patio. He draped his arm around her shoulders, and she took his other hand, threading their fingers together. Looking at her pale fingers entwined with his dark ones, his cock twitched a little. He wondered what his dark hand would look like on her pale breast, and tried not to think about it. Thinking like that would make the agreement they'd made very hard to keep, and he didn't want to rush things. But damn, it would be good to find out.

Looking back up, he found her gazing at him like he was a sundae complete with whipped cream and a cherry on top, but the trepidation in those turquoise eyes made his heart spin. They practically screamed *Don't hurt me*. He thought of all of the lonely nights he'd spent, even with Dottie sleeping beside him, and all the lonely nights Nikki had spent too. He hoped to make all of that a distant memory, but he knew he couldn't do it in a day, a week, or even a month. It would take time. And they might not have as much of that as a younger couple, but they had enough. Taking her chin in his hand and pulling her face to his, he kissed her, a long, sweet, closed-mouth kiss, and he felt something hard and cold inside his chest start to crack wide open.

As he kissed her, Nikki's mind raced. This was it, her last, best chance. This was a kind, honorable man, beautiful and wounded and hungry for something she had plenty of – care, concern, and the love he'd never found in his adult life with a woman who wanted to be with him in every way. Nikki almost felt like she was floating as she realized, *If this guy is being straight with me, and I think he is, I might actually have a shot at a life*. She'd asked for a friend and companion, but she had a feeling she'd found a lot more. If she'd been looking, she might've missed him. But he'd found her, and she was more than glad. She was ecstatic.

"This was the best day I've had in a long, long time." Nikki turned to Tony on the porch. "Want to come in?"

"No. I'd better get going. Work will come early tomorrow morning, and we both need to get some sleep." Tony slipped his arms around her waist and pulled her closer. "But I don't want to go a single day without seeing you if we can manage it, okay?" He planted a sweet little kiss on her mouth.

"I don't want to go a day without seeing you either." She kissed him back. He kissed her again, this one longer and hotter. Her knees felt like spaghetti, and she wanted him to hold her closer, but he pulled back so he could see her precious face and make a mental snapshot to keep it with him until he could see her again.

"I'll call you before bed." He gave her a quick peck on the lips, then turned to wave before he got into the Mercedes. She watched his taillights disappear down the street and out of sight.

Before she could get her makeup off and change into her pajamas, the phone rang.

"Just wanted to say goodnight." His voice was bright. In her mind, she could see his gorgeous smile.

"Thanks." She hesitated, then took a chance and said, "I miss you already."

"I miss you too, sweetie," he told her without missing a beat. "Get some sleep, beautiful girl. Hope I see you tomorrow."

"I hope so too."

Chapter Sixteen

Tony smiled when the text came in the next day. He'd planned to call her when he got home, but this was even better; Marla had sent her home early and she was cooking! Damn, he wished he had something nicer to change into. He didn't know what she was cooking, and he didn't care. It wasn't about the food anyway.

When he got out of his work truck in front of her house he could smell whatever she had on the stove. He bounded up the front steps, but the knob was locked; two seconds later, the door popped open. "Hey, babe! Come on in!" She hugged him around the neck, and he planted a big kiss right on her mouth.

"I tried the knob. I thought the door would be unlocked since I called when I left work." That seemed odd to Tony.

"I never leave my door unlocked. Anybody could just stroll in." *She's cautious; that's good,* Tony thought. He wouldn't have to worry about her if she approached everything so guardedly, and he definitely wanted her safe.

"What's that amazing smell?" He inhaled deeply.

"Let's see . . . a beef roast; roasted beets, turnips, and carrots with beet greens; and boiled okra. Oh, and a mixed greens salad. Hungry?"

"Starving! By the way, thanks for asking me to come over. I really wanted to see you," Tony said, taking her hand.

"I can't think of anything that would make food taste better than to eat it across the table from you." She put her free hand on his cheek. "Let's eat it before it gets cold."

Once in the kitchen, she handed him a plate and pointed to the stove. "I don't get all fancy. Just serve yourself. Eat all you want. If you eat it, I don't have to store it. And, for the record, everything I've fixed is very healthy, so you can pretty much have all you want." She smiled; he could tell she was proud of herself, and he was thrilled. No woman except his mother and the hired help had ever made him a decent meal.

He took the plate and forked out a hunk of roast beef; Nikki handed him a small ladle and he ladled some of the *au jus* over it. He wasn't sure about the vegetables; he'd never had them roasted before, and certainly not beets, but they smelled good, so he took a good-sized spoonful. When he got to the okra, though, he almost balked. Nikki had put a spaghetti server in the pan and, when he scooped up a strainer full, a gooey substance ran down in strings. As he stared at it, Nikki laughed. "Afraid?"

"Um, no. I . . ."

She laughed again. "It's yummy. Just wait – you'll see!" She took her plate, filled it, and sat down at the table with him. "Let's get it over with. Like this." Nikki took an okra pod on her fork and stuck it in her mouth. Tony watched with curiosity as the stem end reappeared between her lips, and she bit it off and put it back on her fork, depositing it on her plate. Then she chewed the pod for a second and swallowed. "Now, you try it."

Tony took his fork and picked up a pod. The stringy liquid dripped from it. He popped it in his mouth, then mimicked her actions and paid close attention as he chewed. It was surprisingly delicious, kind of peppery and sweet. "That's amazing!" he smiled softly at her. "It looks so disgusting, but it tastes so good."

"Wonder how many men have said that over the years?" She smiled down at her plate, then looked up at him from under her brows and broke a huge smirk. That made him laugh. After the okra success, he wasn't afraid of the roasted vegetables. They were very spicy and had a warm, comforting flavor, and the taste of the roasted greens mixed into them was very unusual and sort of exotic.

Everything she'd cooked, every dish, tasted like it was full of hugs, all designed to make the people enjoying them feel cherished and loved. Tony tried to remember anything Dottie had ever cooked that had been edible – nope, nothing. He almost choked as his eyes welled up.

"Honey, what's wrong? Don't be afraid to tell me – is it that bad?" She wasn't sure – had she done something wrong?

Tony put his fork down quietly, then dropped to his knees beside her chair and wrapped his arms around her waist. What could he say to make her understand what this little bit of heaven had meant to him? How could he explain to her she'd just tipped his heart toward her, that she'd spent a small amount of time to do something that made a big difference in his day, in how he saw himself, in how he felt about her? "This is possibly the best meal I've ever had. No woman's ever cooked a meal like this for me – ever." He felt himself choking up again, and he laid his head in her lap. Her fingers danced softly down through his hair, massaging his scalp to calm him, and he felt her hand shaking ever so slightly.

Then he felt her straighten up as she lifted his head and turned his face toward her. "Well, they should have. You deserve to have somebody do nice things for you, cook you good, healthy meals, go the extra mile for you. You deserve to be special to somebody. And you're special to me," she announced. "Now, I want you to sit down and enjoy a meal cooked especially for you. And if I fix something you don't like, you tell me and I'll fix something else until I find something you do like. I'll gladly do it over and over." She kissed his forehead and pointed at his chair.

Tony sat back down and took up his knife, then discovered he didn't need it – the roast was so tender that it fell apart. With every bite, he smiled a bit broader, until he couldn't contain his delight. Nikki was smiling too.

"So, how was your day?" he asked, grinning at her over a forkful of vegetables. It was the most normal thing he could think of to say. And he desperately wanted to enjoy what appeared to be the first normal meal of the first normal relationship of his previously abnormal life.

They talked and laughed for a long time at the table, occasionally touching hands or kissing. By the time he'd helped her clean up the kitchen, it was after eight.

"Want some tea or coffee? A beer?" Nikki asked.

"Nah." Tony walked to the door, then turned and placed his hands on her hips. "Probably need to get going. Work tomorrow and all that. And if I don't leave soon," he murmured, kissing her forehead, "I won't be able to. And I don't know if we're ready for that yet."

Her lower lip popped out in a pout, but she fake whined, "Well, be that way!" Taking his hand and kissing it, she looked at it, really looked at it. His hands were strong but refined, with long, thin fingers, nails perfect and smooth, and a little bit of dark hair on the backs of his hands, which she found incredibly sexy. She thought about how much she'd love to have those hands on her, then reached up and ran her hands through his hair, put her fingers on the back of his head, and pulled his face to her, kissing him long and hard.

Tony couldn't stop himself; he pressed his tongue against her lips, and they parted for him. Finding her tongue, he sucked it into his mouth, then ran his back into her mouth, probing into it over and over and never wanting it to stop. She moaned, a long, low sound of want and longing, and he felt every inch of his body start to tingle. His arms wrapped instinctively around her and pulled her tight to him, and he ran his hands down to her ass and pulled her pelvis against his. Nikki felt his erection against the softness just below her navel, and she moaned even louder and tipped her head, reaching further into his mouth with her tongue. Tony could feel the hardness of her nipples pressing into his chest, and he ran his hands back up her back to the hook of her bra; when his hands touched it, he stopped and pulled back, taking a deep breath and locking his eyes with hers. Their ocean-like blueness scanned his face and she smiled.

"Wow." He couldn't think of anything else to say.

"Uh-huh!" she whispered, then leaned in and softly kissed his chin.

"I, um, probably should go." Never taking his eyes from hers, he reached behind him for the doorknob, waved his hand around until he found it, and turned the knob until the door popped open.

"Yeah, I guess so. I hope you liked dinner and, um, everything." She blushed a little.

"I didn't like it – I loved it. Everything was amazing. Especially you." Tony kissed Nikki on the forehead and turned to the door. "Call you in a bit?"

She smiled. "I hope so." He gave her a quick peck on the lips and closed the door behind him.

On the porch, Tony took a deep breath. God, he'd have trouble falling asleep. He wanted to run right back inside, grab her up, and never let her go. But when he got into the car, a pang of guilt pierced right through his chest. Should he? He decided he had to tell her – he couldn't be that person, the one who held things back, hid things, sneaked around.

He took the front steps two at a time, hesitated, then knocked on the door. He heard a quiet shuffling, saw the peephole darken from the inside, then the security chain rattled and she opened the door. "Uh-oh – did you forget something?"

"I need to talk to you about something. It can't wait." His anxiety level was rising by the minute.

Nikki was confused. What in the world could've happened in that two-minute period? He had an odd, serious look on his face that sort of scared her. Had she gone too far with that last wild, heated kiss? "Sure, okay." She pointed at the sofa.

Tony sat down. She could tell he was nervous, bouncing one heel on the floor.

She waited. "Tony, for the love of god, what the hell?" she finally asked, sitting down beside him.

"I have to tell you something." He took a deep breath. "I have somebody looking into you, your background, doing a check." His face turned deep scarlet and he met her gaze, hoping to see some forgiveness there when she understood what he'd done.

Nikki threw her head back and started laughing. "Well, I would certainly hope so! You have a lot to lose, sweetie. I would hope you'd check out anybody you dated!"

"You're not mad?" he asked, incredulous. He'd expected her to be furious, or indignant, or both.

"Of course I'm not mad! People are so devious these days that if I were one of your family members, I'd definitely want you to do that." Nikki patted his hands reassuringly. "Don't worry about it."

"But, I need to know, is there anything you need to tell me before I get the report? Anything at all? Because I'd rather you told me than for me to find out the wrong way . . ."

"What I'm afraid you'll find out is that I'm the most boring person you've ever met!" She laughed again. "Dull as dishwater. Not a thing interesting about me. I'm not the least bit worried." She saw his shoulders relax.

"You're not dull or boring. But I couldn't keep this from you. I felt so dishonest and sneaky." Tony took her hands in his. "As long as you're not mad . . ."

"No, not at all. But if anything interesting turns up, please share. I'd love to know what it is," she chuckled.

Nikki could never understand his relief. "Okay. I'm really going now. I'm sorry I startled you, took up more of your evening." He turned to leave.

"I'll give you as much of my evening as you want," she replied, following him to the door.

"I'm gonna hold you to that soon – very soon!" Tony leaned over and kissed her lightly, then pulled away. "Talk to you in a bit."

Nikki leaned against the inside of the door, hugging herself. She felt like a kid again, and her heart was slamming like a sledgehammer in her chest. She'd loved Randy and they'd been good together, but Randy had never kissed her with that eagerness or passion. She hadn't felt alive in that way in a long time. Her nipples ached and her panties needed to be wrung out.

She readied herself for bed and climbed in with a book and a tall glass of water. Her ringing phone caused her to drop the book and answer sweetly, "Hi, gorgeous guy!"

"Hi yourself! Snuggled up in bed?" His deep, warm voice was so sexy; it gave her goose bumps and her nipples hardened yet again. Seemed they stayed that way most of the time.

"Yep, book and all. Hey, I'm so glad you came over for dinner. I enjoyed cooking for you so much."

"I enjoyed the food — and the company. You're an amazing cook. Let me feed you tomorrow night, okay? My house? Thai delivery? How does that sound?"

Nikki felt like she'd just won the lottery. "I'd love it. Gym first, then eat?"

"You've got it, beautiful girl. See you tomorrow night. Sleep tight, baby."

"You too, sexy. Night." Nikki hit END and sighed. She was falling, hard and fast. She hoped he was too.

Tony stared at the phone for a second or two, then put it on the charger and climbed into bed. She'd called him sexy; no woman had ever done that. He lay back and thought about the evening, his mind finally resting on the last few minutes before he left her. Remembering her arousal, the fervency of her kiss, her fingers in his hair, made his cock grow more and more rigid until his hardness wouldn't wait anymore. He wrapped his fingers around his shaft and worked unhurriedly, remembering her delicate scent, the softness of her bright hair, her sweet breath against his cheek, her tongue working around and into his. Wanting her, needing her against him, his desperation increased, his hips thrusting upward and his breathing growing shallow as he began to pump furiously. Within seconds, he came with a groan, moaning her name, his desire for her overwhelming.

He was pretty sure he was falling in love with her. He didn't care that it wasn't smart or safe. It was just happening, and he wasn't going to stop it. Besides, he wasn't sure he could even if he tried.

Tony had cleaned up and was climbing back into bed when the phone rang —

Steve. "Talk to me, great all-knowing one. Whaddya got?"

"Nothing. A whole big bunch of nothing."

"Nothing?"

"Nope, not one thing. If this woman is hiding anything, I can't find it," Steve told him. "I've talked to half of that little shithole of a town, which would be about three and a half people, and no one could say one bad thing about her."

"'Zat so?" Tony's face broke into a huge smile. He'd worried for nothing.

"Yep. I now know virtually every medical procedure she's ever had done . . ."

"You got into her medical records?" Tony practically screamed. "How the hell . . ."

"Don't ask. Illegal as hell. And I got a copy of her school records . . ."

"Are you kidding? Shit, Steve, for god's sake!"

"No, not kidding. Did you know her I.Q. is one sixty-two? And she has no college degree, even though she got four full-ride scholarships. Get this — the schools awarding them were never contacted. There was no confirmation that she ever received the notifications." He sounded like he was chewing again. Did the guy eat all the time? "So basically, whoever got the mail at her house didn't want her to go to college."

What kind of people had raised her? Why would anyone hobble their child that way, especially one with that much potential? "So, did you find and talk to her parents?" Nikki hadn't told him about them until after he'd talked to Steve.

"Funny you should ask. Yeah, I found them, or at least I think I did, Calvin and Barbara Wallace. But I called them and asked for her, and they said they didn't know anybody by that name. I know I have the right people; I got their phone number from her cousin." Tony wondered what kind of story Steve had told the cousin to get that information. "So I'm kinda confused by what they said. But whatever — the girl's clean as a whistle."

"Thanks, man. I really appreciate it. Send me the bill." Tony felt the built-up tension drain from his neck and shoulders.

"No problem, bud. Moving forward with it?"

"Definitely. Talk to you soon."

Tony hit END and put down the phone, then turned out the light. Everything was going to be fine.

Chapter Seventeen

When she finished and came out of the locker room the next evening, Tony was nowhere in sight, even though his truck was still in the parking lot. Then she remembered – she'd left her lifting gloves on the locker room bench. Before she could replace her combination lock on the hasp, a hand grabbed her upper arm, spun her around, and pushed her against the locker.

"What the hell is going on? You'd better dish, girlfriend!" Kelly leered into her face.

"What do you mean?" Nikki asked, feigning ignorance.

"You guys are sleeping together, aren't you? I mean, if you're not, well . . . I think you are. 'Fess up!" Kelly laughed.

"Nope. Not sleeping together. Yet."

"Lying!"

"No, I'm not," Nikki said with mock indignation. "But at the rate we're going, it won't be long."

"I knew it!" Kelly laughed and plopped down on the bench. "Spill."

"There's really nothing to tell. We spent most of the weekend together, getting to know each other. I met his kids. We went to dinner, had a picnic, took a little road trip. Nothing overnight, just fun."

Kelly had a dreamy look on her face. "Lucky girl. Wish it were me, but if it's got to be somebody else, I'm glad it's you. Keep me posted, would ya?"

"Oh, yeah." Nikki turned to leave, but when she got to the door, she turned back to Kelly and decided to be a little bold. "Hey, would you like to get a drink sometime, maybe do lunch or something? I don't really have any friends in Louisville."

Kelly looked kind of embarrassed. "I don't either. I moved here eight years ago from Nashville and I still don't know one damn soul. So yeah, I'd like that."

"Good. Let's do that. See you later." Nikki waved as she walked out.

Tony was standing by the door, and he seemed to be waiting for her. "I'm starving. I didn't get any lunch today. It was crazy," he told her as she walked up. "You still up to coming to my house?"

She grinned up at him. "Thought I would, unless I get a better offer." She sauntered out the door, and he followed and took her hand as they walked across the parking lot.

"Then how about we both go home, shower, and you come over when you're done. Call me when you're ready and I'll call out for Thai."

"That sounds perfect!" Nikki gave him a peck on the cheek and broke away to run to her car, but he grabbed her arm and pulled her back, locked his hands onto her waist, and gave her a fast, deep kiss that made her suck in her breath. "At this rate, we'll never get any food!" she laughed as he came up for air.

"Let's go!" Tony gave her butt a playful smack, and they ran to their cars and took off.

"Hands down the best Thai I've ever had." That opinion was pretty obvious, given that she said it with her mouth full. "That stir fry was incredible."

"Yeah, I know. Golden Thai is the best place in the city." Tony's mouth was full too. "And I was so hungry."

"Bad day?"

"Nothing that dinner and an evening with you won't fix." He smiled at her and she felt a catch in her chest knowing that seeing her made him feel better; he had the same effect on her.

After they'd cleaned up the carryout mess, Tony pulled her onto the sofa. "Let's play a game."

"First, tell me: Did I pass the test?"

"The test? I don't know . . . ah, the test." He nodded as her eyes pierced him, looking up at him from beneath her brow. "The test. Yes, you did. Steve said he couldn't find one negative thing about you. And from what he said, it appears you're very smart. As in crazy, wild, unbelievably smart." She blushed a deep crimson. "Nothing to be embarrassed about."

"Guess you're wondering what somebody as smart as me is doing working in a florist shop, huh?" She stared down at the floor.

"Nope. Everybody has a different path. Not my job to judge anybody for the path they're traveling." He watched as her shoulders relaxed and the redness in her face faded. "Now, for my game."

"If it's spin the bottle, I'm all in!" she giggled.

"No. It's better. I'll start."

"I don't know how to play," she protested.

"You'll catch on very fast. Here goes. So, what's your favorite color?"

"Red."

"Now ask me a question."

She thought for a few seconds. "So what's your favorite color?"

"I think, um, gray."

She laughed. "Oh my god, that's not a color!"

"It is if you're in my closet!" he laughed back. "Okay, my turn. Favorite movie?"

"*The Princess Bride*. Your dream car?"

"A Lamborghini Gallardo Spyder, the LP 570-4, in silver. See, you're getting the hang of it. Where would you most like to go on vacation?"

"Hmmmm . . . any small Caribbean island that's not a tourist magnet." Tony made note of that answer. "And I like the Smoky Mountains a lot."

"'Zat so? Well, since you couldn't know, I'll tell you – I have a house there."

"Really? I'd . . ." she caught herself ". . . bet it's beautiful."

"If things keep going the way they are, you'll probably see it pretty soon." He tried to give her his most provocative smile and she threw her head back and laughed, a glorious sound like wind chimes on a breezy day. He couldn't help but think how sexy she looked when she did that.

"My turn," she said. "So, if you could change anything about yourself, what would it be?"

"Physically? Personality-wise? What do you mean?"

"I literally mean anything. Anything at all."

"My nose. It's too big." He pointed at the Aquiline feature that was the dead giveaway to his Italian heritage.

"I think it's a perfectly beautiful nose. I wouldn't do a thing to it." She leaned over and kissed it, and Tony's heart skipped a beat. It was too late to stop it – he'd already fallen for her.

"Question for you. If you only had one more day to live, what would you do with it?" When he saw the dark cloud pass over her face, he wished he could take the question back. What was he thinking, with her history?

He watched her shudder, then she straightened, took a deep breath, closed her eyes, and began to answer in a whisper. "First, I'd watch the sun rise. Then," she said, her voice growing stronger, "I'd spend the rest of the day making love, if I had a willing partner, of course." She smiled and squeezed his hand, then continued. "I eat chocolate, take a walk and listen to the birds." By the time she ended the answer, her voice was strong and clear. It was odd, almost as if she'd thought about it before. Then he remembered what she'd said when she told him about her family: *I ask myself every day why I couldn't have died too.* She'd definitely thought about it, maybe too many times.

A lump formed in his throat; he couldn't lose her. He wanted to see that sadness taken from her, wanted to know that she didn't go home, close the door, and plan ways to leave the world behind. As clearly as if someone had spoken it aloud to him, the thought formed in his mind, solid and complete: *It's my job, from now on, to make sure every day is a day for you to be glad you're alive.* She still sat perfectly motionless, her eyes closed, and he moved silently to her and kissed her eyelids one at a time, then wrapped his arms around her. She pressed her face into his shoulder and wrapped her arms around him. Neither of them spoke. They sat in that embrace for what seemed like forever, him floating along on the scent of her hair, her listening to the beating of his heart and absorbing the heat from his skin like flame consuming dry tinder.

Finally, he moved his hands to her face, drew it to his, and kissed her, a slow, unfurling thing that started out with his lips pressed, closed, to hers, and grew into its own being. His tongue parted her lips and found hers, and danced along its length and breadth; hers responded, going deeper and stronger as it explored his mouth. Taking her hands from his chest, she wrapped her arms around his neck, pulling him even closer. His hands drifted down the sides of her neck, down her chest, and around the sides of her soft, warm breasts, feeling her respond to his lusty touch as she pressed herself against him. Cupping her breasts briefly, he drew his big hands down her sides, latched them onto her waist, and pulled her longingly into him, drawing her hard against him and tilting his stiffening cock against her. The hitch in her breath told him she felt it, wanted it, and she leaned back until she fell onto the sofa and pulled him down on top of her.

"Nikki, baby, I don't know if I can say no to you," he moaned into her neck, his hips grinding into her, hers rising to meet them in an erotic dance.

"Then don't," she whispered. She put her hands on his face and raised his head so she could stare into those warm, melted-chocolate eyes. He saw the need there in her blue-green ones, consuming and mesmerizing.

"No. No – not like this," he told her, coming to his senses and pulling back. "We've got some ground to cover first."

Her face flushed in embarrassment and she tried to squirm out from under him, but he held her firm. "I'm sorry. I guess I got carried away. It's okay." She looked like she'd cry at any moment, her vulnerability raw and exposed.

"No, baby, stop. It's not you. You're fine. You're fucking hot. I want you so bad I can hardly think or breathe," he managed to say, his voice husky and strained with enough longing for them both. "But I don't want to mess this up. It's too important."

"Mess it up? I don't get it." She looked completely confused.

Tony sat up and ran his fingers through his hair, then took her hand and pulled her up to a sitting position. "Remember, Friday night, when you said you thought people should communicate, especially about sex? I think you're right. So let's have our talk Sunday. Whaddya say? Next step?"

He could see that the light bulb had clicked on behind her eyes. "Next step. I think that's a good idea. Let's do this thing right." She licked her lips.

"That's my girl. Now let's both get some sleep. It's been a long day, and this is just Tuesday. Start thinking about what you might like to do Saturday." He smiled and kissed her on the nose. "Come on and I'll walk you out."

After their phone call before bedtime, Nikki reached into her nightstand and pulled out her vibrator, then checked to see if she had extra batteries in the lower drawer. She was pretty sure she'd need them, maybe all of them. And maybe she should get another pack.

Chapter Eighteen

The text notification on Nikki's phone pinged. *What are you doing at lunchtime?*

Eating lunch, I suppose. Why?

Can you get a little extra time? I need a favor, please.

Nikki replied after Marla assured her that she could take a little longer for lunch. Instead of texting her, he called.

"Hey, baby, can I pick you up?"

"That works! See you in a bit." After she hung up, she realized she hadn't asked what the favor was. Couldn't be anything very serious or he would've told her, she was sure.

Once she was in the truck with him, she asked him, "So, is this a big mystery, or can you tell me where we're going?"

"It's not far; we're almost there. Hang on a minute," he said as he wheeled into the parking lot of a large medical building. When he'd parked he turned to her. "Remember, we're having our talk Sunday?"

"Yeah. So what's this about?" She was really getting curious now.

"Well, I was thinking, if we're going to have the talk Sunday, that means we're getting closer to the deed, right? So, let me be really clear about this: I trust you. Completely. No reservations. I believe you when you say you haven't been with anybody since Randy. And I've told you the truth too; I haven't been with anybody in over two years. But don't you think, for peace of mind, that we both should be tested? I mean, get the green cards and show them to each other?" He looked anxious, almost pleading.

But Nikki had a question of her own. "I need to know something. Are you seeing anybody else?"

Tony was taken aback. "No! Of course not!"

"Are you interested in seeing anybody else?" she asked pointedly.

"Absolutely not! I thought I'd made that pretty clear," he stammered, sounding kind of put out.

"So, are we saying we're exclusive? That this is an exclusive relationship?" she asked straight out.

It only took Tony a second to respond with "Yes. As far as I'm concerned, this is an exclusive relationship. I hope that's okay with you."

"Very okay. And in that case, yes, I'll gladly be tested, but I didn't want to be bothered if there was a third person in the mix; would've kinda made it pointless. So, is that why we're here?"

"Yep. I called my doctor. I thought maybe we'd like a little more privacy than a testing center could offer. He said to come on over and he'll have the results by Friday."

"Wow, that's quick! Okay, let's do it. I think it'll be good for both of us," she agreed, climbing down out of the truck.

In the lot across from The Passionate Pansy, he leaned over and kissed her before she got out. "See you at the gym after work?" he asked.

"See you there, sweetie!" she said and went back to work. But she didn't want to. She wanted to stay with him.

Friday night was quiet at the gym. After her post-gym shower, dressing, and driving over to Tony's, Nikki walked into his house and went straight to the kitchen. There, on the counter, was a large manila envelope, and she recognized the name of Dr. Coulter's practice.

"Yep, drove over and picked them up this afternoon." Tony turned from the sink, dried his hands, and picked up the envelope. "Are you ready?"

"Sure. You?"

"Let's do this thing." He opened the envelope; inside were two smaller ones, one with his name on it, and one with hers, and they each took the other's envelope and ripped them open. Both of them pulled the letters out at the same time and opened them.

He looked up at her, and she at him, both of them breaking into huge grins. "Well," Tony announced, "looks like all systems are go, huh?"

She laughed. "That's right, Houston! Looks like we're ready for liftoff."

"I'm home. See you in the morning, baby."

"Yeah, see you then. Hey, Tony?"

"Yeah, babe?"

"I wanted you to know, today was the most fun I've had in a long time." They'd spent Saturday afternoon having lunch, then they went to movies and back to the green space to walk and talk. "It was so relaxed. And there's something I really want to say to you." *It's now or never*, her heart told her.

"Nope. Don't say it." Nikki's heart froze until he said, "That's a face-to-face thing. I want to look you right in the eye, and I want you looking back. Get it?"

"Got it." Her heart trembled; he knew what she was about to say. And he wanted her to say it. That meant that he . . . Oh boy! Yeah, he felt it too!

"I'll see you in the morning, beautiful girl. And by the way, today will be a memory that I carry with me forever. Night, baby."

"Night." Nikki hit END and laid the phone down.

Sweet mother of god, she thought. *I'm in love with Tony Walters. And he's in love with me!*

Chapter Nineteen

"My house or yours?" Nikki asked Tony when they were finished at the gym on Sunday morning.

He stopped at the door of her SUV and thought for a minute. "Let's go to the big house. It's quieter there, and we won't be disturbed."

"Good idea. Can I bring Bill and Hillary?"

"Sure! Make sure they have some toys and something to eat, some snacks or something, because there's nothing there for them and we might not get back until late." Tony opened her door and she slid into the seat. "Buckle up, sweetheart." He leaned down to kiss her. "I'll be over as soon as I'm showered and dressed."

She was almost dressed and ready when she heard him set the alarm on whatever he'd decided to drive. She got a surprise; when she finished getting ready, she found that he'd gone into the kitchen and packed up a zippered storage bag of food for the dogs, found a tote, and put the food and some toys into it.

"Well, you must be in a hurry!" she laughed.

"Actually, I kinda am," he grinned back. "I'd like to get this show on the road."

When they stepped out the front door, Nikki gasped – at the curb was a huge, pearl-white Yukon. The Denali. He'd mentioned it. It was some kind of gorgeous – gold package, the whole enchilada. "Wow. I'm going in style," she said, using her sexiest voice.

"Yeah, I thought it would be quieter, and bigger, since the dogs are with us." He opened the rear passenger door. Nikki was startled to see that he'd put a large blanket across the back seat, and there were a couple of dog toys on the seat.

"You bought those for them?" She couldn't manage to hide the surprise in her voice.

He gave her a sheepish grin. "I thought that would give them something to do while we rode." She wondered at him – he was just full of surprises. It appeared he genuinely liked the two little monsters.

The ride gave them a chance to talk about benign things. He told her his full name – Antonio Luigi Walters – and that his birthday was September nineteenth. She told him her full name – Nicolette Renee Wallace Wilkes – and that her birthday was on September eighth; he was surprised that her parents named her such a French name. He asked her questions about Paganism; she asked him questions about Catholicism. They talked about school, growing up, things they did as kids. It was so quiet and sweet that Nikki almost forgot to be nervous.

But when they turned down the lengthy, winding driveway to the big house, her stomach lurched. This conversation, more than any other, would determine whether or not their relationship would move forward. She felt kind of sick knowing what was riding on it, but she was determined to be honest and straightforward.

Helene was at the big house when they got there, putting the finishing touches on lunch. It was one o'clock and, even though she was a bundle of nerves, Nikki was starving. She noticed Tony seemed anxious too.

Helene set the table, then left them to eat alone. Nikki was getting Bill and Hillary settled when Tony groaned, "My god, that smells good and I'm really hungry, but I'm so nervous I'm not sure I can eat."

So he was nervous! She felt a little better and giggled.

"What's so funny?"

"I wondered if you were as nervous as I am. Guess I got my answer!" She sat down at the table and picked up her fork.

"Probably more. Can you eat?"

"I don't know, but this smells and looks so good that I'm going to try!" The salmon Helene had baked had an aroma like nothing else, and the baby asparagus and roasted red skin potatoes looked like something from a cooking magazine. Nikki hadn't been sure she could eat, but once she tucked into the food, the deliciousness of it all took over and she ate ravenously. Tony seemed to be enjoying his lunch too. He entertained her by telling her about some of the improvements they'd made to the house over the years. When they were finished eating, he poured them both a second glass of wine while Nikki carried all of the dishes to the sink and put away the leftovers.

With the lunch taken care of, Tony handed Nikki her glass of wine and took her free hand. "Let's go sit in the great room. We've got to get this started. It may take awhile, and I don't want us to feel rushed."

He led her over to a huge, overstuffed armchair, filled with soft, brightly-colored toss pillows. He sat on the adjacent sofa.

She pretended to pout. "You're not going to sit with me?"

"If we sit together, we won't get to have a conversation. Things will happen that we don't intend, and, well, this is probably how it should be." Nikki nodded. He was right – that was exactly what would happen. She was already itching to touch him, and having him beside her would mean she wouldn't be able to control the urge.

"So, how do we begin?"

"At the beginning. Why don't you start?" Then he added, "You can start with when you lost your virginity, and we'll work our way up."

Nikki took a deep breath. *This is it*, she thought. "Well, that's a funny story. I had this high school friend, and we decided if we hadn't gotten laid by the time we were fifteen, we'd sleep together. And that's exactly what happened. It was pretty wretched, but at least we could say we weren't virgins anymore."

Tony started laughing. "That's one way to solve that problem!"

"Maybe not a good way, but that's what we did. After that, I pretty much screwed anybody who showed an interest in me." She hadn't meant for it to sound that way, but it was fairly accurate. "I was quite the little slut. I liked sex, and I had a lot of it. Until I met Randy. And I got knocked up almost immediately. But we were crazy mad in love with each other, so we got married when I turned eighteen, and Jake was born a few months later."

"Nikki, I need to know," Tony started, his voice deepening and turning serious, "were you ever unfaithful to Randy?"

Nikki's gaze was unwavering. "No. Never. There was no one after Randy. It was just us, always. I thought he might've cheated on me a couple of times, but he insisted he didn't and, in the end, I believed him. But I never, never, ever cheated on him. I swear."

"Oh, I believe you. But you have to understand how important that is to me. I'll never tolerate that. I've put up with too much to go through that again."

"I'd never do that to you, babe. Never. I'm just not like that. If I were that unhappy, I'd leave. I wouldn't sneak around and hurt you."

Tony seemed relieved. "So," he began again, "what was your sex life like with Randy? Good? Mediocre?"

"It was good – great, in fact. We were both adventurous and liked variety, so we were always mixing it up, you know, new positions, new toys, lingerie, kink . . ."

"Kink?" Tony perked up considerably. "Define kink for me, or your version at least."

"Well, let's just say there sometimes was rope, a blindfold, and/or spankings involved. We liked to go at it occasionally in places where we might get caught. We had a flogger, a cat o' nine tails, and a riding crop. Some restraints. Three or four kinds of nipple clamps. Those kinds of things." She stopped for a minute, then said, "Actually, we more or less had a Dom/sub relationship in private."

Tony was sitting up on the edge of the sofa, listening intently. Then he asked, "So, do you have limits?"

"Well, sure, don't we all?" Nikki sounded kind of put-out.

"So where do you draw the line?"

Nikki thought for a minute. "Well, mine are pretty far out there, but there are some things I just won't do. For instance, if it involves pee or poop it's pretty much out of the question."

Tony made a face. "Me too. Not interested and not going there."

She laughed. "Well, good, because if you wanted to go there, you'd go there alone!"

Tony laughed, then took her hand and pulled her over to the sofa to sit with him. He just couldn't stand being that far away from her anymore, not with the conversation they were having. "So, what will you do? I'm guessing all the standards." Nikki nodded. "Anal?" She nodded again. "Oral?" She nodded enthusiastically; he felt his cock start to stiffen. "Ever been fisted?" She looked mildly surprised, then said, "Yeah, Randy and I tried it, but we never could manage. He just wasn't patient enough."

A hum set up in Tony's mind. He felt like he'd hit the jackpot. It sounded like she was open to pretty much anything, and he was getting too excited thinking about all of the things they could do, or try, together. "So you said restraints. Do you like being restrained?"

"Actually, yes, I do. Can I be completely honest here?"

"I wish you would." He wondered what was about to come out of her pretty, pink, extremely hot mouth that would make him even more glad he was a man.

"Okay, to be completely honest, I like pain with my pleasure. I don't want anything to do with needle or blade play, nothing that draws blood, but I need an ache to have a screamer. Sometimes I want to make love, but most of the time I just want to fuck, and fuck hard and fast. If you're not giving me what I need, I'll tell you. And if I don't like what you're doing, I'll tell you that too." She took a deep breath. "As long as you treat me like a princess everywhere else, you can treat me like a whore in the bedroom and I'll take what you give me and come back for more."

Tony felt like the air was getting heavier and it was getting harder to breathe. Then he realized maybe it was because he was holding his breath. "And how many times a week could I expect this call to action?" He wished he could cross his fingers without her seeing.

She looked at him from under her lashes and said, without hesitation, "Based on past experience, I'd say maybe a couple of times a day, but at least daily. Unless we're both really, really busy." She licked her lips, and he almost came undone. "Anything else?"

Tony was having trouble articulating. He finally managed to breathe out, "Nope. I think that about covers it."

"Are you extremely put off? I mean, does what I've told you change anything?" She looked a little worried. "Are you afraid you've gotten yourself involved with some kind of freak?"

"No, baby. The only thing it's done is to make me even more determined to make this work," he emphasized, taking a deep breath. *Shit, I could really do with a glass of bourbon right now*, Tony told himself. "So now I guess it's my turn?"

"Yep. Run with it."

"Okay. Well, Dottie was my first and only. Sort of." Nikki made a puzzled face. "I've told you how we met. When it came to sex, neither of us knew enough in the beginning. We fooled around before we got married, but we never actually had sex, just lots of heavy petting. Then when we got married, she made it clear on our wedding night that she had limits."

"What kind of limits?"

"Everything. I wasn't supposed to touch her, just kind of hover above her, put it in, thrust a few times, and we were done. There was one position – missionary – and no other. And god forbid I mess up her hair. Which brings me to one of my pet peeves."

"What's that?"

"Do not – I repeat, do not – tell me not to mess up your hair or makeup. Take that shit off before we get into bed. If I'm gonna fuck you, I want to be able to fuck you without worrying about 'messing you up.' I'd like to screw you with wild abandon, not watch out for your hairdo."

Nikki grinned. "You don't have to worry about that. I never sleep in my makeup – I think better of my skin. I was kind of worried about you seeing me without my makeup, but now, based on what you just said, not so much."

"Hey, remember where we met," he laughed, then waited, head cocked to one side.

"Oh, yeah. The gym. I guess if you could see me like that and still want to go out with me . . ."

"Exactly. A moot issue. Anyway, that was the extent of our sex life. In the beginning, we had sex maybe once a week. After the first year, maybe once every three months. Eventually, I just quit asking. Of course, when she wanted to get pregnant, that was different, but the limits still applied." Tony had a pained look on his face, and it bothered Nikki that talking about it still caused him so much grief.

"You realize that was her, not you, right? That the not wanting sex was no reflection on you?" Nikki asked, trying to get him past the pile of garbage memories.

"Well, that brings me to what I need to tell you most. I hope you're still with me when I finish." Worry clouded his beautiful face. "Remember when I said I'd only talked about sex with one other person, and you assumed it was Dottie, and I said no?"

"Yeah?" She couldn't imagine where he was going with this.

"Okay, so here goes." Tony sat back on the sofa and tried to get comfortable, but that was a losing battle. "So, you said it – I wasn't sure it was all her. I thought maybe it was me, my lack of experience, something like that. A couple of years ago, I started to think maybe I'd eventually want to get back into a relationship, even though it seemed like a long shot. And I started to think about the fact that I was over fifty-five and still had no clue about most things sexual. I mean, I watched porn videos and looked at magazines, but I knew most of that stuff wasn't real. And I started trying for a way to learn more. So I did the only thing I could think of – I hired a hooker."

"No shit!" Nikki laughed. "How'd that work out?"

"Better than you'd think." Tony still looked surprisingly serious. Nikki got her giggles over and settled down, so he continued. "I hired an escort from a company there in town, bought a big box of condoms, took her to dinner, and then went to a hotel room. When we got there, she asked me what I wanted, and I told her I didn't have any idea. Then I explained to her why I'd hired her, that I was hoping she could teach me some things about sex."

"And? Did she?"

"No, but she said she knew somebody she'd recommend. She made a phone call, kissed me on the cheek, and thanked me for dinner without taking any money from me, then told me to sit tight and Cinda would be there shortly."

"Cinda?"

"Yeah, I guess it was short for Cinderella; I'm sure that wasn't her real name. Anyway, there was a knock on the door, and I opened it to a woman who was mid-forties and pretty ordinary-looking. She told me her name was Cinda and she'd be glad to teach me whatever I wanted to know. She said she could do ten sessions, and they'd be rigorous – we'd work from ten at night to six in the morning. Eight hours at a time of whatever she thought I needed to know or whatever I wanted to learn. I said yes, so we started right then.

"She started out with an anatomy lesson featuring both of us, then started showing me things about my own body that I never knew. It was totally and completely mind-blowing to me – this woman seemed to have zero shame, and she was willing to teach me. I thought there might be hope for me yet.

"After the show and tell, she asked me what I had and hadn't done. The 'had-dones' was a pretty short list. She said she wanted to get things off on the right foot, so would I like a blow job. I'd never had one, which she thought was pretty amazing, so she dropped to her knees and gave me one right there on the spot, which I thought was pretty amazing. I was standing when she did it, and I damn near collapsed when I came."

Nikki laughed out loud, and Tony grinned. "Anyway," he began again, "when she was finished, she told me it was her turn, and taught me to perform cunnilingus. She scared me to death when she came – I'd never given Dottie an orgasm, so I thought she was dying. She thought it was hysterically funny. We got back up on the bed together and she explained the mechanics of male and female orgasm to me. Before she left that first night, we had plain vanilla sex, and I thought I'd died and gone to heaven. Plus I knew we had nine more sessions to go. You can't begin to understand what that was like for me."

"What else did she teach you?"

"Everything. At least seventy-five different positions. All kinds of ways to give a woman an orgasm, with my hands, tongue, vibrators. Using all kinds of sex toys, lubes, creams, anything you can think of. She taught me about orgasm denial, how it can help a woman who has trouble having orgasms to have huge, earth-shattering ones. Cock rings, penis pumps, things like that. How to use a suction device to enlarge the clitoris, make it more sensitive. The ins and outs, literally, of anal sex; how to prepare a woman who's never had it before, dilating techniques, lubes to use, everything. Some bondage, rope play, safe use of restraints. And she had some really strict rules," he added, taking a deep breath.

"What do you mean?" She noticed that he seemed to be getting tense.

"I don't know exactly how to say it . . ." he mumbled, looking at his hands.

"Just spit it out. If we've come this far, you should've already figured out that you can tell me anything," she told him matter-of-factly, and he believed her. So far, she'd turned out to be the most open-minded person he'd ever met.

"Well, she believed if you were going to do it to somebody, you should allow it to be done to you. And if you wanted it done to you, you should have to learn to do it to somebody else."

"Meaning?"

"She brought a friend in to assist. A male friend." There – he'd said it. Nikki's eyes got a little wider, but she didn't say anything. "She said if I wanted to have anal sex with a woman, I should know what it felt like. So her friend helped us with that."

"Are you trying to tell me you took it up the ass for the team?" Nikki asked, incredulous and, as usual, blunt as hell.

Tony blushed. "Yep. Not as bad as I thought it would be, either. Not sure I'd ever want to do it again, but now I know what it feels like to somebody else if I fuck them in the ass. Great way to drive home a point, pun intended," Tony said, and chuckled a little. He still looked a little embarrassed. "Does that completely freak you out?"

"In a very positive way. I'm trying to imagine, and it's very hot," she practically purred. "And I'm very impressed."

Damn, he thought, *this woman is incredible. I can't believe she's not running for the door, but if she'll hang around now, I guess nothing will scare her away.* "So then she said if I wanted to get oral sex, I should learn to give it, because if I did, I'd know what the giving was like, and I could teach a woman how best to do it."

"And you gave her friend a blow job, too?"

"Yep. Also not as bad as I thought it would be, although I don't think the taste of ejaculate is something I'd want to experience very often."

"I can't say the same thing." Nikki's eyes went kind of glassy. "Frankly, I like the taste of cum. Sometimes I crave it." Nikki nibbled at her lower lip, then closed her eyes and took a deep breath. Tony struggled to stay in control until she told him, "Go on. Please."

He waited a minute, trying to remember where he'd gotten to in the conversation, then started again. "So that's kind of how it went. She taught me to fist her, taught me to do some very basic restraint techniques, some light BDSM stuff, flogging and the like, and nipple torture. We had a three-way with the male friend, and then another night, she brought in a female friend and we did a three-way. She also taught me how to take a woman from giving me a simple blow job to letting me fuck her throat." Tony watched as Nikki instinctively put her hand up to her neck, letting her fingers slide down almost to her cleavage, and he thought he'd come unglued. This was going much better than he'd expected. If he was getting this much of a charge watching her reactions to this discussion, how spectacular would the sex be?

"You have to understand," he said, catching and holding Nikki's gaze, "this wasn't lovemaking. She was a lovely, warm, friendly woman, but it was very clinical, almost mechanical, for her. She was instructing me and I was learning. She asked me on the last night if I felt confident about my abilities. I told her I'd never felt more confident in myself, or more virile, for that matter. Then she said, 'I'll tell you a secret about women that every man should know.'"

Nikki waited; she leaned toward him, and Tony was enjoying watching the look of anticipation on her face. Finally, she blurted out, "Oh, for the love of god, tell me what she said!"

"She said, 'What every woman wishes you knew but won't tell you is that, deep down inside, every woman wants her man to take control of her in the bedroom. She craves it. She wants to be dominated, to be pushed to her limits, to be taken to where she can't stand it anymore and then taken just to the other side. She wants her man to let her choose a safeword, and then she'll try her best to never use it, to take everything he gives her and beg for more. Treat a woman to that raw maleness, that masculinity, and make her enjoy it and feel cherished and loved, like she's the most desirable woman in the world, and she'll feel safe with you and let you do anything with her and to her that you want.'" He stopped for a minute, the questioning in his eyes warming her face, and asked, "Nikki, I have no idea – was she right?"

It took her a minute to catch her breath, then she forced out in a whisper overflowing with longing, "Oh, baby, she was one hundred and ninety-eight percent right." She was pretty sure if she didn't change gears, she was going to come right then and there. Tony watched her squirm; he knew what was going on, and he loved it.

"So, let's talk about deal breakers." Tony attempted to break the sexual tension by taking the throw from the back of the sofa and spreading it over Nikki's lap, and she was definitely glad for the change in the conversation.

"I'm assuming you have some or you wouldn't have introduced the topic?"

He stood. "I do." Before sitting back down, Tony refilled their wine glasses. "My number one deal breaker is cheating on me. I simply won't tolerate it. Period." His tone was stern. He tried to get comfortable on the sofa and started again. "There are far too many things out there now that penicillin won't kill. I'm responsible for too many people, their jobs and their lives, to take chances like that, and I won't be with somebody who exposes me to that kind of danger." Nikki nodded her understanding.

"Number two is being untrustworthy. I have to be able to trust you. I get lying about something like a Christmas gift or a surprise party, but if it's a lie to cover up something wrong or at least questionable, then I'm extremely intolerant. I can't be open and honest with somebody who's not open and honest with me."

"Number three is my family. You've got to get along with them. I know they're not perfect. My youngest brother's wife, Caroline? They were horrible to her when she and Bennie first met; they're still not very kind. I knew it wasn't her; it was them, and Bennie and I called them on it. That wasn't her fault. But if you're being generally rude or hateful to them, bitchy or mean or whatever, that's just not going to fly. If there's a legitimate problem with you and them, then we're going to have a problem, that is, if you've contributed to it."

"And number four is as big as number one. I will never again be in a relationship where sex is withheld. No discussion, no negotiation. If you were in a terrible accident that left you completely debilitated, or had a horrible illness, like cancer, where you were incapacitated or in disabling pain, that would be one thing. But to withhold sex for spite, or meanness, or from general disregard or lack of love, nope. I'm done with that. I lived with it for sixteen years, and I won't do it again."

With that, Tony put his wine glass on the table beside the sofa and asked, "Yours?"

Nikki looked thoughtful for a minute. "I'd say the cheating thing for me too. The fucking everything in sight thing wouldn't bother me that much, but

I'd be terrified you'd come in and tell me you'd fallen in love with somebody else. That would kill me. And even without that, I couldn't take the pressure of the competition. I've always been able to hold my own sexually, and if you found somebody you liked better than me in the sack, well, I can't imagine you could, but I couldn't compete with her if you did. And I guess my second one is like your trustworthiness issue. I couldn't take it day in and day out if I felt like you were sneaking around or hiding something from me, or if you were lying to me all the time. Those are about all I can come up with. I can work with anything else, as long as you're trying. Oh, and by the way, my safewords: Stop is red; slow and question, yellow; and go, green. And I have a hand signal for when I can't speak," she demonstrated, showing him two fingers raised in a "V."

"For when you can't speak? And why wouldn't you be able to sp . . . Oh. Never mind." His cheeks pinked up. "So that's it?" Nikki nodded and took a sip from her glass. "Well, okay then. I think it's all out on the table, except for one more thing we need to get out of the way." Tony poured each of them another glass of liquid courage.

"So, what's that?" she asked, sipping the Kentucky vintage from nearby Willisburg.

"You were about to say something to me on the phone the other night and I stopped you. I told you I wanted us to be looking each other in the eye the first time we said that, not hiding on the telephone. So can I be the first to say it?"

"Oh, well, go right ahead!" She smiled through her relaxation from the wine. She wanted to hear those three words more than anything else in the world.

"Okay. Here goes." He took a deep breath. "Nikki Wilkes, I love you. I love you and I'm in love with you. I don't want to be with anyone else. I want to be with you, completely and totally, emotionally, mentally, and physically. I'm ready for that step. And I want you to think about a long-term relationship with me, up to and including marriage. I'm not proposing, at least not yet anyway; I just want you to think about whether or not that's something you'd be open to. Will you?"

"Absolutely!" She sat up straight and looked straight into his eyes. "My turn. Tony Walters, I love you and I'm in love with you. One look at you makes my knees weak and my heart pound. I want you so bad I can barely stand it, and if we don't have sex in the next couple of weeks, I think I'll lose my mind. And I will think about a long-term relationship with you. I'm not saying I never want to remarry; I'm just saying that this relationship caught me off guard and I hadn't given marriage any thought up to now but, trust me, I have in the last week. I hope you know how crazy I am about you." She stopped, then added, "Oh, and by the way, I love your kids and their significant others. I hope they'll eventually think of me as a kind of mom."

She was startled to see a tear well up in the corner of his eye. He wiped his hand across it and looked down at his lap. "My poor, poor kids," he moaned, shaking his head. "They never really had much of a mom, and from what I've seen, you were a pretty fine one. You have no idea how happy what you said makes me. I'd like nothing better than for them to eventually call you Mom. They deserve to have a woman in their lives who loves them and does the things for them that moms do." He reached over and pressed his hand against her cheek, and she rested her face into it as she put her hand on the back of his. Moving to sit beside her, he leaned down and placed a soft, chaste kiss on her lips, then dropped his forehead against hers. They sat that way for several minutes.

"I probably should get up and go to the bathroom." She stood and took a much-needed stretch.

"I'll get us some more wine. I guess we need to start back in a couple of hours." They'd talked for so long that it had gotten near dark. "But I wanted to ask," he hesitated, ". . . would you like to go away for the weekend with me? Memorial Day weekend, in two weeks?"

"I'd love to!" She kissed him on the cheek. "Where are we going?"

"The house in Gatlinburg maybe?"

"Oh, my god, YES!" She kissed him on the cheek, then ran toward the bathroom.

As he filled the glasses, Tony decided he should check his phone. He'd turned the ringer off when they got to the house, and he didn't often do that. Looking at the screen, he saw calls – lots of calls, mostly from Clayton, one from Vic, his cousin in Lexington who managed their office there, and one from a number he didn't recognize. He pulled up his voicemails, and there was a message from the unfamiliar number.

Tony touched LISTEN and put the phone back up to his ear. "Mr. Walters, this is Detective Marsh from the Lexington Police Department. Could you give me a call, please?" The voice left a number.

Clayton, then Vic, then the police? A sick fear rose in Tony's chest as he hit Clayton's contact and the phone began to ring. Nikki walked back into the room just as Clayton answered.

"Dad! Where the hell are you?" Clayton sounded frantic.

"Clayton, what's going on? I've got calls from you, and Vic, and the Lexington police?" He glanced over at Nikki; she stared at him in alarm.

"Dad, where are you?" Clayton asked again.

"I'm at the big house. Why?"

"Are you alone?"

"No. Nikki's here with me. What's going on?"

"Dad, go sit down. Right now. Make sure Nikki's with you. Do it!"

Tony started to question, then took Nikki's hand and went back into the great room. He sat down, then pulled her down beside him with her ear next to the phone so she could hear too; she could tell he was nearing full-blown panic. "Okay, son, I'm sitting and Nikki's here. What's going on?"

"Dad, I'm so sorry. It's gone. The Lexington office is gone. Those assholes from GoGreen burned it to the ground."

Chapter Twenty

"Clayton, is everybody okay?" Tony was frantic, and Nikki's eyes were wide with horror.

"Yeah. I'm in Lexington. Dad, Zio Vic's totally beside himself. Please, call him and tell him everything's going to be okay. Then get here, please! I'm here with the fire department."

"I'll be there as fast as I can get there." Tony hit END and turned to Nikki. She threw her arms around his neck, hugging him as hard as she could. He wrapped his arms around her and drew her up against him, and her softness and warmth made him feel safe.

When she pulled back, she looked him in the face. "So, what is this GoGreen and what's going on? You'd better tell me. If you don't, Annabeth will."

"Annabeth doesn't know anything about this – yet. Now she'll have to." Tony looked stricken. "I didn't tell you because I didn't want you to worry, but I guess that's over. We don't know who they are. Some kind of ecoterrorism group. They've flattened dozens of tires on our trucks and equipment, broken glass out of our trucks, ruined some hydraulic equipment. They've tried to sabotage a couple of our projects. So far, no one's gotten hurt, but now I'm getting a little worried."

"Who is Ziovic?"

"That's Zio Vic – *zio* is Italian for uncle. My kids have always called him that. He's my cousin. Long story, but he needed somebody and we were there for him. He wound up working for me, and he was so good that when I opened the office in Lexington, I asked him to head it up. He's grown that portion of the business from nothing to a full twenty-five percent of our total assets. I'm sure he's almost in cardiac arrest – that was his baby, and now it's rubble. Of course, there was nothing there that can't be replicated or replaced, but it's just that it will slow us down, you know?"

Concern lined her face. "Why are these people targeting your company?"

"That's just it. I don't have any idea. I don't have any enemies I'm aware of, except for all-bark-and-no-bite Dottie, and there are lots of construction companies out there that aren't as green in operations as we are. We're running our localized trucks off of reclaimed French fry oil, we follow a stricter protocol for waste disposal than the government requires, and we reuse and recycle everything we can. But they're still targeting us and, from what we can tell, only us. It's a mystery to me. It almost seems personal." Even though Nikki had managed to get him to talk about it, he still looked shaken and a little pale under his olive complexion.

He broke away from her arms. "I've got to go. I've got to be there with them."

"I'll go with you."

"No! You stay here where I know you're safe. Do you have to be at work tomorrow?" He suddenly remembered that she needed to get home. "You can drive one of my cars back."

"Don't even think about that. I'll call Marla and tell her I can't come in, tell her what's happened. I know she'll understand. I'm so glad we brought the dogs some food. I'll just plan to stay here tonight." She kissed him softly and added, "And you stay in contact with me. I want to know where you are and what's going on. Mostly I want to know you're safe, and I want to know when you start back so I know when to expect you."

"Will do. Get into my dresser drawers and get yourself a tee and some warm socks. I'll call Helene, ask her to come and help you clean up and find anything you might need." Tony grabbed his keys, stuck his wallet back into his hip pocket, and shot for the door. But he turned around, walked right up to Nikki, caught her up in his arms, and gave her a big kiss. "I love you, baby. I'll be back as soon as I can."

"I love you too, sweetheart. Be careful!" she called after him as he headed out the door. It felt so good to hear those words and to be able to say them back to someone, especially because the someone was him.

When he pulled the truck in, Tony's heart sank. The building was completely gone – everything. One exterior wall stood, teetering inward, waiting to fall. The rest was an ashy heap. He found Clayton and hugged him, and Clayton pointed Vic out, standing off to the side alone.

"Hey, buddy, you okay? Everything's going to be all right, you know?

We've got really good insurance and . . ."

Vic seemed to almost be in shock. "Man, I'm so sorry, really. This office was my responsibility. And look what happened. I wouldn't blame you if you fired me right on the spot."

"Damn, Vic, I don't hold you responsible for this in any way. No way could you have done anything about this. You've got to keep it together – we've got to help the police nail these shitheads. I'm just glad no one was hurt, that's all. It'll be all right, really." Tony put his arm around Vic's shoulder, and the big Italian started to cry like a baby. Vic had been through so much, and now this.

"Come on, cheer up. You hated the color of the walls, remember? Well, now here's your chance to paint the new ones whatever color you like!" Tony laughed. He heard Vic sniff back a sob and then start laughing too. "That's more like it! Chin up," Tony told him, patting him on the back.

"Oh, god, it was so hard to watch and not be able to do anything about it." Vic still sounded a little shaky.

"Yeah, I know. But everything will be fine, you'll see. Let's go talk to the detectives. They probably want to ask us some questions anyway."

Travis sat on the ground in the brush, watching the fire trucks and knowing there was nothing for them to salvage. He'd chosen Sunday afternoon specifically because the building was in an industrial area and there'd be very little traffic on a Sunday. He didn't know who'd noticed the flames, but the call hadn't gone in until the building was completely engulfed.

He dialed the phone, and when she answered, he said, "It's done. It was really pretty too. I left enough calling cards that they'll know it was us."

"Travis, we need to talk." She sighed and proceeded with caution. "I've been doing some research. Did you know Adams Construction and Mechanical dumped five tons of asbestos last year without following proper disposal procedures? That's way worse than anything Walters has done."

Travis let out an irritated sigh. "Autumn, let it go. We've got one objective and only one; make those bastards at Walters Construction pay. Are you with me or not?"

"I'm with you," she replied. She was too scared of him to say anything else.

Chapter Twenty-One

When Nikki woke at about three o'clock in the morning, she had trouble figuring out where she was at first. She squinted around the unfamiliar room; Tony's bedroom. The weight of both dogs was on the bed with her. Looking at the clock, she gasped when she saw the time. Why hadn't she heard from Tony? She checked her phone – nothing – so she hit his contact and waited.

"God, sweetie, don't be mad at me, please. I'm just leaving," Tony said when he answered, adding, "and I'm sorry I didn't call you before now."

"I was so scared when I realized what time it is." Her voice was still raspy from sleep.

"What are you doing up at this hour?"

"I don't know, just woke up, that's all. I didn't know where I was at first. Then I saw the time and got scared because I hadn't heard from you."

"Yeah, sorry about that. I went over to Vic's for awhile. Poor guy, he's really torn up about this, like he could do anything about it."

Nikki rubbed one eye. "Did you tell him that? That it's not his fault?"

"Of course. Didn't matter. It's his baby and he's upset. He has a right to be; I'm pretty upset too. This is getting ridiculous – and dangerous. Somebody could've been seriously hurt, like an employee who'd stopped in or a firefighter, heaven forbid. It needs to stop. I hope the cops can figure out who these clowns are, but this happened in Lex, and most of it has taken place in Louisville, so I doubt they'll get much."

"So, are you headed this way?"

"Yes ma'am. Coming in. Go back to sleep – I'll be there in a little while," Tony assured her. "And before you say it, I'll be careful."

"You'd better be. I love you," Nikki whispered.

"I love you too, little girl. See you in a few."

Tony undressed in the laundry room down to his boxer briefs. Everything, including his hair, reeked of smoke, but he was too bone-weary to shower. He had to have some sleep.

He tiptoed down the upstairs hallway and opened his bedroom door. Bill and Hillary looked up at him but didn't move or make a sound. Tiptoeing across the floor, he slid under the covers next to Nikki.

Even sound asleep, she instinctively turned toward his weight on the mattress, and he put his arm around her and pulled her to his chest. When she laid her face on his chest and threw her arm across him, he buried his face in her hair; it smelled so sweet, like herbs and sunshine, and he kissed her crown, then put his other arm around her and drifted off.

Bill nuzzled her hand; she checked the clock and saw it was well past seven, then realized Tony was still sound asleep. She picked up the two dogs, set them on the floor, and wrapped the robe she'd found on the back of the bathroom door around her to take them outside, very careful to be quiet so he could sleep.

Tony woke to the smell of coffee and an erection the size of a telephone pole. Did Nikki drink coffee? He wasn't sure – he'd never asked – but he sure wanted a cup. Looking at the chair across the room, he saw Nikki's clothes neatly folded and draped across the back. He couldn't help it; he picked up her bra and looked at the tag. 32D – bigger than a walnut, smaller than a basketball, which made them the perfect size. He chuckled at the thought.

"Doing a little detective work, are we?" Nikki grinned at him from the doorway.

He turned a shade of pale pink under his dark complexion, hoping all evidence of his morning excitement had disappeared. One brief glance down told him she had a full view of every inch of him standing at attention. "Uh, yeah, it's so, um, pretty," he said and held up the bra.

"I see. Would you like some coffee, Mr. Walters?" she asked, crossing the room and taking the bra out of his hands. She tossed it onto the chair, then wrapped her arms around his neck and kissed him. "This is a red-letter day – the morning after the first time we slept together!" She laughed when she said it, and Tony grinned at her.

"Oh, it was tempting to assault you in your sleep, but I kept it together," he told her as he slapped her on the butt.

"And I appreciate your effort. Although didn't your daddy ever tell you – you can't rape a willing soul?" She kissed him again, harder. He was trying not to force his tongue between her lips, afraid of where that might lead. And he needed coffee; his head was pounding.

"I've waited this long. I'm planning to wait until our agreed-upon date." He kissed the top of her head. "Is there food down there?"

"Courtesy of Helene. I would've cooked, but I don't know where anything is."

"Well, maybe we should change that, start spending some time here. Whaddya think?"

"That would be fine with me." She took his hand and led him downstairs.

"Doing okay, buddy?" Tony asked Vic on Thursday. It had been three days since the fire, and Tony needed to know if Vic had everything he needed to keep the Lexington office going. Tony and Cheryl had worked late on Tuesday and Wednesday night, making copies Vic needed, and Nikki had even come in and helped them sort through and staple everything together. Nikki had learned quite a bit about the business just from the reading she'd done as she handled all of the documents.

"Yeah, I think I'm okay. Thanks for sending the courier with the keys. The guys are all out now doing their thing. With what's been going on, I don't think we need to use a construction trailer for an office, so I'm heading out to look for some temporary office space. Any requests?"

Tony laughed. "Yeah. Make sure it has a good fire alarm, some extinguishers, and a sprinkler system!" That made Vic chuckled. "But, listen, in all seriousness, be careful. Those fuckers are still out there somewhere. Who knows what they'll try next?"

"My forty-five is on my hip," Vic assured him, "and my shotgun is in my truck. I'm keeping watch."

Chapter Twenty-Two

Sometimes it seemed like their big weekend would never get there, and sometimes it seemed to be rushing toward Nikki. After thirty years of being someone's wife and only five of being alone, she'd never thought she'd get so nervous at the prospect of having sex. Being such a bundle of nerves had turned out to be quite a surprise, and not necessarily the good kind.

Tony, on the other hand, was a different story. The anticipation was making him practically giddy. Everyone was noticing how upbeat he was, not to mention the permanent smile plastered on his face. He thought about Nikki practically every waking moment, and sometimes in his sleep. Wondering what she'd look like undressed, how soft her skin would be, how it would feel to be inside her, kept him up at night and made him greet every day with a new attitude. He had a girlfriend, he was intent on getting laid, and nothing was going to get him down.

It was smooth sailing until after dinner on Monday night at Nikki's house. When she'd gotten the dinner dishes put in the dishwasher and the leftovers put away, Tony dropped the bomb. He'd been uncharacteristically quiet all evening; now Nikki knew why.

"Sweetie, what are you doing tomorrow evening?" he asked innocently.

"Same thing I do every evening – spending it with you – unless you've got other ideas." If he did, she was kind of afraid to hear it.

"Actually, I do." He tried his best to sound nonchalant. "We've been invited to dinner."

But something in his voice set off an alarm, and she turned from the sink to look at him. "Is that so? And where is this dinner?"

He'd been looking at a magazine at the table and, without looking up at her, answered in a placid tone, "My mom's."

Nikki felt her heart sink. Aw, hell – the meeting of the mom. "Do we really have to do that already?" she asked, panic rising in her chest.

"Yes we do, Nik. My mother knows I've been seeing someone special, and she wants to meet you." He looked for all the world like he was lying and knew he'd been busted. "Not to mention I spent Mother's Day with you instead of her. She wants to see exactly who usurped her power," he laughed. With no kids anymore and a mother who didn't seem to care for her at all, Nikki had forgotten Tony actually had a mother and he hadn't spent Mother's Day with her. She had a feeling she had some apologizing to do for that.

"She wants to meet me." Tony nodded at her. "Who ratted us out?" Tony shrugged. If Nikki had to guess, she'd say Annabeth, and probably accidentally. "Your mother wants to meet me," she repeated. "This can't be good." She was trembling slightly when she said it.

"Annabeth thinks she's going to hit you with a Sicilian curse. But I think it'll be fine. You two should hit it off – you're a lot alike," Tony quipped, taking a sip of his wine. Being sarcastic was probably a bad move at that point, but he couldn't help it. There would have to be a trip to the liquor store, because he had a feeling he was going to need more wine before all was said and done, or maybe even whiskey.

Nikki groaned and dropped her head to the countertop. If there was anything she hated, it was having to try to make small talk with someone she barely knew, least of all someone whose son she was dating. It was a damn shame she hadn't had more lead time or she could've gone to the hospital and found someone with the flu to infect her so she could have a legitimate excuse to avoid this.

Tony came over and started rubbing her shoulders. Usually his touch made her feel better, but this time it wasn't working. "Baby, I'll be right there. She might make you miserable, but she can't eat you."

"Okay. I'm going to assume she simply wants to meet me and make friends," Nikki replied with a huge, forced dose of fake cheerfulness.

"Yeah, you go with that." Tony dripped sarcasm again. Then he smiled at her. "Look, I will promise you this; I won't let her get too rough with you. But with Mamma, you have to hold your own. If you let her run all over you, she won't respect you. And that's everything in our family. So you have to stand up to her."

"Oh, thanks. No pressure." Whatever hopefulness she'd managed was completely shot. "I guess it's got to happen sooner or later. Might as well get it over with."

"How do I look? Do I look okay?" Nikki asked for the hundredth time as Tony helped her out of his truck at his mother's.

He smiled. "Baby, you look beautiful. Just the right combination of classy and voluptuous. And you looked beautiful two and a half minutes ago when you asked me the last time. And the time before that, and the time before that."

She was a mess. Her stomach was churning, and she felt kind of dizzy. *God, I hope I don't trip, fall, and make a complete fool of myself,* she thought as they walked up the steps to the front door. Instead of ringing the bell, he opened the door and walked right in. *Of course; that's what people do at their parents' house,* she laughed to herself. She'd forgotten. It had been awhile since she'd had parents.

"Mamma, we're here!" Tony called out. As he took Nikki's purse and placed it in a chair by the door, she heard footsteps and turned.

Raffaella was tiny, barely four feet ten inches and curvy in all the right places, a very attractive woman, and Nikki could tell she'd been a true stunner in her day. She had on a deep green dress Nikki would've guessed cost over five hundred dollars, a pair of what looked like black patent Manolo Blahniks, black hose, and enough jewelry to put Tiffany's out of business. Her hair was perfectly coiffed. Nikki was surprised to notice it was almost completely dark, with only a few white strands here and there, so it obviously wasn't dyed. She smelled of something really, really expensive, like a pricey perfume mixed with money. As Nikki looked at her, she saw Annabeth's features and coloring – the girl looked so much like her grandmother. After greeting Tony with a kiss on each cheek, she turned to Nikki and held out her hand.

"And you are . . . ?" Raffaella asked, pretending to have no clue.

"Mamma, this is Nikki. Nikki Wilkes. Nik, this is my mother, Raffaella Walters." Nikki took her hand, wondering if she was supposed to shake it or curtsy and kiss it. Instead, she gave it a gentle squeeze, and the older woman's other hand enveloped hers. *Off to a good start,* she thought.

"Dinner is ready. Would the two of you care to come and sit at the table?" Raffaella led the way, Nikki followed, and Tony walked slightly behind her, his hand on her lower back. When they neared the table, Tony stepped briskly to pull out his mother's chair, then did the same for Nikki before seating himself.

"I made spaghetti Bolognese, but we'll start with mussels marinara. Oh, no, I forgot the bread!" Raffaella exclaimed.

"Don't worry, Mamma, I'll get it." Tony darted into the kitchen, and Nikki was a little frightened when he disappeared through the door. She really didn't want to be alone with Raffaella – not yet anyway.

"So, I hope you like Italian food," Raffaella purred toward Nikki, "because it is a staple in the Walters family."

"Oh, I love it!" Nikki exclaimed, then worried she'd sounded a bit too enthusiastic through all the nerves. Raffaella's eyes narrowed, scrutinizing her. At that moment, Tony came back through the door with the bread.

"Shall I serve the mussels?" he asked.

"Please do, my son." Raffaella's strong accent practically dripped sugar when she spoke to Tony.

He spooned out several mussels onto Raffaella's plate, then Nikki's, and then served himself. Nikki waited. Raffaella stared directly at her, which made her even more nervous than she already was.

"Well?" Raffaella questioned, continuing to stare at her. "Please try them and let me know how you like them."

Nikki swallowed hard. She'd been waiting, hoping Raffaella or Tony would eat the first one. She had no idea how they ate mussels. She knew how *she* ate them, but . . . she picked one up, broke the upper shell off, and used it to scoop the mussel out of the lower shell, then spooned it into her mouth with the shell.

Raffaella looked at her as though she'd just shot the pope. "My child, we have forks for that," she responded in a biting tone. Tony looked disturbed. "How on earth did you decide to eat mussels that way?"

Nikki couldn't manage more than a whisper. "This is how Martha Stewart said to eat them." It was the truth; that's where she'd seen it, and the reason she'd always eaten them that way. Tony started to chuckle under his breath, and Raffaella choked, sputtering and coughing into her napkin.

"You all right, Mamma?" Tony asked her, still chuckling. Nikki looked at him, desperate, eyes wide, and he grinned and winked at her. *Good answer!*, he mouthed.

"My, well, regardless what Queen Martha says, I think I will stick with my fork, if that is all right with you," Raffaella said sourly and picked up an hors d'oeuvres fork.

"To each his own." Nikki felt a bit better, especially when she watched as Tony picked up a mussel and mimicked her technique. She smiled at him and he grinned again.

"So, Ms. Wilkes . . ." Raffaella began.

"Nikki. Please call me Nikki."

"So, Nikki, where did you meet my son?"

"He came into the florist shop where I work to buy flowers for Annabeth for her birthday. But we also go to the same gym." Nikki was trying to be quick with her answers and still not talk with a mussel in her mouth.

"Ah, you are a shop girl!" Raffaella cried out with glee as though she'd made some huge point. It was lost on Nikki. As far as the younger woman was concerned, work was work, regardless what it was.

"Well, I haven't been one for long. I had to find a job when my, well, my situation changed." She really did not want to share any emotional scrap with the dark-haired, steely-eyed woman.

Raffaella looked at her, waiting for an explanation. Tony answered her unspoken question. "Mamma, Nikki suffered a horrible tragedy. Her husband and children were killed in a terrible accident."

"That is horrible. I am terribly sorry for your loss." Raffaella spoke the words, but they didn't match the cold, hard expression on her face. It appeared to Nikki that Raffaella thought the whole story was a made-up tale for sympathy. "So how many months ago was that?" she asked pithily.

"Mamma, it was five years ago," Tony replied for Nikki, a hint of exasperation in his voice.

"Oh, so you are now sufficiently over it." Nikki stifled any facial expression, but she couldn't believe the callousness in the older woman's voice.

"Mamma!" Tony spat harshly. "That's enough!"

"What? I am only asking because it appears she is moving on." She turned back to Nikki with a smirk on her face, and Nikki could feel herself shrinking. "So how did you decide my son was the one with whom to do this?" Boy, she didn't pull any punches or even slow down. Nikki tried to formulate a clever response, then decided pure honesty was the way to go.

"Because he asked me to take a chance on him," she answered quietly in a tremulous voice. Any hope she'd had of keeping Raffaella from knowing how rattled she was had flown out the window.

"Take a chance on *him*?" Raffaella shrilled, her voice rising. "Young woman, I would definitely think that would be the other way around, wouldn't you?" Raffaella was practically indignant at that point. Nikki thought it was ironic that Raffaella had almost complimented her; it had been a long time since anyone had called her a young woman.

Tony interrupted. "No, Mamma, what she said is true. I specifically asked her to take a chance on me. Nikki hadn't dated anybody since her husband died, and she wasn't sure she was ready. I pursued her; she didn't pursue me." Tony gripped Nikki's hand under the table, and she immediately felt better.

Raffaella seemed surprised. "Is that so?" She turned to glare at Tony, then turned her attention back to Nikki, her eyes practically shooting lightning bolts. "So, is the shop girl willing to take a chance on my handsome, successful, wealthy son? Hmmm?" She drummed her fingers on the table. "And by the way, do not think I do not notice your expensive jewelry and clothing. Antonio, are you already keeping this woman up?"

Tony was starting to panic. He'd expected his mother to go after Nikki, but not so soon, and not so ruthlessly. He turned to Nikki, afraid she'd burst into tears and run from the room; if she did, she'd be done. His mamma would destroy her. And they'd be over before they even began.

To his shock and delight, Nikki did neither. He saw her take a deep breath, straighten her spine, and turn to Raffaella. Her face was expressionless save for one eyebrow that was slightly raised. When she opened her mouth, her voice was even, clear, and very strong. "Mrs. Walters, I've more than taken a chance on your son. I'm in love with him, and he's in love with me. I may only be a retail clerk, but I'm smart, and frugal, and friendly, and kind. I'd do anything for Tony and his children, and I believe he'd do anything for me. And for the record, the jewelry I'm wearing? All gifts from my late husband over the years. And my clothing? If it's anybody's business, which it's not, it all came from Goodwill or a thrift or consignment store. I don't have the money a lot of women in this town have, but I have more love to give than most. Now, I'm going down the hallway to find the bathroom. I don't know where it is, but I can assure you if I come back to the same level of disrespect and disdain I've just experienced, I *do* remember where the front door is." Nikki scooted her chair back and rose. Tony started to rise too, but she put her hand on his shoulder and pushed him back into his seat, then took off down the hall without saying another word.

The bathroom was the second room on the left, and she locked the door behind her. Her lungs couldn't pull in enough breath, and she practically heaved in air. Putting the toilet lid down, she sat and dropped her face into her hands. What had she done? Tony had said to stand up for herself. Had she gone too far? She sat, trying to catch a ragged breath and calm her slamming heart, and then she heard a gentle knock. "Tony, I know that's you. Go away," she snarled, and the knocking stopped.

Tony had sat, glaring at his mother, until he'd gone to check on Nikki.

When she told him to go away, he came back to the table, beyond furious. "Mamma, I . . ." he began.

Raffaella put a hand on his. "Antonio, that young woman has fire. She may not be Italian, but she will definitely be a challenge to you. I am impressed with her tenacity and strength," she told him brightly, taking a huge bite of bread and smiling broadly at Tony.

He stared at her in utter astonishment. "You insulted my girlfriend, no, the woman I love, in every way I could think of and a couple that surprised me, and you're telling me how much you *like* her?" He didn't quite trusting his hearing.

"No. I do not know if I like her or not. But I do admire her."

And that was when Nikki appeared in the doorway. Tony expected her to look shaken and pale; she was anything but. Slightly flushed, she walked into the room, put her hands on the back of her chair, and, gave Raffaella a piercing glare. "May I sit back down? Or perhaps the question would be, should I?"

Raffaella beamed at her. "Please. You seemed to enjoy the mussels. My spaghetti Bolognese is legendary. I hope you will enjoy it as well. Tony, would you please serve?"

"Well, how was that?" Nikki asked, grinning, once they were back in Tony's truck.

"What the hell just happened in there?" Tony shook his head, a bewildered look plastered on his face. "One minute she was trying to tear you limb from limb, and the next, she was eating out of your palm. Woman, you are a true wonder," he whispered, reaching for Nikki's hand.

She broke into a smug smile. After Tony had served the spaghetti, they had talked and laughed the rest of the evening. Raffaella had asked questions about Nikki's childhood, and talked about her own in Italy. She told them stories about Tony's grandparents and about her time in school. Then she spoke with a sparkle in her eye of a young Italian hunk with an odd, decidedly un-Italian last name who'd stolen her heart and dragged her to the United States, where she'd started a new life she never could've imagined and raised five truly amazing, handsome boys who, according to her, were a cross between Superman and Saint Peter. Nikki had listened, riveted, and asked questions here and there to let Raffaella know she was interested in what the older woman was saying. As they'd left, Raffaella had kissed Nikki on both cheeks and said, "Please come again and bring my son with you. He rarely visits." She'd frowned and kissed Tony on both cheeks, then swatted him on the behind as he turned to walk down the steps, catching him off guard with her playfulness. Yes, Nikki thought, the evening had gone quite well.

"So, am I in?" she asked, turning to look at Tony.

"Oh, baby, you are so in. And by the way, I've never wanted to fuck somebody's brains out as badly as I do right now. The way you stood up to her? That really turned me on."

"Really?" He answered her question by taking her hand and placing it between his legs. She could feel his erection, hard as steel, through his jeans and gasped. "Wow. Well, Saturday is almost here. Can you hold out?"

"Saturday? I've got news for you, little girl. I'm calling Carter tomorrow to see if the plane is ready. We're leaving Friday night. I can't wait any more."

Chapter Twenty-Three

Nikki was a wreck on Friday afternoon. Tony told her he usually drove to Gatlinburg, but he didn't want time wasted in travel that weekend. Carter had assured Tony that the plane was ready and waiting, and he'd taken her on Thursday evening after dinner to the mall to pick up things she wanted or that he wanted her to have. They'd even made a trip to Clarenda's, the nearest adult store, to pick up some cute lingerie, some toys Tony wanted, and plenty of lube.

Packing had taken her the rest of the evening until later than she wanted to stay up. She tried to pick out clothes, then chuckled to herself – she was hoping she wouldn't need anything to wear all weekend, just food and maybe clean sheets. Annabeth had shown up early to get instructions on caring for Bill and Hillary, who were staying with her and Katie for the weekend. It seemed everything was falling into place.

Discussion over dinner that night had led to a serious decision – no condoms. Their lack of sexual activity over the previous years and the testing they'd had done made it clear that protection wasn't an issue. That meant they'd be totally and completely together, nothing held back. Neither had thought the other would agree to it, but between their low risk and the impossibility of pregnancy – she'd had a hysterectomy years before – that kind of precaution seemed unnecessary. A quivering sensation flooded through Nikki when she thought about that moment, the familiar warmth and wetness inside her, and she wanted to experience that with Tony.

Marla came out to the front counter and shook her head at Nikki. "Please, for the love of god, would you just go on home? You're making *me* a nervous wreck!" she laughed, hugging Nikki.

"Are you sure?" Marla pointed silently to the door. "Oh, thank you!" Nikki squealed, sprinting out.

"Have a good time!" Marla called after her.

Once she got into her car, she called Tony. "I'm on my way home!"

Nikki gushed into the phone when he answered.

"I've got about thirty minutes here, then I'm on my way too. My bags are in the car." Tony hesitated for just a second, then asked, "Are you as excited as I am?"

"Oh, god, honey, I'm about to jump out of my skin!" she cried in a hoarse whisper.

"Good. I'll see you in a few, baby."

Tony had invited Carter to bring his wife, and had gotten the couple a room at one of the resorts in the Gatlinburg area. Nikki and Carter's wife, Adelaide, chatted on the plane and found they had some things in common, especially their love of healthy cooking. Adelaide was a beautiful young woman, blond and stacked, and Carter was just as adorable and good-looking. Dinner arrangements were made for Sunday evening between the two couples, which sounded like fun to the two ladies. Rental cars picked up at the airport, the Walters and the Carters parted ways.

Since she was familiar with the area, Nikki was surprised when Tony drove out past the Save-A-Lot grocery and turned down Buckhorn Road, her favorite area in town, then kept driving. "Hey, drive slow. There's a house down here I've always wanted to see inside of." She pointed to the left-hand side of the road. "It's down here not too far past the pub. Even though it's dark, maybe they'll have the window treatments open. I've always wanted to catch a glimpse."

She was excited to see that the pub was still there and open – the neon signs advertising beer were glowing, and there was a good smattering of cars parked outside. They had the best bangers and mashed she'd ever eaten, and if they'd closed it would've been a crime. Tony slowed and Nikki watched. Up ahead she could see the lights of the house, and she whispered, "There it is! It's so beautiful! Look at all those windows!"

Tony slowed even more, then turned on the left-hand blinker. "What are you doing?" she cried out, aghast. "We can't drive up there! That's somebody's house!" He drove on up to the front door and shut off the car.

Opening her door, he took her hand, helped her out of the car, and closed the door behind her. Then he pointed at the house.

"What?" she asked, confused.

"Precious," he smiled, his perfectly white teeth glowing in the light from the windows, "welcome home."

The chicken salad in the fridge, bought from one of the local eateries, was especially tasty; Roselle, his property manager, had brought over a few things so they'd have a little something to eat when they got there. A roaring fire fended off the spring nip in the air, and Tony handed Nikki a glass of wine as she enjoyed the fire's warmth. "Like it?" Tony asked, looking around the room.

"Like it? That's like asking if winning the lottery cheered somebody up." She sipped the wine, then pointed at her glass. "Where's this from?"

"One of the local wineries."

"Very nice." She took another sip. "This place is, well, I don't know what to say. I'm stunned. I've been looking at it for years now, wondering what it would be like to have a house like this. It's so beautiful. I can't believe I'm here."

"If you think this is beautiful, wait until you see the bedroom," he said, rubbing her back. Then he leaned over and kissed her ear.

A bolt of sexual energy hit her clit, and she felt herself getting moist. Her nipples hardened immediately, painfully, and she remembered why she and Tony were there. She wanted to strip off her clothes and climb astride him that very minute.

As if he could read her mind, Tony said, "I want to talk to you about something."

"Shoot."

"I want to rip your clothes off and fuck you like a maniac." *At least we have the same idea,* Nikki thought. "But this is our first time together, and I don't want that to be how we remember it. I want us to take our time. I want to make love with you, really connect, you know?" The warmth in his brown eyes made her blush.

Nikki leaned in and kissed him softly. "I agree," she moaned into his lips. "I want to really get to know your body, and I want you to take the time to really get to know mine. Soft lights, no shame, no embarrassment, no holds barred. On the same page with you?"

"Same paragraph, line, and word." He kissed her. "Let's go get ready for bed, unless there's something else you'd rather do."

"Not one thing in this world." She took his hand and he led her up the stairs, then opened the bedroom door. Nikki gasped in wonder.

White – it was everywhere. The room was made up in white, from the white comforter to the white sheets to the white draperies around the bed – the fourteen-foot-tall bed. Soft, impressionistic art was placed here and there on the walls and, in one corner, a huge fireplace had a lovely fire burning in its belly. French doors leading to the balcony were open, their white draperies fluttering in the springtime mountain breeze.

Tony pointed to a door on one wall. "Your bathroom." He pointed to a door on the opposite wall. "My bathroom." He then pointed to a third door, this one on the same wall as her bathroom. "Closet." He wheeled their luggage into it, and she stepped in to find an enormous closest, bigger than her bedroom at home. A door in the closet led into her bathroom. "Make yourself comfortable and I'll see you back in the bedroom." He left her in the closet and went to his bathroom with his luggage.

There was plenty of room, and Nikki went through her suitcase, hanging up some clothes and putting undercloths and personal items in the drawers in the closet system. She pulled out the lingerie she'd bought to wear that night – a pretty black chemise with a shirred bodice and a thong that matched. The thong got tossed back into a drawer. She wouldn't need it; she wouldn't need the chemise either, but she thought it would be nice to see his face when she walked out in it. Finished in the closet, she glided into the bathroom to take off her makeup, brush her teeth, and freshen up. The chemise fell softly over her rinsed-off and lotioned-up skin, and she brushed her hair one last time. She took a look in the mirror.

Looking back at her was someone she hadn't seen in a long time. Her hair was long and shiny. The sadness she'd seen for so long in her own eyes seemed to be gone. She saw the little pudge around her middle and hoped Tony wouldn't mind it; the rest of her was toned and trim, even if her breasts weren't as pert and high as they'd been earlier in her life. This was her, her body, and it was brimming with excitement and desire. She was sure she wasn't about to be disappointed; she hoped Tony wouldn't be either.

Nikki stepped into the bedroom to find the lights on low, the fire glowing brightly, and Tony in the big bed, propped against the huge headboard. The sheet was pulled up to his waist, and his hard, muscled chest made her heart skip a few beats. When he looked up and saw her standing in the bathroom doorway, his eyes widened and a low whistle slipped from his lips.

"Like?" She felt suddenly bashful and uncovered even in the chemise.

"Love." He patted the spot beside him on the bed. "You look amazing."

Get over here, woman. I've got something for you."

"Good, because I've got something for you, too." She slid under the covers with him.

"Is that so? Maybe we can do a trade," he murmured, reaching up to graze her cheeks softly with his knuckles, and her eyes closed.

Tony slid his hands from her face down her neck, around the sides of her breasts, and down her sides until he could wrap his arms around her waist. He pulled her body to his; she could feel his hard, erect cock pressed against her belly, and she hoped he could feel her stiff, burning nipples against his chest. He kissed her, ran his tongue around and over her lips, then sank it between her parted teeth, his heart pounding in his temples. His hand caressed the back of her thigh, reached her tight, firm ass and cupped her curve in his hand, then continued up her side, under the chemise, until he reached her breast. When his finger and thumb squeezed one hard, throbbing nipple, she thrust her tongue into his mouth with an expediency that surprised him, and he squeezed and twisted harder, feeling her pelvis buck against his erection.

He stopped and pulled his hand from under the chemise and covers. "The outfit is beautiful, baby, but I don't need it. I want you, and it's just in my way. Take it off." Sliding out from under the sheet and turning her back to him, she pulled the chemise up and over her head and threw it across the room onto a chair. "Turn around," he ordered.

Panic threatened, and she closed her eyes – the moment of truth. Without opening them, she turned toward his voice and waited, her heart threatening to stop. Even without seeing, she could feel his eyes on her, looking her over, scrutinizing her, and she started to tremble.

Before him in the dim light stood everything Tony could've ever wanted. There was nothing remotely angular about Nikki – every inch of her was soft and womanly. Her slender neck and well-defined collarbone gave way to a beautiful sight; two gorgeous breasts, just heavy enough to pull slightly downward, adorned with the largest and hardest nipples he'd ever seen. His mind reeled and he had one blinding thought: *I want my mouth on those – right now.* Her ribcage dwindled into a narrow waist, and just below its width lay her soft belly, only a slight paunch divulging that it had carried children. Her mound was bare, a thing that almost made him gasp, and he could see her arousal plainly, the lips of her pussy unable to hide her clit, swollen and dark. And those legs – oh, god, those legs! They had the best muscle definition he'd ever seen, and yet they were soft and curvy in an almost indecent way.

But the overall effect was breathtaking. There in front of him was a body that had been loved and made love to, a body that had made love to a man and satisfied him over and over. It wasn't a body he'd expect to see in a men's magazine or a porn video; it was a body a man wanted to keep to himself, cherish and adore, touch and fill. Tony glanced down and found his long-ignored friend had not only made a comeback, but was demanding attention, so hard that a burn had set up, and he wasn't sure he could ever put out the fire. When he looked back up at her, he could see a tremor running through her body.

"Nikki?" Tony's voice was filled with uncertainty. "Baby, what's wrong?"

"Now that you've seen me, do you still want me?" she choked out, teetering on the brink of tears, eyes still closed.

How on earth could she even ask me that?, Tony thought. *She has no idea how beautiful she is.* "Gee, I don't know, angel. Take a look and tell me what you think."

Nikki opened her eyes. Tony lay on his side, head propped on his hand, sheet wadded up at the foot of the bed. She gasped – his enormous cock nearly reached his navel, thick and so engorged that it was almost purple. It looked like it had a pulse of its own, its veins raised and dark. Better yet, it was obvious there'd been some serious manscaping going on there, something she'd heard of but never seen before, and that only served to make what was already large look even larger. She felt her nipples stiffen even more, and there was a gush of wetness between her legs.

"Oh. My. God," she whispered, barely able to catch her breath.

Tony reached for her. "Woman, I told you I had something for you. Come and claim your gift."

She couldn't get back into the bed fast enough. Drawn to his cock like a mouse to cheese, her hand went straight to it, and she grasped its girth firmly in both hands. She wanted to feel it, to see if it was as big and rigid as it looked. No disappointment – it was exactly as it appeared, hard as a tree trunk. Tony's mouth went straight to one nipple and his hand to the other, and within seconds she was moaning and writhing at the onslaught. As she pumped his firmness, he let his other hand meander down her tummy, using his fingers to graze her skin sensuously, making no distinction between the smoothness of her upper abdomen and the softer skin on the lower. She shivered, breaking out in goose bumps under his fingers like in the depths of a Maine winter, but as they moved along her softness they left behind a spreading heat like an August day in the deep south. When he reached her mons, she flexed her pelvis instinctively toward his hand, and he slid his fingers around the side of her mound and down her groin, then down the inside of her thigh and back up to the crease between her leg and her labia.

"Shaved. I love it. God, baby, you're so fucking beautiful," he moaned, his hand cupping her hot folds. He flexed his middle finger and pressed it inside her inner lips. "And god, you're so damn wet," he whispered into her breast, taking her nipple back into his mouth and nipping it with his teeth. Her back arched, thrusting her breasts forward, and he slipped his middle finger into her pussy in a smooth, fluid motion.

She gasped and thrust her hips toward his hand, and when he slid his finger back out and drew it slowly and softly up her slit, across the surface of her clit, she jumped like he'd shocked her. When he repeated the motion her response was stronger than before, and it drove him on. His teeth clamped onto her nipple and he raised his head, pulling outward until her breast was stretched out painfully, then letting it snap back, and her moaning became more frantic. Pulling his finger back out of her, he traced up her slit again, then pressed his finger inside her hood and began to slowly and softly draw his finger around her clit, making sure to make contact with each side in turn. She moaned loudly, whispered his name, and tilted her pelvis toward his hand as a heat like a smoldering coal set up behind her hard nub.

When his free hand made the trip from under her ribs up to the back of her neck, it left behind a trail of white-hot current that almost sizzled. Reaching her hair, he fisted a handful and drew her head back, taking his mouth from her nipple and kissing her, a hard and urgent kiss, his tongue probing her mouth feverishly, her tongue meeting his and dancing against it. His finger continued to circle her clit, increasing in speed and intensity, and she cried out, "Oh, god, Tony, I need to come!" and worked his shaft relentlessly, stoking the flames of her reawakening womanhood with the heat from his hardness in her hand.

"Wait, baby, not yet." His finger continuing to circle her clit, he rolled her onto her back. Keeping up the rhythmic torture, he knelt between her legs. "Knees up, baby. I want to be inside you – I can't wait another minute." Nikki pulled her knees tight to her chest and drew her legs apart as far as she could, opening herself like a butterfly bursting from a cocoon, offering her most private self to him deeply and freely.

Tony took a good, long look, and the sight was dizzying. Her cunt was engorged and a deep rose, her clit swollen, and her juices ran freely out and down like honey in July. It was something he never dreamed he'd see – a woman who wanted him as much as he wanted her. He pressed the tip of his cock into her entrance, then pushed in ever so gently.

Passion and desire collided and, as the head of his cock breeched her opening, she gasped and reached for his waist, pulling him in tighter. As she thrust toward him, he drew back, then forward, pumping into her, slamming into her cervix and causing her to whimper. The whole time, she was watching him above her, the muscles in his shoulders hard and flexing as his strong hands pressed the backs of her thighs down and out, keeping her wide open to him. Those dark eyes drilled into her, serious and smoldering, taking in the sight of his cock disappearing into her warmth and softness.

"Oh, sweet lord, Tony, please," she pleaded. "I need to come. Please!" Her hips continued to buck against him and he set the pace, his rhythm sucking her in and setting her pace as well. He started stroking her clit again, the tension building and swelling somewhere down deep inside her, boiling and rising until she reached the edge. "Oh, baby, I'm coming. Please, Tony, I'm coming – come with me, please? Please!" she begged him, frantic and panting.

"Right here with you, angel," he groaned. He'd done his best to wait, but he felt his balls tense and draw up and knew he only had seconds. Increasing the speed and intensity of his finger stroking her clit, he moaned and she screamed out, the tension too great for her to hold back any longer.

"Tony! Oh, god, ohhhhhh!!!" she shrieked, stiffening as the orgasm took her. Her belly convulsed, her muscles tightened, and her hips churned wildly. The walls of her pussy throbbed around his cock, tight and pulsing, and he was so close to coming that he felt like he was losing his mind. As her orgasm subsided, he slid his hands around her hips to her ass. Gripping her roundness with both hands, he buried his face in her neck and began to ravenously grind into her, his cock hitting bottom in her channel over and over again, his tempo escalating, and she continued to cry out, urging him on. The sensation of his hair brushing her shoulder drove her wild, all of her want and need unleashed.

"Oh, Nikki, come again for me, babe, while I'm inside you. Join me this time," Tony whispered in her ear. Her body responded as he pounded into her mercilessly and she cried out and screamed his name louder than before, her pelvis tilting up at an impossible angle and rocking, begging for more of his cock, her hands kneading the smooth hardness of his pecs as the orgasm hit her down deep, an inferno setting up in her depths. He felt his shaft thicken as he let go, releasing every ounce he had into her, and she felt it all, felt his heat, his wetness, all of the desire he'd been holding in for so long, all of it given to her, his gift for the desire she'd poured into him. As he came, he called out her name, long and low, almost a growl, and the primitiveness of it all ravaged her heart and made her crave more.

He dropped his full weight onto her, wrapped his arms around her waist, pressed his face into the side of her sweet-smelling neck, his lips to her ear, and he whispered softly, "Nikki, I'm so in love with you that it feels like my heart is split wide open." He felt her hands travel up his back and then his neck, finally winding into his hair. She put a hand on either side of his head and lifted it so that their eyes met.

What he saw in those eyes took any fear, any hesitation, any doubts he had, and pulverized them, sending them into the wind like ash and smoke. "Oh, baby, I've felt so empty for so long. I finally feel full." She kissed his forehead. "I love you more than I know how to say," she whispered to him, her face wet with tears of pure joy and delight.

Tony rolled them onto their sides, their bodies entangled, and stared into her face. For the first time in his life, naked and sated, still buried inside a woman, he saw love looking back at him, and he felt a peace he'd never known before take root in his chest. This was his woman, and she loved him as much as he loved her. In that bed, in that room, in that house in a tiny little mountain town, Tony Walters, who had everything a man could want, had finally found what he'd wanted most.

Real love.

"Well, Mr. Walters, was that okay?" she asked with more than a hint of satisfaction in her voice, her face on his chest, her fingers dawdling about through his chest hair and circling his nipples.

"I was just about to ask you the same thing, Ms. Wal . . . Wilkes." He'd almost called her by his last name. Was that what he wanted? Everything was happening so fast. Should he slow it down, put on the brakes? Who the hell was he kidding? He wanted to claim her and do it fast, but common sense said to wait, at least for a little while anyway.

"I'm a satisfied customer, stud. I want more. You?"

"God, yes. Making love with you was lots of things, but I wouldn't say okay. That nowhere near does it justice," he announced and kissed the tip of her nose. "I've never felt like that before in my life."

"Me neither." She pinched his nipple lightly.

"What about with Randy?"

"Nope." She ran her tongue from his chin up the side of his jaw, then up to his ear, where she rimmed the ridge around the outside of his ear. He shuddered and his cock jumped. "Not even with Randy."

He couldn't believe it. "Seriously? In thirty years?"

"Not in thirty years. I don't know what just happened here, but I feel, well, different somehow. Like you've unlocked something really deep down inside me and set it free." She reached down and touched his cock, then wrapped her fingers around it, her hand instinctively beginning to pour the friction on. He hadn't completely softened from the first time, and he stiffened proudly again.

"If you don't stop that," he growled at her, "we'll have to do it again."

"I've got news for you, big boy." She flashed him an evil grin. "I was banking on doing it again anyway."

At four thirty the next morning, Tony sighed and rolled off of Nikki. "Round four, precious. Or was that five – or six? I think I'm done for the night."

Nikki giggled and curled up against him. "Surely you're not tired?"

"And you're not?" he groaned out sarcastically.

"Of course not!" She laughed and added, "Well, maybe just a little . . ."

He rolled back on top of her and started tickling her ribs, and she squealed and pretended to fight him off. Then he stopped and his eyes bored deep into hers with a look that warmed her heart.

She waited, but he didn't say a word. "What?"

He smiled a dreamy smile. "I'm thinking about how much I love you and how happy I am at this very minute." He hesitated, then asked, "Are you happy too?"

Nikki's eyes welled and she answered in a broken whisper, "This moment, right now? It's the absolute happiest of my life. I'm just waiting for the next moment with you, because I'm pretty sure it's going to be even happier."

Tony leaned down and placed a kiss on her lips, a long, sweet, warm, closed-mouth kiss that caused her heart to beat faster and stronger. It was a kiss full of roses and honey and chocolates with toffee, of hopes and plans and prayers. It told her she'd made all his dreams come true, just like he had hers.

He rolled them both back onto their sides and wrapped his arms tight around her. With her body pressed tight against him, her face tucked into his chest, and her arms around his waist, they drifted off to sleep.

God, she was hungry! Nikki checked the clock; nine thirty. Tony had made it to the other side of the king-size bed during the night, so she scooted across and spooned his back, throwing an arm across his ribcage. Reaching back, he grabbed the cheek of her ass and pulled her closer into him.

"Good morning, angel," he said in a voice hoarse with sleep. "Get some rest?"

"Um-hum. And I'm starving."

"Well, I guess we'll have to see what we can do about that." He turned to face her and kissed her on the forehead. "Oh, my god, this makes me so happy."

"What?" A silly grin broke across her face.

"Waking up next to you. I want to do this every day from now on."

"That would suit me just fine." She smiled and dropped a tiny kiss on his cheek.

"Yeah? We'll have to work toward that, if you want to." He brushed a stray lock of hair out of her eyes.

"I do." Then she thought, *Would I like to say "I do" officially?* She had to admit it was becoming a very appealing idea. "I hate to think about when we go back and I can't do this every morning."

"Then don't think about it right now." Tony gave her a little kiss. "Just enjoy it. We can work on that when we get back." He kissed her again, then sat up on the edge of the bed. "Let's pull ourselves together and go to the pancake place in town."

"You know I don't eat that stuff, right?" she grunted, sitting up on her side of the bed and reaching for something, anything, to put on.

"Oh, come on – this is a special occasion. We both got laid last night!" Tony laughed, leaned across, and ruffled her hair. "Besides, you can eat anything you want for one day, can't you? Let's have some fun with food today, diet be damned. I love their pancakes. I bet they have a whole grain pancake you'd like, maybe some plain fruit toppings? Shower and let's go see." He headed for his bathroom, and Nikki watched his tight, muscular ass as he went, a shiver of sexual tension racing through her like a Kentucky thoroughbred. The ache between her legs came back, but this time it was accompanied by a soreness she hadn't expected.

When she stood up, that soreness made itself known in a big way, at least to her. She didn't realize she'd made a noise, but Tony called out, "You okay out there?"

"Yeah." She must not have been very convincing because he stuck his head out his bathroom door and stared at her, frowning.

"What's wrong, baby?"

"Um, I'm kinda sore," she groaned, walking carefully toward the bathroom.

"Really?" He chuckled. "Why?"

"New exercise routine. Must've gotten in a little over my head," she snipped sarcastically, and he laughed at her. She made a face.

"Poor thing. You know what they say: If you get thrown, get right back on the horse." He was laughing outright at that point.

"Oh, yeah, right. Thanks for the tip." She minced her way into her bathroom and turned on the shower. When she turned around, she let out a little squeal to find Tony right behind her.

"Need help?" he asked with a sly little smirk.

"Yeah. I'm not sure I can grip the soap by myself," she snarled, but she was grinning as she said it.

Tony pulled her into the hot water and kissed her, then began to systematically and gently wash her all over, first her face, then her hair, and then her whole body. There was nothing remotely sexual about it; it was a lover caring for the person he loved, and it made her feel cherished and adored. He watched in delight as she shaved everything. Then she turned and began the process for him, and watched him carefully wield his razor to landscape what she now thought of as hers. They took turns toweling each other off, then dressed and took off for the pancake house.

"I think I'm going to take a nap," Nikki announced when they came back from their late breakfast. "Want to join me?"

"That, my dear, sounds like an excellent idea. I'll get us a glass of water apiece and I'll meet you in the bedroom.

Upstairs, Nikki peeled off to nothing but her underwear. When she turned the sheets back, she was surprised to find they'd been changed. Someone was clearly taking care of the house, but they were moving around like a ghost because she'd seen no one. She slid in and plumped her pillow.

Tony appeared and put a glass on her bedside table, then took his to the other side, shucked off his jeans and tee, and slid in beside her. He reached over and pulled her up against him, wrapping an arm around her. She cuddled up against his warmth and, within minutes, they were in dreamland.

Nikki woke to a strange sensation – something pressing into the cleft in her backside. She'd rolled over in her sleep, her back to Tony. Plus she didn't have on her underwear; she could've sworn she'd left them on. Odd. She tried to place the sensation, and then realized he was pressing something against her rosette. "Is that your . . ."

"Yes," he whispered. "How would you feel about that?"

"Condom," she answered.

"Don't want one. Hope you can live with that." He waited while she thought for a second, then nodded her okay. This was about trust, and she wanted to trust him completely. She felt him shift behind her, then heard a pop as he opened a bottle of lube and poured a generous amount onto his fingers. He rimmed her opening, then pushed one finger against her muscles, and she felt the burn as it entered her tightness. After a minute, he pulled his finger out, then pushed two fingers into her. As he pushed, she pressed against him and hissed her pleasure, and he removed the two fingers and gently replaced them with three, waiting to hear her guttural approval. When he realized all three were not a challenge, he asked, "How does that feel?"

"Burns a little, but not bad. Is this what you want?" she asked, breathless with anticipation.

"Very much, baby." He reached for a wipe to clean his hands. "You *have* done this before, right?" She nodded. "Can you handle it? I want this so much – I want to take you every way there is."

"Anything for you, lover," she answered with a smoldering growl. "Take whatever you want. It's yours anyway."

That was all the encouragement Tony needed, and hearing Nikki say those words took his erection from hard to excruciating. He pressed the head of his cock against the tight ring of muscles, and they resisted for only a second or two, then allowed him access through their grip. The velvety head of his cock slid in; Nikki felt it breech her entrance slowly and she moaned, feeling the deliciousness of the stretch. He pushed into her with purpose; she felt the burn as her passage opened to his breadth and in a hoarse whisper, she begged, "Please, baby, more lube!" Tony pulled back, leaving only the head inside her, coated his shaft generously, and glided into her again. Nikki gasped loudly as half of his cock slid into her, stretching her passage.

"Okay? Hanging in there?" he asked.

"Yeah. It's just been a long, long time. But I want it too," she almost begged, and he felt her press gingerly against him again, her movement dizzying him and urging him on.

Tony moved back again, then pushed in farther still, patient but eager to claim her ass as his. Slowly, a little at a time, he buried his entire length in her, and she moaned heartily and pushed against him. "Ready, little girl?"

"Oh, yeah, baby. I'm ready, past ready. I need you so bad . . ."

Tony pulled out, grabbed her around her waist and set her on all fours, then slid into her again, a smooth, graceful motion. Nikki felt every cell in her body light up like a marquee on Broadway, and her skin tingled with the excitement of something she'd missed so much. He set up a gentle rhythm, then reached around her to tease her clit mercilessly with one hand and twist and pull a hard, swollen nipple with the other, trying not to put too much weight on her. But that was why she'd worked so hard in the gym – to be fit and strong. That work paid off as she braced herself to take his weight, enjoying the feeling of him resting on her back as he took her.

Nikki let out a sultry moan, crying out through her arousal. Tony kept up the vigorous pumping deep in her ass and the methodical stroking of her clit, twisting and pulling her nipple with abandon. She kept moaning and crying out in pain and pleasure, feeling the orgasm building in her belly, her pussy aching, wanting to be filled.

"My god, angel, you're so damn tight," Tony choked out, keeping the sensations building in her clit.

"Faster, baby, faster," she urged him on. "I need to come, please? Oh, god, it's so good, I can't stand it."

Tony grabbed Nikki around the waist again and hoisted both of them up to their knees, but she was so overcome with sensation that she couldn't stay upright; she fell forward on the bed, gripping the sheets to hold herself in place, her face and breasts resting on the bed, her round, tight ass in the air for Tony's pleasure. He reached around her, still stroking her engorged clit, and began a boisterous ramming, faster and harder, until she was screaming his name, ecstatic and uninhibited.

"Don't hold it back, love. Come for me – come hard!" Tony shouted, and Nikki's body shuddered under him, her orgasm driving her to scream and grip the sheets furiously, her ass hot and needy, the stretch and friction she felt stealing the breath from her lungs. He felt his body readying and he rammed her wildly as he came, his scorching cum pouring into her until it ran down the insides of her legs.

He stopped everything and straightened up, still on his knees. She was trembling and clutching the sheets, his dick still buried in her up to his balls. She looked so damn gorgeous, her hair a wild mess, her sweet ass in the air, and he raised his hands and slapped her backside. She let out a loud, throaty groan but didn't move a muscle. He pulled out of her slowly and watched his cock reappear, reddened by her tightness, and more cum ran out of her and down her leg.

Falling onto his back on the bed beside her, gasping for breath, he looked over at her. Her face was inches from his, but her eyes were closed in what looked like utter peace, her ass resting on her heels. "I don't think I've ever seen anything so beautiful. My god, you're something," he whispered, but she didn't respond. "Babe, you okay?" He pushed her hair back so he could see her sweet face clearly.

She bit her lower lip coyly and opened her big cerulean eyes. "Yeah, I'm good. Great, in fact. That was awesome. But my pussy is so empty. I need you to fuck me, Tony, please? Fuck me hard. Oh god," she purred, the muscles in her belly knotting in need.

Tony's eyebrows shot up and his eyes opened wide. "Seriously?" he asked. He couldn't believe it – he was sure she'd be done, but she wanted more, was practically begging him.

She closed her eyes again and nodded. Her legs straightened so she was lying face down, and she rolled toward him. "You didn't want a condom, so you'll need to do cleanup – really good cleanup."

Tony reached for more wipes and cleaned himself. Thinking there'd be more action anytime soon was overly-optimistic, though – he was spent. She'd emptied him completely like he'd never been emptied before. "Better?" he asked, pointing at his fading cock for her approval of his cleanup job.

"I don't know. You tell me." Nikki smiled a wicked little smile and, before he could say or do anything else, she slid down, snuggled in between his legs, and took the head of his cock into her rosy mouth. Tony dropped his head back in blessed agony and let out a long, lusty moan as she sucked his cock head for all she was worth, and he felt himself hardening fast to the point of pain, the blood rushing in at an alarming speed. Rimming the ridge around the head with her hot tongue, she moved to tease his frenulum until he started to moan again. Then that sweet tongue meandered down his shaft, and her luscious lips followed, taking in more and more of him until his whole length was in her mouth, her nose sensuously brushing his abs. His manhood hardened and lengthened under her expertise, and she started a hearty stroking down his length with her mouth as she gripped the base of his cock in her hand, tenderly fondling his balls with the other hand.

Tony was bombarded with sensations. She was good – really, really good. It felt like she was sucking an orgasm right out of him like a milkshake through a straw. He flexed his pelvis sacrificially toward her, and she responded by taking her soft lips farther down onto his rigid shaft. His fingers dug into her wild, glowing hair, wrapping it around his hand, and he looked down to watch her sucking him with an eagerness that thrilled him. She was honoring his cock with those soft lips and that raspy tongue, and he couldn't look away – it was too heavenly.

As he watched her, she looked up at him and their gazes locked magnetically. Her eyes seemed to almost flash silver, and the look he saw in their depths spread heat all over his body – the piercing stare of a fierce and hungry tigress devouring her prey. The jolt of pure sexual energy she sent through him with that single look was so strong that it was almost frightening. He tipped his pelvis up again to meet her constricting mouth, and she went down, his cock going past her gag point and down her throat, her eyes watering as she looked into his. Tony felt his balls drawing up tight and he cried out, "God, Nikki, I can't take it – I'm coming!"

"Oh no you don't!" she said matter-of-factly, sitting up abruptly and turning loose of his cock. Tony's mouth flew open to protest but before he could speak, she threw a leg across him and, taking his shaft in her hand, lowered herself completely onto him and began to ride him.

Tony watched her and was blown away. She rode him with total abandon, her hips grinding as she slid downward, moaning every time his stone-hard dick smacked her dead end. As she moved, she growled ferociously over and over, and he slid a hand up the hardening muscles of her torso to her breast, pinching and pulling a nipple as hard as he dared while he tormented her swollen clit over and over with the thumb and fingers of the other hand. Her breasts bounced, and the sight of her, the sensual way she moved, her fervent cries as she stroked up and down on his hardness, made him ache deep down. Her eyes were closed, and she looked like she might pass out from her mounting climax.

She moaned loudly, "Oh, Tony, baby, I'm coming!" Her abdominal muscles drew tight as he watched, and she dropped herself completely onto his cock and shook as she came, her pussy gripping him in ripples.

When her orgasm subsided, Tony flipped them both over. With her feet planted on the fronts of his shoulders, he rose up on his knees and began to administer a relentless, hard-driving pounding to her begging pussy, his hands gripping the backs of her thighs. "God, Tony, more! Faster, harder, baby, please, please!" she pleaded, her whole body convulsing in another orgasm, her impassioned screams filling the room. He felt himself nearing climax; he was having trouble understanding how it could be happening so fast, every muscle in his body tensing in anticipation of the moment the energy building in him would peak and he'd force his essence into her. Her hips continued to flex as she wrung the orgasm out of him, and when she dropped her legs, he fell flat on top of her, gripped her ass, and ground into her, giving her everything he had left.

They both stilled, and he slid his arms up to and around her waist. His face was buried in her hair, and he turned to kiss her earlobe. "Good?" she asked in a whisper, and she wove her fingers through his silky, wavy locks.

He sighed loudly. "God, Nik, are you serious? I've never felt like that in my life," he groaned into her ear, then traced his tongue around its edge. She giggled.

Still inside her, he rolled them onto their sides, and she threw her leg over his hip. He didn't want to pull out of his woman, not now, not ever.

They fucked like rabbits all afternoon, all over the house. It seemed impossible to Tony that he could be so turned on for so long and stay so damn hard, but it was undeniable – she had a powerful, almost magical effect on him, and when her body beckoned to him, his rose to the occasion. Nikki didn't deny him anything; whatever he wanted her to do, or wanted to do to her, she offered up to him like a gift, the best gift anyone had ever given him. When his fingertips grazed her trembling flesh, he felt as if he were touching a treasure to be cherished or abused at his will, one he'd never take for granted or hurt in any way.

As for Nikki, she'd never been with a man who satisfied her as completely as Tony did. He made love to her like she was a fragile china doll and then, ten minutes later, fucked her like she was a lusty bar room whore. Better yet, he seemed to know which to do and when. Whatever he asked for, she gave gladly; when she asked for more, harder, faster, he poured it on, and she took it and pleaded for more. She had never hurt so bad or felt so good, or felt so cherished and so used at the same time, and couldn't explain it, just enjoyed it, loved it, drank it in and wanted more. The simple sight of him stroking into her, the potency of his desire, unwound and unfettered, made her want him like she'd never wanted any other man. Exhaustion and energy mingled inside her, and she decided all she needed in life was sleep, food, and sex – more sex. With Tony, and only Tony.

Chapter Twenty-Four

The rest of the weekend had flown by. Tony had bound Nikki wrist to ankle, splayed her open for his viewing pleasure, and licked her clit with maddening flicks, but wouldn't let her come until she'd screamed out loud that she was his dirty slut. Thirty minutes later, he'd held her tenderly and made love to her like she was the only woman in the world and he was having a worship experience. Blueberries had been consumed off of each other's naked bodies, they'd fucked like animals on the balcony in the dark, and laughed as they told each other old stupid dirty jokes. They'd even managed to pull themselves together for dinner with Carter and Adelaide as they'd agreed to during the flight in, but they both would've preferred to stay in bed, and that's exactly where they went as soon as they got back from dinner.

The flight back on Monday was uneventful. Nikki had trouble walking without everyone knowing how sore she was, and Tony had admitted he didn't know men could get sore from sex, but apparently they could. He'd complained that his dick was raw, and Nikki had told him he sounded like a pussy – her pussy, specifically, which was suffering indescribably. And both had smiled while they were complaining.

They rode home from the airstrip and talked about the sex all the way to Nikki's house. It was refreshing to Tony to see how easy it was to talk about it with her, what they'd liked, what they'd like to do again, what they'd like to try, and it wasn't embarrassing or strained. Matter of fact, he had to admit she was easy to talk to about anything and everything. When they pulled up to the house, they both grew quiet. To him, the thought of leaving her there and not waking up beside her in the morning was almost more than he could consider. And he had more bad news.

She could tell something was bothering him before he ever spoke. "Out with it," she barked unceremoniously as they sat in the car, and he let go a deep sigh.

"Nik, the next month is going to be very hard. I don't know how much time we'll have together. It's the end of the fiscal year for the company, so it's also tax time. That means long work days, pulling lots of records, that kind of thing."

Nikki frowned. "Can I help?"

Tony's eyes widened and he smiled. "Actually, you might be able to, especially when it comes to pulling files, copying documents, sorting, that type of thing. Cheryl and I could always use an extra pair of hands."

"Then I'm your girl!" Nikki smiled.

Tony took her hands in his and gazed down into her face, the love and trust in those turquoise eyes making his heart nearly pound out of his chest. "But know that as soon as the Fourth of July rolls around, things will get better automatically. The tax issues and corporate filings are due June twenty-ninth, the last business day of the month, and my whole family will be here for the holiday. Then I'll be able to breathe. So can you hang in there with me for one month? I promise it'll get better after that."

Nikki leaned in and kissed him lightly. "Hang in there with you? Babe, I'm not going anywhere. I'm yours. Just promise me you won't forget me."

"Not a chance!" He wrapped his arms around her and pulled her to him. "There's no way that could happen."

She broke away from him suddenly and looked at him, her eyebrows almost disappearing into her hairline as his words sank in. "Wait – your whole family? Fourth of July? Is that what you just said?" She hoped she didn't look as terrified as she felt.

"Yeah. Since my mother wasn't born in this country, that's the holiday that's always been most special to her. She makes a big deal out of it, and she expects everybody, and I mean everybody, to be there. We all get together at the big house and have a huge dinner. About the only ones who don't make it are some of my nieces and nephews, but all of my brothers and their wives will be there, along with Mamma. And Vic comes too – as far as I'm concerned, he's as much or more my brother than my actual brothers."

"So, am I . . ." she started to say, then got embarrassed – she never asked to be included in anything, always waiting to be asked.

"Invited?" he finished her question. "You're not invited – you're the hostess." He smiled. "You're my baby!"

"Uh-huh. Your baby. So who fixes all of this food? Your baby?" She was afraid of the answer.

Tony threw his head back, laughing. "God no! Everybody helps. Mamma, Annabeth and Katie, Clayton and Brittany, I barbecue and grill, Bart and Freddie's wives fix food, Helene helps. Everybody pitches in. It's a lot of fun – you'll see. I look forward to it every year."

"That's something to look forward to – I really want to meet all of them," she told him, visibly relaxing.

He patted her knee. "They all want to meet you too. And I want to show you off!"

Changing gears, Nikki asked, "So where do we go from here?"

"We just get up in the morning and start again." He kissed her forehead. "The next month will be tough, but we'll make it. So tonight, let's get a good night's sleep and I'll see you tomorrow. Call you later, tell you goodnight. Going to pick up the dogs?"

"Naw, Annabeth said they were having a ball, so I told her I'd pick them up after the gym tomorrow."

"Sounds good. So let's get you settled in."

After they'd said goodnight and Tony had driven away, Nikki looked around the quiet house – too quiet. It seemed so empty with no Tony, not even the dogs. She puttered around for a little while, putting away this, straightening that, until she ran out of reasons to stay up. As soon as she got settled into the bed with her latest read, the phone sounded off – Tony's ringtone. She picked it up and hit ANSWER.

"Hey, baby, I love you!" she sing-songed into the phone before he had a chance to say anything.

"Hey, baby, I love you too! Would you do me a favor?"

"Yeah, sure! What?"

"Could you please go to the door and let me in?"

Nikki dropped the phone and jetted to the front door. And there he stood on the porch, his gym bag over his shoulder.

"Sorry. I couldn't stand being away from you. Can I come in?" He shrugged his shoulders, a shy smile on his face.

"Get on in here." She pointed into the house and swatted his backside as he walked past her, then closed the door behind them.

"I've got to get you a key," Nikki announced, lying back and gasping for breath. Tony had wrung three crazy orgasms out of her in less than thirty minutes, one with his tongue, the other two with his cock. The guy was insatiable, but so was she, so she wasn't about to complain.

"Yeah, I need to get you one to my place too." He reached over and tweaked her nipple. Shrieking, she tweaked his and laughed when she saw his cock jump. "And I need to show you where the key cabinet is. You need to know where everything is."

He held her face in his hands and she turned one hand over, kissing his palm softly. "You're an amazing lover, Tony Walters. I can't get enough of you."

"You're pretty amazing yourself. I'll be glad when June is over and we can move forward.," Tony snuggled into Nikki. "Morning's coming pretty quick. Nite-nite, princess." He kissed her on the forehead and she sighed as she tucked her head under his chin and drifted off.

"Dad, I need you over at the medical plaza project." Clayton sounded pretty irritated. Tony had only been in the office for about thirty minutes that morning, and already something was going wrong – he could just feel it.

"What's up, bud?"

"None of the equipment over here will run. Not one piece of earth-moving equipment, not a truck, nothing. If one wouldn't start, I wouldn't think anything of it. But everything? Something's not right. What do I do?" Tony could hear the frustration in Clayton's voice, and his heart sank.

"Call Richard, get a crew over there. Maybe he can figure it out." Richard was Tony's mechanic, and he was a whiz-bang at diagnosis. Then something from years back rolled through Tony's mind. "Did you by any chance find a gas cap lying around anywhere?"

"Funny you should ask. Yeah, I did, near one of the end loaders. Why?"

"Sugar in the fuel tanks – oldest trick in the book." Tony reached for his coffee cup and took a swig before standing. "Takes five minutes, ruins everything, sometimes permanently. And if it's not sugar, it's sand; just as damaging. I'll be there in a few minutes, Clayton. You can handle this, but I'll come over if it'll make you feel better."

"Yeah, I could use the moral support. Everybody's looking at me like they expect me to know what to do, and . . ."

"Say no more. I'll be there." Even though he had full faith in Clayton, the other employees didn't; Clayton was still very much in the process of proving himself to all of them.

Tony hit END on his cell and stalked past Cheryl's desk. "Sugar in all of the fuel tanks at the medical plaza project. I've got to go provide moral support for Clayton. When you want to go to lunch, just lock 'er up," he told her. He bounced down the front steps and climbed into the big truck. Cheryl watched him go, sad that he had to deal with the whole GoGreen mess.

By the time Tony got to the jobsite, Clayton had found something for everyone to do to keep them busy. One of Tony's rules: If they're on the clock, they should be doing something. "Richard here yet?" he asked as he walked up to Clayton, who looked frazzled.

"Yeah, and you were right. What do we do? We're at a standstill here."

"We call Sandusky Rentals, rent some equipment. If we can't get enough equipment, send the personnel overages to another site, but keep them busy. Did you call the cops?" Before Clayton could answer, Tony heard a commotion and looked back to see three police cruisers pull up.

The detective who showed up talked to Tony for over an hour. At that point, the police had been called to Walters sites so many times that they knew what to expect. The uniformed officers collected what evidence they could find, which was very little. They didn't even find empty sugar bags, but Richard provided them with fuel samples for analysis. Tony remembered to tell the detective, Keith Ford, about Detective Lynch in Lexington, and asked him to contact Lynch.

When Tony had done all he thought he could do, he turned to Clayton. "Well?"

"They're sending a good-sized fleet over – be here in about an hour. Thanks for being here." Clayton looked far more relaxed than when Tony had first walked up.

"Good job, son. I'm going to lunch. You can handle this – I have every confidence in you." He clapped Clayton on the shoulder and strode back to the truck.

Then he drove straight to The Passionate Pansy. Nikki was surprised when he walked through the door.

"Hey, baby! You're a wonderful surprise!" She came out from behind the counter and kissed him, and he hugged her tight, but her sharp eyes caught the strain in his face, and she frowned. "Everything okay?"

"No. Can you have lunch with me?"

"Um, probably. Hey, Marla!" Nikki called out to the back. "Can I go to lunch now?"

"Yeah, I guess . . . Hey, good-looking!" Marla broke into a huge smile when she saw Tony standing with his arms around Nikki.

"Hey, gorgeous! Can I steal the most beautiful woman in the world away from here for a little while?" Tony laughed.

"Sure! Let me get my purse!" Marla chuckled. "Oh, you mean her? Well, can't blame a girl for trying! Go, you two. Have a good time."

Once in the café with their lunches laid out in front of them, Nikki got straight to the point: "What's wrong?" He took a deep breath and told her about the morning. When he was finished, he took a bite of sandwich and chewed it absent-mindedly, his thoughts a thousand miles away.

"Well, this is getting stupid," she said, forking into her grilled chicken salad.

"I know, but they can't seem to find these people. And I'm not hearing about anybody else having a problem with them. It's starting to feel very personal."

"Yeah, I can see why it would." Nikki patted his hand. "Eat your lunch. We'll figure it out."

The next week passed without incident. Tony, Nikki, and Cheryl worked almost every evening on paperwork, and accounting came in to coordinate, bringing their list of needed documents. Cheryl did most of the work, but Nikki could tell it meant a lot to Tony to have her there and willing to help, and she could also tell why Tony valued Cheryl so much as an employee.

They worked that Saturday and Sunday too, trying to get all of the paperwork done. Even though they were exhausted, Tony and Nikki still managed to make love an hour or more a night; neither was willing to give that up. They'd exchanged keys, and she and the dogs went to his house, or he to hers, every night. They'd made it almost halfway through June, and the light at the end of the tunnel was getting brighter.

Until it just about went out in one fiery burst.

"God, baby, fuck me," Nikki whispered into his ear. The alarm was set for six o'clock, but he'd awakened a little before five with a raging hard-on and found his way into her while she was still half asleep. His firmness slid in and out of her languorously, and she reached down and attended to her clit while he clutched her ass and kept his slow, even rhythm. She started to moan softly and he felt himself readying to come when the phone rang. Without stopping, he looked at the clock – five forty-two. A glance at his phone made his heart almost stop – Clayton.

He speeded up his strokes, came quickly, and called Clayton back. Nikki groaned the groan of the disappointed – loudly. When Clayton answered, he yelled into the phone, "Dad! Oh god, where are you?"

"Nikki's. Clayton, what's wrong?" The panic in Clayton's voice made Tony sit upright in bed. "Are you okay?"

"Yeah, Dad, as good as I can be. But the Colufab project, not so much. It's a total loss."

Tony jumped from the bed, grabbing clothes. "Is anybody hurt?"

"No. Everybody's fine. But, Dad, I don't know what to do! I've never . . ."

At that point, Nikki was wide awake and trying to figure out what was going on. "Clayton, call the cops . . ." Tony started.

"I already have – they're on their way. The fire department is already here." The fire department? Again? Tony's heartbeat jumped to double-time.

"Son, I'll be there as fast as I can get there." Tony hit END and started pulling on clothes.

"What the hell's going on?" Nikki asked, her eyes still sleepy. "Is everybody okay?"

"Yeah, I think so." Tony zipped his jeans and reached for his boots. "But one of my jobsites isn't. Bastards hit us again." The stress in his face scared Nikki. "I love you, baby, and I'll call as soon as I can." He kissed her on the cheek and ran out the door.

Nikki lay back down and threw an arm over her eyes. She wanted to do *something* to help, but she had no idea what.

The smoke was visible from a couple of miles away. Tony felt sick to his stomach, fearful of what he was about to find. But when he pulled up, he was unprepared for the catastrophe that lay before him.

Everything was destroyed. Every piece of equipment was smoldering, as well as the construction itself. Someone had taken one of the earth movers, probably the big dozer, and knocked down the whole structure before setting it on fire. Three months of work, gone. Tony's mind went straight to the bottom line, and he realized their profit margin for the fiscal year was now shot all to hell unless an insurance settlement came through fast.

He found Clayton talking to Detective Ford. When he walked up and put his hand on his son's shoulder, Clayton turned, and the look on his face told Tony everything. "Detective, would you please excuse my son and me? We need to talk."

"Of course. I'll look around, help the uniforms for a little while. You guys take your time." As they turned away, Detective Ford winked at Tony out of Clayton's field of vision, and Tony managed a tiny smile in return.

"Get in the truck," Tony ordered, and Clayton obediently climbed into Tony's big F-250. Once inside, Tony turned to the silent young man, who looked genuinely fearful.

"Son, it's going to be okay." He put his hand on Clayton's shoulder. "*We're* going to be okay."

"But Dad, I'm so frustrated. I don't know what to do." Clayton turned to look out the window so his face was away from Tony.

"Look at me." Clayton turned, eyes downcast. "Hey, son – look at me!" Clayton finally met Tony's gaze, and Tony put both hands on his son's shoulders. "There's no script for a situation like this. I don't know what to do either. But I know this: We've got employees to think about. They depend on us; their families depend on us. We've got customers; they depend on us. And we've got family; they depend on us. So it's up to us. But we've got good people who want to help us, and we need to let them. And we've got our family, all of them. Trust me on this one – it's going to be okay."

Clayton nodded but didn't speak. "Look, son, we've lived through some pretty bad things." Dottie flashed through Tony's mind. "But we've made it out the other side. You're happy with Brit, Annabeth and Katie have each other, and I've got Nikki now; *we've* got Nikki now. No matter what happens to Walters Construction, *we're* going to be okay. Got it?"

Clayton nodded again, and he looked like he was settling down. Problem was, Tony wished he could convince himself that everything was going to be all right because, at that moment, it sure didn't feel that way.

Nikki came from the kitchen and answered Tony's door to find a very tall, very blond Viking of a man standing there. "You must be Nikki!" he drawled.

"Yes. And you're . . ."

He extended his hand. "Steve. Steve McCoy."

"Ah, Tony's attorney! Nice to finally meet you. Please, come in." Nikki gripped his hand tightly and opened the door wider, then stood aside while Steve's six foot four frame glided through the doorway. Nikki couldn't help but think he was one tall, good-looking drink of water. "Tony's not home yet. Want something? Beer? Tea? Wine?"

"Sure! I'll take a beer. Wow – something smells wonderful!"

"My meatloaf. One of Tony's favorites. Could you please stay and eat?" she asked, ever the gracious hostess.

"Oh, no, I couldn't impose . . ."

"No imposition. There's plenty. Please stay – he should be here just any time." Almost as though she'd prompted it, they heard the back door open and Tony strode into the kitchen. He had a worn look to him, and Nikki realized he was still in the previous day's clothes he'd slipped into at her house that morning. "Hey, baby!" she murmured in his ear as she hugged him. The smell of smoke draped over him like a cloak. After several calls from him during the day, she was painfully aware of everything that had happened and how irritated and dismayed, even discouraged, he was.

"Hey yourself," he whispered back, giving her a light kiss, then turned and shook Steve's hand. "Steve, man, glad you could come over."

"I'll do anything I can to help – you know that. Come talk to me." Steve pointed toward the den.

Nikki interrupted, hands on her hips. "Not just yet." She looked at Tony. "Dinner's about fifteen minutes out. Honey, you really need to shower, put on some fresh clothes. Take a break. I'll keep everything warm until you're done. Steve will help me out in here, right, Steve?"

"Yeah, sure!" Steve grinned. "I get to spend time with the pretty girl instead of the grumpy old guy!" Tony glared at him and stalked out of the room, the smell of smoke following him like an angry viper.

"So what do you have in mind?" Steve and Tony had settled into the leather seating in the den. Steve had a beer; Tony had poured himself a bourbon. Nikki was cleaning up the leftovers of the delicious meal she'd served them. Steve couldn't help but think what a lucky man Tony was, at least where Nikki was concerned.

"This whole thing feels like a personal attack to me. I think we need some protection. I want a security company to take over our sites, including the office. And I want my house, Nikki's house, and Clayton and Brittany's place all covered, too. Plus I want somebody specifically on Nikki, twenty-four seven." His hand shook as he raised the glass to his lips; he was exhausted, and it showed, not to mention how frightened he was for her safety.

"Doable. I don't have enough people to watch all of the sites, but we can mobilize your workforce for that. Find some people who are willing to do it and we'll do a little training for them. And I guess you want the guys following her to be, um, invisible?" Steve asked, tipping his head toward the kitchen. She didn't strike him as a woman who would want someone shadowing her.

"Absolutely. Matter of fact, I'm not planning to tell her." Tony swirled the bourbon in his glass.

"Are you sure that's a good idea?" Steve asked. "I mean, invisible is one thing, but without her knowledge? Once she finds out, and she *will* find out, she's going to be really, *really* pissed. Sure you want to deal with *that*?"

"No, but I'll take my chances to keep her safe. If she knows about them, she'll go into evasive mode. She's all about being independent, taking care of herself." Tony stopped for a second, then said, "And see what you can find out about this GoGreen bunch. The cops haven't had any luck, but I know you have your ways . . ."

"Say no more, big guy. I'll see what I can do."

"In the meantime, I'm going to arm her, make sure she knows how to use a gun. And make sure Clayton is carrying his too. I already know Vic's armed."

"Good move," Steve agreed, polishing off his beer. "And you realize that until this thing has played out, you've got to be careful when you're out in public."

"Yeah, I'd already thought about that." Tony sighed. "I'm thinking more about where I go and what I do these days."

"Good. See if you can instill that mindset in Nikki and Clayton. By the way, let me ask you this: Do you have any disgruntled employees? Or former employees?"

"I've thought about that," Tony answered, "but no, no one. I'm really at a loss here."

"What about Bart? Anybody bothering anything of his?"

Tony shook his head. "Not that I'm aware of, and I think he'd call and tell me if that was the case. So I don't think it's the family; I think it's just me.

I mean, I want somebody watching Clayton and Brit because of his ties to the company, but so far even he hasn't seemed to be a target; he doesn't have anything to do with the Lexington office. So I feel like it's personal, just against me."

"Angry, jealous woman?" Steve asked with a smirk.

"Only Dottie, and she's always wanting money, so I don't think she'd sabotage her only possible bank roll."

"See her much?"

"Nope. Not unless she wants something." Tony got a distant, wistful look. "Come to think of it, she's been really quiet lately. Must be lying in wait to strike," Tony said with his own smirk, the closest thing to a smile he'd come up with that evening.

"Like a big ol' bear," Steve growled. Tony nodded, looking down into his glass. "Or a big ol' elephant. You know they never forget." Steve's sarcasm was a welcome comic relief, and it made Tony chuckled. *I should invite him over more often,* he thought with a smile.

After Steve left, making sure to thank Nikki for dinner, Tony and Nikki walked arm in arm to the bedroom. While Steve and Tony had talked, Nikki had turned down the bed, run Tony a tub of hot water, and lit a couple of scented candles. Tony smiled when he saw the trouble she'd gone to for him.

"Go soak. I'll be here when you get out." She picked up her book and settled in the bed. Tony shuffled into the bathroom, stripped off, and dropped into the tub. God, the hot water felt good, and he was so shot.

When the water was tepid, Tony let it out, toweled off, and walked naked into the bedroom. He was at half-staff, and Nikki patted the bed beside her.

"Baby, I'm just not sure I've got it in me tonight," he groaned, trying to relax into the mattress. "What can I do for you?"

"Nothing. Not one thing. I want to do something for you, nothing in return."

"Oh, no, I can't let you . . ."

Nikki had always appreciated Tony's "she comes first" attitude, but not tonight. "You can and you will." Nikki stripped off her gown down to nothing but her panties. "My pleasure – literally. Now, lie back and close your eyes. Do not open them. And no matter what I do, the operative word here is 'relax,' okay?"

"I'll try." Exhaustion was so plain on his face that she couldn't understand how he could *not* relax.

She positioned herself between his legs. "I want your legs bent. Knees up, feet flat on the bed." He pulled his legs up. "A little more. That's good," she said as he moved his feet closer to his hips. Gripping his already-stiffening cock, it grew and hardened in her palm, and she went to work. Once he was agonizingly rigid, she took the head into her mouth and got busy. She found him delicious, musky and sweet-smelling and kind of savory, like fresh grass warmed by sunlight.

She stopped for a second. "I'm about to do something that's going to feel weird, but remember, relax, okay?" Tony nodded. "Keep your eyes closed, baby," she repeated.

She went down on him again, but she was doing something with her hands too – he couldn't tell what. He heard a snapping sound, then something chilly dripped down below his balls. Her hand was moving around and he knew the cold sensation was lube. She pressed something lightly against his entrance, and he tensed.

"Relax, baby. You're going to love this if you'll give it a chance." Tony took a deep breath, and Nikki rimmed the ring of muscles, then pressed firmly into the center. He remembered Cinda and her friend and tensed again. Her finger slipped in gently, then stopped to give him time to become accustomed to the stretch. The sensation was unnatural to him, but not really painful. *Relax*, he kept telling himself, *she won't hurt me*. She gently pulled her finger in and out until he had relaxed the muscles completely.

"Oh my god," he blurted out. "Your nails . . ."

"I told you, relax. Condom. I'm not going to hurt you," she answered. *My girl*, he thought.

Then she pressed her finger farther in, several inches, and he felt her doing something, moving her finger somehow. He wasn't sure what it was but, at first, it felt somewhat weird and uncomfortable. Then something odd happened – he felt himself getting harder, painfully so. Something knotted in his belly, and he recognized it as the tension of an orgasm building, but it didn't feel like it usually did. It had an urgency and power he couldn't have expected and hadn't experienced before. Nikki continued to suck and lick his cock, and she stroked inside him at the same time. It suddenly hit him: She was stimulating his prostate, and he tried to relax and enjoy the sensation. The longer she did it, the more he realized it wasn't really unpleasant, just unfamiliar, and the intensified arousal he felt was unexpected but damn welcome. It was more than her mouth on him; something erotically delicious was happening to him, and he felt warm all over. The vortex deep in his core started to double on itself, and he moaned out loud and wound his fingers into her hair, then held her head and began to fuck into her throat.

"Oh god, Nikki, I'm coming," he whispered hoarsely, then cried out again, "Oh, god, I'm coming!" Just as he felt his balls tighten and draw in, Nikki took her mouth from him and cupped her hand over the head of his cock, stroking his shaft just beneath it with her fingers as she rubbed her palm in a circular motion over its head.

Tony's whole body stiffened; his back arched, and he shook all over. "Ohhhhh, my god, ahhhhh!" he screamed, feeling a strange but wholly satisfying sensation as he felt pure liquid heat shoot from his cock. He gripped the headboard with both hands, and every muscle in his body hardened and strained. It felt like his cock would never stop pulsing.

"Aw, yeah, baby! That's it!" Nikki cried in encouragement. When his muscles finally stopped contracting, she gently drew her finger out of him and stopped stroking him with the other hand. "Honey, look. You've got to see this."

Tony looked down at his belly, and he was shocked – a puddle of cum lay in the middle of his six pack. He realized it probably wasn't as much as it looked like, but at first glance it seemed like a quarter of a cup or more, and it was still dripping from the palm of her hand. "Oh, fuck, did I do that?" he asked, astonished.

"Yeah, baby, you did!" Nikki looked very proud of herself. "How did that feel?"

"Amazing. Weird, but totally amazing. Where did you learn to do that?"

"From Randy's urologist. He said it's very good for men. It's called milking the prostate. Randy would never let me do it." She wiped his stomach with the towel. "Pretty good, huh?" He nodded. She crawled across him and pulled out a couple of the wipes he kept on his nightstand, then wiped his stomach down and cleaned up her hands. "And now," she ordered, throwing the wipes away, "you go to sleep. I hope I've managed to help you relax. This was my early Father's Day gift to you, baby. I want you to get some rest; I'm worried about you."

"Don't worry about me, princess. Just be here with me." Until that moment, Tony hadn't let himself admit how exhausted he was. "And that had to be the best Father's Day gift I've ever gotten," he whispered. Nikki turned off the light and curled up against him. In less than five minutes, he was out like a light.

She felt it building, building, building, until it finally broke, hitting like a tsunami. Wave after wave, the orgasm took her down, down, down . . .

Nikki's rocking pelvis woke her, and a tiny gasp escaped her lips. That didn't happen very often, but it was scrumptious when it did. She wondered what time it was, and opened her eyes to find Tony staring at her, a wide grin lighting up his face in the darkness of the bedroom.

"What are you doing awake?" she asked him, stroking the side of his face.

"You woke me up making some kind of sound. Did you just have an orgasm in your sleep?" he asked with a look of shock and delight.

"Yeah," she answered, sweeping his hair out of his face.

"I didn't know women did that." He started peppering tiny little kisses on her lips.

"Yeah. It. Happens. Sometimes. Not. Very. Often. But. Sometimes," she managed between kisses.

"Wow. I knew guys did that, but not women. That was very cool." He gave her his sexiest smile and added, "And I suppose it would be okay, since your portion of the show is over, if I gave you the grand finale?"

She gave him a sweet little kiss. "That would be awesome. Hey, what time is it?"

"Doesn't matter. It's just whatever time it is. Actually," he told her, pulling her to him, "I think it's time to fuck you, baby." They lay on their sides, and he drew her legs up and around his waist, then slid ever-so-gently inside her like silk on water. His strokes were slow and gentle, and she felt like she was being caressed from the inside out, so tenderly that she almost couldn't feel him moving. She wrapped her arms around his neck and he pulled her close, her breasts pressed against his chest, his arms wrapped around her tightly, and she could feel the possessiveness in his embrace. They passed tiny, warm, lovely little kisses back and forth between them like raindrops falling onto pebbles. She'd never felt safer or more loved, and he'd never loved anyone more in his life. They rocked against each other until they both came in a solemn, reverent swelling of desire, and then lay peacefully, his cock still inside her, until they fell back to sleep.

Chapter Twenty-Five

"Honey, did you hear me?" Tony's blank stare was fixed on something outside the window, and Nikki's voice brought him back.

He spun around in the desk chair and looked at her. "I'm sorry. What did you say?" he asked.

"I said, do you know where the receipts are for your trip to Owensboro in February? I found the entry in your planner, but not the receipts. They're not in with everything else, and I don't know where to look."

He rifled through his desk drawer and pulled out a folder. "Here." He handed her a wad of cash register receipts. "They were in with the information on the location."

She shook her head. "You were a thousand miles away. You okay?"

"Yeah." He motioned for her to come to him, then took her by the waist and pulled her onto his lap. "I'm just concerned. About you."

Her brow furrowed. "Me? What's wrong with me? Is something hanging out of my nose?"

He shot her a look and rolled his eyes. "Nothing's wrong with you — now. But these bastards, they want to get to me for some reason. And the easiest way to hurt me would be to hurt you. I don't want that to happen. If anything happened to you because of me, well, I'd die."

"Oh, nothing's going to happen to me — I'm too damn ornery!" She kissed his forehead. "I'm fine, and I'll stay that way. *I'm* worried about *you*. You're not eating right, not sleeping, just generally off. Look, June is almost over. We'll have the Fourth of July thing, and then let's go away for a weekend, please? Just get away from here?"

Tony smiled, the first time she'd seen him smile, except in bed, in a week. "Yeah, let's do that! I'd love to. We've got three days to get all of this finished up, and then the holiday, and we'll head out. Anywhere you want to go, anywhere at all."

"I'll think on it." She kissed him lightly on the lips, and he wrapped his arms around her waist and reciprocated with a long, deep kiss, his tongue buried in her mouth. She finally pulled away from him and slapped him playfully on the chest. "But if we don't get back to work, we're going to miss the deadline."

They'd missed going to the gym three days in a row, but the financials were almost done. Then they could take a deep breath. In seven days the big house would be full of family and fun. Tony was pretty sure he could hold on until then.

"Well, that's the last of it." Cheryl handed a stack of assorted paperwork-type mess to one of the accounting clerks, who promptly took off out the door.

"Whew! I'm exhausted!" Tony fell back on the sofa in his office. Cheryl plopped down in the chair in front of the desk and turned to look at him. She smacked him on the leg and he grinned.

"Let me tell you something, boss man," she said in her sassiest voice. "That little girl you've found? You'd better hang onto her. She's a keeper."

"Don't I know it! She's turned me upside down and wrong side out, and I keep coming back for more." He smiled so wide that his cheeks hurt. "Isn't she just the most gorgeous thing you've ever seen?"

"You know, Tony, she's not." He frowned at Cheryl's words until she said, "Not in the magazine-type beautiful category, you know? But there's something about her, something from the inside . . . the more you look at her, the more you're around her, the more beautiful she gets. It's like there's something ancient and mysterious in there, something dark and sweet and, I don't know, rich or something. Like she's made of dark chocolate and her blood is pure liquid gold. I hugged her one day and all day I felt warm and energized, like she'd rubbed something magical onto me." Cheryl had a dreamy, far-away look on her face, as though she wanted to say something but didn't quite know how.

"I know exactly what you mean. She has the same effect on me all the time." Tony stared at the ceiling. "I can feel her when she walks into the room. It's like the air changes. Like it's charged with something vibrant and energizing. Like I'm being drawn to her."

"So I take it everything's going good with the two of you? Even, you know . . ."

Tony grinned. "Oh, yeah. Everything's excellent. By the way, since we're here alone, I thought I'd tell you: I'm going to talk to Clayton and Annabeth before the holiday and, if they're okay with it and everything goes well with the family and all on the Fourth, I'm going to ask Nikki to move in with me."

"Oh, god, Tony, that's wonderful!" Cheryl gushed. "I'm so glad! Think she'll say yes?"

"I don't know why she wouldn't. We're together all the time at one house or the other, but I want her there with me, plus she'll be safer and not alone. And I think it's time."

"So you're thinking you want to make this relationship permanent?" Cheryl crossed her fingers.

"Yeah. If things keep going like they have been, she'll be Mrs. Walters by the end of the year if she'll have me."

"Oh, Tony! I'm so happy for you." Cheryl's her eyes welled. "You know I love you like a brother. More than anybody I know, you deserve a chance at happiness. And she's a smart one; she'll never let you go."

"You know I love you like a sister too. Thanks for loving me and supporting me in this. It means a lot. If I hadn't had you, Annabeth, Clayton, Vic, Cal, so many supportive people around me the last few years, I'm not sure I would've made it." Tony sat up straight. "It's been a long, hard journey. I think I'm finally coming to the end of it and maybe starting a new journey on a wider, smoother, better road."

"You've earned it, boss man, if ever anybody has." Cheryl smiled and slapped his knee. "Now, let's get the hell out of here!"

When they left the gym that night, Tony said he'd go to the store on the way to his house and pick up some fresh green beans for her to sauté for him – he loved the way she cooked them – and then he'd be right home. He'd seen the grey sedan sitting nearby, and when they pulled out of the parking lot, the sedan turned and followed Nikki, while Tony turned the other way and he drove straight to the store.

But when he got to the house, no Nikki. Her SUV wasn't there. She should've beaten him to the house with time to spare. He called her – no answer. That was when he started to panic.

He called the number Steve had given him, and a man answered.

"Stokes."

"This is Tony Walters. Who is this?"

"This is Peyton Stokes, sir, Ms. Wilkes' security detail. Where are you, Mr. Walters?"

"I'm at home. Where's Nikki?" A sense of dread had started to creep over him.

"She's about two cars in front of me, sir. I don't know what she's doing. She's been driving around kind of aimlessly for fifteen minutes now."

Tony was puzzled. "Where are you?"

"Just a few blocks from your house. I think she's headed that way now. But she's in my crosshairs, sir. I've got a constant visual on her."

"Okay. She's not answering her phone. I was just, you know . . ."

"I know, sir, but don't worry. She's never been out of my sight."

"Thanks, Stokes." Tony hit END and put down the phone. What in the hell was she doing?

Within minutes, he heard her SUV pull up. She hit the front door like a tornado and ran straight into his arms, shaking all over and dropping her purse smack on the floor.

"Baby! What's wrong? Where in the hell have you been?" He kissed the top of her head and held her tight, trying to stop her shaking.

"Oh, god, Tony! Somebody was following me!" she shrieked. She pulled back to look into his face, and he could see she was terrified. Then she started to cry.

"Yes, honey, someone is following you," He hugged her tight and she cried into his chest. Then he pushed her back and looked at her from under his brows. "Someone is following you, babe – someone I've paid to follow you. They're security. They're there to keep you safe."

Her head snapped back and she looked at him, an unfamiliar, wild look in her eyes. "What do you mean, to keep me safe? You've been having me *followed?*"

"Yeah. They're Steve's people, and they're really good at what they do. Former military, mostly."

"You've been having me *followed?*" she repeated, a little louder this time. "For how long?"

"Since the night Steve came to dinner."

A look he'd never seen before passed over her face, and her cheeks turned bright pink. "You've been having me followed and you didn't show me the courtesy of telling me? Oh, that's just spectacular! What happened to all that bullshit about expecting honesty from each other? You have the right to expect it, but not me? And, pray tell, why exactly is it that you didn't think it important enough, you didn't respect me enough, to tell me this? Why would you do this and not tell me?" She was practically yelling at that point, indignant and furious.

"Well, for exactly this reason. The way you're reacting right now."

The look on her face told him that was not the right answer.

"Oh, I see. Uh-huh. So now I can't take care of myself. So it's okay to have somebody follow me, without my knowledge, and scare the living hell out of me? What the fuck? Uh-uh, no. That's just wrong!" Nikki turned and picked up her purse where she'd dropped it on her way in. "No." She stormed toward the door.

"Nik, wait! Baby, I just want you to be safe, and . . ."

She waved him off and opened the door. "I'm going home. I'll talk to you later." She slammed the door behind her as she stomped out.

Oh, that went well, he thought. He ran to the front door in time to see her open the door of her SUV. She put one foot in, then turned, looked across the lawn, and yelled, "I know you're out there! I'm going home now! I'm sure you know where I live, so you can just follow me there and sit outside my house all night because I'm sure as hell not coming back here!" She got the rest of the way into the SUV, slammed the door, started it, and squealed out of the driveway.

He picked up his phone and dialed her number. It rang once, then went to voicemail; she'd declined his call. He tried again; same thing. *I'll just keep calling until she answers,* he thought. *She can't keep this up forever.* He called three more times, all with the same result. On the next attempt, she answered and screamed into the phone, "WHAT THE HELL DO YOU WANT?"

"I want to talk to you in a rational, calm manner."

"I'm in no mood for rational or calm! And I don't want to talk to you right now – I'm too mad!" She hung up again.

"Well," he said out loud to himself, "I think we're officially having our first fight."

Tony went into the den, poured himself a bourbon, and waited. He'd rather wait a few hours for a mad, live girlfriend to calm down than to wait a lifetime for a dead one to come back to life and blame him for her demise. He wouldn't be able to sleep without her anyway, so he'd just sit there and wait.

Peyton was about to get the jar out of the back floorboard to relieve himself in when he saw Nikki's front door open. She half walked, half stomped down the steps and down the walk, coming straight toward his car. He watched, astonished, as she crossed the street, walked around the front of his car, then knocked on the front passenger window. So much for staying invisible. He put the window down a crack.

"Unlock the door," she said matter-of-factly.

"But, ma'am, I . . ."

"Unlock the damn door," she demanded, her face totally unreadable.

Peyton hit the button; she opened the door and plopped down on the seat beside him, then closed the door behind her. "Here," she said, holding out a plastic container and a big cup. "Lemon and rosemary cookies and some herbal tea. Sorry – I don't have coffee." He didn't dare turn down anything she was offering him. He'd already seen her fury earlier and he sure as hell didn't want to be on the receiving end. If what had gone on inside was anything like the display he'd seen outside, he almost felt bad for Tony, but Peyton believed he'd brought it on himself, even though Peyton couldn't say so.

"Thanks, ma'am." Peyton took the cup and put it in the cup holder, setting the container of cookies in his lap.

"You're welcome. You already know my name – what's yours?"

"Peyton, ma'am. Peyton Stokes."

"Nice to meet you, Peyton Stokes," she said, staring straight ahead. "And I'm sorry. This isn't your fault. You're doing what you've been paid to do, and quite well, I might add. I tried everything I could to shake you, but I just couldn't lose you. Well done."

"Um, thank you, ma'am."

"What is it exactly that you've been paid to do?" she asked.

"Watch you. Actually, there are three of us. We take eight-hour shifts."

"I see. So you're just watching me. Knowing where I am, what I'm doing. That sort of thing."

"Yes ma'am. Making sure you're safe."

"Because?"

"Because Steve told us to. Because there's someone out there trying to hurt Mr. Walters, and the easiest way to hurt him . . ."

"Would be to hurt me. Yeah, yeah, I know, I know. He's already told me all of that. But tell me something: What do you think? You've done this before, right? What's your opinion on all of it?"

"It's not any of my business, ma'am. I've got a job to do. It's not about my opinion."

Nikki let out an irritated sigh. "So let's pretend for a minute that it is your business, and your opinion *does* count because I say it does," Nikki declared with a certain amount of force. "So, let me ask you again – what's *your* opinion?"

Peyton knew to choose his words carefully, but he still wanted to be honest with Nikki. She seemed smart and kind, and she'd been put in a very difficult position. "Well, personally, I think this is a really good idea. Steve's trying to find this group, find out exactly what they're up to, and if anybody can, it's Steve. But it seems to me, from what we know, that this is a personal attack. They're using ecological talking points as a smoke screen to go after Mr. Walters. You could inadvertently be his Achilles heel, if you know what I mean. He loves you, and hurting you would destroy him. And destroying him seems to be what they want to do."

"Do you have *any* leads on these people?"

"No ma'am. I'm afraid this is going to be a long, bumpy ride."

"And exactly whose call was it to keep from me the fact that you guys are following me around?" Nikki asked pointedly.

Peyton decided she didn't deserve to be lied to. "I'm not sure, but I *think* it was Mr. Walters' decision. I think he was afraid you'd do exactly what you did, try to shake me – which, by the way, can't be done." He grinned. "But I will tell you this: That man loves you. He's obsessed with keeping you safe from these people."

Nikki sighed and finally turned to look at him, and he grinned at her again. She couldn't help but notice how dazzling his smile was. "Thanks, Peyton. I appreciate your honesty. I'll probably go back to Tony's in a little while, after I get the dogs gathered up, so consider this your heads-up." She opened the door and got out.

"Yes, ma'am. Thank you, ma'am."

She bent over and stuck her head back into the car. "And that's Nikki to you. Enjoy the cookies." Closing the door, she crossed the street and walked back to the house.

Wow, Tony's got his hands full with that one, he thought as he sampled the cookies. *But if she can bake like this, she's worth it.*

It had been almost two hours when Nikki's ringtone finally sounded on Tony's phone. He braced himself, snatched it up, and answered soothingly, "Hey baby."

"Hi," he barely heard her say in a near-whisper. "Can I come back?" she asked, her voice breaking. "I'm sorry for the way I acted." She started to sob.

"Oh, baby, don't cry!" he said, his tone as gentle as he could make it. "*I'm sorry. Steve said I should tell you, but I knew you'd have a fit. I was hoping this would get resolved and you'd never have to know. I should've listened to him. I should've had more respect for you. I'm just so, well, hell, I'm scared. I'm terrified something will happen to you, and that would kill me." He waited. "Honey, please say something. Forgive me. Please?"

She started to cry harder, and he was afraid for her again. "Baby, everything's all right. Look, don't try to drive. I'll come over there, okay? I'll grab a few things and be there in a couple of minutes. Don't cry. Everything will be fine as long as we stick together. They want to hurt me, and if we're divided, it'll make everything easier for them. We've got to stay focused and on the same page, stick together."

He heard her trying to stop the sobbing, and she managed to say, "Okay." Then she cried out, "Oh, Tony, please, come and hold me!" and started sobbing again.

"Be there in a minute, love. It's all going to be okay."

When he opened the door, she flew into his arms and was still wailing. He held her so tight he was afraid he'd crack her ribs, and she clung to him like a child. When he realized she wasn't calming down, he finally picked her up and carried her to the sofa, choking and sobbing. They sat with her in his lap for what seemed like an hour, his fingers lovingly stroking her hair, her face buried in the warmth of his neck. With his eyes closed, the scent of her made him feel like he was sitting outside in the sunshine on a warm summer day. She finally quieted, with only an occasional sob escaping, more like a hiccup, and he could feel her relax.

Finally, he asked, "You okay?" She nodded against him. "We've got that under our belts now."

"What?" She sounded shaky and tired.

"Our first fight!" he chuckled. She kissed the side of his neck. "That was fun, huh?"

"No!" She sat up and glared at him. "It was awful. I was sick to my stomach. I don't ever want to be that mad at you again." She looked like she was going to start crying again, but Tony pinched her nipple and she smacked his hand. "Oh, no, sex will not get you out of this, buster. You've got some explaining to do."

"No, I don't. You know why I did this."

"Yeah, yeah, blah, blah, blah. Just don't do it again, please? Tell me everything. I don't like being scared for no good reason." She cuddled back down onto his chest.

"Okay, I promise. I'll never keep anything like this from you again. I just want you safe, that's all." He kissed the top of her head. She pulled herself up, faced him, and planted a hot, passionate kiss right on his lips. Then she forced his mouth open with her tongue, and stroked until his tongue met hers. She climbed astride his lap, and Tony felt his cock come to life under her.

He slid his hands under her top, got hold of the bottom edge, and pulled it over her head, then reached around and unclasped her bra, took it off, and threw it on the floor with her top. Attacking one nipple with his mouth, he took the other between his thumb and forefinger and she arched her back and gasped, her breasts swelling and rising toward him, then let out a raspy sigh. His teeth teased her hard peak, and he pinched the other one savagely, making her squirm on top of his growing hardness and moan. After a couple of minutes she put her hands on his shoulders and pushed him back, but Tony didn't let go, and her breasts stretched out painfully, then snapped back, bouncing softly when he released them. Nikki jumped up off his lap, grabbed his hand, and pulled him up off the sofa.

"Let's go." She grabbed her top and bra from the floor and led him toward the bedroom. "Makeup sex is the best. Come on!"

"I'm with you." And with that, he let her lead him down the hallway to heaven.

Did she ever get tired? Tony couldn't believe she was still riding him, or that he was still hard as stone. Even though he felt like he was going to blow his balls, he was concentrating on making her come again. Nikki had already exploded once, and he was determined to wear her out, even though he wasn't certain that could be done. Picking up his pace, stroking her clit as fast as he could, he watched her writhe and go wild, screaming and fucking him with an absence of consciousness that blew his mind. Nikki's pussy clamped down on his swollen shaft, milking his cock of every drop, and then she dropped onto his chest, limp and drenched in sweat.

Tony flipped her over and crawled down between her legs. His cum ran from her slit and down onto the sheets, but he didn't care; hell, he reveled in tasting himself all over her, his scent mingling with hers, creating a heady, intoxicating blend that rendered him very nearly mad. He slid his fingers up her slit, under her hood, and moved it up so her tender nub was completely exposed, then watched with glee as that one simple action caused her pussy to weep profusely. Nikki moaned and wound her fingers in his hair, then tipped her hips up so she was offering herself to him. Instead of using his tongue, Tony wrapped his lips around her clit and sucked. She cried out and shook. He continued to suck, occasionally running his tongue up and over the swelling bud, then sucking again. Knowing it was driving her nearly insane, he kept it up. She pulled his hair ever so slightly, and he attacked with greater gusto, sucking hard, making her hips shiver and buck. As he drew the tiny nub into his mouth, it hardened and lengthened like a tiny cock, and Tony could feel his own hardness readying to take her. He stopped for a minute to adore the root of her arousal and blew on it gently; it was beautiful, an exquisite pearl in its soft, lovely shell. Nikki gasped when his breath hit her sweet spot, then moaned long and low, and Tony went back to work. Her hips started to thrust and her moans turned to a continuous, guttural sound that told him she was getting closer.

Nikki's thrusting became more frantic and she cried out, "Tony, I'm coming! Oh, god!" He could tell she was there – almost. Then he stopped.

Nikki looked down at him, confused. "Whaaaa . . . what are you doing?" she cried out.

"What's wrong, baby?" His voice was as smooth as warm syrup.

"Oh, god, I need it. Please!"

"Okay," he said simply, and started back in, sucking and pulling on her clit, harder and more vigorously than before. Her hips started to thrust again, and her moans got louder. Tony could tell she was right at the edge of her orgasm, and he stopped again.

The look on her face was a mixture of confusion and frustration. "What are you doing?" she practically screamed. "Are you kidding me? Tony, give it to me! Please! I want it so bad."

His voice was cool and detached. "Want what?"

"Sweet mother of god, what are you trying to do to me?" she whined. He watched her belly shake with orgasmic tension.

Tony grinned up at her; she didn't look amused. "What's wrong, sweetheart? Something bothering you?"

Nikki threw her head back on the pillow and arched her back. "Make me come or I'll take care of it myself. I can't stand this."

"Sure that's what you want?" he asked again in an ominous tone.

"Yes! God, yes. I need it," she whimpered.

"As you wish," he replied calmly and tucked into her. He sucked her clit back into his mouth roughly, and she screamed and thrust her hips toward his face. As he sucked, he ran his tongue up and down the center of the enflamed bud, and her screams got louder, her thrusts more violent. Grabbing her hips, he held them down, which made her cry out more frantically and thrash wildly as he continued to suck and lick, hard. Nikki's hands wound into his hair again and she pulled a handful while he sucked as hard as he dared, so hard that his teeth raked her tender nub. Her back arched impossibly high, and she screamed his name as she fought to thrust, her hands grabbing the headboard, her biceps straining, every muscle in her body coiling like a cobra ready to strike. Tony didn't let up, and the waves of her orgasm consumed her, burning through her like wildfire. Nikki shrieked incoherently as Tony continued to tug and suck, and she begged him to stop, to turn her hips loose, to take his mouth off of her, but he wouldn't. Finally, her voice turned to a hoarse whisper, her body convulsing uncontrollably, and Tony stopped.

Nikki didn't move or make a sound. Tony propped himself up on her thighs, leaned down, and kissed her clit, by then swollen and enormous, rising up and out from under its hood. When his warm lips touched it, her hips jumped. He kissed up her soft belly, over her navel, up her ribcage, first one nipple and then the other, and up her chest and neck, watching the twitching as he touched each spot, until he reached her mouth, claiming it with his tongue. Nikki kissed him back and whispered, "Please, baby, I need you inside me."

His dark, hot cock throbbed for her, and he knelt between her legs, wrapped his arms up and under her knees, and lifted her up to him, then slid into her. She was so wet that there was no resistance, and he fell into a perfect rhythm with a singular purpose; to fill her masterfully and forcefully, control her body and soul, and to remind her that, beyond any doubt, she was his and his alone. The sight of his bulging pecs set her heart racing and lit her skin on fire. When she moaned and stiffened, he pumped her harder and faster, smiling with satisfaction as he watched her lose all control. Within seconds the orgasm ripped through her and she came violently, crying out his name over and over and reaching for him. Tony pounded into her until he yelled out, "Oh, baby, fuuuuuck me!" and filled her so full of his hot essence that he was sure he'd soaked the sheets. He fell backward onto the bed, spent to the point that he wasn't sure he could move.

Silence filled the room; only their breathing stirred it. Tony finally pulled himself together enough to crawl up the bed and wrap his arms around her. Nikki kissed his chest and teased the triangle of dark hair there, then buried her nose in it and breathed his scent in deeply.

"Still mad at me?" Tony whispered.

"For what?" Nikki asked, weak and drenched in sweat.

"Best answer in the world." He kissed the top of her head and heard her let out a long, satisfied sigh just before she dropped off.

Tony looked down at the sleeping woman in his arms, her head on his chest, her hair crazy and draped across his arm like fine brocade. Morning light was seeping in around the drapes and blinds in her little bedroom, but the alarm clock hadn't gone off yet, and Nikki was sleeping the sleep of the dead. With great tenderness he pushed a lock of hair off her forehead, and she opened one sleepy eye and looked up at him. The smile he gave her was full of so much adoration that it made her smile back.

"Are you watching me sleep?" she asked in a whisper.

"Yes. You know, this is my favorite time of the day."

"Morning? You like morning best?" She stretched against him.

"Yeah. I love waking up with you in my arms, your head on my chest, your soft, even breathing. It's so quiet and peaceful, and for those few minutes there's no one in the world but you and me. I love it – I love you. There's nowhere else in the world I'd rather be." He kissed her on the forehead.

She kissed his chest. "I love you too. I don't ever want to wake up and find myself without you."

"I wanted to talk to both of you before the holiday." Tony was supposed to be working out in the garage's home gym on Saturday morning, but Clayton had stopped by, and Tony had dragged him into the garage; then he called Annabeth and put her on speakerphone. "There's something I want to do, and I wanted to get your opinions before I do it."

Clayton nodded. "Okay. Let's hear it."

"I'd like to ask Nikki to move in with me. How do you guys feel about that?"

There was silence. Then Annabeth made a sound – was she crying? He looked at Clayton, whose eyes were turning red. Tony's face was crestfallen. "Geez, is it that bad an idea?"

"Oh, Daddy!" Annabeth gushed. "I love her so much. I feel like I might finally have a shot at having a real mom!"

Tony looked at Clayton, and his son managed a hoarse, "Yeah, what she said." He cleared his throat and looked away.

"Well, by god, why didn't you two tell me this before? I'm planning to ask her the afternoon of the party, after everybody's gone. I want to make sure she can handle the whole family. So it's a go for you two?"

"Absolutely." Clayton's answer was strong and clear. "I wish you guys would have us over more often too. I'd really like to spend more time with her. So would Brit. I'm not so sure what kind of grandpa you're going to make, you old fart, but I think she's going to make a wonderful grandma." Tony shook his head and grinned.

"Katie and I feel the same way, Daddy. Please, don't let her get away. Our family needs her," Annabeth sniffled.

Tony was astonished – and very relieved. "Okay, it's settled. You're getting a new mom. I haven't asked yet – it's still a few months away – but I'm hoping we'll be married by the end of the year." Annabeth squealed, and Clayton cracked a wide grin. "And I think she'd love to spend more time with all four of you. She's crazy about you guys, but I think she's kind of hanging back, afraid to get too close because she's not sure where we're going with this. I'll fix that on the Fourth."

One thing was sure: This was going to be a holiday for the Walters family history book.

As Nikki toweled her hair after her shower, she watched Tony dressing in the other room, her heart slamming against her ribs. He had his back to her and his shoulders rippled as he moved, the muscles playing against each other as he pulled a shirt from the closet, looked at it, then put it back and chose another. Watching him move was like watching sunlight on water, or watching a stand of silver maples on a breezy day. It made her sigh with longing and set her pulse dancing. If she lived to be a thousand, she'd never get enough of him.

"Where are we going?" she called out to him. They'd both taken a half day off in anticipation of the holiday. The next day would be prep for the party on the Fourth, and they both needed a little extra time for all of that.

"I'm taking you to the gun range." He buttoned his shirt as he walked toward the bathroom. "I want to teach you to handle a gun. I'll feel better if I know you can protect yourself if you have to."

"Okay." She bent forward with the blow dryer and turned it on. She heard him say something over the racket and turned it off. "Did you say something?"

"Yeah, I asked aren't you going to argue with me about it?" He looked puzzled.

"Why would I do that?"

"Well, I may be a liberal, but you make me look right-wing. I thought you'd be anti-gun." Her heart nearly stopped at the sight of him leaning against the door facing, his arms crossed. Sometimes she still had trouble believing that this man was hers.

"Nope." One simple word. She didn't elaborate, which he thought was very uncharacteristic for her. Something was amiss, but he couldn't figure out what.

"I thought I'd start you out on something small and lightweight, like maybe a nine millimeter or a three-eighty." He stopped and waited for the backlash.

"Okay," she replied again. *Something's just not right here,* he thought. *She's taking this far too well.* But he still couldn't put a finger on it.

Once they'd gotten dressed, Tony pulled the Yukon around to the front and waited. Nikki came out of the house, and she was carrying a good-sized box that looked something like a toolbox. She knocked for him to put the tailgate up and she stowed the box in the back before she climbed into the front seat beside him. "What's in the box?" he asked her.

"Stuff." She didn't say anything else.

The range was quiet for a Monday afternoon, with only one other station in use. Tony led her down the hallway to the door of the range they'd paid to use, and held it for her to go inside. She was carrying the box he'd seen her stash in the back of the Yukon. He asked her again, "What's in the box?"

"Stuff." That was all she said. He couldn't figure out what it could be. It looked like a sportsman's box of some kind, but he wasn't sure what.

Tony had carried in a double-sided pistol case and a carton of ammunition. He opened one side of the case and took out a beautiful Heckler & Koch nine millimeter. Nikki gasped.

"Baby, don't be afraid of it. Guns won't hurt you; ignorance of guns will hurt you. So I'm going to show you how to hold it, how to load it, how to shoot it, and then how to clean it. That's the most important part. It's important to keep your weapon well-maintained so it works properly when you need it."

"Oh, I always keep my weapon clean," she countered with a smirk.

"Yes, you do," he replied, smirking back. She tried to look away, but he saw her grin.

"Okay, watch me." He shoved a loaded magazine up into the grip, racked a round into the chamber, and held it out for her to look at. "Want to try it?"

Nikki looked at him for a second. "Sure." Then she stopped and looked at him pointedly. "But wasn't there a sign about eye and ear protection?"

"Yes. That's important. I thought you might want to practice loading it and chambering a round. But we can go ahead and put on our protective gear if you want to." He opened the case again and produced a pair of safety glasses for her, then handed her some ear plugs. He had some for himself as well and, when everything was in place, he held the gun out to her. "Here you go. All ready for you."

Instead of taking it, she reached into her pocket and laid a full magazine on the bench in front of them. Then, before he could process what was happening, she reached into the back of her jeans, pulled out a pistol, flipped off the safety, took her stance, and started firing at the target. Eight spent shells flew onto the floor. When the pistol was empty, she ejected the magazine, picked up the one on the bench, slammed it in, racked a round into the chamber, and started firing again, sending seven more projectiles into the target.

Tony stood stock still and his jaw dropped. *What the hell?*, he thought. She turned to him and simply said, "No thanks. I have my own."

He couldn't say anything; he couldn't think of anything to say.

"Close your mouth, baby, you're catching flies." Tony hadn't realized his mouth was hanging open, and he snapped it shut. "Now, I'm sorry, honey, what was it you wanted to teach me?"

"Apparently nothing," he answered, embarrassed as hell.

"Okay." She ejected the second magazine and reached into the box she'd brought with her to get more ammo. She started reloading the magazines, keeping an extra round out to replace the one she would chamber.

"Where the hell did you learn to do that?" he asked, still stunned.

"Randy was a competitive shooter. Me, I just like the guns."

"Okay, so what have you got in that box?"

"Oh, stuff. More ammo," she said matter-of-factly, "cleaning supplies, my custom Browning shooting glasses, my favorite ear plugs with strings, things like that."

Everything had happened so fast that he really hadn't had a chance to see what she'd pulled out of her jeans. He reached for the pistol; a Walther PPK-S with custom grips. "Nice piece," he said.

"You've told me that before, darling," she purred. He winced.

"Got anything else in your arsenal?" he asked sarcastically.

"Yeah, matter of fact, I've got another three-eighty, a vintage Browning. I've also got Randy's Smith & Wesson nineteen-eleven which, in case you didn't know, is a forty-five." When she said that, he shot her a dirty look. "Plus a Rossi thirty-eight special rated for Plus P, and a nine millimeter Glock 19. Oh, and enough ammunition to last a couple of years. And I've got middle-of-back carry holsters for everything except the nineteen-eleven. Bastard's too heavy to carry." She looked at the H&K. "That thing's beautiful. Is that your carry gun?"

Tony looked a little disappointed. "No. I carry a nine millimeter Ruger." He pulled it from his holster and showed her, then put it back. "I bought the H&K for you, as a gift. I guess you probably don't want it though."

"Want it? I love it! It's a beaut. Mind if I shoot it?"

He looked relieved. "No, of course not. It's yours if you want it."

She stopped and stared at him for a second. "Tony, that's the first gift you've ever given me. Do you realize how fucked up that is? My first gift from you is a gun to protect myself from some wing-nut who's trying to hurt or kill you and/or me. That's fucked up."

"Yeah, that is fucked up," he agreed. "I take it back. You can't have the gun – not yet. I'll loan it to you now, and you can have it after I've given you something better first."

She laughed. "That's fucked up too. Okay, so you shoot the H&K. I want to see it in action."

Tony pulled the target up to change it. Damn, the girl had fired all fifteen rounds into the kill zone. They hadn't all gone into the bull's eye, but they'd all been in the critical range. He put up a new target and sent it to the wall. Then he pulled the weapon up, stared down the sights, and started pulling the trigger. Casings flew, and Nikki watched with an appreciative eye.

She pulled the target in and took a look. Every shot was well within the inner ring of the bull's eye, and she let out a whistle. "Wow, you're good."

"Thanks. You're pretty damn good yourself. I feel much better now." Knowing she could protect herself gave him some relief.

She grinned up at him. "Good. Let's sling some lead, shall we?" she shoved a magazine into her Walther and sent a target back down range.

After a full hour of target practice, they packed up and headed for the Yukon, stowing their gear in the cargo deck. Tony was about to close the tailgate when impulse hit and, with no warning, he grabbed Nikki by the waist and pushed her up onto the cargo deck, squealing, then jumped in behind her and pulled the tailgate down. "Tony! What the hell?" she laughed.

He grabbed the front of her jeans, unbuttoned and unzipped them in record time, then peeled them off of her and tossed them aside. "Watching you shoot like that made me very, very horny. And I intend to do something about that right now," he snarled, snatching her panties off. She squealed again and laughed. Tony unbuttoned and unzipped his jeans, reached inside his boxer briefs, and pulled out a full-blown hard-on. The look he gave her was so scorching that she felt the heat to her core, and he came after her like a panther on the prowl. He crawled on top of her and pinned her to the deck with his body weight, and she leaned in and bit him on the shoulder. At that little erotic show of power, he ran a hand up her back, grabbed a handful of hair, and held her head still so he could stare into her eyes.

Nikki leveled her gaze at him and growled, "Fuck me, tiger," and Tony tore into her like a hurricane, ramming her with all the force he could muster. She was pretty sure she'd be bruised the next morning, but she didn't care one damn bit. It was so unlike him, so spontaneous, that Nikki was consumed by the pure, raw desire he was pouring into her, and she met his every stroke with churning hips and piercing cries until she was breathless. Wrapping his hands under her ass and pulling her pelvis into him, he pounded her until she screamed out an orgasm and he came deep inside her, winded and trembling.

"Son of a bitch – that was fucking awesome! What came over you?" she asked as he lay on top of her, both of them still panting.

Without looking at her, he wound his hands into her hair, pulled her head back, and kissed up and down her slender neck. "Watching you handle that gun, handle yourself, so forceful and graceful, hit me down deep. I had to take you; I couldn't wait." He kissed on down her neck, then worked his way up her cheek and back down to her mouth. When his lips touched hers, he gave her a solid, searing kiss and stared down at her, looking very proud of himself.

A tiny smile turned up the corners of her mouth. "Can we come to the range every day?"

"Anything you want, princess. Anything you want."

"Where are we going?" Nikki asked Tony as he led her down a small path behind the big house. After they'd pulled themselves together in the parking lot of the gun range, they'd picked up Bill and Hillary and driven to Shelbyville to stay the night; that way they'd already be there the next day for the holiday. Tony held her hand as they walked down a little path in the late afternoon sunlight and, to Nikki, it looked for all the world like he was leading her out into the woods.

"You'll see." They rounded a curve on the little trail and came out into a clearing. Nikki gasped.

A little gazebo, white and pristine, stood at the edge of a glassy pond, the only occasional break in the pond's surface made by water bugs. A few birds were calling in the trees nearby. On the gazebo were two settees, and Tony sat down, then drew her onto his lap.

"I hope you didn't think I'd lost my mind, but watching you at the range today firing that pistol was extremely hot," he moaned, kissing her.

"Not at all. Watching you do *anything* is extremely hot." She kissed him back harder. "So what is this place?"

Tony kissed her again. "I designed this little corner of heaven." When he said it, he had a far-away look on his face.

"Really? Why?"

"Because I had a dream once. I dreamed I was making love with a beautiful woman in a place that looked exactly like this. So I was familiar with the clearing and decided to make the place real, even if I didn't have the woman. I've never brought another soul out here – never. I used to come out here when things were really bad and imagine the woman was here with me.

Sometimes when the kids went to Mamma's, I'd even come out here and sleep just to have some peace. It was my refuge, a place to hide." A softness came over his features. "And look. Here I am, with the woman of my dreams."

"And you're making her dreams come true too," Nikki whispered to him and kissed him.

"I certainly hope so. Mine have definitely come true. I never thought I'd have this, ever. I just wanted to bring you out here, you know, make the dream a reality." Tony pulled her closer, and Nikki rested her head on his shoulder, letting his strong arms soothe her. When he turned his face to her and kissed her again, it reminded Nikki of a high school junior kissing his freshman girlfriend, a sweet, soft little thing full of longing.

They sat like that until almost dark. All of a sudden, he slapped at his arm. "Shit! Damn mosquitos! Guess we'd better get inside before they carry us away."

Nikki stood and reached for his hand. "We need to get some rest before tomorrow's prep anyway. We'll be exhausted by Wednesday night."

"I think everything is as ready as we can get it," Nikki told Tony as she stood in the kitchen on that evening, looking around.

"Then I guess I'll lock up and we'll call it a day," He shuffled off to lock the front door. Nikki turned to lock the back door, then turned off the kitchen lights. As she passed the island in the middle of the kitchen, a pair of strong hands grabbed her around the waist and lifted her onto the island.

"Yeesh! You scared the bejesus out …" she tried to say, but Tony covered her mouth with his and kissed her – hard. When he pulled back, she was breathless. "Wow, that was …" and he gave her a repeat performance, this time running both hands up under her top and peeling it off, then unbuttoning and unzipping her shorts. "You're . . ."

"Determined to have you. Right now. Want it? Say yes, baby," he murmured into her neck, then kissed her again, sucking her lower lip in between his.

"Yesssssss," she moaned, and he dug his fingers into her waist and picked her up. She promptly wrapped her legs around him, her arms clasped around his neck. They made it as far as the dining room table, biting each other's lips, tongues lashing into each other, before he sat her down on it, yanked her shorts off, then peeled off his tee and jeans. He climbed up onto the table with her and stared down at her in the darkness, his eyes intense, almost glowing.

"I should take you right here," he hissed into her ear, then bit her neck. Instead of making it easy for him, Nikki managed to wriggle away from him and took off running, giggling the whole time.

She made it as far as the foyer. Tony caught up with her, grabbed her around the waist, and spun her to look at him. "You're not getting away this time, little girl," he snarled at her. "I've got you and I'm not letting you go." This time, he reached around her and snapped the hooks of her bra loose, then locked his fingers into his boxer briefs, slid them down, and stepped out of them. Nikki purred when she got a glimpse of his cock, hard and waiting. He snatched her lacy hipsters off, then lifted her up again, and she wrapped her long, sculpted legs around his waist.

She wanted to kiss him again, long and slow, but before she could say or do anything, Tony wrapped his hands under her ass, lifted her a little higher, and impaled her on his rigid cock. Nikki stifled a scream as he bored into her pussy and showed no mercy, and Tony groaned and wedged her between his body and the wall, pistoning into her like a four-stroke engine as he held her there. He bit her neck again and, in turn, she bit his shoulder just like she'd done in the back of the SUV earlier in the day. He moaned into her ear, "I just wanna fuck you until I can't fuck you any more. You are so goddamn sexy that you make me crazy for you."

"Then fuck me," she whispered back. "Fuck me hard. Just pound me until I scream for you to stop."

"Like I'd listen," he snickered and tied into her. His mouth found hers, and he kissed her so hard that she was sure he'd bruised her lips, then he latched onto her neck again and kissed, sucked, and bit it until she was nearly mad. He worked fast and hard, enjoying her cries against his collarbone, the pulses of her hot, wet sheath around his cock, and the hardness of her rigid peaks against his chest. He wished he could stop time or at least pause it, make a mental picture of them together, freeze the intensity of the sparks she gave off as her flint and his stone came together, as one's body burnished the other's to brilliance in that moment, so he could always recall it. Wanting to capture it all so he could enjoy it again later, sit in his office and think about it, picture her in his mind while he was at a jobsite, dream about her as she lay beside him sleeping in the night, he listened to her, soaked in the feel of her skin. He waited as long as he could before he poured himself into her in a gasping, moaning thrust that tuned her up until he was sure that Helene could hear them, even down at her house. Hell yeah, he hoped she could.

His possession of her body was too much for Nikki, and she tightened and came around him, screaming out, her fingers in his hair. When he stopped, she leaned in and locked her lips onto his, holding his face against hers until she couldn't breathe. "Sweet mother of god, babe, what's gotten into you today?" she panted when she finally broke the kiss.

"You. You're under my skin. Permanently. And I'm not complaining – not at all!" He laughed, then kissed her again. "I think it's about time I started living a more spontaneous life, stop planning everything out to the letter, start fucking you when I want, where I want, how I want, and making you want it too. And do you want it?" he asked with a seriousness that startled her.

"Want it? God, I crave it. Just cut loose!" She laughed back and kissed him.

He turned and carried her up the steps. "Let's go finish this in the bedroom. I'll show you 'cut loose!'"

Thirty minutes later, she was still overwhelmed with his pressure inside her, his big, dark hands on her pale skin like molten lava, molded to her, pouring over her, twisting and pulling her nipples, flicking and stroking her clit. The sight of him above her drove her to the edge until his eyes closed and she saw that look on his face that said he was lost in ecstasy, lost in her. That look was all she needed; her own need consumed her and, as he buried himself in her over and over, she rasped her clit against his pelvis and came, repeating his name like a prayer. Within seconds, he groaned out his own climax. The liquid fire of his seed filled her and when he dropped down beside her, she fell onto his chest, panting and moaning. His arms encircled her and tightened against her skin, and she'd never felt so desirable or so loved, so satisfied and so hungry for more.

"Are you trying to kill me?" she asked as he burrowed his face into her hair and kissed the top of her head.

"Yes. Death by sex," he chuckled as she licked his nipple.

"Correction: Death by great sex. Big difference," she giggled as he kissed the top of her head again. "But what a way to go!"

Chapter Twenty-Six

"Hi! Where should I put this stuff?" Nikki turned to find a man standing in the foyer on Tuesday morning. He didn't look familiar except for one thing – he was definitely a Walters. Slightly older, what hair he still had white, and even with a beard and mustache, he was still clearly a Walters. He was shorter than Tony and stockier. Picking up on the startled look on her face, he asked, "Nikki? You must be Nikki. Hi, I'm Bart."

"Oh!" Nikki came back to herself. "It's nice to meet you! Let's take it all in the kitchen. Gracious, what is all of this?" She stared at the boxes he carried in.

"Well, let's see." Bart started pulling things out of the boxes after he'd set them down. "Kathy made her potato salad." He dragged out an enormous container of the stuff. "This is . . ." he said, opening a corner of another container, "deviled eggs. And this is her homemade barbecue sauce Tony asked for." He opened the other box and pulled out several stacked trays. "And these are Molly's infamous rolls. She sends them every year. I stopped by their house and picked them up so you'd have them in the morning."

Tony walked into the kitchen and yelled, "Bart!"

"Hey, Tookie!" The two men embraced, then slapped each other on the back.

"Nikki, I assume you've met Bart the Fart?" Nikki grinned – guys!

"Yes, in the foyer." He smiled widely. "Nice to finally meet you." He stuck his hand out, then said, "Aw, hell," and hugged Nikki – he even felt like Tony! She hugged him back. "Kathy is really excited about meeting you, can't wait. We're all so happy for you guys. Well, except for Bennie. And Molly, of course."

Nikki looked at Tony, puzzled. "Don't worry," Tony told her. "It's just Molly. She hates everybody." Bart nodded in agreement. *Great,* Nikki thought.

Bart smiled. "So that's the only reason I came. Long drive for not much, huh?"

"Come on in here and at least have a beer with me." Tony slapped his older brother's back.

"That's really why I came – I was hoping you'd say that! Makes the trip worthwhile." Tony handed him a bottle from the fridge and the two men retreated into the great room.

Nikki looked everything over, then managed to fit all of it into the huge refrigerator. She couldn't help herself – she got a spoon and sampled the potato salad. It was scrumptious, and she decided she couldn't wait to meet Kathy either.

After feeding Bill and Hillary, she cleaned up some of the odds and ends around the kitchen. She was thinking about going on upstairs when she heard Tony and Bart in the foyer. Bart called out, "Bye, Nikki honey – nice to meet you!"

"Same here, Bart. See you tomorrow!" She heard the door close and Tony strolled into the kitchen, empty beer bottles in hand.

"So you've met Bart! What do you think?" he asked her, dropping the bottles into the recycling bin under the sink.

"I think if the rest of the bunch are as nice as he is, it'll all be fine," she smiled, wringing out her dish cloth and hanging it inside the cabinet door.

"Yeah, they are. Well, except for Molly. She's a bitch, but then she's always been a bitch, at least for as long as I can remember, so it's no big deal. Sometimes we actually torment her to bring out more of her bitchiness so we have an excuse to double our efforts." He stopped for a minute, unsure if he should say anything, and then added softly, "And then there's Bennie."

"The youngest, right?" He'd been quizzing her for two weeks on the siblings' and spouses' names, and she was about to get them all down – at least she thought she was.

"Yeah."

"What's that about?"

Tony shook his head. "Wish I knew. Right after I graduated from college and went into the business, and he had started college, he kind of turned on me. When we were together he was at my throat constantly. At first I thought it was just me, but everybody else started noticing it too. I even asked him why he was so mad at me, and he never really answered me, just kind of told me I was nuts. But he can barely stand to be in the same room with me. I've wracked my brain over the years and I can't come up with one single thing

I've ever done to him. To make matters worse, I'm the only person in the family who's ever been the least bit kind to his wife, Caroline. Everybody seems to dislike her except me, Annabeth, and Clayton. You'd think he'd be grateful that I try so hard to be there for her, but it hasn't made things any better at all. He still hates me." Tony was looking at his shoes while he talked, and Nikki realized Bennie's animosity toward him really bothered him.

"Why does everybody despise Caroline?"

"They think she's weird. But she's actually very nice, just kind of quiet and withdrawn. She had a terrible childhood and I don't think she trusts people very much. But she's always been kind and warm to me and the kids. I guess she felt sorry for us, what with Dottie and all. So please, try to go out of your way to be nice to her, okay?"

"Oh, babe, you know I will." She shot him a sad smile. "I know what it's like to feel like you have no one in your corner, remember?" She walked up to him, slid her arms around his waist, and laid her head on his chest. His arms came up and squeezed her tight to him.

"I feel like it's my job to make sure you never feel like that again." He kissed her hair.

"Thanks, baby, and I'm grateful for that. Now, let's pack it in, shall we?"

"Sure. Let me lock up." Tony went into the foyer and armed the alarm system. He looked out the side light and could see the car at the crest of the hill, and he felt better knowing that Peyton, or José, or Laura were out there watching the house for the night.

Nikki woke up before the alarm went off at six o'clock on Wednesday morning and went into the bathroom. She caught sight of herself in the mirror and was startled to see that her belly was flatter than it had been a couple of weeks before. *Must be true,* she thought. *Sex is good exercise, especially for the abs.*

She slipped into the shower and got herself all cleaned up, then went back out into the bedroom to dress. She tried not to wake Tony, but found him watching her as she rummaged through her bags. "Oh my god, you're gorgeous," he purred. She smiled a shy smile.

"How was that quickie last night?" she asked, grinning mischievously.

He laughed. "Pretty damn good for pretty damn quick! We'll have to do that more often."

"If we had sex any more often, we'd never get anything else done!" She giggled. "I've gotta get cookin'. When are you firing up the grills?"

"In about five minutes. I'll get them started, eat breakfast, and then shower." Tony pulled on his boxer briefs and jeans from the day before. No shirt. Everything below Nikki's waist vibrated, watching him walk around shirtless. His shoulders and his chest were just about the most beautiful things in the world to her. Well, those plus that huge cock of his.

By seven thirty, everything was in full swing, the kitchen full of women, and Clayton watched the grills while Tony showered. By eleven o'clock, they'd pretty much made a dent in everything. Tony had said everyone would start arriving about eleven thirty, so Nikki started getting food out, finding serving utensils in the big, unfamiliar kitchen, and filling pitchers with ice water, tea, and juice. She started the coffee pot too, in case anyone wanted hot coffee.

At eleven fifteen, Annabeth scanned the kitchen counters. "Nikki, where are Zia Molly's rolls?"

"What, honey?" Nikki asked, her head coming up out of a cabinet where she'd been looking for a dish.

"Zia Molly's rolls. Where are they? Zio Bart usually brings them by early, but I don't see them." She continued to look around.

"Oh, they're in the fridge," Nikki answered absentmindedly.

"They're where?" Something in Annabeth's voice made Nikki stop and pay attention. "Did you say they're in the fridge?"

"Yeah. I put them in there last night. They were room temp when he brought them, so I put them in the fridge with everything else."

Annabeth's face went white and her eyes got huge. "Please tell me you didn't."

Nikki began to get anxious. "Yeah. I didn't want them to spoil overnight. Was that wrong?"

"Oh dear god," Annabeth started. Katie and Brittany turned, strange looks on their faces.

"What?" Nikki was starting to feel a little panicky.

"They won't rise. If you chilled them, they won't rise. They were supposed to be left out to rise overnight, then we divide them and bake them. If they've been chilled overnight, they're ruined."

Nikki's heart started slamming against her ribs. "Please tell me you're kidding, Annabeth." Annabeth shook her head. "I didn't know, I swear," Nikki whispered. Her heart sank. *What the hell do I do now? I've ruined the Walters family holiday celebration.* She felt absolutely sick.

"We'll have to come up with a plan," Katie announced. "Molly's gonna eat you alive, Nikki." Brittany nodded in agreement.

"Oh, my god, what do I do?" Nikki groaned, frozen in place and in full-blown panic. Tony picked that moment to walk into the room.

"Hey, girls! Everything going okay in here?" he asked, reaching into the fridge for a beer. He stopped for a second, looked at the trays of rolls, and then closed the door.

Nikki felt a tear roll down her cheek. "No, everything's not okay. I've ruined it all." She started to tremble, her hands visibly shaking.

Tony turned and looked at her. "What did you do?" he asked in a mock accusatory tone.

He didn't notice how pale she was turning, didn't see the tear. "I put Molly's rolls in the refrigerator. They won't rise. I ruined them."

Tony still really wasn't paying much attention, and he didn't see how red her eyes were. He continued, in his mocking tone, "Uh-oh, you're screwed. Molly will eat you alive." Katie nodded. "Can't have that. You'd better come up with something." He walked over to her, kissed her on the cheek, and told her, "You're a smart one. You'll figure something out. I have complete faith in you." He strolled to the back door, opened it, and kept on walking.

Oh, my god, I'm so screwed. And he's mad at me. What do I do? All three girls stared at her, and she felt like her head was going to burst into flames. She wanted to run to the bedroom, lock the door, and cry, but there wasn't time. She took out her smart phone and did a search.

"Unless your phone is going to bake rolls, you'd better come up with something else," Brittany groused sarcastically.

Nikki took a deep breath. "Actually, it just might." She found a number for a Kroger on the far eastern side of Louisville and called. "Yes, do you by any chance carry Blackhawk dinner rolls? Really? Do you have any? Yes, I'll hold." She waited. "Oh, thank god. Yes, I need four bags. Yes. Wilkes. Or Walters. Either name. Thanks — thanks so much. I think you've saved my life." She whipped off her apron. "I've got to go. I've got to pick up the rolls."

Annabeth folded her arms across her chest. "They'd better be good."

"They're not good. They're spectacular," Nikki called out, rushing around to leave. "Annabeth, can you . . . Oh, god, I can't leave. I've got too much to do."

"Hello?" a deep male voice called from the foyer.

"In here, Zio Vic," Annabeth called out.

Nikki looked up and her mouth dropped open. Vittorio Vincenzo Cabrizzi stood in the doorway, and she'd never seen anything like him before in her life.

His six foot eight frame filled the doorway, and if his smoky brown eyes hadn't nailed her, his huge shoulders and trim hips would've. His dark, wavy hair hung down over enormous biceps, and he had thighs like tree trunks. For a few seconds Nikki couldn't even move her lips, much less speak. Tony was gorgeous, but this guy was breathtakingly unreal, his features looking like they'd been carved by one of the old Renaissance masters, the scruff on his jaw, his mustache, the soul patch beneath his lower lip, all impeccably sculpted. Annabeth ran to him and wrapped her arms around his waist to hug him, and he picked her up and spun her around in rag doll fashion as she squealed like a child.

He put Annabeth down and closed the gap between himself and Nikki with just a few steps. "Hey, you must be Nikki. I'm Vic. I'm so glad to finally meet you!" In typical Walters fashion, instead of extending his hand, he threw his arms around her and hugged her. His scent almost made her swoon, like a spicy pine grove, and his body, for all the hard muscles, was surprisingly soft and warm, comfortable even. Everything in her told her she'd always be safe if Vic Cabrizzi was around.

"Oh, Vic, it's so good to meet you! Tony's told me so many wonderful things about you," she smiled, pressing her palms to his cheeks. The smile Vic returned was huge and warm. Then he took a good look at her face.

He frowned at her. "You look like you've been crying."

"Oh, it's nothing." She wiped her eyes with the backs of her hands.

"She ruined Zia Molly's rolls," Annabeth blurted out.

"Sweet mother of god! You didn't," he cried out, looking at her out the corner of his eye, oozing mischievousness. She nodded sheepishly. "Molly's gonna eat you alive." Katie shot Nikki her *See, I told you!* look. "Well, we're going to have to fix that, aren't we?" He grinned and chucked her under her chin. She felt like she was about nine years old.

"I think I already have. I just have to go pick up some rolls," she said, breaking away from him.

"Nope. You've got too much to do here and everybody will start rolling in. You let me go get them, okay? I didn't bring anything with me, so it'll be my treat. Just tell me where."

"Oh, Vic, no, I couldn't . . ."

"You absolutely can and you absolutely will. I'm leaving and if you don't tell me where I'm going, I guess I'll just drive around all afternoon!" He wandered back out the door.

"Zio Vic, wait! I want to go with you!" Annabeth called out, running after him.

He stopped at the front door and called to her, "Where, Nikki?"

She sighed. "Kroger on Shelbyville Road at the Snyder," she called back.

"Be back in two shakes." She heard the door close behind him and Annabeth.

Nikki stood there for a second, then asked no one in particular, "What just happened here?"

"Vic Cabrizzi," Katie answered with a wistful smile. "You'll get used to it."

Nikki breathed a sigh of relief. Everyone seemed to be having a good time — everyone except Molly, of course. She alternated between bites of food and glaring at Nikki. Even worse were the rolls — they were delicious, and everyone kept saying so.

"Tell us again, where did these come from?" Freddie asked. Molly was especially ticked that her own husband was going on about them.

"A little bakery in the larger town near the one I grew up in. It's called Blackhawk Bakery. They made these rolls for years, then automated the process and started selling them all over the country. I took a chance that someone here would have some, and they did. And again, I'm sorry, Molly, really."

"Oh, that's okay," Molly retorted. "You can't help it if you don't know your way around a kitchen."

Tony said nothing, just kept eating. She knew he was mad about what she'd done, but he could at least help her out. After all, it wasn't like she'd done it on purpose. Nikki looked down at her plate and pushed her food around. She didn't really feel much like eating.

"They are delicious, aren't they?" Vic said, and Nikki glanced at him to see him wink at her. A little smile tugged at the corners of her lips, and Vic smiled back warmly. *At least he's in my corner,* she thought.

"I think they're fabulous," Bart said.

"Um-hum," Kathy added, her mouth full.

"Molly, maybe you should order these from now on," Mark repeated, and his wife, Victoria, nodded in agreement beside him. Nikki could practically see the steam coming off of Molly.

"Well, I think Daddy outdid himself on the barbecue this year," Annabeth said with pride.

"He certainly did," Nikki said, attempting to make conversation.

"Now how would you know, little girl?" Tony asked her. "You've never had my barbecue before."

Something in Nikki's gut turned. *Oh, god,* she thought, *he's trying to tell me I won't get another chance to find out.* She felt her eyes well. *Don't cry, don't cry, don't let them see you cry,* she repeated in her head. Tony looked over at her, an odd expression on his face, and she turned away. She couldn't take his gaze right then. And all over some stupid dinner rolls. Who would've thought some stupid bread would be her undoing? She tried to breathe, but it was getting more difficult.

"Son, I also think you did a fine job," Raffaella echoed. She sat on the other side of Nikki and, surprisingly, she patted Nikki on the hand. Nikki tried to hide her shock.

"Thanks. I enjoy doing this for everybody. It's my gift to all of you." Tony took another bite, beaming, and looked at his youngest and smallest brother. "Bennie, I'm glad you guys could be here. I've missed you."

Bennie gave a curt, "Thanks, bro." Caroline smiled a tiny smile.

"Well, I, for one, am glad to be included in this family." Vic sat on the other side of Raffaella, and she hugged Vic and kissed him on the cheek. "Thanks, Zia Raffie," he said and kissed her back.

Nikki didn't try to say anything else during the meal. She had no stomach for her food either. Anything she tried to swallow made a knot in her throat and she almost choked, so she resigned herself to going hungry. She grew more heartsick with every passing moment, but she comforted herself with the knowledge that it would be over soon. Of course, then she'd have to deal with Tony's anger with her, and things weren't looking too good in that regard.

Annabeth, Katie, Brittany, and Raffaella tried to help Nikki clear the tables, but she shooed them away. "No, this is your annual family gathering. Go, go. Have a good time, visit with everybody. I'll take care of this." They retreated, and she was finally alone in the kitchen.

She leaned against the countertop and took a huge, heaving breath. The window over the sink looked out over the back yard, and she could see everyone out on the patio, laughing and talking. No one even realized she wasn't there. She'd been so stupid, actually thinking her life could change, that she could be a part of a family like this and be happy and loved. It had been nice while it lasted, but along comes some dinner rolls, and what's a girl to do? She swallowed hard as her heart broke. Then she felt someone near her elbow and turned.

Caroline stood at the counter next to her, latex gloves on her hands, holding a dish brush. The tiny blond scraped food off of the plates into the sink where the disposal was, then stacked them on the counter. Nikki looked at her, and she smiled a sad smile back and kept scraping. Then she peered back out the window, and she heard Caroline say in a small voice, "It's okay. They don't like me either." Turning back to look at Caroline, a tear escaped one of Nikki's eyes and ran down her cheek. Caroline continued to scrape the dishes. The two women stood in silence.

"I like you, Caroline," Nikki finally said quietly. "And so do Tony and the kids; they love you. Thank you for being kind to me."

"I know what it's like to not have one single kind soul to come to your aid. I always try to be kind when I can." She smiled. "What else can I do to help?"

That did it. Nikki began to sob; she couldn't help it. She felt Caroline's hand on her back, and she tried to get herself under control, but she couldn't manage it. Caroline patted her shoulder and told her, "Now, run upstairs and pull yourself together. We wouldn't want them to see you like this. Go on now. I've got this." She went back to work, loading the plates into the dishwasher.

Nikki whispered, "Thanks," then hugged the little blond and hurried to the stairs. As she passed through the foyer, she saw Raffaella coming out of the downstairs bathroom, and Raffaella smiled at her and turned back out toward the patio. *What must she think of me?*, Nikki wondered. She made it to the bedroom and closed the door behind her.

Nikki rinsed her face, reapplied her makeup, and brushed her hair. Looking down, she realized she'd spilled something on her top, so she pulled another one out and changed. As she was getting ready to go back downstairs, the door opened and Tony walked in, closing it behind him.

"Babe, where've you been?" he asked in curiosity. "I was missing you. You weren't in the kitchen. Caroline told me you were up here." She steeled herself for whatever he was going to say, and the fear and uncertainty were plain on her face. That's when his curiosity turned to concern. "You okay?"

Nikki drew in a shuddering breath and straightened as well as she could. "Look, Tony, before you say anything, I'm sorry," she started, but she couldn't hold back the tears. "I'm really, really sorry. I didn't mean to do it. I just didn't know. I know it was stupid. I messed everything up. It won't happen again. Please, please," she pleaded, "please, whatever you do, please don't embarrass me in front of all of them, okay? Wait until they're gone. Then you can say whatever you like to me, do whatever you like, send me away. But please don't humiliate me. Please?" She felt nauseous and had started to shake all over.

Tony's eyes went round, his eyebrows shot up, and his mouth dropped open. "What in the hell are you talking about, sweetie?"

"Oh, Tony, I know I messed everything up. I know Molly's mad – Freddie's probably mad too. I know Bart and Kathy and Vic were just trying to be nice to me. They think I'm an idiot too. And the girls practically tore me a new one – I deserved it. I'm so stupid. But please, oh, god, please don't leave me!" Her knees buckled and she dropped down onto the floor, trembling all over.

"What the . . . baby, what in the hell are you talking about?" Tony dropped to his knees in front of her and gathered her against him. "I'm not mad at you! Why would you think that?"

She sobbed and choked. "The rolls . . . you were mad when you found out. And you didn't talk to me all through dinner. I'm so sorry." She sobbed harder and dissolved in his arms.

"You thought I was . . ." Tony laughed. "I wasn't mad, princess. I was trying to make light of it. I couldn't figure out why anybody was all worked up about those rolls – they're terrible! The ones you bought were fifty times better. I didn't see it as any big deal. It was actually kind of funny. Molly's such a bitch – serves her right."

"But at dinner? You didn't say a word to me . . ."

"I'm sorry, honey." He tried to comfort her by smoothing her hair. "I had no idea you thought I was mad. I was just hungry! I hadn't had anything but beer since breakfast, and I was starving. Clayton was too – did you notice he didn't have much to say either? That's why – that's all. As for the girls? They were just giving you shit, so all I can say about that is, welcome to the family."

Nikki shuddered and took a deep breath, a sob still bubbling in her throat. "So we're okay? I mean, you and me? Okay?"

"Yeah, there wasn't a time when we weren't, honey." He wiped the tears off her face, then reached over to the dresser and grabbed a tissue. "Here – blow." Nikki blew her nose into the tissue. *God, I must be a real mess!*, she thought. "Better?" She nodded. "Okay, well, we've got to get back downstairs or they're going to wonder where we are. And I don't want them knowing you were upset, okay? I want them to know how strong you are. Don't let Molly ruffle you – stand up to her." He stood and pulled her to her feet. "Ready?"

"No! God no. I have to fix my makeup and my hair again. You go on – I'll be down in a minute." Nikki released his hand and he walked to the door. He opened it to go out, then closed it back and turned to face her.

"What?" she choked out, terrified he'd remembered some other mess she'd made.

Tony crossed the room back to her and took both her hands in his. "I was going to wait until later, but I want to do this now." *Oh, god, what now?*, she thought, her heartbeat racing again. "Nikki, will you move in with me? As soon as possible? I don't want to wake up one single morning without you beside me. You don't have to answer right now, just think about it, okay?"

"I don't have to think about it." She took a deep breath. "If Walters Construction has a truck I can use, I'll move tomorrow."

Tony laughed, picked her up, and spun her around, then kissed her. "Baby, I love you so much!"

She threw her arms around his neck and whispered in his ear, "You have no idea how much I love you back."

"Where's Nikki?" Mark asked. "I was hoping we'd all get to know her a little better."

Tony popped the top on another beer and sat down on the end of one of the chaise lounges on the patio. "Got something on her clothes while she was straightening up the kitchen. Changing. She'll be down in a minute." He took a draw on the bottle. He'd noticed she'd changed, so that sounded better than *She was bawling ten minutes ago and she's pulling herself together*. If he had anything to say about it, they'd never know they'd gotten to her, especially Molly. He'd known the stress of the day would get to her, but the thing with the rolls had pushed her over the edge. He hadn't paid enough attention to her, hadn't been supportive enough, and he wouldn't make that mistake again.

They were all chatting and laughing, enjoying the warm breeze coming across the patio. Freddie was telling everyone about a new car he was looking to buy and was in mid-sentence when he dropped his voice and growled, "Holy shit!" Everyone turned to get the same view he had. Vic whispered, "Oh, wow!" Molly scowled. Tony turned too, and a long, low whistle escaped his lips.

Nikki stood on the steps leading to the patio, and she looked unsure as to whether or not she should join everyone. After Tony had left the bedroom, she'd changed again, this time into a black, bustier-type camisole, and she'd pulled a sheer, lacy, red and black top over it. Her black diamond pendant shone against her creamy breastbone, but the guys were mostly staring at her legs, shown off to perfection under some skin-tight capris. Her red toenails matched her top. She'd pulled the sides of her glittering hair back low into an elastic band and tied a black ribbon around it. As she glanced around, she fidgeted with her nails, clicking them together, and she tried to decide what she should do, where she should go. With everyone staring at her, it was even harder to feel comfortable. *Somebody say something,* she thought. *Please!*

"Ah, there's my baby now!" Tony called out, finally coming to his senses. He stood and closed the gap between them in less than a second, wrapped his arms around her, and kissed her as he lifted her off the flagstone. When he set her back down, he took her hand and led her back to the chaise, where he sat down and drew her onto his lap. "Everybody, we've got an announcement to make. Sweetie, why don't you tell them?"

Nikki looked into Tony's face, and he nodded and smiled. She addressed the family in a voice barely over a whisper. "Tony asked me to move in with him."

"And?" Annabeth squealed.

Nikki was beaming. "Oh, I said yes, of course." Tony's arms tightened around her waist, and she hugged them to her.

"Well, it's about time!" Clayton said as Annabeth, Katie, and Brittany jumped up and ran to Tony and Nikki, hugging them, each other, and anyone else who'd hug them back in their excitement. One by one, the brothers and their wives hugged Nikki and Tony and congratulated them.

Then, over the ruckus, they heard the sound of crystal ringing and turned to see Raffaella standing, wine glass raised, gently tapping a spoon from the dessert table against it. When they quieted, she spoke.

"For more years than I can count, I have wished for my sons, all of them, to be happy. It seemed all of them had found happiness – all but one. Today, we celebrate the birth of my adopted homeland and my pride at being a citizen of the greatest nation in the world. But we also celebrate the happiness Antonio has finally found with this lovely woman. Nikki, welcome to our family, and thank you for finally bringing my son happiness." She raised her glass, as did everyone else.

Tony lowered his face to Nikki's and pressed his forehead against hers. "Well, baby," he smiled, "if there was any question before, this locks it – looks like you're in!"

Nikki was enjoying herself immensely. Victoria and Kathy were chatting with her about when they should get together to start the planning for the annual Thanksgiving feast, and were already wheedling her about a wedding date. She tried to tell them that Tony had only asked her to move in, but they were running right ahead and, if she'd been honest, she would've told them she wondered about it too. Would he ever ask her? Was this the beginning, or would living together be the end of the road? She didn't care; as long as she was with him, nothing else mattered.

Vic, Bart, and Tony were in a lively discussion about the economics of the construction industry. Clayton and Mark were talking baseball while Bennie sat with them silently, and Caroline sat next to Raffaella, answering the older woman's questions about the grandkids. The three girls chatted with Molly about summer fashions; Molly ran an exclusive boutique Freddie had bought in Anchorage, the Louisville township where Tony lived, and she always had a leg up on the newest trends, not to mention that the only time she could manage to be civil was when she was talking about herself or something she knew more about than everyone else. It seemed every member of the family was having a very pleasant evening until a voice rang out from inside the house: "Helloooo? Where is everybody? I'm late, but I'm here!"

Nikki heard the voice; she didn't recognize it, but it was clear everyone else did. There was a mad scramble, and Nikki found herself on the move, Vic's hand on her arm. When they reached the back edge of the patio, Vic slipped in behind her and wrapped both arms around her waist.

What the hell was going on? As Nikki watched, Bart, Freddie, Mark, and Tony moved to the front edge of the patio just below the steps, feet shoulder width apart and arms crossed across their chests, with Tony in the forefront.

Raffaella joined the brothers, standing next to Mark. Nikki wasn't sure what was going on, but the five of them looked as imposing as any group she'd ever seen. There was movement at her left, and Clayton pressed himself against her, reaching to take her left hand and hold it tight behind him. Vic's right arm left her waist, and she glanced over to see Annabeth fold into his side and his arm wrap securely around her. From the darkness of the house, a form emerged.

Nikki's eyes went round. It had to be Dottie.

The woman standing on the steps was about five foot six and the biggest mess Nikki had ever seen. She had a head full of wild, dark, unbrushed hair, under which a dark, unkempt unibrow resided, and her face was covered in a mess of makeup the likes of which Nikki had never seen before, so muddled that her features were hard to distinguish. She was dressed in the most gosh-awful junk Nikki had ever been unfortunate enough to witness, dark green drawstring capris that were two sizes too small and a blue and purple wraparound top that barely covered her breasts. Anyone with eyes could see she wasn't wearing a bra, which was a real shame, because having breasts that large and heavy meant she could've used a really good one. She was wearing flip-flops that didn't match each other, and also didn't match her outfit, and a big wad of fifteen different kinds of jewelry, all in a mismatched confusion. Trying to sort her out was impossible. She put her hands on her hips and asked, "So, where's the food? I'm starved!"

Everyone was silent for a few seconds. Then she heard Tony snarl, "Dottie, what in the hell are you doing here?"

"It's the family gathering. I always come. Why wouldn't I be here?"

"Gee, I don't know. Maybe because you haven't been a member of this family for sixteen years?" Mark shot back.

"Yeah, Dottie, why are you here?" Bart asked.

She pointed at Tony. "That man right there is my husband, and I have as much right to be here as anybody else."

"I haven't been your husband legally in sixteen years, and emotionally for a long longer than that. I think you need to leave. Everybody was having a good time before you got here." Tony practically spat the words toward her.

"Oh, honey, you don't mean that. I know you don't," she whined. She walked up to Tony and put her hand on the side of his face. Nikki tried to move forward but she felt Vic's arm tighten around her waist. She looked up at him, and he gave her a look that told her he wouldn't be turning her loose any time soon.

"Yes, I absolutely do mean that," Tony snapped and moved her hand away.

"Mom," Clayton begged, "please leave. This has been a really good day for us. Please don't ruin it."

"Yeah, Mom," Annabeth pleaded in a tiny voice. "Please?"

"Well, there you are – my kids! Hey, guys! I'm so glad you're here! I was hoping to see you." Dottie walked toward them, then stopped and grinned at Nikki. "So, who's this?" She turned her weird smile to the big man standing behind Nikki. "Why, Vic, you old dog, you've got yourself a girl! I was beginning to wonder about you, you know, thinking you were queer or something." Annabeth winced at the vinegar in her words, and Nikki had trouble hiding the disgust she felt just listening to her. She couldn't imagine how badly Dottie had hurt Annabeth over the years.

"Dottie," Vic nodded, digging his fingers into Nikki's waist to keep her still. "You need to run along. Nothing for you here."

"Oh, but there is. I'm still a member of this family and I still want to be here with all of you."

Then Raffaella spoke up. "Dorothea, you are not welcome here. Please go."

Dottie turned to reply to Raffaella, and when she did, she caught Tony's face. Tony was looking straight at Nikki, trying to reassure her without speaking, and Dottie saw it, saw the way he was looking at Nikki, saw the concern on his face, the silent exchange between the two of them, and she knew. She whipped her head around to see Nikki's face and caught all the unspoken emotion directed toward Tony.

That was when Dottie just couldn't manage to behave herself any longer, and she flew at Nikki. "Oh my god, you slut! That's my husband! You bitch!" She reached for the smaller woman, but not before Vic wheeled Nikki around and stood in front of her. Clayton instinctively stepped in front of Dottie, and Tony jetted across the patio in a split second and grabbed Dottie around the waist, heaved her away from Vic and Clayton, and set her down a full ten feet away.

"Dottie, I'm warning you," he barked as she broke free and spun around to face him. "Don't do this! I'll have you arrested, I swear! Now, get out. And don't come back." She stood her ground and glared at him. "I mean it, Dottie. Go!" he yelled, pointing toward the front of the house. Then, since he knew she'd figured out his relationship with Nikki, he decided to lay it all on the line. "And if you bother her, if you touch her, if you so much as look at her funny, so help me god, I'll make you wish you'd never been born." As he spoke, his voice grew in volume. "You hear me?" he shouted at her.

"Whore!" she spat at Nikki, ignoring Tony's warning. "I'll get you, I swear. You can't hide from me!" She struggled to get around Tony, but he, Freddie, and Bart wouldn't let her by. Mark stood protectively next to Raffaella.

Nikki struggled to loosen Vic's arm from around her waist, but he wouldn't budge. She looked up into his face again, but Vic mouthed *No* and wouldn't let go. Clayton took her hand again and held it tight. Annabeth was crying softly, and Katie had come to her side and was stroking her right arm. Brittany was huddled with the wives on the other side of the patio, trying to stay out of the way.

After staring Tony down for what seemed like forever, Dottie shouted, "Okay, fine – I'm leaving! You should all be ashamed, treating me like this. And you," she thundered, turning and pointing at Nikki, "your ass is mine, slut!" She stomped up the steps and lumbered toward the front door.

No one moved for a very long, painful time. Finally, Tony went into the house, then came back and told them all, "She's gone." The whole group let out a collective sigh and visibly relaxed.

Vic put his other arm back around Nikki, hugged her tight, and whispered in her ear, "Sorry, sweetie. I wanted to keep you safe," then let her go. She stood there, not knowing quite what to say or do. Everyone else was speaking low and trying to console Annabeth, who was sobbing uncontrollably. Clayton looked furious, and Brittany was talking to him and stroking his arm and face. Freddie took Raffaella to a chair, then went to get her a fresh drink.

Tony slipped up behind Nikki without her realizing he was there and wrapped his arms around her. At first she thought it was Vic again, but then she felt him sigh against her. She turned to face him and put her arms around his neck. "God, honey, I'm sorry. I never dreamed she'd show up. I hate that you had to see that."

Nikki shook her head. "It's okay; it's not your fault. But holy shit, she's scary-looking. I can't believe you were ever married to her."

"She wasn't always like that, even though it's hard to remember a time when she wasn't. But at least she's gone now." He looked around, then announced, "Hey, bar's still open. Anybody want another drink?"

Choruses of "hell yeah," "absolutely," and "hit me again" rang out, and Tony kissed Nikki and made his way back inside to the bar. All of the men, even Bennie, followed him. Most of the women did too. Nikki crossed the patio to Caroline, curious about something.

"Caroline," Nikki started, "where was Bennie when all of that was going on?"

Caroline turned a nervous eye toward the house, then turned back to Nikki. "I know why you're asking and, honestly, I don't know why Bennie is so hostile toward Tony. He's even admitted to me that nothing has happened between them, but he's openly hurtful to Tony, and he won't tell me why. I'm so sorry." She looked more sad than before.

"Oh, well, I was hoping to get some insight." Then she gave Caroline a kiss on the cheek. "I'm so glad I've gotten to know you a little. I hope I get to know you better."

"Me too." A tiny smile broke at the corners of Caroline's mouth.

Freddie hugged Tony and then Nikki as he and Molly left, and told Nikki once again how glad he was to have her in the family. Molly took Nikki's hand and told her goodbye, but was very cool to her. As she walked away, Tony looked at Nikki and shrugged.

Bart and Kathy had brought Raffaella with them so she wouldn't have to drive home to Louisville by herself after the fireworks. At eighty-three, she was still very independent, but no one would let her drive after dark. All of the out-of-towners were staying at the big house and all four kids had decided to stay too so they didn't have to drive home. After everyone had told Bart, Kathy, and Raffaella goodbye, Tony and Nikki walked with them to the car. Tony hugged his mother and kissed her on the cheek. Then Raffaella turned to Nikki.

She took both of Nikki's hands in hers and looked the younger woman in the eye. "My Antonio clearly loves you – we all see it." She smiled. "You will be good to my son, yes?"

"He's very easy to be good to, Mrs. Walters. He treats me like a queen," Nikki said, tearing up.

"Please, call me Raffaella." Nikki nodded. "We must have lunch one day, you and I. I hope you will be open to this?" she asked in her thick accent.

"Absolutely. My boss is very easy to work with. I'm sure any time you'd like to go would be fine. Just let me know."

"I will do that. And thank you for working so hard today to make everything beautiful for our family." Raffaella stopped, then added, "Your family," and winked at Nikki. Nikki leaned over and gave the older woman a kiss on the cheek, which Raffaella returned.

Vic was the last one out the door. As he walked out, he turned toward them, then turned to leave, then turned back to them again as though he was trying to decide what to do. "Um ..." he started, then reached into his pocket and pulled something out.

Nikki turned three shades of burgundy – it was her panties from Monday night. They'd been lying there, in the foyer, for two days. She wondered who else had seen them before Vic found them. And apparently he'd been carrying them around all day.

"I kinda found these right inside the door and under there; well, Zia Raffie pointed them out to me," he admitted, pointing to the table by the door. Nikki buried her face in her hands and groaned. He handed them to her and fought to keep from laughing. "They were kinda halfway under the table and I, um, I kinda thought you wouldn't want to leave them there. This was the first chance I've had to give them back without a bunch of people around." When Nikki managed to look him in the face, he was grinning with absolute devilment, and then had the audacity to wink. "How they got there? I don't want to know, really." He snickered. "I thought about just keeping them, but they looked expensive. Got the bra to match?" he asked, trying to look serious.

By that time, Tony was laughing so hard he was wheezing, and Nikki didn't quite know what to say. "Um, thanks?" she said barely above a whisper.

"Um, you're welcome?" Vic burst into laughter. He leaned in, punched Tony on the arm, and gasped out, "She's a keeper!" Before she could say anything else, Vic hugged Nikki tight and kissed her on the cheek. "I did not sniff them, swear to god! And by the way, Raffaella didn't find them; I was just kidding about that. Welcome to the family!" He chuckled as he pulled his keys out of his pocket and strolled down the walk toward his car.

Nikki and Tony stood on the steps and waved goodbye, his arm around her waist, Tony still gasping and wiping his eyes. When they turned to go back into the house, Nikki growled, "I thought you picked up all of our clothes yesterday morning!"

Tony had finally regained his composure. "Well, I obviously missed something! I don't know how we missed them before, but leave it to Vic." He chuckled as they closed the door, then slapped her on the ass as she turned to the stairs.

Tony sighed as they lay side by side in the big bed, staring at the ceiling. "Well, I guess there'll be no lovin' for us tonight with a house full of people."

"Yeah, neither one of us can be quiet when we're screwing, so here we are." Nikki smiled to herself. She didn't bother to mention the banging headboard. That thing really bugged her sometimes, but at other times she loved hearing the sound of that headboard amplifying him pounding into her.

"Now that we're alone, I've got one more surprise for you." Tony reached into the nightstand and pulled out a rectangular box. "I hope you like it. I had it custom made for you." He handed Nikki the box.

She took the lid off and lifted out the red velvet box inside. It had a large "C" imprinted with gilt in the red velvet. When she lifted the hinged lid, she gasped and her mouth formed a silent "O." Inside was a bracelet, and it was impressive. It was a bangle, and she wasn't certain but it looked like the band and settings were done in platinum. It was set with diamonds, rubies, and sapphires, all baguette cut and set perpendicular to the band, and each one was about twice the size of a grain of rice. Along both edges of the band were diamonds the size of birdseed. She couldn't begin to guess – altogether, maybe eight to ten carats of stones or more? It was fairly heavy for its size. She wouldn't even venture a guess at its monetary value, but none of that mattered to her. Tony took the bracelet from her, opened it, and put it on her – it fit perfectly on her tiny wrist.

"Wait!" He took it back off her arm and pointed inside the band. "Read the inscription."

Nikki took the bracelet and looked at the inside. It said *Tony & Nikki – Our first Fourth of July. Baby, when I'm with you – FIREWORKS!* She laughed right out loud and hugged him. "Thank you, sweetheart! It's beautiful!" She put it back on her arm and admired it, then looked at Tony. He seemed extremely proud of himself.

"Do you realize this is the first thing you've ever given me?" She looked at the bracelet dreamily.

"No, it's not," he retorted, a small smirk on his lips.

"So what else have you given me?"

"Well, let's see . . . I sent you pink roses."

"That you did."

"And I tried to give you a handgun. And I still will if you want it."

"I want it now."

"And I've probably already given you more orgasms than you've ever had in your life, and that's got to count for something," he answered matter-of-factly.

"You'd better believe it. Best gifts of them all." Nikki winked as she kissed him goodnight.

Chapter Twenty-Seven

Everyone from out of town was staying until the weekend, but Tony and Nikki had to get back to work. Tony got up early, got ready, and took Nikki home so she could get ready there. Regardless of the fact everyone else was at the big house, they'd be staying in Louisville for the rest of the week so they'd be close to work.

Nikki almost put the bracelet away, but then decided to wear it to the shop. She'd had a rule with the jewelry Randy had given her: Enjoy it and wear it, every day if possible. Why should this be any different? Tony had given it to her proudly and with great joy, and she should wear it and let it make her happy.

Marla and Carol were both impressed with Nikki's gift. They kept asking to see it throughout the day and, at one point, Carol wanted to try it on, but it wouldn't fasten on her wrist. Nikki had extremely small wrists, but how had Tony known what size to have the bracelet made in?

Late in the afternoon Nikki texted Tony and asked if he'd be at the gym after work. *Late meeting. Won't make it. Kids are coming over. See you at home.* Home. Their home. She had to get busy packing up her personal stuff so she could move in. She wanted to be at home in her new home with him.

She went into the gym locker room and changed from her street clothes to workout gear. When she walked back onto the floor, Peyton sat at a table in the window in the smoothie café, talking to another man she had never seen before. Nikki walked straight over to them and said, "So, Peyton, who's this?"

The man stood and extended a hand. "José Flores, Ms. Wilkes. I'm Peyton's relief."

"Good to meet you, José. And please, it's Nikki. Might as well warn you, after dealing with me, Peyton definitely needs relief!" Peyton laughed right out loud and shook his head, and Nikki laughed and took José's hand – strong grip. He was positively dangerous-looking, his waist-length, dark hair pulled back into a smooth ponytail, his dark eyes almost black, with an ominous-looking goatee that hung, braided, almost to his breastbone. He was good-looking in an almost sinister way, and so muscled up that his skin looked painful stretched over the tautness of his structure, his dark skin defining every ripple. He had an overall build much like Peyton's, powerful but not tall. But he had a warm smile and almost microscopic smile crinkles in the corners of his eyes.

"Well, I'm out of here. José will take good care of you. Just go on about your workout. I think he's enjoying the scenery anyway." Peyton laughed, punching José good-naturedly on the shoulder as he walked out. Nikki could tell they were pretty good friends.

"Yeah, man, very nice!" José yelled at his back. He leaned toward Nikki and whispered conspiratorially, "I've been trying for two years now to tell him I'm gay, but he just refuses to believe me."

"Is that true?"

"Nah, but he doesn't know for sure. Actually, I'm AC/DC, if you know what I mean," José whispered back, smiling.

"Equal opportunity banger, huh?" Nikki smiled and winked, and José tipped his head back and laughed loudly. "It'll be our secret!" Nikki whispered to him. Growing suddenly serious, she looked up into his face. "Thanks for being here. I'll try to not be too much trouble."

"No trouble at all. You're a great addition to the scenery," he laughed. She playfully slapped his arm and headed back toward the treadmill. Even though she barely knew this guy, she already liked him.

Ten minutes into her walking regimen, Nikki saw something, a brightening of the room, that she couldn't identify. She looked up and across the room at a guy facing her and saw his face literally light up and his eyes widen as he looked out the windows behind her. But before she could turn to see what he was looking at, she felt a hand on her arm, and in the next instant, José was half pushing, half pulling her toward the locker room at a dead run. He ran in without calling out to see if any other women were in there, then hustled her into a restroom stall.

He pointed to the toilet. "Get on it." Confused, Nikki started to sit, but he barked, "On your feet!" She climbed onto the toilet seat. "Crouch!" he barked, and she did it quickly. "Now lock this stall door and don't come out until one of us comes to get you. Understand?" he shouted at her. She nodded, bewildered, and he disappeared.

Nikki leaned forward and locked the stall door. What was going on? She heard lots of voices, then shouting, and then something very loud, a bang of some sort, and the building shook. It seemed like she crouched there forever, and she started to tremble, wondering where everyone was and why no one had come to get her. Her three-eighty was in her gym bag, but it was in her locker all the way across the locker room – not much use to her.

Then it got quiet. Within a few minutes, she heard someone say, "Nikki?" She waited – was it a trick? "Nikki, it's Peyton. Where are you?"

"I'm here, Peyton, in the restroom stall." She scrambled off the toilet seat and threw open the stall door.

Peyton ran to her and looked her up and down. "You okay?" She nodded.

"What happened? Where's José?" She had started to calm down a little as Peyton took her hand and led her from the locker room, but he said nothing.

When they walked out into the main workout area, the scene through the windows was insane. There were police cars, fire trucks, ambulances, every type of emergency vehicle she could imagine, all clustered in the parking lot. And light – a bright orange light. A fire? "Peyton," Nikki asked, her voice rising, "what's happening? Where's José? Is he okay?"

"José's fine, Nikki. Everybody's okay. But your SUV – um, not so much."

Nikki stood and stared at the burned-out frame of her SUV. There was nothing left of it. The explosion when its gas tank ruptured had taken out the windows of every other vehicle in the parking lot; pebbles of safety glass were everywhere. She was glad she'd parked away from everyone else like Peyton had told her to earlier on, or other vehicles would've caught fire as well. He'd told her it would make their jobs easier, making sure no one could hide between vehicles to hurt her when she came out, but she doubted they'd expected anything like this would happen. The ambulances had gone, the paramedics satisfied no one had been hurt, and the police were making reports and talking to other gym members when the big silver Walters Construction truck came racing into the parking lot and slid to a halt. Tony hit the ground running and swept her up in his arms.

"Are you okay?" he practically yelled.

"Yeah, I'm fine! Peyton and José took good care of me." He set her down and looked her up and down like Peyton had. "I promise, honey, I'm fine," she repeated. "I was so scared, though. José left me in the restroom, and I heard this big boom, and . . ."

"Nicolette Wilkes?" Nikki turned to find a uniformed officer standing behind her with a clipboard in his hands. "Ms. Wilkes, that is your SUV, correct?"

She grimaced. "Was. Any idea what happened to it?"

The officer looked at Tony. "Mr. Walters," he said and nodded; seemed like everyone in Louisville knew Tony. Tony nodded back. The officer turned back to Nikki. "It looks like somebody broke out a window, threw an incendiary device into it, and ran; you know, like a Molotov cocktail. We'll know more when the fire marshal takes a look at it. Any idea why anybody would do this?" It was the first time Nikki had taken a second to think about it, and she started to shake and cry.

Tony intervened. "Officer . . ." He looked at the badge. "Hanson? You need to talk to Detective Ford – he's been handling arson cases involving my business. This is the first time something like this has happened, at least with anything of Nikki's, anything personal, in fact, but I have to believe it's related."

"Oh. Yes sir. I'll get with him and get the rundown. Mr. Stokes and Mr. Flores have given me your contact information, Ms. Wilkes. We'll be in touch." Officer Hanson walked away while writing down more notes.

Nikki took a really good look and the reality of the situation sank in. "Oh, my SUV!" Nikki wailed. "And it was paid for!"

"It was old," Tony said, not missing a beat.

"It was mine!" Nikki snarled indignantly. "I loved it."

"You'll get a new one," Tony said simply.

"I'll get a used one. I can't afford a new one." Nikki stared in disbelief and wondered how she'd ever afford something to drive. She'd dropped her comprehensive coverage to save money when the loan was paid off on it, and there wouldn't be replacement cash coming.

"No, you'll get a new one." Tony took her arm and led her to his truck. "Come on, get in. We're going home. We'll get you something to drive tomorrow."

As they drove home, Tony turned a couple of times until they were on Shelbyville Road. He drove down near the malls and turned into the lot of a car dealership, driving right up front to the new models. Nikki looked around; it was a Volvo dealership. Tony parked right behind a brand-new black Volvo XC90 SUV and got out. "What about this one?" he pointed.

Nikki got out and walked straight up to the window with the sticker on it. Her mouth dropped open. "I can't afford this," she whispered.

"But do you like it?"

"Not really." Yeah, she did, but it was easier to say she didn't. It was kind of embarrassing – did he really think she could buy one of those?

"They're the safest cars on the road," he said plainly, walking around it.

She looked at it again. "Tony, I don't have this kind of money."

"Would you prefer another color?" They were looking at a green one, but there was a dark blue one on the other side of two silver ones, and he pointed toward it. "What about that one?"

She pointed at a red one. "What about that one?" It had a sunroof. She walked to the sticker and looked – five thousand more than the first one. "Never mind." She was feeling more hopeless by the minute. She just started walking away.

"But do you like it?" he called after her.

"Doesn't matter. I could never afford it." She got back into his big silver pickup truck.

Once they were rolling again, Tony told her, "I'll take you to work in the morning. Or you can drive the Camaro."

"Can't. I can't drive a straight shift."

"Guess I need to teach you how. You can drive the Mercedes." He reached over and wiped a stray tear off of her face. "It's gonna be okay, princess – I've got your back." He squeezed her hand and she squeezed his in return.

They walked into the house to the smell of something fabulous. Crap – they were supposed to cook with the kids. She checked the kitchen – all of them had been there, cooked, eaten, and left Tony and Nikki leftovers. "I'll call them, make the appropriate apologies, and fill them in," Tony told Nikki. "While I do that, you can fix us some plates. I'm starving."

"You need some stress relief," Tony informed her. He slid down her legs and slipped between them, his face in the apex of her thighs. She stretched and gasped when his tongue found her clit and started to circle it gently. Her folds were already wet, and Tony decided she was the most delectable thing he'd ever tasted, her juices thick and creamy, sweet and tart and salty. She couldn't have tasted better to him if she'd been topped with vanilla bean ice cream. To Tony, this wasn't just a mere sex act – it was intensely spiritual. Fuck the cathedral; this was his place of worship, his sanctuary. Her, her essence, brought him to his knees, held him there, fed him, warmed him, and kept him safe.

All the cares of the day vanished, and orgasmic tension pooled in her abdomen. She felt the ebb and flow of electricity in her pussy as it constricted and released, constricted and released in time with his rhythmic stroking. His fingers crawled up her thighs, up her mons, on up and across her soft belly, and past her ribcage to find her erect nipples and twist them – hard. She felt everything below her waist twist into a blazing knot, and within seconds she was riding an orgasmic wave that had her hips bucking. Tony never let up, never slowed down, never missed one beat of the rhythm.

Before her cries had settled he was deep in her, hammering into her, and her legs came up and around his torso, giving him complete access to her depths. Flipping them both over, he sat them both up and wrapped his legs around and under her bottom as he sat up. He lifted her up and down on his cock, her weight forcing his shaft into her as far as it could go, and she almost screamed at the fullness. He jacked her onto him ravenously, his hands wrapped under her ass, and she pressed her arms into the tops of his shoulders and helped to lift herself up and down on his rigidness, kissing him the whole time, the feel of his skin on hers making her heart sing.

"I wish you could see how you look to me," Tony panted as his cock pumped into her warmth and softness, and he listened to her moan with burning satisfaction. "You're fucking gorgeous. You've got to be the damn sexiest thing I've ever seen," he groaned, looking up into her face.

"If you could see how you look to me, you'd know what sexy *really* looks like," Nikki whispered back. She let her hands slide like quicksilver down his strong neck and shoulders, then to his upper arms, watching his mighty biceps pop with the stress of lifting her up and down. He handled her as if she weighed no more than a sunbeam, and that power over her always tripped every illicit switch in her body. "I wanted you from the first time I saw you," she declared breathlessly, "but I never dreamed I had a chance to be here with you. I thought you were just somebody I'd think about when I met Mr. Okay. I couldn't imagine being here with Mr. Perfect."

"I'm far from perfect, but I love you." Then he added, "And I hope that's all that matters."

"It is." She grinned malevolently. "Well, that and this magnificent cock of yours. Damn, baby, sometimes I think you'll split me wide open. I love you, I want you, I want to fuck you. Sometimes I think I'll die if I don't have you in the next ten minutes. Waiting all day to get back here with you is murder."

"Sometimes all I think about all day is making love with you, precious. I want you so bad I can't breathe." Tony picked up the pace. "Oh, god, baby, I'm gonna come. Are you close?"

Nikki moaned, "I'm right there. Drive it home, babe." His essence bathed her inside and when she felt it, she turned everything loose and came around him, her feminine pulsing drawing every drop of his maleness out and into her. They sat there in the darkness, locked together body and soul, for what seemed like forever before they finally gave in to their exhaustion.

Chapter Twenty-Eight

Nikki turned to the sound of the bell on the door. It had been a slow morning at The Passionate Pansy, and she was relieved to have a potential customer to take her mind off what had happened the evening before.

A young man walked up to the counter. "I'm looking for..." He checked the envelope he was holding: "Nikki Wilkes?"

"That's me," Nikki responded. "How can I help you?"

He held out the envelope with one hand and a set of keys with the other. "You'll have to come and check it out before I can ask you to sign."

"Sign what?"

"The paperwork." He walked to the door. "It's right there." He pointed down the block.

Nikki walked to the door and looked in the general direction the young man's finger was pointing. At the curb was a huge, brand-new Volvo XC90, and red at that. Nikki blinked – she was pretty sure it was the same one she'd looked at the night before. "Oh, no." She shook her head. "I can't accept that."

"It's already paid for. Just go out, inspect it, and sign. It's yours."

Nikki pulled her cell phone from her pocket and dialed Tony's number. He answered in one ring and announced, without even greeting her, "If you're going to say anything other than thanks, don't bother. That's the only word I'll accept right now."

"Tony, I . . . thanks. But I can't take it."

"Yes, you can. And you will. It's safe, it's an automatic, and it's red. What more could you possibly want?"

"I want you to know that I can take care of myself," Nikki said very bluntly.

"I know you can. But last night was scary; god, honey, I thought I'd lost you. I'll feel better if you're driving that thing. Please don't give me any trouble on this, baby. Just don't, okay? I've got enough on my plate right now. I'm already worried enough about you, and this takes care of one worry."

Nikki stopped for a second before she agreed. "Okay, I won't argue right now. But we're going to talk about this later."

"About later." *Oh, god, what now?*, she thought. "I need you to come over here to the office after lunch, say about three thirty? There are some things we need to discuss."

"That sounds scary," Nikki said, holding her breath.

"Nothing scary. Something good – you'll see."

"Okay. I'm sure it'll be fine with Marla; I'll be there. And thanks again. I love you. I'll see you then."

"See you then, babe. And I love you too."

Nikki stepped into Tony's office mid-afternoon. "What's this all about?" She was greeted by the sight of Tony, Clayton, Cal, Steve, and Vic all sitting there, and all apparently waiting for her, and suddenly she felt like she was on the hot seat, maybe even in front of the firing squad. "Is something else wrong?"

"Nope, baby. Just sit down and we'll get right to business. Want coffee? Water? Anything?" Tony kissed her before she sat down.

"No, I'm fine." *I'm not fine. What the hell is going on?*

"All right then," Steve said, starting the ball rolling. "First of all, neither of you are going back to the gym for the time being." Nikki started to protest, but Tony shot her a look. Steve continued by saying, "It's not safe for the others who go there. One of them could've been seriously injured last night if they'd been near your SUV." Nikki hadn't thought about that, but he did have a point. She certainly didn't want that.

Tony responded quickly, "I'd already thought about that and I've ordered some gym equipment for the garage at the house here in town."

"So," Steve asked, "Nikki, can we agree this is the best thing for right now?"

She nodded. "I don't like it, but yes, it is best."

"Good. We've got that settled. Now, Tony, you had something you wanted to tell Nikki?"

"Yes." Tony rose from his desk chair and walked to where Nikki sat on the big white sofa, sitting down next to her. He took both of her hands in his and looked straight into her eyes. "Nikki, do you trust me?"

Nikki was taken aback. "Yes, of course! Completely! Why?"

"To make decisions you don't like but that are for your own good?"

"What's this about?" *Uh-oh, here it comes,* Nikki thought, instantly suspicious.

"Nik, I want you to come to work here at Walters Construction."

"Oh, no, I can't . . ."

"Look, it's partly for your safety, honestly. But otherwise, if you're going to be with me and be part of this family, you should be working here."

"But Tony, what if . . ."

"Stop it," he said abruptly, a look of frustration washing over his features, and she blushed in embarrassment. "You're coming to work here, end of discussion. We'll go this evening and get you work clothes and steel-toes. You can hang out with me to start – there's an enormous amount of stuff I need to teach you before you go into anything else. I've decided I want to groom you to take over as chief operations officer, COO. So what do you think?"

"I think this is a mistake and you've possibly lost your mind." She was pretty sure the top of her head was about to blow off. "First of all, I don't know anything about the construction industry." Tony frowned at her. "And second, don't you feel the least bit bad about letting these people rule our lives this way? Isn't this pandering to them?"

"Well, first, you do know more about the construction industry than you give yourself credit for, and I know this because I've watched you working around the house, not to mention the conversations we have over dinner. You're far from clueless. And second, no – I don't give a rat's ass about those people, whoever they are. I only care about keeping you safe. And there are other aspects you don't know about, but I'm sure my mother will enlighten you soon." Nikki gave him a puzzled look, but he ignored it; it was Tony that Raffaella had called and talked to, not Nikki, so his little girlfriend was in for a big surprise. "You can call Marla tonight and talk to her, tell her you won't be back. Under the circumstances I'm sure she'll understand. As far as their safety goes, she'll probably be relieved."

Nikki started to protest, but Steve broke in. "Nikki, every time you walk into that shop, your coworkers are in danger. Is that really what you want?" Nikki's mouth snapped shut. No, she didn't want anyone getting hurt because of her.

"Good. It's settled." Tony patted her hands and went back to sit behind his desk. "Oh, and by the way, Steve, I want her name put on all of the accounts. All of the business accounts should be me, Clayton, Nikki, and Vic. And put her on my household and personal accounts too, and get her debit cards for everything. And I do mean everything." Nikki opened her mouth, then closed it – nothing she'd said to that point had mattered, so why would this time be any different? Tony hit a couple of buttons on his phone and a voice answered over the speaker: "Central supply. Brandon here; may I help you?"

He picked up the handset and put it to his ear. "Brandon, it's Tony. I need a new truck issued. Ford F-250 Super Duty; exactly like my truck. Outfitted the same, winch, generator, brush guard, everything. Automatic transmission. Lots of chrome." Tony looked at Nikki, then said, "What have they got?" He listened, then said, "The blue one. Walters signage. All the GPS links. When can we have it?" Nikki heard the muffled voice on the other end of the phone, then Tony said, "Being issued to Nicolette Renee Wilkes. I'll get you all the personal information tomorrow. Thanks, Brandon."

He ended the call, then punched a few more buttons. The call was answered almost instantly.

"Hey, yeah, Brenda, this is Tony. Listen, I need a new employee added to payroll and a company credit card issued to Nicolette Renee Wilkes. How soon can we get that?" He listened. "Next Tuesday? Yeah, fine. When it comes, bring it straight to me. Send over all of the employment paperwork and we'll fill it out. Thanks."

He ended that call and wrote something on his desk blotter. Nikki was in shock – he wasn't kidding about this. She wanted to say, *What if you get tired of me? What do I do then?* But she didn't. That should be a private conversation, and this was anything but private.

Tony looked at Nikki, then Clayton. "Can we move her into your office? It's the biggest in the building."

"Sure, Dad. Besides, I've never done anything with it." Clayton turned to Nikki. "Maybe you could do something in there. It looks like a storage space."

"Unless you want to share this office with me?" Tony asked Nikki.

"Whatever you want." She was so confused and bewildered that she really couldn't think. "At least I think that's the answer you're looking for." Tony frowned. Vic cleared his throat and Cal and Clayton both turned away.

"We'll have that conversation at home," Tony said curtly. "But I want to add something here. If anything happens, anything, and I'm not around or not available, you go to Clayton or Vic. If I can't protect you, these two would lay their lives down for you, Nik. No question in my mind." Clayton and Vic nodded in agreement. "You'll always be safe with any of the three of us. Steve too, for that matter."

"Yep," Steve interjected. "Speaking of which, we're installing cameras and motion sensors all over your house and property. I'm adding more employees, and I've decided to incorporate the business into Citadel Security. Are you comfortable with the people I've got on you?" he asked, turning to Nikki.

"I like Peyton and José," Nikki answered. "I haven't really met the lady yet."

"Laura. Laura Butler. She's good. She's, well, not much I can tell you, but she's tough as nails."

"One more thing." Tony pointed at Clayton and Cal. "If I hear anything about any of the guys being disrespectful to Nikki, making rude comments, touching her in any way," he added, a menacing look coming over his face, "I expect you to put a stop to it immediately. I won't have it. First infraction, stern warning. Second infraction, termination. No exceptions." Cal and Clayton nodded their understanding. "Good. Glad we got that straight up front. Okay, everybody back to work. Except you, Vic. Sit tight. Steve, thanks for being here."

"Any time. We've got you covered, big guy," Steve told him as he walked out.

Clayton started out the door, then turned and walked back to Nikki. He hugged her tight, then stepped back with his hands on her upper arms, smiled a huge smile, and kissed her on the cheek before turning and walking out the door. She'd wondered what he thought about all of this, and now she knew. That was the thing with Clayton; he didn't talk much, but he had a way of letting you know how he felt.

Once everyone else was gone, Vic moved over to the sofa beside Nikki and hugged her. They sat with his arm around her shoulder, and Tony turned to both of them. "I wanted to talk to you two together. Nikki, this man sitting here beside you? I'd trust him with anything, even your life. He's easily the most intelligent person I know besides you, and the most trustworthy and loyal. If you need anything, anything at all, go to Vic."

Tony looked at Vic. "This woman is my life. I haven't made this official, and we haven't had the definitive discussion, but I have every intention of making her my wife before the end of the year, if she'll have me." Nikki tried not to look too shocked, but her mind went into overdrive. "If anything happens to me, I expect you to take care of her. That puts both of you in a very difficult position, I know, so I don't even care how far that goes, as long as I know you're involved and she's safe. You and I, we're closer than I am to my brothers, and I trust you implicitly. Please, please don't let me down in this; I really need to know you'll be there for her."

Vic nodded to Tony, then looked at Nikki. "Little girl, I love you too." He gave her a squeeze. "I'd do anything for you." The feeling was mutual; when Vic had returned with the dinner rolls on the Fourth, Nikki knew she didn't ever want to spend too many days without being graced by his presence. Vic turned back to Tony. "You have my word. They'll have to kill me to get to her. You'll never have to worry about her as long as I'm around."

"Well, that's settled. I feel better; well, a little better. I'll feel a whole lot better as soon as we find this bunch of idiots and put an end to this. Vic, want to stay at the house tonight? It's Bennie and Mark's last night here, and we're all going out, even Mamma, so come to dinner with us."

"Sure! I'd love to!" Vic looked positively thrilled.

Great, Nikki thought. *Dinner with everybody. Even longer until I can get him alone and have a long talk.*

And then it hit her – Tony had said *I have every intention of making her my wife before the end of the year, if she'll have me.* He wanted to marry her. Suddenly, everything became crystal clear. She was worried about a lot of things, but Tony and how he felt about her didn't have to be one of them.

Molly was still mad – that was obvious. She was barely polite to Nikki all evening and spent most of her time stewing. Kathy and Victoria chatted with Raffaella. Nikki spent most of the evening trying to engage Caroline, but it was really hard; it almost seemed like she had no life so she had next to nothing to talk about. Kathy, Victoria, and Raffaella had sensed Nikki's efforts and tried to help her out, but it was almost a lost cause.

The guys talked business; well, most of the guys talked business. Bennie hung on the edge of everything and, if he talked to anyone, it was most likely to be Mark. Nikki assumed that was because neither of them lived in Louisville. Tony, Vic, and Bart had the most in common, and at least Freddie also lived in Louisville and knew a lot of the same people, so they had more to talk about.

When dinner was over and some of the family members were enjoying coffee, Tony stood. "I have something to announce." He motioned to Nikki. "Babe, would you join me here please?" Nikki stood awkwardly and moved to his spot at the table, wondering what he was up to. He put one arm around her waist.

"I'd like to let everyone know that as of tomorrow, Nikki will be a full-time employee of Walters Construction. I'll be working her into the position of chief operations officer. She's a very quick learner, and I don't expect it to take her very long before she's making herself invaluable to the company." Nikki had noticed a swarm of servers buzzing around, and she realized it was champagne they were carrying. They served everyone, and Tony raised his glass. "A toast to my lovely girlfriend and newest coworker. Baby, may this be the most perfect job you weren't really looking for."

"*Congratulazioni e buona fortuna!*" Vic called out, laughing. Nikki was truly surprised. She'd expected someone to make some kind of snide comment about how it would never work, but no one said anything unwelcoming. She glanced over at Raffaella, who gave her a small smile and nodded. Even Molly kept her mouth shut. Nikki didn't really know what to make of it, and she hoped no one noticed she wasn't smiling, because she sure didn't feel like smiling.

As the champagne started flowing, everyone was laughing and talking, and Nikki excused herself to go to the restroom. She went into a stall and sat. There, in the quiet, she took a deep breath and tried to get her mind to still, but she was almost dizzy from the way her thoughts were racing. She finished, flushed, and came out of the stall, only to find Raffaella sitting in one of the chairs in the lounge area of the restroom. Nikki washed her hands, then walked over to where Raffaella was sitting, curious as to what the older woman wanted. "Please, sit," Raffaella directed, sweeping her hand toward an empty chair. Nikki sat and waited.

After a minute, Raffaella started hesitantly. "I suppose you wonder why I would come to speak to you in here, but I have no other place. Too many family members around, and I must speak now." If she was looking for Nikki's full attention, she'd gotten it.

"I have four daughters-in-law. They are all lovely women; well, most of them. Molly can be, how you say, trying sometimes." That was sure an understatement. "I must be blunt. Through the years, I have tried in vain to find the qualities in these women that must be present for one of them to become the matriarch of this family. But none of them possess those qualities. You, however, have them all – strong sense of loyalty and family, bravery, intelligence, compassion, and resourcefulness. And more than that, you love my son and his children – this is plain to see." Raffaella took a deep breath. "Nikki, I wish for you to begin to think like *la matriarca* of this family, to do for this family what I would do, to be what I would be. I am not getting any younger. You have the ability to hold it, hold them, together when things get difficult."

Nikki was taken aback. "Oh, Raffaella, I feel so honored, but . . ."

"Then it is settled. I trust your judgment to do or say whatever you need to. And I am sorry it could not wait until a more private setting, but I felt the need to move this forward." Raffaella leaned over and patted the younger woman on the hand. "You are the best thing that has happened to our family in many years. Your love for my son and my family has put my mind at ease, and your character is above reproach. I am sorry our relationship started with such a painful test, but it had to be so. I apologize if I hurt you, but I think you can understand my original concern, which I now realize was totally unfounded. If I can ever help you in any way, please come to me." She rose and, without another word, walked out the restroom door.

Nikki sat and blinked. What had just happened? She stood to go back to the table, but her feet felt like lead. When she got back to the group, Tony took one look at her and helped her get into her seat. "Are you okay?" he asked in a whisper. "You look like you've just seen a train wreck."

"I feel like I've been in one," was all she could manage to whisper back.

"Night, Vic. See you in the morning," Nikki called down the hallway as she closed the door to the master bedroom. Tony was already in bed, sitting quietly propped against the headboard, pillows everywhere. Neither said anything as Nikki went into the bathroom to wash her face and brush her teeth.

Finished, she came out into the bedroom and crawled under the sheets, then reached to turn out the light on her side of the bed. Everyone was settled, dogs and cousin. Mark, Victoria, Bennie, and Caroline were back at the big house, getting a good night's sleep before heading home the next day. The house was finally quiet – really, really quiet.

Tony made no move to touch Nikki or to lie down, just sat with his light on, her back to him. After what seemed like forever, he said quietly, "Please, say something. Anything. Get mad at me. But please don't shut me out."

Nikki rolled to her back and let out a loud sigh. "I'm not shutting you out. I'm just exhausted and I really don't know what to think. I spent the latter part of this day getting railroaded by everybody in my cone of influence until I feel like I've got tire treads up the middle of my face." There – that pretty much described her feelings to perfection. "I was hoping to talk to you this evening, but I really don't think I'm up to a heavy-duty discussion right now."

"Honey, I'm so sorry." Tony's voice was low, and there was a sadness in it she hadn't heard before. She glanced over to see him looking down, a pained expression on his face. "I never meant for all of this to be so harsh and overpowering. And I saw her leave the table too, so I'm guessing my mother caught you in the restroom?"

Nikki sighed again. "Yes, she did. If I wasn't completely beaten down before, that pretty much capped it off. I feel like somebody's taken a baseball bat to me. I'd cry, but I'm just too tired and stressed out."

Tony reached over and took Nikki's hand. "My fault, all my fault. But it had to be done, and I couldn't come up with a better way to do it. I'm so sorry. I just love you so much . . ."

"I know, baby." She reached up to stroke his face. As soon as her fingers touched him, he scooted down in the bed and scooped her into his arms. The relaxing effect was instantaneous, and she curled into his chest and wrapped her arms around his waist. The heat from his skin was soothing, and she was comfortable for the first time all day. "I love you too, and I want to do what needs to be done, but damn, I'm in over my head, you know?"

Tony kissed the top of her head. "No, you're not. You're going to be fine. You're smart and tough."

"It feels like everything's being taken away from me," she whispered as she nuzzled into the hair on his chest. His scent always gave her a peace she couldn't find anywhere else, and she almost forgot everything that had happened since she'd slept last.

"Actually, you've been given a fantastic opportunity. You're a new, rising employee of one of the biggest, strongest businesses in this area. You've got full support of management," he reminded her, kissing her forehead, "a company vehicle, insurance, benefits, a security team at your disposal, and access to all the money you could possibly need. And a guy who loves you more than anything in the world, don't forget that."

"By the way, about this thing with the accounts, why did you do that?"

"Well, I happen to know you haven't had a physical in several years because you didn't have money or insurance to pay for it. I also know you buy most of your clothes at consignment or Goodwill – you admitted that. And I know about all the little things, a magazine or book, popcorn at the movies, a new hairbrush – all things you pass up because you don't have the money. Those days are over for you. If you go out and buy a fifteen carat diamond, I might be upset. But if you go to the mall and spend two hundred dollars on bras, I'm not going to bat an eyelash. Hundred dollar jeans, four hundred dollar boots, whatever you want – go buy it. I've worked hard and, apparently, you're the reason, even though I didn't know it the last thirty-six years. Whatever I have, it's all yours." He stopped for a minute, then added, "And a future mother-in-law who thinks you're the greatest thing since gorgonzola."

Future mother-in-law, huh? "Oh, yeah, and there was that thing you said in the office . . ."

"About being married by the end of the year? Caught that, did you?" He'd known she'd ask about that sooner or later.

"Yeah, that's the one."

"Baby, I'm sorry. I know that's not the dream proposal a girl wants. I plan to do it and do it right later on, but you needed to know right at that moment what I was thinking." He gave her a soft smile. "I don't know for sure what you want, but as for me, I want to spend the rest of my life with you."

"I want to spend the rest of my life with you too." She grimaced. "But if I have another day like today, the rest of my life may not be much longer. Not to mention I'm going to be subjected to driving a monster truck." She frowned.

"I can make it all better." Tony gave her a dreamy smile and scooted down under the covers. Nikki felt him get hold of the top of her panties and pull them down until they were gone, snatched off to that far-away place where panties go when hot guys make them disappear. "Want me to take you far, far away?" he asked, his voice muffled by the sheet and blanket. "I can make that happen, beautiful." He slipped under her leg and, next thing she knew, she was being transported to that wonderful place where only he could take her, face down and making a bedtime snack of her. His tongue probed into her pussy and she sighed; then he lapped at her tender, swelling bud, and she groaned and squirmed while he held her hips down.

Nikki needed it. She didn't care that she was making noise, or that Vic was right down the hall and probably listening to the whole thing. None of that mattered – all that mattered was her and him and right that minute. When she moaned and cried out, "Oh, god, Tony, I'm coming!" he stopped abruptly, drew her legs straight up his torso, and plunged his cock into her, rubbing her clit vigorously with his thumb. Wailing like a banshee, she rode into her orgasm full-throttle until she was out of her head with ecstasy. He pounded away, jarring everything inside her as he drove himself home over and over, the sight of her long, shapely legs and her hard nipples propelling him. She was so out of it, so enraptured, that she vaguely heard him murmur something about how tight she was, and then felt his hot cum flood her. He drew her legs wide apart, fell on top of her unceremoniously, and wrapped his arms around her waist, thrusting two or three times more for good measure, milking both their climaxes for everything he could get out of them.

"Oh. My. God. That was a head rush," she whispered, still panting and wriggling.

He chuckled. "You think that was good, you just wait. I've got a new trick up my sleeve – literally – that I'm going to spring on you tomorrow night."

"Do I have to wait until tomorrow? What about now?"

He laughed. "I thought you were tired and stressed out."

"Well, I was! I think you've got the cure, big boy," she laughed back.

"That's right, baby – the doctor is in."

Chapter Twenty-Nine

Saturday was relaxing, with nowhere they had to be and nothing they had to do. They invited the kids to come over that evening and Tony grilled. After everyone was gone, Nikki told Tony, "I'm so proud of you."

"Huh? Why? What did I do?"

"Because of how hard you work. Because of everything you give back. Because of how you love your family, your friends, this community. I'm so lucky to have you." She was beaming.

"Thanks, baby. I'm pretty proud of you. You've stood up to my family, and you're going to make a great coworker, I just know it," He squeezed her hand and smiled down at her.

"I wish there was something I could do for you so you'd know how much I appreciate you."

He leered at her. "Oh, I think there's something you can do. Let's go down the hall and I'll let you do it."

"Oh, Mr. Walters! Whatever do you mean?" she whined in her best fake southern accent.

"Come on and I'll show you."

Tony had been running it over and over in his mind, and he wanted it so much for her that he hurt just thinking about it. Nikki had done everything he'd ever asked her to do in bed; she'd even offered to do things he'd never thought of. And he knew she wanted this. If he could give it to her . . . he wanted to fulfill every desire she had, felt like it was his duty. He loved her too much not to. Besides, if she were asked who the greatest lover she'd ever had was, he wanted her to honestly be able to say it was him. It was just a damn point of honor.

"Fuck me again, baby," Nikki growled under her breath. "I need you so bad." She reached between her legs and found that huge cock she loved so much right where it had left off, stroking it to keep it hard and ready again. "Please?" She'd found the more he fucked her, the more she wanted him. She was addicted, and she didn't mind that he knew.

"I promised you something else last night, and I aim to deliver tonight, right now." Tony plunged his tongue into her mouth and breathed into her before breaking away. "Ready?"

"I have no idea. I don't know what you're up to," she said, breathless and aching for him. "I just want you back inside me."

"Oh, I'm gonna be inside you all right," he snickered. He got out of bed and stood at the edge of the mattress, then grabbed her ankles and pulled her to the edge while she squealed and giggled. Once she was in place, he shoved a towel under her ass and knelt down in front of her. "Drop your legs open as far as you can." When she'd opened as much as possible, he stopped, admired, and said, "Damn, baby! I think that's the prettiest thing I've ever seen!" She giggled again. "Now, put your feet on the outsides of my shoulders and leave them there." His arms were lying on the mattress, so it was easy for her to rest her feet there, and she waited, wondering what he was up to. "Gonna be cold, sweetie. Hang in there. I have to do this." She heard a *snap* and felt a flood of something cold and wet – lube, had to be. But god, that much of it? Nikki looked down and tried to see what he was doing, but he chuckled and snapped, "Uh-uh! Close your eyes and relax."

She felt him slide a finger inside her, then two, then three. He drove them in and out a few times, and she moaned. Then he put one finger of the other hand in with them, and the stretch was yummy. He added a second on the other hand, and she felt the added stretch and moaned louder. The sounds of her pleasure were exactly what he wanted; every time she made a sound his cock got a little bit harder. When he added the third finger on the other hand, she groaned out, "Oh, god, that feels so good."

"Yeah?" he snickered. "You may change your mind in a minute."

She felt him rotate his hands so that his palms were out and his thumbs down, fingers still inside her. Then everything changed – he was pulling outward with both hands, opening her up farther, and she felt the pressure on both sides of her sheath. It was excruciating and delicious at the same time. He pulled and relaxed, pulled and relaxed, and she wondered where he was going with it.

"How's that?" he asked. "Good?"

"God, yeah. Incredible. But I don't like being empty. At all. I've gotten used to that giant dick. Where is it?" she whined.

"Oh, I've got something to go in there, but I don't know if you can handle it."

She snorted. "I've never backed down before. What makes you think I would this time?"

"This will push your limits, baby. Ready?" Tony asked.

"Oh, yeah, bring it on!"

Tony removed his fingers, and Nikki felt his absence, was maddened by it. Then she felt him push into her again, but this time, it was fuller somehow. The fullness opened her deliciously and grew with each subsequent stroke. Then he asked, "Little girl, remember your safeword?"

"Of course. Red. Will I need it?" *Oh, I hope, I hope, I hope,* she thought.

"Maybe. I'm going to tell you what to do, and you've got to keep your wits about you and follow my instructions. Hear me?" He slapped the inside of her thigh with his free hand to bring her into the moment and get her attention, and she squealed.

"Yeah, okay. What do you want me to do?" she asked to let him know she was listening.

Tony put his free hand just above her mound, right above her pubic bone in the soft hollow of her belly. "Remember when you had your kids?" Nikki nodded. "When I tell you to push, you push like you're pushing something out. Keep pushing until you feel it – there'll be something like a 'pop' and you'll know. Can you do that?" he asked, his hand insistent, the pressure inside her growing.

"Yes," she whispered; she'd just realized what he was doing. She'd wanted it for years, and she and Randy had tried it but never succeeded; then she remembered he'd told her Cinda had taught him how to fist. Her whole body flushed and her mind started to whir. Tony was going to reach inside her, to touch her in a way no other man had. Apparently he wanted it too – the thought made her smile.

"Listen to me: If it hurts too much, say so. I'll die if I hurt you, angel." Tony pressed even harder and deeper into her, and ordered, "Okay, baby, get ready." She heard the lube bottle cap pop again and more of the liquid dripped. He stroked twice more, then instructed, "Okay, babe, push – push hard and don't stop until I tell you to."

Nikki bore down, dropped her knees farther apart and pulled her glutes in tight. The stroking stopped and she felt the pressure from his hand building when, suddenly, there was the sensation he'd described as a "pop" as his hand breeched her pelvic bone. Nikki screamed out, "Ohhhhhh myyyyyyy gaaaawwwwd," and thrust her pelvis upward.

She heard Tony gasp, and then he whispered, "Oh god – wow!" The sensation was unbelievable, so full, so tight, so deliciously painful, a deep ache that sent every nerve ending into overload. "Baby, please," she whined, "please, move inside me, please. Oh, god, please, I can't stand it!"

"Nik, I wish you could see what I see," Tony whispered. "Oh, my god. It's beautiful – you're beautiful. I see it but I don't believe it. Give me your hand." She reached out and he took her hand, then placed it on her belly where his had been. Through her own flesh, she could feel ntedhis hand inside her, feel it moving, and she was overjoyed at the way it connected them, like she and this man, this precious, beautiful man, were linked in a way she'd never been with anyone else. She felt him flex his fingers and make a fist, and she cried out in utter bliss and gave herself over to the sensations.

Even the tiniest movement inside Nikki was intensified by the incredible stretch, and when she felt him start to circle her clit with the fingers of his free hand, she came completely unglued. She cried out over and over at the top of her lungs until, at one point, he asked, "Baby, you okay? Need to safeword?" She shook her head wildly and he kept up the exquisite torment until she finally succumbed to the orgasm and her body convulsed uncontrollably. Tony coaxed her along with, "That's my girl," and "Keep it up, baby, don't stop," until she was a jerking, breathless mess. The contractions around his fist made his cock throb, and the joy in his heart at being able to give her something she'd wanted so badly made the ache even sweeter. He didn't want it to ever end, but he finally straightened his hand inside her, relieving some of the pressure. She wiped her eyes with the backs of her hands and tried to make sense of everything she'd felt.

"Sweetie, I've got to take it out."

"No! God, no! Please?" she pleaded, awash in a sea of satisfaction.

"Yes – have to. Same way it went in. You push and I pull. Ready?" Tony asked. Nikki nodded. "Okay, push, baby – give it all you've got." Nikki bore down again, and she felt a snap, then a heartbreaking emptiness.

With a swipe of the towel to clean her up, Tony had her back up on the pillows and pulled her into him. "Oh, god, baby, that was incredible! I'm so glad I could give you that. Was it good? You liked it?" he asked her.

Nikki started to sob, and she whispered, "Oh, god, Tony. I love you so much," and wrapped her arms around his neck, crying into his shoulder.

"Oh, baby, I'm so hard for you, I want you so bad. Think you can handle it right now? Feel okay?"

"I feel okay, but I need to wait; hurts a little, you know? Like it's supposed to; not bad. And besides, I have other plans." She wiped her eyes again and slithered down his side, then snuggled down into the space between his legs. "I want to do something for you." She didn't waste any time settling her mouth down over his cock, and it was as hard as she'd ever seen it. The ache between her own legs drove her onto him, and she sucked him greedily like a bird pulling at a worm on a warm spring morning. He moaned and thrust into her mouth, and she took him deeper.

Nikki wrapped her arms around his legs and flipped them both onto their sides. In a velvety voice, she purred, "Fuck my throat, baby. Take whatever you want. I'm all yours." Tony's hands wound into her hair and he pulled her to him as he drove his hardness into her mouth, hitting the back of her throat. Nikki relaxed to kill off her gag reflex, and her eyes watered as he slammed harder and faster into her. About every third stroke she tried to remember to swallow around him, and he moaned louder and stroked into her harder. When she thought she'd completely lose her breath and drift into unconsciousness, she felt his balls tighten, and he unloaded into her, his salty cum filling her throat and her mouth and running out the corners of her lips.

Tony released his hold on her hair and his arms dropped in exhaustion. Nikki was gasping for breath as she wiped her mouth with the back of her hand, then crawled up to lie in his arms. In the kiss she gave him he could taste his own saltiness on her lips, and he forced his tongue into her mouth, savoring what she'd done for him, the way he felt at that moment, the way he felt about her.

"Is everybody happy?" he asked her, cuddling her tight.

"Over the moon here. You?"

"Never happier. If you'd told me a year ago I'd find a woman I'd be this much in love with this fast, I'd have told you that you were crazy." He gazed down at her. "Nothing crazy about this. God, I love you. I can't imagine ever being without you." He stopped, then asked, "You'd really let me do anything I want to you, wouldn't you?"

Oddly, Nikki felt herself blush. "Yeah, I guess I would. I trust you completely."

"Precious, I will never take that trust lightly, and I'll never betray it, I promise." He kissed the tip of her nose.

"I know that. And that's why this body is yours to do with as you please."

"I feel the same way. You've never brought me anything but bliss. And I hope I never bring you anything but bliss. That was okay, what we just did? You're okay, not hurt?"

"Sweetie, I've never felt better in my life, more free or more satisfied. And I need to tell you something."

"What's that?" he asked, kissing the top of her head.

"When we first got together and you told me about your history, I was really worried."

"Yeah? Why?"

"Because you'd only been with two women. Because you'd been exposed to so little."

"And now?"

She propped herself up on an elbow to look into his face, "Baby, I've never been with anybody who's been as concerned about satisfying me and as open to trying things as you are. You're pretty fearless. And you're good, too, really good. Plus we can talk about sex and neither of us gets all weirded out, you know? I love that. You're the best lover and best friend I've ever had." She lay back down in his arms, her cheek resting on his chest.

"Good." Tony looked very proud of himself. "All I want is for you to be completely, totally, one hundred percent happy. I just want to give you what you want and need." He stopped for a second. "But you're still gonna have to drive that truck."

Sunday rolled around and Tony decided to go fishing for the afternoon, and made arrangements for Bart and Vic to meet him at Taylorsville Lake. Not Freddie. He never liked that kind of stuff; he didn't like to get dirty. Nikki went to buy her work clothes – carpenter's jeans, tees, an steel-toed boots – and Tony ordered her to use his credit and debit cards and get whatever she wanted.

When Tony came in from fishing, Nikki had been cooking for awhile. He walked into the kitchen to see what was going on because there was so much noise coming from in there.

He stopped in the doorway and tried to take it all in, to let it sink into his mind and his heart. Nikki stood at the sink, barefoot, washing some vegetables. She was wearing a brightly-colored apron she'd bought at one of the boutiques in Gatlinburg while they were there, a pair of tight denim shorts hugging her sweet ass and peeking out from underneath the apron. Tony had bought her a docking station with speakers for her smart phone, and she was playing music, a female singer belting out a cheerful sort of tune; Nikki was part singing, part humming, her hips swaying in time to the music. She dropped the brush and vegetable and danced over to the stove where several pots were steaming, taking lids off and stirring first one, then another. The smell was beyond incredible, and his mouth was already watering just wondering what she was cooking.

She danced back to the sink and started scrubbing the vegetables again and, in that moment, Tony realized he was seeing something most men took for granted. But not him. For Tony, this was something he never thought he'd see in his life – a woman, a beautiful, loving, sensuous woman, singing and dancing happily in his kitchen, their kitchen, cooking a wonderful meal for him, waiting for him to come home, thinking about him with love and passion and joy. He whispered under his breath, "Nikki Wilkes, oh my god, I love you. I love you so much."

As if she'd heard him, she turned gave him a wide smile. "Hi, baby! I didn't see you standing there! I'm so glad you're home!" She bounded across the room and into his arms, and the smell of her, her softness, was almost too much for him. He looked down into her face and couldn't say anything, he was so choked up. "What's wrong?"

He smiled through his tears. "Not a thing – not one damn thing. I'm going to shower. I don't want to make you wait to eat."

"How was dinner?" Nikki asked as she cleared the table.

"You're a dream, sweetie. It was delicious. I'll help you clean up." He started picking up the plates and taking them to the sink. They worked together, side by side, until the whole kitchen was spotless.

"So what did you buy today?" Tony asked her after they'd gotten settled in the den. She showed him the shirts, jeans, and boots.

"I think I got everything I need," Nikki told him. "And I got something for you."

"For me? You weren't supposed to be shopping for me."

Nikki smiled. "Well, you've given me some very nice gifts, but I realized I've never given you anything. I saw something I thought would look good on you, so I got it. It's kind of silly, I know; you actually wind up in the end buying it for yourself. So I guess it was kind of stupid, huh?"

"No, not stupid. I'm really excited. I don't get too many gifts. And it's from my baby, so that's exciting, too!" He actually looked excited, Nikki thought. "Besides, you'll be getting a hefty paycheck in a couple of weeks, so you can pay for it yourself," he told her as she crossed the room and pulled the box from her purse.

"Here. She handed him the box, breathless and fighting her pounding heart. "I hope you like it."

Tony took it and opened it, and the bracelet gleamed in the lamp light. He blinked a couple of times, trying to believe what he was seeing. If he'd picked it out himself, he couldn't have done a better job. Nikki sat and waited, nervous and wondering what he'd say.

"Oh, sweetheart, it's perfect. Just perfect. I've never had anything like this! Thank you so much!" He hugged her, then gave her a big kiss before trying it on.

"You really like it?" The look on her face, the delight there at giving him a gift, made his heart melt.

He gave her cheek a gentle kiss. "I love it. I love it almost as much as I love you!"

"Your truck's ready." Tony put the phone down and looked at Nikki over his sunglasses. "I'm leaving to go to the hospital jobsite. I can take you over to central supply to pick it up."

"Sure. Can we have lunch later?"

"You bet. I'll meet you at Café Mimosa at," he looked at his watch, "twelve thirty?"

"Deal!" She climbed into his truck and, as she did, she looked over at him and smiled – he was wearing his bracelet! It made her so proud.

Even though she was familiar with Tony's work truck, she'd never driven it. When they pulled up and she saw the giant, bright blue truck, she felt funny all over, and not in a ha-ha way. It was really, really blue and really, really big, and the brush guard on the front gave it a positively evil look. One of the guys in the supply office grabbed the keys and came out with them to look it over before she signed off on it. Tony did most of the looking; Nikki mostly stared, wide-eyed.

"Okay, I've gotta go. It's all yours. And by the way, it's diesel, so don't go pulling up to any unleaded pumps, okay?" he grinned. Nikki nodded; she'd never had a diesel vehicle before.

Tony pulled away, and Nikki climbed – literally climbed – into the cab. If anything slid to the other side of the seat, she wouldn't be able to reach it because it was so huge. She looked it over – GPS navigation system, satellite radio, hands-free feature, towing package, everything. The dash was covered in buttons, and she had no ideas what the icons on all of the buttons represented. She wondered if there was a toilet hidden somewhere in the cab.

She couldn't find a place to stick the key into the ignition, so she tried the button on the key, and the truck roared to life, scaring her half to death in the process. She expected some resistance, but the gearshift lever slid smoothly into drive and she pulled out of the parking space and headed for the gate. As she neared the office, Clayton came out the door, popped a startled look onto his face, and grinned and waved as she passed. She stopped at the street, then pulled out into traffic, and she was surprised as she pulled out of the drive at how smooth the ride was. She had deposits to take to the bank – her first official duty, Tony announced – and she rolled out toward Katie's branch of Kentucky Miner's Savings & Loan.

But she almost didn't make it.

She started to switch lanes and heard loud honking. That was when she realized that the truck was so big, she couldn't see small cars in the right-hand lane, even in her mirrors. She tried again, with the same result, just a different car. Nikki felt tears coming to her eyes, and she wondered if she'd ever get over into the right-hand lane when she heard a honk and a man waved her over. She moved right, then waved back to him. *I have to get some bubble mirrors for this thing before I kill somebody,* she thought, making a mental note to herself to take it to the shop when she got back.

The day went pretty smoothly, all things considered. Nikki felt like everyone was watching her, waiting for her to make some kind of terrible mistake, but they were all very nice to her. That afternoon, she went to her house and pulled artwork off the walls, loaded it into the truck, and took it back to the office. It was doing no one any good at her house, since there was no one there to see it, and it would brighten up her and Clayton's office.

Clayton walked in at quitting time to see Nikki's artwork all over their shared office. "Wow!" He gazed around. "This looks great! Hey, what happened to my stuff?" he asked, looking for the boxes he'd piled everywhere.

"All in here." Nikki pointed to a whole bank of filing cabinets. "Every box now has a drawer, and everything is in hanging folders so you can find it. I hope that was okay." The smile she gave him was small and timid.

"Okay? It's great! You've really worked hard. I hope Dad plans to reward you with a nice dinner or something."

"I'm sure he's got something wonderful in store for me." Nikki shot him a dreamy smile. "He always does."

"So, how do you like your truck?"

"I hate the damn thing. It's too big. I feel like I'm in some kind of tactical vehicle."

"Okay, why don't you tell me how you *really* feel?"

"Why can't I just have a normal truck, Tony? Something not so, oh, I don't know, fucking *huge*?"

"Because there'll be times when you'll have to hook up to something and winch it free, or drag something heavy, or power something with the generator, and you'll need that *huge* truck. This ain't no job for sissies, little girl."

"Well, I ain't no sissy. But I am little. And I can't see out of the damn thing. I almost crushed two tiny little cars today because I couldn't see them."

"Then they should stay the hell out of your blind spot. Or better yet, if they were that little, they should stay the hell away from a truck that size. In that thing, you've got the power, sistah."

"Well, hell yeah, I guess I do, huh?" she grinned.

Chapter Thirty

Nikki looked at her checklist for the day. Contracts signed, correspondence done, disaster averted at the university jobsite, and she'd had the damn truck in for its first thousand mile service. She was pretty sure she'd never get used to driving that thing, although it was so huge that the Volvo had started to feel small to her.

They were staring down the barrel of a loaded August, and things were going pretty good. There'd been a couple more incidents at jobsites, some GoGreen graffiti at one, and a couple of pieces of earth moving equipment disabled at another, but nothing major. She felt like she was actually earning some of her pay too, although she still didn't really understand half of what was going on around her. She'd spent some time helping central supply streamline some inventory issues, and she ran lots of errands.

At least one day each week Nikki spent the day with Tony, doing whatever he needed to do, shadowing him to see how he handled things. She had to admit she was impressed and very, very proud when she was with him. Not only did he know exactly what to do in every situation, but he was tactful, diplomatic, and kind, while still being extremely strong and forceful. He got results. She smiled to herself – he had the same effect on her in bed, and she loved it. He was a one man force of nature, and she considered being part of his world a privilege.

She told Cheryl goodbye for the day and strolled to the truck. Tony was at a jobsite on the other side of town – something to do with one of the university buildings – and she didn't know when he'd be home. When she got to the house, she woke Bill and Hillary and sent them outside, then changed into some workout gear and headed to the garage. Tony had ordered an HVAC unit and had it installed, and the workout room in the garage was about as comfortable as they could make it. They had several weight machines, a treadmill, spin bike, and plenty of free weights and benches, plus a rowing machine. It was no commercial gym, but it would do.

When she finished her workout, she showered off quickly, changed into sweats, and started working on dinner. Bill and Hillary were still outside, probably playing in the dirt, their favorite thing to do; baths tonight for sure. It had been odd that they'd been sleeping when she came in, but they'd been alone all day. They'd probably been pretty bored.

She texted Tony: *Coming home anytime soon?* He responded almost immediately: *Leaving the school site now. Be there in fifteen.* She smiled as she roasted the peppers over the open flame of the rangetop, then laid them aside to cool while she cut up the chicken for the stir-fry.

By the time she had everything cut up, Tony had come through the door, kissed her, and changed and headed to the garage. After putting the rice on to steam, she started making the stir-fry sauce, a special concoction she'd come up with years before, and Tony had decided he loved it. She was getting ready to go to the garage and ask when he'd be done when she heard it: Tony bellowed her name so loudly that it made her jump even in the house. Her heart almost stopped, and she dropped the towel she'd used to dry her hands and bolted out the door.

Tony had dropped to his knees in the yard. Bill was lying in front of him, convulsing wildly. Not ten feet from them, Hillary lay still, a puddle of vomit by her face. "What is it?" she screamed, running toward them. "What's happening?"

"I don't know! I found them like this when I started to the house! Quick, run and get some towels to wrap them in – I'll get the truck!" Nikki bounded up the back steps and into the laundry room, grabbing an armload of towels from the dryer and running back outside. Bill had quit convulsing and was lying perfectly still like Hillary. She threw a towel over him and scooped him up, then did the same with Hillary. Both were limp as rags in her arms, and she feared the absolute worst.

Tony had the truck running and she threw both dogs into the front seat beside him, then scrambled in herself. "Everybody's closed now," she wailed. "What are we going to do?"

"There's a twenty-four hour clinic off Westport Road." Tony was trying to keep the panic at bay. "I'm heading there." Nikki held on as he gunned the big truck and she heard the engine whine as the turbocharger kicked in. She touched first one dog, then the other, but they were completely still, and she couldn't tell if they were breathing. *Oh, god, please let them be okay,* she whispered to herself, horrified by what she was thinking.

Tony skidded to a stop in front of the clinic, and he grabbed one dog while Nikki grabbed the other. They ran inside, and the lady at the front desk whisked them into the back, calling to one of the vets as they ran. Within minutes, a team worked on both dogs as Tony and Nikki stood close by, watching and trembling.

They sat in the driveway, neither of them able to get out of the truck. Nikki pressed her forehead to the glass of the window, and tears rolled down her cheeks in torrents.

Finally, Tony spoke. "Baby, we did all we could do." He reached for her, and she choked out a sob and turned to him, collapsing into his arms. Her chest ached so badly that it hurt to breathe, and she remembered the days right after Randy and the kids were taken from her – this felt exactly the same. Those two little dogs had been the only family members she'd had left, their little bodies wrapped in towels and lying in the bed of the truck now. Tony couldn't understand how she felt – no one could. It was like the last connection she'd had to her old life was destroyed, and now there'd be no one but her who remembered it, remembered any of them, knew they'd even existed. She was wracked with guilt. She'd been so busy lately that she hadn't spent much time with them, but she'd tried to give them some attention, even if just a little, every night. How had she let this happen?

"It's my fault." She wept loudly and clung to him. "The vet said they probably drank the first batch this morning, but I didn't notice, I should've been more careful. I thought they were just playing. I should've . . ."

Tony shook his head. "Hey, you couldn't possibly know this would happen. Those bastards are cowardly little shits, to hurt a couple of innocent little things like them. Those two never hurt anybody. What kind of monster does that? No way could you have dreamed they'd do that – you're not wired to think like a monster. It's definitely not your fault, or mine, so we can't beat ourselves or each other up over this, sweetie."

"No, but I should've been more careful! I knew they were still outside. I should've called them in." Nikki cried harder. "Now they're gone. It's all gone. My life is all gone."

Tony ran his fingers through her hair tenderly and asked, his voice almost a whisper, "What about your life with me? Doesn't that count for something?"

Nikki pulled back to look at him. "Of course it does. But you don't understand. They were it – they were all I had left of my old life, of my old family. Now they're gone too."

"But you have a new family, Nik. We love you. I know it hurts to lose them, but you won't ever forget your old family. They'll always be in here." He patted her chest just above her left breast. "They'll always be alive in there. But we're all here, and we love you. I hope that's enough."

Nikki looked into his face to see a huge tear roll from the corner of his eye, down beside his nose, and eventually drip off his chin. "You know, I loved those little guys," he said softly, his voice breaking. "I'm going to miss them too. They were the first dogs I ever had. Well, you know what I mean." He wiped his eyes and blinked hard.

Nikki smiled through her tears and took Tony's hand. "Thanks, baby. That means the world to me." She thought for a minute, then asked, "Can we take them to the crematorium tomorrow? I'd really like that."

"Sure. Whatever you want. We'll get some urns or something. But Nik," he told her, looking out the window instead of at her, "I'm sorry. I'm sorry for all of this. I'm sorry you're being hurt by people who want to hurt me. I'm sorry I ever asked you out, and . . ."

Nikki let loose an anguished cry. "What? Oh, god, no, please don't say that! You're sorry we're together?"

His head whipped around, absolutely horrified. "No-no-no! No, baby! What I meant was, if I'd known somebody would try to hurt you because of me, I might have been slower to get involved, that's all. No, I don't regret a single second we've been together. But I feel guilty that it's my fault you're getting hurt, that's all."

"That's not your fault, Tony Walters. That's those bastards with GoGreen. If I ever get my hands on them, so help me god, I'll . . ." She buried her face in his chest, and he wrapped her up in his arms and squeezed her tight.

"Let's go inside. I'm not really hungry – I'm sure you're not either – but we really need to try to eat something. And then let's try to get some sleep, even though we probably won't be able to. Tomorrow will be another day, and we'll start again. Okay?"

"Okay. I love you, Tony."

"Oh, little girl," he murmured, stroking her hair, "I love you too."

It was late when Tony and Nikki finally got everything taken care of so they could go to bed. Tony put Bill and Hillary's bodies in the basement on the cool floor, thinking that would be the best place for them. In the yard he'd found the bowl with traces of antifreeze in it, just as the vets had suspected. After he'd showered, Nikki had fixed them a salad and they'd eaten it while they waited for Detective Ford to come by and take a statement.

When he was done and gone, they climbed into the big bed together and, for the first time since they'd been together, sex didn't seem like an option. They lay together in the darkness, her head on his chest, his arms around her, and listened to each other breathe. It dawned on Nikki that this was why elderly nursing home patients often married; for the comfort they could take from each other in their distress at being old and sick and weary. Tony's arms around her were more comfort than she'd had in a long time, and she wanted that to last until they were old – old together.

"So you'd mentioned you'd like to go away. Would you like to go to the Gatlinburg house next weekend?" Tony asked out of the blue.

"I think I would."

"So let's work toward that." He hugged her tighter. "I love being there with you. The mountains always make me feel so . . ." he stopped, searching his mind for the right term.

"Fresh and new?"

"Exactly!" he answered, surprised. "How'd you know?"

"They have the very same effect on me. Plus I like making love out on the balcony in the night. I feel so free there." She smiled up at him.

"Well, sweetie, I can definitely take you out there and set you free, no problem!" he chuckled and gave her a soft kiss. "But right now, get some sleep. Things will be a little better in the morning."

"Sweet lord, the tired old woman in me needs the optimist in you," she whispered.

"I'll always be here for you, babe. You can count on it," he promised as he closed his eyes and drifted away beside her.

Chapter Thirty-One

"You won't believe this, but the committee for the Labor Day parade called and asked me to be the grand marshal."

Nikki squealed and clapped. "You said yes, right?"

Tony frowned. "No." Nikki's face fell. "I talked to Steve and he said he thought it was a bad idea. And he's right. That would leave me extremely vulnerable in a very public setting."

"I agree, but I'm still disappointed." Nikki frowned back. She wouldn't have cared if they wouldn't let her ride with him — just seeing him riding in the parade as grand marshal would've been enough to make her heart burst with pride.

"I explained the situation to them, told them I really wanted to do it but my chief of security said it wasn't a good idea. They told me no sweat — next year would be fine. We'd better have this cleared up before then or I'll do it anyway." As he fiddled with his stapler absentmindedly, Nikki could tell he was disappointed too. "Hey, by the way, what have you got going on this afternoon?"

"The usual. Run some errands, some meetings with HR, take those revised plans out to Clayton. Why?"

"I was wondering if you'd go to Lex, see Vic. They've got the new office in pretty good shape, and he could use some decorating tips. Poor guy, that's definitely not one of his strong points." Nikki could see that — Vic's wardrobe was black, black, and more black, with some black thrown in. She shuddered to think what the office might wind up looking like, but then she realized she'd been to his house several times and it was as gorgeous as he was, so she was pretty sure she shouldn't be overly concerned.

"Sure, if you can cover my stuff, I can do that." As she spoke, she grabbed his stapler, took it away from him, and set it pointedly down on the desk. Tony huffed, and she grinned. "When do you want me to leave?"

"Whenever you can. If you could go real soon and take him to lunch, that would be all the better." He reached for the stapler and Nikki playfully slapped his hand, then he grinned wider, snatched it, and put it in his lap. He laughed at her. "You'll have to come and get it if you want it now."

"Pervert!" she laughed back at him. "By the way, I've been meaning to ask you something."

"Shoot."

"What's with Vic?"

"How do you mean?"

"I mean, he's a good-looking, no, gorgeous guy. I mean really gorgeous. Like if-I-hadn't-met-you-first-I'd-follow-him-to-the-ends-of-the-earth gorgeous. But there's no woman. Is he gay?"

Tony chuckled. "No, he's definitely not gay."

"Then what is it? He doesn't have a woman, and he doesn't seem to be interested in having a woman. I've never heard him even mention a woman. What gives?"

Tony motioned for Nikki to close the office door. When she had, he said, "Um, Vic has a problem."

"Erectile dysfunction?"

"No!" Tony answered quickly. "Not that. No, it's more of a, well, an emotional problem, I guess you'd say." Nikki looked at him, puzzled and more curious than before. "He's had girlfriends, had one for awhile, in fact, but something happened."

Nikki waited. She could tell Tony was fishing for the right word or words to describe it. "Oh, out with it, baby," she groaned. "Surely you can tell me."

"Well," he began, "he has a control problem."

"Premature ejaculation?"

"Geez, girl, there's nothing wrong with the guy's dick!" Tony chuckled at her; then his expression turned somber. "He, well, he hurt her. Pretty badly, in fact. Almost got himself thrown in jail."

Nikki's eyes flew open wide. "Vic? He beat her? He's the gentlest guy I've ever met!" That didn't sound like the Vic she knew.

"No, no, he didn't hit her. He hurt her, um, sexually." Nikki looked at him, confused. "When I said he almost got himself thrown in jail, I mean the doctor who examined her almost had him charged with rape."

"Oh, my god! What the hell?" Nikki gasped – Vic?

"He's fine, and then he gets involved in the act, and, well, he gets a little crazy, forgets himself, and gets a little too, shall we say, exuberant? The way he described it, he gets kind of animalistic and just completely loses control.

One minute, they're enjoying themselves; next minute, she's screaming that he's hurting her, she's bleeding, and he can't stop himself. She winds up with serious vaginal tearing and he winds up trying to fend off rape charges. In the end, she forgave him, but she was so afraid of being with him that they couldn't work things out. Very sad."

Nikki was shocked, and it showed. "I'll say. Poor Vic! Has he tried counseling?"

"Actually, he did. The therapist said it had to do with his childhood and all the trauma."

"I knew you said it was bad. How bad?"

"Zia Serafina thought Vic's father loved her when they married, but she found out later that he married her because she was beautiful and would make a good trophy wife, especially considering his position." Nikki didn't know what that meant, but she didn't want to interrupt. "Then he started beating her, and they separated. Vic was about two at the time. They got back together when he was about six, and his father started beating her and Vic. He was drinking, gambling, sleeping around, whatever. It was torture. At least that's the story I got."

"When he was fourteen, my parents sent her tickets for the two of them to come to the states, and they never went back to Italy. Mamma and Papa helped Zia Serafina get her citizenship, and Vic went through naturalization while he was in high school. They lived with us, but he had a lot of problems, truancy, bad grades, discipline problems. He and Bennie are the same age, so he was graduating from high school when I was graduating from college. Mamma and Papa offered to send him to college, but he wanted to join the military. When he started talking about getting out, I sent him word I'd hire him into the company – I was running it by then. By the time he got out of the military, Papa had passed, and I hired Vic and taught him the business. We grew up like brothers, but I guess he really looks at me more like a father than a brother or cousin."

"No wonder he loves you the way he does." Nikki beamed at Tony. "I know you love him too."

"Two straight guys couldn't love each other more than Vic and I do. I've never been as close to another man as I am to him, even to Papa, and we were together every day while he taught me the business. Vic and I just have a solid, strong relationship."

"I'm glad he has you. Seems like he doesn't have anybody else." As they talked, Nikki straightened papers on Tony's desk. It was a habit she couldn't seem to control, the constant straightening and organizing.

"Well, actually, he does. The kids all love him, and my mom does too, and now he's got you. And in case you haven't noticed, he's crazy about you."

"Me?" Nikki looked surprised. "You think so? How nice!"

Tony rolled his eyes. "Oh, good god, Nikki, he's in love with you. I mean stone-cold in love." Tony shook his head in wonder. "You must've realized that."

"Nah!" Disbelief was plain on her face. "He couldn't be, he wouldn't . . ."

"No, he wouldn't. He'd never say anything, and he'd certainly never act on it, but it's true. I can tell when he's around you. He's smitten. Completely, totally, head-over-heels in love."

"Oh god!" Nikki whispered, horrified. "Do you think it's a good idea for me to go there and spend time with him?" She was feeling a bit uncomfortable, and she hoped Tony was wrong.

"I think it's absolutely a good idea. He needs to spend time with you, know we're totally committed to each other and you're not interested, get used to the idea. He'll be fine, honestly. But he needs a woman to give him confidence, and your friendship can do that for him. It'll be all right." Tony stood up and leaned over to give her a kiss on the forehead. "You can handle this. You're a tough girl with a really big truck!"

"Uh-huh. How bad?" There was a long pause. "Well, fuck me. Okay, call me when you know more." Tony hit END on his cell and sighed.

"Geez, what now?" Nikki asked. It had been a beautiful weekend, hot but nice. They'd hiked to a waterfall, then gone to her favorite barbecue place in Gatlinburg. Visits to a couple of local wineries had their cargo deck full of bottles. Nikki had hit a couple of the outlet stores in Pigeon Forge and gotten a very pretty dress to wear to dinner sometime. Then came the phone call, and it looked like all of the rest and relaxation Tony had managed to get was now undone. "GoGreen again?"

"Looks like it. That was Clayton. They went into the hospital project and busted up every porcelain fixture that's been delivered. Over a quarter of a million dollars' worth of fixtures. I don't understand — Cal was supposed to be watching that site. I've got somebody on every site. How did they get in there and do that much damage without somebody noticing?"

"Wait – you've got somebody on *every site*? Watching them? You're kidding!" Nikki hadn't realized it was that bad.

"Nope – have had since your SUV was firebombed. I've been paying employees to take shifts 'round the clock. I didn't say anything because I thought this wouldn't last long, but I was wrong about that." Tony started folding clothes to put them in his bag. "But I'm pretty pissed about this. Cal was supposed to be watching the place. What the hell was he doing?"

"Guess you'll have to ask him when you see him." Nikki rushed around and packed her things too. So much for peace and quiet.

"Well, you can bet I'll be seeing him tomorrow morning. I've had just about enough of this shit."

"Would you care to explain how this happened?" Tony was still livid and about ten seconds from a rip-roaring rant. Cal was appropriately subdued, and that was probably a good thing.

"Boss, I'm so, so sorry. But I guess it happened when I ran home. The kids called and said Jenny was sick, so I went to check. She was just, you know . . ." Cal shrugged. It sounded like a good-enough story; Tony would never know the difference.

"Yeah, I know. You need to get your wife into rehab; our health insurance will pay for most of it. Her drinking is keeping you from doing your job and, much as I like you, working is why you're here, after all. This problem of hers is costing me money, money on the project, and money I was paying you to watch the project." Tony was so angry that he couldn't even look at Cal. The idea of firing him immediately was definitely there, but he knew what it was like to have a spouse who fucked up your life.

"Don't pay me for last evening, boss. I don't deserve it."

"No, you were there most of the night, so I'll pay you. I've never asked any employee to do anything I wasn't willing to pay them to do. But don't, and I mean don't, let that happen again. You understand? Next time I might not be so forgiving. You've been with me for awhile now, Cal, and you've been a good employee. But this is some serious shit. I can't afford another fuckup like this." Tony slammed a desk drawer shut and stood. "Now get your ass back to work. I've got a million things to do, and now this to clean up."

"Yes sir, Tony. It won't happen again." Cal turned and shuffled out of the office, head down and shoulders slumped. If Tony ever found out... Well, he couldn't. They'd just have to be more careful.

"I'm taking a half-day off. Gonna go sit by the pool. When you get done at the dentist's office, why don't you come by and swim?" Tony asked Vic. For reasons nobody could understand, Vic came all the way to Louisville to go to the dentist. If anybody asked why, he said he'd finally found a dentist he wasn't afraid of, so it was worth the drive. Imagining Vic being afraid of *anyone* was nearly impossible.

Vic smiled. "Yeah, I'll be there! I could use some down time. Want me to bring anything with me?"

"Beer." Tony walked out the door with Vic. "That's your ticket to the Walters swimmin' hole."

"Goes without saying. I think I can manage that. Whaddya think, Newcastle?"

"Sounds good. See you in a couple of hours." Tony waved goodbye to Vic, then called Nikki on his hands-free in the truck. "Hey, baby, whatcha doin'?"

"Going over to the hospital site to take some revised plans to Clayton – just picked them up at the architect's office. What's up with you?" she asked as she climbed back into the big blue monster.

"Taking a half-day off, gonna go sit by the pool, do a little swimming, invited Vic over. This GoGreen shit has me completely stressed out. Can you come home?"

"It'll be a little while, but I'll be there. I've got a couple of things to do at the office, then I'll be on my way!" *Um-hum – when the boss offers you the afternoon off, you take it,* she chuckled to herself.

When Tony got home, he changed into his trunks, got a little lunch, and opened a beer. He'd made it down and back the length of the pool several times when Nikki walked out the doors onto the patio. "I'm going to put on my suit. Need anything?"

"Nope. Not a thing." He climbed out and kissed her, slapped her butt as she walked away, then took back his spot on the chaise lounge.

Within a few minutes, Tony heard a car alarm being set. Vic – had to be. He heard the front door open and close and then, a few seconds later, he looked up to see Vic coming out the door onto the patio. Already shirtless, Vic's jeans were lying on the floor just inside the door. "Hey, buddy, you know . . ." Tony started.

"Give it a rest, cousin boss man. Don't wanna talk about work. Just let me get into the water and relax for a second, okay?" Vic peeled his boxer briefs off, dropping them where he stood, and slipped head-first into the pool. He swam the length of the pool and started climbing out at the far end just as Nikki stepped out the back door. Rubbing the water out of his eyes, he turned toward the house and opened them, only to find Nikki standing at the other end of the pool, her face a mess of startled confusion as she stared right at him and held his jeans in one hand, his briefs in the other.

Her eyes went wide and her mouth formed an "O." What she was looking at was beyond her wildest imagination. Even flaccid, Vic had set a new size record for Nikki. She thought only porn stars were hung like that, and she was having trouble pulling air into her lungs from the pure adrenaline surge.

Horrified, all Vic could think to do was jump back in the water, which he did as fast as he could.

Nikki looked at Tony, and he grinned; she grinned back. Vic swam over to where Tony was sitting and snarled, "You could've warned me she was here!"

"I tried, but you made it clear you didn't want me to tell you anything. Besides, in case you forgot, she lives here!" Tony laughed.

"I thought she was at work!"

"Well, she was, but she wanted to come and see you. And she sure did see you!" At that point, Tony was laughing so hard he was having trouble catching his breath.

Vic swam up to where Nikki knelt by the edge of the pool, waiting for him to swim over. He folded his arms onto the edge and looked up at her. Her face was pure mischief. "Sugar, I'm so sorry. I didn't know you were home," he moaned, his dark face scarlet.

"Hey, sweetie, you don't have anything to apologize for; if it doesn't bother you, it sure as hell doesn't bother me! Besides, you know what they say: No good deed goes unpunished!" He knew she was talking about the Fourth and the panty incident. When she pinched his cheek and winked at him, he got even redder, then pushed off and started swimming laps. By that time, Tony had tears rolling down his cheeks.

"You gonna go get him a suit?" Nikki asked as she dropped onto the chaise beside Tony to enjoy the view.

"Nah, not yet. I'll let him stew a bit," he told her, trying to catch his breath. "I'll go get him one in a little while. Serves him right, flashing his boy bits at my girl!"

"Boy? That ain't no boy, darlin', that's all grown-ass man. I will tell you this: You need to help that one right there find him a woman. It's a damn shame that's going to waste. Ummm, damn shame." She grinned as she sipped her glass of wine and watched Vic swim.

"Should I be jealous?" Tony asked, giving her a fake concerned look.

"Well, maybe," she drawled, and his eyes went wide. "Just kidding, baby! But you know, I'm just sayin'." She fanned herself and groaned, "Have mercy!"

Chapter Thirty-Two

"Is there any way I can take tomorrow off?" Nikki asked Tony during dinner on Wednesday night.

"Well, sure, I guess. Got a doctor's appointment or something?" Tony thought it would be odd that she'd have something coming up and not say anything to him.

"No, I just want the day off, that's all." She didn't explain, just pushed her food around on her plate.

"Okay. Not a problem. Got anything that needs to be covered?"

"No. I took care of everything today. It's all good."

He tried again. "Well then, okay. Got big plans?" He forked up another bite of her meatloaf – god, it was always good – and waited.

"Nope." She didn't offer any more information, and Tony wondered exactly what she was up to.

"Boss, you've got a call. It's José Flores," Cheryl called into Tony's office.

"Hey, José, what's up?" Tony rarely got calls from Nikki's security detail.

"Tony, I don't know what Nikki's up to, but she's headed out of town."

"Out of town in which direction?" Tony's instincts had been right – she was up to something, but he had no idea what.

"She's on I-65 headed toward Elizabethtown. Do you have any idea where she might be going?"

Tony thought for a minute. Then something passed through his mind. "Hang on a minute, José. I've got a hunch." He brought up his computer and, in his search engine, typed "Randy Wilkes." Nothing. Then he tried "Randall Wilkes obituary." He got three results, and one of them was the local paper in Murray. And there it was – date of death, August sixteenth. Six years to the day. "Yeah, José, she's going to Murray, where she's from."

"What do you want me to do?"

"Stay on her. I'll call in a few favors. Thanks for letting me know. Call you back in a few."

In forty-five minutes, Tony was at the airport and boarding Frank Simpson's helicopter for Murray. Frank owed Tony a few favors for extras Tony had added during the building of Frank and Becca's house, and Frank had reminded Tony over and over that he was owed a favor whenever it was needed. The Walters' theory of doing right by others and they'd do right by you was paying off.

Tony called José to say he was on his way, then called the only car rental place in Murray and asked for a car to be left at the airport, giving them the address of the cemetery to put into the car's navigation system. After he'd found Randy's obit, he'd used the kids' names to find their obits, which included the burial plans. With all the prep done, he sat back and thought about what he was doing. He was conflicted; she might need some privacy, but she also needed someone there with her. He'd watch her from a distance, then let her know he was there for her if and when she needed him. If she didn't need him, she'd never have to know he'd been there.

He picked up the car at the tiny airport – truly tiny – and drove straight to the cemetery. His last call to José told him Nikki was still some time out. The town was pretty, a typical small Kentucky town, with some old structures and some new, and a little park here and there. A loop through the cemetery turned up some interesting headstones; one appeared to be a big cat, possibly a leopard or panther. Any other time he might've stopped and looked around, but instead, he drove to the very back and waited. He'd stopped at a small grocery on his drive through town and picked up a sandwich and a drink, and he sat in the rental car at the cemetery and ate slowly, wondering when she'd get there.

Had Nikki intended to tell him that evening what she'd done, or would she have made up some story? No, he thought, she wasn't that devious, and she certainly didn't lie. She would've told him that evening; she was probably just afraid he'd try to stop her, and he had to admit he would've. With everything that had been happening, he didn't think her leaving town alone was a very good idea, but she had to have known one of Steve's people would follow her.

Almost on cue, his phone rang: José. "You in place?"

"Waiting."

"We're headed your way." Within minutes Tony saw it – the red Volvo

SUV. He watched as the big vehicle made its way down the narrow lanes in the cemetery. It finally stopped about halfway back. The door opened, and Nikki stepped out. She crossed the large burial area and stopped, then dropped to her knees. Tony's heart broke; even at the distance between them, he could see the anguish on her face, as fresh and raw as the day her children had died.

He was about to start the car and drive toward her when he spotted another car, a large blue sedan, coming in the drive. It pulled up past her SUV and stopped. An older couple got out of the car and started toward the gravesite, but when they saw Nikki, they turned and hurried back toward their car. He watched as Nikki stood and called out to them, then ran toward them, but they ignored her. She made it to their car almost as soon as they did, and he saw her reach out and touch the man's arm.

To Tony's horror, the man pushed her hard enough that she fell on her backside, then yelled something at her and got in his car. Nikki got up, tried the door handle, beat on the window, and followed the car for about twenty feet until it sped up and drove away. She stood in the drive, watching the car drive away, and the look of misery on her face caused his throat to close.

Her parents – had to be.

Tony was beyond appalled. She'd come five hours to stand at the graves of her dead children, only to have her own parents turn away from her, her father shove her, drive away, treat her like garbage. What kind of people would do that? He watched her drop to her knees in the gravel, double over, then curl up like a dying fern and shrivel before his eyes. And he'd had enough.

He started the car and drove around until he was behind the Volvo, then got out and walked toward her. What he heard made him stop and tore the breath from his lungs – a keening, sharp and agonizing, as she cried out in heart-wrenching anguish. Her wailing was so pitiful, so piercing, that he froze. What could he say, what could he do, that would make this better? How could he console her through a pain so unbearable? What could anyone say to someone who's been so wounded and left to suffer that way?

When he worked up the courage to walk to her, he simply knelt beside her and laid his hand on her shoulder. She didn't even look up; she just reached across her body, grabbed his wrist, and continued to heave and sob. He could've been anyone, and he realized in that moment that she didn't care who was touching her; she just needed a tiny little bit of kindness, and it wouldn't have mattered if it came from a stranger.

They sat like that for what seemed like forever, then Nikki turned to look at him. Her eyes were so swollen from crying he wasn't sure she realized it was him. "Sweetheart, it's me," he whispered. "It's me, baby. I'm here." He knelt in front of her and pulled her to him, wrapping his arms around her.

Nikki hugged her arms against her body and folded into him. She cried softly, "They don't love me. My own parents; they don't love me. I'm not sure they ever have. Why don't my parents love me, Tony? What's wrong with me that I'm so unlovable? What did I do that's so terrible that my own family doesn't want me?"

A tear slid down his face as he squeezed her tight. "Oh, baby, I don't know what's wrong with them. But you listen to me: Don't come back here. Ever again. Don't do this to yourself. There's nothing wrong with you, sweetie – nothing, you hear me? It's them, baby, it's not you. It's them." He smoothed her hair, then put his hand under her chin and raised her face to his. "You're smart and beautiful and loving. You have me; you have Clayton and Annabeth and Katie and Brittany; you have Vic; you have Mamma and all of my brothers and their families. Marla and Carol think you're wonderful. The guys at work all think you're super cool, not to mention very, very hot. To hell with these people. You don't need them anymore, and you certainly don't need the way they make you feel. Shake it off, precious. You have a wonderful life now. Live it, love it, and leave this behind."

He took her hand, helped her stand, and walked back to the headstone, a beautiful white granite; Jake and Amanda's names were there, set forever into its face. Tony stood behind Nikki with his arms around her waist. "You'll never forget and after today, I never will either. You know, Nik, I know it still hurts – it always will – but that pain is what helps you remember." He felt her relax against him, and he took her hand and led her toward the Volvo.

After he'd insisted that she eat a sandwich in the grocery store parking lot and they'd taken the car back to the rental place, they met José at a gas station near the parkway and told him they were driving back. He fell in behind the Volvo and followed them to Louisville.

When they pulled into the driveway of the house in Anchorage, the windows were lit up. Katie's little Subaru wagon and Brittany's Lexus sedan sat out front. He looked at Nikki, but nothing registered on her face. She'd said next to nothing all the way back, and he didn't know how she'd react to a house full of twenty- and thirty-somethings after the day she'd had.

"If you want me to send them home, I will," he said quietly as he parked her Volvo. "I know you probably don't feel like . . ."

"No, no, it's okay. I'm fine, just tired. They probably think they're helping." She climbed down out of the SUV and trudged toward the door.

When they stepped inside, they were more than shocked. In addition to the kids, Raffaella was there, and all five of them were sitting in the living room, quietly playing cards. They all looked up and smiled as Tony and Nikki walked into the room.

Raffaella rose and took Nikki's face in her hands, kissed her on the forehead. "Daughter, I am glad my son brought you home. I have pasta e fagioli in the crack pot in the kitchen for you." Nikki knew she meant the slow cooker, and she heard Annabeth stifle a giggle.

"Thank you, Raffaella," Nikki hugged the older woman, who squeezed Nikki back.

"Please, that is Mamma, my dear." She took Nikki's hand and led her toward the kitchen. As they walked away, Tony heard her say, "I also made for you my Italian cream cake. I hope you will like it."

On the counter in the kitchen was an enormous vase of fresh cut flowers with a card from The Passionate Pansy sticking out. Before Nikki could pull it off to read it, Clayton told her, "Marla and Carol sent those to you. They couldn't find you, so they brought them to the office. I brought them home for you." They'd remembered; Nikki teared up at the thought.

Raffaella sat Nikki down at the table and crossed to the stove to ladle out some of the pasta. Even though she'd thought she couldn't eat, Nikki's mouth watered as Raffaella handed the bowl to Tony and he set it in front of Nikki. While Raffaella ladled another bowl out for Tony, Brittany placed a plate of sliced, crusty French bread on the table, and Annabeth pulled the water pitcher from the refrigerator and poured each of them a glass of water, then replaced it and produced two small salads and a bottle of dressing. Nikki couldn't believe it – they'd apparently planned this all afternoon. She looked at Tony, who just smiled and dug into the bowl of pasta. She tried a bite – it was delicious, all hot and savory, and the ditalini was cooked perfectly. Everything – the food, the house – was filled with love. "Aren't any of you going to eat?" she asked.

Katie shook her head and smiled. "We've already eaten. We were waiting for you guys. We haven't had dessert yet, but Nonna wouldn't let us cut the cake until you got here." Despite the day, Nikki had to chuckle, and Tony laughed outright.

After the salad and pasta, Raffaella produced the cake, which looked too good to eat. She cut perfectly sized portions and passed them around, even taking one herself. Nikki put a forkful of the cake in her mouth and almost cried – it was easily the most delicious thing she'd ever tasted. "Raffa . . . Mamma, this cake is, well, I don't know what to say. It's amazing!"

The small woman smiled broadly. "Thank you, dear. It is my favorite to make. My Marco used to say it was better than sex." Nikki almost choked, and Tony started laughing again.

"Wow, Mamma, if I were you I wouldn't tell that on myself!" Tony cackled, but Raffaella looked puzzled as Nikki and all of the kids started laughing too.

"Perhaps it was the flour?" Raffaella said, still confused, and Tony howled. Everyone was laughing except Raffaella, who still couldn't understand what was so funny.

When they'd all calmed down and gotten themselves under control, the usually-quiet Clayton spoke softly. "Nikki, Annabeth and I wanted to ask you something."

"Of course, honey. What is it?" she asked, finishing her cake and fighting the urge to ask for another piece.

"We were wondering, do you think it would be okay if we called you Mom?" he asked, his voice serious and low.

Tony's eyebrows shot up into his hairline – their timing couldn't be worse – but Clayton misread his expression and timidly asked, "Oh, Dad, is that not okay?"

"Oh, no, Clayton, that's absolutely fine with me. I was thinking, though, that this has been a hard day, and maybe it's not a really good time to . . ." Tony said, recovering pretty quickly but still concerned.

Nikki interrupted him. "No, Tony, that's okay. I think it's a perfectly good time to ask that." She sniffed hard to keep the tears at bay and straightened her back, then looked from one young face to another. "You know, I never expected anybody to call me Mom again." She took a deep breath and tried to keep her composure. "If it's ever going to happen, I can't think of anybody I'd rather it be than you guys. I love you both – I love all four of you – and I'll gladly be your mom if you'll have me." Even though she was working hard to keep it from happening, a tear escaped from one eye and meandered down her cheek.

Annabeth started to cry outright and ran to hug Nikki. Clayton reached over and took her hand wordlessly, his eyes welling. Tony decided he'd better say nothing or he'd start to blubber. Then Nikki turned to him, a sob escaping her lips, and cried in an almost childlike voice, "Oh, god – I have a family! A real family, people who love me!" she wailed, and Tony lost it. He pulled her to him and held her tight, so tight he was afraid she might break.

"Baby, I've been trying to tell you that for months. We're all here for you – always. Between me, the kids, Mamma, Vic, and all of my brothers and their families, you'll never be alone again. This is your life now. We love you so much."

"I love you guys too!" Nikki cried out, still sobbing, and pretty soon there was a seven-person Walters pileup going on as everyone hugged everyone. It went on for what seemed like forever until Nikki heard Clayton say, in his usual straightforward Clayton fashion, "Would it be okay if I had some more cake now?"

After his third piece of cake, Clayton announced, "Brit and I have something we want to talk to all of you about." They both got up from the table and walked toward the den. Everyone else followed, looking at each other and wondering what they were about to hear.

When they were all settled, Clayton started. "You all know we've been trying to get pregnant." Everyone in the room nodded. "So we just wanted to ask: What would everybody think about us becoming foster parents?"

Before anyone else could speak, Nikki asked, "How do you feel about getting your hearts broken over and over?"

Not missing a beat, Brittany answered matter-of-factly, "I've miscarried three times. We've lost implanted embryos four times. I don't know how much more broken my heart could be."

"Then if you're prepared for the heartbreak, I think it's a great idea." Nikki looked at Tony. "Baby, what about you?"

"Personally, I think it's a wonderful idea," Tony agreed. "Are you thinking of fostering and then maybe adopting? Is that where this is going?"

Clayton nodded. "We hope so. And we don't care – baby, toddler, small child, teen, Black, White, Latino, Asian – we really don't care. We'd just like to give a home to a child who needs one."

Annabeth and Katie were quiet. Raffaella spoke up. "I think this fostering is a wonderful idea. I would welcome a new great-grandchild." She looked at Annabeth and Katie. "Well," she asked, "what about the two of you? What do you think about this idea your brother and his beautiful wife have?"

"Oh, I think it's great," Annabeth mumbled, sounding decidedly unexcited. "Katie?" Annabeth asked, turning to her partner.

"Yeah, great." Katie looked miserable.

"Something going on here?" Tony asked the girls.

"Yeah." Annabeth tried to work up her courage. "It's just that, well, we want to try artificial insemination, but we can't afford the sperm or the procedures. And no, Dad, we don't want you to help out," she added when Tony started to speak. "We want to do this ourselves, but it's all so expensive."

Everyone jumped when Nikki interjected, "Turkey baster."

"Huh?" Annabeth croaked.

"Turkey baster. People did it for years before anybody had ever heard of artificial insemination. The only problem is, you've got to be careful not to blow any air up your hoo-hah. Otherwise, it's a cheap alternative and it works great." Everyone looked at her like she had three heads except for Raffaella, who looked horrified. "What? You got a better idea?"

"Would that really work?" Katie asked, an odd expression on her face.

"Look," Nikki pointed out, "women have gotten pregnant easier than that throughout time. Hell, it's nothing to hear that a woman got pregnant when her partner ejaculated on her stomach." Raffaella's eyes widened, and Tony was biting his knuckle to keep from laughing. "Well, it's true. Those little guys are pretty focused and strong and they can travel a long distance. So you just prop your backside up with a pillow and tilt your pelvis upward, then drop the, well, you know, in and presto! Baby!" Everyone was still staring at her, and being on the hot seat made her want another piece of cake.

"Wait, this could work?" Annabeth asked. "Really? I mean, that would be awesome!" she whispered reverently. "But where would we get the semen?"

Nikki turned and looked directly at Clayton. "What about you, Clayton? I mean, your sperm is okay, right? Count, motility, all that stuff?"

Clayton turned five shades of burnt orange. "Uh, yeah, but that's just sorta . . ."

"Oh, buck up for your sister's sake, honey. Look, this is simple. You supply the sperm and Katie carries the baby. That way, it's genetically Katie's and more like Annabeth's because of your shared genetics."

"But, but . . . but what about Dad? He's got sperm, right? He could do it," Clayton whined, scrambling and looking at Tony.

Tony choked on his second piece of cake. "Hey, don't look at me! That's just weird."

"Like it's not weird to use mine?" Clayton cried.

"Guys, guys, it's not weird, so don't make it weird." Nikki tried to calm them both, then turned to Clayton. Okay, now she really wanted cake. "Tony's would work, but genetically speaking, yours would be closer to Annabeth's DNA makeup. And you know, down the road, if you and Brittany wanted to have a child of your own, well, Annabeth would make a great surrogate for any embryo you two had. Her body would host it well because of the shared genetics." She stopped. "Easy peasey," she added. Where the hell was that cake?

Katie and Annabeth looked at each other, then Annabeth turned to stare at Clayton but said nothing. "What?" Clayton asked, sounding kind of desperate. No response. "Are you serious?" he cried out. Annabeth continued to stare at him, and Katie joined her. "Oh, my god, you are! Brit?" he moaned, looking at his wife.

"What? I don't see the problem. I'm on board with this. God knows you've got a never-ending supply of sperm," she grinned but feigned disgust.

Tony laughed and slapped Clayton on the shoulder. "Ah, that's my boy – a chip off the old block!" The younger man didn't seem the least bit amused. He glared at Nikki.

"What?" Nikki smiled at him. "Tell your mamma 'thank you,' son."

"Thank you," Clayton growled, his voice dripping with sarcasm. "I'll remember this," he added.

"You'll thank me when you see your sister and Katie with a beautiful little baby you helped them have," Nikki smiled. That was the moment she saw the muscles in Clayton's face start to relax, and then he smiled too and got a thoughtful, calm look on his face.

"You know what, Mom? I think you're probably the smartest woman I've ever met." There was not a hint of sarcasm in his voice, and he kissed her on the cheek.

"Thanks, son. And now the smartest woman you've ever met wants another piece of that awesome cake!"

"God, I love this family," Tony said to no one in particular with a huge, goofy grin on his face.

"You know, little girl, I think that's my only real regret in our relationship."

"What, baby?"

"That we can't have a child together. That I'll never get to see you pregnant with my child, or hold a life we made with our love. I'd give anything to be able to do that."

"Well, it won't be long before you'll be holding a grandchild, changing smelly diapers, cleaning up spit-up, going to tee-ball games and dance recitals and all that crap. And after we've spent our formerly-lovely weekends babysitting a two-year-old who's never still and can't seem to make it to the potty, I'll remember to ask if you still think you'd love to have a baby with me."

"Yeah, uh, no, what the hell was I thinking? Sorry – I must've completely lost my mind for a minute there." He stopped and gave her a wily grin. "But I remember how it's done. Want me to show you?"

"Oh, yeah, I want you to show me. I want you to show me all night long. Think you're up to it, Grandpa?"

"Oh, hell yes. Take a look – I'm already up to it."

"Hell yeah, Gramps – you sure are."

Chapter Thirty-Three

By the last week of August, the float for the Labor Day parade was almost finished. Tony stopped by the shop to see what it looked like, and he had to admit it would make Walters Construction proud. The guys had knocked themselves out to do a good job, and it showed. Cal had volunteered to ride on it, and so had Jeremy, one of the newer employees who had been a jackhammer jockey for the company for the last six months. Clayton had signed on to drive his company truck to pull it, so they were all set.

Nikki wanted to go to the Gatlinburg house for the weekend, but Tony insisted they be back in time for the parade, so he decided they would leave on Friday morning to have more time there. There was no reason they couldn't; Clayton was more than capable of taking care of things.

Everything had been a little better, but GoGreen was still active and doing an irritatingly good job of keeping everyone on edge. It was almost as though they knew where everyone was and when. No one got hurt, but property got destroyed. Trucks and equipment were disabled, supplies burned or otherwise mangled, and fires set. Tony continued to pay employees to patrol at night and on weekends, and Steve's crew kept tabs on Tony, Nikki, and Clayton around the clock. Detective Ford had wearied of taking reports and still getting no leads on who the GoGreen people were, and Steve hadn't had any luck getting any information on them either. Even more maddening, the group never contacted the press, so there was no clue as to exactly what their beef with Walters Construction was.

The constant vigilance could've taken its toll, but Nikki and Tony were careful to not let that happen. And whenever they could, they ran to the Tennessee house. There was no need for security there – the general consensus was that the GoGreen people probably didn't know about the house and, even if they did, it was doubtful they would follow Tony and Nikki all the way there, especially since most of their activity was directed at property. So far they hadn't tried to hurt anyone, except for Bill and Hillary, and they probably hadn't seen them as family members, even though Nikki had.

Tony called Roselle and asked her to do everything she could to get the house ready, lay in food, and set things up so they didn't have to go out to get anything. They wanted to be alone for the weekend, relax, unwind, and enjoy themselves and each other, no interruptions. Nikki seemed especially excited, and Tony was glad the house was finally bringing them the joy he'd intended when he bought it, instead of having it be just a place to run to when things got too crazy at home.

When they got there on Friday afternoon, the first thing Nikki did was change into a thin, lacy gown with nothing underneath and open all the doors and windows to let air and light into the house. Tony stripped down to his boxer briefs, and they had a lovely late lunch of fruit on the back deck, enjoying the sunshine and fresh mountain air.

"I love this place." Nikki closed her eyes and stretched. She moved to the chaise lounge and got comfortable, then reached for Tony. He came over and sat down beside her, stroking her hair and her back as she drew herself to him. She practically purred.

"I love it too. I'd love to retire here, but I want to be close to the kids, especially when we have grandkids."

"Oh, for sure! So I guess this will always just be our special place." Nikki hesitated, then shot him a sexy smile. "By the way, I have a surprise for you later, if you're up for it."

"I'm definitely up for it." *What's she up to now?*, he wondered. He was pretty sure it would blow his mind. That seemed to be her life's mission, and he sure as hell wasn't complaining.

It seemed like Nikki was taking an awfully long time in the bathroom at bedtime. He waited and waited and, finally, he called out, "Hey, baby, what are you doing in there?"

No answer.

"Nikki? Are you okay in there?" Crickets. What in the hell was she doing in there? Tony crossed the room and knocked. Nothing. He opened the door.

Empty. Where the hell was she? Then he remembered: She'd asked him to go down to the kitchen and get both of them a glass of water to have on the nightstands. She must've sneaked out of the bathroom while he was in the kitchen. But where did she go?

He was trying to figure out what to do next and where to look for her when the doorbell rang. It was ten thirty at night. Who in the world would be at the door at that hour?

Tony slipped on his lounging pants and bounced down the steps. When he got to the door, he turned on the porch light, then he peered through the peephole and saw a headful of blond hair. Nikki.

He yanked open the door and, before he could say anything, he got a look at her as she turned. She was wearing a lot more makeup than usual, and her hair had been curled. Even more shocking, she was wearing a trench coat, black stockings, and red patent stiletto heels. As he took in the sight of her standing there, she said, "Oh! Sir, I'm so sorry to bother you, but my boyfriend and I got into a huge fight and he put me out of the car. Could I use your phone?"

Ah-hah! Tony smiled inwardly as it dawned on him what she was doing. *I'll play along and see where this goes.* "Oh, no bother, miss. Please, come in." He stepped aside and invited her in. "The phone's right over there."

She looked around until she spotted it, then went to it and dialed a number. "Damn. His voicemail. Oh, god, I don't know what to do. I don't know anybody else here." She looked at Tony and plumped her lower lip out into a pout.

"Would you like something to drink?" Tony asked. "By the way, my name's Sam. What's yours?"

"Oh, I'm so sorry! I'm Tiffany." She extended her hand. He took it and held it for a few seconds, then turned to get their drinks. "What's in the drink?"

"Just the best bourbon on the market. I don't scrimp on my liquor. I want it to be strong and smooth." He handed her a glass and she sipped, then smiled. "Can I take your coat?"

She looked slightly panicked. "Oh, no, that's okay," she answered, pulling the lapel closer together. "I guess I need to decide what to do and get out of your way. I've interrupted your evening. I hope I haven't ruined anything."

"No. As a matter of fact, I'm glad you're here. I was expecting somebody, but I don't think they're coming." He worked to keep a straight face.

"Oh? I'm sorry. Well, I hate to ask, but could you take me up in town? I'll find a room somewhere, try to figure out what to do next." She looked around furtively, almost as though she was looking for an escape route.

"What's your hurry? I've got nothing going on here. And besides, I've got plenty of room. I suppose you could stay until morning if you'd like."

"Oh, no, I wouldn't want to impose and I could never repay the kindness."

"Hmmm." He walked toward her and took her glass, setting it on the hall table. "I'm sure we can work something out." He stared down at her big turquoise eyes, and she looked positively terrified; god, she was a good actress. "Don't worry – it'll be something you can live with, I promise." He traced the line of her arm from her wrist to her shoulder, and she shuddered.

"I think I should probably go," she whispered, glancing nervously at the door.

"Where? We're a long way from town and I don't think you're going to have much luck walking all the way there in those heels." He ran his hand up her back, her neck, and then into her hair.

"Oh, sir, no, I don't know what you're thinking, but . . ."

"Look, we're both adults here. I'm not a bad guy, but I know what I want, and I think you're here for the same reason, right?" She looked confused. "I saw you at the restaurant earlier. You followed me here, didn't you? Confess," he demanded.

He's getting into this!, she realized. She shook her head hesitantly, then looked down at the floor. "Well, okay, yeah. I don't know why. I've never done anything like this before."

"Oh, you know exactly why, slut," he snarled and grabbed her hair – hard. She gasped as he pulled her head back so he could look down into her face with a menacing glare, those dark caramel eyes of his looking even darker, the gold flecks flashing. "You want a man, and tonight, that man happened to be me. How many times have you done this? Tell the truth," he demanded, pulling her hair harder.

"Oh, god! Please don't hurt me! I don't do this . . ." he tugged even harder, ". . . okay, okay, I do this a couple of times a week! I don't know why, I just need it! Please, let me go, okay? I'm really sorry I bothered you. I won't come back. Please!"

Tony held her hair tight and untied the belt on the trench. She tried to push his hands away, but it wasn't buttoned, so he flipped it open and peeled it back and off her shoulders. Underneath it she was wearing nothing but a black and red bustier, her nipples peeking out the tops of the cups, with a garter belt and thong to match, hot and indecent and so unbelievably fuckable that he could barely think, and his cock started to throb. She scrambled to cover herself, but he turned loose of her hair and grabbed her arms, pulling them behind her and holding them together, making her breasts jut out and up tantalizingly. Her wrists were so small that he could capture both of them in one hand, and he held them while he leaned into her. With his free hand he brusquely plunged two fingers into her folds – yep, soaked. She cried out at his invasion of her most sensitive flesh.

"We're gonna see how much noise you can make," he snarled and threw her over his shoulder. He took the steps two at a time, and she slapped at his back and ass as he carried her up the stairs, yelling and kicking the whole way, her stilettos falling off and tumbling down the stairs.

"Put me down! Please, put me down! Don't do this!" she screamed. He slapped her ass hard and she screamed louder. The house was over five acres away from the others around it, and right then he was really glad he'd bought the extra land.

When he got to the bedroom, he dumped her on the bed like a sack of potatoes. She tried to scramble away, but he grabbed her arms, reached into his nightstand drawer, and pulled out a length of cotton rope, tying her wrists securely and then tying the rope to the massive headboard. *Uh-huh,* he thought, *I had a surprise planned for you too!* She squirmed and started yelling expletives of all sorts alternated with begging. He reached up to her face and pinched her lower jaw with one hand. "Shut up," he growled. "In this room, you will address me as sir. I will do to you whatever I please, and you will beg for more. If you don't, you'll be punished. Do you understand?"

She screamed again, "Please! Don't hurt me! Don't do this! Please, just let me go!"

"Nope, slut. You came here to get fucked, and that's exactly what you're going to get." Tony reached back into his bedside table and pulled out a knife. She gasped when she saw it and got quiet. He used the knife to cut her thong off, and she drew her legs together as tightly as she could.

"Might as well not even try to keep me out of you. Won't work." He put his hands between her knees and pulled them apart. She fought, but he was stronger, and he parted her thighs. "Ah, look at that bare pussy! Very pretty! Now, you hold still, let me do what I want, and I won't have to punish you like the dirty cunt you are." She watched him, wide-eyed, as he spread her slit open with his fingers and consumed her with his eyes, looking her over like she was a sixty-five Mustang and he was checking under her hood. "I'm gonna wear this out. When I'm done with you, you'll know you've been fucked and fucked hard. Don't give me any trouble, you hear me?" She nodded, trembling.

He crossed the room, opened a dresser drawer, and pulled something out. She watched him and shuddered as he came back with something in his hands – nipple clamps. And not just any nipple clamps – clover clamps. *He means business! Oh, god, I want this,* a voice in her head whispered. He looked at her slit, saw her grow visibly wetter simply from the sight of the chain, heard her whimper. Before he climbed back onto the bed and straddled her, he pulled off his pants and boxer briefs and that huge, hard cock she loved so much sprang forward. She gasped, but he noticed she also licked her lips in anticipation. He pulled her nipples up over the edges of the bustier cups, then pinched and pulled them roughly and watched them grow painfully rigid. When he had them so hard and erect that she was moaning and crying out, he put a clamp on one and she screamed out, "Oh, that hurts like a motherfucker!" He attached the second one, and she yelled again.

"How pretty. You've got a nice pair of tits, little one. Do you like the pain? Need it?"

"No! Please . . ."

"The right answer is yes. Say yes, slut."

"Yes!" she wailed.

"That's 'Yes sir,' as you were already told," he snapped, and slapped the inside of her thigh hard. She shrieked.

"Yes sir!"

"Say, 'Yes sir, hurt me, sir!'" She repeated what he told her to say. "That's much better. How's this?" He grabbed the chain between the nipple clamps and pulled until her nipples were stretched to what had to be their limit.

"That feels good, sir!" she screamed. "Please, more, sir! Make it hurt, sir!"

Oh, my god, this is just too good, Tony thought. *I know her safeword, and I know her hand signal. She'll use them if she needs them. Think I'll see exactly where my little wild girl's line is drawn.*

Tony untied the rope from the headboard and dragged her to the edge of the bed, her head hanging off and her arms over her head, and he dropped the rope onto the floor and stood on it. "I need some relief; you've got me so hard that my cock is aching. I'm going to face fuck you. If you bite me, you'll be sorry, whore. And you will swallow, understand?" She nodded.

He moved toward her and put the head of his cock against her lips. She pressed them closed firmly. "Open wide, bitch. I've got a load for you." She shook her head. "Do you want to be punished?"

"No sir! But please, sir, I don't want to . . ."

"What you want is of no concern to me. You came here to fuck me and get yourself used, and that's exactly what's going to happen to you. Now open up or I'll make you scream until your mouth is wide open anyway." He pressed the head of his cock against her lips again, and she parted them slightly. Pushing as hard as he could manage, he forced his cock into her mouth and started to pump gently, then slightly harder. Her eyes rolled back, and he pumped with more force.

As he drove his hardness into her mouth, he reached down and got hold of the chain on the nipple clamps, pulling it tight, and she screamed around his erection. All the while he watched her hands for her hand signal that told him she'd use her safeword if her mouth wasn't full, but she wasn't making it. He held a handful of hair with his other hand, pounding harder and faster until he was ready to pour himself into her. When he shoved deep into her throat he felt his cock head hit the soft, hot flesh at the back of her throat, knew it blocked her airway when it slid in deep, heard her gasping as he pulled back, watched her beautiful neck expand as his hardness rammed down into her throat, her struggle to pull her hands free exciting him beyond reason. He shot his cum down into her, enjoying the sight of her swallowing it as he pumped into her with gusto. He pulled out and watched her lick her lips.

"Tastes good, doesn't it?" he asked her.

"Yes sir," she whispered, panting. "Please sir, please . . ."

"What are you begging for, whore?"

She groaned and writhed. "Please fuck me, sir. Please! Oh, god, I need to be fucked!" she cried out.

"I'm not that done with you yet, bitch." He scooted down her body, then pinched her clit. She screamed and arched her back. "Those clamps still hurt?"

"Yes sir! They hurt so good, sir! Please, fuck me!" she cried out again, bucking her pelvis upward, positively writhing in the heat of her desire, her body out of her control. "I want you to do whatever you want to me, sir. Please!"

"You're not getting fucked yet; you're not getting off that easy." He dragged his hand roughly up her slit, then began to rasp her clit aggressively. She managed a hoarse moan, her throat still swollen from his pounding, and felt her orgasm mounting, but he stopped abruptly, leaving her whimpering, and went back to the dresser drawer. When he turned back, he had a fur-covered paddle in his hand, and he flipped her over with her ass in the air and went to town with it. She cried out each time contact was made, and her ass turned bright pink everywhere the paddle struck. In between blows, he rubbed her reddened cheeks with his hand, and she howled as the heat spread across her glowing skin.

When both cheeks were bright red, he went back to the drawer and came back with a large butt plug and a big bottle of lube. She felt the coolness of the lube, and cried out as the plug breeched her rosette. It popped into place and she groaned.

"My turn. Let's see how much you can take," he laughed, flipping her onto her back again. The way he handled her, manipulated her body like she weighed no more than a speck of dust, made something in her gut twist with need, and she wanted more. He pushed her legs up to her chest and out, exposing her swollen clit to the cool air, and slammed into her, making her scream with the sudden fullness, the plug in her ass making her feel tighter than ever, driving her pelvis to churn. Reaching down, he pulled up the chain between the nipple clamps and grasped it between his teeth, then began to throw his full weight into her, pounding, tugging the chain with every stroke. She screamed loudly, the stretching of her engorged sheath making her nerve endings vibrate, and she bucked and squirmed. He groaned louder than her screaming, then dropped the chain and yelled, "Oh, god, slut, you're a good fuck. So tight! I'm gonna fuck you all night, dirty girl. You like getting rammed hard, don't you? Don't you? Say it, slut! Say it!"

"Yes sir, I want you to ram me, sir! Fuck me hard, sir!" she yowled, and he slammed into her harder than ever. He yanked on the chain again and she cried out, "Oh, god, sir, make me come! Please, make me come!" He reached between the two of them and started stroking her clit vigorously, and she screamed, "Oh, god, sir, I'm coming! I'm coming! I'm coming!!!!" He felt her pussy tighten around his shaft and begin to pulse, and her body convulsed of its own accord, her hips bucking wildly, but he didn't let up, didn't stop aggravating her clit, and she exploded, the orgasm consuming her completely. "Oh, god, sir, stop, please, stop! I can't take any more! Oh, god, please!" but she still didn't safeword, so he kept going. He continued to grate her nub and grind into her, still occasionally pulling the chain. Her eyes rolled to white and her body continued to shake wildly with the sustained orgasm.

He felt himself getting closer and closer, his balls tightening, and he shot his creamy seed into her, ramming down into her depths for all he was worth, listening to her moan incoherently. Even after he stopped stroking her clit, her body kept twitching with orgasmic aftershocks, and he could feel them in her pussy around his cock, the tiny tightenings over and over. She was still panting. When he pulled the chain one last time, she yelled out. He reached down and pinched one nipple behind the clamp as close as he could get to the teeth of the clamp, causing her to cry out, and he held her nipple as he slowly released the clamp. He leaned down to take the rosy, sore bud into his mouth, sucking as he did so and gradually releasing the pinch, allowing the blood flow to come back into it without causing her too much pain. The other nipple got the same treatment.

She was still gasping when he pulled out of her, flipped her over, and pulled out the plug. Just watching her, her post-orgasmic heaving and the jerking of her body, made him swell all over again, and he lubed up his cock, then worked more into her entrance, already open from the plug and calling to his hardness. She moaned loudly, then cried, "Oh, sir, no! Please don't fuck my ass! Oh, please, sir!" and, without hesitation, he drove his shaft into her.

He went to work stroking in and out of her tightness, growling and moaning as he went. "God, you've got a sweet little asshole, you horny little bitch. It's so hot and tight. Has anybody ever fucked you this hard, this long? Answer me," he snarled and smacked her ass cheek.

She squealed. "No sir! Nobody's ever fucked me like this. Oh, my god, I want you to fuck me, sir. Use me up, sir! You've got the biggest dick I've ever had, but I can take it! I need it so bad!"

"I don't think you can take it, whore. I think I'm too big and hard for you. Am I too big and hard for you?"

"You're too big and hard, sir, but it doesn't matter! I'm here for you to use as you see fit, sir! I'll take whatever you do to me, sir! Please don't punish me." *Sweet mother of god, this is incredible,* Tony thought as he closed his eyes and let all the sensations take over. *She fucking drives me wild. I must be the luckiest man in the world.* He dug in again, grinding into her with renewed resolve, his fingers digging into her hips. The way she cried out over and over propelled him, and he wanted to hear her, feel her around him, pour himself into her like there was no tomorrow. He slipped his arms under her thighs and lifted her so he was standing on his knees, pounding into her as she screamed in time with his rhythm.

He'd never felt so strong, so powerful, so raw and virile and so violently sexual. He looked at the woman he was stroking into, and he'd never seen anything so breathtakingly beautiful, so amazing, so vibrant, so vulnerable, and so wanton in his life. Every longing, every yearning, every fantasy he'd ever had, she'd fulfilled them all and then some. She was completely and totally spent, and she was still begging for more of what only he could give her, truly open to him in every way. *My woman. My love. My wife.* The words slammed into his brain and sent a bolt of energy through him, something wholly natural and fierce and primitive. This was his – forever. He wanted to do this with her every day of the rest of their lives, pump everything he had into her, consume her, mark her as his, stake his claim.

"Oh, sir, please, I need to come. Please!" He changed his strokes to long and steady, and she could feel her orgasm building, the need hot and overwhelming.

"You've earned it, whore. No good fuck should go unrewarded." He slid one hand from under her thigh to her slit, and when he dragged his finger across her clit, she came instantly, crying out and straining against him. Her cries made him ready, and he yelled out, "Oh, sweet mother of god, fuck me!" and bored into her one last time, spilling everything he had left before he pulled out of her and dropped her on the bed, then fell on top of her.

They lay there for what seemed like an hour or more, exhausted, and then he heard her whisper, "Red," and giggle. He rolled to one side, and rolled her over to face him. When she pressed the flat of her hand softly against his cheek as only a lover could, he took her hand in his and kissed her palm. Her forehead was damp and her hair was stuck to it, her makeup a mess, and she had a dreamy look in her eyes.

Tony leaned in close and kissed her lips, and marveled at how soft they were, how warm and how sweet, made sweeter by the taste of his essence still on them. She smiled at him, and he smiled back. With his fingers he pushed her hair back from her face, and she reached up for his hand and kissed his knuckles.

"Baby, I don't know what to say. What can I say to you? How can I tell you how much I love you, how much I need you?" he told her in a voice as warm and spicy as tabasco. "You're my everything – lover, whore, baby, friend. If you ever leave me, I'll die. I can't live without you. I mean it – I'm not kidding. I need you like I need air and water." She just continued to look at him with that dreamy gaze and smile. "Nik, say something. You okay?"

She licked her lips before she spoke, and her words were a lullaby to his heart. "Tony, I told you before, and I'll tell you again: You can do whatever you please with my body. It belongs to you. I belong to you. Without you, I don't care to go on. You're my life, my whole world. There's nothing I wouldn't do for you, nothing I wouldn't give you, nothing I wouldn't share with you. I'm yours. Forever. If you want me."

He drew her to him and wrapped himself around her. If he could've drawn her in through his pores, he would've. He wanted to absorb her into him, to meld with her, to find that oneness he craved. It almost wasn't enough to have his body inside hers; he wanted them to mesh somehow, to become one entity, one soul.

"We have somewhere to go tomorrow."

"Where are we going, lover?" She traced the outline of his lips with her fingertip, making him want to make love with her the rest of the night, wild and hot and out of control.

"We're going to look at rings." He waited for her response.

"Sure that's what you want?" she asked, nibbling gently on one of his nipples.

"I think the question is, is that what you want?"

"More than anything in the world," she assured him, kissing him.

He wrapped his arms around her and kissed her back. "I don't care when or where, who's there or what we're wearing, but I want to marry you, and I want to do it soon."

She was so gorgeous, sitting there on the deck in her lace gown, sipping a glass of water with all kinds of berries and fruit floating in it. When she set the glass down, it rested in a late evening sunbeam, the water and glass refracting the light until a rainbow fell onto the tabletop. Tony watched her as she scanned the mountainside behind the house, her eyes searching far away, the light mountain breeze ruffling her hair.

"I'd say we're going to have to wait," Tony had told Nikki as they left the fourth jewelry store earlier in the day. "Tourist areas apparently aren't very good shopping for quality stuff." Tony had promised they'd go during the week to some of the nicer places in Louisville. They'd find something there.

As they sat there on the deck, an idea struck him: "Hey, babe, what would you say to me taking your old rings and incorporating them into a new ring? We could use the diamonds you have and add more, use the gold to make the ring. Would you like that?" She'd told him once that the small diamond on her old engagement ring was the same one Randy had given her when he proposed all those years ago. It seemed to Tony that it might be a nice way to honor their new commitment and the one she and Randy had shared.

Nikki surprised him when she quietly replied, "Oh, no. I don't think so." The far-away look returned to her face, and she turned to gaze into the falling sun. The fading light of the day on her face made her look child-like, and he couldn't help but stare at her, his heart aching with all the love he held there for her.

"Really? I thought you'd like that idea, you know, your old life and your new life merging?"

Without looking at him, she replied in a strong voice, "My old life is gone. My new life is here and now with you, you and my new family. I loved my old family and life, still do, but that's over. I have to move forward. And I choose to do that with you." There was no trace of sadness or grief on her face, just peace and joy.

Tony felt it again – his heart overwhelmed with emotion, something he'd never experienced before her but was learning to embrace daily. He asked quietly, "Angel, what did I ever do to deserve you?"

She turned to him, her eyes bright with promise, her heart full and running over. "You dared to love me. And I'll spend the rest of my life trying to show you how grateful I am for that second chance."

Chapter Thirty-Four

Tony and Nikki had to park several blocks from the parade route, the downtown street being packed with spectators. They made their way to the grandstand; he might not have gotten to be the grand marshal, but Tony still commanded a spot in the grandstand simply by virtue of who he was in Louisville. The brunch at Brisbane had been delicious, and Nikki was glad they had to walk a distance to get in. She needed the exercise.

It was the first time Tony and Nikki had been in a large public venue since they'd been together. She noticed people were turning and looking at them, some speaking to Tony as they passed. He stopped several times and shook hands with people along the way. "Everybody's looking at us," she whispered to Tony.

"Everybody's looking at *you!*" Tony whispered back. "They're curious about you. Everybody knew I was seeing somebody, but no one's really seen us out except in the occasional restaurant. They want to see you, see what you look like. I'm sure the gossip mill is going crazy." He chuckled. "I don't think you're what they were expecting at all."

No, I'm sure I'm not, Nikki thought. They were expecting her to look more like, oh, Molly; someone really pretty and "fixy" and plastic. She was none of those things. But Tony seemed to like how she looked, so it was none of their business.

The parade started a few minutes after they reached the grandstand. Fire trucks from every fire district in the city passed by, then a police cruiser from every precinct. Several labor unions had floats, and they were attractive and well done. Float riders threw candy to the crowd, and several dozen kids scrambled every time candy went flying. "Do we have candy?" Nikki asked Tony.

"Well, of course! What kind of two-bit outfit would we be if we didn't have candy?" Tony laughed and ruffled her hair. "Hey, let's go down on the curb. I want to be down there when the guys go by." He took her hand and they made their way down the grandstand and through the crowd. They stood at the curb, looking up the parade route, waiting for theirs to come around the corner.

"I see it!" Nikki cried out, pointing. "Oh, Tony, look! It's great!" Tony stood on his tiptoes, looking over the crowd.

Clayton spotted them on the curb and waved, then started honking the truck's horn. Cal and Jeremy spotted them too and waved at them. Nikki heard Tony speaking to someone behind them, and turned to see a man talking to him, shaking his hand. The man said something about "good job" and "worked hard," and Tony was smiling and nodding as he spoke. Nikki didn't know anyone, but it seemed Tony knew everyone. She began to turn back to the street, but something caught her eye – a streak of orange, whizzing over the top of the crowd. She opened her mouth to say something, but she wasn't quick enough.

The float burst into flames.

She screamed and Tony turned, his smile dissolving into sheer terror. People were shrieking and pushing backward, but Nikki was already on the move, Tony right behind her, pushing against the crowd and heading straight for the inferno.

Nikki ran right up to the trailer, and the heat was unbearable. Where were Cal and Jeremy? She skirted the back and found them on the other side of the float on the ground. Cal was coughing but seemed fine, but Jeremy's shirt was burning. Cal was trying to put it out and couldn't, so Nikki ran up and fell right on top of him, smothering the flames. Poor Jeremy was screaming and writhing on the ground, and Nikki yelled at Cal, "Help me drag him farther back!" His arms were so badly burned that they each grabbed a leg and pulled until they had him on the lawn of a business, well on the other side of the sidewalk from the burning hulk. She felt a presence on her right side, and Peyton grabbed her arm, looked her up and down, and knelt with her beside Jeremy.

Tony ran directly to the truck, where Clayton had peeled from the cab and was trying to get the trailer unhitched. He was too close: "Clayton! Clayton, get back!" Tony screamed at him. Then he remembered the tools in the bed of the truck, and he climbed up on the bumper and dug around, finally finding a sledgehammer. He jumped out of the truck bed and ordered Clayton, "Get back in the truck and wait for my signal! Be ready!" Tony took the sledgehammer to the trailer hitch, knocked off the latch, and slammed down on the tongue. It broke free, and he threw his arm up in the air, traced a circle, and whistled loudly. The truck lurched as Clayton stepped down on the gas and pulled away from the trailer.

Tony glanced around in panic, and realized José was standing right beside him. Both men scanned the area. Where was Nikki? In the middle of the street, the once-beautiful float sat blazing, destroyed. Parade spectators had stopped running and were coming back toward the scene, staring in disbelief. Tony could hear emergency vehicles, probably the very ones that were in the parade, heading toward the scene. "Nikki!" he screamed, looking around frantically. The last time he'd seen her, she'd been running straight to the flaming disaster. "NIKKI! Where are you?"

He heard a horn blaring and turned to see Clayton standing on the running board of the truck, pointing to the other side of the street behind the float. Tony and José ran around the back of the blaze and were stunned and horrified by what they saw.

Cal, Nikki, and Peyton were squatted down beside Jeremy; the younger man's arms were badly burned and he was twitching and shaking. Nikki and Cal were sooty; Nikki's dress had what looked like burn marks across it. Tony sprinted to them. "Baby! Oh my god, are you okay?" he cried, looking her up and down.

"I'm fine, I'm fine. We need a blanket – he's going into shock. Find something, please!"

Tony ran to the front of the trailer and caught Clayton's eye. "Get a tarp!" he yelled, and he saw Clayton start to rummage around in the bed of the truck. Within a few seconds, Clayton stood by the six of them, unfolding a canvas tarp, a standard issue for all Walters Construction vehicles. Nikki tucked it around Jeremy, whose head was resting in her lap. While they stood waiting for help, Vic ran up, asking what he could do to help, his face anxious and drawn.

It seemed to take forever for EMTs to reach them. One of the ambulances in the parade made it to them first, and they loaded Jeremy in and took off. Two fire trucks fought their way through the crowd and traffic but, by the time they reached the scene, the float was almost completely destroyed, the tires melted and the decking collapsing, so they secured the area and just let it burn. Police officers swarmed in, keeping spectators back and trying to talk to everyone involved.

Detective Ford found the little group standing on the sidewalk. "Oh, for the love of god, not you guys again," he moaned, shaking his head sympathetically. "Is everybody okay?"

"No!" Tony shouted, his face a mask of fury. "One of my employees is on the way to the hospital with serious burns. I think it's time you guys took this seriously and got us some help. It's a miracle no one was killed." Vic reached over and put a hand on Tony's shoulder again to try to calm him down and was surprised to find his cousin shaking.

Detective Ford glared at him defensively. "Mr. Walters, we've *been* taking this seriously, but we haven't been able to get any leads. I understand your own hired gun hasn't been any more successful than we have. So know we're doing our absolute best, okay?"

"Yeah, okay. Sorry. I'm just so damn frustrated." Tony shook his head, his hands on his hips.

Detective Ford pressed on. "So, can anybody tell me anything?"

Before anyone else could speak, Nikki blurted out, "It was a flare gun." The entire group turned to stare at her. "Well, it was," she repeated sternly. "I saw the flash."

Tony couldn't believe it. "Are you kidding? From where?"

"From up there." She pointed at a three-story parking garage in the same block as the grandstand. "It was up high, so it must've come from at least the second floor. You were talking to some guy behind us," she said to Tony. "I turned to see who it was – I didn't know him – and I saw something streak across the sky above the crowd. And then – BOOM! – the fire started."

"Okay, ma'am, take me to where you were standing when you saw this and explain to me what you saw," Detective Ford told her. They both turned to go back to where she had been when the fire started.

"I'm not leaving her," Vic announced, looking toward Nikki, and Tony nodded. Vic took off, following Nikki and the detective.

Tony watched them walk away, then turned to Clayton. "Get a wrecker on its way here. As soon as the fire marshal is done with the investigation, we need to get this trailer out of here and out of the way. Take it to the shop and drop it. And take Cal to his truck." Clayton nodded. "I've got to get to the hospital and check on Jeremy."

"You okay, Tony?" José asked. Peyton walked up on Tony's other side and looked him up and down just as he had Nikki.

"Yeah, yeah, I'm fine." He ran his fingers through his hair. "This is insane, just insane. If we don't find these people pretty soon, somebody's going to be killed. I just don't know what to do anymore."

José put a hand on Tony's shoulder. "It'll be okay. We'll eventually find them."

"I know. I appreciate you guys – Laura too. You're doing a good job of keeping us safe. Clayton's detail too." He clapped José on the back. "I'm grateful, really. Now I've got to go and talk to Nikki; I've got to tell her I'm going to the hospital to check on Jeremy. I want one of you to stay with her until she's done and bring her to me, or have Vic bring her." Tony crossed the street, heading toward the detective and Nikki, as José and Peyton stood watching him go.

José turned to Peyton. "You realize they're in a lot more danger than we thought, right?"

"Yeah. It's gonna take everything we have to keep them both alive." Peyton took a deep breath and sighed. This was going to be one tough assignment, and he hoped they were up to the challenge.

When Tony got to the house, Peyton was in his usual spot across the street in his gray sedan, and Tony waved to the younger man as he turned into the driveway. He walked in to find Nikki in the shower, her ruined sundress on the floor, and the pile of her clothing reeking of smoke. He stripped off his clothes and opened the shower door.

She jumped, and then smiled at him. "Hey, baby! I'm sure glad to see you!" Nikki threw her arms around his neck and kissed him.

"Angel, I'm sure glad to see you. And I'm glad you're okay. You were a hero today," he whispered into her ear, then kissed her back.

"Oh, no, no hero here. I just did what I knew to do." She worked shampoo into her hair, and Tony moved her hands away and took over massaging her scalp. She moaned as he worked it into a lather.

"Uh-uh, sweetheart. I'm hungry. Let's finish up and eat," Nikki told Tony when he got frisky in the shower. She put on a simple shift dress and some flip-flops and fixed them a tasty lunch of homemade chicken salad and field greens. Before they could finish, they heard Clayton and Brittany come through the front door, followed almost immediately by Annabeth and Katie, and Vic brought up the rear. Clayton's first words to his dad were, "You need to call Nonna. She's going to be terrified until she hears your voice."

Nikki heard Tony say, "Mamma, I wanted to call you …" as she asked the kids and Vic if they wanted food, then fed them. The questions started flying, and Nikki was glad when Tony got off the phone with his mother and helped her field some of them. Clayton did his best to fill in the blanks, but

Nikki realized he hadn't seen anything; he'd been busy watching the crowd while he drove the truck.

After about forty-five minutes, Tony announced, "Okay, guys, everybody go home. Your mom and I are exhausted. This has been an awful day. Go home, calm down, have a quiet evening. We've all got work tomorrow and we need to be as rested up as we can manage." There was lots of hugging all around as everyone left.

Clayton turned as he was leaving and walked back to Nikki, wrapping his arms around her. "You scared me, Mom. I don't know what we would've done if you'd gotten hurt. That was really brave of you, to go to Jeremy like that and help him. I know he appreciates it." He stopped, then said softly, "I love you, Mom."

"Oh, honey, I love you too!" Nikki smiled, hugging him again. "I'm okay, don't worry about me. Now you take Brit home and relax. See you tomorrow at work." She kissed him on the cheek and he squeezed her hand as he walked out.

"Night, guys," Vic told them, hugging first Nikki, then Tony. "Call me if I can do anything." Nikki stood on tiptoe and gave him a peck on the cheek, and he kissed her forehead as he left.

"I'm getting a beer and sitting on my ass in the den. Want a glass of wine?" Tony asked Nikki, turning back toward the kitchen.

"Yeah. Meet you on the sofa." Nikki followed him into the kitchen to finish her clean-up.

They sat quietly, holding hands, for the rest of the evening, watching shows they didn't care about and wouldn't remember the next day. When they finally climbed into bed, Tony made love to Nikki as softly as a whisper, listening to her breathe and soaking in the feel of her satiny skin against him. The orgasm he gave her was strong but slow, and instead of crying out, she just gripped his arms and ground gently against him. It was so peaceful and calming that neither wanted it to end.

She lay in his arms, and he breathed into her hair, "I don't know how long it's going to take, but everything's going to be okay. We've got each other."

"I know," she sighed and drifted off to sleep.

Chapter Thirty-Five

The week after Labor Day, Nikki came out of Bart's office across town to find that someone had keyed her truck, both sides, deep. They'd ruined the signage in the process. Two days later, the same happened to Tony's truck as it sat in the parking lot at the courthouse while he was inside taking care of some permit issues. Both trucks had to be painted and the signage replaced. Tony was furious, but at least no one was hurt.

But if he was furious about the damage to the trucks, he was pleased as a peacock with his girlfriend's performance as operations officer. The guys were not only respectful to her, but they commented to him about what a good job she was doing and his good judgment in hiring her. She seemed to enjoy the work too, and it gave them plenty to talk about over dinner every night. He'd given her a special, covert assignment as well; she was trying to talk Annabeth into coming to work for the company.

They fell into a comfortable lifestyle, working together and separately, having lunch two or three times a week, spending time in the garage gym, eating nice dinners Nikki genuinely enjoyed cooking, and having both intelligent conversation and something else Tony hadn't had in a long time – fun. They laughed together several times a day and, even when GoGreen did their worst, he still felt like his world was okay as long as they were together. Tony had never been as happy as he was with Nikki.

On the following Monday, Nikki called Annabeth to invite her and Katie to dinner on Wednesday the nineteenth for Tony's birthday and a late celebration of hers from the eighth, then caught Clayton in the office to ask him the same thing.

"Sure!" Then Clayton hesitated. "Is it okay if we bring a guest?"

Nikki looked at him with curiosity. "A guest? Sure. Who is it?"

"Well, um, that's a surprise." Clayton was expressionless.

Then it hit Nikki. "Oh my god! Are you bringing a little one?"

"I can't say." Clayton worked to mask his expression. "Brittany will kill me. It might fall through."

"Say no more. Mum's the word. I'll make sure there's a place at the table. Oh, this is so exciting!" Nikki gushed.

She called Vic and asked him to come; of course, he let her know he wouldn't miss it for the world. Raffaella was on board, too; she was bringing that divine cake again. *God,* Nikki thought, *being part of this family is probably going to mean I'll end up weighing three hundred pounds!*

She thought about calling Bart and Freddie, but then decided if there really was a child coming, that might be too many people too soon. What would Tony think when Clayton and Brittany walked in with their guest? She couldn't wait for Wednesday to come.

"I'm leaving early," Nikki told Tony. "It's your birthday, and I've got to go home and cook. You're not going to be late, are you?"

"Nope. I'll be right behind you." Tony was already in the process of packing up for the day.

"Good. Think – what would be your request for your favorite birthday meal?"

Tony smiled. "Your meatloaf. I can't get enough of that stuff."

"Great! That's what I was planning to make anyway! So happy birthday to you!" She kissed him lightly on the cheek and skipped out the door.

At home, Nikki started pulling the meal together. Tony came through, kissed her lightly, and went up to shower and dress. Annabeth came in and started helping, watching Nikki make the meatloaf so she would know how it was done. By the time it was in the oven she had asked Nikki for a copy of the recipe, which her new mom took as a great compliment.

About the time Katie showed up, Vic brought in four bottles of nice wine. He also brought in Raffaella. "I thought Clayton was bringing you?" Nikki questioned Raffaella.

Raffaella shrugged. "I thought so too, but Vic came."

"Clayton called me and asked me to pick his nonna up," Vic said. "He didn't say why."

Tony came up the hallway and greeted everyone with hugs and kisses, then turned to Nikki, kissing her firmly on the lips. He looked delicious; she could feel her nipples hardening just from looking at him.

Before they could move into the den, the front door opened and Clayton came in. He held the door for Brittany as she entered, and she was holding the hand of a very small child. Every eye in the house turned and went straight to the tiny face.

The little boy had dark skin that was almost chocolate brown, and his hair was so short that his head was very nearly shaved. Under his thick, black lashes, he had the absolute largest dark brown eyes Nikki had ever seen, and beautiful, soft lips. Finally, Tony spoke: "Well, who do we have here?"

"Dad, Mom, guys, this is Stringer. Say hello, buddy." Clayton took the child's other hand. Almost in unison, the entire group mouthed silently to Clayton, *Stringer?* He shrugged.

"Hi der," the little guy said, then smiled a jack-o-lantern smile so every tooth in his head showed. But the smile was on his lips; it didn't extend to his eyes, which looked more than terrified. The tense look on his face pierced Tony's heart, and the big man dropped to his knees in front of the tiny boy.

"Hi, Stringer! I'm Tony. I'm glad to meet you." He held out his hand, and Stringer took it and shook it vigorously. "Nice grip! You're a strong one, huh?" Tony laughed.

Stringer held up his arm, flexing his little bicep. "Wooka my guns!" he shouted.

"Wow! That's pretty impressive," Tony said with mock seriousness. "Guess you can take care of yourself, huh?"

"You betta bewieve it." Stringer scowled out from under his wrinkled brow.

"Wanna go look around?" Tony took his hand. "I can show you where everything is." He stood and started down the hall, Stringer looking up at him.

"Whaw da baffroom? Das a good fing to know."

"I agree – very important," Tony told him as they wandered down the hall.

"Well, that went better than I expected," Clayton said under his breath, and Brittany let out a sigh of relief.

"Uh-oh." Nikki watched her big guy lead the little one down the hallway. "Your dad is falling in love." Vic laughed. "You know I'm right," she said, frowning at Vic, who nodded.

Clayton grinned. "Yeah, Mom. I think he is."

"I don wike dat." Stringer shoved the meatloaf away.

"Have you tried it?" Tony asked him. Stringer had insisted on sitting next to Tony. That was usually Nikki's spot, but she'd decided she could give it up for one night.

"Nah, but I don wike it," Stringer repeated, making a disgusted face.

"Why don't you try it?" He leaned over and whispered in Stringer's ear, loudly enough so everyone could hear, "You'll hurt Ms. Nikki's feelings if you don't. She made it especially for you." Tony picked up Stringer's fork and loaded it with meatloaf, then held it up to his face. "Then if you don't like it, you don't have to eat it."

To their surprise, Stringer opened his mouth like a baby bird, and Tony shoved the meatloaf in before he had a chance to clamp it shut again. Stringer chewed it a bit, then cocked his head to one side.

"Hey!" he yelled. "Dass pwetty good!" He took the fork from Tony and started eating the meatloaf by himself. Tony looked at Nikki with a silly grin plastered all over his face that made her heart thump faster.

When dinner was done, Stringer had a screaming fit because Clayton and Brittany would only let him have one slice of Raffaella's cake. Nikki had to promise to take him to the nearest fast food restaurant with a playground to get him quiet, and he wanted to know right then when he could expect her to do that. Tony dug around in the closet of the back bedroom and found a box of Clayton's old building blocks, and Annabeth and Katie helped him build something unidentifiable in the den.

Eventually, everyone left, knowing they had to go to work the next day. As he left, Stringer had to hug and kiss everyone. "Bye, ebberbody! Bye, Tony," he yelled out, and kissed Tony on the cheek.

"Bye, buddy! I'm glad you came to my birthday party," Tony told him. "You come back and see me, okay?"

"Okay. I come tomowoe," Stringer declared, then he hugged Nikki and kissed her. "Bye, Nitty. I wike you hayah. Iz vewy pwetty," he cooed, stroking her hair.

"Oh, thank you, sweetie! I'm so glad you were here." She hugged him back. "You be careful going home, okay?"

"I be cayfuw. You be cayfuw too," he said absentmindedly as Brittany led him out the door, distracted by the dollar bill Vic had given him.

Clayton hugged Tony first, then Nikki. "Happy birthday, Dad. I appreciate everybody being so supportive."

Tony clapped him on the back. "Son, that's what we're here for! He's a great little guy. I hope we get to see lots more of him."

Clayton flashed a gentle smile. "I hope so too."

"So, how would you rate this birthday?" Nikki asked as they got ready for bed.

"On a scale of one to ten, with ten being the best, I'd say a thirteen, at least." Tony took off his jeans. "New girlfriend, prospective new grandchild. There's only one thing that would make it better."

"Yeah? What's that?"

Color rose in Tony's cheeks. "Could I get a replay of my Father's Day gift?"

"Oh, I think that could be arranged." Nikki patted the space on the bed beside her. "Come to mamma."

She did the exact same thing she'd done before, except for one thing – she tied his hands to the headboard. That was unexpected, and he argued a bit, even struggled a little, but in the end he gave in and stayed put without too much fuss.

It meant that, when he came, he found himself in a new predicament, and she didn't stop as soon as he came, but kept going until he was jerking, gasping, and begging her to stop. Watching his pecs and biceps strain against the restraints made her so hot and wet that she was almost frantic to get on him. She climbed up to the headboard and straddled his face, lowering her mound to his mouth, and she gripped the headboard while he sucked, licked, and pulled her clit to climax. After she came, she went down on him and teased him back to maximum hardness, then rode him in reverse cowgirl position like he was a bucking bronco and she was a rodeo star before she finally untied him.

When they were both spent and in each other's arms, Nikki giggled. "Wow, baby, you should moonlight as a porn star!"

He let out a hearty laugh. "Funny, I was thinking the same about you!"

Nikki dawdled a fingertip around his nipple. "You and Stringer really hit it off, huh?"

"He's a cute little guy. Wonder what his story is?"

"I've got a feeling we're going to find out tomorrow at the office." Then she chuckled out, "Hey, cowboy, thanks for the ride!" as she kissed him goodnight.

"We aim to please, ma'am," he drawled as he smiled and kissed her back.

"His mom was addicted to heroin. He was born addicted," Clayton explained. "He's got some minor developmental issues because of it, but mostly he's just sad and abandoned."

"Where is she now?" Tony asked.

"Dead. Overdosed. No dad. No one. He's an orphan." Clayton stopped for a moment and looked first at Tony, then at Nikki. "We're hoping . . ."

"One day at a time, son. If it's meant to be, it'll happen," Nikki reminded him calmly.

"I know. And he's fitting in so well, and I think we're doing a pretty good job of adapting too. By the way, as long as he's a foster, any sitters we use have to be approved by the social worker. So do you think maybe you two . . ."

"Send her on over, son." Tony would do anything to help out, and he hoped Clayton knew that. "Not a problem. Do we have to jump through the same hoops you did?"

"No. I'll bring you a sheet of stuff she'll be looking for, though. And thanks — we really appreciate it."

"No problem, honey. We're glad to help," Nikki added.

After Clayton left, Tony sighed. "I really hope this goes through for them." Then he looked into her eyes and smiled. "And I'm really kind of excited, you know?"

"I can tell!" she smiled back. "I am too. He's a cute little fellow, and the two of you really looked very cute together!"

"Yeah? Think so?"

Nikki blushed. "Well, you were cute together, but watching you with him got me really hot."

"No shit! Hmmmm. Who knew grandpas were sexy?"

"No, baby, grandpas aren't sexy; you're sexy. And you might happen to be a grandpa," she laughed.

"Travis, come here and look at this." Autumn stopped the video footage on her computer screen and ran it back. Travis came to look over her shoulder and squinted at the screen.

"What is that? What am I seeing?" he asked, leaning in.

"That's a Walters truck."

"Is that Walters in the truck?"

"No. I don't know who it is. That's the hospital site."

As they watched, the truck pulled up, facing away from the camera. Some other vehicle pulled up beside the passenger side of the truck, out of the range of the camera. They could barely see the activity on the passenger's side of the truck as the door opened and someone got in, then there was some kind of activity inside the truck. They both leaned in and squinted, then Autumn squealed and pulled back.

"Oh my god! They're having sex! Eeeeeewwwwww!!!!!" She turned around, disgusted.

Travis made a face. "Who is that?"

"Damned if I know. I just know it's not Tony Walters. Oh, that's just gross!" She slammed the laptop shut.

"Well, that's really interesting," Travis said. "We'll have to keep an eye on that."

"You go right ahead," Autumn announced. "I don't want to see that ever again!"

Chapter Thirty-Six

I swear, if there's a piece of paperwork that comes through this company, I think it finds its way to my desk, Nikki thought as she shuffled through another pile. She'd been helping out human resources and payroll, and she hadn't been able to get out of the office for three days. Her regular ride-along with Tony had also had to wait. Plus all of the furniture and artwork for Vic's office was in, and she hadn't even been able to take a couple of days to go down and supervise the delivery and installation. She *had* to get that done; Vic's birthday was the next week on October thirtieth, and she wanted it all in place by then.

She'd gotten most of the documents into big envelopes sorted by the offices they went back to when she heard it. The whole building shook, and Cheryl screamed. Nikki jumped up and ran to the front door, and she nearly fainted.

Tony's truck was sitting across the lot, and it was blazing. At the moment she opened the door, the reserve gas tank blew, and fiery pieces of metal shot in every direction. She almost fell to her knees, then, staggering, she threw the door open and started running straight to the truck. As she ran, she shrieked his name, terrified, not hearing or seeing anything around her, just watching as the truck burned, flames shooting twenty feet into the air. She was almost to it when something, someone, grabbed her and lifted her off the ground in mid-stride.

"Whoa, baby, stop! It's me!" Tony yelled as he clasped her around the waist from behind. "I'm fine! Nikki, look at me!" Tony spun her around. Eyes wide, her mouth dropped open, and she couldn't speak or breathe. She felt faint.

"Baby! Hey! It's okay!" Tony shook her – hard. "Stay with me, sweetie!" She sank down, and he swept her up into his arms and carried her back to the sofa in his office. "Breathe, Nikki! Breathe!" She drew in a hard, ragged breath while he poured her a glass of water, but when he handed it to her, she could see that his hands were shaking.

"God, Tony! What the hell?" she screamed and sat bolt-upright, finally coming out of the panic that had thrown her into near-unconsciousness.

"I have no idea. I'd just gotten out of the thing when it blew. Thank god I was inside the shop or I might've really gotten hurt." He grabbed a wad of paper towel, wet it, and went to work patting and wiping her face to cool her down and calm her, then sat and held her, both of them numb.

They were still sitting like that about five minutes later when they heard a commotion as Clayton, Steve, Peyton, José, and Laura hurried into the office. Tony looked up at them, and Steve announced, "We need to have a talk. Now."

Nikki had been trying to rest, but she sat up and moved down the sofa. Clayton and José sat down with her, with Laura perched on the sofa arm; poor Clayton looked like someone had punched him in the gut. Tony took his seat behind the desk, and Peyton and Steve stood with their arms folded across their chests. There was a lot of posturing going on, and Nikki didn't like it one bit.

Then Steve walked straight to Tony's desk, put his hands on the desktop, and leaned forward toward Tony. "If there's anything you need to tell me, out with it, now," Steve growled.

Tony looked shocked. "No! There's nothing, nothing I know of. Don't you think I would've already told you?"

Steve squinted at him. "You're sure?"

"Positive. I got nothin'." Tony looked pretty deflated.

"What about you?" Steve turned to Nikki, almost snarling.

"Hey, watch it!" Tony barked. "You show her some respect!"

"Hell, no. I got nothin' either," she replied indignantly.

"Okay." Steve relaxed a little. "This is getting serious. I was just driving by here with Peyton when that happened. Laura and José were getting ready for shift change, and either of them could've been too close to that. How do you think I felt, seeing that, knowing how many people were endangered?"

"Yeah? Well, you should've been me." Tony leaned back in his chair. "I don't know what to do. What if that had been Nikki? Or Clayton?" He shuddered.

It got really quiet. Finally, Peyton spoke. "Anybody got any suggestions? I'm really stumped. It's almost like somebody's watching. Like they watched you get out of the truck, then detonated it. But we've done multiple sweeps and we haven't found a thing."

"By the way, where the hell are the cops and the fire department?" Nikki asked. "The damn thing is still burning. They should be here." As if to answer her question, a fire truck tore up to the front of the building, then turned and went straight to the burning pickup truck. Two police cruisers pulled in right behind it. They heard the door open, then the thump of boots across the floor, and Keith Ford filled the doorway. He looked around the room at all of them. "Shit."

"Exactly," Tony replied.

"Somebody want to tell me what happened?" Tony started filling the detective in, with help from Steve and Clayton. Nikki looked over at Laura and gave her a half-hearted smile, but the muscular brunette didn't smile back.

When they were done, Tony looked at Nikki. "Give me your keys to your company truck." He held out his upturned palm to her. Nikki fished them out of her pocket and handed them to him, puzzled. "That's it. You're staying here in the office from now on. No site work. It's just not safe." Nikki opened her mouth to argue, then closed it. No point – she always wound up caving to him anyway. "I can use your truck," he added. "No need to order me another one."

Nikki frowned. "What about Vic's office? I'm supposed to go down there and help him with the furniture and decorating."

"Peyton or José can take you. Or Laura," Steve offered. "Yeah, Laura, I think that would be good. You guys work it out amongst yourselves." Nikki could've sworn Laura made a face, but she said nothing. He looked around the room. "So we need some kind of new strategy. What we're doing isn't working. We're missing something here, but I don't know what."

I can't do this anymore. Nikki got up and went to the office she shared with Clayton, the neurons in her brain misfiring in every direction. She put her head on her desk and took a deep breath. The sound of footsteps at the door made her look up to find Peyton standing in the doorway. "May I come in?"

She nodded and pointed for him to sit. "Please."

"I know this is getting to you." His crystal blue eyes were sympathetic. "But it's eventually going to be fine. We'll find these people. In the meantime, we've got to keep both of you safe, that's all. Just hang in there, okay?"

"I'm trying." Nikki was fighting back tears. "I was just so scared. I thought Tony was in the truck, and . . ."

"I know," Peyton said quietly. "I did too." Suddenly, Nikki felt sorry for the younger man. He seemed concerned about them, genuinely concerned.

"Peyton, I'm so sorry. I wish I knew something that would help you guys help us, but I don't know anything."

"That's okay. But listen, if you need anything, anything at all, don't hesitate to tell me, or Steve, or José. Laura too," he added.

Nikki scowled. "I don't think she likes me very much."

Peyton gave her a tiny smile. "She doesn't like anybody. But she's good at what she does, and you can trust her. What you don't know is that it's not just the four of us. Steve's got a whole stable of security people; former military, former law enforcement, former federal agents . . ."

"Which are you?"

"Military. Special Forces, then combat. Had to, um, retire because of my injury." He got up and walked to Nikki's side, then pulled up his left pant leg. His prosthetic was state of the art – Nikki had never guessed by watching him walk that there was anything different about him. "So you see, we've all got our crosses to bear. We just have to make the best of it."

She nodded. "Thanks, Peyton. You've been good to me. I really appreciate it."

"You're easy to be good to. You're a good person. Hang in there – we're all gonna get through this. We just have to stick together." He started out of the office, then turned and looked at Nikki from the doorway. "And if I'm tailing you again, don't ever try to get away from me. Can't be done. I'll follow you to the ends of the earth!" He laughed.

"Duly noted." Nikki smiled at him as he left. What a sweet young man, and so cute too. She hoped he had someone special.

She heard more movement, and Tony appeared in the office door. He leaned against the door facing in his jeans and tee-shirt, arms and ankles crossed, and it was all she could do to stay in her chair – she wanted to grab him and run her hands all over him. "You okay?"

She nodded. "I am now. Peyton came in and gave me a little pep talk. He's such a nice guy. But I'm a little ticked off at Steve. Where does he get off talking to us like that?"

"Hon, he's just frustrated. We all are." Tony sighed and plopped down in the chair where Peyton had been sitting. "I am too. I don't know what to do anymore."

"Me neither." She wadded up a piece of paper and threw it toward the trash can. And she missed.

"So what would you like to listen to?" Nikki asked Laura.

Laura just stared out the window. "Doesn't matter."

"Oooo-kaaaay." Nikki changed the satellite radio to a progressive rock station.

Ten more miles went by in silence. "So, are you married? Got kids?"

"No and no."

Five more miles, and Nikki asked, "So what do you like to do in your spare time?"

"I don't *have* spare time," Laura grunted.

"Right." Fifteen miles later, Nikki got right to the point. "So, why is it that you dislike me so much?"

Laura huffed. "I don't dislike you. I don't like you. I don't have any feelings whatsoever toward you. I'm just doing my job."

Nikki tried very hard to rein in her frustration. "Okay then, well, I'll just pretend I'm alone and you can just sit there and pretend you're an emotionless shell and we'll both have a dandy time." As far as Nikki was concerned, she was finished. She'd done all she could.

They rode in complete silence all the way to Lexington. When they got to Vic's office, Nikki got out of the car and went on inside, saying nothing to Laura. She could come in, or she could sit in the car; Nikki didn't care.

Vic greeted Nikki as soon as she walked in the door. "Hey, baby! It's so good to see you! You doing okay?" He scooped her up and hugged her tight.

"Hey, sweetie! It's good to see you too! I'm good. You?"

"Good. I see you brought a suitcase with you." He frowned and pointed through the door at Laura, who had taken up a position out front.

"Yeah. She's as friendly as a porcupine," Nikki snarled.

"Don't I know it. She's a hot little thing, but I tried to talk to her, and she just shut me down. And this time, I don't think it's me." Vic shook his head, bewildered.

She giggled at Vic. "It's never you, gorgeous. You're almost as hunky as that beautiful cousin of yours! So did you get the delivery arranged?"

"Yeah, they'll be here in about an hour. You're gonna have your work cut out for you."

"As long as the albatross stays out of the way," Nikki said, looking at Laura, "it shouldn't take long to get it all sorted out."

"'Bout done?" Tony asked Nikki when she answered the phone.

"Yeah, I'm probably forty-five minutes from being finished. Vic wants to take me to dinner before I head back. Honestly, I wish I'd brought clothes to stay over at his house, but I didn't. Can you fend for yourself for dinner?"

"Sure. I'll check with Clayton and Brit, see what they're doing. Maybe I could go over there and see Stringer."

"Oh, that would be fun! But let me know what you're doing so I won't worry."

"Hey, same on your end. You and Laura getting along okay?"

"Yeah. Can't *not* get along with somebody who won't talk to you."

"Huh. Guess that's right. Oh, well, love you, baby. See you in a bit. You be careful driving back."

"You bet! Love you too."

Nikki called Tony to tell him that Vic wanted to take her and Laura to dinner before they headed back to Louisville. "You and Laura getting along okay?" he asked.

"Yeah. Can't *not* get along with someone who won't talk to you."

"Do you like sushi?" Nikki asked. Laura sat in the front passenger seat of Nikki's Volvo as they followed Vic to the Japanese hibachi and sushi restaurant.

"Doesn't matter. I won't be eating anyway."

The boss lady in Nikki rose up; she'd had just about enough and she was going to put an end to it. "Actually, yes, you will be eating," she growled in a measured, even, firm voice that let Laura know she wasn't going to tolerate being fucked with. "Vic wants to treat us to dinner, and you will not be rude to him. He's a prince of a guy, and he at least deserves to be treated with kindness and respect. So you're going, you'll eat, you'll be gracious, and you'll thank him when we're done. You got that?"

Laura turned to look at Nikki, but one glance at the fiery blond beside her told her there was no need to try to argue. She'd never seen this side of Nikki, but she had to admit she liked it. The woman looked a little fluffy, but she was tough as steel, and Laura respected that. "Yeah, I got it. Sorry. I don't mean to come across as rude. I'm just trying to be professional."

"Being professional and being cold and distant are *not* the same things," Nikki reiterated, not looking at Laura. "You need to work on your people skills, take some lessons from Peyton and José."

The corners of Laura's mouth turned up slightly. "Point taken." Then she got a little bold. "You're not at all what I thought you'd be."

"Thought I was just some spoiled little hank of hair trying to hook a rich man, huh?" Nikki's smirk drew the corners of her mouth up.

"Something like that."

"Well, you obviously don't know my background or you wouldn't think that. And if you ever decide you want to know about it, just ask. I don't mind talking about it, but I won't bore you if you don't care."

Laura made a note to herself to ask on the way back. Now she was curious.

Vic smiled the smile of the totally smitten as the server cleared the table, and Laura couldn't help but notice how he looked at Nikki. "I hope you enjoyed that, princess."

"Oh, god, it was so good! This place is amazing," Nikki gushed, tinkering with her chopsticks. She'd enjoyed watching Vic eat with his, but she'd never master the things in a million years. He'd tried to give her a crash course, but she was a lost cause.

Vic turned to Laura. "What about you, Laura? Was it good?"

"Very. Thanks so much, Vic." She stared at the table as she dabbed at her mouth with her napkin.

"Wow – five. I think that's the longest string of words I've ever heard you speak. And you're so welcome. I'm glad you enjoyed it." He looked Laura right in the eye when he spoke, and his voice was smooth as satin. She felt something stir in her gut, but she shut it down. Vic Cabrizzi was unbelievably good looking, the hottest guy she'd met in a long time, maybe ever, and he seemed extremely nice too, but she couldn't let him in. She couldn't let anybody in. That was just her life, nothing new.

Nikki and Vic hugged goodbye, and he kissed her on the cheek. He turned to Laura and took her hand in his. Laura tried to pull her hand away, but Vic held it firm. "Thanks for coming to dinner with us. I enjoyed your company," he told her, and she could tell he was being genuine. Matter of fact, she got the distinct impression that Vic couldn't be anything but genuine. He turned loose of her hand, and she snapped it away from him, but she instantly missed the warmth of his skin. She wanted to run and, at the same time, she wanted to run back and touch him. What the hell was wrong with her?

On the way back to Louisville, Laura asked Nikki about her past, and Nikki quietly and simply told her without a lot of details. Listening to her, Laura thought, *We're not so different, she and I. Oh, yeah, different circumstances, but the pain's still similar. I wish I could tell somebody what happened to me, but that'll never happen.*

"And so that's how I got here," Nikki finished up. "I'm no cream puff. I'm used to working hard to take care of myself. Being with Tony is a dream come true. I didn't think I'd ever love or be loved again."

"I don't believe in love," Laura blurted out. "There's no such thing."

"Oh, I can tell you, you are definitely wrong about that. Maybe one day you'll know what I mean," Nikki argued, glancing at her. "I hope you find somebody who changes your mind."

"Not likely." *Especially if I'm not even willing to give it a chance to start.* She stared out the window and watched the miles, and her life, go by.

It had been a long day and they'd been apart the whole time. Tony practically pushed her into the bedroom when she walked through the front door.

"Oh, Mr. Walters, that was amazing! Can we do it again?"

"We can do it as many times as you like, princess."

"You know, you've never spoken Italian to me in bed. I think that would be really sexy."

"Oh really? Well, '*Voglio fare l'amore con te tutta la notte, preziosa.*'"

"Oooooo, that's lovely. What does it mean?"

"I said, 'I want to make love to you all night long, precious.'"

"Oh, yeah, baby, that's what I'm talkin' 'bout."

"Yeah? Well, '*Voglio scopare il tuo cervello fuori, puttana.*'"

"Mmmm, that sounds exciting."

"I just said, 'I want to fuck your brains out, slut.'"

"Ooooo, baby, say something else."

"Uh, um, '*Perché non fare un carico di bucato?*'"

"And?"

"That was, 'Why don't you do a load of laundry?'"

"Oh, my god, Mr. Walters, you can even make laundry sound sexy!"

"Well, it is if you're doing it. Especially if you're doing it naked!"

"I don't know about doing the laundry naked, but there's something else I'd like to do naked."

"Don't you mean, do again naked?"

"No, I mean do over and over naked."

"Well, then I guess we'd better get started, huh, future Mrs. Walters?"

"I'm just waiting on you, Mr. Walters."

"Well, I dunno – think we need to wait?"

"Nope. Feels to me like we don't need to wait; feels like you're locked and loaded."

"Ready to fire, baby."

Chapter Thirty-Seven

"Honey, I'm sorry." Tony cringed as Nikki slammed a cabinet drawer, then stomped out of the office toward the front door.

"I'm sick of this shit," she growled, not caring that Cheryl was staring and hearing every word. "This is bullshit."

Tony caught her by the arm before she got out the door and wheeled her around. "Nikki, I know. I'm sick of it too. But Steve's only trying to keep us safe."

"Well, if I went to some big ol' damn church here in town instead of dancing around an open fire, would he tell me I couldn't go there?" she yelled. She'd told him that she wanted to attend the local Samhain festival on Halloween, but Steve and his crew had nixed that idea immediately.

"Yes, I think he might." Tony looked her in the eye. "But this is even riskier, because it's outdoors and it would be almost impossible to secure. I don't want another vehicle going up in flames just to find out *you* were in it, you hear me? So calm down. They're working on it, but we've got to focus on being safe."

She slumped into a chair in the main office area, and Cheryl made herself scarce. "I know. I mean, intellectually I know, but I still don't like it."

"We don't have to like it; we just have to do it. You with me here?" Tony knelt down in front of her and looked up into her big blue-green eyes. "I'll do anything to keep you safe, including inconveniencing you and pissing you off." He tried to keep from laughing and failed miserably.

She couldn't help it – she started laughing too. "We haven't been laughing enough lately, you know?"

"I agree. We should work on that. In the meantime, can you do your own little celebration at home?"

"Of course. It won't be as much fun, but I can do it."

"Good. Get whatever you need to do that. And I'll give you some privacy. I want to go with Clayton and Brit to take Stringer trick-or-treating."

"Oh, I wanna go too!"

"Whatever you want, beautiful girl."

"Oh my god." Tony stood staring at Nikki with his mouth hanging open.

"What?"

"You are absolutely the most enchanting witch I've ever seen." His eyes watered, and so did his mouth. "God, is that what you wear when you're doing witch stuff?"

Nikki gave a loud huff. "No! This is just a costume! God! Don't be a smart ass."

He shrugged and looked a little hurt. "I'm not! I don't know what kind of things you wear when you do whatever it is that you do," he mumbled.

"Oh, yeah. Sorry. Does it look okay?"

"Look okay? Geez, babe, if you wore that to bed, I'd keep you up all night. Hey, maybe . . ."

"Not a chance, bub – they're expecting us. Where's your costume?"

"Stringer told me he didn't want me to wear one. He said he wanted his to be the best, and I'd mess him up. I'm afraid he's going to be *really* mad at you," Tony laughed.

"Wow! That was fun – look at all the candy I got!" Nikki was laughing when they walked into the house. She skipped down the hall to the bedroom with her pillowcase of goodies.

"Yeah," Tony grumbled, disgusted. "I thought I was going to have to beat up that old guy who put the candy bar in your cleavage."

"Oh, god, honey, he was old enough to be my grandpa! I thought it was cute!" She smiled. "I thought *he* was cute. I was actually thinking about going back later and asking him if he would run away with me . . ."

Tony grabbed her and threw her across the bed, pretending to be mad. "You'd better not leave this grandpa for another old grandpa. I'll hunt you down and snatch you back!"

"Not a chance! Speaking of grandpas, you seem pretty crazy about Stringer. I'm glad you guys have really hit it off. Has Clayton said what's going on with all of that?" Nikki asked, drawing him down on top of her.

"No. I guess I should ask. I hope it's going okay. I'd hate to see them lose that little boy. They're crazy about him." Tony rolled to his back and stared at the ceiling. "Maybe you could do a little spell or whatever it is that you do . . ."

"Already done, sweetie. Now, are you going to enjoy this costume?" she asked, winking at him.

"I absolutely am, starting right now!" he laughed and rolled back on top of her.

"Mr. Walters? Antonio Walters?" Two state police troopers stood in the doorway to Tony's office the next afternoon.

"Yes, officers? What can I do for you?"

"Do you own a red Volvo SUV?" one of them asked.

"Yes. Well, it's my fiancée's vehicle." He suddenly felt sick to his stomach. "What's wrong?"

"Mr. Walters, do you know where your girlfriend is?"

A buzzing started in Tony's head, and his stomach lurched. "She's somewhere between here and Lexington. She went to the Lexington office this morning. Hang on a minute." He pulled out his phone and called Nikki.

After two rings, she answered, "Hey, baby! What's up?"

"Oh, god, Nikki, where are you?" he whispered into the phone, his throat so tight that he almost couldn't speak.

"I'm in a thrift store in Lawrenceburg, Second Best. Why? Is everything okay?"

"Who's with you today?"

"Laura. She's right here." At that, he heard Laura say something in the background.

"Hang on a second, hon." He turned to the officers. "She's at a store in Lawrenceburg. What's up with the SUV?"

"It was involved in a hit-and-run accident on the Bluegrass Parkway just outside Lawrenceburg, and it was found burning a few miles from the accident scene. Responders are on scene, but it doesn't appear there's anyone in the vehicle."

"Nik, did you hear that?" Tony asked.

"Uh, yeah. Hey, Laura," she called out, "go look out the door and check on my Volvo, would you please? Tony, it's here, I'm sure."

"How long have you been in the store?" he asked.

"Maybe an hour? Wait." He heard her say loudly, "What? What do you mean, it's not there?" There was a voice in the background, and she relayed, "Tony, it's gone. What the hell is going on?"

"Somebody took it, drove it like they stole it, and wrecked it. Stay there, tell Laura what's happened, and I'll call Vic, get him to come get the two of you and bring you here. Wait there for him, you hear me? Stay in the store."

"Okay, okay. We'll stay here and wait for him. I love you."

"I love you too, baby. Do whatever Laura and Vic tell you and stay safe. I've got to go and talk to the officers." Tony hit END and turned to them. "Well, she's safe with her bodyguard in a store in Lawrenceburg. Looks like they stole her SUV from the parking lot." Damn – that meant they'd followed her. "Please call Detective Ford. He's been handling all of this crap. He'll need to add this to the file, I'm sure."

"Care to fill us in?" one of the officers asked. Tony launched into the story and, three minutes in, the officer stopped him.

"Thanks, Mr. Walters. We get the picture. This might not be related, but it most probably is. We'll coordinate with Detective Ford and get back to you. Might want to call your insurance company. Where do you want us to have the vehicle sent?" Tony gave them the name of his insurance agent and told them to send what was left of the brand-new Volvo to the shop at the construction company.

"We're going to run out of cars. I'd just gotten used to that one. What do you want me to drive now?" Nikki asked, looking at the key organizer near the back door.

"Take the Yukon or the Mercedes. Your choice." Tony shook his head. "I'd been thinking about selling some of the cars, the ones we don't drive much, but at this rate we're going to wind up needing every one of them."

"What in the hell are we going to do, honey? This is ridiculous." Nikki took the key for the Yukon. That thing was like a tank, and that's exactly what it appeared she'd need for the time being.

"I've got an idea. I've got to talk to everybody, family included, and then I'm going for broke. I hope you'll be on board too."

"I'm with you. Whatever you decide, I'll back you one hundred percent," Nikki assured him and gave him a peck on the cheek.

"God, Autumn, what the hell?" Travis looked her over in the front seat of the stolen, beat-up Toyota he'd followed her from Lexington in. "Shit, you smell like smoke."

"I was so scared." She was crying, her face slick with tears. "I couldn't drive that great big thing. It was awful. Then I hit that other car – I don't know what I did wrong, something with the traction control, I think – and then I lost control of it by that exit. I think I hurt my shoulder," she whined. She pulled down the neck of her tee-shirt and looked at her shoulder – there was a huge red mark across it. "That's going to leave a bruise."

"Nothing's broken," he snapped without even looking at her. "I'd hoped to part that Volvo out at a chop shop, but the damn thing is gone, destroyed like they'll be. That's all that matters." Travis pulled out into traffic from the shoulder of the overpass where he'd picked Autumn up after she'd fled the burning vehicle. He'd seen all he needed to see.

"That's all that matters? I could've been *killed*! Doesn't that matter?" she screamed at him.

"Oh, shut up, stupid. You're fine. It's no big deal." He lit a cigarette and kept driving. Autumn sat there, shaking and afraid – afraid because of what had just happened, and what might happen to her at his hands.

Tony spent hours on the phone until he'd talked to everyone in the family and made sure they were okay with what he was about to do. When he was finished, he sat down and sent an email out to all Walters management people stating that he expected all employees to be in attendance at the next day's meeting, with the exception of those who were sick or on vacation. Then he called Steve, told him to have extra security on hand, and also asked him to call all of the news outlets. After explaining to the kids what was going on, he called Detective Ford and asked him to talk to the police chief.

Annabeth and Brittany helped Nikki pick out something to wear for both purposes, something attractive but also businesslike. Katie wanted her to wear a suit, but that's what Katie wanted everybody to wear because that's all Katie wore, all the time. They talked about how she should wear her hair but, in the end, she pulled it into a ponytail and it was good enough.

The next morning, Tony stood on a flatbed trailer in the materials yard,

Nikki on one side and Clayton on the other, Vic behind him, and Steve and his crew dispersed around the area, watching intently. Several hundred Walters Construction employees stood expectantly, wondering what was going on. They'd heard rumors, but nothing concrete. Tony laid out what was happening to them at the hands of the ecoterrorism group and asked them to keep their eyes and ears open and to be especially careful. When he was finished, they headed downtown to the police station.

Nikki was flabbergasted when they got there. TV and radio stations and reporters from newspapers were everywhere – from as far east as Ashland to the other end of the state in Paducah, even a Nashville station, and Cincinnati and all of northern Kentucky, not to mention from across the river in Indiana. There were microphones and cameras stacked on top of each other.

Nikki was wearing the same thing to both conferences, but Tony had changed; for the first time, she was seeing him in a suit and tie, and she couldn't get over how handsome and distinguished he looked, the epitome of the businessman. The charcoal gray was perfect with his dark hair and skin, and he'd shaved off every bit of his usual fashionable scruff for complete smoothness. No doubt about it – he could've easily been a model.

They walked hand in hand to the podium where he, Detective Ford, and the police chief would be speaking, Clayton and Vic with them. The police chief turned to Tony and nodded. "Ready?" Tony nodded in reply, then turned to Nikki.

"I couldn't do this without you," he whispered to her and gave her a quick peck on the cheek. "Thanks for being here with me."

"Baby, there's nowhere else I'd be," she whispered back.

He said basically the same things he'd told the employees with one exception: He announced the amount of the reward, one hundred thousand dollars. *Well,* Nikki thought, *if that doesn't do it, nothing will.* Her next thought was to wonder how they'd sift through all of the bogus leads to which they'd be subjected.

After only a few questions, most of which were directed at the police chief, the press conference ended. Tony took Nikki, Clayton, and Vic to lunch.

"Well, do you think it'll do any good?" Clayton asked his dad.

"I have no idea, but I don't have a lot of options." Tony forked up a mouthful of salad. "I don't know what else to do."

At four that afternoon, Tony called Detective Ford to ask if there had been any tips called in. Detective Ford wasn't very positive.

"Oh, yeah," he sighed. "Some lady called in and said Jesus told her GoGreen was justified in what they were doing, and there would be more to come, but it could be stopped by giving the reward to her church. One guy said the GoGreen people were really aliens. Another said you were part of the mafia and deserved whatever you got." Tony rolled his eyes. "The one we were most interested in was a short call from a young woman who seemed to want to tell the officer something, but then hung up like she was afraid. We're hoping she calls back."

"I'm disappointed, sure, but hopeful. It's getting people talking. Somebody, somewhere, knows what's going on. Maybe eventually they'll call in. Until then, we'll keep doing what we're doing." Tony sighed. "Thanks for your help. Stay in touch."

"Will do. Hang in there," the detective said as he hung up.

Tony propped his elbow on the desk and rested his forehead on his hand. He was so tired of the crap, but there didn't seem to be an end to it. At least it was almost Thanksgiving, and he was looking forward to the holiday and all of his family being together, his kids, his mom, Vic, and the love of his life. It would be the best holiday they'd ever had.

Chapter Thirty-Eight

Sometimes Nikki felt like she was dreaming. Her life with Tony was so good, it didn't seem real. Oh, yeah, there was that GoGreen shit, but she tried not to focus on that. She knew the holidays were coming up, their first together, and even though she wasn't much for the social aspects of life, she wanted everything to be as perfect as she could manage.

"Who's coming to Thanksgiving dinner?" she asked on the Wednesday evening of the week before. With just a week to go, she had to get her act together fast.

"Just all of us. The kids, Vic, Mamma. Everybody else has their own kids to be with, and my brothers use this as a holiday to spend with their in-laws. Especially this year, because they have to be here for Christmas." Tony cut into his stuffed chicken breast. Oh, god, it was good – that girl could cook!

"Is this here or in Shelbyville?"

"Oh, here. If it's just nine or ten of us, we'll do it here."

"Do I do all of the food?"

"Good god, no! Why do you always ask that? You know I'd never do that to you. Everybody will bring something, even Vic. Just tell him what you want him to bring and he'll do it."

Nikki thought for a second, then nodded. "I'll have him pick up the rolls again. That's easy for him."

"Just find out what everybody is bringing, then see where you need to fill in. Plus we do the turkey and dressing." Tony took more rutabagas – they'd become his favorite. Nikki had introduced him to dozens of foods he would've never tried otherwise.

"Okay – got it. We're good. By the way, what's going on at Christmas?" she asked, forking up some green beans.

"Well, it all depends on what happens on Thanksgiving, but I think it's all going to go as planned. Guess we'll see, huh?" He gave her a wink.

"Guess we'll see." She wondered what he was up to – had her ring come in? Was he going to propose? Suddenly, it didn't matter that she was going to be worn out from cooking – she was excited about Thanksgiving for the first time in a very long time.

"Hey, baby, got the turkey thawed?" Tony asked, standing in the doorway to Nikki and Clayton's office.

"Yep. Got a list of what everybody's bringing. Got the other stuff to make up a meal. Got the house cleaned up. You got holiday coverage arranged for the sites?"

"Yeah. Promised them double time to do it, but it's covered. Why don't you take tomorrow off to get ready? Clayton and I can take care of anything that comes up."

"Thanks. I think I'll do that. I'm a bundle of nerves." She cleaned up her desk and got ready to leave.

"Sweetie, don't be nervous – it's going to be a great day!" He smiled and kissed her as she headed out the door.

"It *is* going to be a great day. I can't wait!"

At ten 'til ten that night, Nikki's phone rang; it was Clayton. "Hey, honey, what's up?"

"Hey, Mom. I've got a favor to ask."

"What's that, honey?"

"Can we bring another guest with us tomorrow?" Nikki looked at Tony and he could tell she was suddenly excited about something.

"Sure, honey. Who's coming with you?" she asked, hardly able to contain her excitement.

"It's a surprise. A Stringer-type surprise. Happened thirty minutes ago. We'll just need an extra seat."

"No problem, hon. We'll see you tomorrow. Love you."

"Love you too, Mom."

"Okay, turkey's in the oven, vegetables are prepped, drinks are iced. Oh, I hear Vic – bread's here." Nikki was ticking everything off out loud while Tony set the table.

"Hey guys! Happy Thanksgiving!" Vic called out, then dropped the rolls on the counter, grabbed Nikki, and spun her around before dropping a kiss on her cheek. She laughed like a ten-year-old.

"Hey, Tookie, how's it going?" he asked as he ruffled Tony's hair.

"Going good, Goliath! Glad you're here!" Tony gave Vic a big hug. "Clayton called last night and said they had a surprise for us today."

"Another kid, I hope?"

"Wouldn't say – we'll see. And thanks for being there with me last week at the conferences. I appreciated it."

"Nowhere on earth I'd rather be. You know I always have your back, bro." Vic nibbled on a carrot stick from the crudités Nikki had put out with a spicy dip.

Annabeth and Katie came in with Raffaella, and within a few minutes, Clayton and Brittany drove up. The front door burst open and a little voice yelled, "Tony! Tony! Whaw aw you?"

"I'm in here, buddy! The kitchen!" When Stringer ran into the room, Tony dropped to his knees and scooped the little boy up. Stringer planted a big wet kiss on Tony's cheek, and Nikki nearly cried when she saw the expression on the big guy's face – he looked like he was in heaven.

Clayton walked into the kitchen and announced, "Everybody, we'd like you to meet someone. This is Ella Jane." Brittany stepped into the kitchen, holding the hand of a small, pale child of maybe seven or eight. She had a large bruise on one side of her face, her hair was thin and brittle-looking, and she was wearing mismatched clothes and run-down tennis shoes. What struck Nikki and Tony both was the sad expression on her face. She looked like nothing had gone right for her in her entire life.

"Hi, Ella Jane. I'm Nikki. I'm so glad you're here. Welcome to our house. Can I get you anything?" Nikki asked, bending down to her level.

The little girl looked around, then timidly said, "This is a really pretty house. Do you have a bathroom?"

"Of course, sweetie. Come with me." Nikki led her down the hall.

Tony chuckled under his breath. "Everybody wants to know where the bathroom is. Story?" Tony asked when Nikki and the child were out of earshot.

"They brought her last night a little after nine. Mom's boyfriend assaulted her and beat her, and it wasn't the first time it had happened. Mom's a junkie. Boyfriend's a pimp. Dad's not in the picture, grandparents have written the whole bunch off. She's got problems, to say the least," Clayton said.

"She's afraid to go to sleep," Brittany told him. "If she does, she has terrible nightmares. It's awful."

"And she wets the bed," Clayton added. "It's all emotional – there's nothing physically wrong with her."

"You guys can handle it. I have faith in you." Tony hugged Brittany. "You both know we'll do anything we can to help you."

"Yeah, us too," Katie said as Annabeth nodded agreement; Vic and Raffaella were nodding too.

After she'd shown the little girl around, Nikki took her back to the kitchen and Annabeth and Katie set about to entertain her and Stringer, who had clung to Tony ever since he'd walked into the house. Tony had to promise to play ball with him later to get him to go with his Zia Annabeth and Zia Katie. Brittany and Clayton both looked like they needed a rest, and Nikki sent them with Vic and Raffaella into the den to wait until dinner was ready.

Tony was impressed; the turkey looked beautiful, and so did his girlfriend. She worked around the kitchen with confidence and grace. He was struck by how different she seemed from the timid, devastated woman he'd met just months earlier. He didn't want to take credit for the way she'd bloomed, but he wanted to think that having someone to love her made at least some of the difference.

Nikki got the food on the table – it was lovely, including the flowers she'd picked up from The Passionate Pansy – and they called everyone to eat. Food flew and drinks spilled and everyone laughed and talked. The girls sent Tony and Nikki to the den afterward to sit down and rest while they cleaned up the kitchen. Ella Jane and Stringer played with the building blocks and some die-cast cars. Nikki beamed at Tony as he played with the little ones, and she thought she'd never seen him look so happy and relaxed.

When the cleanup was done, they all moved to the den and Annabeth and Katie served everyone pumpkin pie with whipped cream, courtesy of Nikki's special recipe. Clayton told Nikki repeatedly how good the pie was. Brittany looked like she was in her element, helping Ella Jane put her headband back on when it came off and retying Stringer's shoes for the fifth or sixth time.

Tony finished his pie before everyone else, and then said, "Well, I guess it's time."

"Time for what?" Annabeth asked. Everyone turned to look at him.

Without ceremony, he stood, looked down at Nikki as she sat on the sofa, then knelt in front of her on one knee and pulled a small box from his pocket. It was red velvet embossed with the same "C" as the box her bracelet had come in; Cavender's, the jewelry store he had taken her to when they shopped for her ring. Nikki smiled and sat up on the edge of the sofa, and Tony looked at her and simply said, "Nicolette Renee Wilkes, I wanted to do this with everyone closest to us here with us. I love you with all my heart – I always will. Will you do me the honor of being my wife?" There was a collective gasp in the room, and all four of the other women whispered, "Awwww!"

Nikki leaned forward and, resting her forearms on his shoulders, replied, "Antonio Luigi Walters, I love you more than life itself, and I would be honored to have you as my husband." He opened the box and, nestled inside, a ring like nothing Nikki had seen before came to life in front of her eyes, the yellow gold gleaming and the big stone twinkling in the afternoon light. Taking the ring from its box, he slipped it onto her left ring finger – a perfect fit. She thought it was the most beautiful thing in the world, second only to the man who'd given it to her.

"Oh, one condition." Tony grinned. "I want to get married on Christmas day."

"Why would that be a problem?" Nikki smiled back. "Sounds like Santa will be giving us a very special gift this year!"

Nikki leaned into him and kissed him. When their lips touched, she thought of the distance she'd gone to get to that moment, all the pain, all the loneliness, all of the things this man had helped to take away, and all the things he'd brought in their place. A home – three, in fact. A family, a huge family, including some things she thought she'd never have; a woman she could call mother, kids to call her Mom, and even grandchildren, or so they all hoped. A job she loved. Security she never thought she'd have. And love, so much love, sweet and hot and never-ending.

All Tony could think of was how miserable he'd been before he'd met her, and how he'd never have to be that miserable again. It was over, all of it. He had the one thing he'd always thought he'd never have – an honest, trustworthy, loving, caring, sweet, sexy, smart woman to share the rest of his life with. It was all he'd ever wanted; she was all he'd ever wanted. His life was complete.

Then it happened. For that one moment, their lips pressed together and their hearts joined, they both felt it – the earth ceased to turn and time stopped for them, and there was nothing, nothing in the world, that meant more than that kiss.

Clayton and Brittany took the kids home to calm down before bedtime, but not before they'd both had an extra piece of pie, which Tony insisted they have. Annabeth and Katie said their goodbyes right after Clayton and Brittany left, and took Raffaella with them. Tony, Nikki, and Vic went to the den to relax and chat. Nikki loved any opportunity to spend time with Vic. He was such a joy to be around, and she appreciated the calming effect his presence always had on Tony. Sunset was on its way, and the three of them got a drink and tried to relax.

It had been a lovely day, and then the door blew open and evil came in on the wind. When it slammed shut, they heard a voice yell, "Hello! Where is everybody?"

Tony and Vic's eyes locked, and Tony whispered, "Dottie."

She stood in the doorway to the den, her presence filling the room with an uncomfortable, nasty energy. "Well, well, well, what's going on in here?"

"Dottie," Tony hissed through clenched teeth. Vic stood beside him. "What the hell are you doing here?"

"I want to talk to you. Now." She twirled her hair and leaned against the door frame. "Can't you get rid of the big ape here?" She glared at Vic. He audibly growled.

"Yeah, well, I want to talk to your ass too." He turned to Nikki. "Sweetheart, go to the bedroom."

"But, Tony, I . . ."

"Now. Go. Stay there until I come and get you. Please?" It wasn't really a question, and he never looked at her, just stared at Dottie.

"Go on, Nikki," Vic told her. "It's okay."

Nikki left the room and walked down the hall, closing the bedroom door behind her. She could hear their voices, Tony's low drone and Dottie's occasional outburst. Where was Vic? Maybe he just wasn't saying anything. She walked to the window and pulled the draperies back; Vic's truck was still there, so she felt a little better. In what was left of the late afternoon light, Nikki watched the street lights twinkle on. Two little girls rode bicycles, one pink, the other purple, down the sidewalk, and across the street, a man sat in a crumpled-up car, waiting for someone in one of the houses. A dog barked; she thought of Bill and Hillary, months gone, and she still missed them so much. Finally, the voices got quiet and, within a few minutes, Tony came through the bedroom door.

"I'm only going to tell you this once: Don't. Come. Here. Ever. Again. I don't want to see your face, hear your voice, hear your name, think of you. I'm done with you, understand?"

"Oh, yeah, you've got that whore now. You don't need old Dottie," she said, smirking.

Tony gritted his teeth and snarled, "You'll speak of my future wife with respect. And you'll stay away from her, from us, from now on. If you come back here, or to any of my properties, I'll have you arrested for trespassing, I swear. Do you understand me?" Vic squeezed his shoulder to try to calm him, but Tony shrugged him off.

"Oh, come on, asshole. You're not going to have me arrested." She stopped. "Wait – did you say future wife?" Dottie's face reddened so much that it looked like it was going to explode. "What the hell? You're not marrying her!" She flew at Tony before either he or Vic could get away, and went straight for Tony's eyes, but he reacted quickly and deflected her hands, then pushed her – hard. She fell backward and her ass landed on the floor. "You son of a bitch!"

She stood again, and this time, Vic grabbed her and threatened, "Dottie, don't. I don't want to hurt you, but I will. Leave him alone."

"Oh, I'll leave him alone all right! He'll be all alone when I get finished with her," she screamed, wresting out of Vic's grip. She snatched a vase from the bookcase and stormed down the hallway. Tony sprinted, grabbed her by her hair, and hauled backward. He dragged her back up the hallway and to the front door that way, with her yelling and swearing the whole time. Vic tried to stop him, but Tony was determined to put her out, and it was as though he was being driven by some unseen force. Vic had never seen him that way before.

When he got to the door with her, he spun her around and got in her face. "You ever touch her, even look at her, and I swear to god, I'll kill you, you understand?" Tony's voice took on a menacing tone, low and hard, his eyes cold. "You hurt Nikki, and there's no one on earth, no one, who can help you. I'll bury you, you mean, evil bitch."

"Oh, right, you worthless bastard! You don't scare me! She says she loves you, but she'll figure it out pretty soon, how worthless and stupid you are, and she'll leave you just like I did! And you'll have nothing, just like me! Just like me!" She gave him a weird grin, and he lost it.

"Get out. Like I said, I'm done with you. I don't care what happens to you, but if you come back, I'll have you arrested." He opened the door and shoved her, then closed it before he could see her tumble down the steps and land on the driveway. She rolled twice, then sat up, brushed herself off, and staggered to her car. Tony and Vic could hear the tires squeal as she left.

An odd sort of quiet settled on the house. "Bud, you okay?" Vic asked Tony.

At first, Tony didn't say anything. He looked around, then wiped his hands repeatedly down the front of his jeans. Finally, he mumbled, "Yeah, yeah. I'm fine. Go on home. She won't be back."

"Okay, if you're sure." Tony nodded at Vic. "I'll call and check on you guys tomorrow, okay?" Vic asked. Tony nodded again.

Vic walked down the steps and went to his car. He hoped Tony would calm down. He'd never seen his cousin like that before, so angry and so, what? Dangerous? Violent? He shuddered slightly, then started the car and headed to Lexington. As he pulled out onto the street, he almost turned around and went back, then decided against it. They'd be fine. They had each other.

"Babe, you okay?" Nikki asked Tony as he disappeared into the bathroom. He didn't answer. She wondered what had taken place. She'd heard the car tires squeal, then saw Vic drive away a few minutes later. They were finally alone and the house was quiet.

She stood by the bed with her back to the bathroom door and took off her jeans, throwing them and her lightweight sweater in a pile in the corner. Before she could do anything else, she felt Tony behind her, and he unfastened her bra, took it off of her, and threw it in the pile with her clothes. Then he pulled her underwear down to her feet, and she stepped out of them; they went into the pile too. He turned her to face him, but there was something on his face, something she didn't recognize. "Babe, what's wrong?" she asked and leaned in to kiss him.

When her lips touched his, he melted into her, then picked her up and carried her to the bed. Once they were both under the covers, he pressed her face to his chest and held her tighter than she could ever remember. She could hear his heart pounding, and there was a tiny tremor all over his body. "Sweetie? Talk to me. Please?" she begged.

In the lamplight, Tony's eyes scanned her face slowly, as though he was searching for something. A tiny little voice, barely a whisper, escaped his lips and he said to her, "I'm so afraid."

Nikki looked down into his face; he truly did look terrified. "Of what, precious?" she asked him, stroking his cheek.

His eyes reddened and he looked as though he was about to cry. "Of tomorrow. Of something happening to you. Of those GoGreen bastards, what they might do to you, to us. Of Dottie finding a way to get between us. Of anyone, anything, that might take what I have now and dash it to pieces, ruin it, snatch it away from me." He choked back tears and added, "I'm so happy here with you. I'm so afraid it'll end." Her heart broke at the frantic look on his face.

"Put your ear right here," she whispered, patting her chest just above her left breast. Tony rested his head there. "Hear my heart beating?"

"Yeah. It's so strong," he whispered back to her, sniffling.

"It is strong. And that beating? It only beats for you. The only way that won't be true anymore is if somebody makes it stop beating. As long as it continues to beat, it beats for you, love. Only you. If you leave me, it'll stop, just go silent. I can't live without you." Nikki kissed the top of his head, and he wrapped his arms around her and sighed. "I love you, and I'll love you forever and a day. Until the last star fades," she sighed into him, and he squeezed her even tighter.

"And I love you too, little girl," he breathed out, his head on her chest. "I'll love you forever, until the sun falls out of the sky."

Tony's phone rang: Cal. "Yeah," he answered, groggy and more than a little grumpy.

"Boss, I hate to wake you, but I had to leave. The girls called and said Jenny is sick again. I'm so sorry."

Tony looked at the clock; one thirty. "Yeah, okay, I'll cover it. Go on home. Later." He hit END and turned to Nikki, who'd stirred to see what was going on.

"Cal's gone; Jenny's drunk again. I've got to go over to the Colufab site and sit until the next shift gets there. Will you be okay?"

"Oh, god, you're kidding. Yeah, José's outside. I'll be fine. You be careful, okay?"

"Will do. Sleep tight, baby," he told her and kissed her.

"I won't sleep without you here," she whispered.

When he'd pulled out of the circular drive, Tony put his window down; José did the same. "I've got to go to the Colufab site – the guy watching it had to go home."

"But, Tony, you won't have security coverage and . . ."

"I'll be fine. I've got my Ruger. Just keep her safe, okay?"

José nodded in agreement. "That's my job. But I wish you'd let me call somebody in to watch you . . ."

Tony shook his head. "Not necessary. I'll be fine."

José shrugged. "Okay, if you're sure. You'll call if you need somebody, right?"

"Of course. You just make sure she's safe," Tony said again as he pulled away.

When Tony got to the site, he settled down to wait until dawn. He'd much rather be in bed beside his sleeping angel than sitting at a jobsite, but business was business.

Chapter Thirty-Nine

Nikki was still asleep when Tony got in at eight thirty. He stripped off his clothes and climbed into bed. Wondering what would happen when he reached out and touched her, he put his hand on her back and, as usual, she rolled toward him and snuggled into his chest. He wrapped his arms around her and kissed her on the forehead, then almost immediately fell asleep.

When he woke and looked at the clock, it was eleven and he was alone. He slipped into his jeans and went down to the kitchen, where he found her happily cooking, making something with the leftover turkey from the day before.

"Tetrazzini," she answered before he could ask. "I figured I'd make it up and freeze it in batches. We'll eventually eat it all."

"Mamma's recipe?"

She grinned. "You know it!"

"You always take her recipes and make them better," he grinned back.

"God, don't tell her that. I'll go from *la matriarca* to *la cagna* in a nanosecond!" she laughed, stirring the sauce and rice together.

"Ah, you're learning some Italian!"

"A little, but absolutely the wrong kind of words, courtesy of Vic. Your cousin is just full of meanness!" she laughed. "You feel okay? You were out there all night. I tried to let you sleep. Anybody bother anything?" She really felt sorry for him. All he wanted was for his employees to be trustworthy and work as hard as he did. She didn't think that was too much for him to ask.

Tony poured himself a cup of coffee and sat back down. "Yeah, everything was okay and I'm fine. I don't know about Cal's wife, though. Apparently her drinking problem is pretty serious. According to him, she was the problem the night the porcelain fixtures were destroyed. I told him he'd better get everything under control, but that's tough. Dottie wasn't a drunk, but I certainly couldn't control what she said or did."

"That's rough for Cal, and especially for his kids." Nikki spooned the tetrazzini into a baking dish. "And how did it go yesterday afternoon with Dottie?"

He pursed his lips and shook his head. "I hope I got through to her, but I doubt it. She's hard-headed, that's for sure."

"Next time," Nikki said, putting everything down and turning to glare at him, her arms braced on the countertop, "do not send me out of the room. I think she needs to see us as a unified force. And I can handle her; believe me, I can. But as long as you keep pulling that 'go away and let me handle this, baby' crap on me, she's going to think she has a possibility of, well, you know . . ." Her eyebrows arched.

"Not a chance in hell!" Tony bellowed. He sat for a minute, thinking, then admitted, "Yeah, maybe that is the approach to take. But I hope there won't be a next time – I was pretty clear about that. I told her I'd have her arrested for trespassing if she came back around."

"I hope she listens. But you need to know – she may be scary-looking, but I'm not scared of her. Never was, never will be."

Tony was in the shower getting ready for work on Monday morning when his phone rang. Nikki reached over to the nightstand and picked it up without looking at it. "Tony's phone," she answered, half asleep.

"Nikki? It's Jason. Jason Miller."

Nikki shook herself awake. "Yeah, Jason, Tony's in the shower. He'll be there in a little while. What's up?"

"Yeah, that's why I called. We need him at the Franklin University site. As soon as he can get here. Please."

"Something wrong?" she asked, picking up on the tension in his voice.

"Yeah. A body's turned up over here. Please ask him to get here soon."

"Oh my god! Of course! Don't worry, Jason – it'll be okay."

"Thanks, Nikki. See ya."

Jumping out of bed, she ran into the bathroom. "Honey, Jason Miller just called. They found a body at the Franklin University site!"

The water stopped, and Tony stepped out, soaking wet and looking incredibly delicious. Nikki drew in a breath and let out a low whistle. He turned to her and grinned. "A body, huh?"

"That's what he said!"

"No biggie. That happens all the time. We start digging and unearth an old burial site. I just hope it's not Native American or the whole thing will get shut down. Sometimes they even revoke the building permits, which is really bad. But I doubt that will happen. I'll get over there and see what's going on. Nothing to worry about." He kissed her as he walked out of the bathroom.

"Having lunch with me?" Nikki asked later as Tony left for the jobsite.

"I don't know. I'll give you a call later when I find out where I'll be." He wrapped his arms around her waist and gave her a big kiss goodbye. "I'll see you at the office."

"Yes sir!" she grinned and saluted him. He was still laughing when he hopped into his truck.

When he pulled up to the jobsite, Jason met him at the truck. "Hey, boss. Sorry to call you so early. The cops were leaning on me to get you down here."

Tony rolled his eyes. "All this fuss for an old skeleton? Don't they have better things to do?"

"This is no old skeleton, boss. This is a fresh body. Well, within the last few days."

That wasn't what Tony expected to hear. A fresh body? He'd had someone out on the sites constantly over the weekend. How could that happen?

When he got closer to where the police officers were clustered, he called out, "Hey, guys, what's up?" They turned, and he recognized Bryson Hawkins, a friend from elementary and junior high. Bryson had become a homicide detective, and seeing him there shocked Tony. Bryson walked toward him at a brisk pace and put a hand on Tony's chest. "What?" Tony asked, puzzled at the expression on his old classmate's face.

"Hey, Tony. Man, I'm sorry about this. You need to prepare yourself." The detective was speaking in hushed tones, and Tony was getting very confused about what was going on.

"Jason says this is a fresh body. I thought it would be just an old skeleton. I don't understand what's happening."

"Yeah. Apparently it was dumped in here Thursday night or Friday morning and when the guys started pouring the concrete this morning, it floated to the top. We need you to identify the body. But be prepared; it's pretty bad."

Identify the body? It was someone he knew? He nodded to Bryson. "Okay, let's do this." The detective walked with him to the tarp on the ground, and the group of officers surrounding the spot parted and let him through.

"Ready?" Bryson asked.

Tony shrugged. "I guess so."

Bryson pulled the tarp back and all the air vacated Tony's lungs. He felt his stomach wrench, and things started to get blurry. Turning away, he ran to the closest trash drum and lost his breakfast, and he couldn't stop heaving and choking. Tears burned his eyes as he heaved over and over.

Then Tony heard a voice: "Hey, Dad, what's up?" He looked up from the drum to see Clayton striding toward him. Clayton stopped and, looking at Tony standing over the drum and clutching its rim, he got a funny look on his face. "What's going on?" Tony didn't, couldn't, speak. "They said they had a body down here . . . Dad? Oh my god, what's going on?" Clayton walked past Tony, but Tony grabbed his arm and tried to hold him. Clayton shook Tony's grip off and walked on.

"Clayton, don't!" Tony ran past him and got in front of him. "Son, please!" He pushed Tony's hands away even as his dad tried to stop him, and walked right up to the body. Clayton took one look and fell to his knees, a silent scream on his lips, and Tony grabbed him and threw his arms around him, shielding him from the sight.

"Oh my god . . ." he managed to gasp, trembling all over as Tony held him.

"Oh, son, I know! I'm so sorry." Tony looked up at Bryson Hawkins and whispered, "I don't believe it. That's Dottie, my ex-wife."

"Nik, baby, I need you to do me a few favors, okay?"

"Sure! Whaddya need?" She'd showered and dressed, so she was ready for anything – within reason.

"I need you to go and pick up Annabeth. Talk to her boss first, then take her to the house. But don't tell her why." Tony's voice sounded strained. "I can't go to her – I've got to stay here with the cops. But Clayton's coming over there, and the two of you can tell her together."

"Cops? What's going on? Tell her what?" This wasn't sounding good.

"Tell her the body they found at the jobsite is Dottie's."

Nikki gasped. "Oh, sweet mother of god! You're not serious?"

"As a heart attack. They want to ask me a million questions, so I'm going to be tied up for awhile. I'm so sorry – I know you probably don't really want to do this, but can you handle it?"

"Yes, sweetheart, I can. Don't you worry about a thing. I've got it covered."

"Thanks. I love you, baby. I'll see you as soon as I can."

"I love you too. Hang in there."

"Will do." Tony hung up and turned back to the huddle of police officers at the site.

Nikki managed to get all of the kids gathered up. On the way, she called Clayton and got a chance to really talk to him. "Are you okay? Son, are you handling this?"

"Yeah, Mom, I'm fine." His voice was flat, and Nikki knew that seeing the body there had to have been traumatic for him no matter what he said.

"Son, I know you spent more time with her than Annabeth did, even if just because of your age. I know you remember some happy times, and that's okay. It's good to remember those. Just promise me if you start having a hard time, you'll talk to me, or your dad, or Brittany – somebody. Don't go this alone – please," she begged him, keeping her fingers crossed.

"I will, Mom, I promise. It was a shock, but I'm kind of relieved."

Later on, he'll feel guilty for feeling that way, Nikki thought. *We need to keep an eye on him.*

When they both got to the house and got the three girls there, Annabeth was worked up, sure something was wrong with Tony. Clayton took responsibility for telling her about Dottie. It concerned Nikki that Annabeth showed very little emotion, but she also knew what they'd been through for all those years, and that everyone handles grief differently. All of the kids asked questions Nikki didn't know how to answer, and she told them Tony would fill them in as soon as he could.

"So who was supposed to be watching this site?" Bryson asked Tony.

"One of my employees. I'm not sure who, but I'll find out." Tony made a call and, in ten minutes, his phone rang. When he hung up, he turned to Bryson. "Well, that was Kenny. He said he was here and another employee called him, told him they were supposed to relieve him even though his shift wasn't over, but they were running late and to go on, they'd be here in a minute. He said it was somebody named Harold, but we don't have an employee named Harold. So for at least a couple of hours, no one was here –

maybe longer than that."

Bryson nodded. "So somebody sabotaged the security, somebody who knew how to find out who was working and get rid of them."

A crime scene technician walked up. "There's no evidence anywhere here, so it looks like this wasn't the crime scene, just the body dump."

"Any trace that might suggest where she was killed?" Bryson asked.

"We won't know until we get into the lab," the tech told them, walking away.

Another detective, a large African American man, joined Bryson. "Tony, this is Detective Emmett Fox. Detective Fox, Tony Walters." Tony extended his hand, and Fox briefly shook it.

"Nice to meet you," Tony said.

"That remains to be seen," Fox replied, then walked away. Tony scowled after him.

"Sorry about that," Bryson offered. "They wanted me to partner with somebody who doesn't know you. Fox is new here, didn't grow up here. They were afraid I wouldn't be objective because I've known you for so long."

"I understand that, but why would that matter? I'm not a suspect." Bryson said nothing, and Tony's mouth dropped open in astonishment. "I'm not a suspect, am I?"

"Well, not right now. But you had a rocky relationship with the victim, so you're definitely a person of interest."

"You're kidding, right? I didn't kill Dottie!" Tony couldn't believe what he was hearing. "If I were going to kill the bitch, I would've done it years ago. I certainly wouldn't have let her torture me all these years!"

A voice behind Tony growled, "Tony, shut up. Don't say another word." Steve walked up to the men and turned to Bryson. "I'm Steve McCoy, Mr. Walters' attorney." Steve turned back to Tony. "We need to talk – now."

"Excuse us, please." Tony walked a distance away with Steve. "Okay, what the hell was that about?"

"I got word; they're looking at you."

"You're not serious!" Tony almost yelled.

"Shhhhhh!" Steve sputtered, looking back to see if the detectives were listening. "Yes, I'm very serious. So watch what you say," Steve whispered forcefully.

"Well, that's just crazy!"

"Yeah, I know, but that's the way it is."

"Excuse me, gentlemen." Bryson was back. "Tony, we'd like to look at some of your personnel records, schedules, things like that. Could we go back to your office?"

"Sure. I'll meet you there." Tony looked at Steve, who nodded and got into his own car to follow.

When they got to the office, it was deserted except for Cheryl. They started into the building, Tony first with everyone else following. A crime scene tech brought up the rear, and he stopped in the doorway.

"Mr. Walters," Fox said, "I need to let you know up front that we don't have a search warrant, but we hope you'll work with us."

Tony shrugged. "Sure. I don't have anything to hide."

"So, where were you on Thursday night?" Fox asked Tony.

"Oh, so you think that's when she died?" Tony asked.

"Just answer the question, sir," Fox replied gruffly.

"Well, I was at home until around one thirty. I got a call from my foreman. He said he had to go home because his wife was sick, and I went to the jobsite to stay until the eight o'clock person showed up."

"Which jobsite was that?"

"The Colufab site, over across town."

"I see. Was there anyone there when you got there?"

"No. Cal was gone."

"So you were there the rest of the night by yourself?"

"Yes."

"So no one saw you arrive?" Fox asked.

Tony's brow furrowed. "No, guess not."

"Anyone else see you?"

"Um, I don't think so. One of Mr. McCoy's people offered to get me some security, but I told him not to bother. Hey, what's he doing?" Tony pointed at the tech, who was swabbing at something dark on the frame of the front door. Steve was one unhappy-looking son of a bitch.

Fox got up and walked over, whispered with the tech, and came back. "Mr. Walters, do you have a bathroom with a shower in this office?"

"Yes, matter of fact, I do." Tony pointed to a door behind his desk. "It's back there."

The tech walked past them and into the bathroom. Fox asked Tony, "So, who has keys to this office?"

"Me. Clayton, my son. Cheryl, my secretary. Cal, my foreman. And Vic, my cousin who lives in Lexington."

"Your girlfriend doesn't have one?" Fox asked.

"Nope."

"Isn't that kind of strange, given that she's the operations officer?"

"No, it's not, given that we've been the target of terroristic activities lately," Tony sniped. "I don't want her here alone at any time for any reason. And if she had a key, I couldn't ensure that. You don't know her; she'd get a wild hair and come over here to work by herself. So I haven't given her a key."

"And of the people who have keys, who of them would have reason to want Dottie dead?"

"Hell, all of them, truth be known. Except for Cal – he didn't really know her. But you can forget it. They were all either at home with their spouses or in a completely different town."

"Except for you," Fox countered. Bryson frowned.

"Well, I, no, I mean, I wouldn't do that. Besides, I was at home with Nikki." Tony didn't like where this was going, and Steve was growing more agitated by the second.

"Except for the time you spent at the Colufab site," Fox continued, "where no one saw when you arrived and when you left, or if you were even there." Tony knew what he was insinuating, and he didn't like it at all.

The tech stepped back through the doorway and motioned for Fox to come into the bathroom. When he returned, he glared at Tony. "Mr. Walters, the substance on the front door frame is blood. We don't know whose, but we'll find out. And there's something else – someone tried to clean your shower, but there's blood trace all over it." The tech walked the path to the front door and sprayed something on the hardwood as he went, then hit it with a light, and blobs of color appeared here and there. "Those spots on the floor? That's blood trace too."

"Well, I'll be damned," Tony whispered, shaking his head. "Who would've . . ."

Fox walked around behind Tony. "Please place your hands behind your back. Antonio Walters, you're under arrest for the murder of Dorothea Walters. You have the right to remain silent . . ."

Nikki and Katie managed to get Annabeth calmed down enough to get her to take a nap in Tony and Nikki's bed. It was the only way she'd settle down;

she said being there made her feel close to the two of them, and that was good enough for Nikki. She'd spent the afternoon railing against Dottie, and Nikki assumed it was to protect herself against caring. When she muttered, "Crazy bitch couldn't even die right," Nikki knew she'd had enough.

Brittany got her sister to come and stay with Ella Jane and Stringer so she and Clayton could come to the house to be with Annabeth and Katie. Clayton was having a difficult time; he'd seen the body as it lay on the ground, and he was so distressed that Brittany couldn't get through to him. Nikki made him a cup of hot tea, and he sipped it and started to tear up. Once the silent tears started flowing, he seemed to be able to express himself a little better, and he and Brit sat and talked quietly. Nikki set about making some cookies to try to tempt Annabeth to eat something when she woke. She was pulling one batch out of the oven when the front door opened.

"Nikki?"

"In the kitchen, Peyton." Nikki started transferring the cookies from the cookie sheet, but something in Peyton's face stopped her cold. "What? What's wrong?"

"Come in here and sit down. I need to talk to you." He went into the den, spoke to Clayton and Brittany, motioned for Nikki to sit, then asked, "Where's the daughter?"

"Annabeth? I'll get them," Nikki said.

"No, I will," Brittany said, sensing something was very wrong.

They sat in silence until the three girls came back into the room. "What's going on?" a groggy Annabeth asked when she and Katie walked into the room with Brittany. She plopped down by Nikki.

Peyton sat down on the ottoman in front of Nikki and took both of her hands. "Nikki, Tony's been arrested."

There was a collective gasp, and Nikki cried out, "Oh, you're not serious? There's got to be some mistake! That can't be!"

"Steve's with him right now. The cops found some blood on the door frame at the office and also in the shower. They don't have any other physical evidence, but that was enough for an arrest. If the blood turns out to be Dottie's, we might have a real problem on our hands."

"No. This can't be happening," Nikki whispered, her mind spinning. "I have to see him. I have to see him right now," she cried, jumping up from the sofa.

"They won't let you see him. He'll be arraigned tomorrow morning. You can go then. But they won't let you see him now."

Nikki sat back down. She didn't know what to do. Annabeth, Katie, and Brittany were crying, and Clayton was staring at the floor, unable to speak. Someone had to call Raffaella; better yet, someone had to go and talk to her. "Has anybody called Vic?"

"I think Steve called him; I'm pretty sure somebody did."

"What about Cheryl?"

"The secretary? She was there when they made the arrest."

Nikki's face clouded. "Why didn't she call me?"

"I asked her not to. I told her I'd come and tell you myself."

"Oh." Then it hit her. "Oh! Clayton! We've got to go!"

Clayton's head snapped up. "Go where?"

"Do you realize we're it? We're all that's going to keep the company running. We've got to get busy. Your dad is counting on us." Nikki ran into the kitchen, turned off the oven, and ran back into the den. "Clayton, I'm not joking here. This is going to hit the news outlets so fast it'll make our heads spin. We've got to pull it together. A lot of people are depending on us, and they'll be watching us too. You with me?"

Clayton looked at the three girls, then back to Nikki. "Yeah. Yeah, I'm with you, Mom. You're right – we've got to get on it." He turned to Annabeth. "Bethie, will you guys go and talk to Nonna, tell her what's going on? She deserves to be told face to face, not over the phone."

"Sure. No problem. Where are you guys going?"

"We've got to go to the office and hope they'll let us in," Nikki told him. "There's got to be a show of competency so the employees don't freak out. That means we'll have to split up and visit every site, make things look like business as usual. Then it's got to be business as usual. The community's got to see that we're behind Tony but we can still keep things moving forward without him. Everything's on the line here."

"We can do this," Clayton agreed.

"God, little girl, are you okay?" Vic's frame filled the doorway, and Nikki ran and leaped into his arms.

"Oh, my god, I don't think I've ever been as glad to see you as I am right now." Nikki cried into his neck as his big arms pulled her to him.

"Vic's here, honey. Everything's gonna be okay. They let you see him yet?"

She sniffled. "No, Peyton says they won't."

"We'll talk to Steve about it. In the meantime, what do you need me to do?"

"We've got to get back to business, instill some confidence in the employees and the community in our ability to keep things going. Clayton and I could use your help."

"Whatever you need, baby. I'm at your disposal." Vic grabbed Annabeth and hugged her tight. "You too, sweetie. Zio Vic will do whatever he can to help you guys. All you've gotta do is let me know what you need."

"Thanks, Zio Vic." Annabeth sobbed and kissed his cheek through her tears. "I love you."

"No matter what happens, I'm here for all of you. You can always count on me," Vic told the girl he considered his niece as he kissed her back.

Nikki clapped her hands together, then lodged them firmly on her hips. "Okay, girls and boys, enough chit chat. We've got a company to run."

Chapter Forty

"Next case, Commonwealth of Kentucky versus Antonio Luigi Walters. Charge, murder in the first degree," the bailiff called out.

The courtroom was full, mostly of curiosity seekers and reporters. Besides Vic, Bart and Freddie had shown up to support Tony; Vic sat on one side of Nikki, holding her hand, and Bart sat on the other with his arm around her shoulders. Nikki's eyes were so swollen from crying that she could barely see.

Tony was led into the courtroom wearing an orange jumpsuit from the corrections department. He turned and scanned the courtroom and, when he saw her, his eyes brightened and he gave her a little wave even in his handcuffs. She squeezed Vic's hand – hard.

Vic leaned down and whispered in her ear, "You okay, sweetie?"

Nikki shook her head and fought off more tears. "No. God, look at him, Vic. He's worn out. I don't know if I can stand this." She choked as she tried to wave back at Tony and give him a little smile, but it was almost too hard.

Bart squeezed her. "I'll be okay, honey. You'll see."

"Doesn't feel that way."

The proceedings were a blur to Nikki. She heard Steve say, "Your honor, my client pleads …" and then, very clear and strong, Tony interrupted and said, "Not guilty, your honor." When it came to bail, Nikki was prepared to pay, but her heart sank when the prosecutor argued that Tony was a flight risk, and the judge denied him bail.

Steve had an idea: "Your honor, I'd request that, considering the number of people my client employs in this area and the contracts his company has to honor even in his absence, he be allowed two conferences per week with key officers from the corporation to keep everything going smoothly and avoid layoffs, thereby avoiding lost revenue for the region."

Nikki held her breath and squeezed Vic's hand again.

"I see no reason to deny that." Steve watched, expecting the prosecutor to have a fit, but he said nothing. "I'll order the jailer to find a secure conference room where up to six people could meet," the judge told the courtroom. This time, Vic squeezed Nikki's hand.

When they led him out of the courtroom, she mouthed *I love you* to him, and he nodded and smiled. Standing to leave, she found Steve at her side. He took her hand and pulled her out into the hall and to a bench, then sat down with her. "You okay? Need anything?" he asked with a hand on her shoulder while Vic watched from a distance, his eyes never leaving Nikki.

"Yeah. I need Tony out of jail. I need to be in fifteen places at once. I need a vacation. God, I need this nightmare to be over."

"How's Mrs. Walters?" Steve asked. "This has got to be hard on her."

"Annabeth said she was really upset. I'm going to check on her tonight." Nikki dreaded that visit.

"What about all of the brothers?"

"I'm letting Vic and Clayton handle them. I can't deal with that right now. I'm under a lot of pressure to keep the company running, and I don't know what the hell I'm doing." She started to cry, and Vic couldn't take it anymore; he walked over, sat down on her other side, and put his arm around her. She sighed and leaned into his shoulder.

"Hey, remember, I've been his attorney for a long time. I know a lot of stuff that might help you. Never hesitate to ask if I can help you with anything. I'll be glad to." She knew that wasn't just talk; Steve meant it. "Tony's not just my client; he's my friend. Now this is personal. It's my job to make this go away, and I've got my work cut out for me."

"Thanks, Steve. By the way, that thing with the conferences? Brilliant. I never would've thought of that. So thanks for that too." Nikki patted his arm.

"Yeah, I thought of that at the last minute. And it worked. It's a miracle!" he laughed. "And I want you to know I think you're one tough, smart lady, and if anybody could keep the company running, it's you. Clayton's a good kid, and he's got a good head on his shoulders. He could do this by himself if he had to. And you've got the big guy here too." He nodded toward Vic, and Vic kissed the top of Nikki's head. "So you're going to be fine, ladybug."

"I appreciate you, Steve, really, I do." His words were the most positive thing Nikki had to hold onto. She was going to have a lot of people looking at her, waiting to see how she'd perform. She couldn't let Tony down. "And I promise I'll call you if I need you."

Nikki had an armload of paperwork; so did Clayton. Both had legal pads full of notes. Vic was with them, and Cal and Cheryl came along. They could have one more employee with them, so they chose Brenda from the accounting office. She was a supervisor, so she could speak to all different kinds of accounting issues.

After the officers had gone through everything they had with them, they all filed into the conference room. They were shown to seats and admonished that they could not touch Tony or each other, or pass anything to or from him and, when they had received all their instructions, he was led in wearing handcuffs and leg irons. It took everything Nikki had to not break down when she saw him like that. There was a tired, worn-down look about him, and all she really wanted was to wrap her arms around him and tell him everything was okay. No one said anything until the guard moved to the door.

"Hi, baby." Nikki was trying her best to not cry. "Are you okay?"

"As okay as I can be in this place. You okay?" Tony asked, as subdued as she'd ever seen him.

"I'm all right." She winked at him and he smiled. "So we've got to keep this company together. That's why we're all here. We've got an hour, and we've got lots of stuff to go over. You up to this?"

He nodded. "Absolutely. Let's do it."

They spent the hour going over projections, schedules, punch lists, anything and everything Clayton, Nikki, Cal, and Vic could think of. Cheryl chimed in a few times, and Brenda answered several questions. It was a good meeting, and they covered a lot of territory and stayed on track.

Eventually, the guard gave them the five-minute warning. They wrapped up the loose ends, and then Tony turned to Vic. "Do you remember what I told you? About if I wasn't there?"

"Of course. And I want you to know I'm doing exactly what you asked," Vic assured him.

"Good. I really don't care about anything else, as long as you do that one thing," Tony reminded him, then turned and looked at Nikki. She smiled as she understood; he was talking about the time when he told Vic to always take care of her if he wasn't around. She was cared for and loved, even if Tony wasn't with her. And he wouldn't be gone long, she was sure. "You listen to Vic," he reminded her. "He knows what he's supposed to do."

"I know, baby," she whispered. "I'm fine; I'll be fine."

"I love you, angel. Never forget that," Tony whispered to her, and an ache set in as he fought to keep from reaching out to hold her.

"I love you too. I'll see you soon." The guard put Tony's handcuffs back on, then took him by the arm and led him away. One turn at the door to look back at all of them, and then he was gone.

Nikki was fighting back tears, but she managed to squeeze out, "Well, that was a good meeting. Clayton?"

"Yeah," Clayton sighed. "I feel better about everything now."

Nikki wished she could say the same.

"Well, well, well! Look at this!" Travis sing-songed as he turned the newspaper around so Autumn could see it. The front page was covered with a large photo of Tony being led into the courthouse, and a small photo of the site where Dottie's body had been found.

"Oh my god! Is that Mr. Walters?" Autumn took the paper from Travis, but he snatched it back before she could get a good look.

"Yeah, that's him, the bastard. Well, looks like our work is done."

"What do you mean? Nothing has changed. The company has the same procedures it's always had." Autumn was confused. "That hasn't gotten any better, has it?"

"You dumb bitch, you just don't get it, do you? We're done. As long as he's in jail, we don't have to do a thing." Travis grinned at the newspaper as though he'd won the lottery. "Maybe he'll be convicted. If that happens, our work is done." He shot her a weird, scary smile, and Autumn shuddered.

Now she was *really* confused. What would Mr. Walters being in jail have to do with anything? After Travis left, she decided to check the video feed logs to see if she could find someone moving a body around in the timeframe they gave. Sure enough, there was a guy dumping something large into a trench, but the guy wasn't Tony Walters. It was someone else entirely, someone smaller and, based on what she could tell from the camera angle, someone bald. But Autumn didn't tell Travis that; she didn't tell anyone. If she told anyone and Travis found out, he'd kill her.

Tony sat, trying to understand how he'd gone from Nikki's arms to a jail cell, and then it hit him: The thing he feared most was upon him, and there wasn't a damn thing he could do about it. He lay down on his cot and pressed his face into the pillow, crying silent tears into it until it was soaked. When he had cried all he could, he flipped it over and fell into a restless, troubled sleep.

"Clayton, I need to ask; have we had any more damage at any of the sites?" It had just occurred to Nikki that if anything had happened, no one had told her.

Clayton shook his head. "Not that I'm aware of. It's been really quiet."

"Your dad thought his being in jail would make it stop, and it looks like he's right. It is personal. But who? And why?" Nikki sat at Tony's desk, working on some figures for a new project, and it looked promising; that was, if her calculations were correct. Tony would know just by looking at them – if he were there, which he wasn't.

"I don't get it." Clayton shook his head. "I don't get any of it."

"Me neither."

"Hello?" Nobody ever called her after ten o'clock at night, and the number was unfamiliar. Nikki was sure it would be a wrong number.

"Hi, baby!"

"Tony! Oh my god! How did you . . ."

"Money talks, babe – literally, in this case. One of the deputy jailers has a burner phone he carries. For five bucks, he'll let me use it for thirty minutes. Guy's making a fortune – he's quite the entrepreneur. Good for me that Steve gave me some cash to hide away, so I'll probably get to call several times a week, especially if I offer him more. Anyway, that's what we've got – thirty minutes. I just wanted to hear your voice."

"God, yours sounds good to me too. Are you okay?"

"Yeah, guess so. Food's terrible, but I'm okay. How are you holding up?"

She signed. "I guess I'm all right. I've been working on the calculations for the Lindon Brothers warehouse. I hope I'm getting everything right."

"I'm sure you're doing fine. Hey, tell me something: Are you in bed?" he asked.

"Yeah. Why?"

"What are you wearing?"

Uh-huh, I know where this is going!, she thought. She looked down at the plain nightgown she had on, then decided to charge him up a bit. "Um, this is embarrassing, but I'm not wearing anything."

"Really? Why is that?"

"Well," she purred, reaching into the nightstand, "I was getting ready to get chummy with my vibrator."

"Oh, is that right? So if I were there, what would you want me to do?"

She pulled her gown up to her waist and ran her finger down her slit. "I'd want you to touch me, stroke my clit." She began to do exactly that, and her breathing quickened.

She heard him chuckle, a low, overheated sound. "And how would you want me to do that?"

"Around and around it, over and over, slowly," she told him, doing the same herself and gasping for breath.

"Uh-huh. So tell me what would happen."

"My clit would start to swell until it got rock-hard and my nipples would be so hard they'd hurt." Hers already were. "Then, if you were here, what would you do to me?"

"Let's see, I'd keep stroking around your clit until you could feel the tension building, slow and strong," Tony whispered, hearing her moan slightly. "You'd try to get me to stop, but I wouldn't – I'd make you go on until you almost couldn't stand it, leave you hanging as long as I could." She moaned louder. "Your back would arch, and your legs would go stiff, and your hips would start to buck, and you'd come and come hard, screaming out my name."

"Oh, god, Tony! I'm coming, I'm coming . . ." she cried out, and her orgasm kicked in, making any other words impossible. "Ohhhhhh, ohhhhhh, ohhhhhh gawd . . ."

"Hmmmm – that sounded delicious. Was it as good as it sounded?" he asked, laughing.

It took her a second to pull herself together enough to talk. "Better. But not as good as what I'd do for you if you were here," she answered, still breathless.

"Is that so?"

"Yes it is," she sighed. "I'd probably start out tracing my finger up and down your shaft until you were stiff as a board. Then I'd run my finger around the rim of your head and straight up the middle across the slit." Tony plunged his hand into his underwear to find his cock hard as stone, and he wrapped his hand around his shaft.

"What then?" *Geez,* he thought, *she's really good at this.*

"Well, I'd lie down between your legs and pop the head into my mouth like a lollipop, and then I'd slide my lips down until it hit the back of my throat. Then I'd swallow." Tony groaned softly. "I'd suck you in and out of my throat and run my tongue up and down the underside of your cock as I went." He was so hard that he hurt, and he dragged his hand up and down his length, imagining her lips on him.

"Then you'd wrap your hands in my hair and fuck my throat, and I'd use my tongue to tease you as you stroked in and out of me. And you'd drive into me hard and slow until your balls tightened, and I'd close down on you to make my mouth really, really tight, and you'd come in my mouth and I'd swallow it all down like the good little slut I am." Tony was trying to be quiet, but he couldn't help but moan as he came, wondering what the jail laundry service would make of his underwear. Hell, he couldn't be the only guy there who was shooting a load into his boxers; they all probably were, except the gay guys, and they were shooting them into each other.

"Awww, baby, that was awesome. God, I miss you." Tony wiped his hand on the sheet, then rolled to his side and relaxed. "I needed that. I need you," he said, still a little breathless.

"I need you too, stud. I miss you like crazy. I'll be glad when you get out of there."

"Me too. Everybody doing okay?"

"Yeah, I think so."

"Honey, what about you? How are you?"

"I'm fine," she assured him. "Vic is taking good care of me. He's like an old mother hen."

"What about the kids? What about the funeral?" he asked, not really wanting to hear.

"Annabeth took care of it. I had to make her do it, but Clayton was so overloaded already, it was the least she could do. Cremation. And they don't have to make a decision about where to put the ashes until they're ready. So it's done." Nikki was glad he'd asked because she hadn't been able to find a way to tell him.

Tony felt a flutter in his chest as it finally soaked in. "Oh my god. I'm free. I'm really, really free of her. I can't believe I hadn't realized that before. She'll never bother us again!" He sounded almost gleeful.

"She can't hurt you – us – anymore. She's gone. I love you, you love me, that mess is over. We'll get you out of there, and then things will be sweet and simple."

Chapter Forty-One

"Hey, buddy, how's it going?" Nikki asked as she answered her phone. She was glad to see Marla's number pop up, especially since they hadn't talked in awhile. Nikki had been extremely busy trying to keep everything going, to see Tony when she could, and to keep everybody happy. And keeping everybody happy was becoming nearly impossible.

"Hi! I've been missing you!"

"I've been missing you too! And Carol. How's she?"

"Actually, that's why I was calling." Marla's cheerful tone turned serious. "I've got a big problem. And I know you've got problems of your own, but I was hoping you could help me. By the way, how's that hunk of yours holding up?"

"He's doing okay. We're all suffering; him, me, the kids, his mom, the business. Everybody. It's going to be okay, but it doesn't feel like it right now." Nikki had tired of trying to sound cheerful, but she was still hopeful.

"You'll be fine. Tell him I asked about him, please? He's such a good guy; he doesn't deserve this. But back to why I was calling you: Carol fell and broke her leg."

"Oh god! Is she okay?"

"She will be. She's in a big cast. Had to have some pins put in."

"So what does that have to do with me?" Nikki was almost afraid to hear the answer.

"I'm in a real bind. It's almost Christmas and Carol can't be on her feet at all, so she really can't work. I've got the weekdays covered – no problem there – and a high school girl coming in during the afternoons to watch the place so I can make deliveries. But I'm exhausted, and then there's Saturday. I hate to ask, but it's just a half day – can you come in on Saturdays through the Christmas season so I can at least have a day off when everything is open? I'm having trouble getting my hair cut and colored because I'm tied up all the time."

Nikki thought for a minute, then said, "Sure! Why not? I love the shop – I've missed it. I don't work on Saturdays here, and all I do is rattle around in the empty house or go bug the kids so I don't miss him so much. It'll be fun. Want me to start this week?"

"Oh, would you? That would be fabulous! You still have your key, right?"

"Yep. I'll just come in on Saturday. Don't give it another thought." Nikki thought about all of the bright blooms and smiled.

Marla let out a squeal. "Oh, thank you! You have no idea how much I appreciate this!"

"Don't mention it. I'm looking forward to it."

"Steve, don't start on me. I won't be endangering anybody – I'll be there alone. Besides, nothing has happened since Tony went to, well, you know." Nikki was working hard at defending herself against the barrage of negativity Steve was throwing at her.

"You should at least check with me, don't you think? After all, it's Tony's orders to keep you safe, and I'd think you'd honor that." Not only was he being rude as hell, but he looked really pissed.

"Please don't throw that up in my face. Look, it's only a half day on Saturdays. Whoever's on duty can watch me as easily there as they can here at home. And it'll give me something to keep me busy. By the way, the next time you see my baby, give him some more money, please. He's got to pay the piper."

"Damn it, Nikki, okay. But don't do anything like this again without talking to me first, hear me?"

"Fine!" she snapped, smacking her butter knife down on the counter. "Now could you at least be useful and open that jar of peanut butter for me since you can't seem to get my jar opener out of the slammer?"

"Steve's mad at me about it, but what do you think?" Nikki asked Tony when he called that night.

"Nothing's happened at any of the jobsites?"

"Nope. Nothing. It's been completely quiet. And I wouldn't be working with anybody; I'd be by myself, so I wouldn't be endangering anybody else. I want to help Marla, but I also need to be busy, you know?"

"I know exactly." Sitting in a jail cell was proving to be difficult for Tony too. He was used to going and doing, being outside, and the only outdoor spot the jail had was a small courtyard that was completely enclosed. It was driving him crazy being confined that way. "If that will help her and help you, I think you should do it. I'll talk to Steve, get him to back off a little. He's just trying to keep you safe. And he was right about one thing – you should've talked to him first, or to me. But it's okay, sweetie."

"Thanks, babe. I just want to survive this with my mental faculties intact, you know?"

"Yeah, I know. Me too."

"So what've we got?" Detective Fox asked the coroner. Bryson stood next to him, arms folded.

"Well, we have a victim who was killed with an execution-type shot. It went in the base of her skull, and traveled up and forward until it came out the front of her head and blew most of the front of the skull out from the supraorbital foramen up past the frontal, bordered by the coronal suture on both sides – basically, the whole upper portion of the front of the skull. The wound is consistent with a forty-five slug, but the slug's not present, so I've got nothing for a ballistics workup. She also had DNA evidence on her – a pubic hair that wasn't hers. No semen, though, but between that and some very mild but fresh vaginal abrasions, it looks like she had sex very shortly before she was killed. There were tiny glass fragments in her hair consistent with auto safety glass." He pushed his glasses back up his nose.

"And the DNA?" Fox asked.

"No match in any of the databases. So it's somebody who's never been in trouble."

"What about Walters' DNA?"

"We got that when he came in for booking, but it doesn't match his," the coroner said.

"Well, all that means is maybe he was jealous she was having sex with someone else," Fox said as they left the coroner's office and walked down the hall.

"You didn't know her. I think that would be unlikely that anyone would care about that." Then Bryson asked, "What did we get from forensics?"

"The bloody print on the trash can in Walters' bathroom? Not his and not in the system." Fox read the report as they walked. "And according to this report, all of the blood was from the vic – none of it belonged to anyone else."

"And we still don't have a real crime scene," Bryson pointed out. "Auto glass. Could be any car in the area."

"If we don't come up with something better than this," Fox told him, "we're going to lose an already shaky case. At least we've got him in custody – he can't run."

"He wouldn't run anyway," Bryson said. "He's not that kind of guy."

"They're *all* that kind of guy." Fox shook his head. "You really believe he didn't do this, don't you?"

"I've *never* believed he did this."

"Well, shows how gullible you are."

Nikki was restless. Tony had been gone two weeks. She was trying to keep the office running, and she was getting really tired and stressed. She put her head in her hands and sighed. What next? Her desk was a mess. There were so many things to do that she didn't know where to start, and she decided she probably needed to come in on Saturday afternoon after she left The Passionate Pansy and try to catch up on some stuff; Tony's office key was at home, so she could get in easily, and whoever was working her detail would probably welcome the chance to sit in Tony's office and watch TV rather than sit in the car. She'd work on Sunday too if she had to.

She stood and stretched. The coffee out front smelled fresh, but she didn't drink coffee; maybe she should start. Sleeping was impossible without Tony beside her, and she was tired all the time. She'd moved into his office temporarily, and she walked to the big window and looked out.

Looking at the yard always helped her keep perspective. From the big window she could see the building where central supply was, and the larger office building with accounting, human resources, and all the operational offices. The mechanics hangar was back there, too, but what she really loved was watching everyone moving around. There were people everywhere, walking back and forth with paperwork, plans, or envelopes of all kinds, guys carrying tools, heavy equipment moving around, and trucks all over the place.

Directly under the window were a half-dozen pickup trucks, but Clayton's wasn't there – it was the only Walters truck that was red, and thinking about how much he liked that made her smile. He was such a good kid, so smart and handsome, and so quiet that any funny thing he said was made that much funnier just because he'd been the one who said it. She stood looking at the trucks and almost cried; her big blue truck was parked there too. If Tony was there, he'd be driving it. But he wasn't.

Then something caught her eye – something on the roof of the white truck right under the window. She squinted and looked at it. What was that? She called out to Cheryl, "Hey, Cheryl, whose truck is twenty-three?"

"That's Cal's truck," Cheryl called back.

"Where is he?"

"He and Clayton went to a jobsite – don't remember which one, hospital maybe?"

"Can you come here for a minute?"

"What's up, boss lady?" Cheryl appeared at Nikki's elbow.

"Look at the roof of that truck. What is that?"

Cheryl squinted at it. "I can't tell."

Tony kept binoculars in his desk to watch the yard with, so Nikki pulled them out and looked at the roof of the truck. It was a piece of duct tape – white duct tape – and it had a strange-looking, protrusion-like lump in the middle of it. The protrusion was round and had rough, upward-pointed edges that were visible even under the duct tape. "You look." She handed the binoculars to Cheryl. "What is that?"

Cheryl looked through the glasses. "I can't tell. It's weird."

"Can you find out if that truck has had glass breakage recently?" Something was bumping around in Nikki's mind, and she wracked her brain to try to remember all the things Steve had told her about the evidence in Dottie's murder.

Cheryl went back to her desk. In a few seconds she came back. "Yeah, we've had twelve in the last month. That one had a windshield replaced."

"When?"

"The day after Thanksgiving. What are you thinking?"

"I'm pretty sure that's a bullet hole underneath that duct tape. I think I just found the crime scene." She grabbed her phone and dialed Clayton.

"Hi! What's up?"

"Clayton, I'm going to ask you some questions. Please, please just answer them yes or no, or something like it. Try to be casual, okay?" Nikki instructed as clearly and emphatically as she could.

"Okay."

"Is Cal still with you?"

"Yes."

"Good. And you're at a jobsite?"

"Yes."

"Okay. Is it the Colufab site?"

"No."

"Is it the hospital site?"

"Yeah."

"That's what, about twenty-five minutes from the office?"

"Something like that."

"So here's what I need. Keep Cal with you. Don't let him out of your sight. Don't let him come back here with anybody else. Keep him busy. Then I'll call you in a little while and tell you when to bring him back. When you do, make sure he has his seatbelt on so it'll take more effort for him to get out of the truck. When you get here, there will be lots of cops here, but it's okay. Can you do all of that for me, honey?"

"Yeah, no problem."

"Thanks, sweetie. I wish I could explain to you what's going on, but I can't if he's with you. I'll call you in a little while. Love you."

"Uh-huh – same here," he replied discreetly.

Nikki hit END, then dialed Bryson. It only took one ring for him to answer. "Hawkins."

"Detective Hawkins? This is Nikki Wilkes, Tony Walters' fiancée?"

"Hey, Ms. Wilkes, what can I do for you?" The detective sounded sort of friendly. "And please, call me Bryson." Nikki was shocked, but she didn't have time to ponder Bryson's personality.

"Um, Detec . . . Bryson, I think I found your crime scene."

"Wha . . . really? Where?"

"We've got a company truck over here that has what looks like a bullet hole in the roof. I mean, I haven't pulled the tape off because I didn't want to ruin any evidence, but that's certainly what it looks like from the window with Tony's binoculars."

"Where is the person who drives the truck? Because this could be dangerous if that individual knows you've figured this out," Bryson warned.

Nikki went over the instructions she'd given Clayton. "Excellent." Bryson was impressed. She was really, really sharp. "Listen, I'll be over with a wrecker and a couple of uniforms in about fifteen. We'll take care of everything – don't touch anything."

"No problem. We're not going anywhere near that truck until you get here. And thanks, Bryson."

"No, thank you, Nikki. I appreciate you calling me. See you in a few."

Now it was just a matter of waiting. Nikki thought about what this could mean. She was getting excited just thinking about the possibilities. After a few minutes, she quieted her mind, then realized she should probably call Steve, and he assured her he'd be there as fast as he could get there.

True to his word, Bryson and a cruiser with two uniformed officers showed up in less than ten minutes. She had Cheryl give him the keys to the truck, and the three of them went out to look at it. Bryson pulled the tape off the roof and, sure enough, there was a bullet hole through the metal. Inside the headliner he found the entry, a tiny slit in the cloth. Using a small metal rod, he stuck the rod through the slit and it went through the hole in the roof at an angle toward the truck's bed. Before he could ask about the windshield, Nikki told him they'd checked and the truck's windshield had been replaced the day after Thanksgiving. The department's wrecker showed up, and Bryson helped them load the truck.

Once it was gone, he turned to Nikki. "Now it's time to call and have your son bring him here."

Nikki made the call, and in less than a half hour, Clayton's red truck pulled into the parking lot. They were all watching through Tony's big window, and she noticed the look on Cal's face as they drove up and he realized his truck was gone. The uniformed officers met them at Clayton's truck, talked to Cal for a few minutes, and then handcuffed him and put him in the car.

Clayton took the steps two at a time and came through the door double-time. "What the hell is going on now?" Clayton asked, looking from Nikki to Bryson and back to Nikki.

When Nikki explained, Clayton dropped down onto Tony's sofa and sighed. "So you think my mo … Dottie was with Cal?" he asked, dazed.

"It sure looks that way," Nikki said.

"Our forensics team will find out for sure, but that's what we're betting," Bryson told him.

He shook his head. "Dad's trusted him for years, and Cal's let him sit in jail? I can't believe it. Do you think he's the one who killed her?"

"No, I'd say not, but he might know who did," Bryson said.

Clayton squinted at Bryson. "Wait — I thought *you* thought it was my dad."

Bryson shook his head. "No — I never said that. Actually, I don't think that at all."

"Oh." Clayton's struggle to process it all was unmistakable. "I'm confused, and I'm not going to ask any more questions. Just let me know when you've figured it all out."

Nikki sat down beside him and took his hand. "Honey, I know this is all crazy, but we're going to get to the bottom of it, I promise."

Clayton stood up and walked toward the door without looking back. "I'm going back to work. I can't think about this anymore."

"He's really having problems with all of this, isn't he?" Bryson asked after Clayton had gone.

"We all are. But Clayton saw Dottie's body at the jobsite, his dad's locked up, and the man they're out there putting in a squad car is somebody their whole family has trusted for years, not to mention that if this doesn't turn out as it should, he'll be responsible for this whole company. This is difficult for us — more so than most people can understand."

Steve appeared in the doorway. "Okay, what's going on? I passed Clayton and he looks like he's stoned or something. And is that Cal in the cruiser out front?"

"Long story. Bryson, I'm sure you've got a lot of work to do, thanks to me — sorry! But thanks for coming over," Nikki said.

"No, thank you. Steve, we'll let you know what we find." With that, Bryson strode out the front door.

"Missy, you let the fox into the hen house," Steve growled as soon as Bryson was gone. "This had better be good."

When Nikki answered her cell later that afternoon, Steve said, "Nikki, Bryson just called me."

"And?"

"He said the bullet hole is a forty-five, and there's blood all over the inside of the cab. Cal tried to clean it up, but it can't be done, not completely. There are shards of glass in the cab that are the same kind as the glass taken from Dottie's hair, and there are small amounts of brain matter on the back glass. And this gives them probable cause to get a DNA sample from Cal, which I'm guessing will match the pubic hair they found on her body. I'm also guessing the thumbprint from the trash can in the office is his." Then Steve snickered, "To top it off, there's the fact that Cal's singing like a bird."

"No shit? Good. I'm pissed," Nikki seethed into the phone. "I'm here to tell you, if Tony doesn't fire him, I will; I can, and I will. That little shit knows Tony didn't do this, but he's let Tony sit in jail and said nothing to save his own ass. Leave me alone with him for ten minutes and that little cocksucker is mine, I swear to god," Nikki hissed. Steve had never heard her like that, and it was a revelation to him. She wasn't the meek little thing he'd thought. "Not to mention the fact that he was sleeping with Dottie. I mean, what the fuck? I'd love to hear him explain that."

"Oh, I can't wait to hear what he's got to say," Steve snickered again. "But I'll tell you this – if the DNA checks out, the blood is Dottie's, and the thumbprint is Cal's, I'm going to ask that the charges against Tony be dropped."

"Oh, Steve! Do you think that'll work?" Nikki gasped.

"Without any physical evidence against him, they don't have a case. And without a case, they can't hold him." Nikki could tell that, as far as Steve was concerned, this was pretty cut and dried and Tony would be coming home.

"Will you call me when you find out about the evidence?"

"Sure will, hon. I think he's on his way home."

"Your honor, all of the evidence the prosecution has brought forward points in directions other than my client. Based on the commonwealth's inability to provide enough evidence that he was involved in the death of Dorothea Walters, I'm asking that the charges against my client be dropped." It was bright and early on Tuesday morning, and Steve was doing what he loved to do most – working the courtroom. He'd asked for an emergency hearing and gotten it.

"Mr. Holshouser, do you have any new evidence to present?" the judge asked the prosecutor.

"Not at this time, your honor, but the commonwealth requests more time to prepare."

"Mr. Holshouser, if you don't have evidence, you don't have evidence."

"Your honor, the investigation is ongoing. We're asking that Mr. Walters be held while the investigation is completed," the prosecutor stated.

Steve started: "Your honor, the only thing they have is the fact that no one can corroborate my client's whereabouts that evening during the time his ex-wife was killed. I . . ."

"Mr. McCoy, let me interrupt. You don't have to say anything. I will allow the commonwealth to continue their investigation."

Nikki was watching Steve's face and, even though he was obviously frustrated, it was also clear he'd just had an "aha" moment. "Your honor, under the circumstances, would you at least grant my client home incarceration with a monitor?"

The judge thought for a moment, then answered, "Yes, I believe that would be appropriate. Mr. Walters is to be released to his residence with a monitor pending completion of the investigation. Mr. Holshouser, fair warning," he admonished the prosecutor, "you have two weeks to come up with more evidence or the charges against Mr. Walters will have to be dropped. Do you understand?"

"Yes, your honor. Thank you, your honor," the prosecutor replied.

"Thank you, your honor," Steve echoed.

"Bailiff, take Mr. Walters to processing, have them set him up with a monitor, and send him home. Next case."

Tony turned and looked back at Nikki. Tears rolled down her face, and he smiled and winked.

They led him out, and Steve found his way to her through the crowded courtroom. "Well, it's not what I wanted, but it's better than nothing." He was breathless and relief was painted all over his face.

"No, it's wonderful. Thank you so much, Steve. That was brilliant. Can I take him home now?"

"No, it'll take about two hours to process him and get the monitor set up. They'll bring him home in a cruiser. But he's going to need something to wear."

"I packed him a bag before I left this morning. It's in the car." Nikki beamed. "I'll go and get it for you to take to him."

"Are you kidding? You packed it before you came?" Steve asked in surprise.

"Yep. I had faith in you." Nikki hugged him.

Wow, Steve thought, *that's actually pretty amazing. Now I know why he's so crazy about her.*

Bryson and Fox had let Cal sit and stew the rest of the day and spend the night in holding, and then they started in on him bright and early while Steve was in court. Stewing hadn't mellowed him at all.

"So, Mr. Forrester, um, can I call you Cal? We're all friends here, right?" Detective Fox began.

"Oh, yeah, sure, you can call me Cal if you want." Cal fidgeted in his chair.

"So, Cal, when we process the evidence we found in your truck, can I assume it's going to show that Dottie Walters was in your truck?"

"Uh, uh, yeah, uh, she was in my truck," Cal stammered.

"And we found a pubic hair on her body," Fox told him. "Am I to assume it's yours?"

Cal was silent for a minute, then admitted, "Um, yeah, I guess so."

"So you were having sex with Dottie in your truck. Is that correct?"

"Uh, um, yeah, um, I . . ." Cal was becoming more agitated with each question. His hands were visibly shaking, and sweat was popping out on his forehead.

"So would you mind walking us through what happened that night? Because we're a little confused," Fox said calmly, leaning back in his chair.

"Well, I, um . . . so Dottie and me, we were, well, for about six months now we've been sort of seeing each other. And I was watching the Colufab site because of all the, you know, the environmentalist crap that's been going on, them tearing up stuff. I was there alone, so it was easy for her to come over and see me. So she came over Thanksgiving night. She'd bring me some fast food, and then we'd, um, you know."

"Have sex?" Fox asked.

"Yeah. I couldn't take a chance on my wife finding out," he stammered.

"What about Mr. Walters?" Fox asked.

"Tony? I wouldn't want Tony to find out either." He stopped, and a look of sheer terror came over him. "Oh god! He's going to find out, isn't he? Oh, no, oh, he'll fire me. Oh god! I can't do this!" Cal looked like he was going to pass out from the mental overload.

"Cal, let me explain something," Fox told him in a firm tone. "We've got you on multiple charges – failure to report a homicide, obstruction of justice, abuse of a corpse, interfering with an investigation, concealing a homicide, the list is endless – so right now, worrying about what your boss thinks is the least of your worries." Fox pulled out a box of breath mints and popped two. "Mint?"

Cal shook his head. He was trembling all over and so pale that he looked like he might fall out of his chair. "So just answer the questions and we can see where we stand. Because right now, we might even be able to charge you with murder," Fox bluffed.

"Oh, no! I didn't kill her! You can't possibly believe . . ."

"I don't know what to believe. So let's get the facts straight. You were telling Mr. Walters your wife was a drinker, but that wasn't true, was it? It was your cover to sneak off with Dottie, right?"

Cal got visibly upset when he realized the detective thought of him as a habitual, perpetual liar. "Yeah. Jenny isn't a drunk."

"And you told her what?"

"That I had to work – which was true," he emphasized. "But I wasn't working the whole time . . ."

"So back to the original question. Dottie came to you that night, and the two of you had sex. Can you tell me what position she was in inside your truck?"

Embarrassment was plain on Cal's face by that point. "We were in the cab, and she was sitting on my lap, facing me."

"With her back to the windshield?"

"Yeah. And we were, you know, and all of a sudden, I saw something move out of the corner of my eye, and there was this sound, and the windshield exploded and blood went everywhere, and Dottie's face blew off, and I was covered in blood, and . . ." Cal was getting more worked up with every word, and he looked like he was about to have a stroke.

"Calm down, Cal. I know this is hard to talk about. So who was the person who killed her?" Fox asked, leaning forward in his chair.

"I don't know. I didn't see them, just the movement out of the corner of my eye."

"So it could've been Mr. Walters?" Fox asked.

"No, couldn't have been. This guy wasn't tall enough." Cal sounded very sure.

"I thought you didn't get a good look at him," Fox reminded him of his earlier statement.

"No, but I *do* know he wasn't tall enough to be Tony," Cal said with resolve.

Fox sighed; that didn't help his case. "So after she was shot, what did you do then?"

"Well, I knew they'd dug the footers at the university site that day, so I called Kenny – I knew he was over there – and told him to go on home, that my name was Harold and I was his relief. He didn't know any different. Then I drove over there – I took the back streets because my windshield was blown out – and wrapped her up in a tarp. Then I called Tony and told him I had to go home because Jenny was drunk. I waited a little while to make sure if he went by the office, he'd be gone before I got there and we wouldn't run into each other. Then I went to the office to clean myself up and clean up the truck."

Bryson Hawkins listened to all of this through the two-way mirror in the interrogation room, and Steve McCoy stood right beside him. "That's exactly what I thought," Bryson whispered to Steve.

"You mean you used your key, went into Mr. Walters' office, took a shower, and cleaned up the truck?" Fox continued.

"Yeah, well, no, I mean, I cleaned up the truck at a car wash down the street. I went home and, the next day, I called the glass place and had them come and put a new windshield in," Cal explained.

"And the bullet hole in the roof of the truck?" Fox asked, leaning back again. "You put the duct tape over it?"

"Yeah, I didn't want it to leak when it rained." Cal looked down at the table, humiliated.

"And you basically went on, business as usual."

"Yeah, I guess you'd say that," Cal answered. As Steve listened, he shook his head in disbelief. Cal sounded so nonchalant when he talked about just going on like nothing had happened that it pissed Steve off to no end.

"I take it the thumbprint in blood on the trash can in Mr. Walters' office is yours?"

Cal hung his head and said quietly, "Yes."

"One more thing, Cal. What would you say your relationship with Dottie Walters was? Were you in love with her? Did you feel sorry for her? What was it?"

"I don't know, I really don't." Cal started to sniffle. "The sex was pretty good. I wasn't in love with her. I think she was trying to get back at Tony; I'm not sure. But no, it wasn't about love at all. It was just sex." He started to outright cry. "I've thrown my whole life away for sex in my truck, and not the greatest sex in the world, just pretty good. Oh god – what have I done? Tony's never going to forgive me!"

"That's not something you should worry about at this point. Officer," Fox asked the uniform at the door, "would you please arrest Mr. Forrester, read him his rights and the list of charges against him?"

"No!" Cal yelled. "Oh, please, don't do this! I didn't do anything wrong! Oh, please, what will my wife and kids do?" Cal screaming was all that the whole precinct could hear as they led him out the door and down the hall to booking.

"So I guess you get to break the news to Tony," Bryson told Steve. "Man, that's one job I don't envy you."

Steve shook his head. "No shit. He's going to have a coronary when he finds out about this."

"Officer, could you give us a few minutes?" Steve asked the officer who was processing Tony's paperwork. "There's something I need to tell my client."

"Sure. I've got to go retrieve his personal effects anyway. You've got ten minutes."

"Thanks." Steve turned to Tony. "I've got something to tell you, and I don't quite know how to start."

Tony's brow furrowed. "Can't be that bad, can it?"

"Well, actually . . ." Steve started relating Cal's statement and watched Tony's eyes grow bigger with each passing moment. When he was done, Tony looked at him with a mixture of disgust and fury.

"He was fucking my ex-wife? In the company truck I provided for him? On my time? After all I've done for him over the years? That little sawed-off son of a bitch!" he growled, trying to keep his voice down. Steve had never seen Tony angry before; it just wasn't part of his personality, but Steve was surprised. The normally-calm Italian looked like he could break Cal in half. "If I could get my hands on him . . ."

"He was worried you'd fire him," Steve snickered.

"Fire him?" Tony's face was a red mess of boiling indignation. "*Fire* him? He's lucky I don't do worse! Hell yeah, he's fired! Bastard left me to twist in the wind . . . I've been in *jail* for two goddamn weeks, and he's worried about getting *fired*? I'd better not see him . . ."

"You won't be seeing much of anybody unless they come to the house," Steve ordered with a look that told Tony he was way past serious. "You will wear the monitor and you will stay at the house – period. I don't want you to mess this up, hear me? You violate this, and I'm not sure I can help you."

"Yeah, yeah, I hear you." Tony sighed. "But the whole idea of Cal and

Dottie just . . ." He shuddered.

"I know. I was a little grossed out too. But there's no accounting for taste, huh?" Steve laughed.

"No shit. So when can I get out of here?"

"As soon as your processing is done. Nikki sent some clothes for you. A cruiser will take you home. They'll explain how the monitor works," Steve told him. Tony made a disgusted face. "But you'll be at home in your own bed tonight. That counts for something, right?"

Tony broke into a huge smile. "Oh, that counts for a lot more than just something. That's everything!"

Chapter Forty-Two

"So what's going on? Why weren't you at the office this morning?" Clayton asked Nikki when he got to the house. He had gone by and picked up Brittany and Stringer; Ella Jane was in school. Before Nikki could give him an answer, Annabeth, Katie, and Raffaella walked through the door. Vic had reached the courthouse just as the proceedings had ended, and he'd headed straight for the Louisville house as soon as he'd heard.

"I had something I had to do; actually, I was at the courthouse. I have a surprise for all of you." Nikki was almost bouncing in front of them as they all sat around in the den. "Within the next hour and a half," Nikki could barely get out, her excitement about to spill out everywhere, "your dad will be home!"

Annabeth nearly shattered everyone's eardrums with her screaming. Everybody was hugging everybody else except for Nikki; she was standing to the side, watching, when everyone stopped and realized she was standing by herself. Clayton strode across the room and threw his arms around her, hugging her tight. "Mom, I'm so sorry you've gone through all of this. You've been here for everybody, and no one's really been here for you," he told her, suddenly looking like he was about to tear up. Clayton's love warmed Nikki's heart; he was so much like his dad and had such a kind soul.

"I'm fine, honey, really. I just want your dad to come home." Nikki pushed his hair back from his face and stroked his cheek.

"I want to say, in front of everybody, how amazed I am at the way you just put on your big girl panties and jumped in there, Mom. You've done a great job of running a company you knew very little about until just a few weeks ago, and I'm so proud of you. And I know Dad is extremely proud of you. I'm just sorry we haven't been more supportive."

"Yeah, we've given you more to worry about than we helped," Annabeth chimed in. "We should've been more supportive and thought about you more, but we were busy just thinking about ourselves. I'm really, really sorry for that." She looked like she would cry at any minute.

Nikki shook her head. "It's okay, honey. This has been stressful for all of us. We've all done the best we could. And I have had support; somebody's been here for me." She walked to where Vic was sitting quietly and looked down at him with a smile. He took her hand and kissed it. "Your Zio Vic has checked on me every day, taken me to dinner when I thought I couldn't face another evening alone, and looked over my shoulder when I didn't know what to do. He did it quietly so I wasn't embarrassed, and that was important to me so no one knew how shaky I was. I owe him a lot." Nikki put her hand on Vic's cheek, and he closed his eyes and smiled, leaning into her touch.

"You don't owe me a damn thing, little girl. I did it all gladly, and I'd do it again. But I hope I don't have to!" he laughed.

"When Big T be heyah?" Stringer asked, dancing from foot to foot.

"Pretty soon," Nikki smiled, and then the front door opened. Everyone except Nikki ran to greet him. She could hear Annabeth squealing and Stringer using his outside voice, and, over the din, Tony's smooth baritone, laughing and chatting with his family. They came streaming back into the den, all of them crowded around Tony like yippy little ankle-nipping dogs. But when they made it into the den, he came to a dead stop and looked across the room.

Nikki stood by the French doors, midday sunlight framing her slight form and making her hair look like a halo. Her hands were clasped in front of her, and she was standing motionless, just waiting for him to notice her, hanging back like she so often did, looking unsure of her place in all of the commotion. Tony was holding Stringer; he set the little boy down, then ran across the room, arms open, and snapped her up, swinging her around and holding her tight. She threw her arms around his neck and buried her face in his hair, his familiar scent warming her inside and out, from head to toe. "Oh my god, baby, I've missed you so much," Tony whispered to her, working to choke back the tears he'd been holding in for so long. He wanted to stay positive and cheerful for her; she'd been through enough.

"Please don't leave me again," Nikki breathed into his ear.

"I have no intention of it." He pulled back and kissed her. "I'm *never* leaving you again." He kissed her over and over and over.

She finally stopped him and said, "We've got lunch to eat. Want some chicken salad?"

"Your chicken salad? You bet!" Tony put her down, then clutched her hand tight. "I've missed your cooking almost as much as I've missed you!"

Everyone ate and talked. Tony called his brothers and told all of them that he was home. The only one who didn't sound ecstatic was Bennie, but Tony hadn't really expected anything more. After lunch was eaten and Nikki had cleaned everything up, Tony looked at his family with a smile and said decidedly, "Okay, everybody – go home."

"What?" Annabeth cried. "But you just got home, and we've missed you, and . . ."

"And you can come and see me tomorrow. Right now, Nikki and I have some catching up to do. So go home. I love you all, but we . . ."

"Right, right," Annabeth grumbled. "Come on, Nonna. Dad and Mom want to be alone. In the biblical sense, and in the middle of the day. Animals!" But she was grinning when she said it.

"Hey, Tony! I comin' back soon, kay?" Stringer yelled.

Tony stooped to talk to his little buddy. "You'd better, mister! I've been missing you!" he grinned, tapping the end of Stringer's nose.

"I been missin' you too!" Stringer gave him a big sloppy kiss on the cheek and ran out the door.

"We're glad you're home. See you later, Dad!" Clayton called and ran out the door to catch Stringer before he could make it to the end of the driveway. Brittany kissed Tony on the cheek and followed the boys out.

"Brother, I love you. I'm glad you're home." Vic hugged Tony, and Tony hugged him back tight.

"Hey, I just appreciate you being here." He leaned into Vic's ear and whispered, nodding toward Nikki, "And thanks for keeping up with her. I knew she'd be fine as long as you were watching out for her."

"She did really well – you should be very proud. And taking care of her was a pleasure. I love spending time with her – with both of you," Vic whispered back. "Bye, Nik!" he called out. "See you later – love ya!"

"Love you too, sweetie," Nikki called back, waving from the kitchen.

Vic looked at Tony and winked. "Go get 'er, big guy!" he whispered slyly, and Tony grinned and slapped him on the shoulder as he left.

Tony walked back across the room and folded Nikki into him, and she couldn't help but notice the hungry look in his eyes. She didn't know if he could see the same in her face, but she could feel her own hunger, hot and swelling south of her waist, everything tensing and aching, a thirst waiting to be slaked. He stood, tilting his pelvis and pressing his hardness against her, and just losing himself in the depths of those blue-green eyes for a few minutes. His voice was strained with need when he told her, "I'm going to take a shower and wash whatever's left of the jail off of me. Then, if you want..."

"Oh, I want. Trust me – I want," Nikki assured him, leaning in to give him a hot, ravenous kiss. When their lips touched, hers parted, and Tony slipped his tongue into her mouth. Her legs went weak and she moaned. He slapped her backside and grinned.

"I'll be out of the shower so fast it'll make your head swim. I'll set a land speed record in showering," Tony promised and kissed her one last time before he headed up the stairs and disappeared into the bathroom.

"I think you missed me a little," Nikki whispered after their third go-round. Lying on their sides in each other's arms, Tony was still inside her and still hard as marble, and he flowed into and out of her, a slow and gentle rocking, her velvety tightness soothing him like a salve. He cupped her breasts in his hands, his thumbs lazily drifting back and forth across her nipples, and stared at them like they were the most amazing things in the universe. Late afternoon sun was streaming in the bedroom window, throwing a golden light all over the room and across her hair, fanned out over the pillow. She was overcome by his touch, the heat in his hands, and the love he'd breathed into her with every stroke.

His smile was soft and warm. "I knew I missed you, but I didn't realize how much until I undressed you and touched you. That first second, my hands on your skin, almost took me down, precious. I've never wanted anything or anybody so much."

Nikki buried her face in his chest. She'd missed his scent; it was beyond comforting, and it engulfed her. She'd had a security detail following her, not to mention Clayton and Vic watching her every move, and yet she hadn't felt as safe in over two weeks as she felt right at that moment. She ran her fingers softly down his cheek, and he caught her hand and kissed her palm, his stubble tickling her fingertips.

"I missed you more than I can say," she said quietly and kissed him. His lips were soft and warm, and she could taste her own juices on his mouth from the attention he'd laved on her hot, needy folds earlier. She sighed into him; he breathed in her sigh and then sighed back into her. So utterly immersed in him, so breathlessly consumed by her desire, Nikki felt she might lose consciousness.

"Babe, what do you want? I'll give you whatever you want," Tony whispered to her, rolling her nipple between his thumb and finger.

Nikki smiled. "I just want to be here with you, to satisfy you, to make you happy." A tear rolled from her eye and into her hair.

"I am happy." He kissed her again. "I've never been so happy in my entire life."

Nikki spent the next day working, part of the day from the house, and part of the day in the office, even though walking out of the house and leaving him there that morning had been one of the hardest things she could imagine. She got Todd, a young man from accounting who also took care of most of their computer issues, to help her get everything together.

By afternoon, Cheryl got a big surprise. She came back from lunch and powered on her monitor, only to have Tony's face fill the screen and hear him call out, "Hi, Cheryl!" She screamed and jumped back. The commotion got Nikki's attention and she came out to the front, only to laugh hysterically at Cheryl. Tony was laughing at her from the computer screen.

"Welcome to the modern world of work!" Nikki laughed and patted her on the shoulder. "The boss is in the house!"

"You could've warned me!" Cheryl cried out, then started to laugh at herself.

Tony chuckled. "Yeah, I can see you. I can see when you're reading that needlework magazine instead of working."

"I'll have to hide it better, huh?" Cheryl chuckled back. "So you're officially back to work?"

"Thanks to my tech-savvy girlfriend." He pointed at Nikki through the screen. "And you – you'd better get back to work too. I'm watching you!" He looked at her sideways and gave her an evil glare.

"Oh, your bark is sooooo much worse than your bite," Nikki smirked, walking away. "Now you've got to figure out how to switch from Cheryl's camera to mine or you can't . . ." She walked around her desk and there he was, giving her a guess-I've-shocked-you look. "Hmmmm. You're a quick learner," she grumbled with mock sarcasm.

"Guess I'm in business, huh?" Tony laughed.

"Yeah, looks like it. Figured out the fax and scanner yet?"

"Yep. Check your printer."

Nikki looked in the printer tray and found the modified bid packages she'd left for him to review that morning, all edited, redone, and printed off. "Well, you're a quick worker too."

"Hey, I don't fool around," he announced. "Well, I *do* fool around, but only with you. Not with business. And now, business, dearie." And his face disappeared from her screen.

Within ten minutes, he was back, asking her a question about some documents he'd been working on the day he was arrested, so she sent them to him. A little while later, she pinged in to show him some pictures of one of the jobsites, and he weighed in on her questions. At four thirty, she told Cheryl, "Day's almost over. You know, this is working out pretty good."

Cheryl smiled. "Yeah, it's good to have him back, even if it is just on a screen."

"I heard that!" Tony called out from the speakers. "And thanks – it's good to be back."

"Travis, we've got to tell somebody, the police or somebody," Autumn begged, the blood draining from her face.

"You'll keep your damn mouth shut is what you'll do," Travis snarled. He hit the PLAY button onscreen and the video from their surveillance camera rolled again.

Autumn had decided to check some of the video feeds from other sites, and she was appalled by what she'd found. The scene was almost the same as the video they'd seen before; the Walters Construction truck, the passenger door opening, someone getting in, what looked like the truck's occupants having sex. But then a shadowy, crouching figure crept from an unidentifiable vehicle outside the fence, stopped at the front driver's side corner of the truck, raised an arm, and a flash burst out. In the next few seconds of footage, the figure ran away, and one of the truck's occupants practically fell out of the driver's side door and jumped around a bit. Whoever it was seemed to have walked a few feet away, done something that looked like throwing up, and gotten back into the truck before driving slowly away.

"But Travis, we'd already seen the body being dumped, and now we just witnessed the murder! We have to tell somebody. And we have to let them know Mr. Walters didn't do it! He's innocent and he doesn't deserve to go to jail!" Autumn wailed.

"He deserves whatever he gets. I don't want to hear another word about it!" Travis yelled and stormed out of the room.

Autumn reached into her purse and pulled out a flash drive. She plugged it into the computer and downloaded a copy of the video. She had to get it to someone. *I know,* Autumn thought. *I'll take it to Mr. Walters' girlfriend. She'll know what to do.*

Autumn had wracked her brain, trying to figure out how she could get to Nikki. Travis kept tabs on Tony Walters and his girlfriend; while he was at work at the office supply store, she went through his notes. On the newest page of notes, he'd written that the girlfriend worked at the construction office now, but had gone back to her old job at the florist shop on the weekends. She didn't know what their weekend hours were, but she decided eleven in the morning would be a pretty safe bet.

She thought for a few minutes, then decided she'd call to make sure. She dialed the number and waited, then heard a woman's voice say, "Good morning! The Passionate Pansy. How can I help you?"

"Hi. Is Nikki there?" Autumn was trying to figure out what she was going to say if Nikki was there and especially if she was the one answering the phone.

"No, I'm sorry. She only works on Saturdays. Can I help you with something?" the woman asked.

"Oh, no thanks. She called me about something she wanted to buy from me, so I'll call her back another time. Thank you." Autumn hung up – fast. *Whew, that was scary,* she thought. *So Saturday it is. Now I've got to work up some courage.*

"Hi Dad!" Clayton turned to Nikki, smiled, and said, "This is pretty cool!" Turning to look back at the computer screen, he told Tony, "I wanted to show you this order, Dad. Something looks wrong, but I'm not sure what it is. Can you look at it for me?"

"Sure. Send it over and I'll see what's up with it. In the meantime, can you check with the site supervisor over at the university site, see why they haven't gotten the framing done for those front windows for the library building? That should've been done several days ago."

"Okay." Clayton was beaming. "I'm really glad you're back, well, sort of back. You know what I mean," he laughed.

"I'm glad to be back too. Thanks for all your hard work, son. You did a really good job while I was gone. You do a really good job all the time. It's going to pay off pretty soon."

"What do you mean by that?" Clayton asked, one eyebrow cocked in question.

"Oh, nothing. So I'll see you guys this weekend? Bring Stringer and Ella Jane over? Please?" he whined.

Clayton grinned. "Yes, I'll bring your little playmate over, Dad. He's driving us crazy wanting to see you too."

"Ah, that's my boy!" Tony crowed like a proud grandpa. "How's the adoption thing going?"

"Going. I think it's going to go through soon. Plus they're working on getting Ella Jane's mom to sign over parental rights. And since she's the only living relative who has any contact, if she'll do that, we can go straight to adoption."

"Clayton, I want you to know," Tony said, his eyes reddening, "that you're turning out to be a great dad. I'm really proud of you."

"Thanks, but it helps that I had the absolute best teacher in the world." Clayton was getting a little misty-eyed himself. "I just love them the way you've always loved us. That way, I can't go wrong,"

Chapter Forty-Three

Thank god she decided to close this place next Friday. I don't think I could work next Saturday – this has just been too much, Nikki thought. When she'd promised to help Marla out, Tony hadn't been home and she was looking for something, anything, to help her get through the weekend. Now he was back and she was busier than ever. This was just one more drain on her mental and physical resources.

She got out the cash box and turned on the OPEN sign, hoping it would be a slow morning. Through the front window she could see the familiar sedan across the street; looked like it was Laura this morning. If she waved, Laura probably wouldn't wave back. Even though Nikki felt she'd made some progress, the pretty brunette still had the personality of a twice-dead zombie.

Nikki took several phone orders for poinsettias and miniature Christmas trees, and one order for a dozen red roses for someone whose birthday was, bless their heart, on Christmas Eve. After watering everything, she swept up some dropped leaves and cleaned the customer restroom. Then she went to the workroom and cleaned out the refrigerator. A lady came in to see if they had any paper-white narcissus, but they were completely out. *Oh, god, this morning is going so slow,* Nikki thought. She was still so tired; maybe she could take a nap in the afternoon while Tony watched a game on TV. As she dusted she daydreamed, thinking about lying on the sofa with her head in his lap as he twisted his fingers into her hair while he watched the game.

At five after eleven, a young woman walked by the glass, looked in, and went on past. In a few seconds, she came back and walked in. Nikki greeted her with, "Good morning! Can I help you with anything?"

"Um, I hope so. Could I borrow your phone? My car won't start. My phone's battery ran down and I need to call my brother to pick me up," the young woman explained.

"Sure!" Nikki handed her the shop's cordless phone, but she shook her head.

"Oh, he has a cell with a long-distance number. I wouldn't want to do that. Do you have a cell phone?"

"Well, yeah." Nikki fished her phone out of her purse. She never let anyone use her phone, but this girl looked scared. "Here you go." She handed over her phone.

Nikki watched as the girl dialed a number, then waited and hit END. "Straight to voicemail, and his inbox is full. I can't even leave him a message. Oh, well," the girl sighed, "guess I'll start walking."

"Can I call you a cab?" Nikki asked.

"No, thanks, I'll be fine. Thank you."

"You're welcome. Hope your day gets better, hon."

The girl had only been gone a few minutes when Nikki's phone rang. She looked at the screen; an unfamiliar number. *Must be the brother calling back,* she thought, expecting to tell the stranger what his sister had wanted. Instead, before she could say "hello," a woman's voice said, "Nikki?" Nikki recognized the voice – it was the girl who'd been in the shop just minutes before. How did she know Nikki's name?

"Yes, this is Nikki?" What was going on? The girl had said her phone was dead, but apparently she'd called it from Nikki's phone to get Nikki's number.

"I have something to prove Mr. Walters is innocent. I'd like to give it to you, but I'm scared to do it there; too much glass and too much of a chance of somebody walking in. You'll have to meet me somewhere. Please, god, don't bring anybody with you."

The room seemed to tilt as Nikki tried to think. "You tell me where and when and I'll meet you." She knew it was crazy and dangerous, but she had to try. What if the girl had something that really would help? That was a chance Nikki couldn't pass up.

"Now. I'll text you the address. But you have to come alone."

"I will – I promise. I'll leave now. Text the address to me and I'll be right there."

"Okay. I just want to help, you know?"

"Yes, I understand, hon. I'm on my way," she assured the girl, already pulling the cash drawer.

Nikki hit END, then stopped for a minute. Laura was sitting in the car across the street, but she couldn't know what was going on. Nikki locked the door but didn't turn off the OPEN sign. She grabbed her purse and dashed out the back door as the text notification on her phone chimed with the address. Looking at the location, she knew by the general area it would take about twenty minutes to get there; hopefully, Laura wouldn't notice she was gone until she was already there.

She programmed the address into her navigation system and took off. The Yukon was parked far enough down the block that Laura hadn't noticed her leaving, and Nikki took a deep breath. What she was doing was risky, but it had to be done. If there was a chance someone had something to help Tony, she had to find out.

The longer she drove, the seedier the area looked, until she was genuinely frightened. An abandoned café was at the address the girl had given her, and Nikki circled around to park on the opposite side of the street. The entire block looked dilapidated and grimy, full of nothing but empty industrial-type buildings, and the windows on the old café building were so dirty that she couldn't see inside. But when she tried the door, she found it unlocked, and she opened it as quietly as possible and slipped inside.

"Hello?" Nikki called out in little more than a whisper.

"In here," the girl's now-familiar voice called back.

Nikki walked through the front of what had apparently been the dining area, past several banks of tables, and found the girl sitting in a more private area to the rear of the counter where the cash register had been. "You got here really quick," the girl said, motioning Nikki toward the chair opposite her. Nikki sat down at the table and pulled herself up, only to stick her hand in some gum under the table's edge; even though it was probably fifteen years old, it was still sticky, and Nikki couldn't help but think how gross people could be. The girl looked her over, then craned her neck to look out the dirty front window. "Anybody with you?"

"No. You said come alone, so I did," Nikki assured her.

"Good. You'll find everything you need to help your boyfriend on here. Travis said to not give this to you; he'll kill me if he finds out I've given it to you. But I couldn't stand to see Mr. Walters go to jail for something he didn't do. I remember him, and he's a very nice man." From her jeans pocket she produced a small object she handed to Nikki, and Nikki looked at it in her palm – a flash drive. It was tiny, less than half the size of a regular pack of gum, and half as thick too. Nikki was struck by the marvel of technology, how something so small could keep Tony from spending the rest of his life in prison, or worse. Just as she started to slip it into her own pocket, a voice rang out from the hallway that came from the back of the building.

"Autumn, you bitch, what have you done?"

The girl's face blanched and Nikki's pulse doubled just seeing the fear there. "Travis, please . . ."

"You know, I hate to do this, but you've got it coming," the young man growled and pulled a gun from his waistband. He had a weird look in his eyes, his dark hair was wild and unkempt, and his appearance was just generally dirty and disheveled. "You were a crappy girlfriend anyway."

"Travis, no, I . . ." He pulled the trigger and, to Nikki's horror, the projectile went straight into the girl's forehead between her eyes and she dropped like a stone.

It took Laura about five minutes to realize something was amiss; she couldn't see any movement in the shop, so she crossed the street and tried the door. It was locked. She looked behind her at the other side of the street; Nikki's Yukon was gone.

Laura picked up her two-way radio and pressed the button. "Wendy," she said to the tech working in the security company's office that day, "does Nikki have one of the Walters key fobs for the Yukon with her?"

"Yep," Wendy replied. "Steve made sure Mr. Walters gave her one. They have one for every vehicle they own. Need a location?"

"Yes, please." Laura was fuming. She didn't even know which direction she needed to go. Damn that hard-headed blond!

"Straight toward downtown and west. Pulling it up and sending it to your device now," Wendy told her.

Laura followed the directions to find Nikki, and Wendy let her know when the Yukon became stationary. She barely knew the area, and was surprised to find it got more and more desolate as she drove. She pulled up across the street and in front of the building next door to the location showing on her device; sure enough, there was the white Yukon. Laura pulled out the rifle scope she kept in her gadget bag instead of binoculars; no infrareds or night-visions would work because even glass has a heat signature, and she'd found that rifle scopes were very clear, small, and easy to use. Not much chance of finding the wrong location, though. There was no one in these abandoned buildings except for the one right in front of her. Through the scope, she could make out two people, and they appeared to be sitting.

Then, from out of nowhere, she saw a third person, and saw the third figure raise an arm; that hand had to be holding a gun. Before she could process the whole scene, she heard a "pop" and one of the figures at the table fell to the floor. She hit the button on her two-way radio and yelled, "Get me some backup here – whoever you can find – and do it fast. And we're probably going to need a bus," she added, thinking someone would wind up needing an ambulance before this played out. As she opened the door of the sedan, she heard a gunshot. She dropped the radio and leaped out of the car.

When Autumn hit the floor, Nikki looked down and saw her face, the vacant eyes, and her mind went into hyperdrive. She looked back up at the young man. "What have you done?" she shrieked.

"Give me whatever Autumn gave you," he ordered, pointing the gun at her, "and I won't kill you."

"She didn't give me anything – she just wanted to talk to me! You didn't give her a chance to do that, now did you? You go to hell!" Nikki screamed, and he fired.

Nikki tried to drop to the floor fast, but she felt a sharp pain in the left side of her chest and fell backward. When she hit the floor, taking the table with her, it felt like all of the air had escaped her body and she couldn't catch her breath. She lay on the floor, gasping, and then, without warning, there was a sound like the whole world exploding around her.

Laura had a decision to make, so she pointed her weapon at the upper right corner of the huge window and fired. If she'd guessed right, it was safety glass, and she wasn't disappointed. It exploded with a sound like a cannon blast and fell away, pebble-like pieces dropping in piles. The young man with the gun turned toward her and fired, and she leaned around the edge of the window opening and returned fire. He fired twice more, and Laura felt a searing pain in her left shoulder.

It was now or never, and Laura moved from her sheltered location and started firing. She couldn't tell if she'd hit him, but the man returned fire, and Laura felt a burning, knife-like sensation in her lower left abdomen. She tried to fire again, but she felt herself sinking, and he took two more shots, hitting her with both. Just as she hit the ground, she heard a woman's voice shout something.

Nikki heard the gunfire and knew someone was firing from outside the building toward Travis. She also knew when he finished firing at the person outside, he'd turn back to her and finish her off, so she did the only thing she could think of; she pulled her Walther three-eighty out of the back of her waistband, flipped the safety off, took aim, then yelled, "Travis!"

When Travis stopped firing and turned toward her, Nikki pulled the trigger. The look on his face was pure disbelief, and he pointed his weapon toward her, but she pulled the trigger on the small semi-automatic twice more, and he fell. She wondered if she'd wounded him enough to keep him down, and she tried to sit up, but the pain was too much and she couldn't breathe.

Fighting unconsciousness, Nikki tried to think. Where was her phone? Who had been outside? Then she heard shouting; male voices. Someone yelled, "See to Laura; I'm going in." Nikki heard movement and footsteps getting progressively closer. The voice outside said, "She's alive, but she's in pretty bad shape. I've got to apply pressure to this wound or she'll bleed out. Where's Nikki?" The first voice answered, "I don't know. Nikki?" Then she could tell there was movement right beside her, and a voice cried out, "Nikki! Oh my god! Where are you hit?"

Nikki forced her eyes open and looked up – a headful of curly blond hair and bright blue eyes. Peyton. "I. Don't. Know. Peyton. Please. Help. Me. I. Can't. Breathe."

"José, I found her; sucking chest wound." Nikki heard the static of a radio. "Wendy! Laura and Nikki both are seriously wounded. There's a dead girl here and the gunman is wounded, and I don't think he'll make it. Where the hell is that bus?"

"ETA of two minutes, Peyton; got two in route. Hang in there," a female voice replied, and in seconds Nikki could hear a siren.

"Nik, hang on, please! They're coming," Peyton pleaded, and she searched his face, looking for reassurance. There were things she needed to tell him, but she couldn't get enough breath to say anything. "Don't try to talk. They'll be here in a minute and we'll get you some help. You'll be okay," he repeated, his hand pressing on her ribcage.

Nikki felt cold, and it started to get dark around her, a buzzing sound setting up in her ears. She tried to make a sound and kept moving her mouth, making the shape of the word even if she couldn't get her voice to work.

"I'm sorry, Nik. I don't understand. Just try to stay calm – the EMTs are right down the block." He watched her continue to mouth something. "What, hon?" he asked and put his ear to her lips.

Nikki tried one last time: "Gum." Then everything got fuzzy, and she was out.

"Hey, baby, where've you been? I made us . . ." Tony rounded the corner coming out of the kitchen, only to find Steve and a pale, shaken Clayton standing in the foyer. "What the . . ."

"Tony, you need to sit down." Steve was very matter-of-fact, but he had a very odd look on his face, and even the air around him felt crackly and strange. Clayton's face was ashen.

"What's going on? I thought you were Nikki coming in from . . ."

"Sit down, Dad," Clayton ordered. "Now."

Tony felt a chill come over him. "What's going on? Where's Nikki?" He sat down in the chair in the foyer. "What?" he practically screamed.

"Dad, Nikki's at the hospital. She's been shot," Clayton stammered, his face contorted in pain.

Tony sat for a minute, unable to sort through those simple words. How had that happened? She was at the shop; Laura was watching her. What they were saying, that couldn't be right. "Are you sure it's Nikki?" He didn't want to believe it.

Steve nodded. "Tony, it's Nikki. She's been shot, and it's not good. Laura's in worse shape. There's a dead girl and a dying gunman. The cops are still trying to sort everything out. But the doctors are working on Nikki now; she'll be in surgery in a few minutes."

Tony jumped up from the chair. "I've got to go. I've got to get to the hospital. Nikki needs me, and I need to be there with her."

Steve shook his head. "Vic and Bart are on their way, and Freddie's coming. Clayton's going back to the hospital. You're under home incarceration; you have to stay here."

"Like hell! I'm going to the hospital!" As Tony ran to the bedroom he heard the doorbell ring. When he came back out with his shoes, Bryson Hawkins was standing in the foyer. "Bryson, goddamn it, I'm going to the hospital! Get this thing off me!" he yelled, pointing at the monitor.

"Tony, you know I can't do that. If I do . . ."

"Look, it's like this." Tony put his hands on his hips. "You either take it off me, or I'm cutting it off and heading out this door. That's the bottom line. Help me or get the hell out of my way, because regardless what anybody says, I'm going to that hospital. Now." He set his jaw, and Bryson could tell he had every intention of cutting the monitor off his ankle. Short of shooting him, he'd be unstoppable.

"Aw, hell, I knew . . . okay, okay, I'll take it off and I'll take you to the hospital. Man, I'll lose my job over this," Bryson moaned, pulling the specialty tool for the ankle monitor's lock out of his pocket and bending down to grasp it and take it off. "But you listen to me and listen good; you're my responsibility. You stay with me. You give me any trouble, I'll take you straight to the jail myself. Understand?"

"Completely," Tony agreed, rubbing his ankle before he put his shoes on. "I won't give you any trouble. Just get me there, please. I have to be with her."

"Come on." Bryson opened the front door and pointed at his car. "I'll use the lights and siren; we'll be there in a few minutes."

"Wilkes family?" A doctor in bloody green scrubs stood in the doorway of the waiting room, looking around.

Tony rose. "I'm her fiancé. How is she?"

"We think she'll be fine. The bullet grazed a rib and went through her lung, then lodged in the inside of a rear rib. We got the bullet out, and she'll most likely be okay. She's lost a lot of blood, and we intubated her to help her breathe because her lung collapsed and the pain will be so bad she'd have problems breathing otherwise. It's just going to take some time, and she's not out of the woods yet, but I think she'll make a full recovery."

"Can I see her?" Tony reddened and filled with tears.

"She's in recovery now, and she'll probably be there for another hour or two. One of the nurses will come and get you when you can go back. But you've got time to take a nap or get something to eat if you want. I've got to get back, but don't hesitate to ask if you have any questions."

Tony extended his hand, and the doctor shook it. "Thanks for saving her, for taking care of her."

"You're welcome. Take a deep breath – if everything goes as it should, she's going to be fine."

"And Laura? How is she?" Tony was afraid of the answer.

"There's a team still working on her. It doesn't look too good right now, but you never know."

"Thanks. Please ask somebody back there to keep us updated on her too."

"Will do," the doctor promised, waving as he hurried back into the surgical area.

After the doctor had gone, Bart and Freddie tried everything they could, but Tony wouldn't leave the waiting room to eat, even though Vic promised to stay right there and wait in his place. Annabeth and Katie had come to sit with him too, then offered to go to Clayton and Brittany's to stay with her and the kids and fill her in on Nikki's condition. Tony couldn't sit still; he stood and paced, then sat, then stood and paced again, up and down, over and over.

"Dad, you're making the rest of us nervous," Clayton told him, but Tony didn't respond. His mind was churning out of control, and he was terrified, terrified of losing her, not to mention trying to figure out what had happened, mostly why she had been where she was and what she was doing there. The only person who could answer those questions was lying in a recovery room with a tube down her throat, and she wouldn't be talking anytime soon.

When Tony noticed that Bryson sat quietly in the corner, having to be there but looking as though he felt very out of place, Tony walked across the room and sat down beside him. "Thank you for sticking your neck out and bringing me here. You didn't have to do it, but you did anyway, and I'm grateful," Tony told him. Bryson felt bad for him; he looked so sad and vulnerable. "And I know you're one of the people responsible for me sitting in that jail cell, but I know that you know I didn't do it."

"You're welcome, and you're right – I know you didn't. I just wish I knew who did so I could get the charges dropped once and for all," Bryson told Tony. "And I've learned something else; I thought Fox was trying to hang you. I thought he was a piece of shit, but I've gotten to know him, and he's really an okay guy. He just wants to see justice done."

"Justice won't be served by convicting me – I didn't do it." Tony sighed and closed his eyes, leaning back into the chair.

Minutes later, a nurse appeared in the waiting room doorway. "Wilkes?" Tony sat bolt upright, then practically sprinted across the room.

"Yeah, that's me. I'm her fiancé."

"You can come with me. She's going to a room, but it'll be a few minutes." They started down the hall together. "She's not conscious yet, but she'll be waking up soon. The doctor wanted you to be there when she wakes up to try to keep her from pulling at the breathing tube. They all do that when they first wake up."

They passed through the intensive care unit reception area until they reached the room in the back corner. Tony wasn't prepared for what he saw; tubes and wires snaked everywhere, and Nikki lay in the bed, pale as death, still and quiet, looking tiny and frail, a tube down her throat and a nasal cannula strapped around her face. Dropping into the chair beside her bed, Tony took her hand and stroked it. It was cool and limp, and he kissed the blue veins on the back of it, his tears dropping onto her skin. A hand touched his shoulder. "There are documented instances of comatose patients being able to hear people talking to them, so go on, talk to her," the nurse whispered to him. "It might help."

Tony swallowed hard; she might hear how upset he was, and he couldn't have that. It was important he sound positive to her. He took a minute to pull himself together, then whispered to her, "Nik, it's me, baby. Look, we've only got a little over a week until Christmas, and you promised me you'd marry me on Christmas day. I don't want to get married in a hospital room, and I need help with planning it all. So you've got to get better, you hear me?" He waited, but there was no response, no indication she'd heard him, and his heart sank. She was still motionless and silent.

"Dad?" Tony turned to see Clayton standing in the doorway of the cubicle. "I have to go home to Brittany and the kids, but they told me I could come back for a few seconds. Is she okay?" He came to stand beside Tony and placed his hand gently on his dad's shoulder.

"They say she will be, son. They told me to talk to her in case she could hear me. Say something to her before you leave."

Clayton very gingerly approached the hospital bed. He leaned over and kissed Nikki's forehead, then leaned down to her ear. "I love you, Mom. You have to get better, especially for Dad – he's lost without you. I'll see you soon." He turned, hugged Tony, and his face clouded up.

"It'll be okay. She won't leave us this soon. We need her too much." Tony patted his son's back, and Clayton spun and grabbed his dad, hugging him tight. "Go home to your wife and kids," Tony told him, hugging him back. "I'll call if there's any change."

Clayton was too overcome with emotion to speak, so he hugged Tony again and left. Sitting alone with Nikki in the tiny room, Tony thought about all of the fun he and Nikki had during the summer and fall, and all the long, sweet nights they'd spent together, whispering and laughing, making love until they were so spent they could barely move, then falling asleep in each other's arms. And that night in Gatlinburg – thinking about it made him smile. That couldn't end; it just couldn't. He'd waited so long to find her. A hand on his shoulder brought him back to the present, and he turned to see Vic standing behind him.

The big guy looked pale and frightened. "God, that personality of hers makes her seem larger than life, but she looks so little in that bed," Vic whispered, sniffing hard.

"I know, bud. I'm scared," Tony admitted, his voice shaky. He would never dare say that to anyone but Vic.

"Don't mind telling you, I am too." Vic squeezed Tony's shoulder. "Hey, Laura's here somewhere. Do you know what's going on with her?"

"I have no idea. There was no one in the waiting room for her. Might want to check that out."

"Think I will." Vic turned to the door. "I'll be back in a bit."

Tony rested his forehead on the rail on Nikki's bed. If she didn't make it, what would he do? He felt something on his head and looked up.

Nikki's hand rested in his hair, and he took it in his hands and kissed it. Her eyes fluttered, then stayed partially open.

"She's awake!" he yelled to anyone who could hear him. "She's waking up!" He pressed the call button on the bed and a nurse came rushing in. "Look! Her eyes are open!" he burst out, too excited to contain his joy just from seeing the tiny slits between her lids.

"Well, good for her! Hey, honey, know where you are?" the nurse asked Nikki.

Nikki tried to think, but her brain was fuzzy. She remembered the dead girl and the guy with the gun. And where was she? Then she blinked and focused, and all she could see was Tony's face. She felt like she was choking, but she kept looking at him, trying to make sure he was real.

"Hey, baby! It's me! How do you feel? Clayton was here. Vic's here, and Bart and Freddie are down in the waiting room. Steve and José are helping the police, and then they'll be here too. Peyton came in with you, and I'm pretty sure he's been here the whole time." She made a face, and he added, "I don't know where Laura is; she's here somewhere. Vic went to check."

"Can you tell me anything about her condition?"

"Are you a relative?" the large nurse asked Vic.

"No. Just a friend."

"Then no, I can't tell you anything."

"Where are her people?" Vic asked.

"What people? No one's been here for her," the nurse told him as she bent to monitor some drains. *No one's been here?*, Vic thought. Before he could ask anything else, the nurse asked, "So how well do you know her?"

Vic thought for a minute, then chuckled, "About as well as anybody, I suppose." No one really knew Laura. He wasn't even sure how much Steve knew about her.

The nurse didn't catch his sarcasm; she thought he was being serious. "So how 'bout those scars? Horrible, huh?" she asked.

Vic decided to play along; maybe he'd learn something about Laura. "You mean the ones on her arms?" he asked, making something up.

"No – the ones all over her chest. They're horrible, aren't they?" The nurse shuddered. "Wonder how that happened."

"I believe she said it was a car accident," Vic bluffed, trying to bait the nurse into saying something else.

"Wow. I've never seen accident scars like those. They're crazy." She shook her head and made a face. "Call us if she wakes up while you're here," the nurse added, leaving the room.

Vic looked at the pretty brunette lying so still in the hospital bed. Scars all over her chest? He wondered why she never talked about what had happened. How bad could they be? Hopefully she would be okay so he could ask her someday. Maybe that was why she was such a loner; something horrible had happened to her, and she wouldn't open up.

If Laura were awake, she'd jerk her hand away, but she was unconscious, so Vic could hold it and there wasn't a damn thing she could do about it. He took it in his, and marveled at its warmth and softness. It was tiny compared to the hugeness of his hand, and he held it for at least ten minutes, hoping she'd wake up. When she didn't, he stood, leaned over her, and kissed her on the forehead before he left. "Bye, sleeping beauty," he whispered to her. "I'll be back later."

"When will you be taking the tube out?" Bryson asked the nurse.

"Probably in a couple of days if she does well," she replied.

"I really want to ask her some questions, but she can't answer." He stopped and looked down into Nikki's face. "Nikki, be thinking what you'd like to tell me. I know you saw everything. And I know you were the one who shot the shooter. You were really brave, and you're lucky to be alive. You saved yourself, and you probably saved Laura's life too."

Nikki's eyes went wide, and she sounded like she was choking, even with the tube in. "Calm down, baby; you've got to stay still so you'll heal," she heard Tony say. But instead of calming, Nikki looked like she was in a panic. She made a gesture Tony couldn't understand; she pinched together the first two fingers and the thumb of her right hand and pounded them into the palm of her left, rubbing them back and forth.

"We don't understand, Nikki," Bryson said.

"Honey, calm down. We don't understand. You'll be able to talk in a couple of days," Tony kept telling her. But Nikki got more agitated and kept making the gesture. "Please, baby! We don't know what that means." Tony turned to Steve and Peyton, who were standing in the doorway. "Did you guys find anything in her things? Or anything missing?"

Steve shook his head. "No, nothing. All she had were her keys. She'd left her purse in the Yukon."

Nikki kept frantically making the gesture, and they all looked at each other, bewildered. Clayton walked up to the doorway and asked, "What's going on? Why's she so worked up?"

Tony pointed at her gestures. "She's doing this and we don't know what it means."

Clayton took one glance, shot them a look, and said, "Seriously, guys?" They shook their heads. "Oh, good god, that's easy." He left the doorway, then returned in less than a minute with a note pad and a pencil. "She's trying to tell you she has something to write down. Here, Mom." He put the pencil in her right hand and the notepad in her left. "Write away."

Nikki grew visibly calmer, then held the notepad up and tried to make the pencil work. The pain in her chest made it hard to move her left arm, but she was determined. After a couple of false starts, she scribbled something and waved the pad toward Tony. When he took it and looked at it, cryptically scrawled on the pad was one word: GUM.

"What is it?" Steve asked.

"It says 'GUM,'" Tony said, puzzled.

"Hey, she whispered that to me at the scene before she lost consciousness!" Peyton told the group. "I have no idea what it means though."

Nikki waved a hand, and Tony handed the pad back to her. She tried to focus her eyes again and scribbled something else, then handed it back.

"TABLE," Tony read. "I don't get it, honey. I'm sorry." Nikki grew agitated again and motioned for the pad, so Tony handed it back. She started scribbling again, then waved it at him. "FLASH." He stared at the pad, trying to make some sense of it. "'GUM, TABLE, FLASH.'" He shook his head. "Baby, it's just going to have to wait until you can talk. It'll only be a couple of days."

At that, Nikki got really worked up and started pulling at the tube; Tony jumped up and grabbed her hands and tried to hold them, and Clayton darted to the nurses' station to get someone to come and sedate her so she'd be still and quiet.

Suddenly, Bryson yelled, "Wait! I get it!" Nikki fell perfectly still, and Tony noticed there were tears running from the corners of her eyes. Bryson stood and walked to the bed so he could look down into her face. "Nikki, look at me. Gum, table, flash. When you say flash, do you mean a flash drive?" Nikki nodded vigorously. "There were tables at the scene. Was there gum under one of the tables?" Nikki was nodding even more vigorously.

Everyone looked lost except Bryson. Then he turned and looked at Steve. "McCoy, I need you to come with me. We're going back to the scene." Bryson looked back down into Nikki's face, and he saw relief wash across it. "We're going to find it, you hear me, hon? It's going to be okay." He looked at everyone else. "That girl gave her a flash drive, and she stuck it in some gum under a table to keep it safe. Our job now is to find it."

"See anything?" Bryson asked Steve as they looked around the scene.

"No, looks like the techs picked it clean." Steve looked at the underside of every table as they went along. Bryson was looking too.

"Where exactly were they?" Bryson asked Steve.

"Back here," Steve told him from behind the old counter. "Wait!" He pushed a table over and pointed, and Bryson walked over to look. In a wad of gum on the underside of the table was a perfect impression of a small, rectangular object. "It was stuck here. But it's not here now. Think the techs found it?"

"Not a chance or we would've heard. It's here somewhere . . ." Bryson said, dropping to his knees.

The two men looked for several minutes, then Steve pulled out a small flashlight and shined it under the edge of the old counter. Bryson heard Steve say, "Ah, come to papa!" as he reached under the edge of the counter and pulled out a small royal blue and black flash drive. "Let's take this back to the office and look at it." Steve held it up like a prize.

"Office?" Bryson shook his head. "Hell with that! I've got my laptop in my car – let's look at it right now!"

"Who the hell is that?" Bryson asked as they watched the video for the tenth time. They stopped it every time, staring at the little man running toward the front of the truck.

"I don't know who it is, but it sure as hell isn't Tony." Steve squinted at the screen, trying to make out the figure. "I think it's time to drop the charges against him, wouldn't you say?"

"Yep," Bryson nodded. "Now we've got to figure out who that little guy is. But it definitely isn't Tony."

Chapter Forty-Four

"Ready to go?" Tony asked Nikki as Clayton and Annabeth packed up the last of her things. She'd only been in the hospital for six days, but it seemed like a lot longer. Strange how things piled up so fast. She'd come into the hospital empty-handed, and it was taking three of them now to carry everything home.

"Yep, let's go" she whispered. Her throat was still sore from the breathing tube; she'd only had it out for a couple of days.

"I've got a surprise for you." He squatted down in front of her wheelchair to meet her eyes. "Steve, Bryson, and Detective Fox are coming to the house when we get home. We've got a lot to tell you, honey."

Nikki wondered what it could be. She could recall going to the old restaurant and a little bit about what had happened, but not much more. Tony had asked her what she remembered, but it was all so fuzzy. What she did remember clear as a bell was the girl with the bullet hole in her forehead; she'd been having nightmares about that.

On their way out, Tony wheeled her into another room. Nikki looked at the bed and smiled – Laura. She turned to look at Nikki and Tony as they came up to her bed.

"How are you, little lady?" Tony asked her, taking her hand.

"They tell me I'm doing pretty well, but I feel like I got stepped on by an elephant," Laura replied, her voice sagging with weakness. "How are you doing, Nikki? You look pretty good."

"Thanks," Nikki whispered hoarsely. "I don't remember a lot about what happened. But if the little I know is true, I need to apologize to you."

Laura smiled and pointed at Tony. "I still don't believe in love, but if I had a man like that one I would've done the exact same thing. And it's good you don't remember much. It was pretty awful, but you were a trooper. I hear you're also pretty much a hero, at least to this guy."

"We're going to talk about all of that when I get my baby home. And you," he said, pointing at Laura and pretending to be stern, "you take care of yourself. We'll be checking on you. If you need a place to stay when you get out, where somebody can help you, you're welcome to come and stay with us."

Laura gave him a tired smile. "Thanks, Tony. You know, I just might take you up on that."

"Good. You're always welcome. See you soon!" Tony called back as he wheeled Nikki out into the hall.

"Hero?" Nikki whispered.

"All in good time, sweetie, all in good time," he answered her as Clayton and Annabeth held the elevator car and they all got in.

"What floor?" a lady already in the car asked.

Tony laughed. "Home!" The lady smiled and pushed the button for the first floor.

Nikki's chest hurt. It felt like a hot poker had been thrust into it, but she fought the urge to swallow pain medication and decided to tough it out. She'd just managed to get comfortable in the den when the doorbell rang. Getting up took too much energy and she couldn't.

Tony caught a glimpse of her struggling to rise and barked, "Oh, no! You sit right there! Don't you dare try to get up!" He rocketed past through the den and to the front door.

There was a muddle of voices, and then Steve, Bryson, Detective Fox, Peyton, and José filed into the room. Steve, Peyton, and José hugged her; Bryson took her hand and asked how she was. Detective Fox merely nodded at her.

After everyone was seated, Tony said, "Well, let's get started. Baby, you went through a lot. Are there any questions you need answered? I know things are kind of spotty for you."

Nikki had a question that had worried her ever since she woke. "Are you going back to jail because you came to the hospital?" She started to tear up, afraid of the answer.

Tony reached over and took her hands. "Honey, I'm never going to jail again. Don't you know?" He looked at Steve and told him, "She doesn't know. No one told her." Steve smiled, and Tony turned back to Nikki. "Baby, the flash drive you got from that girl had video footage on it of

Dottie's killer, and it's not me, plain as the nose on your face. The charges against me have been dropped." He took her face in his hands. "You did that. You risked your life to get me out of this. There's nothing I could ever say or do to thank you. I owe you my life." He took her hands in his again and kissed them.

Nikki didn't know what to say, but she was thinking how everything she'd been through, all the pain and fear, had all been worth it – all of it. Then she thought of something else. "Hey, how did Laura know where I was?"

Tony reached into his pocket, pulled out his key ring, and dangled it in front of her face. It had a leather tag with a Walters Construction emblem on it. "You have one of these. Every person who has a Walters vehicle has one of these. Every one of our family members has one of these. All of Steve's people have one of these." From the look on her face, he could tell she still didn't understand. "They all have microchips in them, GPS locator chips."

"Oh! That's brilliant!" she whispered hoarsely. She thought for a few seconds, then shook her head. "I don't have any other questions."

"Well, we have some questions for you," Detective Fox said. "For starters, do you know the people you met with?"

"What do you mean?" Nikki asked; it seemed almost like Fox was accusing her of being in collusion with them. "No – I'd never met them before. Well, I'd met the girl a little while earlier in the day when she came into the shop."

"She came into the shop?" Steve asked. "What exactly happened?"

Nikki told them the whole story, how the girl had come in, the phone call, the location, the way the guy had shown up so quickly. She told them how the guy had shot the girl first, then her, and then there was gunfire from elsewhere; she now knew it had been Laura, trying to get to her before the man could shoot her again.

After she'd told the story, Bryson asked, "Did she tell you her name?"

"No. But he called her Autumn, and she called him Travis. And she said something about remembering Tony and that he was a very nice man." She glanced at Tony, and he shrugged and looked completely baffled. "That's all I know. What about the cars they were driving?"

Bryson shook his head. "We checked the plates, but no luck. They were stolen. Their fingerprints weren't in the system; neither was their DNA. But there was something odd." He turned to Tony. "His DNA was somewhat similar to yours. Had some of the same genetic markers."

Tony looked shocked. "I don't know anybody named Travis, much less have a relative by that name. Sure there's no mistake?"

"Nope. Here's his photo. Recognize him?" Fox handed Tony a photo. Tony shook his head.

Fox recapped the results of the investigation so far. "Okay, so we've got two dead people with no identification. We've got two people wounded. And we've got a video of a killer no one can recognize. We're no closer to solving this than we were before." He sighed. "But one thing is clear; these people were GoGreen. I think your vandalism and harassment are over."

"Good." Tony breathed a sigh of relief. "Please let Detective Ford know that. He may have some leads that would help you identify them."

While Tony was speaking, Clayton walked in. When he sat down on the other side of Tony, he looked down at the ottoman in front of them and saw the photos lying there. "Hey, why do you have a photo of Autumn Landers?" he asked. Then he looked sideways at the photo, and his eyes went wide. "Wait – is she dead?"

All heads jerked in his direction. "You know that girl?" Bryson asked.

"Yeah, of course I know her." They all stared at him. "Dad, remember when I dated that girl named Audrey? In high school?"

"Yes," Tony said slowly, trying to place her face, then suddenly he knew. "Hey, that's her little sister, isn't it?"

"Sure looks like her."

"Same name, too," Nikki said. "That's got to be her."

"Okay, I've got a lot of work to do," Fox told them, jotting notes in his little notebook.

"And the guy said she was a terrible girlfriend, so they were involved," Nikki told them. "Find people who knew her and you'll find out who he was." She thought for a second, then turned to Tony and added, "Wonder if he chose her because she knew something of you?"

"You mean maybe she's dead because she knew somebody from my family?" Tony looked so sad that Nikki wanted to wrap her arms around him and hug him. "I hope that's not the case. That would be horrible, but it's a possibility."

"So I guess if you can find his identity, you can find his residence. And if you find his residence, we'll get a lot of questions answered. Problem is, the biggest one still isn't answered," Steve said. "Who was the man in the video?"

They talked back and forth, but no one had any good ideas. Out of the blue, Nikki looked at Bryson and asked, "Can I see the video?"

"Oh, that's right, I forgot – you haven't seen it! Sure. Let me get my laptop." Bryson left the room and came back with his laptop case. In a minute, he had it out and ready. He put it on the ottoman and hit PLAY on the video utility, and the scene played out in front of Nikki.

She watched and when it was over, she played it again. Something about the video was bothering her, but she couldn't quite decide what. She looked at Tony and asked, "Hey, can this thing be played on the television somehow?"

"Sure." Tony reached into a drawer in the bookcase and took out an HDMI cable. He linked the laptop and the TV and set the appropriate input, then Bryson hit PLAY again.

Nikki watched carefully. When it ended, she asked Bryson to start it again. She saw the truck; someone got in, activity, then a car pulled up. It was shadowy and grainy, but she saw the man get out of the car and come toward the truck. Suddenly, she yelled as loud as her whispery voice would allow, "Stop! Stop the video!" Bryson hit the PAUSE function and Nikki leaned toward the screen.

It wasn't the man; it was the car. And it wasn't really the car; it was the dents in the car. Nikki stared at the image – where had she seen that car before?

"Oh, damn," she finally whispered. "I know where I've seen that car."

"You've seen it?" Tony asked. "Where?"

"Across the street."

"From here? It's one of our neighbors?"

"No, I don't think so," Nikki answered. "I saw it on Thanksgiving day. You sent me to the bedroom while you dealt with Dottie. I stood and looked out the window. That guy, he was sitting in that car across the street. I remember the dents. I thought he was waiting for somebody to come out of a house across the street." In a blinding flash, she understood. "But he wasn't waiting for anybody; he was watching Dottie. And he made it look like he was waiting for somebody in one of the houses, so you guys didn't pay any attention to him," she told Peyton, wanting him to know that the team wasn't at fault.

"So the guy who killed Dottie was watching her," Bryson said, deep in thought. "Hey, has anybody ever seen this Hector guy she said she was married to?"

Tony, Clayton, and Steve all shook their heads. "I'd lost count of her husbands," Tony said, "and I'm not even sure they were actually married.

Matter of fact, I don't even know his last name, just Hector."

"So we need to check marriage records, see if we can find one for her and a Hector. If she married him, when would it have been?" Fox asked.

"She came skulking around last, oh, September maybe? Asking me for money for a divorce from, uh, Clayton, what was that guy's name?"

"You mean Wally? Wally Benton?" Clayton asked.

"Yeah, that was him," Tony nodded. "She divorced him last fall, so this guy would've been after that."

"Okay, that gives us somewhere to start." Bryson watched Fox jot down the information. "Of course, if we find Hector and he's obviously not the guy in the video, we're back to square one. But at least we do know one very important thing." Bryson grinned.

"Yeah." A little smile crept onto Tony's face. "We might not know who killed Dottie, but we know who didn't, and that would be me."

"Let me see everyone off. You sit right here; don't move. If I come back in here and find you standing in the kitchen, I'm gonna be really pissed, hear me?" Tony admonished, and Nikki nodded back.

"Steve, I need to talk to you for a minute," Nikki heard Tony say as they were all walking out the front door. She sank into the sofa and closed her eyes, not realizing until the room was quiet exactly how exhausted she was. This wasn't sleepy tired; this was bone weary. It didn't matter to her that she was stuck on the sofa. She was just happy to be home, in this house, with Tony. And he wasn't going back to jail. He was staying with her forever. She smiled to herself.

"What are you smiling about?" Nikki opened her eyes to find Tony grinning at her from the doorway.

"I was thinking about how you're not leaving me. You get to stay here." The joy on her face made him sigh, and he joined her back on the sofa.

He put his arm around her and pulled her close, but she gasped in pain and he turned loose as he shrieked, "Oh, god, baby, I'm sorry!" He stroked her cheek. "You know, you should probably go to the bedroom and lie down. Come on, let's get you settled in. It's been an exhausting day for you." He helped her stand, then put his arm around her waist and walked her down the hallway to the bedroom.

It took a whole two minutes for her to fall asleep while Tony caressed her hair and face. She slept without moving for several hours until it was almost dark outside, waking to a delicious aroma. Trying to sit up, she found she was stronger than she'd been when she lay down, and she managed to get up to a sitting position on the side of the bed and put on her slippers before Tony opened the mostly-closed door and sat down on the side of the bed beside her. "Hi! Feeling better, beautiful girl?"

"Yeah." She was surprised to find her voice was stronger than it had been. "What's that delicious smell?"

Tony sat down on the side of the bed. "The kids are all here. Brittany is cooking. Stringer and Ella Jane are being very good; we explained to them that you weren't feeling very well. Stringer keeps telling Clayton he wants to see your bullet hole," Tony chuckled.

"Cute!" Nikki laughed. About that time, Vic walked in and sat down on the other side of the bed, then reached for her hand. He lifted it to his lips and kissed it, and she drew his back to her and kissed it too.

"They all wanted to come over and see you. Bart and Freddie both have called about you; Mark and Victoria, too. And Caroline called the other day and wanted to know if you could have company, so I think they're planning to come in early. Of course, that would be Caroline's idea, not Bennie's." Tony and Vic helped her to her feet and they walked down the hall toward the kitchen, one on either side of her, their arms wound around her waist.

"There you are!" Annabeth cried out and ran to hug her. Katie was right behind her, and it was hard to tell which of the girls was happier to see her.

"I'll hug you in a minute; I can't let this sauce burn!" Brittany called out, laughing. Tony passed Nikki off to Clayton, who kissed her on the cheek and helped her sit down on a bar stool at the island. Tony set a large glass of ice water in front of her, and she drank it in gulps; she hadn't realized how thirsty she was, and it helped to almost completely dissolve the soreness still in her throat.

Annabeth's face took on a serious look. "Soooo, we wanted to talk to you about Christmas."

"Oh my god!" Nikki screeched. "I completely forgot about Christmas!" She looked at Tony, her eyes filling with tears. "This is our first Christmas together, and there's no tree, there aren't any gifts, nothing! Oh, I'm so, so sorry!" She started to cry outright.

Tony looked horrified. "Baby, don't worry about any of that! Nobody cares. All we care about is that you're safe and getting well and we're all together. None of that other stuff matters." He turned her to him and wrapped his arms around her, and she buried her sobs in his chest.

"Mom, oh, god, no! That's not what we were talking about at all!" Annabeth dropped what she was doing and ran to Nikki, taking her hand. "No, no, we were talking about the wedding!"

It was Nikki's turn to look completely horrified. "Oh sweet lord, Tony, I promised you I'd marry you on Christmas Day, and it's not going to happen! I've screwed up everything!" She started crying even harder.

"Shhhhhh, baby, listen to Annabeth."

"Yeah, Mom, listen." Annabeth knelt in front of Nikki, put her hands on Nikki's knees, and looked up into her face. "I've taken care of everything. I've got flowers coming courtesy of Marla, and a cake, and something for you to wear. It's all taken care of." Annabeth stopped, then added, "If you still want to do it."

Nikki squeezed Annabeth's hand. "Of course I still want to do it." She tried to stifle her sobs. "I want to marry this man more than anything in the world."

"Then you will," Clayton announced. "Plus we have something else very exciting to do on Christmas Eve, and all you have to do is be strong enough to show up. So you'd better get some rest. You'll kick yourself later if you have to miss this!"

Chapter Forty-Five

Christmas Eve dawned bright. It was a cold Kentucky morning, but not unbearable. Frost was everywhere, on the roofs, on what was left of the grass, and birds smothered the bird feeder Nikki had put out earlier in the season. Tony had tried to keep it filled, and Nikki smiled at their chatter.

Tony helped her shower and dress, and she struggled with putting on her makeup. There was nothing wrong with the arm, but even though she'd been out of the hospital for four days, lifting her arm made her chest hurt so badly that it took her over an hour to finish up. It was worth it; when she walked out into the bedroom, he whistled long and low at her and crossed the room to pull her into his arms and kiss her.

"You're breathtaking, do you know that?" Tony whispered into her hair. "I want you so bad, girl, you have no idea."

"I want you too, but the doctor said no sex until I go back to see him," she whispered back. "I don't know how I'm going to stand it. We're going to have one very boring honeymoon," she pouted.

"Yeah, but at least we'll be together." He smiled down at her, and his handsome face made her heart skip a beat. Flitting through her mind was the knowledge of all she'd almost lost, and she was so relieved that she had to fight to keep from crying, but she didn't want to mess up her makeup – it had been too hard to put it on. "Now let's get going," Tony told her. "Being late is not an option. This is going to be a wonderful day for our family. I'm so excited!"

"Me too!" She managed to get her shoes on, and he walked her to the door.

The courthouse had Christmas decorations galore, big greenery wreaths with huge red bows adorning every door and window, and poinsettias in marble niches in the walls. Tony and Nikki entered the main doors and passed through security to meet Clayton, Brittany, and the children in the mezzanine area. Stringer was dressed up in a suit that fit him perfectly, and his tiny striped tie made Nikki smile. He ran to her, grabbed her around the knees, and asked, "Hey, can I see you buwwet hoe? Pweaze?"

Nikki laughed. "Not here, buddy, but maybe later, okay? Ella Jane, you look beautiful today!" Nikki cooed.

"Thank you. My dress is new," the little girl sing-songed as she twirled around and tapped about in her favorite black patent shoes. The time she'd spent with Clayton and Brittany had completely rejuvenated the child, and her once-brittle, shabby hair was lustrous and golden.

"You look like a princess!" Tony told her, and she blushed.

Annabeth and Katie rushed up to greet all of them. "Mom, you look gorgeous!" Annabeth said, kissing Nikki on the cheek.

"Thank you, sweetie! It was hard work." *And I'm exhausted from the effort,* Nikki wanted to tell them, but she just smiled.

Tony beamed. "It took her awhile, but it was absolutely worth it. She looks great, doesn't she?"

Brittany hugged her. "You look like you feel a lot better."

"I do. I feel so much stronger. I think a lot of it has to do with actually getting some sleep! No one sleeps in a hospital," Nikki laughed. "So what do we do now?"

"Well, we go up and check in with the judge's secretary, and then we wait to be called in." Clayton motioned to the group. "Come on. We'd better get up there."

They all made their way up to the second floor. Clayton checked in at the judge's office, and they all hung out in the hallway, Tony making sure Nikki was sitting. After what seemed like forever, the judge himself came to the door and called out, "Walters?"

"Yes sir. Ready?" Clayton asked, looking at Stringer.

"Weddy!" Stringer cried out, and they stepped through the doorway.

They found themselves in the judge's chambers. Before anything else could happen, Clayton asked the judge if they could get Nikki a chair, while she argued that it was okay and she didn't need one. But the judge seemed to be familiar with what had happened to her and found her a chair himself. *Uh-oh,* Nikki thought. *Did all of that wind up in the news?* She didn't know; she hadn't been watching the news, but she would have to remember to ask when they left.

"Clayton and Brittany Walters?" the judge asked when they were all settled in.

"Yes sir," they answered in unison.

"Stringer DeWayne Foster?" he then asked.

"Dass me!" Stringer cried out in his loudest voice. Everyone, even the judge, laughed.

"Well, it appears we are here today to adjudicate the adoption of Stringer DeWayne Foster by Clayton Lewis Walters and Brittany Ann Norton Walters. Over the years, I've learned that a lot of formality is nonsense on a day like this. Everyone involved wants it or they wouldn't be here, so let's cut the rhetoric and get down to it," the judge said. Nikki looked at his desk name plate: Judge Richard Thornton. He seemed like a very pleasant man.

Suddenly the door opened and a slight woman popped in. "Oh! I'm so sorry I'm late!"

"Ms. Beech. Glad you could join us." Judge Thornton invited her to take a seat. She had on a name tag that read "*Joanna Beech, Social Worker.*" "Now, as I was saying, I just have a few questions. Mr. and Mrs. Walters, are you prepared to care for the aforementioned child for the rest of his life as his parents, to take responsibility for his physical, educational, and emotional needs, and to love him as any parent would love their biological child?"

"Yes, we will," Clayton answered.

"And I see you have family here; will you encourage his bonding experience with extended family and friends?"

"Yes, your honor," Brittany answered.

"And to all of you," the judge said, directing his question to the rest of them, "will you join with this couple in ensuring this child has the best life they can possibly offer him, and enhance his life with your love and support?"

"Yes!" Annabeth and Katie answered in unison.

"Yes we will," Tony answered for the two of them, and Nikki nodded.

"Then I see no reason why I shouldn't sign the adoption order. I see there is a name change requested also. Young man," he said, turning to address Stringer directly, "come here for a minute." Stringer went straight to the judge and, to their astonishment, climbed up onto the austere man's lap. The judge looked a bit shocked at first, then smiled. "I see here you'd like to change your name. Is this your idea, or theirs?" he asked, pointing to Clayton and Brittany.

"Iz my idea, mistaw judge. I wanna change it," Stringer stated clearly.

"And what do you want your name to be?" the judge asked him.

"Iz gone be Tony!" Stringer practically shouted and grinned all over his face. Nikki heard a sound and turned to find Tony choking back tears.

"It says here you want your name to be Anthony Lewis Walters. So that would be where you got Tony?" he asked.

"No, dass whaw I got Tony!" Stringer exclaimed, pointing at Tony, who now had a tear rolling down his face. "He my gwampa." Nikki reached over and squeezed Tony's hand, and he smiled down at her. "And dass my neenee!" he shouted, pointing at Nikki. It was her turn to lose it, and she choked a sob and felt the waterworks start. "And dems my Zia Beffie and my Zia Katie," he said, pointing at the two young women. Annabeth and Katie were crying too, and Brittany's eyes turned red. Clayton kept clearing his throat; he was fighting back tears. Stringer, however, was unfazed. "I not gone be Tony. I gone be Widdow T. And dass gone be Big T," he told the group and pointed to Tony, who started to laugh.

"Well, that's probably the best rationale for a name change that I've ever heard," the judge said, starting to laugh. "And so, I'm going to sign this adoption petition. Young man, your name is now Anthony Lewis Walters, and Clayton and Brittany Walters are now your mom and dad."

"Well, fank you, mistaw judge! I needin' a mama and daddy. Now I Widdow T!" He grabbed the judge's face and kissed him right on the lips, then hopped off his lap and ran to Brittany, grabbing her around the legs and growling as he hugged her knees hard. The whole room erupted in laughter.

"I can honestly say I've never been through an adoption proceeding where I've been met with such enthusiasm," Judge Thornton grinned.

A small voice pierced the merriment. "Your honor, may I have a moment?" the tiny woman asked.

"Yes, Ms. Beech. Please, go right ahead," Judge Thornton seemed to already know what she was going to say.

"Thank you. I haven't had the pleasure of meeting the rest of you, just Clayton and Brittany," she said.

"And me!" Little T yelled. "And huw," he reminded her, pointing at Ella Jane.

"That's right, String . . . um, Anthony." He glared at her. "Little T." The little boy smiled. "But I have something everyone needs to hear." She took a deep breath. "Ella Jane's birth mother has relinquished her parental rights. If you still want to go through with her adoption and your attorney can get the paperwork drawn up, I see no reason why the adoption can't be finalized in the next two months."

There was an enormous amount of shrieking and squealing, mostly from

Annabeth, and even the judge said, "That's fantastic!"

"I get to be adopted! I get to be adopted!" Ella Jane was screaming, and Brittany grabbed her and hugged the little girl to her chest.

"Well, I have to say, this is the happiest thing I've gotten to be a part of in a long time. Mr. and Mrs. Walters, thanks for being here today and giving these children a loving home. Have a great Christmas!" Judge Thornton told them, shaking hands all around. He bent to shake Nikki's hand and whispered in her ear, "You feel better, okay? And have a great holiday season. I hope to see you again."

"Thank you – you too!" Nikki replied. *He hopes to see me again? What an odd thing for him to say*, she thought, then put it out of her mind while she watched her family enjoy the moment.

When they got to their vehicles, Little T said, "Hey, Neenee and Big T, guess what? Santa gone come tonight. Bwitty and Cway say he comin'." He turned to Brittany and Clayton and asked, "Hey, can I caw you Mama and Daddy now?"

Nikki had seen Clayton get teary several times, but for the first time since she'd known him, she saw the quiet, stoic young man she now saw as her son completely break down. Sobbing, he went down on one knee in front of the little boy and whispered, "Son, that would be the best Christmas present you could give us." Little T leaned into his arms and Clayton hugged him close. Then Clayton turned to Ella Jane and told her, "Sweetheart, you can call us Mama and Daddy too if you want."

"That would be awesome!" Ella Jane whispered.

Brittany wiped her own eyes and, taking Ella Jane's hand, said, "Let's go get some lunch, baby."

The kids scampered off to Brittany's new minivan, and she hit a button on her clicker to open the doors and let them get into their restraints. "See you at the restaurant?" she asked everyone else.

"We're right behind you," Tony called out, grabbing Nikki's hand and pulling her toward the Mercedes.

They hadn't gotten more than two blocks away from the courthouse when Tony turned to look at Nikki and saw she was sobbing. He pulled over and reached for her hand. "Baby, please tell me those are happy tears," he said, wiping one off her cheek.

She nodded silently, then sniffled. It took everything she had to pull herself together and get the words out. "I never thought I'd be anybody's grandmother. No one could've given me anything that would've made me happier than that little boy calling me Neenee."

"Yeah. And I'm Big T. I think it suits me, don't you?" he asked, grinning.

"It truly does, precious."

"So, Neenee, let's have a happy day with our grandchildren. I don't know about you, but this is going to be the best Christmas I've ever had." He kissed her hand and then said, in mock seriousness, "That is, if you're still going to marry me."

"Absolutely!"

"Good. Because I really didn't want to have to put you out of the car to let you walk back and think about it some more." He cut his eyes toward her, and it made her laugh. "And I would too!" he told her, laughing at the way she was laughing.

"Do you still want to marry me?" She looked up at him from under her lashes.

"More than anything in the world." Nikki could see that he was struggling to keep his composure.

"Then it'll be the best Christmas I've ever had too," she told him and watched a single tear roll down his cheek. "Tomorrow we'll be forever linked. And I can barely wait."

"Are we packing up to go to Shelbyville tonight?" Nikki asked on the way home from the restaurant.

"Yep. We need to be there tomorrow morning. It's going to be a very busy day."

"What are we going to do about Christmas gifts? You've been in jail, so you have a legitimate excuse."

"And you've been in the hospital. I'd say that's a legitimate excuse if I've ever heard one."

"But . . ."

Tony shook his head. "Baby, don't worry about it. That's just extraneous nonsense. We're together. Our kids are happy. As of today, we have a grandchild and another on the way, in a manner of speaking. And tomorrow every dream I've ever had is going to come true when you come down those stairs and say those vows to me."

"Oh, god!" Nikki whispered. "I don't have any vows written!"

"You'll have time to do that tonight. I know you; it'll be fine," Tony smiled and chucked her chin. "It's probably mine you need to be worried about!"

Nikki woke on Christmas morning to the sound of squealing and laughing. She pushed herself up into a sitting position and realized she was alone in the big bed. It took her a few minutes to go to the bathroom and get her robe on and, in that small amount of time, the squealing and laughing had gotten even louder.

She managed to get herself down the stairs of the big house to find wrapping paper everywhere and the little kids running wild. Little T had on some god-awful superhero outfit and was shooting a toy gun at Ella Jane, who was bouncing around in princess attire. Everyone was laughing and talking and barely noticed her until Tony looked up and yelled above the din, "Good morning, beautiful!"

"Hey, morning, Mom!" somebody shouted, and someone else yelled, "Hey, sleepyhead!"

Nikki couldn't believe her eyes. "Where did all these gifts come from?" she asked Tony as he helped her onto the sofa.

He just laughed. "Why, Santa, of course! What's wrong with you?"

"Seriously," she whispered into his ear. "Where did you get them all?"

"You won't believe it, but my mother did all of this," he whispered back. Then she noticed the tree; it was huge and covered in beautiful blue, lavender, and silver ornaments. "I think she did a good job, huh?"

"No, she did a great job! Where is she, by the way?"

He nodded toward the other room. "In the kitchen fixing everybody breakfast. That's her thing; she does this every year."

When Raffaella announced that the food was ready, everyone went into the kitchen, got a plate, and served themselves. Tony got Nikki a plate and filled it, then made her sit at the dining table to eat. Ella Jane wanted to sit beside her, and Little T worried at Tony until the big man let the little boy sit on his lap to eat his breakfast.

Nikki looked around the dining area. So much love. So much joy. All things she thought she'd never have. She looked at Tony, sitting patiently with Little T on his lap, trying to eat while the littlest family member asked questions and generally worried the snot out of him. She smiled. Her family; this was it, this was her life, her wonderful new life.

"Oh, Mom, we've got to get busy getting you ready!" Annabeth told Nikki abruptly.

"Annabeth, nothing fancy, please? Just dress me and point me in the right direction."

"Oh, no you don't! We're going to do your hair and nails, and I'll help with your makeup," Annabeth told her firmly. "You're going to look beautiful."

"Too late," Tony grinned, eating the last bite of his breakfast while Little T tried to snatch it. "She's already beautiful. You can't improve on perfection."

"How sweet!" Nikki gave him a peck on the cheek. "But really, more than makeup and all that stuff, I need a nap and a shower."

Katie busied herself at the sink and she ordered, "Then get on upstairs and nap. We'll be up in awhile." *Katie looks different,* Nikki thought, *but I'm not sure how.*

Tony helped her upstairs and, before she could get to sleep, Little T was there at her bedside. "Can I see you buwwet hoe now?"

"Yes, baby, come here." Nikki pulled up her pajama top to just under her left breast and untaped the dressing. "See, you can't really tell anything about it because they had to cut me open, so there's lots of stitches."

"Why dey cut you open?" There was a look of horror on his tiny face.

"To take out the bullet," Nikki told him and took his hand to reassure him that she was okay.

"Did it huwt you, Neenee?"

Nikki frowned. "Still hurts, baby."

"Oh, I sowwy. You and you boo-boo need a nap." He kissed her cheek, then trotted out of the room and down the stairs. Nikki couldn't help but laugh.

"Before you drift off, I've got something for you." Tony pulled a folded envelope out of his back pocket.

"My Christmas gift?"

"Christmas, wedding, you name it. I think you'll like it."

Nikki opened the envelope and took out the papers inside it. It took her a few seconds to understand what she was seeing. There was a date, April 24, and a bunch of other numbers, and then it hit her: Rome. Tony was taking her to Italy! "Oh my god!" she shrieked as much as her throat and lungs would allow. "We're going to Italy? We're going to Italy!" she yelled, hugging him and ignoring the pain in her chest.

"I thought April would be good. By then you should be back to one hundred percent. I didn't want to take you when you didn't feel well. We'll have a real honeymoon then!" Tony held her tight.

"Am I going to get to meet some of your relatives?"

"Sure! We're going to be staying near Vic's Nonna Moretti for a week, then Rome for a week, then on to my Cabrizzi relatives' home. I thought you'd like to sightsee in Rome, then actually do some Italian everyday life with them for a few weeks."

"I can't wait! Oh, this is so exciting! Thank you, honey!" Then her face fell. "I didn't get you anything."

"Yes you did — your smiling face. It's been awhile since we've had much to smile about, and I think it's time we did a lot of it, don't you?"

"This will be a day of nothing but smiles, sweetheart. I'm marrying the man of my dreams today," Nikki grinned, snuggling down in the bed. "Now let me take a nap so I feel like getting married!"

Vic stood at the top of the stairs, waiting. Everyone was waiting. All of the Walters brothers had gotten there in plenty of time with their wives in tow. Raffaella stood with Vic, and Annabeth came out the bedroom door. "Wait 'til you see. She's so beautiful!"

The bedroom door opened, and Katie held Nikki's hand until Nikki could get hold of the stair rail. Vic's heart nearly stopped. The gown Annabeth had brought to her was a pale blue satin, corseted in the back with hourglass straps and a sweetheart neckline. The skirt was pleated and fell from underneath the bustier-type bodice, and it dropped at a graceful angle in all directions. Nikki had fought and won; her hair was down, looking like it usually did except for the tiny blue and silver flowers Katie had pinned in it. Her nails were pale pink and her toenails matched in the peep-toe pumps the girls had bought. She had an enormous but very delicate woven silver neckpiece around her elegant neck, and the silver dangles that matched it glittered as she descended the stairs. The only thing that looked unusual about her was her lipstick; it was a deep, dark red, and her face looked like it was illuminated from within.

Vic swallowed hard. *Oh my god. I'm taking her down the stairs and into that room to marry my cousin.* He wondered if anyone could hear his heart breaking as she came toward him. *How do I come back from this?*

Raffaella was wearing a darker dress of the same shade, and when Nikki had joined them, she murmured, "My daughter, you are a vision. My son is a very lucky man."

"Oh, thank you, Mamma!" the younger woman whispered and kissed Raffaella on the cheek.

Vic held out his arm. "Ready?" She couldn't help thinking how breathtaking he looked in his black suit, black shirt, and black tie.

She beamed up at him. "One hundred and fifty percent!"

When the door to the great room opened, Tony took one look at Nikki and his knees went weak, his heart soaring right out of his chest. Even with a sling around her neck and her arm sticking out of it, she was still the most breathtakingly stunning thing he'd ever seen. And he wasn't deaf to the collective gasps around him; everyone was surprised to see her looking the way she did at that moment. They were used to a plain, utilitarian Nikki; this woman was anything but plain and utilitarian. Her hair was spun gold and she radiated a light that was all her own.

Nikki glided into the room on Vic's arm, with Raffaella at her elbow on the side of her injury, helping to keep her steady. They walked right up to Tony, who stood at the big French doors, Clayton and Annabeth at his side. She was glad Annabeth hadn't ordered her a bouquet, because it was taking every ounce of strength she had, with Vic's help, to make it to Tony, and she couldn't have held Vic's hand and a bouquet too with one good arm.

When she got within six feet of him, Tony could see the strain on her face, even though she was trying hard to mask it. When Vic handed her off, instead of taking her hand, Tony put an arm around Nikki's waist. "Sweetie, you okay?" he whispered to her.

She gave him a weak smile. "I am now. But I'm really tired."

"This will only take a few minutes," he assured her and turned to the official who would perform the ceremony. Nikki looked up to a pleasant surprise – it was Judge Thornton! No wonder he'd said he hoped to see her again.

The judge beamed. "Well, hello there, Neenee!" he whispered to her. "I'm getting to do all kinds of happy things for your family these days, huh?"

"You sure are! And we appreciate it too," Nikki whispered back.

Everyone settled in for the usual opening comments of the ceremony, and then the judge asked if anyone had any objection to their union. No one said anything, but it took everything Vic had to keep his mouth shut. *I walked her in here and gave her away,* he thought, a burning ache setting up in his chest. *What I'd give to be the one standing there with her. Do I say something? Should I tell her? Tell them all?* And just like that, the moment was gone and the judge went on with the ceremony, leaving Vic sitting beside Raffaella, his heart broken in two.

The judge droned on, had them repeat the usual, and then announced, "Tony and Nikki have written their own vows, and they'd like to share them with you now. Tony, you first."

Tony started to reach into his jacket pocket, but took a look at Nikki's face and then turned to the room. "You all know how difficult the last two weeks have been for us. I'm far more concerned about Nikki's wellbeing than our vows. So we'll keep them to read to each other later and move on with the ceremony, if that's okay with everyone." He looked down at Nikki, who smiled and nodded. "Your honor?" he turned, questioning.

"Under the circumstances, I think that's more than appropriate," Judge Thornton agreed. They exchanged rings, and the judge made the usual pronouncements, then said, "Please kiss each other as a sign of your commitment to your new life together." Tony grinned, then leaned down and placed a soft, warm kiss on Nikki's lips, and she felt herself falling into him while the room exploded in applause. When they parted, he looked down into her face and whispered, "We made it!"

"Yes we did! I knew we would – I had complete faith in you." She gave him a dreamy smile, her face glowing.

Then Judge Thornton said the magic words: "And now, ladies and gentlemen, I present to you Mr. and Mrs. Antonio Luigi Walters. May their life together be long and happy!"

"I wish she felt better. I'd sure like to have a dance with her right now," Tony told Vic, sipping on a scotch and soda. Vic was silent. The emotional pain he felt was so excruciating that he wasn't sure he could even make a sound. "You okay, cuz?"

"I think I'll go. Please tell the bride congratulations for me, would you?" Vic set his glass down on the table nearest him and headed for the door.

Tony followed, then stepped in front of him and stopped him with a hand on the doorknob. "Vic, you okay?" Vic didn't answer. Tony took a deep breath and said, "Vic, I know."

"Know what?" the big Italian asked, feigning innocence.

"I know," Tony repeated with a look that pierced right through him. Vic's shoulders fell. "I'm not going to apologize for loving her and marrying her, but I will apologize for the pain it's causing you. I'm so sorry." He looked so sad that Vic actually felt bad for him.

"That's just how it is, cuz. It's fine, really." Vic hugged Tony. "I'm happy for you both. You're obviously meant for each other. Just give me some time, okay?"

"Absolutely. I love you, buddy. You're one of the most important people in my life. Please don't let this ruin our relationship. And please don't leave."

"Ruin our relationship? Not a chance, bro," Vic sighed as he opened the door. "I love you too, and I'll never let that happen. But I don't think I can stay here one more minute."

"Antonio, your bride is beautiful," Raffaella told her middle son.

Tony's smile was a mile wide. "Thank you, Mamma. She is, isn't she?"

"Yes. Now, my son, I have asked all of your brothers to be here tomorrow at two o'clock. I hope this is fine with you. Clayton and Vic too," Raffaella said flatly.

"Well, yeah, that's fine, but for what?"

"We need to have a talk. There is something I think you all should know."

Something in her voice and face made him panic just a little. "Mamma, are you sick?"

"No, no, my son, nothing like that. Just something you need to know, that is all," she said, stepping away.

That's odd, Tony thought. Then Bart walked up and asked him something, and he completely forgot about what Raffaella had said.

"Thank you for coming, everyone. You made our day special. And I wanted all of you to know: In April I'm taking Nikki to Italy for our honeymoon!" There were shouts of excitement all over the room, and everyone started buzzing about the trip.

Before they could all get quiet, another smaller, decidedly feminine voice piped up. "Everybody!" Annabeth shouted. "We have an announcement to make too!"

Tony looked at Nikki, confused, but in that moment, Nikki knew what Annabeth's announcement was. "Katie is pregnant – we've having a baby!" Katie stood beside her, her face aglow.

Tony grabbed Nikki and squeezed her tight, only to hear her squeal and have him cry out, "Oh my god, baby, I'm sorry! Are you okay?"

"Yeah, yeah, I'm good! You just got a little carried away! But I'm so excited!" she replied breathlessly.

When they'd all had a few moments to digest the news, Annabeth told the group, "We didn't want to steal you guys' thunder, but we did want to announce it while everybody was here. And we've got a couple of people to thank. First of all, Mom," she laughed, turning both thumbs up, "you were right – it worked!" Nikki squealed and laughed out loud while everyone but the seven who'd been involved in that conversation looked extremely confused. "Second, my loving, generous, and very handsome brother who contributed to the cause. This baby will be beautiful *and* a Walters because of you, Clayton. We love you – you and Brittany! Thanks for talking him into it, Brit – we owe you!" Clayton's cheeks burned bright pink.

"And I bet you'll pay me back by 'allowing' me to babysit, huh?" Brittany snickered.

"You've got it!" Annabeth laughed back. "And I want to thank my mom again for finally talking me into coming to work for the business. Working there will let me make enough that Katie can stay home with the baby, which is something we both really want." She stopped, then started bouncing up and down and cried out, "Oh! I'm just so excited!" Everyone started laughing.

A male voice rang out: "A toast! A toast!" Mark climbed onto a chair and lifted his glass high. "To my brother and his lovely new bride; to my niece and her lovely partner and baby; to my nephew and his lovely wife and their two new children; and to our large and extremely fortunate family. May we all be as happy in the years to come as we are on this day! *Salute, felicità e amore!*"

Health, happiness, and love indeed, thought Raffaella. *After tomorrow, I wonder how they will all feel?*

A hush came over the big house; all of the out-of-town guests had booked rooms at the Shelbyville Road exit because they wanted the newlyweds to be able to have the evening to themselves. Even though it would be a chaste night, Nikki was glad they'd all left because she was exhausted. The day had drained her.

"How are you feeling, princess?" Tony asked her when they got upstairs. "Want me to help you undress?"

"Yes, please," Nikki groaned. "I don't think I can do it by myself. I don't have any energy left and it's hard to get my arm all the way up."

Tony helped her get undressed and into a gown, then loaded her toothbrush and, after she was finished brushing her teeth, he brushed her hair for her, carefully removing the tiny flowers the girls had put in it. With the day washed off and brushed out, she slipped under the covers he'd turned back and scooted up against him.

Then he remembered: "Hey, Mamma told me she'd invited all of the brothers over here tomorrow at two o'clock."

"Yeah, she told me she wanted me in the mix too. She said she has something to tell all of us?" Nikki asked.

"And Vic, and Clayton too. Did she say what?"

"No. Not a clue. Did she give you any clues?" Nikki asked.

"None. I asked if she was sick or something, and she said she wasn't. I can't imagine."

"Me neither. But I can tell you, if I'm as tired then as I am now, I won't care."

"I hear you, Mrs. Walters. Get some sleep. Maybe you'll feel better tomorrow."

"Don't think I could feel any worse, Mr. Walters. Mrs. Walters . . . that sounds soooo good!"

"I love saying it. And I love you, precious."

"And I love you too."

"Wait a minute!" Tony reached down and slipped his wedding band off. "I forgot – you had something inscribed in here, didn't you? I didn't think about it until now." Nikki smiled as he tried to read the tiny lettering. "What does it say?"

"It says," Nikki answered, tearing up, "*Infinity – this ring – our love.*"

"Infinity," Tony repeated and kissed her forehead.

"Exactly."

Chapter Forty-Six

Nikki was pleasantly surprised. The day after Christmas dawned and she actually felt much better. She stretched in the bed and it didn't hurt very much, so she tried putting her arm over her head and found that, even though there was some discomfort, it wasn't unbearable. She'd take any improvement she could get.

Helene had come in early and made them a nice breakfast, but before they could finish it, Annabeth and Katie came trotting through the front door, bags of groceries in their arms. "Need some help?" Tony asked, bewildered. He looked at Nikki; she shrugged. They watched the two young women run in and out, bringing in the rest of the groceries.

"Bethie, what in the world are you girls doing?" Tony finally asked.

"We're not sure. Nonna said all of my zios were coming over this afternoon at two, and she wants us to have a meal ready when she's finished with whatever it is she's doing with you guys," she replied.

"Huh. Well, okay, cook away." He looked back at Nikki. She shrugged again. What in the hell was Raffaella up to?

Tony offered to help Nikki with her shower. She told him she thought she could manage, but she asked him to sit in the bathroom and stay close if she needed him. The only time she wound up needing him was to wash her back; she did pretty well with everything else. Even better, her incision was healing up nicely. The only reason she'd need a bandage now was to protect the stitches.

She took her time and managed to dress by herself while he showered, and when he came out and saw her dressed he told her how proud he was of her. He had to help her a little with her makeup and hair, but she did most of it on her own and felt good about her progress.

They got finished pulling themselves together in time to have chicken salad-stuffed tomatoes for lunch. Tony had just gotten Nikki settled in the den when Raffaella came strolling in. She greeted them both with a kiss, but there was something odd, some kind of undercurrent, in her voice. Nikki couldn't figure it out but, based on the look on his face, she could tell Tony felt it too.

No one was late. At two o'clock, all five of the brothers, plus Vic, Nikki, and Clayton, were in the great room. At five after, Tony looked at Raffaella and asked, "Well, what's this all about?"

"We should wait," she replied curtly. "I'm expecting one more person."

They all looked at each other; everyone was accounted for. Then the doorbell rang. Tony glanced through the peephole, and when he opened the door, his couldn't believe his eyes.

On the front steps was John Henry Henson. Tony hadn't seen him since they were in their twenties and, although he was older and heavier, Tony recognized him immediately. "John Henry?"

"Hi, Tony," the man said nervously. "This is awkward, huh?" Tony nodded, still staring. "Is your mom here? She asked me to be here today."

"Uh, yeah, she's here." He thought for a minute, then said, "Please, come in." He didn't want to ask John Henry in, but he didn't know what else to do. Why would Raffaella invite him there?

As the two men walked into the den, everyone turned and stared, mostly because they had no idea who John Henry was. But Raffaella said, "John Henry, thank you so much for being here." She crossed the room and hugged him.

Tony was dumbfounded. "Mamma," he asked slowly, "would you like to tell me why he's here?"

"Yes, my son, I would like to tell all of you why he is here." She motioned for John Henry to sit beside her on the loveseat.

Tony introduced John Henry to everyone in the room, with Nikki last. "And this is my new wife, Nikki." Tony took a deep breath. "John Henry worked for Walters Construction years ago."

"Nice to meet you, ma'am." John Henry shook Nikki's hand.

"And you as well," Nikki responded. "And please, it's Nikki. How are you?"

"Not very well, ma'am, um, Nikki. I buried my son yesterday." A sad look settled behind his eyes.

"Oh dear! I'm so sorry!" Nikki cried out. "I know exactly how that feels! What happened to him, if you don't mind my asking?"

"Oh, no, I don't mind. You shot and killed him."

Nikki was stupefied, and the blood drained from her face. She heard

Tony say softly, "What the fuck?" and a low murmur went around the room.

John Henry bowed his head and softly said, "I'm sorry. That was pretty tactless of me. None of that was your fault."

Nikki still couldn't manage to compose herself. She looked at Tony, horror-stricken, and he patted her hand, then turned to his mother and John Henry and said quite forcefully, "Okay, well, the two of you came into my home and dropped a bomb like that on my wife – I think maybe you'd better explain yourselves pretty quick. I've been warm and welcoming, but based on that exchange, I think my good humor's worn off."

"My son, I understand. I'm sorry this has to be done, but it's time. After what you and my new daughter went through over the last few months, you deserve an explanation." Raffaella looked around the room, then added, "All of you do. Our secrets nearly cost two of you your lives."

Raffaella took a deep breath, shook herself, and jumped in. "I'll start by telling you that I loved your father dearly. He was my husband – a good husband – and a good father to you boys." Nikki could've sworn she heard Bennie snort. "But he was a man, just an ordinary man, and he made mistakes that men make. And he made one shortly before Bennie was born. Do any of you remember Martha, the lady who used to watch you?" Freddie shook his head no, but Mark, Bart, and Tony nodded. "Well, your father had an affair with Martha, and she became pregnant."

Nikki watched Tony's face as the truth of the revelation sank in; he looked appalled, the other four brothers looked pretty much the same, and Vic didn't look much better. "So are you trying to tell us . . ." Tony began.

"Yes," Raffaella interrupted. "John Henry is your half-brother." John Henry looked at the floor, embarrassed.

"You're fucking kidding me, right?" Tony bellowed, startling Nikki, and Raffaella visibly shrank. "This guy is my brother? Do you know why this piece of shit no longer works for Walters Construction?" He looked around the room, then started in again. "It's because he *stole from us!* And now I'm supposed to just say, 'Oh, well, he's family.' Well, no, I can't do that! Tell them, you shit!" Tony yelled at John Henry. "Tell them what you did!"

John Henry wore a look of total humiliation. "I did – I stole from Walters Construction. But not because I needed money. God knows you paid me well."

"Damn right I did," Tony snarled. Nikki patted his hand.

John Henry launched in. "My growing-up years were hell. When I was born, my father knew I wasn't his child, and he started drinking. He beat my mother and later, me. I didn't have anybody to turn to. Then, when I was in high school, about sixteen, my mother told me who my real father was, and insisted I meet him. Then I got to see you guys, the way your parents sent you to Europe to go to school, sent you to college. I never had any of those advantages, and I got pretty bitter.

"So I knew Marco was my father, but he told me I could work for the company only if I never told anybody that he was my father. It hurt to know that he was ashamed that I even existed. So stealing from the company was my way of getting what I believed was my portion of the business. I knew I'd never be a partner, or even be part of the family, but at least that way I felt like I was getting something. It was still wrong, though, and I've always appreciated that you didn't call the law on me, Tony. That would've been horrible." John Henry shook his head sadly. "It was bad enough as it was. I lost my job, and everything went to hell."

Suddenly, Nikki felt bad for the man. She understood how he felt, having a family who didn't care for him. Even though the reasons were different from hers, she still knew how badly it hurt. "What happened?" she asked him.

John Henry nodded to acknowledge her question, then turned to Tony. "Well, when I lost my job, I started drinking. I was a mean drunk, too; I beat up my wife on a regular basis. When Travis was born, I left. I came back when he was four, and I beat my wife *and* my son. It was horrible; I wound up acting just like the person I despised the most, which made me drink even more." Tony watched Vic's face and saw the agony there; Vic was nothing like his father, but John Henry's story brought back memories of painful days for Vic.

Nikki watched Tony as John Henry spoke, saw his face softening, saw the thoughtful way he was listening to John Henry, who continued. "When Travis turned sixteen, he ran away and we didn't know where he was. My wife died early last year – cancer. By then, I'd turned my life around, been sober for years, turned into a good, well, pretty good husband, I'd like to think. But Travis never forgave me. Even though he hadn't been around us in years, when he lost his mother, he kind of lost his mind. He knew the story about me and my family background, and I think that's why he started targeting you and the business, but primarily you." He turned to Tony. "He saw you, your family, you firing me, as what caused all the problems, and he was taking it out on you. And for that, I'm really sorry. If I'd had any idea what he was doing, I would've stopped him, or at least tried. I would've gone so far as turning him in to the police. At least he'd still be alive." John Henry stopped, steeling himself against the thunderstorm of angry words he was sure he'd hear, especially from Tony.

Tony was hearing all of it, but it was such a shock that he was having trouble taking it all in. "God, John Henry. Your life has been a mess." He looked at the floor and shook his head. "And all because Papa couldn't keep his pants zipped. I'm sorry all of this happened to you. If I'd had any idea . . ." He sat for a moment, still looking at the floor, then looked up and reached a hand toward John Henry. The man took Tony's hand in both of his and just held it, a sad, hopeless kind of clinging that made Tony's heart sink.

At that very moment, Bennie let loose; he just couldn't hold it in anymore. "So you're telling me you didn't know any of this?" he shouted at Tony. "And I'm supposed to believe that?"

Tony turned to Bennie with his eyes wide and brow furrowed. "No! What the hell? How could I have known?"

"Well, I knew!" Bennie shouted, looking around the room; everyone else was shrugging too. "I knew for years. I found out when I was sixteen. I overheard them talking, Papa and Mamma, and I knew what was going on! And YOU!" he yelled, pointing at Tony. "You worshipped him! Idolized him! And he was an unfaithful bastard! He cheated on our mother and fathered a child with a paid servant!"

"I didn't idolize him!" Tony yelled back, leaping to his feet. *Uh-oh, this is falling apart pretty fast,* Nikki thought, watching Tony's face closely; pain was written all over it. "I worked alongside him. I worked to learn the business, since nobody else seemed interested in it. And if it makes *you* feel any better, all I heard was how he thought Mark would want to run the business, or Bart, or Freddie, but no, it was *me*. He was disappointed that it was *me*. And I spent *three years,* the last three years of his life, trying to make him glad it was me, but he never was. I never felt like I was good enough or that he was happy that I was doing everything I could to build the business." Now Tony was shaking, angry, and hurting. "And he wasn't a very good businessman."

"I was there, and Tony speaks the truth; Zio Marco was a *terrible* businessman," Vic agreed quietly. "The business, all the money, all the success? That's all been Tony. It would've failed without him."

"Thanks, Vic, and yeah, Papa almost let the business go under. And it turns out . . ." Tony stopped and, looking at the floor, shook his head and let out a sarcastic chuckle, "it was because he was preoccupied with keeping his secret instead of paying attention to his work. I worked *hard* to keep it going, and I think I did a pretty good job, especially considering what I was dealing with at home. And I didn't do it just for me and my kids; I did it for *all of you*, your wives, your kids, your futures. And I'd do it all again."

He plopped down beside Nikki. She put her hand on his back and rubbed his shoulders; they were knotted tight, and he took a shuddering, deep breath. "So no, I had no idea. And I assume that's why you've been treating me like shit for all these years? You were mad because I wasn't mad at him? Punished me because I didn't punish him? Oh, that's spectacular, Bennie; just great." Tony buried his face in his hands, and his shoulders shook. Nikki leaned over and kissed the back of his neck, and he grabbed her hand and held it tight.

The room got quiet. Mark, Bart, and Freddie hadn't uttered a word, but Bennie was nowhere near finished – he took a deep breath, then started in again. "So, Mamma, you let him just continue on? Stayed with him? How could you do that? Didn't you have any self-respect?"

"Hey!" Mark jumped up, getting in Bennie's face. "Lay off her! She did the best she could – she had four little boys to take care of! God, you ass, how could you even go there?"

"My sons, let's not . . ." Raffaella began. Vic shot Mark a look, and he sat down immediately.

"No!" Bart yelled, leaping into the middle of the fray. "Mark's right – we're not going to let him talk to you like that! *You* were a victim too!"

"I didn't feel like a victim," Raffaella said timidly. "I just hurt because my husband had been unfaithful with another woman." Everyone got very still and listened to her. "And it's true; I had four small boys and no way to care for them. I felt I had no choice. He promised it would not happen again and, to my knowledge, it did not."

"But you had another child with him, Mamma. Why would you have another child with a man who had done that to you?" Bennie shouted, his face twisted in agony and fury.

"I didn't," Raffaella very nearly whispered as she stared at the floor.

"Yes, you did! You had me!" Bennie stated matter-of-factly.

"Yes, I had you." She hesitated, then told him softly, "But I did not have you with Marco."

Every head in the room snapped toward Raffaella, and the shame on her face was painful. Bart got up, walked to where she was sitting, sat down in the floor beside her, and took her hand. Before anyone could ask, she explained. "When Marco's infidelity became known, I was so distraught that I could not stay with him. I went to stay with my family in Italy. Do you boys remember when Zia Angelina came to stay with you?" The three oldest sons nodded; Papa's sister had stayed with them for six months while their mother was away. Freddie was too young to remember, but Tony could remember crying for his mother every night before he fell asleep.

"She stayed with you while I went to see my family. I was a wreck, as you say. While I was there, I was reacquainted with a man I'd known as a child there in the village. He and I laughed and talked and, well, one thing led to another. After I'd been there for about five months, I realized I was pregnant. I didn't tell him; I didn't tell anyone. I just went home and told Marco." A tear slipped down the face of the toughest woman Nikki had ever met, and her heart went out to Raffaella.

Bennie turned pale; Tony started to say something to him, then thought better of it and closed his mouth. Everyone else sat in stunned silence. Raffaella then said, "When I got home, I told Marco of my indiscretion. I told him I did not do it as retaliation toward him; I was only trying to comfort myself at his betrayal. He told me he understood. He was not angry or blaming, only said each of us had made a mistake, and one cancelled out the other. Then he promised he would raise my child as his in such a way that no one would know the difference. And to my knowledge, no one ever knew, am I right?"

"I'd say that's right, Mamma," Freddie told her quietly.

Raffaella held up a small, yellowed photo. "Benecio, do you remember this photo?" Tony recognized it immediately; it was a photo of Mamma, Papa, and a man they'd introduced as Papa's cousin. He'd come to visit them when Tony was in high school. "This man? His name was Arturo. He came to see us, you, when you were ten."

"Yes, Mamma, I remember when . . . oh, god, was he . . ."

"Yes, my son. That man was your father. Someone in my family told him about you. He wanted to see you, know you were well. He had no other children."

"Could I . . ." Bennie started.

"Oh, Benecio, I am so sorry. He died about two years ago."

Bennie was silent, staring at the floor with an indescribable look on his face, his shoulders slumped.

"And so, Benecio, while you punished Antonio for things he could not have known, you yourself had a secret of which you were unaware. I believe you owe your brother an apology, my son."

Bennie looked at Tony, who had tears streaming down his face. "Tony, I, I . . ."

"Forget it, brother. Water under the bridge." Tony's lower lip trembled and he wiped his eyes. "We're brothers; we'll always be brothers. Regardless how you've treated me over the years, I've always loved you, always tried to be good to you, always tried to include you even when you acted like you hated me." Tony stopped and, in a painful, broken voice, asked, "Do you think you could try to love me, just a little bit?"

Bennie got quiet, then crossed the room and knelt down in front of Tony. "I'm so, so sorry." He looked up into Tony's face, tears pooling in his own eyes. "You deserved my love and respect, even my thanks, and I spat on you. It'll never happen again." Bennie reached up and wrapped his arms around Tony's shoulders and pulled him close.

Tony rested his head on Bennie's shoulder and quietly said, "Brother, we start over today. If you'll try, I'll try too." When they broke their embrace, Bennie sat down beside Tony.

Then Vic spoke up. "I want all of you to remember that, regardless what Zio Marco did, he was like a father to me. He took me and my mother in when we had nowhere else to turn, and I regret every day the problems I caused him. He was a good man who made a mistake. That in no way negates all of the good things he did for all of us."

Then he turned to Tony. "Cousin-brother, I want you to know that Zio Marco was very proud of you. After I came to work for the company, I heard a contractor say Zio Marco had told him, 'If my son Antonio tells you something is a certain way, you can take that to the bank. He's an honest, hardworking man who does right by his family, and he's one helluva businessman.' He should've told you himself; he didn't, but that man was kind enough to tell me, and I'm telling you now. I don't think he wished one of your brothers had come on board *instead* of you; I think he wanted one or more of them to come on board *with* you to help you. I'm just thankful there was a spot with Walters Construction for me; you've helped me be the man I am, and I'll always be grateful for that."

"I'm grateful for you too, Vic. I never would've made it without you," Tony said as Vic reached over and grabbed his hand.

Tony turned to John Henry. "So now you're a Walters brother."

John Henry shrugged. "My name's not Walters though."

"Neither is Vic's, but that doesn't make him any less a brother to us.

You're part of this family now, if you want to be," Tony told him.

"We really hope you want to be," Mark added. Bart and Freddie nodded, and Bennie extended his hand to John Henry, who took it hesitantly, then shook it heartily.

"I'd like that. I'd like it a lot. I've never had any siblings. And Nikki, I'm so sorry for what happened with Travis. Are you doing okay?"

She gave him a warm smile. "I'll be fine. I'm feeling stronger every day. I'm sorry about Travis too. He didn't leave me with an option, or he'd be alive today. If you want to apologize to somebody, it should be Laura Butler. She's still in the hospital."

"Speaking of Laura, I need to go by and check on her," Vic said.

John Henry chimed in, "I'd like to go with you, if that's okay."

"I think she might like that," Vic replied.

The whole room and everyone in it seemed rung-out and exhausted, then Freddie spoke up. "Well, while we're all here together and confessing all of our sins, I guess I'd better tell you myself."

"Oh, god, what?" Bart groaned.

"I've asked Molly for a divorce," Freddie blurted out. There were several gasps around the room.

"What the hell?" Tony asked.

"Well, you know my assistant, Felicity? She used to babysit the kids next door." He paused. "She's twenty-six." He blushed deeply. "But I started sleeping with her when she was sixteen." Tony groaned loudly, and Mark, Bart, and Bennie looked at Freddie like he'd lost his mind. Vic shook his head and looked at the floor. *This just gets better and better*, Nikki thought sarcastically.

"Man, what the hell is wrong with you?" Tony growled. "Have you completely lost it?"

"No, she makes me happy."

"Dirty old man," Bennie mumbled.

"Hey, no judgments, okay?" Mark countered.

"Thanks, Mark," Freddie told his oldest brother. "Anyway, I made her my assistant at work so we could spend more time together. But it's not enough. I want to marry her; she wants to marry me too. So I asked Molly for a divorce."

"And are you still sleeping with Molly?" Tony asked. "Does she know about Felicity?"

"Yeah, she knows, and yeah, I'm still sleeping with her," Freddie answered sheepishly.

"So you're unfaithful to your wife with your mistress, and you're unfaithful to your mistress with your wife. Holy shit, man, that's some kind of fucked up," Tony told him. Vic nodded.

Nikki looked at Freddie. "I've got a question."

"By all means, jump right in there," Tony groaned. "I'd say don't make things worse, but I'm not sure that's possible."

As usual, Nikki cut directly to the chase. "So are you screwing around with this girl because Molly is a bitch, or is Molly a bitch because you're screwing around with this girl? Which came first, you know, the chicken-slash-egg thing?" Nikki asked. Everyone nodded and looked at Freddie, who was now firmly implanted on the hot seat.

"Um, she's a bitch because I've been screwing Felicity."

"Is she going to give you the divorce?" Nikki asked.

"Yeah, looks like," Freddie answered.

"And the boutique? It belongs to you, right?" Nikki asked, the wheels turning in her brain.

"Yeah. And the bank has a policy against employees dating or marrying, so I'm giving Felicity the boutique to run," he replied without a hint of emotion.

"Uh-huh, high and dry. Just what I thought." Nikki turned and looked at Tony. "I want you to give Molly a job with the company. She's going to need a way to make herself a living, and we can do that for her."

"I still need an assistant," Vic piped up. "She's welcome in my office."

"Good." Nikki turned and smiled sweetly at Freddie.

"You mean you're going to give my ex-wife a job with Walters Construction? How could you do that to me?" he wailed.

"Because, my brother, unlike you, most of the Walters men believe when they make a commitment to a woman, they should keep it. This is a way our family can at least keep the commitment you made to Molly. You'll just have to live with that," Tony smirked at him.

Freddie shut up, and so did everyone else. After a few minutes, Tony said, "So, since this day has been so lovely, does anybody else have *anything* they'd like to get off their chest before we take a deep breath and relax?" He looked at Bart, Mark, and Bennie; they all shook their heads. He glanced Nikki's way. "Honey?"

"I got nothin'," she smiled. "My life's an open book."

"Vic?"

"Well," Vic started hesitantly, "no, nothing I should say out loud." Nikki gave Tony a knowing look, and he shot back a sad smile.

"Clayton?"

"Aw, hell no. My lesbian sister's wife is having my baby, my new four-year-old son is Black, and my wife is expecting an eight-year-old. Plus I just found out one of my uncles is just my half-uncle, I have a new half-uncle, and I had a cousin who was shot and killed by my mother. Unless some dead relative comes back to life or I'm a zombie and nobody's told me, those damn soap operas got nothin' on me. Nope, I think I'm good over here," he said, looking kind of shell-shocked.

Tony leaned over and patted Clayton on the knee. "You okay, buddy?"

"Yeah, I'll be okay. I just need a quiet corner to process all this in, that's all," Clayton told him, not looking at anyone.

"Anybody? Anything else?" Tony asked. Everyone looked around at each other, then at the floor. "Well, I've got one last thing."

"Sweet lord, don't tell us you've been abducted by aliens," Clayton moaned. "I don't think I could take it."

Tony grinned. "No, son. Better than that." He straightened, then turned to Nikki. "Honey, I'm sorry I haven't gotten a chance to talk to you about this first. I was going to make the big announcement on New Year's Eve, but this seems like the right time, so bear with me and don't get mad, okay?"

"Shit, babe, what now?" Nikki asked, that horrified look coming back to her face.

"No, no! It's good, I swear!" He looked around at everyone, then said, "As of January first, I'm retiring from Walters Construction; well, semi-retiring."

"What?" "When did you decide this?" "You can't do that!" Questions started coming at him from all angles. Nikki stared at him like he had an arm growing out of his forehead.

"Hey, guys, hey! Give me a minute! I've given this a lot of thought, and I've had Steve working on the paperwork to see how we could work the whole thing out. And he's come up with a workable plan. But it's like this," he said, turning back to Nikki. "I love Walters Construction; I really do. I've loved working with you over the last few months, sweetheart. And I love working with you guys," he said, looking at Clayton and Vic, then turning back to Nikki. "But, baby, most couples get married, and they daydream about growing old together and when they'll celebrate their fiftieth wedding anniversary. I'm a realist; we're never going to celebrate our fiftieth. We'll be lucky if we're still healthy enough to enjoy our twentieth. But I want us to be able to spend as much time together as we can while we're healthy, active, and fit. I have some ideas for what I want to do. I'm not going to stop working altogether, but I want to do something that will let me spend all the time I can with you. Does that sound crazy?"

"No," Nikki whispered, tears in her eyes. "That sounds wonderful!" She kissed him and hugged him tight. "I'm so happy!"

"But Dad . . ." Clayton started, sheer terror in his eyes.

"No buts. We're going to work this out. It's all going to be okay; I won't leave you guys twisting in the breeze, I promise. I'm still planning to work two or three days a week. Can everyone at least support me in this, even if you don't agree? It's important to me."

Tony went around the room, and everyone either agreed or nodded. When they were done, he looked at John Henry. "And I'd like you to come back to Walters Construction. Clayton and Vic will need help, and we'll all be glad to show you the ropes."

John Henry nodded. "I'd like that very much. And I kept working in the construction industry, so I have quite a bit of experience. I'd love a chance to make up for the damage I did all those years ago."

"Good! It's settled." As far as Tony was concerned, they were done, really once-and-for-all done. "We'll find you a spot, something we need filled and you'll enjoy, and it'll be settled." He took a deep breath, let it out, and said, "And now, I'm finished, not to mention exhausted, by all of this. So if no one else has anything, I smell something delicious in my kitchen courtesy of my girls, and I think we need to eat."

Everyone got up and started to the dining room; everyone except Nikki. Tony got all the way to his seat before he realized he'd left her behind. He went back to the great room and found her still sitting there, looking kind of dazed.

"Hey, baby," he whispered, steeling himself to apologize.

"Hi," she replied in a low voice.

"You okay? I forgot to bring you with me. I'm sorry. You hungry?"

"I'm not sure I can eat." She seemed foggy. "I'm still kind of in shock."

"The retirement thing?" he asked.

"Everything." She was bone-weary. "I need a nap."

He smiled and took her hand. "Eat first. Then I'll nap with you."

She smiled back. "Just make sure I don't wind up face-down in my plate."

"If you do and you drown, I'll give you mouth-to-mouth," he grinned.

"Oh, I feel so much better knowing that," she responded sarcastically, getting up under her own steam. "Whatever would I do without you?"

With a sudden seriousness, he told her, "I hope you never have to find out."

She looked at him with an equally serious expression. "I hope I never have to either."

After they'd eaten, all of the brothers went back to their wives at their hotels in Louisville, and everyone got teary-eyed as they were leaving. Bennie promised he and Caroline would come and stay with Nikki and Tony soon so they could start over. Tony, Vic, and Clayton told John Henry they'd like to have lunch with him during the next couple of weeks to make some plans, and Tony invited him to come over and watch bowl games on New Year's Day; John Henry said he'd really enjoy that.

The women sat at the table in the cleaned-up kitchen, talking about Katie's pregnancy and which room they'd use for the nursery. Tony played with Little T and Ella Jane, and Clayton and Vic watched a show on TV about mummies. Nikki was trying to get to the bedroom for the nap she needed, and she'd made it as far as the base of the stairs when the doorbell rang. She waited, but nobody made a move to answer it, so she decided she'd get it, hoping Tony wouldn't get mad at her when he found out she was stirring around by herself. But with everything that was running through her head, she forgot to look through the peephole, and she opened the front door to a short, bald man pointing a snub-nosed five-shot revolver at her. "Close the door," he snarled at her.

What the hell do I do now?, she thought. Her Walther wasn't in her waistband; she hadn't been carrying it because she couldn't maneuver well enough to even put the holster in her pants. She looked at the man, and then she recognized him: This was the man who'd killed Dottie. Everyone in the house was busy doing something. Would anyone even notice she hadn't come back from the door? Had anyone else even *heard* the doorbell?

"What do you want?" she asked him. He seemed nervous, maybe strung out? His eyes were red-rimmed, and his nose was flushed. "I don't have any money."

"I don't want your money, bitch. I want you. I'm gonna kill you. My

Dottie is dead because of you," he whispered menacingly.

If I can keep him talking, maybe somebody will find me, she thought. "How is that my fault?" Nikki asked.

"Because!" He seemed confused, looking for what he wanted to say. Then he screamed, "Because everything was fine until you came along! Then she got all crazy and wanted me to go. She was okay as long as he was alone, but when he found somebody, well, she couldn't stand it. It was pretty obvious she was still in love with him. So she was taken from me, and I'm going to take you from *him*!"

"But *you're* the one who killed her!"

She instantly wished she hadn't said that. He started to shake, then cocked the hammer on the gun and waved it around. By then Nikki was very sure he was high on something. "Get down on your knees with your back to me. I don't want you watching me when I shoot you!"

"I'm not getting down on my knees," Nikki said matter-of-factly. "I can't. I have an arm in a sling, in case you haven't noticed."

"Your damn arm isn't going to make any difference!" he screamed. "You'll be dead in a few minutes so it won't matter!" At that point, he got exceptionally worked up. "Now I said get down on your knees!" he shrieked.

"What was that?" Clayton asked Vic, his head cocked, listening. "Wait – who was at the door? I heard the bell."

"I don't know, but I heard it too." Vic got up and went to the kitchen; somebody was missing. He ran up the stairs calling Nikki's name, then ran back into the great room. "Nikki's not in the house."

Tony heard Vic say Nikki wasn't in the house, and a chill ran through him; he called out, "Girls, keep the little ones close. Something's wrong." He ran to the foyer to find Clayton pointing at the peephole, obviously terrified. Tony looked through the peephole, and his heart froze. By the time Vic made it into the foyer and looked through the peephole, Tony had pulled his nine millimeter Ruger from the back of his jeans; Vic produced his Ruger forty-five, and Clayton had already drawn his three-eighty SIG Sauer. "Clayton, around from the back to the right; Vic, same to the left. When you're in position, Vic, try to get her attention, let her know to drop. When she drops, I'll yank open the door. Stay to the sides so I don't wing you if I have to shoot him."

"Got it," Vic nodded, and he and Clayton took off.

Tony stood at the door, looking through the peephole. He could tell Nikki was stalling the guy, hoping someone would notice she was gone. In a matter of seconds, Tony saw Clayton to his right in the peephole, and Vic to the left. He saw Vic raise one hand, and do a quick three-two-one downward-point hand signal. Then Vic nodded, counted down, and Tony saw Nikki's head disappear from the peephole.

He jerked the door open and leveled his weapon at the man's head, and the guy looked genuinely surprised to see a gun pointed directly at him. In a steady voice, Tony told him, "There are three weapons trained on you right now. It would be in your best interest to drop your gun." Never moving his gaze, he told Nikki, "Sweetheart, crawl past me and into the house, then close the door and call the cops." For once, he got no argument out of her. Even though it was a struggle for her, she made it through the door in record time.

"What's it going to be?" he asked the man, who was becoming visibly agitated. "I don't want you to die, but if I have to shoot you and I don't kill you, one of the other two guys will. So please, put the gun down. I really, really don't want to shoot you. I'm just not that kind of guy."

It seemed to take forever for the man to make up his mind, but he finally dropped the gun he was holding and put his hands on the back of his head. Clayton ran forward and grabbed his wrists, forced him to the ground, and placed a knee in the middle of his back. Within minutes, two cruisers pulled up.

Nikki was watching through the sidelights, and she came out the door when the cruisers pulled up. She told Tony, "It's him – Hector. He admitted it; he killed Dottie."

"Wonder where the car is?" Tony mused, looking down the driveway as far as he could see.

"What's going on here?" the uniformed officer asked.

"Officer, this man held a gun on my wife," Tony told the uniform. "If you'll call Detective Bryson Hawkins of the Louisville Police Department, he'll tell you all about it; this man is wanted in the murder of Dorothea Walters in Louisville. By the way, did you see a gray car with the side all dented in on your way in here?"

"Yes sir, the other side of the hill there, off the side of the drive. Is that significant?"

"Very. Please have it towed to Louisville as well. I'm sure they'll want it for evidence. And please, get him out of here." Tony looked at Vic and Clayton. "Everybody all right?"

"Yeah, we're both okay." Clayton turned to Nikki. "Mom, you okay?"

"Yes, honey, I'm fine. And thanks for finding me. I was afraid no one would know I was out here."

"I heard something and that's how I figured out something was wrong. Then we started looking for you and couldn't find you. I was so scared." Clayton hugged her tight. "I just got you forever; I sure don't want to lose you."

"Well, that was Bryson," Tony told Nikki after he hung up the phone. "That guy is Hector Ramirez. He confessed to killing Dottie. So it's all over." The look of relief on his face was a blessing to her.

"So what's next?"

"I have some press releases to send out in five days about the retirement issue, and then we step into our new life. And I've got some surprises for you, Mrs. Walters!"

"Oh, Mr. Walters, I can hardly wait!"

Chapter Forty-Seven

"So she's released? Completely?" Tony asked Nikki's doctor.

"Yes, completely. You can resume all normal activities," Dr. Jessup told Nikki, then smiled at Tony. "*All* normal activities. But you might want to work up to *normal*. Just keep it within reason."

Tony let out a belly laugh. "Gotcha. I'll take it easy on her."

"See that you do! She's still got some healing to do. And good luck to both of you. Stay safe," Dr. Jessup ordered as he walked with them to the door.

Once Tony had helped Nikki into the Yukon and was in the driver's seat, he told her, "Well, that's that! I guess we have something to celebrate, huh?"

"Yep! I can't wait!"

"Me neither. I might just drag you into the back of this SUV . . ."

"Oh, no, buster! Not out here in the parking lot of the medical plaza! I'm too damn old for that," she laughed.

"No you're not. But I'll humor you this time and wait until we get home."

When they walked through the door, Tony scooped Nikki up and took her up the stairs two at a time. He practically threw her on the bed, stripped her down in a matter of seconds, shucked all of his clothes, and was on her and in her so fast she didn't have time to catch her breath. He stroked in and out of her tenderly for a few minutes, then pulled out and took a minute to trail his lips down her neck, down her breast, and down to the scar on her ribcage. She wound her hands in his hair, and he kissed the scar over and over. Finally, he said, "You're going to wear this for the rest of your life, and all because of me. Baby, I'm so, so sorry."

She pulled his head up and the love he saw in those clear, turquoise-kissed eyes made his heart sing. "The only people who will ever see it are you and members of the medical profession. And if you don't care about it, I don't care what they think. So it doesn't matter. It's all over and we're moving on. Now, make love to me and don't stop until I'm screaming, okay?" she smiled.

"Oh, I can definitely do that," he moaned, kissing back up to her mouth and burying his shaft in her warmth and wetness. He lay his full length on top of her, wrapped his arms around her, and put his hands on her ass, pumping into her with an edginess that made everything inside her flair until it all blazed. She moaned and kissed him, forcing herself into his mouth until their tongues met. They made love like that for hours, coming over and over until neither of them could move. Lying in each other's arms, they dozed as the dinner hour got closer and closer.

When they woke, they were lying side by side in the dusk. "So, have you got the plans all drawn up?" Nikki asked him without opening her eyes.

"Yeah, and we're not enlarging the present barn. You can have it; I know you want it."

"Yay! I was so hoping you'd say that! I want to get us a couple of saddle horses. Please?"

"Sure! We'll do that. As for everything else, it's all coming together. I can't wait until we can break ground, probably this summer." Tony kissed the tip of her nose.

"Woo-hoooo!" You're really excited about this, aren't you?"

"Well, yeah! It's going to be such a big leap from what I'm used to doing. But I'm going to love it – you will too."

Nikki trailed a fingertip down his chest. "Shouldn't we at least tell the family?"

"Naw. I don't want to. I did tell Vic, though; I'm going to let the Lexington office do all of the work. It'll get done fast and right, and I won't have to look over everybody's shoulders, just spend my time enjoying being with you."

Nikki snuggled into him. "That, Mr. Walters, sounds like an excellent idea."

"God, I love these wasabi almonds." Vic took another handful. "Nik, did you make these?"

"Yeah, but the ones I get from Trader Joe's are much better."

"I don't see how they could be any better." While Vic kept at the almonds, Tony and John Henry were practically scuffling over the cheddar popcorn. Nikki hadn't made that; she'd cheated and bought it.

"I love New Year's so much." Clayton stuck his hand in the bowl of m&m's. "I love the bowl games. I love the parades. I think it's the best holiday ever."

"Daddy, can I has a cupcake?" Little T asked.

"Go ask your mommy," Clayton told him, not really paying him much attention.

"She said ask you!" The little boy whined and stomped his foot in frustration.

"Then yes, you can have a cupcake. And bring me one," Clayton told him.

"Me too, little man," Tony seconded.

"Der won't be none foe me if you eat dem aww," Little T pouted.

"Then have mine." Tony turned to him and gave Little T his full attention. "I love you, buddy. I want you to eat mine, okay?"

"Okay, Big T! I eat you cupcake!" He ran to the kitchen. Tony beamed, and Clayton chuckled, watching his dad get so mushy over the little guy.

"You let him get away with murder," Clayton snarled. "You didn't let us do that shit."

Tony laughed. "Yeah, well, you were cute, but you weren't *that* cute!" Clayton threw an m&m at him.

Nikki came into the great room with a huge platter of hot wings and a roll of paper towels under her arm. "Here, guys. Have at!"

When she set it down, Tony grabbed her around the waist and pulled her into his lap. She squealed and kissed him. "You look like you're feeling a lot better!" he grinned at her.

"I do. I feel really good. I think it's that therapy I'm getting," she said, nibbling on a pretzel.

"Therapy? What therapy?" Tony asked her, puzzled.

"The therapy! You know . . ." she repeated, her eyebrows raised.

"Oh, *that* therapy!" he laughed. "Yeah, it's doing wonders for me too!" Vic groaned, and Clayton made a barfing sound. John Henry looked really, really confused.

"Okay, I'm going back to the kitchen with the girls now. You guys have fun and try to not make a huge mess, please?"

"As soon as you leave the room, we're going to start throwing food," Vic told her straight-up. "You should probably just get ready for it."

"Thanks," Nikki snarked, shooting him a look. He laughed and threw a marshmallow at her back as she walked out of the room.

Vic looked over at Tony. He'd never seen his cousin as happy as he was right then. "Hey, cuz, is life good for you?"

Tony turned and looked at Vic thoughtfully. "I didn't think it was possible for a human being to be as happy as I am. Every day is like a huge gift. I don't think it could get any better. I'm not just happy; I'm having fun. She's such a joy." Then he leaned in and whispered, "Plus she makes me feel like a *man*, something I've never had before."

"Good, 'cause you're one helluva man, the finest man I know. And she seems pretty damn happy with you! You're both so lucky," Vic told him and winked.

"No luck – fate. We were meant to be together. Now we've got to work on *your* life. I firmly believe that there's someone for everyone, and there's someone for you out there, Vic. You've just got to find her." The doorbell rang, and Tony called out, "I'll get it."

When he looked through the peephole in the front door, he was surprised at the view. "Hey, stranger! I didn't know you were coming!"

"Nikki invited me. I brought these." Laura tried to hand him a container of something.

"Just take that on into the kitchen; all of the girls are in there. Here, let me take your coat." She slipped it off while he held the container, then they swapped.

As she walked through the kitchen door, Nikki cried out, "Laura! You came! I'm so glad to see you! How are you feeling?"

"Pretty good. Still pretty sore, but pretty good. Thanks for inviting me." She handed the container to Nikki. "I made these. I hope they're good."

Nikki opened the container – white chocolate macadamia nut cookies. All of the girls sampled them; they were past yummy.

"Hey guys! Have some cookies!" She took them into the den, and every one of the guys took one.

"Oh my god, these are delicious," Vic mumbled, his mouth full, and he reached for another one. "Where'd you get these?"

"Laura made them."

Vic's head swiveled to the doorway where Laura stood. She gave all the guys a small wave. "Laura! Hey, how are you?" Vic called to her around the cookie in his mouth.

"Good." She hesitated for a second. "Thanks for coming to see me at the hospital," she said shyly.

"Thanks for what you did for Nikki. We all owe you." Vic grinned at her, then turned back to the container. "Hey, put that back!" he yelled at Tony, who was taking his third cookie.

"Share, big boy! If we eat them all, she'll make more. Right, Laura?" Tony laughed.

"I guess I will," Laura chuckled, but when Vic had spoken to her, she'd noticed that same weird feeling she'd had before.

Nikki watched closely. There was some kind of chemistry between Vic and Laura, but she wasn't sure what. She decided she'd have to keep an eye on that.

The clock struck midnight and everyone in the big house cheered. Tony kissed Nikki, Clayton kissed Brittany, Annabeth kissed Katie, and Vic kissed everybody, everybody except Laura, who pushed him away and barked, "I don't think so." Nikki couldn't help but notice how hurt he looked. *Wonder if I can do something to push that along?*, she thought.

They'd all agreed to stay at the big house for the night so no one would be driving after their adult refreshments. When everyone started to calm down, Tony announced, "I have one more surprise for everybody. Come with me."

He started up the hallway toward the living room, and it hit Nikki. "Is this what I think it is?" she asked him quietly.

"Yeah. It showed up yesterday. I went ahead and hung it. I was sure you'd seen it. Didn't look?"

"No. I noticed the door was closed, but I really didn't think anything of it. Shoulda been more curious, huh?" she smiled.

"Oh, wait 'til you see. It's amazing."

Tony stopped at the door to the living room and everyone gathered around. "We did this the day after Thanksgiving, before our whole world went to hell. I'd completely forgotten about it until they delivered it yesterday. I know what I think about it, but I'd like to hear what everybody else has to say." He ceremoniously threw open the doors and everyone stepped inside the room.

There was a collective gasp, and then a hush came over them as they took in the portrait. Every Walters who'd lived in the big house over the years had sat for a painting or photo, but this one was different from anything the family had ever seen.

"Wow." For once, that was all Annabeth could get out.

Above the fireplace was a photo portrait of Tony and Nikki. Taken from a low angle, the setting was one of their jobsites, with three stories of steel rising in the background. In the foreground sat Nikki's big blue F-250, its front driver's side corner facing the camera so that the brush guard, Warn winch, and massive grill were exposed, the angle emphasizing its length. The sun was setting behind the jobsite, and the sky looked like it was on fire.

Standing at the corner of the truck was Nikki and behind and beside her stood Tony, his hands on her shoulders, her right hand on the truck, and her left up on his left, arranged in such a way that the eye was drawn to the rings they wore; they'd put them on just for the portrait. They were both wearing their steel-toed boots and each had on a pair of form-fitting jeans. Tony had on a black tee-shirt with a black and green plaid flannel shirt over it, and Nikki had on a red tee-shirt with a red and navy flannel shirt over her tee. The colors were vivid and bold while still fitting in with the background and the theme of the photo.

But it was them, their countenances, that made the photo remarkable; they were striking. In typical Walters portrait fashion, neither was smiling, but their expressions were heart-stopping. Tony's eyes were deep and smoky, and he had a seriousness about him that was both alarming and comforting. Nikki's expression was far more steely and fierce. Her gaze was intense but warm, her eyes narrowed ever so slightly, and one eyebrow was slightly raised. She looked like she was poised for battle against anyone who threatened the people she loved. Lit from the back by the setting sun, Tony's hair had an auburn sheen to it, while Nikki's looked like golden silk falling around her face and down to the tops of her breasts. The overall appearance, however, was astounding – one look, and the viewer knew that these were two people who knew exactly who they were, exactly who they loved, exactly who loved them, and exactly where they were supposed to be and what they were supposed to be doing. They knew their path was correct, and they were comfortable with each other and comfortable in their own skin. The sense of power and confidence was breathtaking.

"I see it, but I don't believe it. That's really you guys. I don't know who took this photo, but they captured it – what we all see when we look at you." There was a reverence in Vic's voice that took Tony and Nikki by surprise.

"Dad," Clayton choked out, "that portrait makes me proud to be a Walters."

"Me too," Annabeth murmured.

Leaning down to whisper in Nikki's ear, Tony asked, "Well, whaddya think, baby?"

"Oh my god," Nikki whispered back, her eyes round. "Look at us. We look like . . ." she stopped and let out a shuddering sob, "like we belong together."

Tony already had his arms around her, and he pulled her closer. "We do, baby. Forever. Happy New Year."

"Happy New Year to you too, my love." She turned and kissed him like they were the only two people in the room.

The big house was quiet, everyone in their rooms for the night, and Tony walked back into the kitchen to help Nikki finish cleaning up, but it was spotless and she wasn't there. He went to the great room, but it was empty too, so he continued up the hallway, looking around, until he came to the living room. When he looked in, he saw her standing in front of the fireplace, gazing up at the portrait again. Quietly moving nearer to her, he saw her face was wet with tears, and he wrapped his arms around her.

"Whatcha doing, babe?" he whispered into her neck, then kissed it ever so lightly.

"I can't believe that's us. I can't believe that's *me*," she whispered back, her voice coarse with tiny sobs.

"Why can't you believe it?"

"That woman in the photo, she looks confident and smart and strong. She looks like she doesn't have one question in the world about her tomorrows." She turned and looked at Tony. "What do you see when you look at it?"

"I see everything you said, and I see you." He pulled her closer and kissed the other side of her neck. "When I met you all those months ago, I saw a shy, quiet, simple woman with a good, kind, strong heart. But when I got her, I got so much more. I got everything a man could want or need in a woman, and surprises I didn't know I wanted but I've come to love."

"Like?"

"Like the fact that you're the most complex person I've ever met. You're a fabulous mom, and an even more fabulous grandma. You're brave, and gutsy, and determined – when you set your mind to something, you make it happen. You've got the touch of a light spring breeze and the power of a hurricane. And you love me – you really love me, not to mention that most men would kill for a lover as hot as you. You are absolutely the best thing that's ever happened to me in my life. This is the first time I've ever felt really happy, and I hope it never ends."

"So," Nikki giggled a little, "do I rock your world?"

He turned her to him and laughed. "Oh, beautiful girl, you definitely rock my world – every second, every minute, all day, every day, twenty-four seven, three sixty-five! What about you? Have you got what you want? What you need?"

"You *are* my world." She pressed her cheek against his chest. "I love you so much. I just want to go upstairs, make love with you and fuck you like there's no tomorrow, but we've got a house full of guests," she sniffled.

"Yeah, I know," he said, kissing the top of her head. Then he grabbed her and looked down at her, a huge, naughty grin spreading across his face. "But there's nobody in the barn! And there's all kinds of rope, and riding crops, and plenty of hay . . ."

Nikki grinned back at him. "Grab a blanket and let's go!" she squealed, breaking away and running for the back door.

Tony snatched a throw off the sofa and ran after her. "Right behind you, Mrs. Walters!"

AUTHOR'S NOTE

The Love Under Construction series consists of a prequel and four novels, the prequel and first novel of which are now available as a combo volume (although the prequel can still be had alone and free). You'll learn the backgrounds of the characters by reading the introductory volume, and then see them continue on in the remaining books. These books are not stand-alone stories; while they can be read independently, there will be aspects of each that will not be clear unless they've been read in order. Enjoy them fully by reading them that way.

Introductory volume:
The Groundbreaking – Summer 2013 (still free as an ebook)

Book 1:
The Groundbreaking & Laying a Foundation – Summer 2013

Book 2:
Tearing Down Walls – Fall 2013

Book 3:
Renovating a Heart – Spring 2014

Book 4:
Planning an Addition – Fall 2014

ABOUT THE AUTHOR

Deanndra Hall lives in far western Kentucky with her life partner and three crazy little dogs. She spent years writing advertising copy, marketing materials, educational texts, and business correspondence, and designing business forms. After reading a popular erotic romance book, her partner said, "You can write better than this!" She decided to try her hand at it. In the process she fell in love with her funny, smart, loving characters and the things they got into, and the novel became a series.

Deanndra enjoys all kinds of music, chocolate, kayaking, working out at the local gym, reading, and spending time with friends and family, as well as working in the fiber and textile arts. And chocolate's always high on her list of favorite things!

On the Web:
http://www.deanndrahall.com

Email:
DeanndraHall@gmail.com

Facebook:
facebook.com/deanndra.hall

Twitter:
twitter.com/DeanndraHall

Blog:
deanndrahall.blogspot.com

Substance B:
substance-b.com/DeanndraHall.html

Mailing address:
P.O. Box 3277, Paducah, KY 42002-3277

NIKKI'S MEATLOAF

This recipe makes two. If you only want one, half it.

6 banana or 3 bell peppers – your choice

1/2 sweet onion (I like Vidalias)

2 teaspoons minced garlic

2 Tablespoons olive oil

2 gallon zippered storage bag

1 gallon zippered storage bag

2 pounds meat (I use one pound of ground beef and one pound of ground turkey)

2 eggs

1 stack soda crackers (I prefer unsalted tops, but it doesn't matter)

1/2 cup ketchup or barbecue sauce

2 Tablespoons Worcestershire sauce

1 teaspoon ground ginger

1/4 teaspoon nutmeg

1 teaspoon celery salt

1 box/2 packets onion soup mix (any brand, total of about 4 ounces)

Ketchup to taste

4 bread heels (optional)

Cut up peppers and half an onion into small pieces. On medium, heat the olive oil in a sauté pan; put in garlic. When hot, put in peppers and onion. Sauté and stir until they're cooked down and soft and the onion is translucent. Put them into a bowl and into the fridge to cool while you follow the next steps.

Preheat the oven to 450 degrees. Put the soda crackers in the gallon zippered storage bag. Take a large spoon and beat the daylights out of them until they're crushed. It would be tempting to use bread crumbs here, but trust me, it won't be the same.

Put the meat into the 2 gallon storage bag. Smush it around until it's completely mixed together. Throw in the eggs, soda crackers, 1/2 cup ketchup or barbecue sauce, Worcestershire sauce, ginger, nutmeg, celery salt, and onion soup mix. Smush all of that around until it's mixed thoroughly. Then take the pepper, onion, and garlic mixture from the fridge, pour it in, and smush it all thoroughly again.

Divide the mixture into two parts. If you have meatloaf pans, use them; otherwise, put it into a loaf pan that has two bread heels in the bottom (soaks up any grease). Bake for 50 minutes at 450 degrees, then remove from the oven, spread however much ketchup you want on them, and put them back in the oven for 10 minutes. Let sit for about 10 minutes before cutting.

If you want to freeze some of it, slice it first and put it in individual bags. Makes a great sandwich!

Here's a sneak peek at *Tearing Down Walls,* Book 2 in the *Love Under Construction series:*

The club was starting to fill up, and the bar was busier than usual. Laura was drawing a couple of beers from a tap when she heard a woman at the bar say, "Holy shit, who's that? That's one extremely tall, dark, and hot Dom. Wonder if he's got a sub?" Laura turned to see who she was talking about and nearly fainted.

It was Vic Cabrizzi. And it was a Vic Cabrizzi she'd never seen before.

The mild-mannered man who'd sidled up to the bar and tried to make small talk with her was nowhere in this guy. Vic was six feet and eight inches of pure, dark, steaming sex in leather. He had the top half of his elbow-length black hair pulled up in a half-tail with a leather wrap, and his torso looked like it was trying to escape through the skin-tight black tee he was wearing. As he made his way toward the bar, the crowd parted to let him through as though they were in awe of the masculinity gliding across the room like a panther. Her eyes couldn't help but be drawn to his ass, and it looked especially fine under those leathers, not to mention the more-than-obvious bulge in the front of them. The room started to get spotty, and Laura realized she'd been holding her breath. *What the fuck?* was all she could get to run through her mind.

"Well! Guess by the look on your face that you approve of our newest service Dom!" Steve walked up to the bar and took a stool. Even in the dim lighting, Steve could see Laura's face turn three shades of red.

"Cabrizzi? Are you kidding?" she asked, incredulous. "You can't be serious!"

"Look at him, Laura. Tell me you don't want that," Steve grinned.

"No. I don't." *Do I?*

"Liar. Have a fun evening. I'll check on you in a bit." Steve walked away and left Laura to stew.

"Hey, can I get a diet soda?" Vic asked as he leaned backward against the bar. Laura hadn't seen him come up, and she jumped about a foot. "Damn, woman, I just want a drink. I'm not gonna slap you or anything. Calm down," he snapped, not even cracking a smile.

"Don't you want your usual beer?" she asked, surprised that he'd asked for a soft drink.

"Nope. Against the rules."

"Whose rules?" Laura asked.

"Mine." She sat the drink in front of him and he picked up the glass. She couldn't help but notice how elegant his hands were, long, strong fingers with just the lightest dusting of dark hair across them. Looking at them made her feel odd. "Can't drink alcohol and keep my wits about me with a sub."

"You're serious about this, aren't you?" Laura asked, her mouth hanging open.

The new Vic Cabrizzi looked into her eyes and asked, "And what would make you think I'm not?" The low growl in his voice made her insides quiver, and she had to look away. "That's exactly what I thought." He finished the drink and smacked the glass onto the bar, then walked away. *What the hell?*, Laura thought. She looked down at her hands – they were visibly shaking.

Several of the unattached women in the club spent most of the evening talking to Vic, but most of them wanted to be collared by a Dom – right that minute. And Vic was not interested in that at all. They could flirt all they wanted, but it got them nowhere. He made it clear: He was a service Dom, and he'd be glad to meet their needs, but that was it.

"Oh my god! He's so gorgeous!" one woman was gushing as she and another woman walked up to the bar. "Can I have a Bud Light?" she asked Laura, who pulled it and sat it down in front of her.

"I'd take him on in a New York minute," her friend said. "I needed a sign that said 'slippery when wet' just standing there talking to him!" Laura wanted to hurl.

"I want to climb up there and let him spank me good, but he's so damn big, he's kinda scary," the first one said. *Ha! Wish he could hear that!*, Laura thought.

But that left her wondering why she wanted him to fail. He'd obviously worked hard to train with Alex. She should be happy for him, that he was more confident and looked better, happier, than she'd ever seen him. Why did seeing him looking and feeling good make her feel so bad? *Maybe I'm the bitch that José said I am.*

Laura felt her phone vibrate in her pocket and she pulled it out to see an unfamiliar number on the screen. She'd advertised to try to find a roommate, and she hoped that someone was responding. When she answered the call, a male voice said something, but the club was too loud. "Hang on just a minute, please. I can't hear you." She looked around – no Steve. "Hey, Vic!" she yelled. Vic broke away from a beautiful, bare-breasted brunette and came over to the bar. "Hey, I've got a phone call. Can you watch the bar for just a minute?"

"Yeah, but just a minute. Get your ass right on back here," he said. He'd never talked to her like that before, and she was taken aback, but she didn't have time to worry about that.

Jetting out the side door behind the bar, she put the phone back up to her ear. "Yeah, sorry about that. Can I help you? Are you calling about the ad for a roommate."

"No." Something about the voice made her feel odd. "Laura? Laura Billings?" Her hands went cold and a buzzing started in her ears. "Billings?"

"Who the hell is this?" she growled into the phone.

"Laura, I'm so sorry to call you and drag all of this up. This is Brewster. Please don't hang up on me."

"DON'T CALL ME AGAIN!" Laura screamed into the phone, then hit END and dropped the phone on the ground. It promptly rang again; same number.

She stared at the phone. Everything was coming at her in a rush, and the earth seemed to tilt. She hit ACCEPT and asked through gritted teeth, "What the hell do you want?"

"Laura, please, don't hang up. I need to talk to you. I want to make this right; we all do. Well, almost all of us. I hear a lot of noise in the background. Can I call you later? Or tomorrow? It's important."

"I can't believe you'd have the nerve to call me. How did you find me?" she was whispering, feeling so weak that she could barely speak.

"Billings, I know it's hard to believe, but I want to make this right. It's eaten at me for years, ruined my life and I'm betting yours too, and it's time to man up. Please. Let me do this, me and the others. Please?"

Laura's head was spinning and she felt like she was going to throw up. It was a little late for an apology, but it was more than she'd gotten over the last sixteen years, sixteen years of sheer hell. "Call me tomorrow. Ten o'clock tomorrow morning. That's Eastern Daylight Time."

"Okay. Ten o'clock tomorrow morning. Will do." The phone went dead. Laura stood staring at the phone, her hands trembling so violently that she could barely hold it. After a minute or two, she walked back through the side door and up to the bar.

"Where the hell were you?" Vic barked. Then he got a good look at her face. "God, Laura, what's wrong?" She stared at the bar, and Vic grabbed her arms and spun her to look at him. "Talk to me. What is it?"

Laura shook his hands off. "Don't touch me. Leave me alone. Nothing's wrong." She grabbed the towel and started wiping.

She heard Vic say, "That's a lie. I don't believe it for a minute. And when you decide you need someone to talk to about whatever just happened, find me. I can't speak for anyone else, but you can *always* trust me. I'd never hurt you, not in a million years." Laura turned to apologize to him for the way she'd talked to him, but he was gone.

Vic walked into the men's locker room and leaned against the wall. He knew damn well something had happened, but the ice princess wasn't going to tell him what or take any help from anyone. And he was done with trying to get someone who didn't want to be around him to open up to him. That was a dead-end street, and he'd walked down too many of them already.

Here's a sneak peek at *Renovating a Heart*, Book 3 in the Love Under Construction *series:*

José Flores couldn't believe his eyes when he looked up from the computer screen and through the office window on Thursday night – it was Kelly Markham walking through the door at Eden's Gate!

"Hey lady! How are you?" he smiled at her.

"I'm good! It's great to see you, José. You work here too?"

"Yeah, in the evenings. Gotta make a few extra bucks. You coming to visit tonight?"

Kelly nodded. "Steve invited me. Is he here?" She glanced around nervously. The entry looked kind of plain and uninteresting. She wondered what the inside of the club would look like.

A door beside the little office opened and Steve popped out almost like he'd been waiting there for her. "Kelly! Glad you came! Come on in and let me show you around."

When Kelly stepped through the door, her heart sang and she felt warm all over.

She was home.

This was the place she'd been looking for. Everything was posh and well-appointed. The marble-topped bar with its multi-colored pendant lights gleamed, the wood warm and glowing. She recognized the guy manning the bar – Doug Benton, one of Steve's security employees – and waved to him. He waved back. *God, he's cute!*, she thought.

"We encourage fetwear here. I see you brought a bag," Steve said to her as he led her through the big commons area. Kelly had never seen such a beautiful performance area for scenes. It was well lit and spacious, and there were nice groupings of expensive leather furniture for conversing and relaxing. "Come on back. There's a locker room where you're welcome to change if you want." The look that had passed over Kelly's face hadn't been lost on Steve; pure bliss, like she'd walked straight into heaven, and he could tell she appreciated all the work he'd put into the place. "I'll wait out here for you and finish showing you around when you come out."

Steve leaned against the wall, wondering what she'd be wearing. He hoped it was something appropriately scanty. There were already at least a dozen bare-breasted subs walking around out in the large room, but he didn't dare dream that she'd come out like that.

He didn't have to. When Kelly walked out of the locker room, she was wearing a lacy thong and a matching flounce-skirted garter belt, its satin resplendently iridescent in pinks, fuchsias, yellows, and golds, with white lace trim and a pair of white fishnet stockings attached to the gold-plated clips. On her feet were a pair of peep-toed, white patent pumps with gold, five-inch heels, and her legs were deliciously curvy. And all of that was from the waist down. From the waist up . . .

Nothing.

A lump formed in Steve's throat. This woman was barely Nikki's height, maybe not even that, and her breasts had to be a G-cup. They were huge. And she had the hardest nipples he'd ever seen, no doubt about it. It was work to keep his hands to himself, and he almost failed at least twice just standing there.

"Do I look okay?" she asked shyly.

"Uh, yeah, you look, well, amazing," he stammered and turned pink. *Good god, McCoy, pull it together!*, his brain screamed.

"Thanks. It feels funny . . ." She put her hand to her neck. "This is the first time I've ever been in a club without a collar." At the thought of her in a collar his knees went weak, and her face was so sad that he was tempted to pull her to him and hug her.

"I'm so sorry, Kelly. If I can do anything . . ."

She smiled. "Just show me around. Maybe I can at least have a little fun."

"Oh, you can absolutely do that around here!" He took her down the hallway beyond the locker room to show her the private rooms, then took her down to see the dungeon in the basement.

When they came back upstairs, Kelly smiled up at Steve again. "Thanks for showing me around. I really appreciate being able to come here tonight. I can't afford a membership, but . . ."

"You can have one if you want it. I know your situation, and it's my pleasure." *It's most definitely my pleasure*, he sang to himself.

"No, I couldn't let you do that."

"I insist. Go on out there and have a good time. Tell Doug I said to give you a drink on the house. I'll be out again in a little while to check on you."

He wasn't sure why he did what he did, but he leaned down and gave her a timid little peck on the forehead. When he looked down into her face, there was a glow about her that surprised him.

"Thanks. See you in a bit," she called over her shoulder and sashayed out into the big room. *That man is gorgeous. I wonder if he'd . . . nah. He wouldn't be interested in me, especially if he knew everything*, she told herself as she headed to the bar for that drink.

Steve slammed the door to his office closed and locked it. He pulled a bottle of lube out of the desk drawer, dropped down into his chair, unzipped his leathers, and slicked up his stiffened dick. No need to wait – he was already so hard that he was aching. Something about Kelly . . .He stroked his cock religiously, taking his time, enjoying thinking about those beautiful nipples and that tiny waist. He wished she hadn't had the thong and garter belt on – he would've loved to get a glimpse of that pussy. If it was anything like the rest of her, well, that would be one fine cunt.

Before he could even take a deep breath, he came with a groan and shot a stream of cum out that would've put most men to shame. It had been a while since a woman had that effect on him, but he liked it. He was between subs, and he wondered . . . nah, she probably wouldn't be interested in him. But he certainly planned to find out.

Here's a sneak peek at Planning an Addition, Book 4 in the Love Under Construction series:

"Can we just pull over here?" Molly whined on the way back from the drugstore.

"No! Let's at least do this right, okay?" Peyton was having a hard time driving. He couldn't concentrate. There was a woman in the front seat beside him who was intent on fucking him as soon as she could, and that made her more than a little distracting. "I'd like to at least get back to your bed, if that's okay."

Molly sighed. "Okay. How slow are you going?" she asked, trying to see the speedometer.

"I'm doing five miles an hour over the speed limit already! I think you'll live!" he laughed.

"I dunno. There are parts of me that are on fire right now." She giggled.

"Good. I've got the hose to put them out." That made her laugh right out loud.

Peyton couldn't believe his eyes. They walked in the front door and she had her dress unzipped and over her head in a split second. She kicked off her heels as they walked down the hallway and by the time they got to the bedroom, she was in nothing but her bra and panties. Peyton had already started unbuttoning his shirt, and when they got to the bedroom, he pulled it off and dropped it on the floor.

Molly gasped. His chest was broad and smooth, with a generous blanket of blond, curly hair across his pecs and trailing down the center of his torso. She wanted to see where that happy trail ended, oh yes she did. He was built exactly as she'd suspected – broad, thick, powerful shoulders, huge biceps, and it all tapered to a narrow waist. "Get those pants off," she barked. "I want to see if your ass is as fine as the rest of you."

Peyton chuckled and rolled his eyes. "Yes, ma'am. I hope you're not disappointed." Then he realized he didn't have his crutches. What in the hell was he going to do? He started to panic. He wasn't prepared. He didn't have what he needed to get by. What now? She was going to see him as a cripple, as an incomplete excuse for a man.

It took Molly about three seconds to pick up on the fact that something was going on in his head. "What's wrong? Hey," she said, her fingers lifting his chin so his gaze went from the floor to her. "What's going on in there?" she smiled, her fingers grazing his temples.

"This was a bad idea." He froze.

"Why?" She watched his face. "Baby, what's wrong? What changed?"

"Molly, I . . ." He didn't know what to say. "I don't have my crutches." There. She'd just get dressed and show him out and the humiliation would be over.

She disappeared and came back in a couple of minutes with a pair of aluminum crutches. "Todd broke his leg a few years back in a skiing accident. I kept these in his closet. I didn't know why until just now." She handed them to Peyton as he sat there on the edge of the bed. "They may not be adjusted correctly for you, but they'll work, won't they?"

For the first time in years, Peyton fought back tears. She really didn't care that his leg was gone. It didn't matter to her. This was really happening. A woman wanted him, and wanted him badly enough to forget that he wasn't whole. "Yeah, they'll work," he managed to whisper. When he'd gotten the words out, Molly moved to stand between his knees and pulled his face into her chest.

"So, Peyton Stokes, get those damn pants off." She reached down and undid his belt, then unbuttoned and unzipped his slacks.

Peyton slipped his slacks off and let them fall to the floor. Once they were off, he worked his below-the-knee prosthesis off and put it to the side. He waited. What would she say?

Before he could utter a sound, Molly pushed him back onto the bed and climbed on top of him. Her dark hair fell around her face and down into his, and she leaned down and kissed him, her lips warm and tender against his, a sensation he hadn't known in years. A minute later, he wrapped his arms around her waist and rolled her until he was on top of her. He knew she could feel his erection, hard as steel, pressed against her mons and into the softness of her belly. "Why, Mr. Stokes, I think you're looking forward to something!"

Peyton started to relax. She really was okay with it, with him, and she still wanted him, even though she'd watched him remove his hardware. He wanted to enjoy this, to enjoy her, and see her enjoy him. "I am, Ms. Walters.

I'm looking forward to this immensely." He slid his hands under her torso and unsnapped her bra with one hand. "Let's get rid of this, shall we?" As he kissed her again, he drew the bra off and threw it in the floor, then pressed himself upward on his palms to look down at her.

Her breasts were beautiful. He found the way they sagged ever-so-slightly to be beyond erotic, a primitive, lovely thing. Molly's skin wasn't dark, just a light to medium shade, and her large areolas were a deep, rosy pink, with big, hard nipples puckered tight. It had been so long since he'd touched a woman's breasts that he didn't know if he could remember what to do with them. But when he leaned downward and drew a nipple into his mouth, it all came back in a rush. And he was pretty sure if it hadn't, the moan she turned loose with would've reminded him quite nicely.

Something inside Peyton Stokes came back to life with that one moan. He felt alive, strong, powerful. He felt like a man, the man he'd been before that bomb blast had jerked his dreams out from under him, not the shell of one he'd seemed to be for the past too many years. All of the heat and lust rushed into his system in a flood, and he heard himself growl, "Take those panties off. I want to see what I'm about to get myself into, baby. Literally."

Molly had never dreamed something like that would come out of Peyton's mouth, and everything between her legs went wet. It had been a long, long time since she'd been that turned on – maybe never. She scooted up into the bed; Peyton followed on his hands and knees with a look and cadence like a tiger stalking his prey. When she made it up to the pillows, she hooked her fingers in her panties and pulled them off like a pro. Peyton growled. "Spread 'em, beautiful."

All of a sudden, she felt shy and embarrassed as she pulled her feet up toward her ass, then let her bent knees fall to the sides. She was open, wide open, her folds glistening with the juices that were running freely from her sex. Peyton fell down onto his elbows and stared, his face inches from her arousal. Then she heard him groan out the magic words: "God, baby, you're so beautiful and so damn wet."

Molly didn't know whether to smile or cry. No man had ever told her that. She'd always thought genitals were ugly and dirty, and Freddie had certainly never looked at her that way. He'd always kept the covers pulled up and worked under them. She thought for a second, and realized she wasn't sure she'd ever really seen his genitals in all the years they'd been married. He'd just poked around down there in the dark until he hit the spot, then the two-pump chump finished and left her wanting. Even when she'd sucked him, he'd kept the covers over her, and she never really saw his cock or what she was doing, just felt her way around, and he hated it when she so much as accidentally brushed his balls. She wanted to see what Peyton looked like. It was exciting, after being married to a man all those years who was so closed off, to finally be with someone different.

She swallowed hard and whispered, "Peyton? Can you take off your briefs? I want to see you too."

He wouldn't make her wait. Peyton rose up on his knees and worked his briefs down to his knees – he'd take them the rest of the way off in just a few minutes, but if she wanted to see his cock, he wanted her to see it too.

And it was impressive. Molly took a good, long look. It was just like the rest of him, not especially long, but thick. Before he had a chance to even ask what she thought, she was up on her hands and knees and facing its beautiful purple knob, licking her lips and wondering if she should ask or just go for it. To answer her unspoken question, Peyton whispered, "I want your lips on me, but not now. I want the first time I'm inside you to be filling your womanhood, not your mouth." He stopped. "Molly, I don't do this. I don't just go home with a woman and fuck her. I'm not interested in one night stands or screwing around for fun. If you don't want a relationship, you need to let me know now. We can still do this, but you need to know that for me it's a building block, not just a fun kind of thing. I don't want us to be awkward around each other when we're around everyone else. Tell me: What do you want?"

"I want you." Her voice was strong and clear. "I want you right now, and I want you tomorrow too. I want to get to know you and find out if we can have something that will last. I need a man who's strong and knows what he wants, someone who'll take charge, and I think you can. And I'll let you, I will, I swear. Is that what you want? A relationship like that?"

Peyton felt ten feet tall. This was a woman whose needs he could meet. He could definitely build something with her. He dropped to the mattress beside her and drew her to him, then kissed her, a deep kiss full of longing and need. The feel of her nipples pressed against his chest made him ache for her softness and warmth, and she responded by running her fingers through his hair, her nails gently scratching his scalp and making his spine tingle.

As he kissed her, Peyton's hands started to drift over her body, and everywhere he touched felt alive to her, like her skin was waking from a coma. Molly burned deep inside, a painful need, the muscles in her pussy clenching and releasing, longing for something to fill them. She wanted him to touch her, and when he tweaked and rolled a nipple between his thumb and forefinger, she groaned loudly. His mouth replaced his fingers so his hand could continue to wander, and when it made its way to her folds, his fingers dipped into her cunt, leaving him marveling at how wet and hot she was for him. When he pumped two fingers into her, she cried out over and over, her hips thrusting to meet his hand, wanting more, needing more.

Leaving her softness, his hand trailed up her slit until his finger found her clit, hard and waiting, and he began to stroke it gently, so gently that she could barely feel his touch. As it grew harder, his stroking became more insistent, and Molly had trouble hanging on. She needed to come, and the clawing sensation building behind her swollen bud made her rising arousal almost unbearable. She worked at holding off, at making it last, but Peyton whispered, his breath warm in her ear, "Come for me, baby. I want you to lose control."

That was all the encouragement she needed. She shuddered and her hips began to thrust, each flex of her pelvis in time with a stroke of his finger. When she cried out, "No more!" Peyton rose above her and slid into her with one purposeful, powerful stroke.

The stretch was almost unbearable. Like all of the Walters men, Freddie had been well endowed, but this was different. Peyton's girth stretched her sheath almost to bursting, and she shrieked out, "Oh my god! It just hurts so damn good." As her hips rose over and over to meet his thrusts, Peyton dropped his face to her neck and nipped her lightly over and over.

He couldn't believe it; he couldn't believe *her*. What in the world had Freddie Walters wanted with a sixteen-year-old when he had *this* at home? She was incredible, warm and tight and wet, and every touch from his hand set her in motion until he was so hard that he thought he'd die. As he pumped into her, he thought about all of the months and years he'd been alone, and how this woman just might be the one he'd been waiting for. She wanted him. She needed him. And he needed her too.

Sooner than he would've liked, Peyton moaned, "Oh, angel, I can't hold back. I just can't. I'm sorry."

"Don't be. Please, Peyton, come inside me. Please?"

Peyton fell onto Molly, ran his hands around to grip her ass, and hunched her like a wild animal. As his speed increased, so did the friction, and within seconds Molly was crazed and begging, "God, Peyton, please, please, fuck me, oh god, fuck me, oh god, fuuuuuck me, baby." He shuddered and slammed into her three more times, filling the condom and as he poured himself into her, his heart hammering in his chest. Just as he finished stroking, he felt her contract around him and she soared into her own climax as he held onto his hardness to help her finish.

He lay on top of her, panting, and her arms wrapped around his neck. "God, baby, that was soooooo good," she whispered, then kissed his lips lightly, and he squeezed her waist and kissed her back, not as hard as before, but a firm, solid kiss that let her know he didn't want it to be over.

"It was. It was so fucking good, princess. Oh my god, I want to do that again!" he chuckled, and she laughed too.

"We can. We can do whatever we want," she told him, looking into his eyes. "I want more. Stay? Sleep here? Wake up with me tomorrow morning?"

He smiled down at her. "There's nothing I'd like more in this whole wide world.

I hope you enjoyed these excerpts from the remaining novels in the **Love Under Construction** *series. Check your favorite online retailer for the format that works with your electronic device.*

Connect with Deanndra on Substance B

Substance B is a new platform for independent authors to directly connect with their readers. Please visit Deanndra's Substance B page where you can:

- Sign up for Deanndra's newsletter
- Send a message to Deanndra
- See all platforms where Deanndra's books are sold
- Request autographed eBooks from Deanndra

Visit Substance B today to learn more about your favorite independent authors.

Made in the USA
Charleston, SC
24 September 2015